W9-AFJ-985

FORTRESS

围城

BESIEGED

Qian Zhongshu with his wife Yang Jiang in Beijing
Photo courtesy of Dominique Bourgois

FORTRESS

BESIEGED

QIAN ZHONGSHU

Translated by Jeanne Kelly and Nathan K. Mao

With a Foreword by Jonathan Spence

A New Directions Classic

Copyright © 1947 by Qian Zhongshu
Copyright © 1947, 2004 by Yang Jiang
Copyright © 2004 by New Directions
Translation copyright © 1979 by Jeanne Kelly and Nathan K. Mao
Foreword copyright © 2004 by Jonathan Spence

All rights reserved. Except for brief passages quoted in a newspaper, magazine, radio, or television review, no part of this book may be reproduced in any form or by any means, elec-
tronic or mechanical, including photocopying and recording, or by any information storage
and retrieval system, without permission in writing from the Publisher.

Fortress Besieged is published by arrangement with Yang Jiang and the translators.

The Publisher would like thank to Kathi Paton, Joanne Wang, and Dominique Bourgois
for their help in making this edition possible.

The translators wish to dedicate their translation to Petey and to Nathan's children.

Manufactured in the United States of America
New Directions Books are printed on acid-free paper.
First published clothbound in 1979 by Indiana University Press
First published as a New Directions Classic (NDP966) in 2004
Published simultaneously in Canada by Penguin Books Canada Limited

Library of Congress Cataloging-in-Publication Data

Qian, Zhongshu, 1910-1998
[Wei cheng. English]
Fortress besieged / By Qian Zhongshu ; translated by Jeanne Kelly and
Nathan K. Mao, with a foreword by Jonathan Spence.
          p. cm. — (A New Directions Classic)
ISBN 0-8112-1552-0
I. Kelly, Jeanne. II. Mao, Nathan K. III. Title. IV. New Directions
classics.
PL2749.C8W413 2004
891.1'352--dc22
                    2003017221

New Directions Books are published for James Laughlin
by New Directions Publishing Corporation
80 Eighth Avenue, New York, NY 10011

Contents

A NOTE FROM THE PUBLISHER ON THIS EDITION

The translators of *Fortress Besieged*, Jeanne Kelly and Nathan K. Mao, used the Wade-Giles romanization system for Chinese characters in their translation, which they first published in 1979. According to this romanization scheme, the author's name is spelled Ch'ien Chung-shu. Since the year 2000, all libraries and bibliographic services in the United States have joined the international community in using Pinyin, rather than Wade-Giles, as the standard romanization style for Chinese characters. In this edition, New Directions provides the Pinyin spelling of the author's name, Qian Zhongshu, as a cataloguing reference but, in order to keep this edition affordable, throughout the text the publisher has kept the translators' original Wade-Giles transliteration of Chinese names and places intact.

Foreword by Jonathan Spence

1937 was a hellish year for China. After years of threats and corrosive expansion into Chinese territory, the Japanese finally moved to all out war, first in the Peking region, and soon after in Shanghai. In the north, Japanese armies moved swiftly to consolidate the region under a collaborationist government and the following year—despite a Chinese effort to slow them down by blowing up the dikes on the Yellow River—pressed southwest to the strategic rail and river junction of Wuhan. In the Shanghai region, Chinese resistance was far fiercer, and casualties on both sides were enormous. But by the late fall of 1937, the Chinese troops had crumbled, and the Japanese advanced triumphantly through the largely abandoned defensive lines to the Nationalist capital of Nanking. There, in December 1937, the infamous "Rape of Nanking" brought death or agonizing humiliation to hundreds of thousands of Chinese men, women and children. In 1938, the Japanese established a collaborationist regime in Nanking, echoing the one already set up in the north. Having lost Wuhan to the Japanese, the Chinese Nationalist armies retreated still deeper upriver through the Yangtse gorges, establishing a new national capital at Chungking in Szechwan province.

It is into this bleak setting that Qian Zhongshu unceremoniously tosses his hapless hero Fang Hung-chien. Fang has been somewhat aimlessly studying literature and philosophy in Europe for a year or so, living comfortably off cash gifts from relatives, but never assembling a valid number of course credits. Pressured to get his degree, he finally creates his own diploma by adapting a phony one from a fraudulent correspondence college. In 1937, he returns to China on a French boat via Singapore and Hong Kong with neither goals nor prospects, having learned a little about this and that but nothing about life itself. His family, meanwhile, has sought shelter from the widening war by moving from the countryside to the area of Shanghai known as the "Foreign Concessions," controlled by French and British interests, which the Japanese had bypassed, restricting their assaults to the Chinese-controlled areas of the huge city. But weighted by his fake degree, and with no real skills or source of income, in mid-1938 Fang leaves Shanghai for a teaching job at "San Lü," a small university he has never heard of, deep inland in Hunan province. There he gets engaged to be married, but also loses his job. Disconsolately, he returns again to Shanghai, after a hurried wedding in Hong Kong, only to watch bemusedly as his marriage collapses.

Fortress Besieged is an intricately crafted comic picaresque novel that—like any major work of art—operates on a whole series of levels at once. One level is clearly autobiographical. Qian Zhongshu, like his fictional protagonist Fang, was also from a scholarly family in central China, and went abroad to study in Oxford and Paris in the mid-1930s, returning to China in early 1938. Unlike Fang, Qian was an accomplished scholar of both Chinese and English literature, and had obtained his B.Lit. degree at Oxford with a thesis on the depictions of China in seventeenth- and eighteenth-century British literature. But like Fang, Qian Zhongshu taught for a time early in the war in the interior, joining a group of refugee scholars from Shanghai and Peking who had set up a university-in-exile in the southwestern city of Kunming. After a stint there, and another at a college in Hunan, Qian returned to Shanghai (in 1941) where he taught and wrote until the end of the war. After the bombing of Pearl Harbor, in December 1941, the Japanese took over the former foreign concession areas, and interned the foreigners. Qian thus lived and wrote in an area controlled by the collaborationist Nanking regime, but he seems to have avoided—like the fictional Fang—becoming either a member of the resistance or a collaborator. Instead he kept his profile low and wrote and studied in the privacy of his home—together with his wife, the distinguished playwright and translator Yang Jiang—and consorted with a small group of highly educated Chinese scholars and artists. (In 1949 he and his wife decided to stay in China, and spent the rest of their lives under communist rule.)

Another level at which the novel operates is historical. Though Qian keeps the war offstage throughout most of his book, and there are no battle scenes, and no dramatic confrontations with guerrilla forces, collaborationists, or the Japanese themselves, the war remains everywhere. The effects of war are most subtly conveyed in the magnificent chapters that recount the journey made by Fang and four companions, as they travel by bus, boat, on foot, and by sedan chair, for several weeks in their quest to find the presumed haven of San Lü. Though Qian does not emphasize the topics, the alert reader will observe numerous examples of civilian profiteering, military graft, the ripple-effect of the needless destruction of Changsha, and the constant threat of being arrested and interrogated that

Fang and his companions face. Elsewhere in the novel, one can also find references to the dreaded interrogation center run by the Japanese and their collaborators in the suburbs of Shanghai, and note the pressures on journalists and writers to conform to the collaborationist party line. Underlying these themes, at least for many Chinese readers, would have been the fact that the phrase "Fortress Besieged" (Chinese: "Wei Cheng") had been most prominently used by a Chinese poet back in 1842 to describe the city of Nanking when it was besieged by the British after their defeat of China in the first of the so-called "opium wars." Thus shame and national humiliation would have been very much in people's thoughts.

At a third level, the book is about Chinese intellectuals, and about the baleful effects of the excessive adaptation of Western literary and aesthetic theories that Qian felt had corroded the integrity of the Chinese, compounding the disarray of their culture which was already reeling under the collapse of the Confucian value-system. Fang himself is innocent in the sense that he always claims he knows too little to give informed opinions on cultural matters, but such inhibitions are not felt by any of his friends and colleagues. Fang is surrounded by puffed-up pedants and phony scholars, whose self-important diction and mindless comments drive several of the funniest sections of the novel. Many of the people whom Fang encounters on his travels can be readily recognized as real figures from the Chinese literary and academic world of the time, but in his own preface to the novel Qian counsels the reader not to see *Fortress Besieged* as a roman à clef.

At yet another level, this is a book about the relationships between men and women, and about sex and marriage. Fang's agonized and disastrous romances, crammed as they are with misunderstandings and absurd expectations, are brilliantly rendered and often heart-breaking despite their satirical coloration. The last fifty or so pages of the novel are surely one of the finest descriptions of the disintegration of a marriage ever penned in any language. One critic has observed that Qian was led into his particular mode of anti-romantic pessimism by his broad reading of British novels during his time at Oxford, especially the works of Evelyn Waugh and Aldous Huxley, and there is surely some truth to that. It may also be pertinent that while Qian was working away at *Fortress Besieged* one of his closest friends in Shanghai, an expert on Flaubert, was completing his translations of both *Madame Bovary* and *L'education sentimentale*. At the same time, we must acknowledge that the details of the botched relationships, and the weight of a variety of family pressures on the indecisive Fang, remain recognizably and strictly Chinese in flavor.

Lastly, and perhaps most off-puttingly, *Fortress Besieged* is awash, almost from the first page, with images of bile, vomit and phlegm. Human bodies—and not just Fang's—are continually revealing their fallibility through their mouths and their nostrils. There is seasickness, airsickness, carsickness, drunken vomiting, babies' spittle and drool, and snot, and there is nothing the reader can do but wince and move on. One might argue that there are some deliberate echoes of Jonathan Swift here, and that may be true, since Qian was indubitably an expert in British eighteenth century literature as well as modern. But often there is more than satire in these moments. Qian seems determined to remind us of the impossibilities of human purity, and of the fact that our ecstasies are forever doomed to conjure up their opposites.

When *Fortress Besieged* was published in 1947, although the Japanese had been defeated, China was once more enmeshed in a vicious civil war that ultimately brought the communists to victory. It was a time of cruelty and chaos, as the late 'thirties had been. But Qian had completed his task. He had created a novel of originality and spirit, of wit and integrity, one that clearly has earned its place amongst the masterworks of twentieth-century Chinese literature, and can be read on its own merits within the most demanding of global contexts. It has been long out of print in English, and New Directions has rendered a true service in making it available once again to fresh circles of readers. *Fortress Besieged* may not be able to tell us where China is heading now, but it can certainly tell us what China went through on the way.

Jonathan Spence
Yale University
September 6, 2003

Author's Preface

In this book I intended to write about a certain segment of society and a certain kind of people in modern China. In writing about these people, I did not forget they are human beings, still human beings with the basic nature of hairless, two-legged animals. The characters are of course fictitious, so those with a fondness for history need not trouble themselves trying to trace them out.

The writing of this book took two years altogether. It was a time of great grief and disruption, during which I thought several times of giving up. Thanks to Madame Yang Chiang, who continuously urged me on while holding other matters at bay, I was able through the accumulation of many small moments to find the time to finish it. This book should be dedicated to her. But lately it seems to me that dedicating a book is like the fine rhetoric about offering one's life to one's country, or handing the reins of the government back to the people. This is but the vain and empty juggling of language. Despite all the talk about handing it over, the book remains like the flying knife of the magician—released without ever leaving the hand. And when he dedicates his work in whatever manner he chooses, the work is still the author's own. Since my book is a mere trifle, it does not call for such ingenious disingenuousness. I therefore have not bothered myself about the dedication.

December 15, 1946   CH'IEN CHUNG-SHU

Translators' Preface

Ch'ien Chung-shu ranks among the foremost twentieth-century Chinese novelists, and his novel *Wei-ch'eng* (*Fortress Besieged*) is one of the greatest twentieth-century Chinese novels. After receiving extensive treatment of his works in C. T. Hsia's *A History of Modern Chinese Fiction* in 1961, Ch'ien was largely neglected until recently. The present translation of *Wei-ch'eng* reflects that renewed interest, and it is hoped that it will generate even greater interest in Ch'ien Chung-shu and his works.

This translation is the cooperative effort of Jeanne Kelly and Nathan K. Mao. Whereas Jeanne Kelly did the first draft of the translation, Nathan K. Mao revised it; in addition, Mao wrote the introduction, refined the footnotes, and prepared the manuscript for publication. Despite our divided tasks, this book is our joint responsibility.

We wish to thank Professor Joseph S. M. Lau of the University of Wisconsin and Professor Leo Ou-fan Lee of Indiana University for their expert editing assistance, patience, and encouragement; Chang Hsu-peng for help in the first draft of the translation; James C. T. Shu of the University of Wisconsin and Professor Mark A. Givler of Shippensburg State College for reading the entire manuscript and offering their advice; Mr. George Kao of the Chinese University of Hong Kong for permission to reprint chapter one, published in *Renditions* (No. 2, Spring 1974); and lastly Professor C. T. Hsia of Columbia University for supplying us with biographical and bibliographical information on Ch'ien Chung-shu.

We also wish to express our gratitude to Mr. Ch'ien Chung-shu himself for reading the biographical part of the Translators' Introduction as well as the Author's Preface during his visit to the United States in April-May of 1979. He clarified several items of biographical detail and made some corrections. We are deeply honored that this translation has the author's full endorsement and support.

Chevy Chase, Maryland   JK
Chambersburg, Pennsylvania   NKM

Le mariage est comme une forteresse assiégée;
ceux qui sont dehors veulent y entrer, et
ceux qui sont dedans veulent en sortir.

Marriage is like a fortress besieged: those
who are outside want to get in, and those
who are inside want to get out.

—French proverb

FORTRESS

围城

BESIEGED

1

༺༺

THE RED SEA had long since been crossed, and the ship was now on its way over the Indian Ocean; but as always the sun mercilessly rose early and set late, encroaching upon the better part of the night. The night, like paper soaked in oil, had become translucent. Locked in the embrace of the sun, the night's own form was indiscernible. Perhaps it had become intoxicated by the sun, which would explain why the night sky remained flushed long after the gradual fading of the rosy sunset. By the time the ruddiness dissipated and the night itself awoke from its stupor, the passengers in their cabins had awakened, glistening with sweat; after bathing, they hurried out on deck to catch the ocean breeze. Another day had begun.

It was toward the end of July, equivalent to the "san-fu" period of the lunar calendar—the hottest days of the year. In China the heat was even more oppressive than usual. Later everyone agreed the unusual heat was a portent of troops and arms, for it was the twenty-sixth year of the Republic (1937).

The French liner, the *Vicomte de Bragelonne*, was on its way to China. Some time after eight in the morning, the third-class deck, still damp from swabbing, was already filled with passengers standing and sitting about—the French, Jewish refugees from Germany, the Indians, the Vietnamese, and needless to say, the Chinese. The ocean breeze carried with it an arid heat; the scorching wind blew dry the bodies of fat people and covered them with a frosty layer of salt congealed with sweat, as though fresh from a bath in the Dead Sea in Palestine. Still, it was early morning, and people's high spirits had not yet withered or turned limp under the glare of the sun. They talked and bustled about with great zest. The Frenchmen, newly commissioned to serve as policemen in Vietnam or in the French Concession in China,[1] had gathered around and were flirting with a coquettish young Jewish woman. Bismarck

3

once remarked that what distinguished French ambassadors and ministers was that they couldn't speak a word of any foreign language, but these policemen, although they did not understand any German, managed to get their meaning across well enough to provoke giggles from the Jewish woman, thus proving themselves far superior to their diplomats. The woman's handsome husband, who was standing nearby, watched with pleasure, since for the last few days he had been enjoying the large quantities of cigarettes, beer, and lemonade that had been coming his way.

Once the Red Sea was passed, no longer was there fear of the intense heat igniting a fire, so, besides the usual fruit peelings, scraps of paper, bottle caps, and cigarette butts were everywhere. The French are famous for the clarity of their thought and the lucidness of their prose, yet in whatever they do, they never fail to bring chaos, filth, and hubbub, as witness the mess on board the ship. Relying on man's ingenuity and entrusted with his hopes, but loaded with his clutter, the ship sailed along amidst the noise and bustle; each minute it returned one small stretch of water, polluted with the smell of man, back to the indifferent, boundless, and never-ending ocean.

Each summer as usual a batch of Chinese students were returning home after completing their studies abroad, and about a dozen of them were aboard. Most were young people who had not as yet found employment; they were hastening back to China at the start of the summer vacation to have more time to look for jobs. Those who had no worries about jobs would wait until the cool autumn before sailing leisurely toward home. Although some of those on board had been students in France, the others, who had been studying in England, Germany, and Belgium, had gone to Paris to gain more experience of night life before taking a French ship home. Meeting at a far corner of the earth, they became good friends at once, discussing the foreign threats and internal turmoil of their motherland, wishing they could return immediately to serve her. The ship moved ever so slowly, while homesickness welled up in everyone's heart and yearned for release. Then suddenly from heaven knows where appeared two sets of mahjong, the Chinese national pastime, said to be popular in America as well. Thus, playing mahjong not only had a down-home flavor to it but was also in tune with world trends. As luck would have it, there were more than enough people to set up two tables of mahjong.[2] So, except for eating and sleeping, they spent their entire time gambling. Breakfast was no sooner over than down in the dining room the first round of mahjong was to begin.

Up on deck were two Chinese women and one toddler, who didn't count as a full person—at least the ship's company did not consider him as one and had not made his parents buy a ticket for him. The younger woman, wearing sunglasses and with a novel spread on her lap, was elegantly dressed. Her skin would be considered fair among Orientals, but unfortunately it looked stale and dry; and even though she wore a light lipstick, her lips were a little too thin. When she removed her sunglasses, she exposed delicate eyes and eyebrows, and when she rose from the canvas lounge chair, one could see how slight she was. Moreover, the outline of her figure was perhaps too sharp, as if it had been drawn with a square-nibbed pen. She could be twenty-five or twenty-six, but then the age of modern women is like the birthdates traditional women used to list on their marriage cards, whose authentication required what the experts call external evidence, since they meant nothing in and by themselves. The toddler's mother, already in her thirties, was wearing an old black chiffon Chinese dress;[3] a face marked by toil and weariness, her slanting downward eyebrows made her look even more miserable. Her son, not yet two years old, had a snub nose, two slanted slits for eyes, and eyebrows so high up and removed from the eyes that the eyebrows and the eyes must have pined for each other—a living replica of the Chinese face in newspaper caricatures.

The toddler had just learned to walk, and he ran about incessantly. His mother held him by a leather leash so that he could not run more than three or four steps without getting yanked back. Bothered by the heat, tired, and irritable from pulling, the mother, whose thoughts were on her husband who was gambling down below, constantly scolded her son for being a nuisance. The child, restricted in his movements, turned and dashed toward the young woman reading the book. Ordinarily the young woman had a rather conceited, aloof expression, much like that of a neglected guest at a large party or an unmarried maiden at a wedding feast. At that moment her distaste for the child surfaced so much so that not even her sunglasses could hide it. Sensing all that, the child's mother apologetically pulled at the strap and said, "You naughty child disturbing Miss Su! Come back here! How studious you are, Miss Su! You know so much and still you read all the time. Mr. Sun is always telling me, 'Women students like Miss Su give China a good name. She's beautiful and has a Ph.D. besides. Where can you ever find such nice people?' Here I went abroad for nothing and never even cracked a book. I keep house, and I forgot everything I'd learned as soon as I had him. Hey! You pest! I told you not to go over there. You're up to no good. You'll get Miss Su's clothes all dirty for sure."

Miss Su had always scorned the poor, simple-minded Mrs. Sun and detested children, but when she heard all that, she was quite pleased. Smiling pleasantly, she said, "Let him come. I love kids."

She removed her sunglasses, closed the book she had been staring at vacantly, and with utmost caution she clasped the child's wrist before he could wipe his hands all over her clothes.

"Where's Papa?" she asked him. Without answering, the child opened his eyes wide and went, "Poo, poo," at Miss Su, spitting out saliva in imitation of the goldfish blowing bubbles in the tank in the dining room. Miss Su hastily let go of his arm and pulled out a handkerchief to protect herself. His mother yanked him away, threatening to slap him. Then sighing, she said, "His father is gambling down below. Where else? I can't understand why all men like gambling so much. Just look at the ones on this boat. Every last one of them is gambling his head off. I wouldn't mind so much if it brought in a little something. But my husband, Mr. Sun, he's already gambled away a tidy sum and he just keeps going. It makes me so mad!"

When Miss Su heard these last petty remarks, she, in spite of herself, felt a renewed contempt for Mrs. Sun. "You know, Mr. Fang does not gamble," she remarked coldly.

Mrs. Sun turned up her nose and sniffed. "Mr. Fang! He played too when he first got on the boat. Now he's too busy chasing Miss Pao, so naturally he can't spare the time. Romance is the big event of a lifetime, far more important than gambling. I just can't see what there is about that Miss Pao, coarse and dark as she is, to make Mr. Fang give up a perfectly good second-class berth for the discomforts of the third class. I see those two are getting on gloriously. Maybe by the time the boat reaches Hong Kong they'll get married. It's certainly a case of 'fate bringing people together from a thousand *li* away.' "[4]

Miss Su felt a painful stabbing in her heart when she heard that. To answer Mrs. Sun and to console herself, she said, "Why, that's quite impossible! Miss Pao has a fiancé; she told me so herself. Her fiancé even financed her studies abroad."

Mrs. Sun said, "She has a fiancé and is still so flirtatious? We are already antiques. At least we've learned something new this time. Miss Su, I'll tell you something funny. You and Mr. Fang were classmates in China. Does he always say whatever he pleases? Yesterday Mr. Sun was telling Mr. Fang about his poor luck in gambling, and Mr. Fang just laughed at him for having been in France all these years and not knowing anything about the French superstition; Mr. Fang said that if the wife is unfaithful and has an affair, the husband is sure to take first prize if he buys a lottery ticket, and he is sure to win if he gambles. And he added that if a man loses at gambling, he should take it as a consolation. When Mr. Sun told me all that, I scolded him for not asking that Fang fellow just what he meant. Looking at it now, it seems Miss Pao's fiancé could certainly take first prize in the aviation lottery. If she became Mr. Fang's wife, Mr. Fang's luck at gambling would have to be good." The viciousness of a kind, simplehearted soul, like gritty sand in the rice or splinters in a deboned fish, can give a person unexpected pain.

"Miss Pao's behavior is just too unlike a student's. And the way she dresses is quite disgraceful—" Miss Su remarked.

The toddler suddenly stretched his hands behind their chairs, laughing and jumping about. The two women looked around and saw that it was none other than Miss Pao coming toward them, waving a piece of candy at the child from a distance. She was wearing only a scarlet top and navy blue, skintight shorts; her red toenails showed through her white, open-toed shoes. Perhaps for a hot day in the tropics, this was the most sensible attire; one or two non-Chinese women on board dressed exactly like that. Miss Su felt that Miss Pao's exposed body constituted an insult to the body politic of the Chinese nation. When men students saw Miss Pao, they burned with lewd desire, and found some relief by endlessly cracking jokes behind her back. Some called her a *charcuterie*—a shop selling cooked meats—because only such a shop would have so much warm-colored flesh on public display. Others called her "Truth," since it is said that "the truth is naked." But Miss Pao wasn't exactly without a stitch on, so they revised her name to "Partial Truth."

As Miss Pao approached, she greeted the two women, "You're sure up early. On a hot day like this, I prefer to loaf in bed. I didn't even know when Miss Su got up this morning. I was sleeping like a log." She had intended to say "like a pig," then on second thought decided to say "like a corpse." Finally, feeling a corpse wasn't much better than a pig, she borrowed the simile from English. She hastened to explain, "This boat really moves like a cradle. It rocks you until you're so woozy all you want to do is sleep."

"Then you're the precious little darling asleep in the cradle. Now, isn't that cute!" said Miss Su.

Miss Pao gave her a cuff, saying, "You! Su Tung-p'o's little sister,[5] the girl genius!" "Su Hsiao-mei" (Su's little sister) was the nickname the men students on board had given Miss Su. The words, "Tung-p'o" when pronounced by Miss Pao in her South Seas accent sounded like *tombeau*, the French word for tomb.

Sharing a cabin with Miss Pao, Miss Su slept in the lower berth, which was much more convenient because she didn't have to climb up and down every day; but in the last few days she had begun to hate Miss Pao, feeling Pao was doing everything possible to make her life miserable—snoring so loudly she couldn't sleep well, and turning over so heavily it seemed the upper berth would cave in. When Miss Pao hit her, she said, "Mrs. Sun, you be the judge of who's in the right. Here I call her 'precious little darling' and I still get hit! To be able to fall asleep is a blessing. I know how much you enjoy sleeping, so I'm always careful never to make a sound so I won't wake you up. You were telling me you were afraid of getting fat, but the way you like to sleep on the ship, I think you must have gained several pounds already."

The child was yelling for the candy, and as soon as he got it into his mouth, he chewed it up. His mother told him to thank Miss Pao, but he paid no attention, so the mother had to humor Miss Pao herself. Miss Su had already noticed that the candy cost nothing. It was just a sugar cube served aboard the ship with coffee at breakfast. She despised Miss Pao for the way she put on. Not wanting to speak to Miss Pao anymore, she opened her book again, but from the corner of her eye she caught a glimpse of Miss Pao pulling two deck chairs over to an empty spot some distance away and arranging them side by side. She secretly reviled Miss Pao for being so shameless, but at the same time hated herself for having spied on Miss Pao.

At that point Fang Hung-chien came on deck. As he passed by Mrs. Sun and Miss Su, he stopped to say a few words. "How's the little fellow?" Mrs. Sun replied curtly, not paying much attention to him.

Miss Su said with a smile, "You'd better hurry. Aren't you afraid some-one will get impatient?"

Fang Hung-chien blushed and gave a silly smile, then walked away from Miss Su. She knew perfectly well she couldn't keep him back, but when he left, she felt a sense of loss. Not a word of the book sank in. She could hear Miss Pao's sweet voice and laughter and couldn't resist looking at her again. Fang was smoking a cigarette. As Miss Pao held out her hand toward him, he pulled out his cigarette case and offered her one. Miss Pao held it in her mouth, and as he made a gesture with his fingers on the lighter to light it for her, she suddenly tilted her mouth upward, and touching her cigarette with the one he was smoking, breathed in. With the cigarette lit, Miss Pao triumphantly blew out a puff of smoke. Miss Su was so furious that chills ran through her body. *Those two have no sense of shame whatsoever*, she thought. *right in full view of everyone using cigarettes to kiss.* Unable to bear the sight any longer, she stood up and said she was going below. Actually she knew there was no place to go below the deck. People were playing cards in the dining room, and the sleeping cabins were too stuffy. Mrs. Sun was also thinking of going down to her husband to see how much money he had lost that day, but she was afraid if he had lost badly he would take it out on her as soon as she asked him, and there would be a long quarrel when he returned to the cabin. Thus, she didn't dare get up rashly and only asked her son if he wanted to go down and pee.

Miss Su's condemnation of Fang Hung-chien for being shameless was ac-tually unjust. At that moment he was so embarrassed that it seemed to him that everybody on deck was watching him. Inwardly he blamed Miss Pao for being too overt in her behavior and wished he could have said something to her about it. Although he was now twenty-seven and had been engaged be-fore, he had had no training in love. His father had passed the second-degree examination under Manchu rule[6] and was a prominent squire in his native dis-trict south of the Yangtze.[7] Nine out of ten of the emigrants from this district living in big cities were now either blacksmiths, bean-curd makers, or sedan-chair carriers. The most famous indigenous crafts were clay dolls; and for young men entering college, civil engineering was the most popular discipline. The intractability of iron, the insipidity of bean curd, the narrowness of sedan chairs, and in addition, the smell of earth could be called the local traits; even those who became rich or high officials lacked polish.

In the district a man named Chou had become wealthy from a blacksmith shop he opened in Shanghai. Together with some fellow villagers in the same business, he organized a small bank called the Golden Touch Bank,[8] serving as manager himself. One year, remembering the saying about returning home clothed in glory, he chose the Ch'ing Ming Festival[9] to return to his district to offer obeisance at the family temple, attend to the ancestral graves, and make acquaintances with local notables. Since Fang Hung-chien's father was one of the respected men in the community, in due time Chou paid him a visit. Thus they became friends and went on to become in-laws.

While Fang Hung-chien was still in high school, in compliance with his parents' decision, he became engaged. He had never met his fiancée; merely viewing a bust photograph of her had left him feeling indifferent. Two years later he went to Peking to enter a university and had his first taste of coeducation. Seeing couple after couple in love, he grew red-eyed with envy. When he thought how his fiancée had quit school after one year of high school to learn housekeeping at home in order to become a capable daughter-in-law, he felt an uncontrollable aversion toward her. Thus, bewailing his fate and feeling resentful toward his father, he went about in a half stupor for several days. Then suddenly he woke up, and mustering his courage, he wrote a letter home asking for release from the engagement.

Since he had received his father's guidance in literary composition and placed second in the high school general examination, his letter was couched in an elegant style without incorrectly using any of the various particles of literary Chinese. The letter went something like this: "I have of late been very restless and fitful, experiencing little joy and much grief. A feeling of 'autumnal melancholy'[10] has suddenly possessed me, and every time I look into the mirror at my own reflection, so gaunt and dispirited, I feel it is not the face of one destined for longevity. I'm afraid my body can't hold up much longer, and I may be the cause of a lifetime of regret for Miss Chou. I hope you, Father, will extend to me your understanding and sympathy and tactfully sever the ties that bind. Do not get angry and reject my plea and thus help bring me everlasting woe."

Since he felt the wording of the letter was sad and entreating enough to move a heart of stone, he was quite unprepared for the express letter which came from his father. It gave him a severe scolding:

> I did not begrudge the expense of sending you hundreds of miles away to study. If you devoted yourself to your studies as you should, would you still have the leisure to look in a mirror? You are not a woman, so what need do you have of a mirror? That sort of thing is for actors

only. A real man who gazes at himself in the mirror will only be scorned by society. Never had I thought once you parted from me that you would pick up such base habits. Most deplorable and disgusting!

Moreover, it is said that "When one's parents are still living, a son should not speak of getting old." You have no consideration for your parents, who hold you dearly in their hearts, but frighten them with the talk of death. This is certainly neglect of filial duties to the extreme! It can only be the result of your attending a coeducational school—seeing women around has put ideas in your head. The sight of girls has made you think of change. Though you make excuses about "autumnal melancholy," I know full well that what ails you are the "yearnings of springtime."[11] Nothing can escape this old-timer's sharp eye. If you carry on with this foolishness, I will cut off your funds and order you to discontinue your studies and return home. Next year you will get married at the same time as your brother. Give careful thought to my words and take them to heart.

Fang Hung-chien was shaken to the core, never expecting his father to be quite so shrewd. He wasted no time in getting off a reply begging forgiveness and explained that the mirror was his roommate's and not something he had bought himself. Within the last few days, after taking some American cod liver oil pills and German vitamin tablets, his health and spirits had taken a turn for the better, and his face had filled out, he assured his father, except that the high cost of medicine had been more than he could afford. As for his marriage, he would like to ask that it be postponed until after his graduation. For one thing, it would interfere with his schooling; for another he was still unable to support a family and would not feel right about adding to his father's responsibilities.

When his father received the letter, which proved that the father's authority had reached across several hundred miles, his father was extremely gratified. In high spirits, his father sent him a sum of money so he could buy tonic medicine. From then on, he buried his feelings and dared not indulge in vain hopes. He began reading Schopenhauer and would often say wisely to his classmates, "Where is romantic love in the world? It's entirely the reproductive urge." In no time at all he was a senior in college and was to marry the year following his graduation.

One day an express letter came from his father. It read as follows: "I have just received a telegram from your father-in-law. I was greatly shocked to learn that Shu-ying was stricken with typhoid fever, and due to the negligence of a Western-trained doctor, she passed away at four o'clock in the afternoon on the thirteenth of this month. I am deeply sorry. Marriage was so close at hand; all good things have unexpected setbacks. It is all due to your lack of good fortune."

The postscript read: "This may be a blessing in disguise.[12] If you had married three years earlier, this would have cost us a large sum of money.

But with a family of such virtue as ours, if the marriage had taken place earlier, perhaps Shu-ying would have been spared this calamity and lived a long life. One's marriage is predestined, and you have no cause to be overly grieved. You should, however, send a letter of condolence to your father-in-law."

Fang Hung-chien read this with the joy of a pardoned criminal. But for the girl whose life had been cut short he felt a tinge of pity. While exulting in his own freedom, he wanted to help lessen others' grief. He therefore wrote a long letter of commiseration to his would-be father-in-law.

When Mr. Chou received the letter, he felt that the young man knew etiquette, and so he instructed the bank's chief-secretary Mr. Wang to send a reply. When Chief-secretary Wang read Fang Hung-chien's letter, he had high praise for his boss's would-be son-in-law, remarking that the young man's calligraphy and literary style were both excellent, and that the expression of his feelings for the deceased was deep and genuine, indicative of a very kind heart and talent that would take him far. Delighted with all this, Chou instructed Wang to reply in the following manner: "Although my daughter was never wed, our in-law relationship will remain unchanged. I had but one daughter and had originally planned to give her a grand wedding. Now I am going to give the entire amount, which I had set aside for the wedding and the dowry, along with the earnings from investments made with your family's betrothal present—altogether a sum of over twenty thousand dollars or one thousand three hundred British pounds—to finance your education abroad after your graduation from college next year."

Even in his dreams Fang Hung-chien had never conceived of such a stroke of good fortune and felt profound gratitude toward his deceased fiancée. He was a worthless sort, who could never learn civil engineering, and while at the university he had switched his major from sociology to philosophy before finally settling down as a Chinese literature major.

It may sound a bit absurd for someone majoring in Chinese to go abroad for advanced study. In fact, however, it is only for those studying Chinese literature that it is absolutely necessary to study abroad, since all other subjects such as mathematics, physics, philosophy, psychology, economics, and law, which have been imported from abroad, have already been Westernized. Chinese literature, the only native product, is still in need of a foreign trademark before it can hold its own, just as Chinese officials and merchants have to convert the money they have fleeced at home into foreign exchange to maintain the original value of the national currency.

During his stay in Europe, Fang Hung-chien did not spend his time transcribing the Tun-huang manuscripts[13] or visiting the Yung-lo collections[14] or looking for relevant documents on the T'ai-p'ing Heavenly Kingdom.[15] Within four years he had gone the rounds of three universities: London, Paris, and

Berlin. He took a few courses here and there, and though his interests were fairly broad, he gained nothing at all in the way of knowledge, mostly dissipating his life away in idleness. In the spring of the fourth year, with only three hundred pounds left in the bank, he decided to return home in the summer.

His father had written asking him if he had received his Ph.D. and when he would be coming home. He replied with a long letter denouncing the Ph.D. title as having absolutely no practical value. His father did not see it that way at all, but now that his son had grown up, he hesitated to threaten him again with paternal authority, and merely said that he knew perfectly well titles were useless and that he would never force his son to get one, but his son had a duty toward Mr. Chou, who had invested a large sum of money on his education. A few days later, Fang Hung-chien also received a letter from his father-in-law, which said in effect: "A worthy son-in-law like you with talent and learning and a reputation extending far and wide does not need to flaunt a Ph.D. But your father passed the Manchu second-degree examination and therefore it seems only fitting that you become the foreign equivalent of the third-degree holder, following in your father's footsteps and even surpassing him. Then I too would share in your glory."

Finding himself pressured on both sides, Fang Hung-chien finally realized the importance of a foreign diploma. This diploma, it seemed, would function the same as Adam and Eve's figleaf. It could hide a person's shame and wrap up his disgrace. This tiny square of paper could cover his shallowness, ignorance, and stupidity. Without it, it was as if he were spiritually stark naked and had nothing to bundle up in. But as for getting a degree at that point, whether by studying toward it himself or hiring a ghost writer to write a dissertation, there was neither time nor money. A Ph.D. from the nearby University of Hamburg was considered the easiest to muddle through, but even it required six months. He could just go ahead and deceive his family by saying he'd received a Ph.D., but then he was afraid that he couldn't fool his father and father-in-law. As one who had passed the old second-degree examination, his father would want to see the official "announcement." His father-in-law, a businessman, would want to see the "title deed." Unable to think of a solution, he was prepared to return home brazen-faced and tell them that he had not obtained a degree.

One day as he was going to the Chinese bibliography section of the Berlin library to see a German friend, he noticed on the floor a large stack of periodicals published in Shanghai during the first years of the Republic of China, including *The Eastern Miscellany*, *Short Story Monthly*, *The Grand China*, and the *Women's Magazine*. Having stopped to leaf leisurely through one, he happened to see an advertisement with Chinese and English parallel texts placed by the "Correspondence Division of the Carleton Institute of Law and Commerce" in the city of New York. It stated that for those Chinese students who had the desire to study abroad but no opportunity to do so, the school had special correspondence courses, upon completion of which certificate equivalents of the B.A., M.A., or Ph.D. degrees would be granted. The brochures would be forwarded immediately upon request by writing to such and such a number and on such and such a street in New York City.

Fang's heart skipped a beat. As a good twenty years had elapsed since the date of the advertisement, he had no way of knowing whether the school still existed or not. *At any rate sending off a letter of inquiry won't cost much*, he thought.

The man who had placed the advertisement was actually a swindler. Since no Chinese was ever taken in, he had dropped it for another line of business and died some time ago. The apartment he had lived in was now rented to an Irishman, with all the Irish irresponsibility, quick wit, and poverty. It is said that an Irishman's fortune consists of his two breasts and two buttocks, but this one, being a tall, thin Bernard Shaw-type of man, did not have much breast or buttocks. When he came upon Fang's letter in his mailbox, he thought the mailman had made a mistake. But the address was clearly his; so full of curiosity, he opened the letter. Greatly puzzled, he mulled over it for a while, then leaped for joy.

He quickly borrowed a typewriter from a tabloid reporter next door and typed out the following reply: "Since you have been studying in a university in Europe, your level of achievement must be quite high, making it unnecessary for you to go through the correspondence procedures. You need only send a 10,000-word dissertation and enclose five hundred U.S. dollars. After evaluating your qualifications, we will immediately forward to you a Ph.D. degree diploma. Letters can be addressed to myself without having to write the name of the school. Signed, Patrick Mahoney." Underneath his name he conferred upon himself four or five doctoral titles.

When Fang saw the letter was written on ordinary stationery without the name of the school engraved on it, and as the contents clearly showed the school to be fraudulent, he put it aside and forgot about it. The Irishman meanwhile grew impatient and sent off another letter stating that if Fang found the price too high, the price could be negotiated. He himself had always loved China, and as an educator, he was particularly averse to profit-seeking. Fang mulled it over for a while, suspecting that the Irishman was undoubtedly up to tricks. If he bought a bogus diploma and went back to dupe other people with it, wouldn't he himself be a fraud? But, remember, Fang had once been a philosophy major, and to a philosophy major lying and cheating were not always immoral. In Plato's *Ideal State* soldiers were justified in fooling the enemy, doctors in fooling their patients, and officials in fooling the people. A sage like Confucius had pretended to be ill in order to trick Ju Pei into leav-

13

ing,[16] and even Mencius had lied to King Hsüan of Ch'i and pretended that he was ill.[17] Since both his father and his father-in-law hoped he would become a Ph.D., how could he, a son and son-in-law, dare disappoint them? Buying a degree to deceive them was like purchasing an official rank in Manchu times,[18] or like the merchants of a British colony contributing a few ten thousand pound notes to the royal exchequer in exchange for a knighthood, he reasoned. Every dutiful son and worthy son-in-law should seek to please his elders by bringing glory to the family. In any case, when later it came time for him to look for a job, he would never include this degree in his resumé. He might as well try slashing the price, and if the Irishman refused, he could then forget the whole thing and avoid turning into a fraud himself. So he replied that he would pay one hundred U.S. dollars, making a thirty-dollar down payment, and when the diploma was delivered, he would send the rest, and that thirty or more other Chinese students were also interested in dealing with "your honorable school" in the same manner.

At first, the Irishman would not agree. Later, realizing that Fang's decision was firm, and having ascertained from local sources that American doctoral titles were indeed fashionable in China, he gradually became convinced that there really were thirty-odd Chinese muddleheads in Europe wanting to buy a degree from him. He also learned that there were a number of organizations engaged in the same business, such as the University of the East, Eastern United States of America University, the Intercollegiate University, and the Truth University, where one could buy an M.A. diploma for as little as ten U.S. dollars, while the College of Divine Metaphysics offered a bargain package of three types of Ph.D. diplomas. All these were formally accredited and registered schools with which he could never hope to compete. Therefore, keeping his objective of low profits but wide markets in mind, he came to terms with Fang Hung-chien. When he received the thirty dollars, he printed up forty or fifty diplomas, filled one out, and sent it to Fang. In an accompanying letter he pressed Fang to send the balance and to inform the others to apply to him.

Fang replied that, after making a careful investigation, he had found no such school in the United States and that the diploma amounted to waste paper. But he would be lenient toward a first offender and not press charges in hopes that the Irishman would repent and reform himself. Nonetheless, he did send the Irishman ten extra U.S. dollars to help tide the Irishman over while changing to another line of work.

The Irishman was so enraged that he cursed without stop, got drunk and red-eyed, and sought to pick a fight with any Chinese he could find. The incident may well mark China's sole victory over the foreigners since she began to have foreign relations or signed her first treaty of commerce.

Afterwards, Fang went to a photo studio, donned the German doctoral robe and had a four-inch picture taken. He sent a copy each to his father and father-in-law. In a letter he reiterated how all his life he had hated the title of doctor and that while this time he could not avoid the convention, it was not worth mentioning his degree to others.

He returned to France where he enjoyed himself a few weeks, then bought a second-class steamship ticket for the return trip home. After boarding the ship at Marseilles, he discovered that he was the only Chinese traveling second class and was lonely and bored. The Chinese students in the third class felt that he, being a student, too, was just flaunting his wealth by traveling second class, and they eyed him with some hostility. Learning of an empty berth in the cabin of a Vietnamese, he made arrangements with the purser to give up his original cabin and go sleep in third class, while still taking his meals in the second class.

Among the Chinese on board, the only one he knew from China was Miss Su, who had studied French literature at Lyons. She had written her dissertation on eighteen Chinese poets of the colloquial style[19] and had just received her doctorate. When Fang and she were classmates at college, she had never even noticed the existence of the little nobody Fang Hung-chien. In those days she valued her affection too highly to bestow it casually. Now, however, she was just like the person who has some fine clothes made and, saving them for good occasions, locks them in a chest. Then one or two years later she suddenly finds their style and design are out of fashion and is filled with disappointment and regret. Before, she had had her heart set on studying abroad and despised those suitors for their lack of prospects, since they were merely college graduates. But now that she was a woman Ph.D., she felt the loneliness of her lofty perch, which was higher than anyone dared climb. She knew a little about Fang's family background; and observing that he was a nice person and didn't seem to lack money, she thought she might use the trip to give him an opportunity to get near her. She never guessed that her cabinmate, Miss Pao, would beat her to him.

Miss Pao was born and raised in Macao and was said to have Portuguese blood. To say she had "Portugese blood" was the same as for the Japanese to claim they have native culture,[20] or for an author who has plagiarized a foreign play to declare in his revised version, "copyright reserved, translations forbidden," since the Portuguese blood had Chinese ingredients mixed in it from the start. But to judge from Miss Pao's figure, her Portuguese mother may also have had Arab blood inherited indirectly from Spain. Miss Pao had a very slender waist, which fit exactly the standard of feminine beauty the Arab poet praised and described at length in *Arabian Nights*: "Her waist was slender, her hips were heavy and did weight her down whene'er she would rise." Under her long eyelashes was a pair of sleepy, seemingly drunken, dreamy, big smiling eyes; her full, round upper lip seemed to be angrily pouting at a lover. Her fiancé Dr. Li, without any sense of prudence, had given her the money to study obstetrics in London by herself. The Portuguese have a saying that for a lucky man the firstborn is always a girl (*A homem ventureiro a filha lhe nasce primeiro*), because when the girl grows up, she will be handy around the house and look after her younger brothers and sisters; thus before her marriage she saves her parents the expense of hiring a maid. Miss Pao was used to being at her parents' beck and call. Being clever, she realized that she would have to find her own opportunity and seek her own happiness by herself. She therefore chose to become engaged to a man twelve years older, so she could have the chance to go abroad. The British are accustomed to seeing fair skin, so when they saw her dark, though not black, color with its rich, spicy attractiveness, they thought she was a true Oriental beauty. She believed herself to be very seductive, so she was very quickly and easily seduced. Fortunately, being a medical student, she did not take these affairs seriously or get into any trouble. After two years in England she was now returning to get married and set up a joint practice with her husband. Once aboard the ship, the Chinese students found out she carried a British passport issued by the Hong Kong government, which meant she was not a Chinese citizen, so they did not quite warm up to her. Since she couldn't speak French and didn't care to talk about home with the third-class Cantonese waiters, she felt terribly bored. She saw Fang was a second-class passenger and thought he might make a good companion to while away the time during the trip.

Miss Su, who pictured herself in the words of the familiar saying, "as delectable as peach and plum and as cold as frost and ice,"[21] decided she would allow Fang to humbly gaze at her in admiration and then prostrate himself to beg for her love. Who would have thought that while the temperature hovered around 100 degrees every day, this sweet, cool ice cream manner of hers was completely ineffective. By merely letting drop one lighthearted remark, Miss Pao had Fang hooked. The day after Fang had moved to the third class, he went up on deck for a stroll and happened to run into Miss Pao, who was leaning against the ship's railing by herself and taking in a breath of air. He greeted her and struck up a conversation. Before he had said more than a sentence or two, Miss Pao remarked with a smile, "Mr. Fang, you remind me of my fiancé. You look so much like him!"

She made him feel both embarrassed and pleased. When an attractive woman says you look like her fiancé, it is tantamount to saying that if she were not engaged, you would be qualified to win her love. A real cynic might interpret this as meaning: she already has a fiancé, so you can enjoy a fiancé's privileges without having to fulfill the obligation of marrying her. Be that as it may, from that point on their friendship grew with the speed of a tropical

16

plant. All the other Chinese men students teased Fang and made him treat everyone to iced coffee and beer.

Although Fang was inwardly critical of Miss Pao for her immodest behavior, he was also feeling excited. When he turned his head and saw Miss Su and Mrs. Sun's empty chairs, he was thankful the cigarette incident had passed without their notice.

That evening it became windy, and the ship began pitching slightly. After ten o'clock only four or five couples were on deck, hiding in the shadows from the gleam of lights, murmuring sweet words to each other. Fang and Miss Pao strolled along side by side in silence. A big wave violently shook the ship, she nearly losing her balance. He then hooked his arm around her waist, and staying close to the railing, he kissed her hungrily. Her lips were ready, her body submissive. This stolen kiss, hurried and rough, gradually settled into a full and comfortable one. She deftly pushed aside his arm, and breathing heavily said, "You're suffocating me. I have a cold and can't breathe. You got away with it cheap. You haven't even begged for my love!"

"I'll make it up by begging for it now, all right?" Like all men without love experience, he considered the word "love" much too noble and solemn to be used casually on women. He only felt he wanted her, not that he loved her, thus this evasiveness in his reply.

"Anyway, you haven't anything nice to say. You can't get away with that same old line."

"When you put your mouth against mine and I say something to you, those words pass right into your heart without having to take the long way around, making a turn, and going in through your ear."

"I'm not going to be fooled by you! If you have something to say, say it like a gentleman. That's enough for today. If you behave yourself, tomorrow I—"

He wasn't paying any attention and again put his arm around her waist. Suddenly the ship lurched sideways. He had not taken hold of the railing and nearly pulled her down with him. At the same time, in the shadows, the other women let out shrill cries. Miss Pao took advantage of the situation and slipped away, saying, "I feel cold. I think I will go on down. See you tomorrow"—leaving him alone on deck.

Dark clouds had already formed in the sky, disclosing here and there a few stars. The storm sounded like a man greedily gulping his food; the broad open sea of the daytime had now been completely digested in the even vaster night. Against this background the tumult in a man's heart shrinks to nothingness. Only a well of hope for the morrow, which has not yet descended into the vastness, illuminates itself like the speck of light from a firefly in the dark depths of boundless, roaring waves.

From that day on, Fang often ate his meals in the third class. Miss Su's attitude toward him visibly cooled, so he asked Miss Pao in private why Miss Su had been snubbing him lately. Miss Pao laughed at him for being such a simpleton, adding, "I can guess why, but I won't tell you so you won't get more stuck up."

He said she was imagining things, but after this, whenever he met Miss Su, he felt even more awkward and ill at ease.

The ship passed Ceylon and Singapore and in a few days reached Saigon. This was the first colony since the start of the voyage that the French could boast of as their own. The French on board were like dogs at the sight of their master's home—their chests suddenly filled out, their actions became more arrogant, and the pitch of their voices was raised. In the afternoon the ship docked and anchored for two nights. Miss Su's relatives, who worked at the local Chinese consulate, sent a car to the wharf to pick her up for dinner, and so, with everyone watching enviously, she was the first one to get off the ship. The remaining students decided to eat at a Chinese restaurant. Fang Hung-chien wanted to eat somewhere else with Miss Pao, but feeling it would be too embarrassing to say this in front of the others, he just went along with them. After eating, the Suns left first to take their child back to the ship, while the others stopped at a coffee shop and Miss Pao suggested they go dancing. Though Fang had paid for a couple of dancing lessons in France, he was hardly a master at it. After one dance with Miss Pao, he retreated to the sidelines and watched her dance with others. After twelve o'clock everyone had had enough and was ready to return to the ship to sleep. When they got out of the rickshaws at the wharf, Fang and Miss Pao lingered behind. She said, "Miss Su won't be coming back tonight."

"My Vietnamese cabinmate has gone ashore too. I heard his berth was taken by a Chinese businessman on his way to Hong Kong from Saigon."

"We'll both be sleeping alone tonight," she said almost carelessly.

It was as though lightning had flashed through his mind and produced a sudden blinding glare. All the blood rushed to his face. He was about to speak, when someone up front turned around and shouted, "What are you two talking about so much? Walking slowly because you're afraid we'll eavesdrop, aren't you?" Without another word, the two hurried onto the ship. Everyone said, "Good night," and went his own way. Fang bathed and returned to his cabin, lay down, and then sat up again. Trying to dispel the thought, once it has lodged there, seems as agonizing as it is for a pregnant woman to have an abortion. Maybe Miss Pao had meant nothing by that remark. If he went to her, he might make a fool of himself. Since cargo was now being loaded on the deck and two watchmen were patrolling the corridors to prevent intruders from slipping in, there was no assurance he wouldn't be spotted by them. He couldn't make up his mind, yet he didn't want to give up hope.

Suddenly he heard light, brisk footsteps, seemingly from the direction of Miss Pao's cabin. His heart leaped up, but was then pressed down by those footsteps, as if each step trod upon it. The footsteps halted. His heart likewise stood still, not daring to stir, as though someone stood upon it. A long moment passed and his heart was oppressed beyond endurance. Fortunately, the footsteps resumed with renewed speed, coming closer. He was no longer in doubt, his heart no longer restraining itself. Wanting to shout with joy, he hopped from his bed and without getting his slippers all the way on, opened the door curtain to a whiff of Miss Pao's usual talcum powder.

When he woke the next morning, sunlight filled the room. By his watch it was past nine. He reminisced how sweet the night's sleep had been, too deep even for dreams. No wonder sleep was called the land of dark sweetness. He then thought of Miss Pao's dark skin and sweet smile; later when he saw her he'd call her "Dark Sweetness," making him think of dark, sweet chocolate. Too bad that French chocolate wasn't any good and that the weather was too hot for eating it, for otherwise he would treat her to a box. Just as he was loafing in bed thinking of that nonsense, Miss Pao tapped on the outside of his cabin, called him "Lazybones," and told him to hurry and get up so they could go ashore and have fun.

When he finished combing his hair and washing up, he went to her cabin and waited outside a long while before she finally finished dressing. Breakfast had already been served in the dining room, so they ordered and paid for two extra servings. The waiter who served them, Ah Liu, was the one in charge of Fang's cabin. When they had finished eating and were about to leave, Ah Liu, instead of clearing away the things on the table, smiled at them gleefully and stretched out his hand. In his palm were three hairpins. Mouthing Cantonese Mandarin,[22] he said in a jumbled roundabout way, "Mr. Fang, I found these just now while making your bed."

Miss Pao flushed crimson and her big eyes seemed about to pop out of their sockets. Mortified, Fang cursed himself for being so stupid as not to have checked his bed when he got up. He pulled out three hundred francs from his pocket and said to Ah Liu, "Here! Now give me back those things." Ah Liu thanked him, adding that he was most dependable and would certainly keep his mouth shut. Miss Pao looked elsewhere, pretending she knew nothing about it.

After they left the dining room, Fang gave the hairpins back to Miss Pao, apologizing as he did so. She angrily flung them to the floor, saying, "Who wants them after they've been in the filthy hands of that wretch!"

The incident ruined their luck for the whole day. Everything went wrong. The rickshaws took them to the wrong place; they paid the wrong amount of money when they went shopping; neither one had any good luck. Fang wanted to go eat lunch at the Chinese restaurant where they went the evening before, but Miss Pao was set on eating Western food, saying she didn't want to meet anyone they knew from the ship. They then found a Western-type restaurant that looked respectable enough from the outside; but as it turned out, there wasn't a single thing edible from the cold dishes to the coffee. The soup was cold, and the ice cream was warm. The fish was like the Marine Corps. It apparently had already been on land for several days; the meat was like submarine sailors, having been submerged in water for a long time. Besides the vinegar, the bread, the butter, and the red wine were all sour. They completely lost their appetites while eating and couldn't hit it off in their conversation either. He tried to amuse her by calling her the affectionate nicknames "Dark Sweetie" and "Miss Chocolate."

"Am I so dark then?" she asked heatedly.

Stubbornly trying to justify himself, he argued, "But I like your color. This year in Spain I saw a famous beauty dancing. Her skin was just a little lighter than a smoked ham."

"Maybe you like Miss Su's dead-fish-belly white. You yourself are as black as a chimney sweep. Just take a look at yourself in the mirror," she answered him none too logically. With that she flashed a triumphant smile.

Having received a thorough blackening from Miss Pao, he could hardly go on. The waiter served the chicken. There on the plate was a piece of meat that seemed to have been donated by the iron weathercock on a church steeple. Try as she might, Miss Pao could not make a dent in it. She put down her knife and fork, saying, "I haven't the teeth to bite into this thing. This restaurant is a total mess."

Fang attacked the chicken with a greater determination. "You wouldn't listen to me," he said through clenched teeth. "You wanted to eat Western food."

"I wanted to eat Western food, but I didn't ask you to come to this miserable restaurant! After the mistake is made, you blame someone else. All you men are like that!" She talked as though she had tested the character of every man in the world.

After a while she somehow managed to bring up Dr. Li, her fiancé, saying he was a devout Christian. Already piqued, Fang became disgusted upon hearing this. Since religious belief hadn't had the slightest effect on her behavior, he'd just have to use Dr. Li to get in a few digs at her, he thought. "How can a Christian practice medicine?" he asked.

Without any idea of what he was driving at, she looked at him wide-eyed.

He added some rice-water "milk" to the scorched bean-husk "coffee" in front of her, and said, "One of the Ten Commandments of Christianity is 'Thou shalt not kill,' but what does a doctor do but professionalized killing?"

Unamused, she shot back, "Don't be ridiculous! Medicine saves lives."

Seeing how attractive she was when aroused, he decided to provoke her further. "No one who saves lives could be religious. Medicine wants people to live. It saves people's bodies. Religion saves people's souls and wants them not to fear death. So if a sick man is afraid of death, he'll call a doctor and take medicine. If the doctor and the medicine prove ineffective and there's no escape from death, then he'll get a minister or a priest to prepare him for his end. To study medicine and be religious at the same time comes down to: 'If I can't help a sick man to live properly, at least I can still help him die properly. Either way he can't go wrong by calling me in.' It's like a pharmacist running a coffin shop on the side. What a racket!"

She was greatly incensed: "I suppose you won't ever get sick and have to call a doctor. Your big mouth and glib tongue are spouting all kinds of nonsense. Well, I study medicine too. Why do you malign people for no reason?"

Alarmed, he apologized. She complained of a headache and wanted to return to the ship to rest. All the way back he was very apologetic, but she remained in low spirits. After seeing her to her cabin, he slept for two hours himself. As soon as he got up he went to her cabin, tapped on the partition, and called her name, asking if she felt any better. To his surprise, the curtain opened and Miss Su came out saying Miss Pao was sick, had thrown up twice, and had just fallen asleep. He was at once chagrined and embarrassed; he said something lamely and beat a hasty retreat.

During dinner everyone noticed Miss Pao's absence and teased Fang, asking him where she was. He mumbled, "She's tired. She isn't feeling well."

Gloatingly, Miss Su said, "She ate with Mr. Fang and came back with an upset stomach. Now she can't keep a thing down. I'm just afraid she's contracted dysentery!"

The callous men students laughed heartily and spouted all sorts of nonsense, asking, "Who told her to eat with Little Fang[23] behind our backs?"

"Little Fang is a real disgrace! Why can't he pick a clean restaurant when he asks a girl out to eat?"

"It couldn't be the restaurant's fault. Miss Pao was probably too happy and ate so much she couldn't digest it all. Right, Little Fang?"

"Little Fang, you didn't get sick? Oh, I get it! Miss Pao's beauty is such a feast to the eye,[24] and you got your fill just looking at her and didn't have to eat."

"I'm afraid what he feasted on wasn't beauty but—" The speaker was going to say "cooked meat"; then suddenly thinking the words would be inelegant in front of Miss Su and might be passed on to Miss Pao, he picked up a piece of bread and stuffed it into his mouth.

Fang actually hadn't had enough to eat during lunch but now could no longer stand everyone's teasing. Without waiting for all the dishes to be served, he took off, causing the others to laugh even harder. As he stood up and turned around, he saw the waiter, Ah Liu, standing behind him and giving him an understanding wink.

Miss Pao stayed in bed for a day or two; then she finally got up. She still toyed with Fang but not as freely as before. Perhaps because they would be reaching Hong Kong in a few days, she had to cleanse her mind and body in preparation for meeting her fiancé.

Three or four students and the Suns were going to disembark at Kowloon to take the Canton-Hankow train. With departure imminent they gambled away for all they were worth, only lamenting that lights were not permitted in the dining room after midnight. On the afternoon before arrival in Hong Kong, they exchanged home addresses and made repeated promises to see one another again, as if the shipboard friendship was never to be forgotten.

Fang was about to go on deck to look for Miss Pao when Ah Liu furtively called him. Ever since the day he had given Ah Liu the three hundred francs, he felt uneasy whenever he saw Ah Liu. Hardening his expression, he asked Ah Liu what the matter was. Ah Liu said that among the cabins he took care of there was one vacant; he asked Fang if Fang wanted it for the evening, saying he would only ask six hundred francs for it. With a wave of the hand, Fang said, "What would I want with that?" and bounded up the steps two at a time, with Ah Liu laughing scornfully behind him. He suddenly realized what Ah Liu had had in mind and his face burned with shame. He went up to sputter out the incident to Miss Pao, cursing that scoundrel Ah Liu. She gave a snort, but as others were coming up, there was no chance to say anymore.

During dinner, Mr. Sun said, "Today, to mark our parting, we should live it up and gamble through the whole night. Ah Liu has an empty cabin which I've reserved for two hundred francs."

Miss Pao threw Fang a contemptuous glance, then immediately stared at her plate and ate her soup.

Mrs. Sun, feeding her child with a spoon, asked meekly, "We'll be going ashore tomorrow. Aren't you afraid of getting tired?"

Mr. Sun said, "Tomorrow I'll find a hotel and sleep for days and nights on end. The engines on the ship are so noisy, I've not been sleeping well."

Meanwhile, Fang's self-esteem had deflated like a rubber tire under Miss Pao's glance. After dinner Miss Pao and Miss Su were unusually intimate, going about arm in arm and never leaving each other's company for an instant. He followed them lamely onto the deck. As he watched them talk and laugh without letting him squeeze a word in edgewise, he felt silly and humiliated; he was like a beggar who, after running after a rickshaw for some distance without getting a cent, finally has to stop but is reluctant to give up. Looking at her watch, Miss Pao said, "I'm going down to sleep. The ship will dock before dawn tomorrow so we won't be able to sleep well in the morning. If I don't go to bed early, I'll be all tired out and will look a wreck when I go ashore tomorrow."

Miss Su said, "You're so concerned about your looks. Are you afraid Mr. Li won't love you? If you look a little weary, it'll make him dote on you so much more!"

Miss Pao said, "Is that the voice of experience? Just think. Tomorrow I'll be home. I'm so excited I am afraid I won't be able to fall asleep. Miss Su, let's go on down. We can lie down in the cabin and talk more comfortably."

With a nod to Fang they went down. He burned with such rage inside that it seemed enough to set the end of his cigarette aglow. He could not understand why Miss Pao had suddenly changed her attitude. So was their relationship to end just like that? When he was at the University of Berlin, he had heard the lecture on Eros by Ed Spranger, a professor well known in Japan, and so he understood that love and sexual desire are twins which go together but are different. Sexual desire is not the basis for love, and love is not the sublimation of sexual desire. He had also read manuals on love and other such books and knew the difference between physical and spiritual love. With Miss Pao it wasn't a matter of heart or soul. She hadn't had any change of heart, since she didn't have a heart. It was only a matter of flesh changing its flavor over time. At any rate, he hadn't suffered any loss and may even have had the better of it, so there should be no cause for complaint. He tried to console himself with these clever phrases and careful calculations, but disappointment, frustrated lust, and wounded pride all refused to settle down, like the doll which always rights itself when pushed over and even wobbles about more vigorously.

At the crack of dawn the next day, the ship reduced its speed and the sound of its engines altered rhythm. Fang's cabinmate had already packed his things, while Fang lay in bed, thinking that since he and Miss Pao would never meet again, he would see her off with due courtesy, no matter what. Ah Liu suddenly entered with a woeful look and asked for a tip.

"Why do you want money now?" asked Fang angrily. "It'll be several days before we reach Shanghai."

Ah Liu explained in a hoarse voice that Mr. Sun and the others playing mahjong had been too noisy and had been caught by the French who had raised cain. He had lost his job and in a little while would have to pack his bedding[25] and get off the boat. Fang secretly rejoiced at this piece of good fortune, then sent Ah Liu off with a tip.

During breakfast those disembarking were in low spirits. Mrs. Sun's eyes were red and swollen and the corners seemed saturated with tears; they were like the dew on flower petals on a summer morning, and the slightest touch of the finger would cause them to drop. Miss Pao noticed there was a new waiter on duty and asked where Ah Liu had gone, but no one answered her.

Fang asked Miss Pao, "You have a lot of luggage. Would you like me to help you off the ship?"

In a distant tone of voice she answered, "Thank you. There's no need for you to bother. Mr. Li is coming aboard to meet me."

Miss Su said, "You can introduce Mr. Fang to Mr. Li."

Fang wished he could have crushed every bone in Miss Su's thin body to lime powder. Miss Pao ignored Miss Su and, after drinking a glass of milk, rose hurriedly, saying she still hadn't finished packing. Heedless of everyone's jesting remarks, Fang put down his glass and followed her. Miss Pao didn't even glance around, and when he called her name, she said impatiently, "I'm busy. I don't have time to talk with you."

He did not quite know how to show his anger. Just at that moment Ah Liu appeared like a ghost and asked Miss Pao for a tip. Miss Pao's eyes exploded with sparks as she said, "I tipped you yesterday for waiting on the table. What other tip do you want? You don't take care of my cabin."

Ah Liu silently reached his hand into his pocket and after a long time pulled out a hairpin. It was one of those Miss Pao had flung away the other day. While sweeping the floor he had found only one of the three. At first Fang wanted to scold Ah Liu, but seeing how seriously Ah Liu had pulled out this magical object, he couldn't help laughing.

"You think it's funny?" Miss Pao snapped. "If you think it's so funny, you give him some money. I don't have a cent!" And with that she turned and strode off.

Afraid that a disgruntled Ah Liu might run his mouth off to Dr. Li, Fang gave Ah Liu some more money, charging it up to his bad luck. Fang then went on deck by himself and watched disconsolately as the ship drew up to the Kowloon wharf. Other disembarking passengers, both Chinese and non-Chinese, also came up. He hid himself in a corner, not wishing to see Miss Pao. On the wharf, policemen, porters, and hotel agents who had come to greet passengers were clamoring noisily; a group of people were waving handkerchiefs at the ship or gesticulating. He was sure Dr. Li was among them and wanted a closer look at him. Finally, the gangplank was lowered, and after the immigration procedures were completed, friends of departing passengers swarmed aboard. Miss Pao rushed into the arms of a balding, dark, pudgy man in big glasses. So this was the fiancé he was supposed to resemble! He looked like that? Well, of all the insults! Now he understood everything. That remark of hers was nothing but a "come-on." Up to this time he had been quite pleased with himself, thinking she had taken a liking to him. Who would have thought that having been tricked and made use of by her, he was even being secretly ridiculed by her. What was there to say except that adage, which was so old it had grown a long white beard and so stale it was moldy: "Women are the most dreadful of all!" As he was leaning against the railing and thus lost in thought, Miss Su's soft voice unexpectedly came from behind him, "Are you staying on board daydreaming, Mr. Fang? Somebody has gone and left you! You have no one to keep you company!"

He turned around and saw Miss Su dressed with elegance and charm. Without knowing what possessed him, he said, "I'd like to keep you company, but I'm afraid I haven't the good fortune or the qualifications!"

Having made this rash remark, he braced himself for a polite rebuff. A spot of red appeared on Miss Su's cheeks beneath her lightly applied rouge, spreading out like oil stains on a piece of paper, covering her face in an instant and making her look bewitchingly bashful. As if barely able to raise her eyelids, she said, "Who, me? I don't think I'm important enough!"

Spreading out his hands, he said, "Just as I said, you wouldn't give me the honor."

"I want to find a hairdresser to have my hair washed. Would you like to go with me?" she said.

"Splendid!" he said. "I was just about to go get a haircut. When that's taken care of, we can take a ferry to Hong Kong and go up to the Peak[26] to have some fun. When we come down, I'll take you to lunch. After lunch we can have tea at Repulse Bay[27] and in the evening see a movie. How's that?"

With a smile she answered, "Mr. Fang, you've really thought of everything! You've planned for the whole day." She didn't know Fang had only passed through Hong Kong once on his way abroad and couldn't even remember the directions.

Twenty minutes later, Ah Liu took his bag of clothes to the dining hall to await the French supervisor to clear him for going ashore. Through the porthole he caught a glimpse of Fang Hung-chien behind Miss Su, descending the gangplank with his hand around her waist. He couldn't repress a feeling of surprise and admiration as well as scorn. Unable to express these complicated feelings in words, he spat a mouthful of thick saliva into the spittoon with a loud "Tsui!"

2

IT IS SAID that "girl friend" is the scientific term for sweetheart, making it sound more dignified, just as the biological name for rose is "rosaceae dicotyledonous," or the legal term for divorcing one's wife is "negotiated separation by consent." Only after Fang Hung-chien had escorted Miss Su around Hong Kong for a couple of days did he realize that a girl friend and a sweetheart were actually two completely different things. Miss Su was the ideal girl friend, with the brains, the status, the poise, and looks of a girl of good family. Going to restaurants and theaters with her was no cause for disgrace. Though they were quite close, he was confident his friendship with her would develop no further. Like two parallel lines, no matter how close they are, or how long they are extended, they will never join together. Only once—during that moment before they had gone ashore at Kowloon and he saw her blush—had his heart suddenly gone limp and lost the power to beat. Afterwards there was no recurrence of that feeling. In many ways, she had a very childish temperament, he discovered. For instance, she could be mischievous and she could play dumb, traits he had never expected of her. Yet for some reason, he always felt this "little-girlishness" did not quite suit her. It had nothing to do with her age; she wasn't much older than Miss Pao. Besides, in the presence of the man she loves, every woman has the amazing power of rejuvenation. One could only say that it was out of character: For example, we think it's funny to watch a kitten go around in circles chasing its tail, but when a puppy follows suit and turns hectically around after that stubby tail, then it isn't funny any more.

When the other students on board saw that Miss Pao had no sooner gone than Little Fang took up with Miss Su, they teased him unmercifully. Miss Su, however, was very generous to him. During the five or six days before the

26

ship reached Shanghai, she didn't once mention Miss Pao and became much warmer toward the others. Though Fang never spoke with her on intimate terms and never held her hand except for helping her up and down the gangplank when they got on and off the ship, her occasional gestures made it seem as though their relationship went far beyond the stages of proposal, engagement, or newlyweds. Her nonchalance made him apprehensive, giving him the feeling it was a demonstration of confidence secured by love, just as the sea stays calm after a storm while underneath its tranquil surface lies the power to rise up in a rushing torrent.

After the ship left Hong Kong, he and Miss Su were on deck eating the fruit they had bought there. Patiently tearing off the skin of a juicy peach, he remarked, "Why aren't peaches made like bananas? It'd be so much easier to peel them! Or else simply like apples. A few wipes with a handkerchief and you can eat them, peel and all."

She peeled and ate a few lichees; then, before eating anything else, she offered to peel the peach for him. He wouldn't agree under any circumstances. After he ate the peach, telltale marks were left on his cheeks and his hands. She looked at him and laughed. Afraid the peach juice would stain his trousers, he stuck his little finger into his pocket to hook his handkerchief. After two attempts, he managed to pull it out and was wiping his hands when she, in a voice full of alarm and disgust, cried out, "Oh! How did you get your handkerchief so dirty! How could you? Hey! You can't wipe your mouth with that thing. Here, take mine. Go ahead and take mine. I hate being refused."

Reddening, he took her handkerchief and lightly dabbed at his mouth, saying, "I bought a dozen new handkerchiefs before I came on board, but the laundry man lost half of them. Since these little things are so easily lost and it takes so long to get them washed, I thought I'd wash them myself. In the last couple of days when we were ashore, I didn't have time so all my handkerchiefs are dirty. I'll go wash them after a while. Let me wash this one of yours for you before I return it."

"Who wants you to wash it?" she said. "You won't get it clean anyway! It looks to me as if your handkerchief wasn't ever clean in the first place. Those grease spots are probably souvenirs accumulated all the way from Marseilles. I just wonder how you washed them." At this she giggled.

Shortly afterwards they went below. Picking out one of her handkerchiefs and giving it to him, she said, "Use this one for the time being and give me yours to wash."

Alarmed, he said again and again, "You can't do that!"

Puckering her lips, she replied, "You really are being silly! Is it such a big deal? Give them to me."

Left with no choice, he returned to his cabin and took out a bunch of wrinkled handkerchiefs. In an apologetic tone, he said, "I can wash them myself! They are very dirty. You'll hate them when you see them."

She grabbed them and shook her head. "How did you ever get so sloppy? Did you use them for wiping apples?"

This incident left him fearful and uneasy for the rest of the day. He thanked her again and again, only to have her call him "Granny."[1] The next day he moved a lounge chair for her and the strain popped two buttons from his shirt. She jokingly called him "Little Fatso" and asked him to change his shirt later and let her sew on the buttons. His protests were in vain. Whatever she said must be. He just had to submit to her benevolent dictatorship.

The whole situation with Miss Su made him feel uneasy. Washing handkerchiefs, mending socks, and sewing on buttons—these were the little chores a wife performed for her husband. On what basis was he enjoying these privileges? Enjoying a husband's privileges meant by definition that he must be her husband, for otherwise why was she willing to perform these duties. Was there anything in what he had said or done that could make her mistake him for her husband? When he started thinking about all that, he shuddered in horror. If the engagement ring were a symbol of the trap one had fallen into, button-sewing was likewise an omen of being tied down. He had better watch out! Fortunately they would be arriving in Shanghai in a day or two. After that there would be no more chance for them to be so close as this, so the dangers would decrease. But during those one or two days, whenever he was with her, he'd either be afraid of suddenly tearing a hole in his sock or worried a button somewhere would come loose. He knew that her services were not to be taken casually; every time she sewed on a button or mended a hole, the moral obligation to propose to her increased by one point.

Sino-Japanese relations were worsening every day, and the news from the ship's radio made everyone nervous. On the afternoon of August the ninth, the ship reached Shanghai. Fortunately the war had not yet erupted. Miss Su gave Fang Hung-chien her address and asked him to come see her. Readily he promised that after going home to see his parents, he would certainly come to Shanghai to visit her. Miss Su's elder brother came on board to meet her, and before Fang could hide, she introduced her brother to him. After sizing him up a moment, her brother warmly shook hands with him and said, "I've heard about you for a long time."

Hell! thought Fang Hung-chien. *An introduction like that may as well be her family representative's official approval of me as candidate for son-in-law!* At the same time he wondered why her brother had said, "I've heard about you for a long time." She must have often mentioned him to her family, a fact which rather pleased him. He then left the Su brother and sister and went to have his luggage inspected. After walking a few steps he turned his head and saw Miss Su's brother smiling at Miss Su, who blushed half in pleasure and half in anger. Thinking they must be talking about him, he felt a little embarrassed.

Soon he ran into his brother Fang P'eng-t'u, who had gone looking for him in second class. Meanwhile Miss Su knew someone in customs, so she breezed through customs without having her luggage inspected. While Hung-chien and his brother were still waiting for inspection, she came over especially to shake hands with him and urged him repeatedly to come see her. When his brother P'eng-t'u asked him who she was, he replied her name was Su.

"Oh, the one with a French doctorate," said his brother. "I read about her in the newspaper."

Fang Hung-chien laughed, scornful of women's vanity. He hurriedly sorted out the luggage that had been inspected, then called a taxi; he was to spend the night at Manager Chou's and return home the next day. P'eng-t'u was a clerk in a bank. Because the war rumors had become stronger in the last few days, he had been kept busy moving the bank's valuables from one place to another and he got off the taxi along the way. However, before he took off, Hung-chien had told him to send a telegram home indicating the train he would be taking the next day. Considering that a needless expense, P'eng-t'u merely made a long distance telephone call instead.

Fang Hung-chien's in-laws were overjoyed at seeing him. He gave his father-in-law a rattan cane with an ivory handle purchased in Ceylon; his mother-in-law, an avid mahjong player and a Buddhist, a French handbag and two Ceylonese Buddhist religious books; and his fifteen-year-old brother-in-law, a German fountain pen. His mother-in-law, then remembering her daughter who had died five years ago, said sadly with tears in her eyes, "If Shu-ying were alive today, how happy she'd be to have you come back from abroad with a Ph.D.!" Choking back emotion, his father-in-law said that his wife was being silly and that she should not say things like that on such a happy day.

Fang's face was grave and sorrow-ridden; inwardly he felt ashamed, for during the last four years he had never once thought of his fiancée. Her large photograph, which his father-in-law gave him as a memento when he went abroad, had been stowed away in the bottom of a trunk, and he didn't know whether its color had faded or not and wanted very much to atone for his sins and make up for his wrongdoings. In any case he would be taking the 11:30 express train the next morning, and he'd have time to go to the International Public Cemetery. Thus he said, "I am thinking of visiting Shu-ying's grave the first thing tomorrow morning."

With that Mr. and Mrs. Chou became even more fond of him. Mrs. Chou showed him his room for the night, which was none other than Shu-ying's old room. On the dressing table were two large photographs placed side by side: one of Shu-ying; the other, an enlarged picture of himself in a doctoral robe. At the sight of them, he felt dazed, as though he had died along with Shu-ying. It was a gloomy, dismal feeling, like that of the departed soul returning after death.

During dinner when Manager Chou learned that Fang still hadn't found a job for the rest of the year, he reassured his son-in-law, "That's no problem. I think you should try to find a job in Shanghai or Nanking. The situation in Peking is very critical, so you mustn't go there. Go home for a couple of weeks, then come back and stay here. I'll put you on the payroll at the bank. You can drop in during the day and in the evening tutor my son while looking for a job. How's that? You needn't take your luggage with you. In this heat, you'll have to wear Chinese clothes when you go home anyway."

Genuinely grateful, Fang thanked his father-in-law. His mother-in-law brought up the subject of marriage, asking him if he had a girl friend. He quickly said no.

His father-in-law said, "I knew you wouldn't. Your father gave you a good upbringing. You're a gentleman and not the type to get mixed up with any free courtship. Free courtship never comes to a good end."

"Hung-chien is such a simple-hearted soul; he won't be able to find a girl for himself. Let me watch out and make a match for him," said his mother-in-law.

"There you go again," said his father-in-law. "As if his own father and mother couldn't take care of him. We mustn't interfere."

"Hung-chien went abroad at our expense," argued his mother-in-law. "He certainly can't push us aside when he gets married. Would you, Hung-chien? Your future wife must certainly be my adopted daughter.[2] And let me make this perfectly clear. Once you have new relatives, don't forget the old ones. I've seen too many such ungrateful people."

Fang could only smile resignedly and say, "Don't worry. I'd never do that," while inwardly to the image of Miss Su, he said, *Hear that? You want to take this woman as your adopted mother?[3] Lucky for you I don't want to marry you.*

As though picking up his inner thoughts, his little brother-in-law asked, "Hung-chien, there's a returned student named Su. Do you know her?"

He was so flabbergasted that he nearly dropped his rice bowl. *American behavioral psychologists can prove that "thoughts are a soundless language,"* he thought. *What are this kid's jug-ears[4] made of? How did he overhear all my silent, private remarks!*

Before he could answer, his father-in-law said, "Oh, yes! I forgot. Hsiaoch'eng, go get that newspaper. When I got your picture I had Chief-secretary Wang write up a news item for the newspaper. I know you don't care to

show off, but this is something to be proud of. You don't have to hide it."
When these remarks were added, Fang paled.

"That's right," said his mother-in-law. "After putting up so much money, why not get a little honor!"

Fang's face had already turned red with shame and indignation. By the time his brother-in-law brought the newspaper and he had glanced at it, the redness had passed from the back of his ears and the nape of his neck down his spine to his very heels. It was an early July Shanghai newspaper, with two small photographs in the educational news column. The plates were as blurry as the picture of a ghost taken at a divining altar. The caption under the first picture read, "Wen-wan, daughter of Political Councilor Su Hung-yeh, is returning home with a Ph.D. from Lyons." The caption under the second picture was twice as long: "Fang Hung-chien, the gifted son-in-law of Chou Hou-ch'ing, a prominent local businessman and general manager of the Golden Touch Bank, recently received his doctorate of philosophy from Carleton University in Germany after pursuing advanced study abroad under Mr. Chou's sponsorship at the Universities of London, Paris, and Berlin in political science, economics, history, and sociology, in which he made excellent grades and ranked at the top of his class. He will be touring several countries before returning home in the fall. It is said that many major organizations are vying for him with job offers."

He wished he could have ripped the paper in two and seized what's-his-name, Chief-secretary Wang, by the throat, just to see how many more of those sickening clichés of resumé writing could still be wrung out of him. No wonder Miss Su's brother had said, "I've heard about you for a long time." No wonder when his brother P'eng-t'u heard him say her name was Su, his brother knew she had a Ph.D. from abroad. And at the time he had even laughed at Miss Su for being so conventional! The item about himself was in such supreme bad taste that the stench was enough to make the reader hold his nose. Besides, Miss Su was a real Ph.D. What was he supposed to be? While on the ship he had never discussed degrees with her, but when she saw this item, she would conclude that he was a deceitful braggart. Whoever heard of a Carleton University in Germany? In his letter to his father-in-law he hinted vaguely that he had received a degree. But because the letter had been posted from Germany, his father had assumed it was a German university. When those who knew about such things heard of it, they'd laugh their heads off! He had become a fraud and would never be able to face people again!

Noticing how her son-in-law kept holding the paper before his face, Mrs. Chou said to her husband with a smile, "See how pleased Hung-chien is. He's read the item several times and still can't put it down."

Their son Hsiao-ch'eng said mischievously, "Hung-chien is getting a close look at that Su Wen-wan. He's thinking of marrying her to take Shu-ying's place."

Fang couldn't help from blurting out, "Don't talk nonsense!" and barely managed to stop himself from flinging the paper to the floor. Though he prevented his anger from showing on his face, his voice was hoarse.

When the Chous saw his unsmiling countenance and his pale face, they were a little bewildered. Then suddenly exchanging glances with each other as though they understood their son-in-law's state of mind, they scolded their son Hsiao-ch'eng in unison, "You deserve a spanking. Who told you to interrupt when adults are talking? Your brother Hung-chien just came back today. Of course, he's unhappy at the thoughts of your sister. Your joking can go too far. From now on, you're to keep your mouth shut. Hung-chien, we know you have a kindly nature. Pay no attention to the child's nonsense."

Fang Hung-chien again blushed crimson. Puffing out his cheeks, Hsiao-ch'eng thought resentfully, *Don't you put on! If you were any good, you'd never get married for the rest of your life. I don't care about your pen. You can just take it back.*

When Fang returned to his room, he discovered Shu-ying's picture was missing from the table. He thought probably his mother-in-law, afraid that he'd be reminded of Shu-ying by the picture and become too grief-stricken, had come especially to remove it.

It had been only six or seven hours since he left the ship, yet everything that had happened there seemed to belong to another world. All his excitement about going ashore having evaporated, he felt small and weak, thinking a job would be hard to find and romance difficult to achieve. As he had pictured it, returning home after study abroad was like water on the ground turning to vapor and rising to the sky, then changing again to rain and returning to the earth, while the whole world looked on and talked about it. His return home from thousands of miles away hadn't raised a single fleck of froth on the sea of his fellow countrymen. Now, thanks to all the blather spewing out of Chief-secretary Wang's pen, he had been blown up into a big soap bubble, bright and colorful while it lasted but gone at a single jab.

Leaning against the window screen he gazed outside. The stars filling the sky were dense and busy. They remained completely still, yet watching them made him think the sky was bustling noisily. The crescent moon seemingly resembled a girl that is not yet full-grown but already able to face the world unabashed. Its light and contours were fresh and sharp, gradually standing out against the night setting. The tiny insects in the garden grass hummed and buzzed, engaged in a nocturnal conversation. From somewhere a pack of frogs croaked hoarsely, their mouths, lips, throats, and tongues working in unison as though the sound waves were being stewed over a fire until they bubbled: "*Brekekey Coky Coky*," like the chorus in Aristophanes' comedies, or of Yale University's cheerleaders. A few fireflies gracefully passed to and fro, not as if flying but as though floating in the dense atmosphere. A dark area beyond the reach of moonlight was suddenly lit up by a firefly's speck of light, like a tiny greenish eye in the summer night. This was the scene familiar to him before going abroad; but now when he saw it, his heart suddenly contracted in pain, his eyes smarted on the verge of tears, and then he understood life's beauty and goodness and the joy of coming home. Such things as the item in the Shanghai newspaper were no more worth troubling over than the hum of insects outside the screen. He sighed comfortably, then yawned broadly.

When he stepped off the train at his home district station, his father, his youngest brother Feng-i, as well as seven or eight uncles, cousins, and friends of his father were all there on the platform to meet him. He was quite dismayed, and greeting each in turn said, "On such a hot day as this, I've really imposed on you too much." And observing how his father's beard had grayed, he said, "Papa, you shouldn't have come!"

His father, Fang Tung-weng, handed him his folding fan, saying, "You people in Western suits won't need this antique, but it's better than fanning yourself with a straw hat." When he saw his son had traveled second class, he praised him. "Such a fine lad! He came back on the boat in second class, so I thought for sure he'd go first class on the train, but still he went second class. He hasn't become haughty and proud and changed his true nature. He already knows how to conduct himself." Everyone echoed his praise.

They had jostled their way out of the ticket gate when suddenly a man wearing blue glasses and a Western suit caught hold of Fang Hung-chien and said, "Hold it, please! We're taking a picture." Bewildered, Hung-chien was just about to ask him what for, when he heard the click of a camera, and the man in blue glasses let go of his arm. There facing Hung-chien was another man pointing a camera at him. Blue Glasses pulled out his card, saying, "Did you return to China yesterday, Dr. Fang?" The man with the camera came up and he too pulled out his card. Hung-chien saw at a glance that they were reporters from two local newspapers in the district.

The reporters both said, "You must be tired from your journey today, Dr. Fang. We'll come to your residence tomorrow morning to learn more from you." They then turned to pay their compliments to Mr. Fang and accompanied the Fangs and others out of the station.

Feng-i said laughingly to Hung-chien, "You've become a celebrity in the district."

Though Hung-chien hated the way the reporters kept calling him "Dr. Fang," which grated on his ears, seeing people so respectfully regard him as a man of importance made him swell up in mind and body and feel truly great.

Now realizing the advantage of living in a small town, he only wished he had put on a better suit and carried a cane. With the big fan waving about in his hand and his face bathed in sweat, the picture they had taken could not possibly turn out very well.

When he got home and saw his mother and two sisters-in-law, he distributed the gifts he had brought back.

His mother said with a smile, "It takes going abroad to learn such thoughtfulness. He even knows how to buy things for women."

His father said, "P'eng-t'u mentioned a Miss Su over the phone yesterday. What's that all about?"

"It's just someone who was on the same boat," said Hung-chien crossly. "There's nothing to it. P'eng-t'u—he likes to talk a lot." He was about to upbraid his brother for spreading rumors, but caught himself when he saw P'eng-t'u's wife was present.

His father said, "We'll have to work on your marriage. Both of your brothers were married long ago and have children. Matchmakers have already suggested several prospects, but you don't need disgusting old creatures like us to make decisions for you. As for Su Hung-yeh, he does have a bit of reputation, and apparently held a few government posts in his day—"

Hung-chien thought to himself, *Why do charming girls all have fathers? She can be hidden away all by herself in one's heart to cuddle, but when her father, uncle, and brother are dragged along with her, the girl stops being so cute and carefree and it's not so easy to conceal her away in your heart anymore. Her charm has been mixed in with the dregs. Some people talk about marriage as though it were homosexual love. It's not the girl they fancy, but her old man or her elder brother they admire.*

"I don't approve," said his mother. "It's no good to marry an official's daughter. She'll want you to wait on her instead of waiting on you. Besides, a daughter-in-law should come from the same village. Girls from other districts are always a bit unsuited in temperament. You won't be happy with her. This Miss Su is a returned student, so she couldn't be very young." The faces of his two sisters-in-law, who had never graduated from high school and who had been born and raised in that district, both bore an expression of agreement.

His father remarked, "She's not only studied abroad but has a Ph.D. I'm afraid Hung-chien couldn't manage her," as though Miss Su were some sort of hard object like a brick which would take the stomach of an ostrich or turkey to digest.

"Our Hung-chien has a Ph.D., too," protested his mother. "He's not inferior to her, so why isn't he a match for her?"

Stroking his beard, his father said with a smile, "Hung-chien, that's something your mother just couldn't understand. Women who've done a little

34

book learning are the hardest of all to handle. The man has to be a step above her, not an equal. That's why a college graduate should marry a high school graduate, and a returned student should marry a college graduate. As for a girl who has studied abroad and received a Ph.D., no one but a foreigner would dare marry her. Otherwise, the man would have to have two doctorates at least. I'm not mistaken about that, am I, Hung-chien? It's the same idea as 'Marry a daughter into a greater family than your own, but take a wife from a lesser family than your own.'"

His mother said, "Of the girls suggested by the go-betweens, the Hsus' second daughter is the best. I'll show you her picture later."

The matter is taking a serious turn, thought Hung-chien. All his life he had detested those modern girls from small towns with outdated fashions and a provincial cosmopolitanism. They were just like the first Western suit made by a Chinese tailor with everything copied from a foreigner's old clothes used as a model down to the two square patches on the sleeves and trouser legs. No need to protest now. In a few days he would make his getaway to Shanghai.

His father also said that there would be many receptions given in his honor, and with the weather so hot, he should be careful not to stuff himself. He must make courtesy calls to all family elders, for which his father would let him take his rickshaw. When the weather cooled off a little, his father would take him to perform the rites at his grandfather's grave. His mother said she would have the tailor come the next day to fit him for a silk gown and pants, and for the time being his brother Feng-i had two gowns and could lend him one to wear when he went visiting.

For dinner that evening, his mother herself prepared fried shredded eel, chicken wings in soy sauce, stewed chicken with melon, and shrimps cooked in wine—all his favorite local dishes. She picked out the best pieces for his bowl, saying, "How terrible it must have been for you, living abroad for four years with nothing to eat!"

Everyone laughed and said she was at it again. If a person ate nothing abroad, how could Hung-chien keep from starving to death?

She said, "I can't understand how those foreign devils stay alive! All that bread and milk. I couldn't eat them if they gave them to me free."

Hung-chien suddenly felt that in this family atmosphere the war was something unbelievable, just as no one can think of ghosts in broad daylight. His parents' hopes and plans left no room for any unforeseen circumstances. Seeing them thus so firmly in control of the future, he too took heart and thought that maybe the situation in Shanghai would be eased, and there would be no outbreak of hostilities. And if there were, they could be brushed aside and ignored.

When Fang Hung-chien rose from bed the next day, the two reporters had already arrived. When he saw the newspaper they had brought along with the item, "Dr. Fang Returns Home," and the full-length picture taken the day before beside it, he felt so ashamed he couldn't bear to look at it. Blue Glasses' hand gripping his right shoulder showed clearly in the picture, added to which, the side view of his own startled expression made it look exactly like a photograph of someone catching a thief.

Blue Glasses, a man of great learning, said he had long heard that Carleton University was the most famous institution of higher learning in the entire world, on a par with Tsing-hua University.[5] The reporter carrying the camera asked Hung-chien what observations he had on the world situation and whether a Sino-Japanese war would break out. Fang Hung-chien finally managed to send them on their way, though not before he had written two inscriptions: "The Mouthpiece of the People,"[6] for Blue Glasses' newspaper, and "The Mirror of Truth,"[7] for Camera's newspaper.

Just as Hung-chien was about to go out visiting, his father's old friend, Principal Lü of the district's provincial high school, came to invite his father, him, and his brother to breakfast the next morning at a teahouse and later asked him to give a lecture to the summer school students on "A Reevaluation of the Influences of Western Civilization on Chinese History." Hung-chien dreaded giving lectures and was going to beg off on some pretext. Then to his chagrin his father readily accepted the invitation for him. He could only stifle a snort. *In such hot weather, to have to put on a long gown and vest, speak rubbish and stink with sweat, if it isn't a living hell, what is it?* he thought. *Educators sure have a different mentality from ordinary people!*

Mr. Fang, hoping his son would win praises for his "scholarly family background," dug out from a chest several volumes of string-bound Chinese texts, such as *Wen-tzu t'ang-chi,*[8] *Kuei-ssu lei-kao,*[9] *Ch'i-ching lou-chi,*[10] and *T'an-ying lu,*[11] instructing Hung-chien to look through them carefully for his lecture material. Hung-chien read all afternoon with deep interest, greatly broadening his knowledge. He learned that the Chinese were square and honest by nature, so they said the sky was square. Foreigners were roundabout and cunning and therefore maintained that the earth was round; the heart of the Chinese was located in the center, while a Westerner's heart tilted slightly to the left. The opium imported from the West was poisonous and should be banned. The nature of the soil in China was mild, therefore opium produced there would not be addictive. Syphilis, that is, smallpox, came from the West, and so on. Such a pity that while these items of information were all very interesting, they could not be used in the lecture. He would have to read something else.[12]

That day after returning home from dinner at his uncle's house with his eyes blurred from drink, he flipped through four or five history textbooks and worked up a draft of over one thousand words with a couple of jokes inserted. This kind of preparation did not tax his brains any, though he did lose some blood to the mosquitoes.

The next morning at the teahouse, after he had the usual soup noodle—the fourth snack-dish to be served, Principal Lü paid the bill and urged Hung-chien to start off. Each hurriedly took his long gown from the waiter and departed. Feng-i stayed with Mr. Fang for a cup of tea.

The school auditorium was already filled with students—over two hundred boys and girls. Accompanied to the stage by Principal Lü, Fang Hung-chien felt his whole body tingle and itch from having so many eyes focused on him, and walking became difficult. After he had seated himself on the stage, the haze before his eyes lifted, and he noticed that those sitting in the front row seemed to be the faculty. At the recording secretary's desk set close to the stage was a girl student, the waves of whose new permanent were so stiff that they seemed to have been painted on. Everyone in the auditorium was whispering back and forth, appraising him with great curiosity. He silently enjoined his cheeks, *Don't blush! You mustn't turn red!* He regretted having removed his sunglasses when he entered. With two pieces of black glass in front of his eyes, it would have seemed as though he too were hidden in heavy darkness, and he would have felt less embarrassed.

Principal Lü was already delivering his introduction. Hung-chien hastily reached into the pocket of his gown to feel around for his lecture notes only to find they were missing. He broke out in a nervous sweat. *Oh, no!* he thought. *How could I have lost something so important? When I left the house I distinctly remember putting them into the pocket of my gown.* Except for a few opening sentences, he, in his fright, had forgotten the rest of his speech. He searched his memory for all he was worth, but it was like trying to hold water in a sieve. Once he grew panicky, he couldn't focus his attention. His threads of thought would get knotted up, then come loose. A few vague facts remained, but it was like waiting for a person in a busy place. You catch a glimpse of someone in the crowd who looks like him, only to find he's gone when you go over to get him. Just as his mind was playing "hide-and-seek," Principal Lü bowed and asked him to speak. This was followed by a round of applause. He had just stood up when he noticed Feng-i rushing into the auditorium, breathless. Seeing that the lecture had already begun, Feng-i found an empty seat and sat down in despair. Hung-chien suddenly realized that as he was leaving the teahouse, he had put on Feng-i's gown by mistake. Both gowns belonged to Feng-i and were of identical color and material. Such being the case, he'd just have to screw up his courage, brace himself, and spout some nonsense.

When the applause had died down, Fang Hung-chien forced a smile and began, "Principal Lü, members of the faculty, and students: Though your applause was well-meaning, it is actually quite unjustified. Applause indicates satisfaction with the speech. Now before I have even begun, you have already applauded with satisfaction. Why should I have to go on? You should all listen to the lecture first, then clap a few times as you wish, letting me leave the stage with dignity. Now that you've clapped at the start, if my lecture can't live up to such enthusiastic applause, it'll put me in the embarrassing position of having been paid without being able to deliver the goods."

The audience roared with laughter. The recording secretary was also smiling as her pen flew across the paper. Fang Hung-chien hesitated. What should he say next? He still remembered a few of the points and views put forth in the string-bound texts, but as for the history textbooks he had skimmed through after dinner, there wasn't even a trace left. *Those confounded textbooks! It's amazing that I could have learned all that stuff for examinations when I was a student! Ah, now I have it! At least it's better than nothing.* "As for the influence of Western civilization on Chinese history, you can find that in any history textbook. There's no need for me to repeat it. You all know that the first time China officially came in contact with European thought was in the middle of the Ming dynasty [1368–1644]. For this reason Catholics always refer to this period as the Chinese Renaissance. Actually, the science brought by the Catholic priests of the Ming dynasty is now out of date, while the religion they brought has never been up to date. In the last several hundred years of overseas communication, there are only two items from the West which have been lasting in Chinese society as a whole. One is opium, and the other is syphilis. These are what the Ming dynasty assimilated of Western civilization."

Most of the audience laughed, a small number gasped in astonishment, and a few of the teachers scowled. The recording-secretary's face flushed crimson, and her pen stopped, as if by hearing Fang Hung-chien's last remark her virgin ears had lost their chastity in front of the audience. Principal Lü uttered a warning cough behind Hung-chien. By this time Fang Hung-chien was just like a man getting out of bed on a cold winter morning. Having managed after the greatest of efforts to hop from the covers, he just has to bear the cold long enough to dress. There was no backing out now.

"Opium was originally called 'foreign tobacco'—" Hung-chien noticed one of the teachers, who seemed to be an old instructor of Chinese, fanning himself and shaking his head, and he quickly added, " 'Foreign' refers, of course, to the 'Western Ocean' of 'Cheng Ho's Voyages to the Western Ocean,'[13] for according to the *Ta-Ming hui-tien*,[14] opium was an article of tribute from Siam and Java. But in the earliest literary work in Europe, Homer's *Odyssey*"—the old man's bald pate seemed to be overwhelmed by that last foreign word—"there appears what is said to be this very thing. As for syphilis"—Principal Lü coughed several times in succession—"it is without doubt an imported commodity from the West. Schopenhauer has said that syphilitic sores were the most distinctive feature of modern European civilization. If you have not had the opportunity to read the original, you can very easily read Hsü Chih-mo's[15] translation of the French novel *Candide* to learn something about the origins of syphilis. The disease was brought by Westerners after the Cheng-te period of the Ming dynasty.[16] The ill effects of these two things were of course unlimited, but, nonetheless, one cannot dismiss them out of hand. Opium inspired many works of literature. Whereas ancient poets sought inspiration from wine, modern European and American poets all find inspiration in opium. Syphilis transmits idiocy, insanity, and deformity by heredity, but it is also said that it is capable of stimulating genius. For example—"

At this point Principal Lü coughed himself hoarse. When Hung-chien had finished speaking, and while the clapping in the audience was still going strong, Principal Lü, with a long face and a hoarse voice, said a few words of thanks: "Today we have had the honor of hearing Dr. Fang tell us several novel views. We have found it highly interesting. Dr. Fang is the son of an old friend of mine. I watched him grow up and I know how much he enjoys telling jokes. It is very hot today, so he has intentionally made his lecture humorous. I hope in the future we will have the opportunity to hear his earnest and solemn discourse. But I'd like to tell Dr. Fang that our school library is filled with the spirit of the New Life Movement.[17] It certainly has no French novels—" With this he struck the air with his hand.

Hung-chien was too embarrassed even to look at the audience.

Before the day was over many people had learned that Fang's son, just returned from study abroad, publicly advocated smoking opium and visiting brothels. When this came to Mr. Fang's ears, he did not realize it was the result of his having instructed his son to look through the string-bound texts. Though he did not approve of what his son said, he could not very well get angry over it. The fighting at Wusung on August 13, 1937,[18] occurred soon afterwards and Fang Hung-chien's prank was mentioned no more. Those interested in making him their son-in-law, however, could not forget his lecture, and they assumed he had led a life of profligacy while abroad. If they went to the Matchmaker's Temple at West Lake to draw lots before the idols, they would probably end up with tally number four, which read, "That this man should have this disease. . . ."[19] Such a young man would never do as a son-in-law. One after another they deferred discussion of marriage on the grounds that the times were unstable and asked the Fangs for the return of their daughters' pictures and horoscopes. Extremely disheartened by it all, Mrs. Fang could not get the Hsüs' second daughter off her mind. Hung-chien, however, was quite unperturbed.

Now that fighting had broken out, Mr. Fang, a prominent squire in the village, was in charge of local security matters. Remembering the "January

28th Incident"[20] when the district had not suffered enemy bombing, the inhabitants of the district assumed that this too was nothing important and were not particularly alarmed.

After he had been home for a week, Fang Hung-chien felt as if he had not left home at all; his four years abroad were like water running over a lotus leaf leaving no trace behind. The people he met after his return were the same ones of four years ago, still doing and saying what they had done and said four years ago. There was not even one person among all his acquaintances who had died off. Only his wet nurse, who always used to say she would wait till he got married and had a son, then come look after him, was now ill and bedridden. As far as he was concerned, he had not missed the village during those four years at all. Not a single tear or sigh could the village fetch from the wandering son upon his return.

On the sixth day after the outbreak of the war, when Japanese planes bombed for the first time and destroyed the train station, everyone at last realized that the war had really reached them and many fled with their families to the countryside. Later, the planes kept coming in much the same manner as the peerless beauty whose "one glance could conquer a city and whose second glance could vanquish an empire."[21]

Mr. Chou wired Hung-chien urging him to come to Shanghai as soon as possible before all communications were suspended and he himself was stranded at home. Feeling that under the circumstances his son should leave home and look for job possibilities, Mr. Fang let him go.

What happened during the next four months, from the retreat from Shanghai to the fall of Nanking, should be recorded in history, as Friedrich von Logau[22] put it, with a bayonet dipped in the ink of fresh blood upon the paper made from the skin of the enemy. Despondently, Fang Hung-chien read dozens of newspapers and listened to just as many radio broadcasts daily. Exhausted hope, as though sifting sand for gold, tried to find some crack in the news in which to revive itself. His brother P'eng-t'u and he guessed that their house had already been destroyed and didn't know what had happened to their family.

At the end of the lunar year, they finally heard some news of them. Mr. Fang's friends and relatives in Shanghai contributed money to help them get out and rented a house for them in the foreign concessions. The family reunited amidst much weeping. Mr. Fang and Feng-i were clamoring to buy shoes and socks. While en route in a small boat, they met two deserting soldiers. They took Mr. Fang's wallet; and as they were about to make off, they forced both father and son to take off their wool socks and cotton shoes and exchange them for their own stinking cotton socks and tattered canvas shoes. The whole Fang family had traveled on empty-handed. Only a sum of two or three thousand dollars in paper currency sewn in Mrs. Fang's padded cotton jacket had gone undetected by the two soldiers. The businessmen living in Shanghai who were from the same village, having long respected Mr. Fang's reputation, gave him a considerable sum of money so that once again he was able to maintain a household.

Seeing how crowded it was in the small house, Hung-chien decided to stay on at the Chous, dropping in on his parents every second or third day to pay his respects. Every time he went home he heard them talk about all the frightening and amusing experiences they had had during their escape. Their narrative and descriptive skills seemed to improve with each retelling, while Hung-chien's attention and sympathy decreased slightly after each hearing. Since Mr. Fang had rejected the offers of Japanese collaborators in his home district, he could no longer return home; yet the government had given him no recognition, making him feel that, while he loved his country, his country did not love him. He felt the same resentment as a young widow who, despite maintaining a chaste widowhood, finds no favor with her parents-in-law. Hung-chien was very bored at the Golden Touch Bank, and since there were few opportunities in Shanghai, he considered going into the unoccupied interior[23] as soon as he had a chance.

The lunar New Year arrived. The well-to-do in the concessions of Shanghai felt that they had suffered enough alarm for their country. Since the country hadn't fallen, they found no need to play the part of survivors, and once again started up the usual bustle and activities of the New Year.

One day Mrs. Chou told Hung-chien that someone was making a match for him with the daughter of a Mr. Chang with whom Hung-chien and Manager Chou had once sat at the same table at a social gathering. According to Mrs. Chou, the Changs had asked for Hung-chien's horoscope and requested a fortuneteller to match it with Miss Chang's. The forecast for the couple was "A union made in heaven, full of great fortune and prosperity."

Hung-chien asked with a smile, "You mean in a cosmopolitan place like Shanghai, people still ask fortunetellers to determine a marriage?"

Mrs. Chou replied that one could not but believe in fate, and since Mr. Chang had invited him over for dinner, it wouldn't hurt to meet his daughter. Hung-chien, who held to some of the principles typical of the prewar scholar class,[24] remembering that this Mr. Chang was a comprador in an American firm, wanted nothing to do with such a vulgarian. But then he reflected, hadn't he himself, from the time he went abroad until now, been using a philistine's money?[25] At any rate one visit could do no harm. Whether he decided to get married or not depended entirely on whether or not he took a liking to the girl. No one could force him. So he agreed to go for dinner.

Mr. Chang was from the coastal area of Chekiang. His given name was Chi-min, but he preferred people to call him *Jimmy*.[26] For over twenty years he had worked for an American firm, the Stars and Stripes Company, rising from a clerk to become a comprador, and he had amassed a sizable fortune. He had but one daughter and had not spared any expense in her upbringing. She had acquired all the foreign skills and ways that the church schools could teach or instill, and all the foreign hairstyles and makeup that beauty salons and hairdressers could create. She was just eighteen and had not yet graduated from high school, but Mr. and Mrs. Chang, who held to the traditional view of their hometown, thought that a girl was old by the time she was twenty, and if she passed this age still unwed, she could only be put in a museum of old relics to be viewed with nostalgia.

Mrs. Chang was very strict in her choice of a son-in-law, and though many people had proposed matches, none of them had made it. One of these was the son of a well-to-do businessman and a returned student to boot. Mrs. Chang was favorably impressed with him and held high hopes for a marriage, but after one dinner, she never mentioned the matter again. During the meal they began talking about the fact that because of the war the concessions were under a blockade and vegetables were hard to get. Mrs. Chang turned to the son of the well-to-do businessman and said, "With so many people in your family, the daily cost for food must be quite high, I should think."

He replied that he was not quite sure, but thought it was so much money per day.

Mrs. Chang exclaimed, "Then your cook must be both honest and re-sourceful. Our family isn't half as large as yours, yet our cook spends the same amount every day!"

He was quite pleased at hearing this, but after dinner was over and he had left, Mrs. Chang said, "That family lives on peanuts! They spend so little on food a day! Since my daughter is used to comfort, she couldn't take such hardship!" The question of marriage was dropped at this point.

After a few deliberations, the husband and wife decided that they could never rest easy about marrying their precious daughter into another family. It would be far better to adopt a son-in-law into their own.[27] The day Mr. Chang met Hung-chien at the party he mentioned him later at home, saying he found him well qualified: the family background and qualifications were quite good. Furthermore, since he was now already living at the home of his nominal father-in-law without ever having actually become his son-in-law, taking him into the family would be as easy as turning the palm. What made it even better was that since the Fangs had lost so much in the war, they couldn't put on any of the presumptuous airs of a country squire, and the son-in-law would live submissively at the Changs. In the end, Mrs. Chang wanted Hung-chien to dine with them, so she could take a look at him.

Since Mr. Chang had invited him to come early for a chat, Fang Hung-chien went over in the afternoon right after work at the bank. Along the way he passed a foreign fur goods store where he saw in the window a Western-style fur overcoat. It was on sale at only $400 during New Year's. He had always wanted an overcoat like that but had never dared buy one when he was studying abroad. In London, for instance, a man who wore such an overcoat but did not own a private car, unless he looked like a Jewish usurer or a Negro boxer, would be suspected of being a circus performer, or else a pimp who ran a brothel. It was only in Vienna that fur coats were commonly worn, and ready-made fur linings were sold to travelers to line their coats. After returning to China, he had seen many people wearing fur, and now he was even more stirred by the display in the window. After some calculations, however, he could only heave a sigh. His $100 salary at the bank was already considered handsome and ample spending money, and since his father-in-law was providing both room and board and he didn't have to pay a cent, how could he ask Mr. Chou for money to buy a luxury item? He had dutifully presented forty of the sixty-odd pounds left after his return home to his father to buy furniture. The rest had been converted into a little over $400. It would hardly do to sink all his money at once into that coat. In a time of national austerity, one had to economize in everything, and since the weather would be warming up soon, he might as well forget it.

When he arrived at the Changs, Mr. Chang gave him a hearty welcome, "*Hello, Dr. Fang!* Haven't seen you for a long time!"

Mr. Chang was used to dealing with foreigners and his speech had a special characteristic—perhaps in a foreign firm, the YMCA, the Rotary Club, or other such places, this was nothing unusual—he liked to sprinkle his Chinese with meaningless English expressions. It wasn't that he had new ideas, which were difficult to express in Chinese and required the use of English. The English words inlaid in his speech could not thus be compared with the gold teeth inlaid in one's mouth, since gold teeth are not only decorative but functional as well. A better comparison would be with the bits of meat stuck between the teeth—they show that one has had a good meal but are otherwise useless. He imitated the American accent down to the slightest inflection, though maybe the nasal sound was a little overdone, sounding more like a Chinese with a cold and a stuffy nose, rather than an American speaking. The way he said "*Very well*" sounded just like a dog growling—"*Vurry wul.*" A pity the Romans never had a chance to hear it, for otherwise the Latin poet Persius would not have been the only one to say that "r" was a nasal in the dog's alphabet (*sonat hic de nare canina litera*).

As Mr. Chang shook hands with Hung-chien, he asked him if he had to *go downtown* every day. When the pleasantries were over, Hung-chien noticed a glass cupboard filled with bowls, jars, and plates and asked, "Do you collect porcelain, Mr. Chang?"

"*Sure! Have a look-see.*" Mr. Chang opened the cupboard and invited Hung-chien to inspect them. Hung-chien picked up a few pieces and noticed they were all marked with such reign periods as "Ch'eng-hua," "Hsüan-te," or "K'ang-hsi."[28] Unable to tell whether they were genuine or fake, he merely said, "These must be quite valuable."

"*Sure!* Worth quite a lot of money, *plenty of dough.* Besides, these things aren't like calligraphy or paintings. If you buy calligraphy or paintings which turn out to be fakes, they aren't worth a cent. They just amount to *wastepaper.* If the porcelain is fake, at least it can hold food. Sometimes I invite foreign *friends* over for dinner and use this big K'ang-hsi 'underglaze-blue-and-colored ware' plate for a *salad dish.* They all think the ancient colors and odor make the food taste a little *old time.*"

Fang Hung-chien said, "I'm sure you have a good eye. You wouldn't ever buy a fake."

Mr. Chang laughed heartily and said, "I don't know anything about period designs. I'm too busy to have time to sit down and study it. But I have a *hunch* when I see something, and a sudden—*what d'you call?*—inspiration comes to me. Then I buy it and it turns out to be quite *OK.* Those antique dealers all respect me. I always say to them, 'Don't try to *fool* me with fakes. *Oh yeah,* Mr. Chang here is no *sucker.* Don't think you can cheat me!' " He closed the cupboard and said, "Oh, *headache,*" then pressed an electric bell to summon the servant.

Puzzled, Hung-chien asked quickly, "Aren't you feeling well, Mr. Chang?"

Mr. Chang looked at Hung-chien in astonishment and said, "Who's not feeling well? You? Me? Why, I feel fine!"

"Didn't you say you had a headache?" asked Hung-chien.

Mr. Chang roared with laughter. At the same time he instructed the maid who entered, "Go and tell my wife and daughter the guest is here. Ask them to come out. *Make it snappy!*" At this he snapped his fingers. Turning to Hung-chien, he said with a laugh, " '*Headache*' is an American expression for 'wife,' not 'pain in head!' I guess you haven't been to the *States!*"

Just as Fang Hung-chien was feeling ashamed of his ignorance, Mrs. Chang and Miss Chang came out. Mr. Chang introduced them to Hung-chien. Mrs. Chang was a portly woman of forty or more with the dainty little foreign name of "Tessie." Miss Chang was a tall girl of eighteen with a fresh complexion, trim-fitting clothes, and a figure which promised to be just as ample as the capital in her father's foreign company. Hung-chien did not quite catch her name. It sounded like *Wo-Ni-Ta* (I-You-He). He guessed that it was either "*Anita*" or "*Juanita.*" Her parents called her "*Nita*" for short. Mrs. Chang spoke Shanghainese better than her husband, but her native accent often showed through like an undersized jacket that doesn't cover up the gown underneath. Mrs. Chang was a Buddhist and said that she recited the "Goddess of Mercy Chant"[29] ten times a day to beg the Bodhissattva to protect China's army in its fight for victory. This chant, she said, was very efficacious. When the fighting in Shanghai was at its worst, Mr. Chang had gone to the export company to work while she stayed at home reciting incantations and, sure enough, Mr. Chang had come through without being hit by any stray bullets.

Hung-chien thought to himself, Mrs. Chang enjoys the latest gadgets of Western science and yet she still holds to such beliefs, sitting in the living room heated by hot water pipes to recite Buddhist chants. Apparently "Western learning for practical application; Chinese learning as a base" was not so hard to implement after all.

Miss Chang and Hung-chien had little to talk about, so he could only ask her which movies she liked best. Two guests arrived next, both of whom were Mr. Chang's sworn brothers.[30] One of them, Ch'en Shih-p'ing, held a high position in the Euro-American Tobacco Company. Everyone called him Z. B., like the abbreviation in German for the words, "for example," *zum Beispiel*. The other, Ting Na-sheng, whose foreign name was not *Tennyson*, the poet, but *Nelson*, the admiral, worked in a British steamship company. Mrs. Chang said that since there were enough people for a game of mahjong, why not play eight rounds[31] before dinner? Fang Hung-chien was quite an amateur at gambling, and since he had little money with him, didn't care to join in. He would have preferred to chat with Miss Chang, but unable to withstand Mrs. Chang's repeated prodding, he finally agreed to play. Contrary to his expectations, by the end of the fourth round, he alone had won over a hundred dollars. He suddenly thought that if his luck held out, there was hope for the fur coat yet. By this time he had completely forgotten the French superstition he had told Mr. Sun on the boat. All he wanted was to win money. At the end of the eighth round, Fang Hung-chien had won nearly three hundred dollars. The three other players, Mrs. Chang, "For Example," and "Admiral Nelson," all stood up and got ready to eat without paying a cent or mentioning a word about paying. Hung-chien reminded them with the remark, "How lucky I've been today. I've never won so much money before."

As though waking from a dream, Mrs. Chang said, "Why, how stupid of us! We haven't settled with Mr. Fang yet. Mr. Ch'en, Mr. Ting, let me pay him, and we can settle it among ourselves later on." She then opened her purse and handed the notes over to Hung-chien, counting them out one by one.

They had Western food. "Admiral Nelson," who was a Christian, rolled his eyes up toward the ceiling and thanked God for bestowing the food before he sat down. Because he had won so much money, Fang Hung-chien was full of talk and banter. After the meal everyone sat about smoking and drinking coffee. He noticed a little bookcase next to the sofa and supposed it contained Miss Chang's reading material. Besides a big stack of *West Wind* and *Reader's Digest* in the original, there was an unannotated, small-type edition

45

of *The Complete Works of Shakespeare* in the original, the Bible, *Interior Decorating*, a reprint of *The Biography of Madame Curie*, *Teach Yourself Photography*, *My Country and My People* [by Lin Yutang], and other immortal classics, as well as an anthology of a dozen screen plays, one of which, needless to say, was *Gone with the Wind*.

There was one small blue volume with the title in gilt letters on the spine: *How to Gain a Husband and Keep Him*. Hung-chien could not resist taking it out and skimming through it. He came across a paragraph which read: "You must be sweet and gentle to the man in order to leave a good impression deep in his heart. Girls, never forget always to have a bright smile on your face." As he read this, the smile transferred itself from the book to his own face. When he looked again at the cover, he noticed the author was a woman and wondered if she were married. She should have written "Mrs. So-and-So," then the book would have obviously been the voice of experience. At this thought his smile broadened. Raising his head, he suddenly noticed Miss Chang's gaze on him and hastily replaced the book and wiped the smile from his face.

"For Example" asked Miss Chang to play the piano, and they all echoed the request in unison. When Miss Chang had finished playing, in order to rectify the misunderstanding which had caused his smile, Hung-chien was first to say "Wonderful," and called for an encore. He stayed for a while longer, then said goodbye. Halfway home in the rickshaw, he remembered the title of the book and burst out laughing. *Husbands are women's careers. Not having a husband is like being unemployed, so she has to hold tightly to her "rice bowl."*[32] *Well, I don't happen to want any woman to take me as her "rice bowl" after reading that book. I'd rather have them scorn me and call me a "rice bucket."*[33] *Miss Wo-Ni-Ta, we just weren't meant to "raise the bowl to the eyebrows."*[34] *I hope some other lucky guy falls in love with you.* At this thought Hung-chien stamped his foot and laughed loudly. Pretending the moon in the sky was Miss Chang, he waved goodbye to her. Suspecting he was drunk, the rickshaw puller turned his head and asked him to keep still, for it was hard to pull the rickshaw.

After all the guests had left, Mrs. Chang said, "That Fang fellow isn't suitable. He's too small-minded and values money too highly. He showed his true colors the moment I tested him. He acted as if he were afraid we weren't going to pay him off. Isn't that funny?"

Mr. Chang said, "German goods don't measure up to American ones. Some doctor! He's supposed to have studied in England, but he didn't even understand a lot of the English I spoke. After the first World War, Germany fell behind. All the latest designs of cars, airplanes, typewriters, and cameras are American made. I don't care for returned students from Europe."

"Nita, what do you think of that Fang fellow?" asked Mrs. Chang.

Miss Chang, who could not forgive Fang Hung-chien for his smile while reading the book, replied simply, "He's obnoxious! Did you see the way he ate? Does he look like someone who's ever been abroad! When he drank his soup, he dipped his bread in it! And when he ate the roast chicken, instead of using a fork and knife, he picked a leg up with his fingers! I saw it all with my own eyes. Huh! What kind of manners is that? If *Miss Prym*, our etiquette teacher, ever saw that, she'd certainly call him a *piggy-wiggy!*"

When the affair of marriage with the Changs came to naught, Mrs. Chou was greatly disappointed. But when Fang Hung-chien was young he was brought up on the *Romance of the Three Kingdoms*, the *Tale of the Marshes*, *Monkey*,[35] and other such children's literature that were not in line with basic educational principles for children. He was born too soon to have had the good fortune to take up such fine books as *Snow White* and *Pinocchio*. He remembered the famous saying from the *Romance of the Three Kingdoms*, "A wife is like a suit of clothes," and of course clothes also meant the same as wife. He now had himself a new fur coat. The loss of a wife or two wasn't about to worry him.

3

PERHAPS BECAUSE so many people had died in the war, the unspent life energy of all those who had died in vain merged into the vital force of spring. The weather that spring was especially beautiful. Stirred by the invigorating spring, men, like infants cutting their teeth, somehow itched painfully from the budding of new life. A boomtown, Shanghai had no scenic spots in which spring might rest its feet. In the parks and lawns the grass and trees were like the wild beasts confined in iron cages at the zoo—restricted and lonely; there simply was no place for spring to release its full splendor. Lodged only in the minds and bodies of men, spring brought an upsurge of illnesses and infections, adulteries, drunken brawlings, and pregnancies. Since the wartime population needed replenishment, pregnancies were a good sign. But according to Mrs. Chou, children born in that year were really the souls of all those who had died prematurely in the war hurrying to be reborn so that they could live out the allotted years of their lives. Consequently, she believed, they wouldn't live long.

For the last few days, Fang Hung-chien had been drowsy during the day but wide awake at night. When he woke up at dawn and heard the birds chirping in the trees outside his window, for no reason at all he felt happy, full of inexplicable expectations. Also his heart seemed to have become lighter, giddy, floating, but it was an empty joy. Like the balloon released by a child, it would rise no more than a few feet and then burst into nothing, leaving only an indefinable sense of loss and disappointment. He was restless and eager for action and yet lethargic. He was like willow catkins floating about in the spring breeze, too light and too powerless to fly far. He felt this indecisive and confused state of mind was exactly like the mood evoked in the spring-time poetry[1] describing the longings of maidens secluded in their chambers.

48

Since women themselves no longer bothered with such springtime senti-ments and he, a man, was still afflicted with such thoughts, he felt ridiculous. A woman like Miss Pao, for instance, would never have time for springtime longing, but Miss Su? It would be hard to tell, for she seemed to be the model of the traditional beauty of sentiments. He had promised to visit her, and why shouldn't he visit her once? Although he knew the visit might lead to com-plications, he also realized that life was too terribly boring and there were so few ready-made girl friends. He was like an insomniac disregarding the ill effects of sleeping pills and thinking only of the immediate relief.

When Fang Hung-chien arrived at the Sus' residence, he imagined Miss Su dashing into the living room, full of laughter and noise, and chiding him for not having come sooner. Instead, her doorman served him tea, informing him, "Miss Su will be right out."

In the Sus' garden, the peach, the pear, and the lilac trees were in full bloom. It was only the end of February by the lunar calendar, but the flowers were already in bloom. He wondered what would be left of the spring scene by the time of the Ch'ing Ming Festival in early April. One of the windows in the living room was open, and the fragrance of flowers baked by the sun was thick enough to stuff one's nose and warm enough to make one drowsy. The fragrance of flowers resembles the odor of garlic and onions: both are scents from plants but smell meaty and not much different from the thick smell of human hair at a summer dance. Among the wall scrolls was a poem by Huang Shan-ku,[2] calligraphed by Shen Tzu-p'ei. The first line read, "Flower scent overcomes man, making him wish to break Zen."[3] He was amused by the line, thinking that if a monk had been affected by the fragrance outside the window, the monk had already violated his principle of total concentra-tion and this transgression was similar to a monk's eating meat. After looking at the scrolls and antiques in the room for more than three times, he was struck by the thought that the foot stroke of Shen Tzu-p'ei's character for "man" closely resembled the tiny bound foot of an elderly Peking maidserv-ant. The top part of the leg character was stiff and bulky while the bottom part suddenly came to a tiny point and ended. Some foot that was!

Just then Miss Su appeared. Her faint smile was like an overcast sky on a cold dreary day. As she shook his hand, she said, "I haven't seen you for a long time, Mr. Fang. What brought you here today?"

She shook my hand with such warmth at our parting last year but now grasping her hand is like clutching a cold-blooded shark fin. We were on such good terms when we parted, so why this reserve today? Hung-chien won-dered. Like a student who has crammed for an examination but finds he has forgotten everything after a night's sleep, Hung-chien could only lie, saying that he hadn't been in town for more than a few days and had made a point of coming to see her. Miss Su courteously thanked him for "honoring her with a visit," and asked him where he was "making his mark." He stammered that he had not yet found a job, was thinking of going to the interior, and for the time being was helping out at a bank run by a relative.

Eyeing him, she asked, "Isn't the bank run by your father-in-law? Mr. Fang, you are really something! When was the wedding? Here I am, an old classmate from years back, and yet you kept your wedding all to yourself and didn't breathe a word about it. You were coming home to get married after you got your Ph.D., weren't you? That's really a case of having your name on the golden rolls[4] and figured candles in the nuptial chamber—what they call double happiness. I haven't had the honor of meeting Mrs. Fang."

Fang Hung-chien felt so ashamed that he wished he could hide somewhere. Remembering the news item in the Shanghai paper, he said quickly that she must have obtained that information from a newspaper. Roundly cursing the paper, he briefly recounted, in the manner of the *Spring and Autumn Chronicles*,[5] the full story behind his having an adoptive father-in-law and a fake doctorate. By purchasing a fake degree he was thumbing his nose at the world, he said; by accepting an adoptive relative, he was conforming to tradition, he argued. Then he added, "When I saw that item in the paper, first I thought of you, of how you would ridicule and despise me. I even got into a big row with my so-called father-in-law about the whole news release."

Her expression gradually changing, Miss Su said, "What for? Why naturally all those insufferable, vulgar businessmen expect a return on their money. You can't expect them to understand that true learning doesn't depend on a degree. Why quarrel with him? After all, this Mr. Chou is your elder and he does treat you well enough. He has the right to put the item in the paper. Anyway, who's going to notice it? Those who do will forget it the moment they turn their backs. You thumb your nose at the big things, yet you take the trivial things so seriously. This contradiction is hilarious!"

Fang Hung-chien sincerely admired Miss Su for her eloquence. He replied, "When you put it that way, I don't feel so guilty anymore. I should have come and told you everything earlier. You are so understanding! What you said about my getting hung up on trivialities is especially perceptive. The world's major issues can always be dealt with in one way or another; it's the minor issues that can't be treated carelessly. Take a corrupt official, for instance. He would accept millions in bribes but would never steal a man's wallet. I suppose I am not consistent enough in my cynicism."

Miss Su felt like saying, *That's not true. He doesn't steal the wallet because it isn't worth stealing. If there were millions in the wallet and stealing it were as safe as taking bribes, he'd steal it too.* But she kept her thoughts to herself, eyeing Hung-chien momentarily; then staring down at the designs on the rug, she said, "It's a good thing that cynicism of yours doesn't apply to everything. Otherwise your friends would always be afraid that while you

50

were humoring them on the outside, you were laughing at them inwardly."

Hung-chien quickly went out of his way to assure her how much he valued friendship. In their conversation, she revealed that her father had already gone to Szechwan with the government,[6] that her brother had gone to work in Hong Kong, that her mother, her sister-in-law, and she herself were the only ones at home in Shanghai, and that she was thinking of going to the interior. Fang Hung-chien said perhaps they could again be travel companions going to the interior. Then she mentioned she had a cousin who had finished her first two years of college at their alma mater in Peking, and that since the university had moved to the interior because of the war, her cousin had quit school and stayed home for six months but was planning to resume her study again. It so happened that the cousin was at the Sus' that day, so Miss Su went in to get her to meet Hung-chien. They all could become travel companions in the future.

Miss Su led out a cute little girl of about twenty and introduced her to Fang, "This is my cousin, T'ang Hsiao-fu." On Miss T'ang's charming, well-proportioned, round face were two shallow dimples; one look at her fresh and natural complexion, which most girls would have had to spend time and money to imitate, was enough to make one drool and forget his thirst, as though her skin were a piece of delicious fruit. Not especially large, her eyes were lively and gentle, making the big eyes of many women seem like the big talk of politicians—big and useless. A classics scholar, upon seeing her lovely teeth when she smiled, might wonder why both Chinese and Western traditional and modern poets would want to turn into the pin in a woman's hair, the belt around her waist, the mat on which she slept, or even the shoes and socks, that she wore, and not think of transforming themselves into her toothbrush. Her hair unwaved, her eyebrows unplucked, and her lips unadorned by lipstick, she appeared to allow nature to take its own course with regard to her looks and had no wish to amend it in any way. In short, she was one of those rarities of modern civilized society—a genuine girl. Many city girls who put on all the precocious airs cannot be considered as girls; then there are just as many others who are confused, silly, and sexless, and they too don't deserve to be called women. Fang Hung-chien immediately wanted to impress her, while she called him "elder senior schoolmate," a respectful term of address.

"That won't do," he protested. "When you call me 'senior,' I feel like a prehistoric relic. Why do you add the word 'elder'? It's my misfortune to have been born too early. Not being lucky enough to go to school at the same time you did is something I regret. If you call me 'senior' again, you're just deliberately reminding me that I'm old and out of date. That's too cruel."

Miss T'ang said, "Mr. Fang, you are too concerned with insignificant details. Forgive me. I'll first retract the word 'elder.' "

51

At the same time Miss Su said lightheartedly, "Aren't you ashamed? Do you still want us to call you Little Fang like they did on the boat? Hsiao-fu, ignore him. If he can't accept the honor, then simply don't call him anything."

Fang Hung-chien noticed that the trace of a smile lingered on Miss T'ang's face when she was not smiling, like the last few notes that float in the air after the music has ceased. Many women can smile just as sweetly, but their smile is only facial muscle calisthenics, as if a drill master were barking the order, "One!" and suddenly the whole face would be wreathed in smiles, then "Two!" and just as suddenly the smile would vanish, leaving a face as blank as the screen in a movie theater before the movie starts.

Trying to make conversation, he asked what Miss T'ang's major at college was. Miss Su, on the other hand, wouldn't let Miss T'ang tell and insisted that he guess.

Fang Hung-chien said Miss T'ang's major was literature, which was wrong; he then said it was education, which was also wrong. When he found chemistry and physics were both wrong, he resorted to one of Chang Chi-min's English expressions: "*Search me!* Don't tell me it's mathematics. That would be too much!"

Miss T'ang then told him. It was actually quite a common subject—political science.

Miss Su said, "It's still too much. In the future she will be our ruler, a lady official."

Fang Hung-chien said, "Women are natural political animals. Political tactics, such as saying yes and meaning no, retreating in order to advance, are what they know from birth. For a woman to study political science is really developing the innate through the acquired; it is as superfluous as adding flowers to embroidery. In Europe when I attended Professor Ernest Peygmann's lectures, he said men have the capacity for creative thought and women for social activity. Thus, men's work in society should be turned over to women, so that men can seclude themselves at home to think at leisure, invent new science, and produce new art. I think that makes a lot of sense. Women don't need to study politics, but if present-day politicians want to succeed, they should all imitate women. In politics roles are being reversed."

Miss Su said, "You're just purposely spouting weird ideas. You like that sort of thing."

Fang Hung-chien said, "Miss T'ang, your cousin really doesn't appreciate the respect I'm showing her. I speak of women participating in government, yet she turns around and laughs at me for purposely spouting weird ideas! You be the judge as to who's right. As the old saying goes, 'The house must first be put in order before the kingdom can be ruled and the country pacified.' How many men, may I ask, can take care of domestic chores? They rely on women to manage the house, yet they go around boasting about how great men will run the country and bring peace. If they can't be bothered with trivial little domestic chores, then it's just like building a house by first positioning a roof in midair. There are several advantages in handing over the state and society completely to women. At least it would reduce the chances of war. Maybe diplomacy would become more complicated and there would be more secret treaties, but women's biological limitation would make them shun war. And even if a war started, since women aren't as mechanically minded as men, they would probably use simple weapons and apply basic military maneuvers such as pulling out the hair, scratching the face, and pinching the body. In such cases damage would be insignificant. At any rate, the new women today have already balked at raising a lot of children. By that time they'll be so busy managing the affairs of the state that they'll have even less time to procreate. With the population down, wars probably won't even occur."

Miss T'ang sensed that Fang Hung-chien was saying all that to attract her attention. Laughing to herself, she said, "I can't tell whether Mr. Fang is insulting politics or women. At the least, it's not complimentary."

Miss Su said, "Oh, great, you spend all day beating around the bush trying to flatter her and she not only doesn't appreciate it, she doesn't even understand it. I suggest you save your breath."

"It's not that I don't appreciate what he said," said Miss T'ang. "I am truly grateful that Mr. Fang is willing to show off his eloquence. If I were studying mathematics, I bet he would have some other viewpoints and say that women are natural calculating animals."

Miss Su said, "Maybe he would say that if someone like you wanted to study mathematics, he'd stop hating mathematics from then on. Anyway, no matter how you put it or how ridiculous the arguments get, it's all just talk. I never knew he had such a glib tongue. I guess I found that out on the boat returning home. When we were classmates in college, his face would turn scarlet whenever he saw us co-eds from a distance and get redder the closer he came. It was so red that we'd get hot and uncomfortable all over just looking at his face. We used to call him 'The Thermometer' behind his back since his facial coloring indicated his relative distance from girls. It was so much fun. I never would have thought that once he'd gone abroad he'd get so thick-skinned and brazen-faced. Maybe he got his training from running around with girl friends like Miss Pao."

"What rubbish!" said Hung-chien nervously. "What's the point of bringing all that up? You co-eds are really something! You act serious in a person's presence, but as soon as his back is turned, you tear him apart. You really have no sense of decency!"

When Miss Su saw how distressed he had become, her displeasure at seeing him show off in front of Miss T'ang completely vanished. She said with a smile, "Look how upset you are! You yourself are probably guilty of fancy talk in front of people while belittling them behind their backs."

At that moment a tall, thirtyish, imposing-looking man walked in. While Miss T'ang greeted him as "Mr. Chao," Miss Su said, "Oh, good, you're here. I'll introduce you: Fang Hung-chien, Chao Hsin-mei."

Chao Hsin-mei shook hands with Fang Hung-chien, superciliously glancing at him from head to toe as if Hung-chien were a page from a large-type kindergarten reader to be glossed over at one glance. He asked Miss Su, "Didn't you come home with him on the boat?"

Hung-chien was dumbfounded. How did this Chao fellow know who he was? Then it suddenly occurred to him that Chao might have seen the item in the Shanghai paper, and the thought made him feel uncomfortable. Chao Hsin-mei looked smug to begin with, and after hearing Miss Su confirm that Hung-chien indeed came home with her on the same ship, he acted as if Hung-chien had turned into thin air and ignored Hung-chien completely. If Miss Su hadn't bothered to speak to him, Hung-chien would really have felt that he had thinned into nothingness, like a phantom of early dawn upon the cock's crowing or the Taoist truth, which can be "looked at but not seen, expounded but not grasped."

Miss Su explained to Hung-chien that Chao Hsin-mei was a family friend, a returned student from the United States, a former section chief of the foreign office who had not gone with the office to the interior because of illness. She added that he was at the moment a political editor at the Sino-American News Agency. She did not, however, recite Hung-chien's background for Chao Hsin-mei, as if Chao already knew all about it without being told.

With a pipe in his mouth, Chao Hsin-mei lounged on the sofa; looking at the ceiling light, he asked, "Where do you work, Mr. Fang?"

Somewhat annoyed by the question, Fang Hung-chien felt he must answer it. And since the "Golden Touch Bank" didn't sound impressive, he answered vaguely, "For the time being I'm working at a small bank."

Admiring the smoke ring he had blown, Chao Hsin-mei said, "A great talent gone to waste. Such a pity! Such a pity! What did you study abroad, Mr. Fang?"

"I didn't study anything," said Hung-chien crossly.

Miss Su said, "Hung-chien, you studied philosophy, didn't you?"

Chortling, Chao Hsin-mei said, "In the eyes of those of us engaged in real work, studying philosophy and not studying anything amount to one and the same."

"Then you'd better find an eye doctor right away and have your eyes examined. Eyes that see things like that must have something wrong with them," said Fang Hung-chien, purposely guffawing to cover up his ill feelings.

Chao Hsin-mei, quite pleased with the wisecrack he had made a moment ago, was for the moment unable to say anything in reply and puffed away furiously on his pipe. On the other hand, Miss Su tried hard not to laugh, though she was a little ill at ease. Miss T'ang, meanwhile, sat with a distant, aloof smile on her face, as if she were watching a fight from the clouds. It suddenly dawned on Hung-chien that Chao's rudeness toward him had stemmed from jealousy, for Chao had obviously taken him as his love rival. All of a sudden, Miss Su began calling Fang Hung-chien Hung-chien instead of Mr. Fang, as though she wanted Chao Hsin-mei to know her intimacy with Fang. *Having two men battle over her must be a woman's proudest moment,* Fang reflected. *Well, why should I make myself Chao's enemy for nothing. Let Chao go ahead and love Miss Su!* he decided.

Unaware of Fang Hung-chien's intention, Miss Su thoroughly enjoyed the battle of two men over her, but she was worried that the exchange might get too fierce and in a moment separate the victor from the vanquished, leaving only one of the two as the sole survivor and terminating all the excitement around her. She was even more worried that the vanquished might be Fang Hung-chien. She had tried to use Chao Hsin-mei to rouse Fang Hung-chien's courage, but perhaps Fang Hung-chien, like the war news in the newspapers for the last few days, had been "maintaining the present strength through strategic retreats."

Chao Hsin-mei's and Su Wen-Wan's fathers had been colleagues and had rented a house in Peking together during the early years of the Republic. Hsin-mei and Miss Su had been friends since childhood. When Mrs. Chao was pregnant with Hsin-mei, everyone thought she would have twins. By the time he was four or five, he was as tall as a seven- or eight-year-old, so that whenever the servant took him on a trolley car, the servant would always have to argue with the conductor over the "no fare required for children under five" rule. Though Hsin-mei's body was huge, his head, resembling a large turnip with nothing in it, was not. In grade school he was the butt of his classmates' jokes; for with such a large target, no shot could ever miss the mark. With Miss Su and her brother and sister, he used to play "cops and robbers." The two girls, Miss Su and her now married older sister, could not run very fast, so when it came their turn to play the "robber," they insisted on being the "cop." When Miss Su's elder brother played the robber, he refused to be caught. Hsin-mei was the only one who would be a good little robber and take a beating. When they played Little Red Riding Hood, he was always the wolf, and when he ate up Miss Su or her sister, he would pick them up and make a strange expression by rounding his eyes and opening his mouth wide. In the part where the woodcutter kills the wolf and cuts open the wolf's stomach, Miss Su's brother pressed him into the mud and tried to dig at his stomach. Once Miss Su's brother did really cut through his clothes with scissors.

While Hsin-mei was amiable by nature, it didn't follow that he therefore must have a poor mind. His father believed in physiognomy, so when he was thirteen or fourteen, his father took him to see a famous woman physiognomist who praised him for his "fire planet square, earth shape thick, wood sound high, cow's eyes, lion's nose, chessboard piece's ear, and mouth shaped like the character for 'four.' " And she said his physiognomy fit the description of a high official according to her Hemp Robe fortunetelling book.[8] Moreover, she predicted that he would achieve great fame and high political status surpassing that of his father. From then on Hsin-mei considered himself a statesman.

When Hsin-mei was little, he had a secret crush on Miss Su. One year when Miss Su was critically ill, he overheard his father say, "Wen-wan is sure to recover. She is destined to be an official's wife and has twenty-five years of a 'helpmate's fortune.' " He henceforth concluded that she would be his wife since the woman physiognomist had predicted he would be an official. When Miss Su returned from abroad, he thought he would renew their childhood friendship and propose to her at an appropriate time. But to his surprise, when Miss Su first came home, every other word she said was Fang Hung-chien, a name which she abruptly dropped after the fifth day. The reason was that she had discovered an old issue of a Shanghai newspaper and her sharp eyes had noticed an item in it that others had overlooked.

It must be said that her long years of friendship with Hsin-mei did not add up to love, just as in winter no one can add today's temperature to yesterday's to come up with a warm spring day for tomorrow. It must also be said that Hsin-mei excelled in making speeches in English; his resonant and fluent American speech, resembling the roll of thunder in the sky, when oiled and waxed, would slip halfway through the sky. Speeches, however, are delivered from a podium, with the speaker looking down at his audience. On the other hand, a marriage proposal has to be made by the person stooping down to half his height and earnestly entreating the other with an uplifted face. And since Miss Su was not his audience, he never had a chance to exercise his talent.

Though Chao Hsin-mei was jealous of Fang Hung-chien, it was not an it's-either-you-or-me type of enmity. His haughty rudeness was an imitation of Mussolini's and Hitler's attitude toward representatives of small nations during negotiations. He thought he could overwhelm and scare off Hung-chien with the forbidding mannerism of Mussolini or Hitler. But when he encountered a retort from Hung-chien, he could neither pound the table nor roar like the Italian ruler or raise a fist in a shout of authority like the German leader. Fortunately he knew the diplomat's secret of using a cigarette to create a smoke screen if he found himself temporarily at a loss for words. When Miss Su came to his rescue and asked him about the war, he proceeded to recite from memory the editorial he had just written. Continuing to ignore Fang Hung-chien, he kept up his guard against Fang; his attitude resembled that of a person toward germs when inquiring after the health of someone with a contagious disease.

Hung-chien was not interested in Hsin-mei's talk and thought primarily of striking up a conversation with Miss T'ang, but Miss T'ang was listening to Hsin-mei with rapt attention. He prepared to wait for Miss T'ang to leave, then he would get up himself and ask her for her address when they left together.

Hsin-mei finished analyzing the current war situation, looked at his watch and said, "It's now almost five o'clock. I'll run to the newspaper office for a while and then come take you to dinner at the O Mei-ch'un. If you want Szechwanese food, that's the best Szechwan restaurant. The waiters all know me there. Miss T'ang, you must join us; Mr. Fang, if you are in the mood, why not come join the fun? I'd be glad to have you."

Before Miss Su could answer, Miss T'ang and Fang Hung-chien both said it was late and they had to go home. They declined the invitation but thanked Hsin-mei, nonetheless.

Miss Su said, "Hung-chien, stay a while. There's something I want to talk to you about. Hsin-mei, my mother and I have a social engagement today, so let's eat at the restaurant some other day, all right? Tomorrow afternoon at four-thirty, all of you are invited to come here and have tea with Mr. and Mrs. Shen, who've just returned from abroad. We can have a good chat."

When Chao Hsin-mei saw Miss Su detain Fang Hung-chien, he left in a huff. Fang Hung-chien rose and intended to shake hands with him but had to sit down again. "That Chao Hsin-mei is strange. He acts as if I had offended him in some way. He hates me so much that it shows on his face and in his speech."

"Don't you hate him too?" asked Miss T'ang with a sly smile.

Miss Su blushed and scolded her, "You're awful."

When Fang Hung-chien heard Miss Su's remark, he dared not deny hating Chao Hsin-mei but merely said, "Miss Su, thanks for inviting me to tea, but I don't think I will be coming."

Before Miss Su could open her mouth, Miss T'ang said, "You can't do that? It's all right for the audience not to show up, but you're one of the principal actors. How can you not come?"

Miss Su said, "Hsiao-fu! If you utter any more nonsense, I'm not going to pay any attention to you. Both of you must come tomorrow!"

Miss T'ang left in Miss Su's car. Hung-chien, face to face with Miss Su, tried his best to say something that would dilute or clear the thick and stifling atmosphere of intimacy. "Your cousin has a sharp tongue. She seems quite intelligent too."

"That girl is very capable for her age. She has a slew of boy friends that she fools around with!" Hung-chien's disappointed look sent a twinge of jealousy through Miss Su's heart. "Don't think she's naive. She is full of schemes! I always thought that a girl just entering college who is already involved in love affairs can't have much of a future. I mean, how can someone who runs around with boys and leads a wild mixed-up life still have time for study? Don't you remember our classmates, Huang Pi and Chiang Meng-t'i? Who knows what's become of them now?"

Fang Hung-chien quickly said he remembered them. "You were quite popular yourself in those days, but you always looked so arrogant. We could only admire you from a distance. I never dreamed that we would be such good friends today."

With that Miss Su felt better. Then she brought up some old school matters; and when Hung-chien saw she really had nothing important to say, he said, "I'd better be going. This evening you still have to go out with your mother on a social engagement."

Miss Su said, "I don't have any engagement. That was just an excuse, because Hsin-mei was so rude to you. I don't want to make him any more arrogant."

Hung-chien said nervously, "You're too kind to me."

Miss Su glanced at him; then lowering her head she said, "Sometimes I really shouldn't be so kind to you." The tender words he was supposed to say at that point squirmed in the air and rushed to the tip of his tongue to be spoken. He didn't want to say them, yet he couldn't remain silent. As he saw Miss Su's hand resting on the edge of the sofa, he reached out and patted the back of her hand. She drew back her hand and said softly, "You go now. Come a little early tomorrow afternoon." She walked him to the door of the living room. As he crossed the threshold, she called, "Hung-chien." He turned around and asked what was the matter. She said, "Nothing. I was just watching you. Why did you dash forward without even turning your head? Ha, ha, I have become such an unreasonable woman. I wanted you to grow eyes at the back of your head. Come early tomorrow."

When he left her, Fang thought he had become a part of spring, at one with it in spirit and no longer the outsider of two hours ago. As he walked along, his body felt so light that it seemed the ground was floating upward. Just two small matters bothered him. First, he should never have touched Miss Su's hand; he should have pretended he didn't understand what she meant. Being too softhearted, he had often catered to women without intending to, because he didn't want to offend them. In the future he'd just have to talk and act more decisively and not let things get serious. Second, Miss T'ang had many boy friends and might already be in love with someone. So vexed by this fact, he struck his cane violently against a roadside tree and decided he'd better quash all hope from the very start. What a disgrace it would be if he were to be jilted by a teen-age girl!

Disconsolately, he hopped on a trolley car and saw a young couple sitting nearby whispering tender words to each other. On the boy's lap was a pile of high school textbooks; the girl's book covers were all decorated with pictures of movie stars. Though she was no more than sixteen or seventeen, her face was made up like a mask kneaded out of gobs of rouge and powder. *Shanghai is certainly avant-garde culturally. The phenomenon of high school girls painting and plastering their faces to attract men is rare even abroad, he* reflected. But this girl's face was so obviously faked, for no one would possibly believe that powdered wafer cake pasted on her face could be her own. It suddenly occurred to Fang that Miss T'ang did not use any makeup. *A girl who works hard at making up either has a boy friend already and has discovered a new interest or value in her body, or else she's looking for a boy friend and is hanging out a colorful eye-catching signboard to attract a man's attention. Since Miss T'ang dresses plainly, she obviously doesn't have a man in her life,* he concluded. His conclusion had such a profound psychological basis and had followed such precise logical reasoning that he couldn't sit still in his seat.

When the trolley car reached his stop, he rushed ahead and jumped off without waiting for the trolley car to come to a stop, nearly falling down as he did so. Luckily, by supporting himself with his cane and pushing against a utility pole with his left hand, he managed to check his downward momentum. He broke out in a cold sweat from the scare, and a layer of skin was scraped from his left palm. He was also rebuked by the trolley car attendant. When he reached home he applied some tincture of merthiolate to his palm, blaming Miss T'ang for his mishap and promising to get even with her later. Like foam, a smile floated up from his heart to his face, and the pain was immediately forgotten. It didn't occur to him, however, that the scrape might have been punishment for his having put his hand on top of Miss Su's a while ago.

The next day when he arrived at the Sus, Miss T'ang was already there. Before he had sat down, Chao Hsin-mei came. Chao greeted him and then said, "Mr. Fang, you left late yesterday and came early today. This must be a good habit you developed in the banking business. Your diligence is commendable. Congratulations."

"Thank you, thank you." Fang Hung-chien had thought of saying that Hsin-mei's early departure and late arrival must be in the bureaucratic tradition of a *yamen* mandarin,[9] but he changed his mind and kept the thought to himself. He even smiled pleasantly at Hsin-mei. Hsin-mei, on the other hand, had not expected him to be so meek and was startled to find that he had struck at thin air. Meanwhile, Miss T'ang looked surprised and so did Miss Su at the lack of drama. However, Miss Su assumed that Fang's meekness was the magnanimity usually demonstrated by the victor, and since Hung-chien knew she loved him, Hung-chien felt no need to quarrel with Hsin-mei.

Mr. and Mrs. Shen arrived. While introductions were made and pleasantries exchanged, Chao Hsin-mei picked the sofa nearest Miss Su and sat down. The Shens sat together on a long sofa, and Miss T'ang sat on an embroidered couch between the Shens and Miss Su. Next to Mrs. Shen, Hung-chien sat by himself. He had no sooner seated himself than he regretted it immensely, for Mrs. Shen had an odor about her for which there is an elegant expression in classical Chinese as well as an idiom in Latin, both using the goat as a comparison: *yun-ti* and *olet hircum* (smelling like a goat). Mingled with the scent of face powder and the fragrance of flowers, this smell was so strong that it made Fang Hung-chien queasy, yet he was too polite to smoke a cigarette to dispel the stench. Here was a woman just returned from France all right, bringing back to China a whole "symphony of foul odors" from the Paris marketplace. Fang never ran into her while in Paris, and now of all times there was no escape from her; the explanation seemed to be that Paris was big while the world was small.

Mrs. Shen was rather odd-looking and very heavily made up; the two black bags under her eyes were like round canteen bottles, filled probably with hot, passionate tears; the thick lipstick had been washed into her mouth and colored the yellowish, rough ridges of her teeth red, making her teeth look like hemorrhoids dripping with blood or the clues to a bloody murder in a detective yarn. Her speech was full of French exclamations such as *"Tiens!"* and *"O la la!"* as she squirmed her body around into various seductive poses. Each twist of the body let off a fresh wave of the smell. Hung-chien wished he could have told her that it was quite enough if she'd just talk with her mouth and be careful not to twist herself in two.

Mr. Shen's lower lip was thick and drooping. One could tell at a glance that he was a man who spoke much and quickly as though he had diarrhea of the mouth. He was describing how he had propagandized the war to the French and how he had won the sympathy of quite a few people for China's cause. "After the withdrawal from Nanking,[10] they all said China was finished. I said to them, 'During the war in Europe, didn't your government also move the capital out of Paris? Yet you were the final victors!' They had nothing to say to that, no sir, not a thing."

Hung-chien was thinking, *Governments may be able to move their capitals, but I can't change my seat.*

As though offering an expert's opinion, Chao Hsin-mei observed, "An excellent answer! Why don't you write an article about it?"

"Wei-lei [Mrs. Shen] put those remarks of mine in the foreign correspondence column in a Shanghai paper. Didn't you see it, Mr. Chao?" asked Mr. Shen with a touch of disappointment.

Mrs. Shen twisted around and gestured at her husband, saying with a coquettish smile, "Why bring up that thing of mine? Who'd ever have noticed it?"

Hsin-mei said quickly, "Yes, I did see it. I was very much impressed. Now I remember, it had the part about relocating the capital."

"I didn't see it," Hung-chien interrupted. "What was it called?"

Hsin-mei said, "You philosophers study timeless questions, so naturally you don't read newspapers. It was called—uh—it's on the tip of my tongue. Why can't I think of it just now?" He had never read the article in the first place but couldn't pass up the chance to humiliate Hung-chien.

Miss Su said, "You can't blame him. He probably was in the country at the time the article appeared, and he might not have seen any newspapers. Right, Hung-chien? The title is quite easy to remember: 'Some Letters to My Sisters in the Motherland.' At the top was a headline in large type which went something like this, 'A Verdant Island of Europe in the Azure Blood of Asia.' Mrs. Shen, is my memory correct?"

"Oh, that's right," said Hsin-mei, slapping his own thigh. " 'Some Letters to My Sisters in the Motherland' and 'A Verdant Island of Europe in the Azure Blood of Asia.' Beautiful titles. What a good memory you have, Wen-wan!"

Mrs. Shen said, "Gee, you even remember that silly thing of mine. No wonder all the people who know you say you are a genius."

Miss Su said, "If it is something good, you don't have to remember it. It'll leave a deep impression by itself."

Miss T'ang said to Hung-chien, "Mrs. Shen wrote her article for us women to read. You're one of the 'brothers in the motherland,' and you can be forgiven for not having noticed it."

Since Mrs. Shen was not young and since her letter was not addressed to her "nieces and grandnieces in the motherland," Miss T'ang, by reading it, had been elevated to the status of Mrs. Shen's sister.

To make amends for his forgetfulness, Hsin-mei flattered Mrs. Shen, saying that the Sino-American News Agency was going to publish a women's magazine and asking for her help. The Shens grew even more friendly toward Hsin-mei.

The servant drew the curtain separating the dining room from the living room, and Miss Su invited everyone to step inside for refreshments. Hung-chien felt like a criminal having been granted a pardon. When he finished eating, he returned to the living room and quickly sat next to Miss T'ang.

Mrs. Shen and Chao Hsin-mei were so deeply engrossed in their conversation that they could not be separated; since he had a stuffy nose and a cold Hsin-mei didn't mind being close to Mrs. Shen. Meanwhile, Mr. Shen was dropping hints to Miss Su with the intention of having Uncle Su[11] find him a position in Hong Kong. On the other hand, Fang Hung-chien decided his luck that day had turned for the better, as in the expression "After the bitter comes the sweet," and he asked Miss T'ang in a whisper, "You didn't eat anything just now, as if you didn't feel well. Are you better now?"

"I ate quite a bit," said Miss T'ang. "There is nothing wrong with me."

"I'm not the host; you needn't be polite with me. I clearly saw you drink a mouthful of soup, then frown and play with the spoon without eating anything else."

"What's so interesting about watching someone eat? Is it polite to keep staring at someone? I didn't like you watching me eat, so I didn't eat. That's what you did to me—Ha, ha, Mr. Fang, don't take it seriously. I really didn't know you were watching others eat. Tell me, when you were sitting down next to Mrs. Shen, why did you turn your face away and hold your mouth tightly shut as if under torture?"

"So the same thing happened to you!" Fang Hung-chien and Miss T'ang laughed intimately, having now become comrades in adversity.

Miss T'ang said, "Mr. Fang, I'm a little disappointed today."

"Disappointed? What were you hoping for? Wasn't that smell strong enough for you?"

"It's not that. I thought for sure that there'd be a lot of fireworks between you and Chao Hsin-mei. Who would have thought there'd be nothing."

"I'm sorry that there wasn't any nice drama for you to watch. Chao Hsin-mei misunderstands my relationship with your cousin. Maybe you are under the same misunderstanding. I just let him be the provocateur today, while I sit back without returning his salvos to let him know I have nothing against him."

"Is that true? Wouldn't a mere indication from my cousin clear up the misunderstanding?"

"Maybe your cousin has her own ideas. Dispatching a general on a mission isn't as effective as challenging him to do it as a mission impossible. There has to be a major adversary before Mr. Chao's ability can come to the fore. Too bad this tired old soldier can't live up to the fight and for that matter isn't interested in the fighting."

"Why not be a volunteer?"

"No, it'd be like dragging in a conscript." As he said this, Fang Hung-chien regretted having spoken so flippantly, since there was no guarantee that Miss T'ang wouldn't pass all this on to Miss Su.

"But often the underdog gets more sympathy from the bystanders."

62

Realizing that this remark could be misconstrued, Miss T'ang blushed. "I mean, my cousin might be aiding the smaller, weaker people."[12]

Hung-chien was so overjoyed at hearing this that his heart skipped a beat. "That's her business. Miss T'ang, I'd like to invite you and your cousin for dinner tomorrow at the O Mei-chun. May I have the honor?"

Miss T'ang hesitated and before she could answer, Hung-chien went on, "I know it's very presumptuous of me. Your cousin told me you have many friends. Though I am unworthy, I'd like very much to be included among them."

"I don't have any friends. My cousin was talking nonsense. What did she say to you?"

"Oh, nothing in particular. Just that you are very good at socializing and know quite a few people."

"That's ridiculous. I am just an ignorant country girl!"

"You're being polite. Please come tomorrow. I wanted to go to that restaurant but didn't have a good excuse. I'm using you two as a pretext so I can enjoy myself. Please oblige me by accepting the invitation."

Miss T'ang said with a smile, "Mr. Fang, there's something behind everything you say. If that's the way it is, I'll certainly come. What time tomorrow evening?"

Hung-chien told her the time. Relaxed and happy, he heard Mrs. Shen speak in her sonorous voice, "The time I attended the World Conference of Women, I observed a widespread trend. Women all over the world are now going in the direction of men." Hung-chien was both startled and amused, thinking, *It's been like that since ancient times. Mrs. Shen shouldn't have to attend a women's conference now to find that out.* Meanwhile, Mrs. Shen continued, "All the occupations that men have held, such as members of parliament, lawyers, journalists, airplane pilots, women can hold and perform just as well as men. A Yugoslav woman sociologist gave a lecture at the conference in which she said that with the exception of women who were willing to be virtuous wives and mothers, career women could be called 'the third sex.' Though the women's liberation movement is a recent development, already there have been such outstanding achievements. I would venture to say that in the near future the distinction between the sexes will become an historic term."

Chao Hsin-mei said, "You're right, Mrs. Shen. Women today really are capable! Wen-wan, take Miss Hsü Pao-ch'iung, for instance. Do you know her, Mrs. Shen? She helps her father manage a dairy farm and handles major and minor chores herself. Outwardly she looks so dainty and refined. You could never tell what she does."

Hung-chien said something to Miss T'ang, whereupon Miss T'ang burst out laughing.

Miss Su said, "Pao-ch'iung is more clever than her father and is actually the behind-the-scenes manager." Disgusted by Hung-chien's closeness to Miss T'ang, she asked, "Hsiao-fu, what's so funny?"

Miss T'ang just shook her head and laughed.

Miss Su then said, "Hung-chien, if there's a joke let us hear it."

Hung-chien too shook his head and said nothing, making it even more apparent that he and Miss T'ang were sharing a mutual secret. Miss Su became quite vexed, and Chao Hsin-mei, putting on his most supercilious expression, said, "Maybe the great philosopher Fang was expounding some optimistic philosophy of life, which made Miss T'ang so happy. Right, Miss T'ang?"

Ignoring Hsin-mei, Fang Hung-chien said to Miss Su, "I heard Mr. Chao say he couldn't tell by looking at Miss Hsü that she runs a dairy farm. Maybe Mr. Chao thinks Miss Hsü ought to grow two horns on her head so that people could tell who she is at one glance. Otherwise, you could never tell what she does, no matter what she looks like."

Chao Hsin-mei said, "That makes no sense. If she grew horns on her head and turned into a cow herself, how would that show she's a dairy manager?" While he was speaking, he looked around the room and roared with laughter, feeling he had trounced Fang Hung-chien again. Determined not to be the first one to leave, he entrenched himself deeper into the sofa.

Having achieved his aim, Fang Hung-chien did not care to stay any longer and wanted to leave while there were still enough people present to make his parting from Miss Su a little easier. Since he hadn't been near her that day, Miss Su made a point to see him to the hallway. Her reasoning was similar to warming one's hands in front of the stove before stepping outside on a cold day.

Hung-chien said, "Miss Su, I didn't have a chance to talk with you much today. Are you free tomorrow evening? I'd like to invite you to dinner at the O Mei-chun. I don't care to have Chao Hsin-mei invite me. I just wish I were an old customer. I probably can't order the dishes as well as he can."

The fact that Fang was still at odds with Chao Hsin-mei gave Miss Su an uplift in spirit. She said with a smile, "Fine. Just the two of us, then?" As soon as she said this, she felt a little embarrassed, having realized that the question was unnecessary.

Fang Hung-chien said hesitatingly, "No, your cousin is also coming."

"Oh, she is. Have you invited her?"

"Yes, I did. She promised to come—to accompany you."

"All right then, goodbye."

Miss Su's parting manner dampened Fang Hung-chien's high spirits. He felt the situation between him and the two women was too difficult to handle and prayed that he would be able to handle it smoothly and cleanly and let Miss Su's affections toward him die a painless death. He heaved a sigh for Miss

Su. Though he didn't love her, he had become softhearted because of her. *It's just too unfair! She is too scheming. She shouldn't be so easily hurt and she should bear the situation without complaint. Why does love have to lower one's mental resistance and make one so weak that one can be easily manipulated? If God really loved man, He would never be the master of man,* he thought. If his thoughts had been made known to Chao Hsin-mei, Fang Hung-chien would have had to listen to Hsin-mei's abuse about how "the philosopher is up to tricks."

That night Fang's sleep was fitful, like rice-flour noodles without elasticity or stretchability. His joy burst from his dreams and woke him four or five times. Each time he awoke, he seemed to see T'ang Hsiao-fu's face and to hear her voice. Her every word and gesture during the day he tried to impress upon his heart. Moments later he would drift to sleep only to awake with a start a moment later, feeling his joy had been robbed by sleep. Once more he would mentally review the day's happiness. When he finally awoke and got up, he found the sky dull and grey. He had not chosen a nice day for a dinner party, he thought, and wished he could have pressed blotting paper against the pale rain clouds to dry them up.

Monday was usually the busiest day of the week at the bank. Fang wouldn't be able to leave the office until after six o'clock in the evening. Since he wouldn't have time to come home and change before going to the restaurant, he got dressed in the morning before leaving for work. Imagining he were Miss T'ang, he judged his appearance in the mirror through her eyes. In less than a year since his return from abroad, he had acquired more wrinkles on his forehead, and since he hadn't slept well the night before, his complexion and eyes were dull and lusterless. His acquisition of a new love two days ago had made him meticulously aware of every last blemish in his appearance in the manner of a poor man with only one dress suit who knows its every spot and patch. Actually, to other people, his complexion looked the same as ever, but he found himself particularly ugly that day. Thinking that the color of his necktie made his sallow complexion greenish, he changed neckties three times before going down for breakfast.

As usual, Mr. Chou was still in bed, so Fang ate with Mrs. Chou and Hsiao-ch'eng. As Fang was still eating breakfast, the telephone outside his bedroom upstairs rang. At home, he seldom had a moment's peace and quiet, and when irritated by the phone, he would often think his fiancée's life had been snatched away by that "soul-snatching bell" of the telephone. The maid-servant came down to say, "Telephone, Mr. Fang. It's someone named Su, a woman." As she spoke, her eyes passed the message to Mrs. Chou and Hsiao-ch'eng, whose eyes were so busy that they resembled ripples in a spring pond in the breeze. Hung-chien had never expected Miss Su to call, and he was sure Mrs. Chou would quiz him about the call. As he bounded up the stairs to answer the phone, he heard Hsiao-ch'eng remark in a loud voice, "I bet it's Su Wen-wan." The other day in his history class Hsiao-ch'eng had incorrectly identified the family name of the Manchu rulers Ai-hsin Chiao-lo[13] as Ch'in-ai Pao-lo (Dear Paul); for his mistake he had received a severe reprimand from his teacher, and the reprimand had so infuriated him that he was playing hooky and staying home that day. On the other hand, after seeing Miss Su's name once, he had it memorized.

As Hung-chien picked up the receiver, he felt the entire Chou family were listening in with bated breath. "Miss Su?" he said softly. "This is Hung-chien."

"Hung-chien, I thought you'd still be home so I called you up. I'm not feeling well today, so I won't be going to the O Mei-chun this evening. I'm very sorry. You mustn't get mad at me."

"Is Miss T'ang going?" As soon as the words came out of his mouth, he regretted having said them.

Incisively, she said, "I have no idea." Then in a distant tone, she went on, "Of course, she will be."

"What's wrong with you? Is it serious?" He knew his inquiries were already too late.

"It's nothing. I just feel too tired to go out." The implication was obvious.

"Well, I am relieved to hear that. Take good care of yourself. I'll certainly see you tomorrow. What do you like to eat?"

"Thank you. I don't want anything." Pause. "Well, then, I will see you tomorrow."

After Miss Su hung up, it occurred to Hung-chien that as a matter of courtesy he should cancel and schedule the dinner for another day. Should he call Miss Su and ask her to tell Miss T'ang about the postponement? But he really didn't want to. Just as he was pondering over the matter, Hsiao-ch'eng came running and jumping along, yelling at the top of his lungs all the way, "Dear Miss Su, have you come down with lovesickness? What do you love to eat? I love baked sesame buns, fried puffs, five-spice beans, dried bean-curd strips, dried mucus, stinky salt-preserved fish."

With a yelp, Hung-chien grabbed Hsiao-ch'eng, cutting short his proposed menu and frightening him into begging for mercy. Hung-chien gave him a light pat and dismissed him. He then went downstairs to finish his breakfast. As expected, Mrs. Chou was waiting to query him in detail. "Don't forget, you must make me your adopted mother," she said.

"I'm waiting for you to get an adopted daughter. The more daughters you get, the wider is the selection for me. This Miss Su is only an old classmate. Nothing serious between us, so don't worry," Hung-chien quickly answered.

66

The sky gradually cleared up, but because of the phone call that morning Hung-chien's high spirits had been considerably dampened. He felt unworthy of such a beautiful day as he had planned it, and he felt as if a tent were about to collapse on him. Miss Su was up to mischief, no doubt. And if she didn't come, so much the better as that would leave just Miss T'ang and himself. But without a third person, would Miss T'ang come? he wondered. He hadn't asked Miss T'ang for her address and telephone number the day before, so he couldn't find out if Miss T'ang knew about Miss Su's not coming to the party. Miss Su would surely let Miss T'ang know. What if Miss T'ang had asked Miss Su to tell him that she wasn't coming either. That would be disastrous!

At the bank he assisted Chief-secretary Wang with letter writing. His mind preoccupied with his own affairs, he made a few errors in the drafts of letters he wrote. Wang corrected them for him, chuckled, and said, "Brother Hung-chien,[14] the eyes of this old clerk are still pretty sharp."

By six o'clock when he still hadn't received any word from Miss T'ang, he began to get nervous but didn't dare call Miss Su to ask about Miss T'ang. Around seven, he briskly walked over to the O Mei-chun and engaged a private dining room, preparing to wait for Miss T'ang until eight-thirty. If by that time she still hadn't come, then he would have to eat alone. Waiting patiently and never raising his hopes too high, he lit a cigarette and then snuffed it out. The evening was too chilly for him to open the windows, yet he was afraid the odor of smoke might fill the room and offend Miss T'ang. He opened the book he had brought to the bank to read during his spare time but not a single sentence made any sense. When he heard the waiter greeting a customer outside, his heart fluttered. The dinner was for seven-thirty, and it was just seven-forty-five by his watch. She couldn't possibly be coming this early, but suddenly the curtain was drawn, the waiter stood aside and in came Miss T'ang.

In his heart what Hung-chien felt was gratitude, not joy. After greeting her, he said, "I am sorry Miss Su couldn't make it today."

"I know. I almost didn't make it myself. I tried calling you but couldn't get through."

"Then I'm grateful to the telephone company. I hope their business prospers and their lines get so busy that telephone calls to make last minute changes of plan won't get through. Did you call the bank?"

"No, I called your house. This is what happened. Early this morning my cousin called me saying she couldn't come to dinner and had already informed you. I said I wouldn't go either, in that case. She wanted me to tell you myself and gave me your phone number. I dialed and asked, 'Is this the Fangs' residence?' A woman answered in your native dialect—I couldn't imitate the way she said it—'This is the Chous' residence. There is only one person named

Fang here. Are you Miss Su? You want to speak to Fang Hung-chien. Hung-chien's not in. I'll have him call you when he gets back. Miss Su, you must come visit sometime when you're free. Hung-chien often says how pretty and talented you are,' and she went on and on in the same breath. I meant to explain, but I couldn't get in a word. I thought all that rice gruel was being poured down the wrong ear,[15] so I very rudely hung up on her. Who was that?"

"That's my relative, Mrs. Chou, the wife of the general manager of the bank where I work. Your cousin had called just before I left the house, so Mrs. Chou thought the call was from her again."

"Oh, no! What a mess. Mrs. Chou surely blames my cousin for being so rude. I hadn't hung up for more than five minutes when my cousin called again to ask whether I'd talked to you. I said you weren't home, and then she gave me your office number. I thought you were probably on the way there, so I might as well wait a while before calling. Then of all things, my cousin called me fifteen minutes later for the third time. I was getting a little mad. When she found out I hadn't yet got in touch with you, she told me to hurry and call you before you'd reserved a table. I said if he's reserved a table then I will go. What difference would it make? She said that wouldn't be good and invited me to her house for dinner. I replied that I wasn't feeling well either and wasn't going anywhere. Later I thought my cousin was just too silly. I decided to accept your invitation and not make any call."

Hung-chien said, "Miss T'ang, today you haven't just honored me with your presence, you've been a real savior. As host I am more than grateful. I'll have to invite you out many more times. If none of the invited guests shows up, it means the death sentence for the host as far as his social life is concerned. Today was a close call!"

Hung-chien ordered food enough for five or six people. Miss T'ang asked if there would be any other guests, for how could two people eat so much. He said it really wasn't that much, prompting her to remark, "You noticed I didn't have any refreshments yesterday, so now you're testing to see if I'll eat anything, aren't you?"

He knew she wasn't one of those dainty women who will screw their mouth up to the size of the tip of an eyedropper at a dinner party, so he replied, "This is the first time I've been to this restaurant and I am not sure which dishes I like best. If I order a few extra, then I'll have a wider choice. If this one isn't any good, then there's that one. I won't starve you this way."

"That's not eating, that's more like the Divine Farmer[16] testing a hundred varieties of herbs. Isn't that a little extravagant? Maybe all men like to be extravagant in front of women they don't know."

"Maybe. But not in front of all women they don't know."

68

"Just in front of stupid women, right?"

"What do you mean?"

"If women weren't fools, they'd never be impressed by a man just because he is extravagant. But don't worry, all women are foolish, just as foolish as men expect them to be. No more and no less."

He wondered whether these remarks came from naïve candor or from what her cousin had called her social experience. When the food was served and they were eating, he asked her for her address, suggesting she write it on the blank page at the back of the book he had brought along to read, as he never liked the idea of carrying little address books around. When he saw she had written down her phone number, he said, "I won't be calling you up. I hate talking to friends over the phone. I'd much rather write a letter."

"Yes, I feel the same way. Friends should enjoy seeing each other face to face. Talking over the phone is considered having contact, but you haven't seen each other, and what you say over the phone can't be kept like a letter to be taken out and read over several times. A phone call is a lazy man's visit or a miser's letter, not what you would expect from a friend. Besides, did you notice that a person's voice over the phone often sounds unrecognizable or unpleasant?" she said.

"You are right, Miss T'ang. At the Chous where I live, there's a phone right outside my room. The noise gives me a headache every day. Often at the most unreasonable hours, such as in the middle of the night or in early morning, someone will call. It's such a nuisance. Luckily televiewing isn't in wide use; otherwise it'd be even worse. There'd be people spying on you when you're in the bathtub or in bed. As education becomes increasingly widespread, the number of people writing letters decreases. Unless it's an important business matter, people are afraid to write letters, and they'd rather call on the phone. I think that's because it's easy to make a fool of yourself in writing a letter. People in high positions can often speak quite well but can't handle a pen effectively. But with a phone call a person can dispense with a visit from someone repulsive or hide his poor writing ability. So the telephone has been considered a great gift to mankind."

Fang Hung-chien babbled on happily, urging Miss T'ang to eat from time to time. He, on the other hand, ate very little. By the time they had their fruit for dessert, it was nine o'clock. She wanted to leave, and he didn't dare keep her. After paying the bill, he asked the waiter to call a taxi to take her home. He told her he had promised to go see Miss Su the next day and asked if she was going. She replied she might but doubted Miss Su was really sick. He then asked, "Should we tell her about our dinner tonight?"

"Why not? No, no. I got mad a while ago and told her I wasn't going anywhere today. All right, whatever you decide. In any case you can't go to her place until after work tomorrow, and I will go a little later."

"I was thinking of visiting you the day after tomorrow. Would you mind?"

"I'd be glad to have you. It's just that our house is very cramped, nothing like Miss Su's Western-style house with a big garden. If you don't mind visiting a modest home, come by all means."

"May I meet your father?" he asked.

"Not unless you have some legal questions to ask him. He usually stays in his law office and doesn't get home until late in the evening. My parents have absolute trust in my sisters and me. They've never interfered with or checked up on our friends," she replied.

The taxi arrived as Miss T'ang was speaking, and Hung-chien helped her into it. On his way home in the rickshaw, he thought the day had turned out to be unexpectedly perfect. But Miss T'ang's parting remark about "our friends" made him jealous as he conjured up visions of a huge throng of young men secretly surrounding her.

When Miss T'ang arrived home, her parents teased her, "Well, our social butterfly is home." She went to her room and was changing her clothes, when the maid said Miss Su was on the phone. She went downstairs to answer the phone, but halfway down the stairs she changed her mind, stopped, and instructed her maid to say, "Young Lady[17] isn't feeling well and has gone to bed." Indignantly, she thought, *That must be my cousin checking up to see whether I'm home or not. She is such a bully. Fang Hung-chien isn't hers, and he doesn't need her to look after him like that! The more she interferes, the closer I will let him get to me. I can never love Fang Hung-chien; love is a grand and complicated emotion, and it's never so simple and easy. If I could fall in love with someone that easily, then I can't either believe in or submit to love.*

The following afternoon Hung-chien bought some flowers and fruit and went to the Sus. The moment he saw Miss Su, he burst out without giving her a chance to speak, "What happened yesterday? You got sick, she got sick. Was it anything contagious? Or were you afraid I'd poison the food? Was I ever mad! I just went to eat by myself. I could have cared less that you weren't coming. All right, all right, now at least I know what a couple of stuck-up girls you are. Next time I won't risk a refusal."

Miss Su apologized, "I really was sick. I felt better by afternoon but didn't call you up for fear you'd scold me for playing jokes on you, changing my mind from one moment to the next. When I told Hsiao-fu I was sick yesterday, I didn't tell her not to go. Let me call her up and ask her over. It's all my fault. Next time I will be the host."

She then called up Miss T'ang to ask if Miss T'ang felt better and invited her over, saying that Hung-chien was at her house. After she hung up, she took the flowers Hung-chien had given her and smelled them, instructing the servant to arrange them in the vase in her bedroom. Turning to Hung-chien, she asked, "When you were in England, did you know a Ts'ao Yüan-lang?"

Hung-chien shook his head.

"He studied literature at Cambridge. He's a new-style poet who's just returned from abroad. His family and mine have been friends for generations. Yesterday he came to see me, and he's coming again today."

"Oh, so that's it," said Hung-chien. "No wonder you didn't show up yesterday. All that time you were discussing poetry with someone. We're uncouth, just not worthy of your acquaintance. This Mr. Ts'ao hails from the illustrious Cambridge University, while we are nominal students from newly established colleges. How could we ever qualify to make friends with him? Tell me, since your *Eighteen Poets of the Colloquial Style* doesn't seem to mention him, are you planning to include him in the next edition?"

Miss Su was half angry and half amused. Waving her finger at him, she said, "You like being jealous, and it's over nothing." Her expression and implication frightened Fang Hung-chien so much that he became wordless, and he blamed himself for having done too well at feigning anger.

Presently Miss T'ang came in. Miss Su said to her, "Such airs you put on! I called up yesterday to ask about you, and today you didn't even return the call. Now you wouldn't come until I invited you. Mr. Fang was asking about you."

"Am I good enough to put on airs?" said Miss T'ang. "I keep getting bossed around; is it so strange that I don't come until summoned? If I refuse to come after being invited, then you can call me self-important."

Afraid that Miss T'ang might say something about her three telephone calls the day before, Miss Su quickly put her arm around Miss T'ang's waist and said placatingly, "Look at you. I was joking and you take it so seriously." She then peeled an orange Hung-chien had brought and shared it with him.

The doorman showed in a perfectly round-faced man, announcing, "Mr. Ts'ao." Hung-chien gave a start. How did his last year's shipmate, Mrs. Sun's child, grow so big already, he wondered, and nearly called Mr. Ts'ao "Brother Sun." Mrs. Sun's child and the guest did resemble each other a great deal, and somehow Fang felt that it was inappropriate for a poet to have such a plump face and big ears, as if those features would mean that his poetry couldn't be any good. Then he suddenly remembered that the T'ang poet Chia Tao[18] noted for his poetic leanness, was also round-faced and squat in stature, and he shouldn't judge Ts'ao Yüan-lang by his appearance. When the introductions and pleasantries were over, Ts'ao Yüan-lang took a redwood-bound copybook from his briefcase and solemnly presented it to Miss Su, saying, "I brought this today especially to ask for your opinion."

Hung-chien then realized it was not a copybook but a notebook of fine

Hsüan calligraphy paper in a deluxe mounting put out by the Jung-pao Printing House.[19] Miss Su took the notebook and leafed through it, saying, "Mr. Ts'ao, let me keep it so I can study it. I will return it next week. OK? Hung-chien, you haven't read Mr. Ts'ao's work, have you?"

Hung-chien was just thinking what wonderful poetry this must be to be recorded in such a fancy notebook. Reverently he took it from Miss Su; he found standard-type-face characters written very evenly with a brush. The first poem of fourteen lines was entitled "Adulterous Smorgasbord," with the small number "1" beneath it. After studying the poem carefully, he discovered that the poet's annotations were on the second page. This "1," "2," "3," "4," and so on indicated the sequence of the annotations. Note "1" was *"Mélange adultère."* The poem read as follows:

> The stars of last night tonight stir ripples on the wind
> swirling into tomorrow night (2).
> The full, plump white belly of the pregnant woman is
> pasted tremblingly to the heavens (3).
> When did this fleeing woman who had maintained a chaste
> widowhood find a husband? (4)
> Jug! Jug! (5) In the mud—*En ange e il mondo!*[20] [sic] (6)
> a nightingale sings (7),

Hung-chien skipped to the last couplet:

> The summer evening after the rain is saturated and
> washed; the earth is fertile and fresh.
> The smallest blade of grass joins in the soundless outcry.
> *"Wir sind!"* (30)

At the end of the poem the sources of the words and phrases were carefully noted, including excerpts from the poetry of Li I-shan,[21] T. S. Eliot, Tristan Corbiere, Leopardi, and Franz Werfel. Hung-chien surmised that the "belly of a pregnant woman" referred to the moon; the "fleeing woman," to Ch'ang O;[22] and the "nightingale in the mud," to a frog. He did not have the stomach to read any further and put the book down on the tea table, saying, "There's not one word without a source. It's almost like what traditional poets call 'scholar's poetry.' Isn't that style neoclassicism?"

Ts'ao Yüan-lang nodded and repeated "neoclassic" in English. Miss Su asked which poem it was and then she read through "Adulterous Smorgasbord." When she finished reading it, she exclaimed, "Such a marvelous title. There's one phrase that's especially good: 'the soundless outcry.' Those words truly capture summer's bursting, squirming vitality. How wonderful that Mr. Ts'ao was able to express everything so well!"

Upon hearing this, the poet was so delighted that his plump face, as round

72

as the T'ai-chi diagram,[23] was flooded with butter. Hung-chien suddenly had the alarming suspicion that Miss Su was either a big idiot or a superb liar.

Miss T'ang also went over the poem and said, "Mr. Ts'ao, you're too cruel to us unlearned readers. I can't read any of the foreign words in the poem."

The poet said, "The style of this poem is such that those who can't read the foreign words can appreciate it all the more. The title is an assortment, a mixture of different ideas. You just have to note how each person's poetic phrase is used. Naturally the mixture of foreign words with the Chinese gives it a random, disorganized impression. Miss T'ang, didn't you get this haphazard, mixed-up feeling?"

Miss T'ang nodded her head in agreement. Like the surface of a pond at the drop of a pebble, Ts'ao Yüan-lang's face was wreathed in smiles. He said, "Then you've grasped the essence of the poem. There's no need to look for its meaning. If the poem has any meaning, so much the worse for it."

Miss Su said, "Excuse me, all of you wait here a minute. I will show you something."

When Miss Su had gone, Hung-chien said, "Mr. Ts'ao, when Miss Su's second edition of the *Eighteen Poets of the Colloquial Style* comes out, it'll certainly include you as the nineteenth."

Ts'ao Yüan-lang said, "Not a chance. I'm much too different from the other poets; we don't go together. Miss Su told me yesterday that she wrote that book to get her degree. Actually she doesn't think much of their poetry."

"Oh, really?"

"Mr. Fang, have you read her book?"

"I did, but I don't remember much." When Miss Su gave him a copy, he had merely flipped through it to see who the eighteen poets were.

"In the preface she quotes a parable by Jules Tellier about a man whose hair was falling out. The man went to get a haircut, but the barber told him he needn't bother because his hair would all fall out by itself in a few days. For the same reason, most of modern literature is not worth criticizing. That parable is quite apt."

"I guess I didn't notice that," Hung-chien could only say, thinking to himself: *Good thing I don't want to marry Miss Su; otherwise, I'd have to read her book just as carefully. Too bad Chao Hsin-mei's French is not good enough to read books; otherwise, he could certainly make Miss Su happy the way Ts'ao does now.*

Miss T'ang said, "The poets my cousin discusses in her book are like eighteen strands of fallen-out hair; in the future Mr. Ts'ao will be like the single strand of hair that the miser refuses to part with."[24]

They all laughed. Miss Su returned to the room carrying a purple sandalwood fan case. Winking at Miss T'ang who smiled and nodded, Miss Su removed the case's lid, took out a woman's carved garu-wood folded fan, handed it to Ts'ao and said, "There's a poem on it. Please read it."

Yüan-lang opened the fan and read it aloud in the tone of a monk begging alms or an actor reciting the spoken part of opera. Hung-chien couldn't make out a word, for the chanting of a poem, like a dying man talking in his sleep, was in the native dialect. After reading it aloud, Yüan-lang then read it once more to himself, his lips puttering up and down in the manner of a cat chanting the sutra. Then he exclaimed, "Very good! It's simple and sincere and has the flavor of an ancient folk song."

Seemingly bashful, Miss Su said, "How sharp you are, Mr. Ts'ao! Tell the truth. Is the poem any good?"

Fang Hung-chien took the fan from Ts'ao Yüan-lang. As soon as he saw it, he was filled with disgust. On the perfectly good gilt-flecked fan was the following poem written askew with a fountain pen in purple ink:

> Surely I've not imprisoned you?
> Or have you taken possession of me?
> You burst into my heart,
> Shut the door and turned the key.
> The key to the lock was lost
> By me, or maybe by you yourself.
> Now there's no way to open the door.
> Forever you are locked in my heart.

Below in small characters were: "Autumn, twenty-sixth year of the Republic (1937), an old work copied for Wen-wan. Wang Er-k'ai."

This Wang Er-k'ai was a well-known young politician, a middle-level official in Chungking. Miss Su and Miss T'ang meanwhile both looked at Fang Hung-chien, anxiously waiting for his reaction to the poem. He put down the fan and with a wry face said, "The palm of whoever wrote those characters should be spanked. I've never seen fountain pen writing on a fan; well, at least, he didn't write anything in English."

Hastily Miss Su said, "Never mind the calligraphy. What do you think of the poem?"

Hung-chien said, "Could someone as ambitious as Wang Er-k'ai for high political office write good poetry? I'm not asking him for a job, and there's no obligation for me to flatter him," totally unaware that Miss T'ang was frowning and shaking her head at him.

"You are so obnoxious!" fumed Miss Su. "You're completely prejudiced. You shouldn't be discussing poetry." With that she took the fan from him.

Hung-chien said, "All right, all right, let me read it again calmly and objectively."

Miss Su pouted and said, "I don't want you to," but she let him have the fan again.

74

Suddenly pointing at the poem on the fan, Hung-chien exclaimed, "Oh, terrific! This poem was cribbed."

Miss Su's face livid, she said, "Don't be ridiculous! How could it have been cribbed?"

Miss T'ang opened her eyes wide in amazement.

"At the very least it was borrowed—a foreign loan. Mr. Ts'ao was quite right when he said it had the flavor of an ancient folk song. Remember, Miss Su? We heard the professor talk about this poem in the history of European literature class. It's a German folk song of the fifteenth or sixteenth century. When I studied German with a tutor before I went to Germany, I came across it again in a beginning reader. It started out, 'I am yours, you are mine,' and the rest of the poem went something like, 'You've been shut in my heart. The key is lost, and you can never get out.' I can't remember the exact words but I couldn't be mistaken about the general outline. There could never be such a coincidence."

Miss Su said, "I don't remember this poem ever being discussed in the history of European literature class."

Hung-chien said, "How could you not have? Maybe you didn't pay close attention in class. You didn't have to jot down everything the way I did. You can't be blamed for that. You were attending classes in your own major and your not taking notes just showed how knowledgeable you were. You knew everything the professor said, but I was an auditor from the Chinese literature department; if I didn't keep my pen busy in the classroom, I'd have been laughed at by you for being so ill prepared for the course that I couldn't understand the lecture well enough to take notes."

Miss Su became wordless; Miss T'ang just lowered her head. Ts'ao Yüan-lang guessed that Fang Hung-chien's knowledge of German was about as good or as bad as his own. Besides, Fang was a Chinese major, so he couldn't be too brilliant. For in a university, science majors look down on humanities majors, foreign language majors on Chinese majors, Chinese majors on philosophy majors, philosophy majors on sociology majors, and sociology majors in turn on education majors. Since education majors have no one to look down on, they can only despise the professors in their own department.

Immediately Ts'ao Yüan-lang blurted out, "I knew the poem had a model. Didn't I say it had the flavor of an ancient folk song? But Mr. Fang's attitude is contrary to the spirit of literary appreciation. You Chinese majors all have the nasty habit or even obsession of textual authentication. If a poem has allusions, it means more to someone who can recognize them; reading it will bring to mind countless others which can set it off in contrast.[25] Mr. Fang, if you read T. S. Eliot's poetry, you'd realize that every phrase in modern Western poetry has its source, but we never accuse those poets of plagiarism. Do we, Miss Su?"

Fang Hung-chien wished he could have said, *No wonder your honorable work is such a hodgepodge. You experts don't find it at all strange, but we laymen feel obliged to report to the police when we have nabbed the thief and recovered the goods.* Instead, he merely said with a smile, "Don't take it too hard. Gifts to women are rarely one's own; it's nothing more than borrowing flowers to offer to Buddha. If the donor is an official, you can assume that the gift was fleeced off someone else." As he spoke he wondered why Miss T'ang was not paying much attention.

Miss Su said, "I don't like your cutting remarks. So Fang Hung-chien is the only intelligent person in the world."

Hung-chien stayed a little longer; with no one in the mood for more conversation, he said goodbye and left before anyone else. Miss Su did not try to keep him. After he'd left the house he was vaguely uneasy, aware that his remarks might have offended Miss Su, that Wang Er-k'ai must be one of her worshipers. But remembering he was to visit Miss T'ang the next day, he, in anticipation, forgot everything else.

When Fang Hung-chien arrived at the T'angs the next day, Miss T'ang's maid told him to wait in Miss T'ang's study. When Miss T'ang saw him, she said, "Mr. Fang, you made a terrible mistake yesterday. Did you know that?"

Fang Hung-chien reflected for a moment; then he said with a smile, "You mean your cousin is mad at me because I criticized that poem?"

"Do you know who wrote the poem?" She saw his blank uncomprehending look and went on, "It was written by my cousin, not by Wang Er-k'ai."

"What!" he exclaimed. "Don't put me on. Didn't it plainly say on the fan, 'An old work copied for Wen-wan'?"

"It was Wen-wan's old work that was copied. Wang Er-k'ai knows my uncle and was Chao Hsin-mei's boss. He's married, but last year when my cousin returned from abroad, he was trying to ingratiate himself with her. He made Chao Hsin-mei so angry that Chao lost weight. Usually, when a person is filled with rage, he swells up and gets fat, don't you think? Later the executive offices of the government all moved to the interior. Anxious to be an official, Wang finally cast my cousin aside and went to the interior, too. This is why Chao Hsin-mei refused to go there. The fan was Wang's present to my cousin, and he had someone specially carve the design on it. And the poem was my cousin's favorite piece."

"That moron, two-bit politician. The inscription on the fan was so ambiguous that it got me in trouble. Damn! What do I do now?"

"What do you do? Luckily, you are a smooth talker. A few sentences should be enough to clear the matter."

Pleased and humbled by this remark, he said, "It's such a mess now; I am afraid it won't be easy to remedy the situation. I'll go home and write a letter of apology to your cousin immediately."

"I'd really like to know how you'd write such a letter. Let me learn how and maybe I can use one someday."

"If it proves very effective, I'll certainly make a copy of the letter for you. Did they criticize me much after I left yesterday?"

"The poet said all kinds of things, but my cousin didn't say much. She said your Chinese is very good. So quoting a friend of his, the poet said that nowadays if someone wanted to have good Chinese, he'd have to study foreign literatures. Before, people majoring in Western science had to know foreign languages, and now people in Chinese literature have to be well versed in Western languages first. This friend of his is supposed to be returning from abroad soon, and Ts'ao Yüan-lang wants him to meet my cousin."

"Oh, another jerk! If he's a friend of that poet, he couldn't have much on the ball. You saw that poem of his, something about the 'smorgasbord and adulterer.' You can't tell what it's all about. And it's not honest, unpretentious incoherence, but presumptuous, arrogant, and shameless. It insults the reader's intelligence."

"I'm too ignorant about such matters; I am not qualified to comment, but it seems to me somebody who has studied at a prestigious university abroad couldn't be as bad as you say. Maybe that poem of his was meant to be funny."

"Miss T'ang, studying abroad today is like passing examinations under the old Manchu system. My father used to say that if a man failed the third-degree examination, no matter how high an official he became, he'd carry that regret around for the rest of his life. It's not for the broadening of knowledge that one goes abroad but to get rid of that inferiority complex. It's like having smallpox or measles, or in other words, it's essential to have them. Once a child has had the smallpox or measles, he can grow up protected, and if he comes in contact with these diseases later on, he has no fear of them. Once we've studied abroad, we've gotten the inferiority complex out of the system, and our souls become strengthened, and when we do come across such germs as Ph.D.'s or M.A.'s we've built up a resistance against them. Once we've had smallpox, we can forget about ever having caught it; similarly, someone who's studied abroad should also forget about ever having gone abroad. People like Ts'ao Yüan-lang can never forget that they have studied abroad; everywhere they go they have to brag about their Oxford or Cambridge backgrounds. They are like those people who have contracted smallpox and got pock-marked and brag about their faces as if they were starred essays."[26]

Smiling, Miss T'ang said, "If people heard you say all that, they'd just say you were jealous because their universities are more famous than the one you went to."

Unable to think of a reply, he gave a silly smile. She was glad that she sometimes caught him speechless. She then said, "Yesterday I wondered why you didn't know that the poem was my cousin's. You must have read her poems before."

"I came to know your cousin on the boat coming home. It's been a very short time. We'd never even talked before. Remember that day when she said my school nickname was 'The Thermometer'? I am not interested in new-style poetry, and I don't think it's worth getting interested in it just for your cousin's sake."

"Hmm, if she found that out—"

"Miss T'ang, listen to me. Your cousin is a very intelligent and talented woman, but how should I put it? An intelligent and talented woman was born to make a stupid man swoon before her. Since he himself has no talent, he looks upon her talent as something mysterious and wonderful, and so he prostrates himself before her in worship the way a penniless pauper idolizes a rich man."

"In other words, someone as intelligent as Mr. Fang would prefer a stupid, illiterate woman."

"Woman has an intelligence all her own, and it is as nimble and lively as her person. Compared to that kind of intelligence, talent and scholarship are sediments. To say a woman is talented and scholarly is like praising a flower for balancing on the scale with a cabbage or potato—utterly pointless. A truly intelligent woman would never try to become a genius. She'd just find clever ways to loaf around."

"What if she wanted to get a Ph.D.?" she asked with a smile.

"She'd never think of getting one in the first place. It's only women with talents like your cousin who want a Ph.D."

"But nowadays even to graduate from a run-of-the-mill university, you have to write a thesis."

"Then the year she is to graduate, there'd be a change in the world situation. The school would hold its commencement exercise early, and they'd let her graduate without requiring a thesis."

She shook her head in disbelief and dropped the subject. They quickly exhausted their topics of conversation, for pleasantries bear no repetition once they have been spoken. Though the words that lovers speak to each other are inexhaustible, Fang Hung-chien and Miss T'ang were not lovers. He felt that every subject that could be safely mentioned had been spoken, and he could not say any more if he were not to step beyond the bounds of propriety. Noticing his silence, she said with a smile, "Why don't you say something?"

Responding with a smile, he said, "Well, why don't you?"

She told him that in the courtyard of her country home were two cinnamon trees, each over a hundred years old. When she was little she often noticed that a whole flock of noisy sparrows in the trees would suddenly fall

78

silent; then after a brief pause just as suddenly they would start up all at once. And she commented that it was the same way with human conversation.

On his way home Fang Hung-chien mentally drafted the letter to Miss Su, convinced that it would be more appropriate to write it in the classical style, since its ambiguity contained a terseness that would make it an excellent tool for glossing over or playing down an error.

After dinner he wrote a rough sketch, amazed at his greatly increased ability to write the untruth. Worried that the joke might have gotten out of hand, he lay down his brush halfway through the letter; but when he thought how Miss T'ang would appreciate and understand the letter and how the lies would bring smiles to her lips, he continued on happily. The letter read as follows:

Yesterday when you showed me the poem on the fan, I was vexed at seeing that such a beautiful piece of writing had been composed by none other than a vulgar common official. In my surprise and resentment, I made the unfair accusation that it must have had a model. Though I derived momentary pleasure, I really felt uneasy. I am beholden to you for your kindness. I deserve a stern rebuke.

At the end of the letter he backdated it to the day before and then added two more lines:

P.S. After writing this letter, I left a whole day and night go by before sending it to you. Suffering such a defeat in front of Mr. Ts'ao was most upsetting. I hated it.

He then put down the day's date. He read the letter twice again with complete satisfaction. In his imagination, it was not Miss Su but Miss T'ang reading the letter.

The next day when he arrived at the bank, he dropped the letter at the mail section to be delivered to Miss Su by a special messenger. In the evening he went home and had just reached his bedroom when the telephone rang. He reached over and answered it.

"The Chous' residence. Who's calling, please?"

He heard a woman say, "Guess who this is."

Hung-chien said, "It's Miss Su, isn't it?"

"Right." Crisp laughter.

"Miss Su, did you get my letter?"

"Yes, I did. You are childish. I don't blame you. Don't I know your temperament?"

"You may be willing to forgive me, but I can't forgive myself."

"Oh, is it worth getting so upset about such trivia? Tell me, do you really think that poem is good?"

Making every effort not to let the smirk on his face slip into his voice, Hung-chien said, "I just wish such a good poem hadn't been written by Wang Er-k'ai. It's too unfair!"

"Let me tell you something. It wasn't."

"Then who wrote it?"

"I wrote it just for fun."

"What? You wrote it? Well, I'll be damned!"

He was thankful that they were talking by telephone and not by television. Otherwise, the interesting combination of the glee on his face and the alarm in his voice would have certainly made Miss Su suspicious.

"You were entirely justified in saying that the poem had a model. I got the idea from Tirsot's collection of old French folk dance tunes and felt it was fresh and interesting, so I wrote a poem in imitation. According to you, there's a similar German version. It's obviously very common."

"Yours is more lively than the German poem."

"You mustn't flatter me. I don't believe you!"

"That's not flattery."

"Are you coming over tomorrow afternoon?"

Hung-chien answered quickly that he was, and since she still hadn't hung up, he didn't hang up either.

"Yesterday you said men don't give their own things to women. What did you mean by that?"

He laughed apologetically and replied, "Because his own things are so lousy, he's ashamed of them, so all he can do is borrow someone else's things to offer. For instance, in inviting a lady out for dinner, if his house is too cramped and the cook's no good, then he has to go to a restaurant and make use of its facilities and cooking."

Miss Su giggled and said, "OK, you win. I'll see you tomorrow."

His head damp with perspiration, he wondered whether it was from nervousness or from his hurried walk home.

That evening Fang Hung-chien copied out a draft of the letter, enclosed a short note with it, and sent it to Miss T'ang. He wished he could have written in English, since the tone of a letter in literary style was so impersonal, while the tone of a letter in colloquial style too easily turned into obnoxious familiarity. Only a letter in English would permit him to write openly, "My dear Miss T'ang," and "Very truly yours, Fang Hung-chien." These common terms of address in Western correspondence only sounded offensive and sickening in Chinese. He was well aware that his English was imbued with the spirit of the free speech of the British and the Declaration of Independence of the Americans in not being bound by the rules of grammar. Otherwise, were he really to depend on a foreign language to "dear" Miss T'ang, it would be like a political offender carrying out his activities while hiding in the foreign concessions in China.

In the next month or two he saw Miss T'ang seven or eight times, wrote her a dozen or so letters, and received five or six replies from her. The first time he received a letter from her, he read it once before going to sleep, then put it next to his pillow, and when he awoke in the middle of the night, he turned on the light to read it again. When he had read it through, he switched off the light and settled back down; then mulling over what the letter had said, he couldn't resist turning on the light again and reading it once more. Later on the letters he wrote gradually became a day-to-day collection of random notes, which he took to the bank with him. Whenever he came across a subject of interest or thought of a phrase, he would pick up his pen and carry on a private, intimate talk with Miss T'ang on paper. Sometimes even when he had nothing to say, he would still want to write something such as, "Today at the bank I drafted several letters and now at last I can catch my breath, stretch, a-a-a-ah! Can you hear my yawn? The waiter came to say lunch is ready. I'll talk to you later. Maybe you're having lunch now. May you 'Eat a bite more and live till 9994,' or, I still have more to say in this letter I'm about to send you, but as you can see, the page is already full. There's only this tiny space on the paper and I can barely squeeze in the sentence from my heart, which is still too shy to look you in the face. Oh! The page—"

He always considered letter-writing a small comfort which, while better than nothing at all, couldn't compare with the joy of meeting her face to face. Then when he did see her, there was so much he couldn't bring himself to say; he would then think it was still better to have written a letter. However, seeing her soon became an addiction. At first, a date with her could "wonderize" the day before and the day after by virtue of their association. Gradually he wished he could see her every day and even every minute. Once he had written and sent a letter off, he would be forever worrying about it, afraid that when it, like a flaring arrow, reached its destination, it would be nothing but dead ashes by the time she received it.

Miss Su and Miss T'ang saw less of each other than before, but Fang Hung-chien, caught between Miss Su's alternating threats and kindness, had no choice but to go to the Sus often. Waiting for him to make his formal declaration of love, Miss Su inwardly faulted him for being so frivolous and tardy; he, on the other hand, was waiting for a chance to explain that he did not love her, and wished he weren't so tenderhearted and could be courageous enough to cut the Gordian knot. Every time he went to the Sus, he came away reproaching himself for having gone one more time and talked so much again. He gradually realized that he was what Westerners called a "moral weakling," and was worried that Miss T'ang would detect this major flaw in his character.

One Saturday afternoon after returning home from having tea with Miss T'ang, he saw on the table an invitation from Chao Hsin-mei for dinner the next day and was struck with the horrible thought that this might be Hsin-mei's engagement party. That would be disastrous. Miss Su would start concentrating her affections on him all the more. Miss Su called to ask if he had received the card or not and Hsin-mei had asked her to invite him; moreover, she told him to see her the next morning.

The next day Miss Su said that Hsin-mei had insisted that he come, as a chance for everyone to get together. At first he was going to ask why Hsin-mei had invited him, but the words shrank away from the tip of his tongue. Not wishing to mention Hsin-mei's antagonism toward him any more for fear of deepening Miss Su's misunderstanding of him, he asked instead if any others were invited. She said two of Hsin-mei's friends had also been invited.

"Is that little fatso and big poet Ts'ao Yüan-lang included? If he is, they can save on the food. Just looking at that meatball face of his will make people feel full," he said.

"Probably not. Hsin-mei doesn't know him. I know how petty both you and Hsin-mei are. Hsin-mei would start quarreling the moment he saw Yüan-lang. Well, my place here is not a battlefield, and I am not going to let the two of them meet. Yüan-lang is a very interesting fellow. You're so biased; I think your heart must be way over in your armpit. Since that time, I haven't let you and Yüan-lang meet so as to avoid any squabble."

He was going to say, "Actually it makes no difference to me," but under her doting gaze, he couldn't say anything. At the same time, he was greatly relieved to learn that Ts'ao Yüan-lang had been added to the list of Miss Su's worshipers.

"What do you think of Chao Hsin-mei?" she suddenly asked.

"He is more capable than I and has a very dignified bearing. He is sure to be a success in the future. I think he is in fact an ideal—uh—man."

If God had praised the devil or a socialist had eulogized the petty bourgeoisie, Miss Su could not have been more astonished. She was all set for Hung-chien to ridicule Hsin-mei, whereupon she was going to uphold justice by arguing in Hsin-mei's defense. She then said with a sniff, "The guest is already praising the host before he's even had a bite of food! Hsin-mei's been writing letters to me almost every other day. I needn't repeat what's in the letters, but they all say he's losing sleep. I get so sick of reading them! Who told him to lose sleep? What's that got to do with me? I am not a doctor!"

She knew perfectly well his losing sleep had quite a bit to do with her without having to ask a doctor's opinion.

"As the poem from the *Book of Odes*[27] goes, 'The noble young lady,/ Waking and sleeping he sought her;/ He sought her but could not find her,/ Waking and sleeping he longed for her.' His letters are a manifestation of genuine Chinese culture," Hung-chien said with a grin.

Glaring at him, Miss Su said, "Isn't it a pity he doesn't have your good fortune! You don't know how lucky you are. All you do is make fun of people with your wisecracks. I don't like that about you. Hung-chien, I wish you'd learn to be more kind. I'm really going to get after you about that in the future."

He became speechless with fright. Miss Su had business to attend to at home, so she agreed to meet him that evening at the restaurant. He went back home and for the rest of the day remained glum and despondent, feeling he could no longer go on as before and must clarify his position to her as soon as possible.

When Hung-chien reached the restaurant, the other two guests were already there. One was hunchbacked with a high forehead, large eyes, and a pale complexion. He was wearing a gold wire-rimmed pince-nez and a Western suit with cuffs covering his fingers. His face smooth, with neither a mustache nor wrinkles, he resembled an infantile old woman or an elderly child. The other guest had a very proud bearing. His nose was straight and high; his profile gave the impression of a ladder propped against his face. The bow tie at his neck was so large and neat that Hung-chien was struck with hopeless admiration. When Hsin-mei saw Hung-chien, he greeted him warmly. During the introductions, Hung-chien learned that the hunchback was the philosopher Ch'u Shen-ming and the other was Tung Hsieh-ch'üan, a former attaché at the Chinese legation in Czechoslovakia. Transferred back to China, Tung had not yet been assigned a new post; he wrote excellent old-style poetry and was a great literary talent.

Ch'u Shen-ming's original name was Ch'u Chia-pao. After attaining fame he found Chia-pao (literally, family treasure) unsuitable for a philosopher and changed it, following the precedent set by Spinoza, to Shen-ming (literally, careful and clear), taken from the expression "consider carefully and argue clearly." He was known as a child wonder, though some wondered about his sanity. He had refused to graduate from grade school, high school, or college, for he felt no teacher was good enough to teach or test him. He harbored a special hatred for women, and though extremely nearsighted, he had refused to be fitted for glasses for fear of getting a good look at women's faces. He always said that man's nature was composed of a natural humaneness and an animal disposition, and that he himself was all natural disposition. He was an avid reader of foreign philosophical journals, and if he came across the addresses of any world-renowned philosophers, he would write them saying how much he enjoyed their works. He culled his praise of their works from the review sections of philosophy journals and added a word here or deleted a word there and passed everything off as his own opinion.

In the intellectual world, Western philosophers are the biggest whiners; they don't wield the experts' authority as scientists nor do they enjoy as much popular fame as men of letters. So, when suddenly from thousands of miles away came a letter of praise, needless to say they were so thrilled that they nearly forgot philosophy. China, as they saw it, was a primitive country, heaven knows how mean and backward, and yet here was a Chinese who wrote with sense. In their replies to Ch'u Shen-ming, they praised him as the founder of a new philosophy of China and even sent him books. If he wrote them again, however, he rarely received any more replies. The reason was that these vain old men would show off his first letter among their colleagues only to find that everyone else had received a similar letter and had been similarly called "the greatest philosopher of modern times." Inevitably they became angry and disappointed.

With some thirty or forty of these replies, Ch'u Shen-ming had awed innumerable people. One wealthy, talent-loving official spent ten thousand ounces of gold to send him abroad. The only Western philosopher who did not respond to his letter was Henri Bergson, who dreaded having strangers come pester him and kept his address confidential and his telephone number unlisted. After Ch'u Shen-ming arrived in Europe, Ch'u, in a last-ditch effort, sent a letter to Bergson to make an appointment for a visit, but to his chagrin the letter came back unopened. From then on, he bitterly hated Intuitivism. On the other hand, Bergson's rival, Bertrand Russell, was willing to humor the Chinese and therefore invited him over for tea. From then on Ch'u studied mathematical logic.

When Ch'u went abroad, for the sake of convenience, he had to wear glasses, and so it happened that his attitude toward women gradually changed. Though he loathed women and could smell them three doors away, he desired them, which was why his nose was so sharp. His mind was filled with them. If he came upon the expression *a posteriori* in mathematical logic, he would think of "posterior," and when he came across the mark "X" he would think of a kiss. Luckily he had never made a careful study of Plato's dialogues with Timaeus; otherwise he would be dazed by every "X" mark. Now he was translating into English a work on the Chinese view of life written by the official who sent him abroad. Every month he drew out a sum of money from the National Bank for living expenses and lived a very leisurely life.

Tung Hsieh-ch'üan's father, Tung I-sun, was an old scholar who had served as an official for the Republic of China but had not forgotten the former Manchu regime. Hsieh-ch'üan himself was quite gifted and wrote old-style poetry in the same way his father did. A country of active scholar-generals, China is unlike France, which, if it had one or two generals capable of wielding a pen, would want them to be revered at the National Academy. While Hsieh-ch'üan's military strategems were not too different from those of most scholar-generals, his poetry, even if it hadn't been the work of a scholar-general, would still have been considered quite good. But writing can reduce one to poverty. He never had much luck as an official, even though this was not necessarily a misfortune for the soldiers. As a military attaché, instead of discussing military affairs, he criticized his superiors and peers for their literary incompetence, and for this reason he was transferred back to China. Shortly after his return, he decided to look for another job.

Fang Hung-chien viewed Tung Hsieh-ch'üan as a very distinguished individual, so when he heard Chao Hsin-mei say Hsieh-ch'üan was the son of a famous father, he was overwhelmed and said, "Mr. I-sun is well known both at home and abroad. Mr. Tung lives up to his distinguished heritage—a man of both literary and military talents." He thought this would be considered the highest form of praise.

Tung Hsieh-ch'üan said, "My poetic style is different from my father's. In his youth he followed wrong models. Even now he still hasn't gotten away from the styles of Huang Chung-tse and Kung Ting-an[28] of the Ch'ien-lung and Chia-ch'ing periods.[29] I started right off writing in the style of the T'ung-chih and Kuang-hsü periods."[30]

Fang Hung-chien didn't dare venture a word. Chao Hsin-mei asked the waiter for the menu he had submitted the day before and gave it a final scrutiny. Tung also asked the waiter for a brush and ink stone, took the menu from the tea table, and quickly leafed through it. Fang Hung-chien was perplexed.

Ch'u Shen-ming sat silently and stiffly, smiling as though contemplating something interesting in the depths of his subconsciousness. His enigmatic smile would make that of the Mona Lisa amount to nothing. Hung-chien tried to talk to him. "Mr. Ch'u, what philosophical questions have you been studying recently?"

With a nervous expression, Ch'u shot a glance over at Hung-chien and then turned to Chao Hsin-mei. "Old Chao,[31] Miss Su should have been here by now. Waiting for a woman like this—this is the first time in my life."

Hsin-mei gave the menu to the waiter, turned around and was about to agree, when he saw Tung Hsieh-ch'üan writing something. He asked quickly, "Hsieh-ch'üan, what are you up to?"

"I'm composing a poem," replied Tung, without raising his head.

Relieved, Hsin-mei said, "Write all you want. I don't understand poetry, but I like yours. My friend Miss Su writes excellent new-style poetry and has a great appreciation for old-style poetry. Later on, we can show her yours."

Tung stopped writing, tapped his forehead with his finger as if searching for a phrase, then continued writing, observing as he did so, "There's no comparison between new- and old-style poetry. The day I was at Lu-shan[32] chatting with our old family friend Mr. Ch'en San-yüan,[33] we happened to start talking about poems in the colloquial style. It turned out the old fellow had read one or two new-style poems. He said Hsü Chih-mo's poetry is interesting, but it's only about on a level with such poets as Yang Chi[34] of the Ming. Just too pitiful. Women's poetry is second-rate at best. Among birds it's always the male which can sing, such as the cock."

Hsin-mei protested, "Why do Westerners always refer to the nightingale as female?"

Ch'u Shen-ming proved to be quite learned on the subject of the sex of birds. He said coldly, "The female nightingale can't sing. It's the male nightingale which sings."

Just as he was speaking, Miss Su arrived. Exercising his prerogative as host, Hsin-mei preempted the right to bestow his attentions on her in front of Hung-chien. After shaking hands with her, Hsieh-ch'üan did not look at her directly, for he had adopted the manner toward women of the old class of scholars, which was either unrestrained funmaking—the dallying behavior toward prostitutes—or eyes directed at the nose and the nose pointed toward the heart, not daring a level gaze—the courtesy toward the female members of a friend's family. Philosopher Ch'u eyed Miss Su greedily, his pupils nearly imitating the German philosopher Schelling's "Absolute," which was "like a bullet shot from a pistol" (*Das Absolute sei wie aus der Pistole geschossen*), bursting from his eyesockets with double-barreled action and shattering his glasses.

Hsin-mei said, "I also invited Mrs. Tung, but Mr. Tung said she was too busy to come. Mrs. Tung is a beauty and a good painter. She and Hsieh-ch'üan make a perfect couple."

Hsieh-ch'üan observed objectively, "My wife is rather pretty, and her painting is quite professional in style. The inscription on her painting, the 'Setting Sun Buddhist Temple,' can be found in many collections owned by the older generation. When we returned from a visit to the Dragon Tree Temple, she painted a scroll of it on which my father inscribed two *ch'i-chüeh* poems.[35] The best two couplets were:

'Who remains of the scholars of Chen-yüan times?[36]
On countless Buddhist huts shines the setting sun of old.'

Indeed, the old masters grow fewer by the day, and there seems to be a decline of talented writers.

'No need to go back to the time of K'ang-hsi and Ch'ien-lung.
Turn around and already the T'ung-chih and Kuang-hsü seem lost.' ''

As he spoke he shook his head and sighed sadly.

Never having heard anything like this before, Fang Hung-chien was quite intrigued, though he wondered how someone that young and Westernized could sound so much as though he lived in a bygone era. Maybe it came from imitating the poetry written in the T'ung-kuang style.

Hsin-mei invited everyone to go in and be seated. He poured Miss Su a glass of French grape juice and said laughingly, "This is exclusively for you; we have our own liquor. Today at the table we have Shen-ming, a philosopher. You and Hsieh-ch'üan are both poets. Mr. Fang is a philosopher and a poet—both combined in one, which is even more impressive. I myself don't have any talent. All I can do is drink a few swallows of wine. Mr. Fang, I'll drink two catties of wine[37] with you today. Hsieh-ch'üan has a big drinking capacity, too."

Fang Hung-chien gave a start and said, "Who said I am a philosopher and poet? And I can't drink either, not a single drop."

With his hand on the liquor bottle, Hsin-mei scanned the table and said, "Today whoever declines out of politeness will be fined two glasses. All right?"

"Agreed!" said Hsieh-ch'üan. "With such good wine as that, they're getting off easy."

Finding he was unable to put a stop to it, Hung-chien said, "Mr. Chao, I really can't drink. How about giving me some grape juice, too?"

Hsin-mei said, "Whoever heard of a returned student from France who can't drink? Grape juice is a lady's drink. Shen-ming doesn't drink because of his neurasthenia. He's an exception. Don't be polite."

With a smile, Hsieh-ch'üan said, "Since you don't have 'a face that could overthrow a kingdom or topple a city' like Miss Wen-wan, and your body isn't 'full of aches and pains' like Mr. Shen-ming, I think you should 'get drunk while there's wine.'[38] All right, empty one glass first. If not a glass, then half a glass."

Miss Su said, "Apparently Hung-chien doesn't drink. Since Hsin-mei is so insistent, why not oblige him by drinking just a little bit?"

When Hsin-mei sensed Miss Su's protectiveness of Hung-chien, he wished every drop of liquor in Hung-chien's glass would turn to kerosene.

Though Hsin-mei's wish did not come true, Hung-chien, after just one swallow, already felt a line of fire stretching from the tip of his tongue down to the middle of his diaphragm. Shen-ming was only drinking tea, and his cup was still empty. The waiter brought a large bottle of Grade A P'o-nai milk and said that the milk had already been warmed in water.

Hsin-mei gave the bottle to Shen-ming. "You pour your own. I won't stand on ceremony with you."

Shen-ming poured out a glass, and pursing up his lips he took a taste of it. "Neither too hot nor too cold, just right," he said. He then took out a bottle of some kind of foreign medicine from his pocket, counted out four pills, put them in his mouth, and drank them down with a swallow of milk.

Miss Su remarked, "Mr. Ch'u really knows how to take care of himself."

Shen-ming heaved a breath and said, "How much nicer it would be if a man had no body but was all mind. I'm not really guarding my health. I'm just babying it so it won't give me any trouble—Hsin-mei, this milk is quite fresh."

Hsin-mei said, "I didn't tell a lie, did I? I know you. After the milk was delivered to my home, I kept it cold in the refrigerator. Since you take fresh milk so seriously, when I get a chance, I'll take you to see our friend Miss Hsü, who runs a dairy, and ask her to let you suck your fill every day directly from the cow. I brought all the grape juice, wine, and milk we're having today myself rather than ask the restaurant to provide them. Wen-wan, after dinner, I have a box for you. Something you like."

Miss Su said, "What is it?—Oh, you're going to make me get another headache."

Fang Hung-chien said, "I didn't know what you liked. Next time I can get some for you too."

"Wen-wan, don't tell him," said Hsin-mei in a haughty, jealous tone.

Miss Su apologized for her special taste. "When I was abroad I had a yen for Cantonese duck gizzard, but it wasn't easy to get. Last year when I got back, my brother bought some for me. I chewed so much that my temples became sore for days. Now you want to tempt me again."

Hung-chien observed, "Chicken and duck gizzards are never used in Western dishes. In London I saw whole boxes of chicken and duck gizzards selling so cheaply they hardly cost anything. People bought them to feed their cats."

Hsin-mei said, "The English don't eat half the stuff Americans do. When it comes to food, foreigners are cowards; they don't dare take risks, not like we Chinese, who'll try any kind of meat. The main thing in their cooking is seasoning, while ours is frying, together with other vegetables. This is why their soups are so tasteless. They'll boil chicken for a while, then throw out the soup and just eat the meat. It's really a joke."

"Isn't it a shame?" said Hung-chien. "When tea first went abroad, people would put a whole pound of it in a pot of water and bring it to a boil, then throw out the water, add salt and pepper, and just eat the leaves."

They all laughed. Hsieh-ch'üan said, "That's just like the joke about Fan Fan-shan using chicken broth to make Lung-ching tea.[39] That old family friend of ours, while serving as an official in Peking during the early years of the Kuang-hsü reign [about 1875], received a can of coffee from someone who had just returned from abroad. He thought it was snuff and rubbed off the skin of his nostrils with it. There's a poem in his collection about it."

Hung-chien said, "Mr. Tung does indeed come from an illustrious family! We're hearing all kinds of anecdotes today."

Shen-ming pressed down his pince-nez, cleared his throat, and said, "Mr. Fang, what was it you were asking me that time?"

"When?" asked Hung-chien, bewildered.

"Before Miss Su came."—Hung-chien could not recall—"It seems you were asking me what philosophical questions I was studying, weren't you?" To this usual question, Ch'u Shen-ming had a pat answer. Since Miss Su had not yet arrived, he had waited until now to show off.

"Oh, yes, yes."

"Strictly speaking, your statement has a slight fallacy. When a philosopher encounters a question, his first step is to study the question. Is it a question or not? If it's not, then it's a pseudo-question which needn't and can't be solved. If it is a question, his second step is to study the solution. Is the traditional solution correct or should it be revised? You probably meant to ask not what question am I studying, but what question am I studying the solution of."

Fang Hung-chien was astounded, Tung Hsieh-ch'üan was bored, and Miss Su was confused. "Marvelous!" exclaimed Hsin-mei. "A truly thorough analysis! That's wonderful, wonderful! Hung-chien, you've studied philosophy, but you should be quite willing to take a back seat today. After such an excellent discussion, we should all have a glass."

At Hsin-mei's insistence Hung-chien reluctantly took a couple of swallows, saying, "Hsin-mei, I just muddled my way through a year in the philosophy department by reading a few assigned reference books. Before Mr. Ch'u I can only humbly ask for instruction."

Ch'u Shen-ming said, "I'm unworthy! From what you say, Mr. Fang, it seems you were taking the individual as a unit in reading philosophical works. That is only studying philosophers. At best it's studying the history of philosophy, not philosophy itself. At most such a person could be a philosophy professor, but never a philosopher. I like using my own mind, not other peoples', to think. I read works of science and literature, but I never read works of philosophy unless I have to. A lot of so-called philosophers these days don't really study philosophy at all; they just study personalities or works in philosophy. Strictly speaking, they shouldn't be called philosophers, but rather 'philophilosophers.' "

" 'Philophilosophers?' " said Hung-chien. "Now that's an interesting term. Did you coin that yourself?"

"It's a word someone saw in a book and told Bertie about, and Bertie told me."

"Who's Bertie?"

"Russell."

Here was a world-renowned philosopher, who had just recently become an earl, and Ch'u Shen-ming was on such familiar terms with him as to call him by his nickname. Even Tung Hsieh-ch'üan was impressed as he asked, "Do you know Russell well?"

"You could call us friends. He respected me enough to ask my help in answering several questions." Heaven knows Ch'u Shen-ming was not telling a lie. Russell had indeed asked him when he would come to England, what his plans were, how many sugar cubes he took in his tea, and other similar questions that he alone could answer. "Mr. Fang, have you ever studied mathematical logic?"

"I know that's quite difficult, so I've never studied it."

"There's a fallacy in your statement. If you've never studied it before, how can you 'know' it's difficult? What you mean is, 'I've heard that it's quite difficult.' "

Hsin-mei was about to say, "Hung-chien lost. He's fined a glass," when Miss Su protested on his behalf, "Mr. Ch'u is really too sharp! He's made me too scared to open my mouth."

Shen-ming said, "It won't do you any good not to open your mouth. If at heart your thinking is still confused and illogical, the cause of the disease still hasn't been rooted out."

Miss Su pouted and said, "You're really dreadful! You even want to deprive us of the freedom of our hearts. Well, I don't think you have the ability to probe into someone else's heart."

This was the first time in Ch'u Shen-ming's life that a beautiful young woman had ever spoken to him on matters of the heart. He was so excited that his pince-nez splashed right into his glass of milk, splattering his clothes and the tablecloth. A few drops even fell on Miss Su's arm. Everyone burst out laughing. Chao Hsin-mei pressed the button to call the waiter to come clean up. Miss Su did not dare frown as she lightly dabbed with her handkerchief at the splattered drops on her arm. Blushing scarlet, Ch'u Shen-ming wiped his glasses dry. Fortunately they had not been broken, but he would not put them on right away for fear of getting a good look at the lingering smile on everyone's face.

90

Tung Hsieh-ch'üan said, "Well, now. Though 'water was poured before the horse,'[40] still, the 'broken mirror was made round again.'[41] Shen-ming's future marriage will certainly be full of vicissitudes. It should be worth watching."

Hsin-mei said, "Everyone drink a toast in advance to the good wife of our great philosopher. Mr. Fang, you drink too, even if only half a glass."

Hsin-mei was unaware that great philosophers have never had good wives. Socrates' wife was a shrew and poured dirty water on her husband's head. Aristotle's mistress rode on him like a horse, telling him to crawl on the floor naked, and even making him taste the whip. Marcus Aurelius' wife was an adulteress, and even Ch'u Shen-ming's pal Bertrand Russell had been divorced several times.

Hung-chien in fact remarked, "Let's hope Mr. Ch'u won't go through three or four divorces like Russell."

Shen-ming's face stiffened and he retorted, "That's the philosophy you've studied!"

Miss Su said, "Hung-chien, I think you've had too much to drink. Your eyes are all red."

Hsieh-ch'üan roared with laughter.

"Such impudence!" exclaimed Hsin-mei. "Such remarks demand a fine of one glass!"

So far Hung-chien had been required to take only one or two swallows when he drank a toast. Now he was fined a glass and, knowing he was in the wrong, he braced himself and gulped it down. Gradually he began to feel as if some other being had occupied his body and was doing all the talking.

"As for Bertie's marriages and divorces," said Shen-ming, "I've talked with him about them. He quoted an old English saying that marriage is like a gilded bird cage. The birds outside want to get in, and the birds inside want to fly out. So you have marriage and divorce, divorce and marriage in endless succession."

Miss Su said, "There's a French saying similar to that. Instead of a bird cage, it's a fortress under siege (*forteresse assiégée*). The people outside the city want to break in and the people inside the city want to escape. Right, Hung-chien?" Hung-chien shook his head to indicate he did not know.

Hsin-mei said, "You needn't ask. You sounded as if you could be wrong!"

Shen-ming said, "Whether it's a bird cage or a besieged fortress, someone like me who's detached from everything has no fear of a siege."

Under the influence of alcohol, Hung-chien had lost his self-control, as he blurted out, "Anyway, you could always pull the 'empty-town bluff.' "[42] Hsin-mei fined him another half glass of wine, while Miss Su warned him not to talk so much.

Hsieh-ch'üan, deep in thought, said suddenly, "Oh, yes. Among Chinese philosophers, Wang Yang-ming[43] was henpecked." This was the first person he had not referred to that day as an "old family friend."

Hsin-mei quickly cut in, "Weren't there any others? Mr. Fang, you tell us. You've studied Chinese literature."

Hung-chien said hurriedly, "That was a long time ago, and I was never very good at it in the first place."

Hsin-mei gave Miss Su a happy wink; she suddenly looked very dumb, appearing to see nothing.

"Who were your Chinese professors in college?" Hsieh-ch'üan asked without interest.

Hung-chien searched his mind for the names of his Chinese teachers, but couldn't think of a single worthy one, like Bertie or Ch'en San-yüan, names which could be rolled around on the tongue and shown off like a quality Havana cigar. "They were all nobodies," he said, "yet much too good to teach such a lousy student as myself. Hsieh-ch'üan, I really don't know the first thing about poetry. I read it now and then, but if you were to ask me to write a poem, I wouldn't know where to begin."

Miss Su hated the way Hung-chien had debased himself and wanted very much to make him look good.

Smiling scornfully, Hsieh-ch'üan asked, "Did you read the poetry of Su Man-shu[44] and Huang Kung-tu?"[45]

"Why?"

"That's what an ordinary returned student can appreciate, the poetry of the *ehr-mao-tzu*.[46] Students returning from Japan worship Su Man-shu; Western returned students admire Huang Kung-tu. Am I wrong? Of the two, Huang Kung-tu is slightly better than Su Man-shu, whose Japanese flavor is as thick as the hair oil in Japanese women's heads."

Miss Su said, "I'm an ordinary returned student, too, and I don't know who writes the best old-style poetry today. Tell us something about it, Mr. Tung."

"Ch'en San-yüan is of course number one. In the last five or six hundred years, he stands way above the rest. I always say the great poets since the T'ang can be grouped under geographical terms; the hills (*Ling*), the valleys (*Ku*), the mountains (*Shan*), and the plains (*Yüan*). There are three Lings: Tu Shao-ling, Wang Kuang-ling, and—do you know him?—Mei Yüan-ling; two Kus: Li Ch'ang-ku,[47] and Huang Shan-ku;[48] four Shans: Li I-shan, Wang Pan-shan, Ch'en Hou-shan, and Yüan I-shan;[49] but only one Yüan, Ch'en San-yüan." He raised his left thumb as he spoke.

Hung-chien asked sheepishly, "Couldn't you add a bank (*P'o*)?"

"Su Tung-p'o. He's a bit lacking."

Hung-chien clicked his tongue in surprise. *If Su Tung-p'o's poetry doesn't meet with his esteem,* he thought, *heaven only knows how superb this man's poetry must be.* He asked to see the poems Hsieh-ch'üan had just written, and so did Miss Su, for only someone who writes old-style poetry would ever say he doesn't read new-style poetry, and a new-style poet never willingly admits that he doesn't understand old-style poetry.

Hsieh-ch'üan distributed four or five sheets of paper among those at the table and leaned back haughtily in his chair, feeling nonetheless that none of these people understood poetry and could not possibly appreciate the subtle nuances in his lines. Even if they praised him, their praise wouldn't be sincere or to the point. Yet he was waiting for their praise, despite the knowledge that he wouldn't be satisfied with it; it was like finding a pack of cigarettes when one craves opium.

On the sheets were seven or eight modern poems written in a familiar tone. The poem on returning home after his resignation as military attaché went as follows: "Happily I write a poem on returning home to see my wife's dimples,/ Remorseful that the sound of my name stops my son's tears." His poem of indignation over the Sino-Japanese War read: "Keep suspecting that heaven is still drunk,/ And wants to perish with the sun [Japan]." In addition, there were the following:

> The fresh breezes need not be bought,
> The gay rain is just enough to close up ten thousand homes.
> .   .   .   .   .

> Cold currents rinse over jagged rocks.
> Evening breezes flow through billowing pines.
> .   .   .   .   .

> Not permitted to escape men, I think of escaping the world,
> Alone I maintain a lingering intoxication and delight in the
> withering flowers.

But then there were a few lines like,

> Washed out eyes, bright and empty, provide the sleeping
> duck.
> The squirming bosom, strange and mysterious, lures the
> hidden snake.
> .   .   .   .   .

> Several companions are carried seeking historical
> landmarks.
> The wailing reeds and bitter bamboo shine on mournful
> sorrow.
> .   .   .   .   .

> In the autumn air, light of body, a goose is passing.
> Temple hair, flickering shadows, ten thousand crows
> are peeking.

The meaning was quite obscure. Hung-chien had never read *San-yüan Ching-she shih*,[50] and he racked his brains for the etymological sources of these lines. *The reeds and bamboo certainly hadn't caught fire, he thought, so it wasn't very likely they could shine on anything, and besides "mournful sorrow" was something not even a searchlight could illuminate. "Several companions" clearly indicated the friends weren't children, so how could they be "carried?" If ten thousand crows took a liking to the poet's few strands of grey hair, surely it wasn't so "tousled like a crow's nest" that they would want to roost on his head.* He was quite puzzled but did not dare ask questions for fear Hsieh-ch'üan would laugh at his ignorance.

Everyone duly praised the poems. Hsieh-ch'üan responded with bored politeness, like a ruler being welcomed by the people.

Hsin-mei said to Hung-chien, "Why don't you write a few poems to show us what poetry is?"

Hung-chien replied emphatically that he could not write poetry. Hsieh-ch'üan said if Hung-chien really couldn't, they needn't force him. Hsin-mei said, "Then everyone drink a toast to Hsieh-ch'üan's fine poetry."

Hoping to give the wine an unobstructed passage over his tongue and down his throat, Hung-chien gulped it straight down as though letting it pass toll-free. It felt as if everything in his stomach had been churned up by that swallow of wine and was about to come rushing up, like an already plugged toilet given an extra flush. He hastily set down his glass and tightly clenched his teeth together, trying to use his will power to suppress the flow.

Miss Su said, "I've never seen Mrs. Tung before, but I can imagine she must be very beautiful. Mr. Tung's poem, 'I returned home and saw my wife's dimples,' vividly pictures Mrs. Tung's charming smile and her two deep dimples."

Chao Hsin-mei said, "It isn't enough for Hsieh-ch'üan just to have a lovely wife. He has to flaunt his good fortune in his poetry so we bachelors go red-eyed with envy when we read it." With that he looked shamelessly at Miss Su, emboldened by the wine.

Ch'u Shen-ming said, "He's the only one who can see the dimples on his wife's face. Now that he's written about them in his poem, we can all look at them as much as we want."

Hsieh-ch'üan could not very well show his irritation. Stiffening his expression, he said, "There's no point discussing poetry with such ignorant people like you in the first place. I used two allusions in that couplet, one from Mei Sheng-yü[51] in the first line and another from Yang Ta-yen[52] in the second. If you don't know the original source, don't try to force an interpretation on it."

Hsin-mei poured the wine as he said, "Sorry, sorry! We'll fine ourselves a glass. Mr. Fang, you should have recognized the allusion. You're not like

94

us! How come you didn't have the faintest idea about it either? You're fined two glasses. Come on."

"That's nonsense," snapped Hung-chien. "Why should I know it any more than you?"

Since Hsieh-ch'üan's rebuke about their ignorance had included her, Miss Su was quite peeved and said, "I don't have the vaguest idea about it either, but I'm not going to drink that glass of wine."

Affected by the wine, Hsin-mei would brook no restraint from Miss Su, insisting, "You can ignore the fine, but he must drink a glass. I'll drink with him." As he spoke he poured Hung-chien a full glass, picked up his own, drank it down in one gulp, then held up the empty glass for Hung-chien to see.

Hung-chien said resolutely, "I'll finish this one, but beyond that I won't touch another drop even if you kill me."

He lifted the glass and poured it straight down his throat. When it was all gone, he held the glass up to Hsin-mei, saying, "It's—" Before the word "empty" had left his mouth, he clenched his teeth together and rushed and stumbled to the spittoon. With an "Augh" the food and wine gushed from his mouth. He never thought there could be so much in his stomach, and the vomiting continued till he was out of breath. Out came mucus, tears, and stomach juices, and he was occupied with the thought, *What a disgrace! Thank God Miss T'ang isn't here.* Though he had cleared his stomach, the feeling of disgust did not stop. He sat down at the tea table unable to raise his head. His clothes were splattered with drops of dirty spittle. Miss Su was about to approach him when he wearily made a gesture to stop her. While he was in the worst throes of vomiting, Hsin-mei had patted his back for him. Hsieh-ch'üan called the waiter to clean the floor and bring a towel, while he went ahead and poured a glass of tea for Hung-chien to rinse his mouth. Holding his nose, Ch'u Shen-ming opened all the windows. An expression of scorn showed all over his face, but inwardly he was rejoicing at the thought that Hung-chien's vomit had washed the incident of his spilt milk from everyone's memory.

When Hsieh-ch'üan saw Fang Hung-chien was a little better, he said with a smile, "Spitting by the railing no one knows its fragrance.[53] Here you haven't even finished eating and you're already in a hurry to give a return dinner! Never mind! You'll throw up for all you're worth a few more times; then you'll learn to hold your wine."

Hsin-mei said, "He's proved he really can't drink. Let's just hope it's not true that he can't write poetry or that he doesn't understand philosophy."

Miss Su declared heatedly, "You just make light of everything. It's all your fault; you made him drunk. If he gets sick tomorrow, then we'll see what a disgraceful host you are. Hung-chien, how do you feel now?"

She felt his forehead with her fingers. While watching them, Hsin-mei regretted he never took up Chinese boxing; otherwise, he could have given Hung-chien a fatal injury when he slapped Hung-chien on the back.

Turning his head away Hung-chien said, "It's nothing. I have a slight headache. Hsin-mei, I'm sorry about today. I've spoiled it for everyone. Please go on eating. I'll go home now. In a few days I'll go to your place and apologize."

Miss Su said, "Stay a while. Wait until your headache stops before you go."

Hsin-mei wished he could have thrown Hung-chien out then and there. He then asked, "Who has some Tiger Balm?[54] Shen-ming, you carry medicine around with you. Do you have any Tiger Balm?"

Shen-ming pulled out a bunch of bottles and boxes from the pockets of his trousers and overcoat. Among them were pills, tablets, and plasters for soothing the throat, improving the brain, strengthening the lungs, aiding digestion, easing constipation, inducing perspiration, and killing pain; Miss Su picked out the Tiger Balm, dabbed a little on her finger and applied it to Hung-chien's temples.

The wine in Hsin-mei's stomach turned to sour vinegar in his jealousy. Momentarily restraining himself he asked Hung-chien, "Feel any better? I better not keep you today. Some other day I'll ask you out again to make up for it. I'll have someone call a cab to take you home."

"No need to call a cab," said Miss Su. "He can go in my car. I'll take him home."

Hsin-mei's eyes widened in surprise and he stammered, "You're, you're not eating? There's still more food."

Hung-chien limply implored Miss Su not to see him home.

Miss Su said, "I've had enough. There are so many dishes today. Mr. Ch'u, Mr. Tung, please take your time. I'll go on. Thank you, Hsin-mei."

With a sad face Hsin-mei watched Miss Su and Hung-chien get in the car and drive off. His plan to make a fool of Hung-chien in front of Miss Su had almost been a complete success, but that success only confirmed his defeat.

Hung-chien leaned back against the car cushions. Miss Su asked him if he wanted his tie loosened, but he shook his head. She told him to close his eyes and rest a bit. From his self-imposed dark world, he felt Miss Su's cool fingers touch his forehead and heard her mutter in French, "*Pauvre petit!*" He hadn't the strength to jump up in protest. When the car reached the Chous, Miss Su ordered the Chous' doorman to help her chauffeur take Hung-chien inside.

By the time Mr. and Mrs. Chou had come dashing out all agog to meet Miss Su and to invite her in for a moment, her car had already sped off. They had no way to satisfy their curiosity and could not very well question Hung-chien, who lay in bed with his head covered. Instead, they gave the doorman a thorough interrogation; annoyed that he lacked any power of observation, they reproached him for not being able to use his eyes. Why hadn't he given Miss Su a careful scrutiny?

The next morning, Fang Hung-chien woke up early, with a sawing pain in his head, and his tongue feeling like the coir doormat for wiping one's shoes before entering the house. He lay in bed until the afternoon when he finally got out of bed and his mind cleared enough to write Miss T'ang a letter. Skipping the events of the day before, he merely wrote he was ill; and thinking back on the events of yesterday, he began to feel very awkward with regard to Miss Su. She had called in the morning and again in the afternoon to ask about him. After dinner, he decided that since he had been inactive all day, he would take a moonlight stroll. Then Miss Su called once more to ask if he felt better and if he would care to go to her house in the evening for a chat.

It was the fifteenth day of the fourth month by the lunar calendar. The late-spring, early-summer moon was for lovers, while the autumn-winter moon was for poets. A full moon in the sky, Hung-chien wished he could have gone to see Miss T'ang. Instead he went to the Sus. Miss Su's mother and sister-in-law had gone to the movies, and the servants for a walk, leaving Miss Su and the doorman at home. When she saw Hung-chien, she said that she had intended to go to the movies too and told him to have a seat while she went upstairs to put on an extra piece of clothing, so they could go into the garden to admire the moon.

When she came down, he caught a fresh whiff of a fragrance he had not smelled a moment ago and noted that she not only had changed her clothes but had also put on some makeup. She led him into a small sextagonal pavilion; they sat down against the railing. Suddenly he realized how compromising the situation was. He mustn't let himself get caught in the trap that day and end up regretting it ever after. He thanked Miss Su again. She inquired once more about his sleep and appetite. After the bright, white moon overhead had been praised three or four times, there was little else to say. They continued to gaze at the moon. He stole a glance at Miss Su's face, which was so bright and pure that it seemed the moonlight splashed over it would slide right off. The moonlight was flashing in her eyes too. Her red lips, undimmed by the aura of the moon, appeared moist and dark in the shade. She knew he had his eyes on her and turned to smile at him. His determination to resist this seductive force was like a fish out of water, which flaps its head and tail about on the ground but can't get anywhere. He stood up and said, "Wen-wan, I must go."

"It's early yet. What's the hurry? Stay a while," she said, pointing to the spot next to her where he had just been sitting.

"I'm going to sit a little further away. You're too beautiful! The moon might trick me into doing something foolish."

Her light, smooth laughter gave his heart a painful twinge.

"Are you so afraid of doing something foolish? Sit down. I don't want you sitting so stiff and proper. We're not in church listening to a sermon. Tell me, what would it take for an intelligent person like you to do something foolish?" she turned toward him and asked mischievously.

He lowered his head, not daring to look at her. But his ears and nose were irresistibly full of her, and the image of her smile floated in his mind like a leaf spinning in a whirlpool. "I haven't the courage to do anything foolish."

She smiled triumphantly and said in a low voice, *"Embrasse-moi!"* As soon as the words were out of her mouth she was at once abashed and surprised at her own courage to be foolish, but then she only dared order him to kiss her while hiding behind a foreign language. Having no way to escape, he turned his head and kissed her. The kiss was so light and covered such a small area, it was like the way a Mandarin host brushed his lips against the brim of the teacup as a subtle hint to a guest who had overstayed his welcome in the Ch'ing Dynasty, or else it was like the way a witness taking the oath in court in the West touched the Bible to his lips. At most it was similar to the way female disciples kissed the Living Buddha of Tibet or the Pope's big toe—a kind of respectful intimacy. When the kiss was over, Miss Su pillowed her head on Hung-chien's shoulder and breathed a gentle sigh like a child sleeping sweetly. He didn't dare move an inch. After a long while, she sat up straight as if waking from a dream and said with a smile, "That queer old moon. It's really turned us all into fools."

"And it tempted me into committing an unforgivable sin! I can't stay any longer."

His one and only fear at that moment was that she might bring up the subject of engagement and marriage and start discussing future plans with him. What he didn't know was that in the joy and triumph of love, women never think of such things. There must be doubts before they will demand the man to hurry along with the engagement and marriage so their love will have a safeguard.

"I won't let you go—well, all right, go ahead. I'll see you tomorrow."

When Miss Su saw the expression on Hung-chien's face, she thought his emotions were so stirred up that he might lose his self-control and so did not dare keep him. He sprinted out the gate, still believing that his kiss on her lips a moment ago had been so light, it could not possibly be construed as evidence that he loved her, as though kissing were something to be measured by weight.

Miss Su's eyes followed him out, while she remained seated in the pavilion. With joy in her heart and not a single well-formed thought except the two lines "Full moon in the sky,/ And half the month gone by" in her mind, she wasn't sure if it was an old saying or her own inspiration of the moment. It was the middle of April. What would happen by mid-August? she wondered. "The belly of a pregnant woman pasted to the heavens," she recollected a line of Ts'ao Yüan-lang's poem with an irrepressible feeling of disgust. Hearing the maids return, she rose and instinctively pulled out her handkerchief to wipe her mouth, as if the kiss might have left some mark behind. She felt the rest of the evening was just like standing on the edge of a diving board by the sea, and she could plunge into the next day's happiness with one leap. She was trembling with excitement.

Fang Hung-chien arrived home, locked the door of his room, and tore up five or six drafts before he wrote out the following letter:

Dear Wen-wan,
I can't bring myself to see you again, so I am writing you this letter. Everything that has happened in the past right up until tonight is entirely my fault. I have no excuses and no way to explain. I couldn't ask for your forgiveness. I only hope you will quickly forget this weakling who lacks the courage to be frank. Because I sincerely respect you, I couldn't bear to insult your friendship. I don't deserve the kindness you have shown me in the last few months, but it will forever remain a cherished memory.
Best wishes.

He felt shameful; he could not sleep well the whole night. When he arrived at the bank the next day he had a special messenger deliver the letter. He remained on pins and needles, fearful of further complications. Around eleven o'clock a bank trainee came to call him to the telephone, saying a Miss Su was on the phone. His legs went limp. As he picked up the receiver, he expected Miss Su's abuse would be heard by everyone in the bank.

In a very soft voice Miss Su said, "Hung-chien? I just got your letter. I haven't opened it yet. What does it say? If it's something nice, I'll read it; if not, I won't. I'll wait and open it in front of you to embarrass you."

He was so horrified that his forehead nearly shrank into his eyebrows, as his eyebrows rose up to his hairline. He realized she had mistaken it to be a letter of proposal and was being pettish to give him a hard time. He said quickly, "Please read the letter right away. I beg you."

"In such a hurry! All right, I'll read it then. You wait. Don't hang up. . . . I've read it, but I don't understand what you mean. Come and explain it to me later."

"No, Miss Su, no. I don't dare see you—" Unable to cover it up any longer, he said in a low voice, "I have another—" *How should I say it? Hell! The other employees are probably all listening in*—"I have another—another person." He finished as though getting rid of a heavy burden.

"What? I can't hear you."

Hung-chien shook his head and sighed. In his agitation he began speaking in fractured French. "Miss Su, let's speak French. I—love someone—love another woman. Understand? Forgive me. I beg a thousand pardons."

"Why, you—you rotten egg!" Miss Su cursed him in Chinese. Her voice seemed to have a quaver in it. Hung-chien felt as if her abuse had given him a heavy slap on his ear and in self-defense, he hung up the receiver.

Miss Su's voice continued to jar his consciousness. At noon he went to eat at a small Western-style restaurant in the neighborhood, afraid to speak to anybody. It suddenly occurred to him that she might kill herself from frustrated love, and he became too upset to eat. He hurried back to the bank and wrote a letter begging her forgiveness, asking her to take care of herself. He gave himself a thorough smirching and declared he wasn't worth a copper. He entreated her not to keep loving him. After sending the letter, he relaxed a little and began to feel hungry, so he went out again to get something to eat. At around four or five o'clock when his colleagues were all getting ready to leave, he decided he was in no mood that day to go see Miss T'ang.

Meanwhile, the mail office gave him a telegram, and he was terrified, thinking it must be Miss Su's suicide note. Who could be sending him a telegram? He opened it and found that it had been sent from P'ing-ch'eng, which seemed to be a county in Hunan. His alarm abated but his curiosity increased. He quickly got a telegraph code book and transcribed it as follows: "Offer position as possessor. Monthly salary $340 plus travel expenses. Please ware reply. National San Lü University President Kao Sung-nien." "Possessor" was a mistake for "professor" and "ware reply" must be "wire reply." He had never heard of San Lü University. It must be a new university established since the war. He had no idea who Kao Sung-nien was or in which department he would serve as professor. But the fact that a national university did not consider it too far to go a thousand miles to offer him a job was a real boost to his status; for after only one year of war, a national university professor still held an enviable position among the salaried classes.

He learned from Chief-secretary Wang that P'ing-ch'eng was indeed in Hunan. Wang asked to see the telegram and congratulated him for getting the recognition he deserved, observing that the Golden Touch Bank was a small place, and "the flood dragon is no mere creature of the ponds." Wang also said that a professorship at this National San Lü University was equivalent to the presidential appointment rank in the civil service. When Hung-chien heard this, his spirits rose. This news signified a real change of luck, he thought. He should have no trouble getting Miss T'ang to marry him now. That day certainly deserved to be commemorated as the end of old entanglements and the beginning of new opportunities.

That evening Hung-chien told Mr. and Mrs. Chou about his job offer. Mr. Chou was pleased, his only reservation being that P'ing-ch'eng was too remote. Hung-chien said that he hadn't made up his mind. Mrs. Chou said she realized he would have to ask Su Wen-wan's permission first; she remarked further that a traditional couple as close as Hung-chien and Miss Su were would have gotten married long ago. The modern couple who were full of the "Oh, my heart, my flesh," sort of intimacy before ever getting married probably found that once the initial sweetness wore off, things didn't turn out so well after marriage. Hung-chien laughed at her for only knowing about a Miss Su.

"Don't tell me there's someone else besides?" she asked.

Beaming with satisfaction, Hung-chien replied glibly that he would tell her more within three days.

A pang of jealousy for her deceased daughter made her say, "I can't see how someone like you could be such a sought-after piece of juicy meat!"

Hung-chien did not bother to counter this coarse remark, and returning to his room he wrote the following letter:

Dear Hsiao-fu,
The letter of two days ago has probably reached you by now. I've completely recovered from my illness. If you wrote a letter inquiring after my health it will still be as welcome as an extra dose of medicine after sickness. Today I received a telegram from National San Lü University offering me a position as professor. The school seems a little remote, but it's still a good opportunity. Please help me decide whether to go or not. What are your plans for the rest of the year? If you want to go to Kunming to continue your studies, I can find a job there. If you enter a university in Shanghai, then Shanghai will be the place where I long to be. In short, I possess you, bind you, follow you like the spirit of a ghost that's been wronged, and will not leave you in peace. For a long time I've thought of me—oops! Instead of "you," I accidentally wrote "me," but there's good reason for such a slip of the pen. Do you know why? To put it simply, I've already practiced that sentence a thousand times in my head. I just wish I could invent a fresh and fleeting expression that only I could say and only you could hear, so that after I've spoken it and you've heard it, it would vanish and in the past, present or future there would never be another man using the same expression to another woman. I'm so sorry that to you who are without equal in the whole world, I can only use clichés which have been worked to death for thousands of years to express my feelings. Will you permit me to say it? I really don't dare be presumptuous. You don't know how much I fear your anger.

Early the next morning, Hung-chien told Mr. Chou's chauffeur to deliver the letter. In the afternoon he left the bank and went to the T'angs. As the rickshaw reached the door, he saw to his horror and dismay that Miss Su's car was there also. Miss Su's chauffeur tipped his cap to him, saying, "You've come at just the right time. Young Lady arrived not more than a few moments ago."

Hung-chien lied, "I was only passing by. I won't go in." And he turned and went home. *A lie of glass, thin and transparent,* he thought. *The chauffeur must certainly be laughing to himself. Would Miss Su spread malicious tales and ruin everything for me? But she doesn't necessarily know I am in love with Miss T'ang. And anyway, she would only disgrace herself by telling everything that has happened in the last six months.* Consoling himself in this manner, he stopped worrying.

The next day he waited in vain, for there was no letter from Miss T'ang. The day after when he went to see her, the maid said she was not in. By the fifth day when there was still no letter, and two fruitless visits, he became so nervous he lost both his sleep and appetite. He recited his letter over and over ten or fifteen times, weighing each word carefully in his mind, but could find nothing that might give offense. Maybe she still wanted to go back to college. He was eight or nine years older than she, and if he fell in love, that meant he'd want to get married right away. He couldn't wait for her to finish college. Maybe that was what made her hesitant. If she would just say she loved him, then whenever she wanted to get married would be fine. He could certainly "keep chaste." All right, he'd write another letter and ask to see her on Sunday, the next day. Everything would be as she decreed.

That night it grew very windy, and the next day a light rain fell, followed by a heavy downpour which continued without let-up into the afternoon. Hung-chien, bracing himself against the rain, went to the T'angs. To his surprise, Miss T'ang was at home. He sensed something strange in the maid's manner but ignored it. As soon as he saw Miss T'ang he could tell she was very aloof and without a trace of her usual smile. In her hand was a large paper bundle. His courage completely gone, he said, "I've come by twice, but you weren't home. Did you get my Monday letter?"

"Yes, I did. Mr. Fang,"—her reverting back to the original form of address made him breathless—"I heard you also came by on Tuesday. Why didn't you come in? I was home then."

"Miss T'ang,"—he too returned to the old form of address—"how did you know I came by on Tuesday?"

"My cousin's chauffeur saw you and was surprised you didn't come in. He told my cousin and she told me. You should have come in that day; we were talking about you."

"What's there to discuss about me?"

"We weren't just discussing you; we were studying you. We found your behavior quite mysterious."

"What's so mysterious about me?"

"You don't think you're mysterious? Of course, to naïve girls like myself, you're inscrutable. I've known about your gift of gab for some time.

102

You undoubtedly have a very convincing explanation for everything you've done. At the least, you'll just say, 'I have no excuses and no way to explain,' and people will certainly forgive you. Isn't that so?"

"What?" he asked with a start. "You saw the letter I wrote your cousin?"

"My cousin showed it to me. She also told me everything that happened from the boat trip up until that evening."

Miss T'ang looked indignant, and Hung-chien did not dare look her straight in the eye.

"What did she say about it?" he managed to ask. He was sure Su Wen-wan had exaggerated everything, saying he had lured her and kissed her, and he was prepared to counter lies with facts.

"You mean you don't even know what you yourself did?"

"Miss T'ang, let me explain—"

"If you have some 'way to explain,' then go tell it to my cousin first."

Ordinarily Fang Hung-chien liked Miss T'ang for her quickness. Now he only wished she were slow-witted and less overbearing.

"My cousin told me a few other things about you too, Mr. Fang. I don't know if they're true or not. The Chous, with whom you're now living, apparently aren't any ordinary relatives. They're your in-laws. You've been married before." Hung-chien tried to interrupt, but Miss T'ang was not the daughter of an attorney for nothing. She knew the secret of interrogating a witness in court and that's never let him argue—"I don't need an explanation. Are they not your in-laws? If so, then that's all there is to it. Whether or not you were in love during the years you were abroad I have no idea. But on the boat trip home, you took a fancy to a Miss Pao and got on so well with her that you never left her side for a moment. Right?"

Hung-chien lowered his head and said nothing.

"Once Miss Pao left, you immediately went after my cousin, right up until—I needn't go on. Moreover, it seems that while you studied in Europe, you got an American degree—"

Hung-chien stamped his foot in anger. "Have I ever boasted to you about my degree? That was a prank."

"You're an intelligent person. You have a little fun now and then, but dunces like us take all your jokes seriously." When Miss T'ang heard Fang Hung-chien choke back a sob, her heart softened. But at that moment the greater the pity she felt in her heart, the more resentful she became and the more she felt like really attacking him. "Mr. Fang, your past is too rich. I want to be able to occupy the whole life of the man I love. Before meeting me, he would have had no past and would be waiting for me with a clean slate."

Hung-chien kept his head down and remained silent.

"I hope you will have a bright future, Mr. Fang."

Hung-chien's mind and body went numb as though an electric current had passed through him. Only aware that Miss T'ang was speaking to him, he was in no state to try to comprehend the meaning of her words. It was as though his mind were covered with a layer of oilpaper, and her words were like raindrops. Though they couldn't soak through the oilpaper, it still shook under the beating rain. The last remark made everything hopelessly clear to him, and he raised his head, his eyes brimming with tears like a big child who has been spanked and scolded—a face in which the tears have been swallowed into the heart. Miss T'ang's nose suddenly stung.

"You're right. I am a fraud. I won't argue any more or come to bother you again."

He stood up to go. Miss T'ang wished she could have said, *Why don't you defend yourself? I would believe you.* But, instead, she merely said, "Well, goodbye, then." She saw him out, hoping he had something else to say. It was raining heavily outside. As she reached the door, she seriously thought of asking him to stay until the rain died down. Putting on his raincoat, he glanced at her and was too benumbed to shake her hand. When she noticed his glistening eyes that had been washed over by his tears, she lowered her eyes, unable to look at him. Mechanically, she stretched out her hand and said, "Goodbye."

Sometimes "Won't you stay a while longer?" will drive a person away; sometimes "Goodbye" will hold him back. Miss T'ang couldn't hold Fang Hung-chien back, so she added, "I wish you *bon voyage*."

She returned to her bedroom. The rage of a moment ago having completely vanished, she felt tired and remorseful. The maid came in and said, "Mr. Fang is acting strange. Standing on the other side of the street, he's getting drenched in the rain."

She hurried to the window to look. Sure enough, Hung-chien was standing with his back to the road outside the bamboo fence of the house diagonally opposite. Like whips of water, wind-blown lines of rain from all directions lashed at his unresponsive body. As she watched, her heart melted into bitter water. If he, after another minute, still stood there, she thought, she would risk the ridicule of others and tell the maid to invite him back in. The minute lasted forever, and she could hardly wait it out and was just about to give the order to her maid when Hung-chien suddenly whirled around. Like a dog shaking out its hair, he shook himself as if trying to shake away all the rain in the vicinity and strode off.

Miss T'ang regretted having believed her cousin so much and in her anger spoken with such finality to him. She also began to worry that Hung-chien would become so despondent he might get run over by an automobile or trolley car. She checked her watch a few times; after an hour, she called up the Chous to ask about him. Hung-chien hadn't come home yet. Alarmed, she grew more apprehensive. When dinner was over and the rain had stopped, not wishing her family to overhear, she slipped out to a neighborhood candy store to use the telephone. Confused and upset, she first dialed a wrong number; dialing a second time, all she heard was the telephone ringing at the other end. For a long time no one answered. The three members of the Chou family had all gone out visiting.

Hung-chien, who had been sitting in a stupor in a small coffee shop up until this time, finally went home. The moment he entered the house the maid told him Miss Su had called. He turned hot with rage and awoke from his benumbed state. He was just changing into dry clothes when the telephone rang. He ignored it. The maid ran up to get it and had no sooner picked it up than she said, "Mr. Fang, Miss Su is on the phone." With his sock half on and his left foot bare, Hung-chien ran from his room, grabbed the receiver, and not caring whether the maid heard or not, in a hoarse voice—unfortunately he had caught a chill from his drenching in the rain and already had the beginnings of a stuffy nose, so his throat had lost its vigor—said, "We're already through, through! Do you hear? What's the point of calling up again and again? It's really disgraceful! You're just making trouble! I doubt if you'll ever get married—" He suddenly realized the other party had already hung up and nearly called Miss Su up again to force her to listen to his invective through to the end. The maid, who had been listening with great interest at the turn of the stairs, hurried into the kitchen to report.

When Miss T'ang heard "It's really disgraceful," she quickly hung up the receiver, feeling faint. Barely managing to fight back the tears, she returned home.

That evening as Fang Hung-chien thought over what had happened that day, he was swept by intermittent fever. He could hardly believe it was all real. After being picked apart piece by piece by Miss T'ang, he felt too vile and despicable to be a man.

The next morning just after he had gotten up, Miss T'ang's rickshaw boy came with a paper bundle, saying that Miss T'ang had asked for a package in return. He recognized the bundle as the one he saw yesterday. There was nothing written on it, but he guessed it was the letters he had written her. He knew very well she wouldn't, yet he still hoped she had written a few lines, using the final moment of farewell to let their friendship draw out one more breath. He quickly opened the bundle which contained his old letters. Dejectedly he wrapped up her letters in the same paper and handed them to the rickshaw boy, who then departed.

When Miss T'ang received the box wrapped up in the paper, she opened

105

it with considerable curiosity. It was the gold-papered box of chocolate wafers, which she had sent Hung-chien. She knew her letters were in the box but didn't want to open it, as if not opening the box meant she still hadn't completely severed relations with him, and opening it would prove beyond a doubt that she had broken off. She sat in a daze like this she knew not how long—perhaps only a few seconds—then opened the box and saw the seven letters she had sent him. The envelopes had all been torn and repaired with cellophane tape. She could imagine how in his impatience to read her letters he had torn the envelopes and then clumsily patched them up. An unbearable pain pierced her heart. She also discovered, lining the bottom of the box, a piece of paper with her address and telephone number on it and recalled writing them on the last blank page of his book when they first had dinner together. He had cut it out and stored it away like a treasure.

As Miss T'ang sat musing over this, it suddenly occurred to her that his remarks over the telephone the day before might not have been meant for her at all. A month ago when she called him for the first time, one of the Chous had mistaken her for Miss Su, and the person answering her two calls the day before had known right away they were for Hung-chien without even asking her name. Now that their breakup had reached this stage, was this conjecture still worth verifying? Oh, just forget about Fang Hung-chien. But deep down she could not forget him. It was like the gum left empty and aching after a tooth is extracted, or like a small tree in a flower pot. To pull it up roots and all, one must smash the pot. Proud by nature, she preferred to endure the pain until she fell ill.

During her illness, Miss Su visited her and kept her company everyday, telling her that she had become engaged to Ts'ao Yüan-lang. In the throes of happiness Miss Su confided how Ts'ao Yüan-lang had proposed to her. As the story went, at the age of fifteen Ts'ao Yüan-lang had resolved never to marry. The moment he met Miss Su, however, his views on life for the past fifteen years became shattered like a Japanese house during an earthquake. "He himself said that at the very beginning he hated and feared me, and wanted to hide from me but—" giggling, Miss Su twisted around and did not finish the sentence. The proposal had gone like this: When Ts'ao Yüan-lang saw her, he behaved in a very pitiful manner, and suddenly stuffing a velvet box into her hand, he fled with an expression of panic on his face. Miss Su opened the box and found inside a gold necklace with a large piece of jade. A letter was stuck underneath the necklace. When Miss T'ang asked her what the letter said, Miss Su replied, "He said at the very beginning he hated and feared me, but now—oh, you're such a naughty child, I won't tell you."

When Miss T'ang recovered, her elder sister and brother-in-law invited her to spend the summer in Peking. At the end of August when she returned to Shanghai, Miss Su asked her to be the maid of honor at her wedding. The best man was no other than Ts'ao Yüan-lang's friend, the returned student. When he met Miss T'ang, he showered her with attention. Annoyed, she ignored him. Imitating a British accent, he said to Ts'ao Yüan-lang, *"Dash it. That girl is forget-me-not and teach-me-not in one, a redress which has somehow turned into the blue flower."*[55] While Ts'ao Yüan-lang praised his unsurpassed beauty of expression, he thought this remark should be passed on to Miss T'ang, but four days after the wedding she went with her father to Hong Kong and from there to Chungking.

4

WHEN FANG HUNG-CHIEN returned the letters to Miss T'ang, he was dazed and stupefied; some time later, he finally awoke as though from a faint, feeling a continuous pain in his heart. It was like the prickly pain a person feels when his limbs, after having gone numb from being curled up, are stretched out and the blood is once again circulating. The day before he hadn't had time to feel the hurt he had swallowed in one lump. Now, like a cow chewing its cud, he chewed up in bits and pieces the deep, bottomless aftertaste. The sofa and desk in his bedroom, the trees and lawn outside his window were the same, and the people he met every day all went on as usual, seemingly unaware of his traumatic hurt and humiliation. But strangely enough he felt at the same time the world had become dull and colorless, and his own world, at least, had changed its appearance, with his private world severed from the public world. Like a lone ghost cut off from the world of the living, he gazed at its joys of which he could not partake and at its sun which did not shine on him. While he could not enter the world of others, anyone could come into his. The first to enter it was Mrs. Chou. No member of the older generation is ever willing for the young to keep their secrets; it's the older generation's duty to coax or force out those secrets.

After the T'angs' chauffeur had left, Fang went upstairs to wash his face. Midway down the stairs, Mrs. Chou met him face to face and thought of asking him right there and then about what the maid had told her the night before. She, however, managed to keep quiet, proving she was not only duty-conscious but had forbearance as well. Instead she went into the dining room to wait for him to come down. Her son Hsiao-ch'eng, usually a very quick eater, dawdled around that day, waiting for her to question Hung-chien. By the time Hsiao-ch'eng had worn out his patience and had gone off to school, and she had still not seen Hung-chien come down for breakfast, she asked the maid to summon him. Only then did she learn that he had already left. When she found her self-restraint had been in vain, she was furious, calling him a rotten scoundrel. *Even staying at a hotel, one should say a word to the bellboy when he goes out. Here he eats our food, stays in our house, earns our money, and yet he carries on outside behind my back and leaves early in the morning without so much as a word of greeting. No respect for his elders. What kind of behavior do you call that? And he's even the son of a scholarly family. Well, the Book¹ says, "In the morning when you rise, pay respects to your parents." Hasn't he ever heard that? He's gone and lost his head over some girl. No gratitude whatsoever. I don't suppose he ever stops to think if it weren't for our support, what Miss Su or Miss T'ang would ever take a fancy to him!*

Mrs. Chou had no idea Hung-chien knew a Miss T'ang. Because of the given term "*chih-ma su-t'ang*" (sesame seed bar), the word "t'ang" follows naturally after "su." By blurting the words as they came to her, she had hit the nail on the head. The prophets who foretell the future are all like that [i. e., they hit the nail by accident].

In order to avoid Mrs. Chou, Hung-chien had actually left without break-fast. While wary of being interrogated, he felt even more wary of being pitied or lectured to. The new wound in his heart gave him pain whenever anyone "touched" it. Some people when jilted will immediately display their broken hearts in public and drip with blood like a beggar's scraped legs to stir pity. Or else, after the whole affair is over, they will pull up their clothes in the manner of a veteran and point it out like an old battle scar to arouse awe and wonder. Hung-chien only hoped he could conceal his scar in the dark recesses of his mind, like the infected eyes which shun the light or the torn flesh which fears the wind. Thus at first he decided to act as if nothing had happened and not let anyone discover his secret. If he could just keep it from Mrs. Chou, then no one else would meddle in his affairs. But, then, it is no easy matter to keep a man's anguish from showing on his face, while women may use cosmetics to cover up theirs. By applying rouge a little thicker and dabbing on powder a little more heavily, they can effectively use the red and white to hide their inner misery. For a man who did not usually go about looking disheveled and dirty, Hung-chien, besides his usual hair-combing and shave, had no special way of making up to show that he was the same as al-ways. Unable to deal with Mrs. Chou on such short notice, he decided the best thing to do was to slip away.

At the bank Hung-chien mechanically went through his chores, too con-fused to think. The telegram from San Lü University came to mind. Heaving a sigh, and without the least enthusiasm, he wired his acceptance of the offer. No sooner had he told the messenger to send the telegram than someone from the manager's office summoned him to the manager's office.

When Manager Chou saw him, he asked with a frown, "What's with you? My wife's having a gastric attack. When I left the house, Mama Wang[2] was calling the doctor."

Hung-chien quickly explained that he hadn't seen Mrs. Chou all morning.

With a sad face Manager Chou said, "Well, I can't figure out your affairs, but since Shu-ying passed away, your mother-in-law has never been in very good health. The doctor said her blood pressure was too high and instructed her not to let herself get upset. If she does, it may be dangerous, so I always give in to her three parts of the way. So don't you, don't you give her any trouble." He let out a breath when he finished as though releasing a heavy burden. He cowered a little before his nominal son-in-law, a squire's son and a returned student. Today's talk was a distasteful but unavoidable duty.

From the day he married his wife, he had always yielded to her every wish. The year his daughter died, he had considered taking a concubine to mitigate his grief at losing his daughter in middle age. When his wife learned of his plan, she had fallen ill and in tears begged for death, "I'll die and be gone; then someone else can come take my place." Her threat of death frightened him so much that he thought no more of seeking consolation and became even more compliant toward her. The "three parts" referred to in "give in to her three parts" was not the "three parts" of "three parts water, seven parts dust," but rather the "three parts" as in "There are but three parts moonlight in all the world," which simply means total surrender.

"I'll be sure to remember it," said Hung-chien forcedly. "I wonder if she's any better now? Should I give her a call and see how she is?"

"No, no, don't call her! She is angry at you now. No use asking for trouble. Before I left, I told the maid to call me and report after the doctor's visit. Your mother-in-law is getting on in years. Twenty years ago, before we came to Shanghai, she already suffered gastric attacks. When they occurred, she didn't call the doctor to give her a shot or take painkiller pills; there weren't any pills even if she wanted them. Someone urged her to take a few dregs of opium, but she refused for fear of addiction. The only other alternative was our country remedy. She had to lie down on the bed and have someone thrash her with the door bar. I was always the one who did the thrashing, because it's something only someone close in the family can do. No one else could realize how painful it was and would have been so rough it would have been like beating her with a club. But she can't take that anymore. The method is very effective though. Maybe you city folks don't believe in it."

Hung-chien, wondering whether a nominal son-in-law was considered

110

"someone close," replied quickly, "Oh, we do, we do! It's a way of tricking the nerves, diverting attention from the place that hurts. It makes a lot of sense."

Manager Chou acknowledged that his explanation was correct. Full of misgivings, Hung-chien returned to his desk. *If Mrs. Chou's attitude toward me gets any worse,* he thought, *I can't stay on much longer, and I'll have to leave Shanghai as soon as possible.*

After lunch at home, Manager Chou returned to the bank. He summoned Hung-chien for another talk, asking immediately whether or not Hung-chien had replied to the telegram from San Lü University. Hung-chien suddenly realized what Chou was getting at, and a wave of anger roused him from his stupor. He stood stiffly and straight in an arrogant pose, which made Chou want to avoid looking at him, and in fact, what Chou saw was a section of his shirt in front of the desk slowly filling out and expanding and his tie and belt both rising above the desk.

Chou said, "It would be best for you to accept the appointment. Really, there's no sense for you to waste your talent here." He then asked Hung-chien "not to get the wrong idea."

Hung-chien replied with a grating, scornful laugh and asked if his employment was terminated as of that day.

Manager Chou tried feebly to assume a stern air. "Hung-chien, I told you not to get the wrong idea. You have a long trip ahead of you. Of course, you'll be too busy with your own affairs to come to the bank. Fortunately, there's nothing very urgent to do here. I'm giving you your freedom. You needn't come every day. As for your pay, you'll still receive—"

"Thank you very much, but I can't accept the money."

"Now look here. I'll have the accounting department give you four months salary in a lump sum. You won't have to ask your father for traveling expenses—"

"I don't want money. I have money." By the way Hung-chien spoke, it almost sounded as though he were carrying all four major national banks around in his pocket. Without waiting for Manager Chou to finish, he strode out of the office with head held high. A pity that the manager's office was so small, for in less than two strides his proud back was out of Manager Chou's view. Furthermore, without looking he stepped squarely on the foot of a messenger standing outside the door. He apologized. Lifting his foot, a painful smile on his face, the messenger said perfunctorily, "It's all right!"

Manager Chou shook his head, thinking, *Women just don't understand how things work. All they can do is blow their tempers at home, making it that much harder for their husbands to carry on outside.* He had taken great pains to work up a rough draft of the conversation, intending to go from the subject of Hung-chien's travel expenses to Hung-chien's father, and then while on Hung-chien's father, would quickly change his tone and say, *Since you came back, you haven't been very close to your mother and father. Now that you're about to go far away from home again, it seems you ought to go back home for a month or two and look after them a bit. My wife and I would like to have you stay with us for a long time, and Hsiao-ch'eng will hate to see you go, but if I keep you with us and don't let you go back home and fulfill your filial duties, your parents will come over and curse us.* At this point, he would laugh heartily and pat Hung-chien on his hand, arm, shoulder or back, depending on which "pattable" part of his body happened to be within reach at the time. *In any case if you drop over often, won't it be just the same? If you never come, then I won't agree to it.*

He was confident his little speech was tactful and proper, especially the last part, which had been sewn together as flawlessly as "a divine suit of clothes"; it would achieve his objective in every way, what Chief-secretary Wang called as naturally and effortlessly as "pushing a boat downstream." The letters Wang himself wrote were probably no better than this. How vexing that this nice little speech should have been so garbled up in the delivery. He had panicked and lost his composure. That damned little Hung-chien with the disgruntled look of one who has just been slapped in the face. He had given Hung-chien a chance to save face, and instead Hung-chien had to go and scratch it apart and quarrel with him. Hung-chien had no appreciation of the kindness extended to him; no wonder his wife detested him. The part that was hardest to say still stayed pent up inside him, like phlegm stuck in the throat, as vexing as an itch that can't be scratched. Symbolically, he coughed to clear his throat. He had wasted his money educating Hung-chien, who obviously didn't amount to much. His wife had just said that recently when she asked someone to have his horoscope analyzed it had turned out that every sign of his was very rough-edged. The marriage would never have come off. Shu-ying had fallen under Hung-chien's death curse[3] before she'd even married him! Now that Hung-chien was having a love affair, there was sure to be trouble. It would be wisest to let Hung-chien go home to be under Squire Fang's strict guard. That would free himself from any involvement as an elder. But it was rather awkward to be chasing Hung-chien away so suddenly today. Ai, the way his wife used her illness as an excuse to vent her anger was really more than he could take! With a sigh he put the matter aside, and picking up the business correspondence on his desk, pressed the buzzer.

Not wanting his co-workers to see the shame and anger on his face, Hung-chien ran out of the bank in one breath. He cursed Mrs. Chou, considering her the instigator of his troubles. A husband who let his wife make all the decisions like Manager Chou did was pretty despicable himself! The funny thing was that even now he still didn't understand why Mrs. Chou had suddenly made such a tempest in a teacup. He was sure he hadn't offended her in any way! But there was no point trying to figure out her reason. If they wanted him to leave, then he'd leave. He wasn't about to hang around, nor would he bother disputing with them over who was at fault. To please her, he had even thought of buying and bringing home some of her favorite delicacies! When she learned he was seeing Miss Su, she had changed her attitude and began making nasty remarks. On the other hand, Hsiao-ch'eng had never cared much for him to begin with. Helping Hsiao-ch'eng with his studies seemed to mean acting as his ghost writer. Hsiao-ch'eng wanted to bring all his classwork home for him to do, and if he refused, Hsiao-ch'eng resented him for it. Besides, the little rascal liked to meddle in other people's business. Fortunately, every precaution had been taken, and none of the letters had fallen into Hsiao-ch'eng's hands. Why, of course! it must have been the T'angs' chauffeur coming for the letters this morning that had aroused Mrs. Chou's suspicions. But she didn't have to get so upset over that! It really made one wonder! Well, let it be, then! When his luck was rotten, it was rotten to the core, rotten all the way through. Yesterday he had been jilted by his sweetheart; today he was thrown out by his father-in-law. Being jilted followed by losing his job, or rather, losing his job because of being jilted. A true case of "skinning the nose while falling on the back!" or "Good luck never comes in pairs, while misfortune always takes a company."

So let it come. Let the very worst of his luck come. He couldn't stay at the Chous for another day. He'd just have to go back and crowd in with his parents for a few days, like a dog that's been given a beating outside and comes running back home with its tail between its legs. But how could he admit to his family that he'd been thrown out without losing face? In the last two days he'd gone numb with anger. It seemed as if a drumstick wrapped with cotton had been beating on a drum in the back of his brain. There was a heavily muffled, throbbing pain. He could think of no wholly satisfactory way of covering his shame that would not arouse his family's suspicions as to why he should suddenly want to come home and live in discomfort. His family still didn't know about the telegram from San Lü University. What if he announced this to his parents? They would certainly be pleased, and in their joy they might be more magnanimous and not probe and question him very much. He was too lazy to ponder it further and so, with this piece of good news to go on, he braced himself to go home and watch for the right moment to speak. After he had explained everything to his family, he would stay on until quite late before returning to the Chous to sleep in order to avoid meeting Mr. or Mrs. Chou. Then he would pack up his three suitcases and slip out early the next morning, leaving a goodbye note. In any case, he couldn't face the Chous any more than they could face him. It would really save a lot of trouble. He would not be staying at home long, just until San Lü University wired his traveling expenses; then he would find a few traveling companions and set off. Since he didn't have to go to the bank any more, he could have fun for a few days, enjoying whatever leisure provided. The idea of leisure somehow reminded him of Miss T'ang; he hurriedly forced the thought out of his mind like one skating over thin ice. His heart also managed to dodge the pain, which luckily had not yet started up.

Hung-chien arrived at his parents' home some time after four o'clock. As soon as she opened the door, the old maidservant yelled, "Eldest Young Master is here! Madam, Eldest Young Master is here! No need to invite him here any more."

Entering, Hung-chien saw his mother sitting by the old round dining table, holding and feeding Ah Hsiung with powdered milk. Ah Ch'ou was fussing nearby. The old maidservant shut the door and hurried back to cajole Ah Ch'ou, "Don't make a fuss and greet Eldest Uncle like a nice boy. Eldest Uncle will give you candy."

Ah Ch'ou shut his mouth and stared up wide-eyed at Hung-chien. As no candy seemed to be forthcoming, he went back to Mrs. Fang to continue jumping and yelling about as before.

Ah Ch'ou, P'eng-t'u's son, was four years old. His face was so ugly at birth that one had to laugh at it. P'eng-t'u, still unaccustomed to being a father, and feeling neither the pride of the creator nor the partiality of the owner toward this lump of red flesh barely possessing the five organs and seven orifices,[4] bounded into his father's study and announced, "A freak's been born."

Old Fang Tun-weng, eagerly awaiting a grandson, had just divined a lot from the *I Ching*.[5] It was the *Little Beast* lot: "Dense clouds, no rain." "The spokes burst out of the wagon wheels. Man and wife roll their eyes." "Blood vanishes and fear gives way, no blame." He looked disconsolately at the words of the *I Ching* divination lot, thinking that it must mean his daughter-in-law would either have a difficult birth or else a miscarriage. Piously, he was just about to cast another lot when he heard his son's outburst. He jumped with fright, "Don't talk such nonsense! Has the child been born?"

Seeing how serious the old man looked, P'eng-t'u quickly replied in a very correct manner, "It's a boy. The mother and son are both fine."

Containing his delight, Fang Tun-Weng warned his son, "You're a father now, yet you speak so frivolously. How will you ever teach your son in the future!"

P'eng-t'u explained, "The baby's face really is ugly. Please give him a name."

"All right, since you say he's ugly, then call him Ah Ch'ou (Ugly Boy)." Remembering that Hsün Tzu[6] had stated in his chapter "No Face"[7] that the faces of all great saints and sages of antiquity were very ugly, Fang Tun-weng simply gave his grandson the school name of "No Face."

114

Mrs. Fang understood nothing about any face or no face, but she didn't care for the name "Ugly Boy" and insisted, "The boy has a fine face. All newborns are like that. Who says he's ugly? I think you'd better find him some other name."

This brought out Fang Tun-weng's entire stock of long-accumulated knowledge. "You can't appreciate that. If Hung-chien were here, he'd understand it." So saying he went to the bookshelves in his study and picked out two or three volumes, which he opened up and gave his son to read since Mrs. Fang could only make out a few characters.

Fang P'eng-t'u read, "If one wishes to facilitate the raising of one's child, he should give him a lowly name as his childhood name, such as dog, goat, or horse." He also learned that Ssu-ma Hsiang-ju's childhood name was Chuan-tzu (dog), Huan Hsi's childhood name was Shih-tou (stone), Fan Yeh's name was Chuan-er (brick), Mu-jung Nung's name was E-nu (despicable slave), and Yuan I's name was Yeh-i (underworld messenger).[8] There were also "Striped Beast," "Bald Head," "Tortoise," "Badger," and so on. He realized then that for his son to be called "Ugly Boy" was actually rather respectable.

When Fang Tun-weng went to a teahouse that day and told everyone about it, his fawning tea companions, besides repeatedly offering congratulations, all praised his choice of a name, saying it was novel and fitting, not only elegant but also resonant. Only Mrs. Fang, while playing with her grandchild, would often rub her face against his and protest on his behalf, "Our face is so pretty! We're a lovely little precious darling. Why accuse us of being ugly? Grandpa is so unreasonable, you go and pull his beard off."

While abroad, Fang Hung-chien also wrote home voicing his opinion of his nephew's school name. The two vanguard brothers in the novel *The Investiture of the Gods*,[9] he said, were called Fang Pi and Fang Hsiang (Fang Face). The name Fang Fei-hsiang (Fang No Face) seemed to be "colliding" with the younger brother and should be changed as soon as possible. Fang Tun-weng had ignored him. Last year a few days after the war had started, the wife of the third son, Feng-i, had her first child. Fang Tun-weng, feeling deeply their "shared misfortune of war" and moved by his experiences, named him Ah Hsiung, giving him the school name "Fei-kung" based on Mo Tzu's "Nonaggression" chapter.[10] By this time Tun-weng had become addicted to giving names. He'd already thought up a whole series of a dozen or more names and merely waited for his daughters-in-law to give birth to a succession of children to come take them. A boy, for example, would be called "Fei-hsiung" (No Bear) after the story of Chiang T'ai-kung,[11] and a girl would be called "Fei-yen" after a T'ang *ch'uan-ch'i* tale.[12]

During their escape from their home, the two little boys, Ah Hsiung and Ah Ch'ou, had proved to be no small burden. When that insensitive bachelor, Hung-chien, heard his parents tell about the ordeals of the escape, he inwardly faulted his two sisters-in-law for making his parents suffer, because they had not managed their children properly. It irked him now to see Ah Hsiung and Ah Ch'ou pestering their grandmother, while their own mothers were nowhere in sight.

Mrs. Fang had played the role of a filial daughter-in-law for too long. Now when it was her turn to be the mother-in-law, she simply didn't know how to do it properly. In Western families the fighting between mother and son-in-law is an old custom preserved to this day. In Chinese families, the animosity between mother and daughter-in-law has a history no less lengthy. But when the daughter-in-law becomes pregnant, since it is on her that the mother-in-law must rely for elevation to the position of grandmother, the mother-in-law begins to make accommodations. When the daughter-in-law gives birth to a genuine, honest-to-goodness son, the mother-in-law has to make further concessions. Mrs. Fang was meek by nature, while the two young mothers were both quite shrewd. When Ah Ch'ou was born, it had been more than twenty years since the Fangs had heard a baby cry. The old couple couldn't help but dote on and spoil him.

As a result the daughter-in-law's arrogance secretly increased, while the grandson's temper visibly worsened. Feng-i's wife's stomach "did its part," and her firstborn was also a boy. From then on the two sisters-in-law's secret rivalry intensified. The Fangs did their best to appear fair to both, but behind their backs, the daughters-in-law each complained of their partiality. When Hung-chien first came back to China, the house was spacious and Ah Ch'ou had a wet nurse to look after him, so that Ah Ch'ou did not become a nuisance. After their escape, Ah Ch'ou's wet nurse was dismissed.

Since Ah Hsiung was born at the start of the war, Third Daughter-in-law had never used a wet nurse. When they came to Shanghai, she wanted to hire one in order to gain equal footing with Second Daughter-in-law's Ah Ch'ou. According to an unwritten rule in old families, grandparents were expected to pay for the grandson's wet nurse. After their flight from the occupied area, Fang Tun-weng's circumstances were greatly reduced. He had to scrimp on small expenditures and would not hire a wet nurse for his second grandchild. In speaking to Third Daughter-in-law, however, he never mentioned a word about finances, saying only that Shanghai wasn't like their village but a disreputable place where very few of the lower-class girls were clean. Maids had children by the chauffeur or the rickshaw boy, then hired out as wet nurses. All such women carried disease, making them unfit for nursing a child. Besides, the general moral climate of Shanghai was much too debased. A wet nurse would always be asking leave to spend the night out, and if the milk underwent any changes, it wouldn't be suitable for the child and could very well cause "lifelong regrets." Seeing that her father-in-law expected her to take care of the baby herself, Third Daughter-in-law's pent-up resentment swelled and so did her stomach, while her appetite diminished and her limbs grew weak. The doctor was called in and she was given some medicine. Meanwhile Ah Hsiung became the sole charge of his grandmother. The doctor had finally verified only a week ago that Third Daughter-in-law was not ill but nearly four months pregnant.

Second Daughter-in-law, supporting her quivering belly now into her sixth month of pregnancy, said privately to her husband with a scornful smile, "I'd already guessed as much. She knows perfectly well what her stomach is up to. She just wanted to trick that dumb mother of yours. All this about a swelling, an infection of the spleen. Humph, she can't fool me!"

In a large family daughters-in-law usually have to have small stomachs for food but big ones for frustration. Once they become pregnant and their stomachs get big, they can enlarge their stomachs for food and reduce their stomachs for frustration. The bodies of these two young wives were by now like two large spiders which have just feasted on flies. Both had reached the state where the capacity of the house had become visibly smaller. Mrs. Fang was left with more work than she could handle, and the two maids decided this was a good time to fuss about a raise, which they got.

Because of Third Daughter-in-law's illness, Fang Tun-weng developed an interest in the study of family medicine. Unlike when they lived in the country, he had few visitors in Shanghai. Next door there lived a quack doctor from his village who admired Fang's reputation and found time off between killing people to drop by occasionally for a chat. In his village this quack had truly "practiced medicine for three generations and won fame in four quarters." The people in that quarter must at least have had strong resistance not to have been exterminated either by his grandfather's or his father's medicine, leaving three of the four quarters.[13] Like all lettered men of the older generation, Fang Tun-weng believed that he knew something about medicine: "If not a good official, then a good doctor,"[14] as the saying went. The quack, thinking Fang had a wide range of contacts and hoping Fang would introduce some customers to him, inevitably began to flatter Fang. Such "rice gruel" is like alcohol. Everyone has a different capacity for it. Fang Tun-weng's capacity had never been very great, but he was fed so much of it that he had almost become intoxicated, and he quite forgot himself. By coincidence Third Daughter-in-law provided him an experimental subject, and so he wrote quite a few prescriptions. When she found the medicine from her father-in-law and the neighbor doctor ineffective, she raised a fuss with her husband and insisted on calling in a doctor trained in Western medicine.[15] Tun-weng was inwardly displeased when he first found out about this, but when he heard that the Western-trained doctor had diagnosed she was not ill, his displeasure nearly erupted. When the Western doctor announced the happy news that she was pregnant, he, however, could not very well get angry. Instead he just had to keep it to himself, while he looked for some other way to restore honor to his medical skills and the good name of Chinese medicine.

Mrs. Fang took Hung-chien into his father's bedroom. On his desk were spread *The Flowers in the Mirror*[16] and the tenth edition of the Commercial Press's revised and enlarged edition of *Proven Remedies*. He was planning to excerpt the wonder remedies in *The Flowers in the Mirror* and record them on the blank spaces of *Proven Remedies*.

When Tun-weng saw his son, he said, "Oh, you're back. I was just going to call you over for a talk. You haven't been here for about a month. You must come home more often. As a father I've been too lenient with all of you. None of you knows your manners—" and leafing through *Proven Remedies*, he said to Mrs. Fang, "Mother, since Third Daughter-in-law is expecting, I think she could use this prescription. It's to be taken twice a day, each dose consisting of a soup made with one whole piece of bean-curd skin—don't cut it up—soy sauce, and sesame oil. It's not bitter-tasting and she can take it with her meals. There's nothing better. It won't hurt Second Daughter-in-law to do the same. This prescription is very sound: bean-curd skin is smooth, as is sesame oil. If the placenta in the womb is smooth, the baby will come out more easily and the mother can avoid a difficult birth. Let them take a look at this prescription. Now, don't go yet. Listen to what I have to say to Hung-chien—Hung-chien, you're almost thirty now. You should know how to behave yourself. You shouldn't need outdated 'antiques' like us prattling on. But—Mother, if we fail to discipline our son, someone else will do it for us. We can't allow such a disgrace, can we? Your mother-in-law telephoned this morning and said you were fooling around and carrying on with women. Now, don't argue. I'm not stupid. I don't believe everything she says." He held his hand out toward his son with palm down as a signal to quash any arguments. "But you certainly must have done something improper, which has come to her attention. You should of course have been properly married by now. It's my fault. I've been overly indulgent toward you. From now on I'll just have to handle everything for you. I think you'd better move back home so as not to make a nuisance of yourself, and so I can keep you under my supervision. You should put up with the hard life of 'coarse tea and plain rice' we have here at home for a while. Young people expect nothing but comfort. They get soft and never amount to anything."

Fang Hung-chien seethed with shame and rage. Several dozen sentences rushed all at once to his lips, but he managed to say only, "I was thinking of moving back tomorrow. My mother-in-law is being ridiculous. She just likes to make a fuss over nothing, the goddamn—"

"Now, that is no attitude to take," fumed Tun-weng. "I can see you're getting more and more rude and ill-mannered. Maybe she did exaggerate, but she meant well as an elder. You young people—" Fang Tun-weng did not finish his sentence, indicating words were inadequate to describe these disgusting, ill-mannered youths.

Seeing the ugly look on Hung-chien's face, Mrs. Fang feared a clash between father and son, and asked quickly with sly timidity, "What about that Miss Su? If you really do like her, Papa and I will go along with your wishes. We only want you to be happy."

Hung-chien could not keep his face from reddening as he replied, "I've long since stopped seeing her."

The red face did not escape the old couple's notice. They exchanged knowing glances, and with a thoroughly understanding smile Tun-weng said, "You quarreled and broke up, didn't you? That's very common among young couples. Affections grow stronger after every quarrel. Both of you have already regretted it inside but remain resentful and ignore each other. Am I right? At a time like that there has to be a third party to intercede. You won't give in and admit you were wrong, so the only thing is for this old fellow to act as mediator and write her a nice, tactful letter. She's sure to go along for my sake." The naughtiness in Tun-weng's smile and tone was ponderous enough to have caved in the floor.

Hung-chien, who dreaded his father's humor and would rather he get angry, blurted out recklessly in alarm, "She's already engaged."

The look that passed between husband and wife deepened in meaning. Tun-weng grew solemn and said, "Then, you've been—you've been what they call 'jilted.' Well, that's not worth letting yourself go to pieces for! You have a long life ahead of you."

Tun-weng not only forgave but pitied his son for having suffered humiliation at the hands of a woman.

Hung-chien felt even more uncomfortable. True, he had been "jilted"— the word sounded awkward and unnatural on his father's tongue—but not by Su Wen-wan. His parents' sympathy was misdirected. It was as though one had suffered a wound in the flesh only to have the sympathizer dress and bandage a perfectly healthy part instead. Should he tell them about Miss T'ang? They would never understand, and his father might even take up his brush and directly propose to Miss T'ang on his behalf. He was quite capable of doing something ludicrous like that. Hung-chien spouted some nonsense to cover up, then showed his father the telegram.

As Hung-chien expected, the business with Mrs. Chou was forgotten. His father said that this job at last was something worthy of a returned student, much better than eking out a living as a petty bank clerk. "Though P'ing-ch'eng is a little remote," his father went on, "the Fangs should have someone in the unoccupied interior, so I can keep in touch with the people there. When you go to the interior, you can tell the appropriate authorities about my activities since my home area fell to the Japanese." After a pause, Tun-weng said, "In the future you should send me a third of your monthly salary. It's not that I want your money, but it's to instill in you a sense of responsibility toward your parents. Your two brothers both help out with the family expenses."

At the dinner table that evening Mr. and Mrs. Fang clearly sided with their son, criticizing the Chous for being so petty and intolerant that they had to find some excuse to chase Hung-chien out. "Businessmen are always the same. They see that we Fangs have lost our influence. Well, we've no need for relatives who are such stingy, snobbish parvenus as that."

Hung-chien's parents settled it that Hung-chien would return to the Chous that evening and pack his bags. The next day Mrs. Fang would go inquire after Mrs. Chou's health, thanking her on Hung-chien's behalf for all her trouble. This would make it easier for them to get the bags away.

After dinner, Hung-chien didn't feel like going straight over to the Chous, so he went by himself to a movie. When the movie was over, he waited until he thought that Manager Chou and his wife had gone to bed before he finally strolled back. Entering his bedroom, he noticed on his desk Hsiao-ch'eng's English grammar textbook with a note stuck between the pages: "Brother Hung-chien, I can't wait for you any longer. I have to go to bed. Please do grammar exercises nos. 34 and 38 as fast as you can. Also there's a Chinese composition on any topic. Just write two hundred words on something. If you could do three hundred, that'd be even better. Just any which way, don't make it too good. It has to be handed in tomorrow. *Thank you very much*."[17] Beside the book was a large plate of loquat seeds which Hsiao-ch'eng had evidently eaten to pass the time while waiting for him. With a snort Hung-chien packed his bags, then lay down and dozed for a while. Early the next morning he left the Chous.

Mrs. Chou had actually regretted everything that same afternoon. Having tasted the hollowness of victory, she was merely waiting for Hung-chien to come meekly back and apologize and then she would rescind all her orders. When she discovered the next morning that Hung-chien had left without saying goodbye, and her son was jumping and cursing about, wanting to skip school for the day, she was so infuriated she began muttering incessantly. When Mrs. Fang arrived, she nearly found herself an actress in an impromptu performance of "Cursing Relatives." At lunchtime a messenger from the Golden Touch Bank delivered Hung-chien's salary for four months to the Fangs. Fang Tun-weng accepted the money for his son.

Fang Hung-chien's life at home was quite boring. Every day he wrote letters for his father, copied prescriptions, and whenever he had a spare moment took a walk. Each time he left the house he was always secretly hoping that on the street, in a rickshaw, or in front of a movie theater he would accidentally run into Miss T'ang. And what if he did? Sometimes he imagined himself proud and aloof, staring through her as though she weren't there, making it unbearable for her. At other times he pictured himself smiling serenely and being exasperatingly courteous toward her, while she herself completely lost her composure. Sometimes his imaginative powers took even greater leaps, and he saw himself walking arm in arm with someone more beautiful than Miss T'ang, when suddenly he found himself face to face with Miss T'ang, who still had no boy friend. But if Miss T'ang were to show the slightest sign of hurt or disappointment, he would immediately drop the other girl and reconcile with Miss T'ang. The Miss T'ang of his imagination sometimes chided him for being "cruel," and other times she suppressed her feelings and turned her face away to hide the tears on her eyelashes.

After he had been home for nearly ten days and the Dragon Boat Festival[18] had come and gone with still no word from San Lü University, he began to worry. One day early in the morning a special messenger came with a letter from Chao Hsin-mei. The letter said that the day before Chao Hsin-mei had gone to the Golden Touch Bank to see him but had not found him there. If he were free this afternoon, could he please drop by after four for a chat? Hsin-mei had something important to tell him, adding, "What happened before grew out of a misunderstanding. I hope you will not take it to heart." Strangest of all Hsin-mei called himself "Hung-chien's lovemate." After he had read the letter, he was greatly perplexed. Since Chao Hsin-mei was now engaged to Miss Su, what would Hsin-mei want with him? Hsin-mei certainly wouldn't be asking him to be best man at their wedding.

Shortly afterwards the newspaper came, and Third Daughter-in-law immediately grabbed it and began reading. Suddenly she asked, "Your girl friend's name is Su Wen-wan, isn't it?"

Aware that she was watching his face with great interest, Hung-chien hoped he wouldn't blush. In confusion, he asked her why. She pointed to an announcement in the newspaper for him to read. The announcement, placed by Su Hung-yeh and Ts'ao Yüan-chen, was intended to inform the readers that the daughter of Mr. Su and the brother of Mr. Ts'ao had on that day become engaged. Hung-chien was so astonished that he could not suppress a cry. This must be that "something important" Chao Hsin-mei had referred to in the letter. If Su Wen-wan could marry Ts'ao Yüan-lang, then there was really no limit to the stupidity of women. What a pity for Chao Hsin-mei!

What Hung-chien didn't know was that after accepting Ts'ao Yüan-lang's proposal, Miss Su had said, "Poor Hsin-mei. He's going to complain about how cruel I am."

In his great joy the poet Ts'ao's usually minute understanding of the female psyche was completely forgotten, and he blurted out, "Don't worry about that. He'll find someone else. I hope everyone can be as happy as I, and

I wish him quick success in romance."

When Miss Su's face fell and she grew quiet, Ts'ao Yüan-lang realized his mistake. Having always concentrated on new-style poetry, he had never noticed the two lines from Yüan Wei-chih's poem:

> He who has seen a great ocean cannot content himself with
> a pond.
> Having viewed the clouds over Wu Mountain, he will call
> nothing else a cloud.[19]

Ts'ao was filled with remorse. Miss Su of course felt that anyone who had once fancied her could not easily be attracted to another woman. While she wasn't marrying Chao Hsin-mei, subconsciously, perhaps, she expected him to remain celibate and wait patiently for Ts'ao Yüan-lang to die, so he could step in and fill his place.

Ts'ao Yüan-lang hurried home and wrote a love poem to send to Miss Su, first to commemorate the happy occasion and second to make up for his blunder. The general idea of the poem, other than condemning the evils of private property, was that he shared his mind and body with Miss Su. Being so ardent in his emotions and having made a few extra trips into the intense heat of the summer sun, he had developed two small sores on his head, and on his face a layer of pimples had broken out. All these of course he also shared with Miss Su.

At exactly five o'clock, Fang Hung-chien found the Western-style apartment[20] house where Chao Hsin-mei lived. Even before he entered the apartment complex, he could hear the radios of several apartments in the building blaring out the popular tune, "The Love Song of Spring." The air was ripped to pieces by the shrill voice of the universally acclaimed Chinese female movie star:

> Spring, spring, oh why has it not come?
> The flowers in my heart already are in bloom!
> Oh, my love—

The logical conclusion to this was of course that before summer came her body had already borne fruit. There was a turgidity in the sharpness of the star's sweet voice, which seemed for the most part like something blown out from the nose—greasy, sticky, and soft, the characteristics of mucus, the main product of the nose. But it must have been at least as long as the nose in order to hold that endless, whining sound.

He walked up to the door of the Chaos' apartment on the second floor. The song was playing inside there too. As he pressed the bell, he thought, *Hell! Listening to a song like that is like looking at pornographic books or pictures. It's a sign of intellectual backwardness and mental abnormality.* He had never expected Chao Hsin-mei to sink so low after being jilted! The maid opened the door, took his name card, and went inside. The radio was turned off.

The maid came out and invited him into the small sitting room, which was exquisitely furnished and had several large framed pictures on the walls. Among them was a large photograph of Chao Hsin-mei's late father, a large photograph of Chao Hsin-mei in his master's gown with his diploma in his hand, and an autographed picture of Chao Hsin-mei's American professor. In a group picture of the Summer Conference of Returned Students from America, Chao Hsin-mei was seated on the ground in the front row. In order to make it easier for the viewer to pick him out, he had marked a cross on the top of his head in red ink, which was also on the torso of the person standing behind him, making it look as though that person had performed Japanese *harakiri* on him. Most striking of all was a long, narrow color photograph of Miss Su with a stick in her hand herding a flock of sheep. She had a kerchief tied around her head and was dressed like a shepherdess in a classic, romantic, rustic setting. Unfortunately she did not seem to be wholly occupied with tending the sheep but was looking out of the picture frame and smiling slyly at the viewer. The two lines of inscription on the edge of the picture indicated that it was taken in the French countryside where Miss Su had gone to escape the summer heat. She had had the picture enlarged and given it to Hsin-mei after returning from abroad. In spite of himself Hung-chien felt a slight twinge of jealousy. Miss Su had never shown him this fine photograph. Besides these photographs of the principal relationships—including family, teachers, friends, and women—there was a poem and a painting both written especially for Hsin-mei. The poem was by Tung Hsieh-ch'üan written in the Nine-palace calligraphy style:[21]

> Still lacking a Mandarin duck society,
> Not noisy from geese and duck neighbors.
> My good friend Hsin-mei,
> Unmarried at thirty
> Like the Man of Tao in Li Tung-ch'üan's poem.[22]
> He moved and asked for a few lines,
> So in fun I wrote these to clutter his wall.

The painting, by Mrs. Tung Hsieh-ch'üan, was inscribed, "A hut in the zone of human habitation."[23] Hung-chien was just about to take a closer look when Hsin-mei came out, his clothes, thrown on in haste, remained unbuttoned. It was hot, and perhaps he may have been feeling a little embarrassed, for his face was as red as a tomato.

Hung-chien said quickly, "I'd like to take off my clothes. Do I have your permission?"

Hsin-mei said, "By all means."

The maid took their clothes out to hang up and brought in some tea and cigarettes. Hsin-mei told her to go fetch some cool refreshments. Hung-chien admired the elegance of his apartment and asked how many people were in his family. Hsin-mei replied that there were only his mother, himself, and three servants, while his brother and sister-in-law lived in Tientsin. Eyeing Hung-chien he said solicitously, "Hung-chien, you've lost a lot of weight."

With a wan smile Hung-chien replied, "It's all from getting sick that day you made me drunk."

"Please, don't bring all that up again!" exclaimed Hsin-mei hurriedly. "We wouldn't have known each other if we hadn't had a fight. We'll be together for a long time later on, so we should try to be good friends. Tell me, when did you find out that Miss Su was in love with Ts'ao Yüan-lang?"

"I just learned about it this morning when I read her engagement announcement in the newspaper."

"Oh"—Hsin-mei's voice revealed satisfaction—"I found out three days ago this morning. She told me herself and even consoled me with lots of kind words. But I still don't know what sort of guy that Ts'ao fellow is."

"Well, I've met him before, but I never thought Miss Su would go for him. I thought for sure she'd marry you."

"Don't you know it! And I thought for sure she'd marry you. Who'd have thought there was this Ts'ao fellow! That girl sure is something. We were both taken for a ride. Objectively speaking, I admire her for it. But enough of that. We're now co-sufferers and we will be co-workers in the future."

"What? You mean you're going to San Lü University too?"

Thereupon Hsin-mei opened up and explained the whole affair from beginning to end. San Lü University had just been founded this year. Kao Sungnien was a former professor of his. Originally Kao had asked him to head the political science department, but he had not wanted to leave Miss Su. Then he suddenly remembered hearing her say that Hung-chien was anxious to find a position with a national university, so he sent a telegram to recommend Hung-chien to Kao, hoping to get Miss Su away from Hung-chien. But Kao wasn't willing to let him go and instead sent one telegram after another asking him to come. Three days ago he had received his walking papers from Miss Su and had wired his acceptance as soon as he left her house. In the last letter Kao asked him to have Hung-chien send a resumé and said that there were others in Shanghai who had also accepted jobs at San Lü University. Kao wanted him to arrange for all of them to set off together, and would forward the traveling expenses and itinerary to him.

All was now clear to Hung-chien. He said, "I have to thank you for finding me a job."

"Not at all!" said Hsin-mei. "People in the same boat should help each other."

"I forgot to ask you. In your letter you called me 'lovemate.' What do you mean by that?"

Hsin-mei said with a grin, "That's something Tung Hsieh-ch'üan thought up. He says people who study under the same teacher are called classmates, and people who go to the same school are called schoolmates, so people who are in love with the same girl should be called 'lovemates.' "

Hung-chien burst out laughing and said, "That's very clever. Unfortunately your lovemate is Ts'ao Yüan-lang, not me."

"You're being too dishonest!" exclaimed Hsin-mei. "We're fellow sufferers now. I've been jilted and so have you. You needn't put on a front or try to save face around me. Don't tell me you aren't in love with Miss Su?"

"I'm not in love with her. I'm a fellow sufferer but not with the same person."

"Then who jilted you? Can you tell me?"

The secret could be kept no longer. "Miss T'ang," said Hung-chien dejectedly in a low voice.

"T'ang Hsiao-fu! You have good taste, all right! How stupid of me."

At first, when it seemed that Hsin-mei and Hung-chien had both suffered the same misfortune, Hsin-mei had tried his best to outdo his friend in his expression of pain and misery, not daring to let Hung-chien alone get a name for being brokenhearted. Now that he realized he and Hung-chien were not in each other's way, his attitude toward Hung-chien changed considerably, and his voice recovered its usual resonance. He made Hung-chien wait while he called up Tung Hsieh-ch'üan to ask him over. The three of them went out for dinner together.

Hsieh-ch'üan knew all about Hsin-mei's being jilted. After dinner they began discussing Miss Su's engagement to Ts'ao Yüan-lang. Hsin-mei remarked magnanimously, "It's for the best. They have similar interests. Both have studied poetry."

Hung-chien and Hsieh-ch'üan disagreed, maintaining that people in the same line of work were least suited for each other. Both being experts, neither one could dupe the other. The husband would not boundlessly worship his wife, and the wife would not blindly worship her husband. So the marriage would not have a firm foundation.

Smiling, Hsin-mei said, "There's no point telling me all that. I just hope they'll be happy."

They said Hsin-mei was so serene and even-tempered that he could be a saint. The saint laughed and said nothing. Then after a long pause he took out his pipe and with a mischievous twinkle in his eyes, said, "Ts'ao Yüan-lang will at least have Miss Su to read his stuff, and Miss Su will at least have Ts'ao

Yüan-lang to read hers. Neither will lack a reader, so won't that work out nicely?"

They laughed and said Hsin-mei was no saint yet but would still do as a friend. Hung-chien no longer felt lonely after this, and the three of them often got together.

Three weeks later Hsin-mei invited his new colleagues to a teahouse for breakfast, so that everyone could get acquainted. There were three others besides Hung-chien. The chairman of the Chinese Literature Department, Li Mei-t'ing, an old colleague of Kao Sung-nien, was in his forties. He had on a pair of dark glasses and looked haughty, paying little attention to anyone and showing a contemptuous disregard for the weather as well, for though it was mid-June, he still wore a black wool Western-style jacket. Hsin-mei asked him to take it off, but he adamantly refused, so Hsin-mei perspired for him. His white shirt looked like it had a case of yellow fever. Another, Ku Er-chien, a distant relative of Kao Sung-nien, had apparently never dreamed of being offered a position as associate professor in the History Department, and his happiness overflowed onto the whole table like boiling water. He was particularly courteous to Messrs. Chao and Li. He was a wizened man of nearly fifty, who had the sweet innocent air of a young girl. His smile was a good thirty years younger than his face and was made especially bright and dazzling by two gold front teeth. Miss Sun Jou-chia was the daughter of a senior colleague of Hsin-mei's at the newspaper office. She had just graduated from college, and being young and ambitious, she did not want to stay in Shanghai. Her father had asked Hsin-mei to get her a job as a teaching assistant in the Department of Foreign Languages. She had a long face with slightly freckled cheeks, which resembled the color of aged ivory. Her eyes were too wide set, giving her a perpetual look of astonishment. She was dressed very plainly and was too shy to utter a word, but her face flushed in successive gushes. When she came into the teahouse, she greeted Hsin-mei as "Uncle Chao."[24] Hsin-mei quickly asked her not to address him in that manner. Hung-chien smiled to himself.

By the time Hsin-mei returned from taking his mother to Tientsin, it was already the beginning of September and time to set off, as San Lü University was scheduled to open at the beginning of October. Hsin-mei wanted to call everyone together for dinner again to decide on the departure date. A man who loved eating at restaurants, he was always finding some excuse to invite people out. If a friend had a favor to ask of him, he would have to discuss it with him at the dinner table. It was as though he had remembered only two sentences from his study of politics and diplomacy while abroad: Napoleon's instructions to diplomats, "When having company always serve good food" (*Toujours une bonne table*), and Lord Stowell's principle for handling business, "A dinner lubricates business."

But this time Hung-chien protested, saying that this was a matter concerning everyone, and they shouldn't always let Hsin-mei pick up the tab. It was thus changed to a dinner gathering. During dinner it was decided that they would take an Italian ship to Ningpo on the twentieth of September. Hsin-mei said he would buy five first-class tickets and they could pay him later. Li and Ku said nothing to this. When the waiter brought the bill after the meal, Ku grabbed it and insisted on paying it himself, adding that he had always wanted to treat his colleagues and there could be no better time than today. After one look at the bill Ku insisted no more, merely saying, "Such a trifle, why divide it up? You really ought to let me be the host."

Hsin-mei paid the bill, and while he was waiting at the counter for his change, Ku went to the lavatory, followed by Li. When they said their good-byes outside the restaurant, Li asked Hsin-mei if he had any friends at the steamship company to help buy the tickets. Hsin-mei replied that he would ask the China Travel Agency to take care of the tickets.

Li said, "I have a friend who works at the steamship company. Would you like me to ask him to buy them? We've already put you to so much trouble. This is something I can help with."

"Well, that would be fine," said Hsin-mei. "Please get five first-class tickets."

That afternoon Hung-chien took Hsin-mei and Hsieh-ch'üan to a coffee shop and talked about their three traveling companions. "If you ask me, that obnoxious little Li Mei-t'ing doesn't amount to anything. How can he be chairman of the Chinese Literature Department? You should have recommended Hsieh-ch'üan."

"Hsieh-ch'üan?" sputtered Hsin-mei. "You think he'd want to go? If you don't believe me, ask him yourself. Nobody but a pair of jilted rejects like us would be willing to go there. Hsieh-ch'üan has a beautiful young wife at home."

Don't be silly," said Hsieh-ch'üan with a smile. "I've no interest in teaching. As they say, 'If I had three hundred *mou*[25] of paddy fields, I wouldn't be a monkey king [i.e., teacher] next year.' Why don't you both go to Hong Kong with me and look for something there?"

Hung-chien said, "That's right. Coming back home has meant unemployment, so I don't mind teaching. But Hsin-mei has several options open to him. He can either work for the government or run a newspaper, but instead he's going to go sit on a cold bench.[26] I feel sorry for him."

"Running a newspaper is a way to enlighten the people," said Hsin-mei, "and teaching is, too. Both are 'spiritual mobilization,' the one just as much as the other. In terms of influence a newspaper is broadest, but in terms of the degree of influence teaching goes deepest. I'm gaining experience through this trip."

"Such high-flown talk," said Hsieh-ch'üan with a smile, "should be saved for your editorials to dupe your readers."

"I'm not trying to deceive anyone with big talk," said Hsin-mei impatiently. "I really believe it."

Hung-chien said, "You're so used to duping people with big talk that you've even duped yourself into believing it—a very common psychological occurrence."

"You don't understand," said Hsin-mei. "One can engage in politics through teaching, too. Look at the great Chinese statesmen at present. They all started their careers as professors. It's the same in Europe, like the first president of Czechoslovakia or the present prime minister of France. Politicians who begin by teaching can first of all get a firm grasp of the minds of the young, and second, they can train their own cadres. It's the same as a newspaper creating public opinion."

Hung-chien said, "That's not a great professor engaging in politics. It's a petty politician running education. The former policy of keeping the masses ignorant prevented the people from getting an education. The current policy of keeping the masses ignorant only allows the people to get a certain kind of education. The uneducated are fooled by others because they're illiterate. The educated are taken in by printed matter like your newspaper propaganda and lecture notes on training cadres because they are literate."

Hsin-mei remarked sarcastically, "Listen, everyone. Mr. Fang Hung-chien's views are so penetrating! He's only twenty-eight and has just had an unhappy love affair, yet he sees through education, he sees through politics, he sees through everything. Humph! Well, I see through you! All because of a downy-haired lassie, you turn into such a cynic. What a lot of fuss over nothing."

Hung-chien banged down his glass. "Who are you talking about?"

"I'm talking about T'ang Hsiao-fu, your beloved. She isn't a downy-haired lassie?"

White with rage, Hung-chien called Su Wen-wan Old Lady Hsü.[27]

Hsin-mei said, "Whether she's Old Lady Hsü or not is all the same to me. I don't go defending her the way you do T'ang Hsiao-fu. If she knew you were still so hung up on her, she'd probably try to put back the pieces. Right, Hsieh-ch'üan? So spineless! Would you like me to send her a message?"

Hung-chien was speechless. He stood up, but Hsieh-ch'üan pulled him back down to his seat, saying, "Calm down, calm down. People are watching. I'm embarrassed for you. In any case you're both in the same boat. It seems

Hung-chien hasn't been himself lately. How could anyone who calls himself a man get so upset over a girl—"

In a rage Hung-chien stalked out of the coffee shop without listening to his friend. He returned home and was just sitting down in a huff when the telephone rang. It was Hsieh-ch'üan, who said, "Why get so angry?"

Hung-chien was about to reply when Hsin-mei came on the line and said, "Hey, old chap, I can apologize all right, but you mustn't put on a show of anger and take off! Today you, the host, ran away without paying the bill, and we guests didn't bring any money with us. Now we're held in custody here in the coffee shop until you come rescue us! S O S. Hurry up! Tonight I'll treat everyone to a round of drinks to apologize."

Hung-chien couldn't help laughing and said, "I'll be right over."

On the afternoon of the nineteenth, Hsin-mei gave Hung-chien the ticket that Li Mei-t'ing had bought for him, and informed him that the ship company had postponed the departure date to the twenty-second. Everyone was to be on board by six-thirty P.M.

In the West in ancient times, whenever someone disappeared, people would say, "He's either died or he's gone to teach" (*Aut mortuus est aut docet litteras*). While Hung-chien did not fear teaching as much as he did death itself, he did feel this teaching job was all a part of his bad luck and was dispirited and out of sorts for days on end, feeling an inexpressible dread at the thought of the long journey. The longer he could put the trip off the better. But when the ship company really did postpone it for two days, he wished it hadn't happened. He would have preferred to go ahead with it as soon as possible. He was taking three pieces of luggage: one large trunk, one bedroll, and one piece of hand luggage.

Mrs. Fang helped get his clothes and bedding ready for him, saying, "Once you're married you won't need me to take care of these things."

Fang Tun-weng said, "I'm afraid he'll still have to trouble you. Women students these days only like to have things done for them. They don't know how to do anything for themselves."

Mrs. Fang thought the early fall weather very unpredictable; so to prevent her son from catching cold on the way she wanted him to take a small bedroll in which he could wrap up the thin cotton quilt and clothes he used at night and wouldn't have to open up his large bedroll every day. Hung-chien was worried that too much luggage would be burdensome and pointed out that Kao Sung-nien had said in his letter that they'd certainly get there within a week at the earliest or within ten days at the most. The weather would not be turning cold yet. If he put a thin wool blanket in his carrying case, that would be enough.

Fang Tun-weng had several parting words of advice, which he instructed his son to remember, all arranged in catchy parallel couplets, such as: "Clench your jaws tight and stand firmly on your heels," or "One can miss home for a long time, but one must not be tied to home for an instant," and so on. Hung-chien knew that while these remarks were said to him, they were intended primarily to be recorded in a diary or in memoirs, so later generations could see how well Fang Tun-weng had brought up his son in accordance with truth and righteousness. Having so much leisure time of late, Tun-weng had suddenly discovered himself, like a child who is fascinated with his image in the mirror as he moves his head from side to side, and gazes at himself from the corner of his eye. This spiritual narcissism had prompted him to write an autobiography and keep a diary. It was like a woman who puts on Chinese and Western dresses of all seasons and all colors, strikes every kind of pose, walking, standing, sitting, lying, supporting chin in hand and twisting the neck, and has a picture taken of each to give her friends as a memento. These records were to prove from every angle and with every kind of fact Fang Tun-weng's noble character. Now whenever he said or did something, he was thinking at the same time how to record it in his diary or his record of deeds and sayings. The records weren't completely concocted out of thin air and were like a water bubble, which leaves a tiny drop of water when it bursts. Students of the psychology of language will recognize this at once as a case of *verbalmania*: People with a desire to lead, no matter whether in the literary, military, commercial, or governmental field, all reveal this symptom.

When friends came, Tun-weng always showed them his diary. Thus their neighbor, the quack doctor, learned that prior to the Dragon Boat Festival the Fangs' eldest son had fallen in with bad women, but after being reprimanded by Tun-weng had "awakened in terror and been filled with shame and remorse because of it." The entry in Tun-weng's diary of the day before yesterday stated how Tun-weng had asked Hung-chien to go to the Chous to say goodbye and how when Hung-chien refused and cursed Mrs. Chou, calling her a stingy snob, he had admonished his son, "A gentleman is severe with himself while being indulgent toward others, and so he does not lose relations or friends." As a result, his son had submissively "fallen silent."

Actually Hung-chien had never cursed Mrs. Chou. It was Tun-weng himself who was dissatisfied with her and who had thus resorted to this veiled manner to disparage her. At first Hung-chien had in fact refused to go say goodbye, but had finally gone in the end; when he found no one at home, he felt as though he'd been granted a pardon. A day later, the Chous sent over four varieties of food as going-away gifts. But the unreasonable Hung-chien became quite angry when he learned of it and wouldn't allow his mother to accept them. Mrs. Fang told her son to go down himself and speak with the person delivering the gifts, but he did not care to see the Chous' chauffeur either. In the end the chauffeur, after getting nothing but refusals at every turn, flung the food down and took off. In his obstinacy Hung-chien refused to eat anything the Chous had sent. Fang Tun-weng added an entry to his diary poking fun at his son for trying to imitate the Chou dynasty recluses Po Yi and Shu Ch'i by "not eating the grain of Chou."[28]

5

⌐⌐⌐

HUNG-CHIEN was to call a cab to take him to the docks, but the shrewd P'eng-t'u said that since the cab fare had doubled several times recently and since Hung-chien was in no hurry and had only a few pieces of luggage, it would be better for him to hire two rickshaws. In any case, their brother Feng-i would be seeing Hung-chien off.

On the twenty-second, around five o'clock, Hung-chien and Feng-i left their house. When the rickshaws came to the French Concession, a French policeman, with two Vietnamese policemen in tow, was rigorously searching passersby, while letting the cars get through easily. Hung-chien noticed immediately that the French policeman was the one who had been on the same ship coming to Shanghai with him. They had spoken a few times on the ship, and the Frenchman still seemed to recognize Hung-chien, for he waved Hung-chien's rickshaw through. Hung-chien thought to himself that those policemen on the boat were all from the French countryside and were leaving home for the first time, and every one of them was pitifully poor. But, in no time at all, this one had become colossal and colorful. His once anemic complexion was now as red as raw beef; his eyes were completely woven over with red silk threads, and his stomach protruded like a puffed-up frog. The French are known as "frogs" internationally and it is most appropriate. What was so frightening was that the French policeman had now taken on a vicious, beastly look. Shanghai is like the Island of Circe in Greek mythology. It can turn a perfectly decent fellow immediately into an animal.

The Vietnamese policemen looked even more ridiculous. There are no Orientals as puny and ill-suited to wearing a uniform as the Vietnamese. In the case of the Japanese, it's merely that their legs are too short for carrying sabers. The gaunt, emaciated Vietnamese, on the other hand, with their parched skin and black teeth looked like born opium addicts, and the policemen's sticks in their hands even resembled opium pipes. One of the Vietnamese policemen seemed to read Hung-chien's thoughts; he stopped Feng-i's rickshaw, which had fallen behind, and spitefully searched Feng-i from top to bottom, cutting open the cracker box and the fried pork can, and even stealthily stuck out his hand to demand three dollars. The bedroll at least remained intact. Along the way, Hung-chien, busy looking after the large and small trunks, couldn't easily turn his head; when he alighted from the rickshaw at the dock and did not see Feng-i, he spent several anxious moments waiting.

Hung-chien and Hsin-mei shared a cabin. They found Miss Sun, but neither Ku nor Li. When the ship sailed off with still no sign of them, Hsin-mei's whole face broke out in a nervous sweat. Hung-chien and Miss Sun shared his alarm. Just when they were getting anxious, an attendant ran up to say that a passenger in the third class wished to speak to Hsin-mei. Since the passenger could not go up to the first class, the passenger had to ask Hsin-mei to come down. Hung-chien went with Hsin-mei and there they saw Ku, who was waving his arms and stamping his feet to call them down.

"What about Mr. Li?" they both asked quickly.

Ku said, "He shares a cabin with me and he's washing his face. Mr. Li's friend could get only three first-class tickets, so Mr. Li and I gave them to you and we took a berth."

They were both quite dismayed by what they heard.

Ku said, "The berth is comfortable enough. I'll show you around."

They followed him into the cabin, which was filled with suitcases. Li was there washing his feet. Hsin-mei and Hung-chien formally thanked Ku and Li for the cabins.

Ku cut in, "At first only two first-class tickets were available, but Mr. Li asked his friend over and over and finally was able to get three."

Hsin-mei said, "Actually those two tickets should go to you older gentlemen. We young people should put up with a little discomfort."

Li replied, "It's only twelve hours at the most. That isn't much. I have gone first class before; it is not that much more comfortable than cabin."

After dinner the ship was pitching slightly. Hung-chien and Hsin-mei sat in the lounge chairs, which were nailed to the deck. As Hung-chien listened to the sounds of the wind and water and gazed out at the dark expanse of the sea and the sky, he recalled many scenes from last year's trip home. Since they seemed almost identical with those of this evening, he was filled with sentimental thoughts. Hsin-mei, who was smoking a large pipe, a gift from Hung-chien, suddenly remarked, "Hung-chien, I have a suspicion and it's really low. If I'm wrong, then it'll prove that I'm petty and see others with a small mind."

"Go ahead and say it, as long as I am not the one you're suspicious of."

"I've a feeling that Li and Ku were both lying. They certainly could have gotten five first-class tickets. They wanted to save money, so they made up the whole story out of thin air. Look, that day Li Mei-t'ing insisted on taking care of the tickets, but before we came on board, he didn't say a word about having any trouble getting them. If he had, I could have sent someone over to take care of it. There's definitely something funny about this whole matter. What gets me is that after having pulled this, they still expect us to be grateful."

"I think you are right. If they had wanted to save money, why didn't they say so? We could have taken second-class cabins, too. Besides, didn't the school wire every one a hundred dollars for a travel allowance? In his letter Kao Sung-nien said that the sum would be more than enough. What's the point of saving a few dollars?"

"That's not true though," said Hsin-mei. "We have no family to support; they're older and have kids. Maybe they have to take care of family expenses. What Kao Sung-nien said isn't necessarily so. Traveling these days isn't like what it was during peacetime. Expenses can't be accurately estimated. It's better to take a little extra. How much money did you bring?"

Hung-chien said, "I brought along all my unspent pocket money, plus the travel allowance Kao sent. One hundred sixty or seventy dollars in all."

"That's enough. I brought two hundred. I'm afraid that Li and Ku left most of the school's travel allowance at home. They brought so much luggage. If by some chance we run out of money along the way, it'll mean trouble for everyone."

Hung-chien sighed and said, "I think they must have packed their entire families in their luggage—wives, sons, and even their houses. Did you notice? Li Mei-t'ing's metal trunk is as tall as a person. They didn't have to leave any money at home."

Chuckling, Hsin-mei said, "Hung-chien, I'm going to change my ways on this trip. I'm more apt to spend money on good food and luxuries than you. Li and Ku probably see us as a couple of ignorant kids who don't know anything about bad times or who have no sensitivity toward others' problems. From now on I won't make any decisions; I'll leave all questions of food and lodging up to them, so we won't be choosing expensive hotels and restaurants and forcing them to spend money along with us. This business with the tickets is a good lesson."

"Chao, ol' boy, you're wonderful! You really have the democratic spirit. You'll make a great president some day. We've already involved Miss Sun in the buying of the tickets. She's such a shy young girl that she hardly says a word. As her 'uncle' you must take good care of her."

"True, besides, the school didn't give Miss Sun any travel allowance. I forgot to tell you."

"Why not?"

"I don't know. In his letter Kao Sung-nien indicated clearly that he wanted her to come, but he just sent expenses for us four. Maybe a teaching assistant's position is so low that the school feels she doesn't warrant any travel allowance and that there are loads of people like her around."

"That's ridiculous! We're already under salary and could have managed without the travel allowance. But this is Miss Sun's first job. How can they expect her to put up the money? Once you get to the school, you should bring up her case with the authorities."

"I was thinking the same thing. There shouldn't be any problem getting compensation."

"Hsin-mei, let me say something. Don't get angry. This is the first time we've ever taken a trip like this, and transportation is poor. People like us with no traveling experience can barely look after ourselves, so why did you bring a delicate little Shanghai girl along? If she can't take the hardships and gets sick on the way, won't she be a burden? Unless you have something else in mind, then it's—"

"What nonsense! You think I don't know about the troubles involved? It's all because I couldn't say no to a friend. She will be in foreign languages and I will be in political science. Once we get to the school, she'll be someone else's *office wife*, and we won't have anything to do with each other. Besides, I told her at the start that the trip would be hard, that it wasn't like Shanghai, and she said she didn't mind."

"If she can take the hardships, then the trip will be easy for you."

Hsin-mei, gesturing as if he wanted to brush his pipe against Hung-chien's face, said, "You want me to introduce her to you, don't you? Well, that's easy enough."

Protecting his face with his hand, Hung-chien said with a grin, "To tell you the truth, I've never taken a good look at her. I couldn't say for sure whether her face is round or flat. We sure are rude! During dinner we talked among ourselves without ever paying her any attention. Then after we ate we ran off to the deck and left her by herself. She's away from home for the first time. Being alone and deserted must make it even harder to bear."

"Having recently been jilted by women, we are like birds afraid of the bow; we're frightened even by a woman's shadow. But those tender feelings of yours have already planted the seed of love in your heart. Let's go and tell her, 'Mr. Fang is concerned about you.' "

"Relax. I'm certainly not going to be your 'lovemate.' If you have any wine, save it until it's time for me to drink at your and Miss Sun's wedding!"

"Don't talk nonsense! What if she hears us? I recently decided that I won't ever again go for a city girl with a college degree. I had such a hard time waiting on Su Wen-wan; from now on I want women to wait on me. I'd rather marry a simple, honest country girl. She needn't be well-educated, just as long as she's in good health, has a good temper, and will willingly let me be her 'Lord and Master.' I don't think love has to play such an important role in life. A lot of people don't have any romance and they go on living just the same."

"If my father heard you say all that, he'd certainly say, 'The lad can be taught.' But if you want to become an official later, a country girl doesn't have what it takes to be an official's wife. She couldn't help you entertain and advance your career."

"I'd rather that I be an official and she be unworthy to be an official's wife; I don't want her to be an official's wife and insist that I become one of those corrupt officials. If I'd married Su Wen-wan, for instance, I wouldn't be able to go with you now to San Lü University. She'd have forced me to go wherever she wanted to go."

"Do you really like going to San Lü University?" asked Hung-chien, surprised. "I admire your spirit. I'm not like you. You have more conviction than I do about marriage and work. I still remember that time Ch'u Shen-ming or Miss Su said something about a 'fortress besieged.' Lately, I've been having that feeling about everything in life. For instance, I really wanted to go to San Lü University, so I accepted the appointment. But lately the more I think about it the less interest I have in it. Now I really hate myself for not having the guts to turn around and return to Shanghai on the same boat. After my last fiasco with Miss T'ang, I don't know when I'll ever get married. But I think if you'd married Miss Su, you'd have found it isn't anything special. Remember the old saying that a dog loses the juicy bone in its mouth when it goes after the reflection of the bone in the water? When your dream comes true and you marry your sweetheart, it's as though the bone has entered your stomach and you then pine for the never-to-be-seen-again reflection in the water. Tell me, after Ts'ao Yüan-lang's marriage, what did his wife force him to do? Do you know?"

"He is a department head in the Commission of Wartime Resources. It's a post his new father-in-law got for him. You can call it part of Miss Su's dowry."

"Oh boy! The country, the country belongs to the family! If you'd married Miss Su, wouldn't that prestigious post be yours?"

"Phooey! If a man has to hold onto a woman's apron strings to advance himself, then he has no will of his own."

"Some people might say you are like the fox who couldn't reach the grapes and complained that they were sour."

"I'm not at all envious. I will tell you something. The day Miss Su got married, I went to the wedding—"

Hung-chien exclaimed, "Ah?"

"The Sus invited me, so I sent a gift—"

"What did you send?"

"A large basket of flowers."

"What kind?"

"In any case I had the florist send them. What difference does it make what kind they were?"

"You should have sent apricot blossoms to show your love for each other or else narcissus to imply that her heart is too hard. If you add mugwort to the narcissus, it shows that you'll suffer for the rest of your life because of her. You should also include some carnations to emphasize your underlying meaning."

"What nonsense! Where would you get apricot blossoms or narcissus in the summer? You're nothing but an armchair strategist. All right, since you are such an expert, why don't you do that yourself the next time someone gets married? My reason for going that day was to see if I had the courage to watch the woman I loved for more than ten years marry someone else. Ai! When I went, I found it didn't bother me at all. I'd never met Ts'ao Yüan-lang, so at first I thought if Miss Su saw something in him, he must be a lot better than I; I was quite upset at having been bested by someone else. But when I saw that oddball, I thought, how could she have fallen for him? To tell you the truth, a woman with taste like that doesn't deserve to marry me, Chao Hsin-mei. I can do without her."

Hung-chien slapped Hsin-mei on the thigh and exclaimed, "Well said, well said."

"They hadn't been engaged for more than a few days when Mrs. Su came to call on my mother. She was apologetic, mentioning what a stubborn child that Wen-wan was and how she had tried in vain to prevail on Wen-wan, even saying how this might ruin the friendship of two generations between the Su and Chao families. What was even more amazing— you will laugh when I tell you—every morning afterwards when Mrs. Su lit incense in front of the Bodhisattva, she made a silent prayer for my happiness." Hung-chien burst out laughing. Chao went on, "I asked my mother why Mrs. Su didn't read a few sutras to free my soul from suffering. My mother thought I was very concerned about the whole matter and found out all sorts of silly things to tell me. She said the father, Su Hung-yeh, had business to attend to in Chungking at the time and couldn't make the wedding, but he wrote to his daughter that he wanted her to be happy and that everything was up to her. Furthermore, my mother said that Miss Su and her fiancé were very Westernized and wouldn't choose an auspicious date according to the traditional weddings but chose a Western date. May, the couple said, was the least favorable time to get married. June was the most appropriate, but they had already become engaged in June, so they postponed the wedding until the beginning of September. From what I heard, they were very particular about the day of the week, too. They said Monday, Tuesday, and Wednesday were good days to get married, especially Wednesday. Thursday, Friday, and Saturday were progressively worse, so they ended up choosing Wednesday—"

Hung-chien laughed. "That devil Ts'ao Yüan-lang must have been the one to dream all that stuff up."

"In short," said Hsin-mei, smilingly, "you returned students from Europe are the most annoying; you have all the funny schemes and ideas. Well, the Wednesday of their wedding turned out to be an 'autumn tiger,' a real scorcher. On the way there I thought, thank God I'm not the bridegroom today. The church was air-conditioned, but Ts'ao Yüan-lang was wearing a black wool tuxedo and was so busy and hot that his whole face was perspiring. The stiff white collar he had on was yellow and limp from the sweat. I was afraid his whole plump body would melt into sweat, the way wax candles melt down to a puddle of oil. Miss Su was also a nervous wreck. During the wedding ceremony, the bride and groom looked as though they couldn't laugh or cry. It wasn't like a happy occasion at all but more like—no, not like they were ascending the guillotine—oh, of course, like the expressions on the faces of hardened criminals in those pictures under the 'Beware of Pickpockets' signs in public places. It suddenly occurred to me that even if it were my own wedding ceremony, I couldn't help looking like a captured pickpocket either under all those thousands of staring eyes. That made me realize that all those happy wedding pictures of joyful, smiling faces were never taken on the spot."

"A great discovery! What I'd like to know is what happened when Miss Su saw you that day."

"I hid so she couldn't see me and just talked a little with Miss T'ang—"

Hung-chien's heart gave such a heavy thump that it sounded like a package hitting the ground when cargo is being unloaded from a truck. He wondered how Hsin-mei could not have heard it.

"She was a bridesmaid that day. When she saw me, she asked if I'd come to pick a fight and said that when the ceremony was over and everyone was throwing confetti on the bride and bridegroom, I wouldn't be allowed to make a move for fear I might use the chance to throw a hand grenade or sprinkle acid. She asked my plans for the future, and I told her I was going to San Lü University. I thought probably she wouldn't want to hear your name, so I didn't say a word about you."

"Yes, that's best! Don't mention anything about me. Don't mention me," said Hung-chien mechanically, feeling like a prisoner in a darkened cell who has come upon a match and lit it, only to have it go out immediately while the space before his eyes slips back into the darkness before he has gotten a good look at it. It was like the moment when two ships scrape by each other in the darkness of night and someone in one ship glimpses an unforgettable face from his dreams in the light of a cabin in the ship opposite, but before he has time to call out, both are already far apart. That one split second of proximity seems instead like an unbridgeable gap. At that point Hung-chien could only wish that Hsin-mei weren't so stupid.

"I didn't talk to Miss T'ang much anyway. The best man, a friend of Ts'ao Yüan-lang's, kept following her and wouldn't let her leave his sight for a second. I could see he was very interested in her."

Hung-chien suddenly hated Miss T'ang so much his heart stung as though pressed against a thorn. Suppressing the quaver in his voice, he said, "I don't care to hear about such people's affairs. Don't talk to me about them."

Hsin-mei was momentarily taken aback by the abruptness of these remarks; then suddenly understanding, he put his hand on Hung-chien's shoulder and said, "We've been sitting here long enough. It's pretty windy now. Let's go back to the cabin and turn in. We'll be going ashore early tomorrow morning."

He yawned as he spoke. Hung-chien followed him. Just as they had rounded the corner, Miss Sun rose from a bench to greet them. Startled, Hsin-mei hurriedly asked her how long she had been on the deck by herself and whether or not she minded the cold, since it was quite windy. She explained that her cabin mate's child was crying and carrying on so much it had gotten on her nerves, so she had come out for a change of air.

Hsin-mei said, "It's a little rough now. Do you feel seasick?"

"I'm all right," she said. "You and Mr. Fang must have seen a lot worse storms than this when you went abroad."

Hsin-mei said, "Very bad ones. But Mr. Fang and I didn't go the same way," and with that he nudged Hung-chien as a hint for him to say something instead of remaining so rudely silent. Hung-chien's heart seemed at that moment to be in a race with the pain inside it, trying to run fast enough to keep the pain from catching up. He rattled off a few irrelevant remarks as though to throw out some obstacles, which would temporarily block the pain's pursuit. He talked about all kinds of things, which had happened on his cruise abroad. When he mentioned flying fish, Miss Sun was quite intrigued and asked if he had ever seen a whale. Hsin-mei felt the question was naïve beyond a doubt.

Hung-chien replied, "Yes, I did. Quite a few of them. Once our boat nearly got stuck between a whale's teeth."

As the lamplight shone on Miss Sun's astonished eyes, which were as round as circles painted by Giotto, Hsin-mei's suspicions deepened, and he said, "Listen to that nonsense!"

Hung-chien said, "I'm telling you the absolute truth. The whale was taking its afternoon nap after lunch. You know, Miss Sun, some people listen, speak, and see all with their mouths. They open their mouths to listen, to see, and even to sleep. This whale had a stuffy nose from a cold, so it was sleeping with its mouth wide open. Luckily the crevices between its teeth were stuffed up tightly with bits of meat. Otherwise, our boat would really have been in danger."

Miss Sun said, "You're fooling me, Mr. Fang. Isn't he, Mr. Chao?"

Hsin-mei gave a disdainful snort.

Hung-chien said, "There really was a case where a big ocean liner slipped in between a fish's teeth. If you don't believe it, I can check for you."

"Don't be ridiculous," interrupted Hsin-mei. "We'd better go down and sleep. Miss Sun, your father entrusted you to me. I must make you go back to your cabin or you'll catch a chill—"

Hung-chien said with a laugh, "What a good 'uncle' he is!"

Hsin-mei took the opportunity, while Miss Sun wasn't paying attention, to give Hung-chien a hefty punch in the back, saying, "Mr. Fang here loves to tell lies. He's fooling you with fairy tales."

Lying in bed, Hung-chien felt the pain in his heart bearing directly down on him and tried to save himself by chatting with his friend. "Hsin-mei, it still hurts where you hit me!"

"You are shameless," said Hsin-mei. "I saw everything clearly just now from the sidelines. Miss Sun—Ai! Is that girl ever sly? I was a fool to bring her along—Miss Sun is just like that whale. She opens her mouth and you, you stupid idiot, you go right on in like that boat."

Hung-chien, rolling over with laughter, said, "You're too paranoid! Just too paranoid!" When his real laughter had subsided, he continued with simulated laughter in order to scare away the pain in his heart.

"I'm sure that girl overheard everything we said. It's all your fault. You were talking so loud—"

"You were. Not me."

"Can you imagine a college graduate being that naïve and innocent? 'Mr. Fang is fooling me, isn't he?' "—Hsin-mei constricted his throat, giving

140

what he considered a flawless imitation—"Well, I won't be taken in by her! Only a fool like you would! I'll tell you something, you can't judge people by their appearances. Did you notice when I said you were telling her nothing but fairy tales? If I hadn't said that, she'd certainly have asked you to lend her the book to read—"

"I don't have it even if she did."

"That's not the point. Everyone knows women won't spend their money on books. Men will buy candy, dress material, or cosmetics to give to a woman, but in the case of books, they'll lend them to her, never buy them as presents. And women don't want them to either. Why? Once borrowed, it has to be returned. It's borrowed once, then returned once. One book can be an excuse for the two of them to meet twice, and it leaves no trace behind. That's the first step toward romance a girl and a boy have to take. Once the book is lent, complications follow."

Smiling, Hung-chien said, "You're a real terror! But what you say about Miss Sun is complete rubbish."

Smiling smugly at the cabin ceiling, Hsin-mei said, "Not necessarily. OK, enough. Don't talk any more. I want to sleep."

Hung-chien knew that sleep, like Miss T'ang, would evade him. Thinking of the long and troublesome night ahead, he felt the dread of the lone traveler crossing an open plain in the depth of night. He tried to find something to say to Hsin-mei, but Hsin-mei ignored him. Left without aid or resistance, he let the pain of his affliction nibble and gnaw away at his heart.

The next morning the ship did not enter the harbor. Instead, shortly before noon, the steamship company dispatched two launches to the ship to take the passengers ashore. The first- and second-class and some of the third-class passengers boarded the first launch, whose deck was five or six feet lower than the deck of the third-class cabins, so the passengers had to jump down. Every slight surge of the water would separate the launch and the ship by more than a foot; the space seemed like an open mouth waiting for someone to fall in. The passengers cursed the company in unison, but everyone went ahead and jumped regardless of the peril. Surprisingly, no mishaps occurred. Quite a few must have hurt their stomachs in the jump, as they all massaged their stomachs, frowning and wordless. Hung-chien was worried lest he get appendicitis. With so many people jammed onto the little launch, in the air were the cries of "The boat's tilting. A few people on the left move over to the right." "No! Too many on the right! You want to stay alive?" The yelling of each remark rolled over people's tongues like a snowball, getting bigger and clumsier as it went and passing from one end of the boat to the other.

Meanwhile someone told Hung-chien that it would be difficult to find a hotel on shore and that nine out of ten of the rooms would be filled.

Hsin-mei said since there were several hundred passengers arriving with Li and Ku on the second launch, and if they waited for everyone to get ashore before looking for a hotel, they'd probably spend the night outdoors. It was decided that when the launch docked, Hsin-mei and Miss Sun would take the luggage and go find a hotel; Hung-chien would wait for Li and Ku on the dock, and when Hsin-mei had found a hotel, he would come and get them. As soon as Hsin-mei left, suddenly the air raid sirens sounded. Hung-chien grew apprehensive, thinking how misfortune always came in pairs. With the bad luck he'd been having, there was no assurance he wouldn't be killed by a bomb. He was even more worried about Li and Ku aboard the ship. Then it occurred to him that since the ship was the property of the Italians, allies of the Japanese, it wouldn't be bombed. It was, however, more important for him to run for his own life, but he noticed that no one else on the dock was running, so he stayed back. Fortunately the emergency alarm wasn't set off. After an hour or so, the air raid watch was over and Hsin-mei came hurrying up. Shortly afterwards, the second launch approached the dock in pitch blackness amidst the buzzing of voices. Hung-chien caught sight of Li's huge metal trunk, which was set off against the small, narrow prow of the launch; the trunk was like a large nose or enormous mouth on a small face, giving the startling impression of the part being larger than the whole, as if violating the rules of geometry. That such a huge trunk could have been transported off the larger ship was even more of a miracle of physics. Without his dark glasses on his face, Li's large, white eyes looked like two shelled hard-boiled eggs. Hsin-mei hurriedly asked him where his glasses were. Li pulled them from his pocket and put them on, explaining that he had put them away so they wouldn't slip from his nose and get broken while they were jumping onto the launch.

Li and Ku had not made the first launch because of their luggage, but Li implied by his tone that the terror he and Ku had just experienced on the ship from the air raid was on account of Hsin-mei and the others. If he had not given the first-class tickets to them, he too would have had the priority to board the launch and would not have been caught between fire and water or suffered a "shock to the nerves." Hsin-mei and Hung-chien's skills at pretense and flattery literally went bankrupt at this point, and they really could find no way to express their gratitude. Ku Er-chien's enthusiasm, however, was undimmed.

"What a lucky day!" Ku cried. "We really escaped from the very jaws of death! I never thought we'd see you two again. I think everyone on the ship today was depending on Mr. Li's good fortune—Mr. Li, you were on the boat so the airplanes didn't pay us a visit. And that's not just nonsense. I believe in fate. As Tseng Kuo-fang[1] once said, 'Believe not in heaven but in luck.' "

At first Li seemed like a cold-blooded animal in hibernation, but Ku's praise in front of everyone sent the warmth of spring into his body, and he wriggled with the signs of life. With a smile unexpectedly gracing his features, he said, "People engaged in great enterprises all believe in fate. Before I left home this time, a friend read my fortune. He said my luck was now changing. 'Along the way bad luck will turn to good.' "

Ku clapped his hands and said, "Hasn't it, though? I was quite right."

Hung-chien could not help remarking, "I had my fortune told, too. My luck has been terrible this year. Aren't you all afraid of getting involved in my bad luck?"

Ku's head shook like a child's hand rattle as he replied, "Nonsense! Nonsense! Ai! We've been so lucky today. People living in Shanghai go around in a dream world. How could they know there are such dangers on the road? One shouldn't miss coming to the interior. We should find a restaurant this evening and celebrate a little. It is my treat."

They rested awhile at the inn and then went out to eat. After a few glasses of wine, Li Mei-t'ing had fully revived. Whereas before he had been but an insect of early spring, now he was an insect of Dragon Boat Festival time. He plied Miss Sun with questions and made all sorts of silly comments.

Hsin-mei and Hung-chien shared a room. After returning to the inn, they lay on their beds and chatted. Hung-chien asked Hsin-mei if he had noticed Li's unseemly behavior toward Miss Sun.

Hsin-mei replied, "I could tell long ago he is a lecher. When he came ashore without his dark glasses on, I took a good look at his eyes, which have more white than black—the sign of debauchery. I often heard my father say that when I was little."

Hung-chien said, "I'd rather he be lewd. At least that makes him somewhat human. Otherwise there's really nothing human about him."

Just as he was speaking they suddenly heard a woman's hoarse voice in Li and Ku's room next door. The walls of most Chinese inns are very thin, and though one's body may be in one room, it seems as though one's ears are staying next door. As usual, the inn had blind, opium-smoking women soliciting business from room to room and inviting guests to pick numbers from Shaohsing operas[2] for them to sing. While Li was bargaining with them, Ku drummed on the wall and invited Hsin-mei and Hung-chien to come over and listen. Hsin-mei said he could hear the music through the wall just as well and wouldn't go over.

Ku said with a laugh, "You're taking advantage of us. You have to pay as well. Ha, ha! Gentlemen, that's a joke."

Hsin-mei and Hung-chien both pouted their lips and made wry faces without replying. Hung-chien had not slept well the night before and was very tired. Despite the intermingling sounds of stringed instruments and singing in the adjoining room, sleep painted everything pitch black. From the moment his head touched the pillow he slept until dawn, feeling that all the weariness curled up within his body had been pressed flat by sleep, the way wrinkles and creases in clothes are pressed out with an iron. It occurred to him that if he wanted to be a true jilted lover who gave up food and lost sleep, it really wouldn't be easy. The pain of the day before yesterday was so fierce it seemed to have uprooted the source of his injured feelings. All the pain had been eradicated, and he was left too numb and weakened to suffer any more for T'ang Hsiao-fu.

From his bed Hsin-mei yawned and exclaimed, "What a living hell! After the Shaohsing opera was over, you started snoring your head off! It's sheer luck the roof wasn't blown off by your nose. I didn't get to sleep until just before dawn."

Hung-chien, who had always assumed himself a very quiet sleeper, said in embarrassment, "Really? I don't believe it. I've never snored before. Maybe the person next to us was snoring, and you thought it was I. You know how thin these walls are."

"You dirty rat!" said Hsin-mei angrily. "Why don't you just say I snored and blamed you for it? I just wish I could have gotten a recording of your snoring."

If a recording really had been made, it would have been a thunderous racket, like the roaring of waves or the gobbling and gulping of wolves or tigers, accompanied by a thin, sharp thread of sound in the middle that rose and fell abruptly without stop. Sometimes the thread rose higher and higher, getting thinner and thinner like a kite-string about to snap. Then for some reason it would descend and stabilize as if reaching a peak. Hsin-mei was so keyed up that his nerves climbed and fell with it. Now as he thought back on it, he still wished he could twist off Hung-chien's nose as a warning for him to be careful next time.

"All right," said Hung-chien. "Don't keep trying to get back at me. I was tired yesterday. But if you're going to be so unforgiving, heaven will punish you with a wife who snores like thunder. She'll blow a bugle by your pillow every night."

"To tell you the truth," said Hsin-mei, laughing, "last night when I heard you snoring away, I was thinking that I should add another item to the list of standards for choosing a mate I was telling you on the ship: 'Must not snore while sleeping.'"

Hung-chien also laughed. "But to figure out a way to test it out before marriage—"

144

"Don't say it," said Hsin-mei. 'I think you can tell by a person's face whether or not he snores."

"Oh, of course," said Hung-chien. "If you marry a woman with a rotten nose there won't be any question about it."

Hsin-mei jumped up from his bed and tried to pinch Hung-chien's nose.

They went from Ningpo to Hsikou the next day, boarding a boat and then riding in rickshaws. On the boat, it began to drizzle, sometimes one or two drops at a time, drops which didn't seem to be coming from the patch of sky above their heads. Then, when one took a closer look, there was no more. A while later the raindrops became denser, but it still wasn't like rain, just several droplets of water making mischief in midair, rolling and jumping about until tired, then falling to the ground at the right time. Hung-chien and his colleagues, huddling together at the prow of the boat keeping watch on the luggage, hurriedly took out their raincoats. All except Li, who said the rain wasn't heavy and that it wasn't worth opening his trunk to get out his raincoat.

The rain grew bolder as it fell, the drops linking together to form a thread. The surface of the river seemed to have broken out with smallpox, as countless pockmarked eddies continuously came and went. When the rain became denser, it seemed as though hair were growing from the smooth, glossy surface of the water. Li prized his new raincoat so much he had been reluctant to wear it during the trip; then he bewailed his own stupidity, saying he shouldn't have put it away in the bottom of the trunk. If he opened the trunk now, all his clothes would get wet. The thoughtful Miss Sun said she had a rain hat and lent him the small green silk parasol she was holding. It was actually a parasol used to shield herself from the sun. Worried that the spokes might get broken if it were packed in her suitcase, she always carried it with her.

After they had gone ashore, Li went into a teahouse and collapsed the parasol. Everyone gave a start, then burst out laughing. The rain had wet the green silk and caused the colors to run; Li's face also turned from yellow to green, and the green stains on the front of his white shirt looked like a ruined water color painting. Miss Sun blushed and hastily apologized. Li said reluctantly that it didn't matter; Ku called the waiter to get water for Li to wash his face. While Hsin-mei was bargaining with the head rickshaw boy, Hung-chien took care of the parasol for Miss Sun, instructing the waiter to squeeze out the water and set it in front of the stove to dry. Looking up at the gray sky, Li remarked that the rain had stopped, so there was no more need to carry an umbrella.

After having some refreshments, they all got into the rickshaws. The waiter handed Miss Sun the parasol, which was now steaming hot as well as dripping wet. It was already two o'clock in the afternoon. They urged the rickshaw boys to hurry. Less than half an hour later, they came to a steep, rocky incline. Encumbered by the heavy load and trying to make his way on the slippery road, the rickshaw boy pulling Li's huge metal trunk tripped on his way down the slope and fell, overturning the rickshaw. In alarm, Li jumped from his rickshaw screaming, "You bashed the trunk!" and calling the puller a worthless scamp. The rickshaw boy pointed to the blood dripping from his knee, and asked Li to take a look. Li then said no more. After some difficulty, they paid off this rickshaw puller and found another rickshaw. When they reached a long bridge fastened with rattan strips, everyone got out and walked. Without any railing, both sides of the bridge caved downward in the shape of a long, thin saddle.

Hsin-mei was the first to step onto the bridge, but after two steps, he retreated, saying his legs had gone limp. The rickshaw boys laughed at him and urged him on.

Ku said, "Let me go and show you how it's done," and with that he strode nonchalantly across; he then stood on the bridge's buttress and called to the others to come over.

Li mustered his courage, took off his glasses, and cautiously inched his way across. When he'd reached the other side, he called, "Mr. Chao, come on over. Don't be afraid. Miss Sun, would you like me to come back and help you across?"

Ever since that night on the boat, Hsin-mei had grown very cool toward Miss Sun. Now he was afraid there was no shirking his duty as her "uncle" to give help to those in danger and distress. Why not give this chivalrous job to Hung-chien? And so with his heart in his mouth, he made his way across.

Realizing Hsin-mei's intention, Hung-chien silently cursed his own cowardice, afraid he'd only make a mess out of it if he tried to help her. All he could do was smile ruefully at Miss Sun and say, "That leaves just us two cowards."

"Mr. Fang, are you scared?" asked Miss Sun. "I am not. Would you like me to go in front? If you follow me, you won't have to look at the void below and you won't have the feeling that the bridge is endless. This way you would have more confidence."

Hung-chien was struck with admiration. *Women are strange creatures*, he thought. *When they want to be considerate, they really can go all the way; they can even make the pores of your skin feel their tenderness.* As he followed her onto the bridge, the smooth surface gave way slightly under his feet, then bounced back again. The inky green color of the water far below showed through the countless cracks in the rattan. He

146

fixed his eyes on the back hem of Miss Sun's Chinese dress [*ch'i-p'ao*] and didn't dare glance to either side. Fortunately, the bridge soon came to an end. Miss Sun turned and smiled triumphantly. Hung-chien hopped down from the bridge's buttress, yelling, "I've already been condemned to walk the Bridge of No Return without even entering hell! Are there any more bridges like this ahead?"

Ku was about to say, "You people who've been abroad aren't used to Chinese roads," when Li asked Hung-chien in a stage whisper if he'd ever read *Literary Games*, in which there was a marvelous eight-legged essay[3] entitled "Helping the young maid across the bridge."

Hsin-mei smiled and said, "Miss Sun, were you leading him from the front or was he looking after you from behind?"

It suddenly occurred to Hung-chien that other people hadn't necessarily caught on to what a useless coward he was, since following behind Miss Sun could be interpreted in two different ways. He quickly said, "Miss Sun was leading me across the bridge." Miss Sun knew this to be true, while to the others it just sounded as though he was being polite. His vanity had led him to cover up the facts with a true statement. Miss Sun, who had apparently caught on to his intention, just smiled and said nothing.

The sky gradually darkened at the approach of a storm. The rickshaw pullers quickened their pace, saying the weather was about to get worse. The sky seemed to have overheard their remark and responded with a thunderous roar from the air as though several dozen brass drums were rolling on the floor of the heavens. Ever since morning the air had been oppressive, as though it were holding its breath. Suddenly the sky sprang an opening at some point, and the wind outside came rushing in gusts. The yellowing vegetation awoke momentarily from its slumbers, sighing gently and rustling softly. The earth seemed like a steam cooker when the lid is lifted. The rain followed, fresh and joyful, not like the afternoon rain, which had seemed like sweat oozing from the hot, stuffy sky. The rain came down harder and harder, as though the drops were scrambling to get to the ground first, too impatient to line up in rows. Pushing and shoving, they united in solid blocks of cold water, which splashed down in wild confusion. The rickshaw boys would run a few steps, then mop the water from their faces with their soaking sleeves. The heat generated by their running did not equal the force of the rain. Shivering, they said to one another that they'd have to get a good drink of warm wine later and asked the passengers to lift themselves up, so the pullers could get at their dry clothes underneath the seats. The passengers curled up in balls, wishing they had some extra clothes handy to put on. Li borrowed Miss Sun's parasol again.

The rain thickly dyed the night. As the water brought blackness down with it, the sky also became darker by the minute. The procession hurried along in what seemed like a bottle of black ink. The night had turned such a dense black that a person literally could not see the fingers on his outstretched hand! On such a night even a ghost would stub its nose turning a corner. Cats would wish all their whiskers were like the antennae of insects. The rickshaw pullers all had matches, but only two rickshaws had lamps. Lighting the lamps in the wind and rain was no easy matter. The matches had all become damp. Striking several at once only kindled the fire inside. By then the barren plain resembled the world before the birth of Sui-jen Shih.[4]

Hung-chien called out hurriedly, "I have a small flashlight." He pulled it out from the handbag he was carrying and beamed it at the ground, producing a circle of yellow light the size of one's palm. Countless beads of rain rushed into the circle of light like moths toward a flame. Miss Sun's large flashlight shone with snowy brightness for more than a foot, digging a tunnel through the heart of the darkness. Hsin-mei then got out of his rickshaw, took the flashlight from Miss Sun and asked Hung-chien to get out also. With one person on either side unevenly illuminating the way, the eight rickshaws followed the lights along the ridges between the fields as though it were a funeral procession. After a long while Li and Ku stepped from their rickshaws to exchange places. Hung-chien returned to the rickshaw and dozed off from exhaustion. He was suddenly roused by a disturbance; gazing out wide-eyed, he saw a white path of light lying on the ground and heard Li screaming. The rickshaws came to a halt. Li had been carrying the parasol in his left hand and the flashlight in his right. After some distance, he said, his arms had grown sore, and while he was changing hands, he had tripped and fallen into the field and couldn't get out. They helped pull him up from the mud and told him to get in the rickshaw. It was then up to Hung-chien again to guide the way. After walking on for some time, he began to feel as if the rain would never stop and the road would never end. His shoes became heavier and heavier. Exhausted, he merely trudged on mechanically, not daring to stop; for once he did, his legs would never move again. Hsin-mei also relieved Ku.

After a long, long while they arrived at a hamlet, stopped at an inn, and paid the rickshaw pullers. When the four of them removed their shoes, there was enough mud on them to make up for all the land fleeced by corrupt officials. Li looked as though he had taken a mud bath. The back of the pants and the vests of the other three were completely splattered with mud. Everyone's wearied eyes had turned pink from exposure to the rain. Miss Sun's lips were a pale purple from the cold. Outside the rain had stopped, but the sound of the wind and rain kept roaring in everyone's head. Hung-chien had something hot to eat, and at Hsin-mei's insistence drank a little warm wine, then asked for some hot water to wash his feet. He fell sound asleep the moment his head hit the pillow. Hsin-mei was also very tired but was afraid Hung-chien's snoring would disturb him. Just as he was worrying over this, sleep caught him off guard and like a club suddenly knocked him into its dark bottom, a sleep strained of all dreams, pure and complete.

When they awoke, the sky was clear and bright as if nothing had ever happened. Only the yellow earth, sticky on the surface while hard at the core like toffee half-melted in the summer heat, making it slippery under-foot, showed that there had been a heavy rain. They all agreed that since they were tired out from walking so much the day before and their clothes were still damp, they should rest a day and continue on the next day. Ku Er-chien, whose enthusiasm was like a cork floating on water that even a heavy downpour couldn't knock over, suggested they take a walk in the Hsüeh-tou Mountains in the afternoon. After they returned from their walk in the mountains, Hsin-mei inquired about the purchase of bus tickets. The innkeeper said that bus tickets were very hard to get. One had to crowd into the bus station before dawn, and even then couldn't get any unless he was a government employee with an I.D., in which case he could buy tickets early through special arrangement. None of the five had any I.D., since it had never occurred to them that they would need one on the trip. At that time very few people from Shanghai ever went deep into the interior by this route. Most people went to Kunming via Hong Kong. Thus, before setting off they had never heard anyone mention it and were merely following the itinerary drawn up by Kao Sung-nien. Miss Sun had brought her diploma, but that was useless. Li returned to his room, opened his trunk, and took out a box of name cards, saying, "I wonder if this could be considered an I.D."

They all crowded around for a look. The card had three titles printed on it: "Chairman, National San Lü University," "Dean, Journalism Research Institute" and one listing him as the former secretary of such-and-such provincial branch of some political party. The cards were of fine quality paper with elegant lettering, clearly the deluxe print of the China Publish-ing Company. On the back in ornate lettering were the English words: "*Professor May Din Lea.*" Li explained to them that "The Journalism Research Institute" was in reality a sort of tutorial school he and some friends ran in Shanghai, and the two words "Chinese Department" had been omitted in the first line to make it even in length with the second and third lines. Hung-chien asked why Li hadn't used the already existing foreign name of *Lee*. Li Mei-t'ing replied, "I asked a friend of mine who's well-versed in English to choose a word which is similar in sound and has a meaning. Each word in a Chinese name has its own meaning, but there's no point in romanizing it because a foreigner won't be able to remember it easily when he sees it anyway. It's just like foreign names when they are translated into Chinese. The word for George (*Chiao-ch'ih*) is not as easy to remember as *Tso-ch'ih* (help rule). The word for Chicago (*Chih-chia-ke*) is not as easy to remember as *Shih-chia-ku* (poet's valley), because the one has both the sound and a meaning while the other is pure sound."

Ku nodded his head and sighed in agreement. Hsin-mei furiously bit down on his lips, for it occurred to him that the word "*mating*" was also homophonous with "*Mei-t'ing*" and had a meaning as well.

Hung-chien said, "This card should work. It should really impress the stationmaster. I'll go with Mr. Li right now."

Hsin-mei gave Hung-chien a look, and said with a smile, "You can't go like that. I'd better go with him myself. I'll go up and change my clothes."

Hung-chien hadn't shaved or combed his hair for two days. His hair, after having been thoroughly drenched in the rain the day before, was clumped together here and sticking up there in lofty, towering peaks. His suit had been soaked, so he was wearing one of his father's old lined Chinese robes which barely covered his knees and showed more than half a foot of trouser leg. Everyone looked at him and laughed.

Li Mei-t'ing said, "Hsin-mei is so conscious of his appearance. The clothes I have on look even worse, but I'll go anyway."

Li's old flannel overcoat, which had undergone a soaking and baking dry, the two disasters of water and fire, was limp, puffed, and in addition "paralyzed." His trouser legs were thick and perfectly rounded without a single crease, and they could have stood up by themselves like the two hollow pillars of a nation. The imitation wool "wrinkle resistant tie," shrunk by the water, was thin and twisted like an old man's pigtail in Manchu times. When Hsin-mei came down after changing his clothes and shoes, Li lamented that it was as unnecessary as wearing brocaded clothes at night.

Ku clicked his tongue in admiration, "You two will have to work hard. We, members of your party, can only enjoy the fruits of your labor. Truly a case of 'the capable ones are the busiest!' I wish you immediate success."

Hsin-mei said mischievously to Hung-chien, "Keep Miss Sun good company."

Hung-chien found himself momentarily at a loss for words. Miss Sun's blushing face suddenly reminded him of the cold water on the tables in France for mixing drinks. Since he couldn't drink, he would just add a little red wine to the water, watching the red liquid diffuse in the white liquid, giving it a foggy appearance. In another instant the whole glass of water had turned a pale red. He thought that perhaps the first time a girl

150

had a boy friend, her state of mind was like red wine mixed with water—not really love, just a kind of lukewarm excitement.

Hsin-mei and Li returned more than an hour later. Li had a long face. Hsin-mei, all smiles, said that the stationmaster had specially reserved two tickets for the following day and three for the day after next. Of the five, who was to leave first? It was finally decided that Li and Ku would go first to Chinhua the next day. Li finally regained his spirit after a few drinks at dinner. It was told that when Hsin-mei and Li arrived at the station and asked for the stationmaster, there was a long wait before the messenger brought the stationmaster to them. His face perspiring from running, the stationmaster rushed right up to Hsin-mei and addressed him as "Mr. Li" and "Dean Li," completely ignoring the presence of Li Mei-t'ing and even asking Hsin-mei if he weren't also a newspaper editor. Hsin-mei told him truthfully that he was an editor at the Sino-American News Agency. The stationmaster then said, "That's a very fine newspaper. I often read it. There's much room for improvement in the way our station here is run. I hope you will offer me your advice, Mr. Li," and with that the stationmaster jotted down his own name and gave it to Hsin-mei, tacitly requesting that Hsin-mei commend him in the paper.

Hsin-mei burst out laughing when he got to this part, explaining that for the sake of the bus tickets, he had no choice but to pose as Mr. Li for a while.

"That snobbish little rascal," declared Ku indignantly. "He only values the clothes and not the man himself! Of course Mr. Chao is a prominent figure in society too, but Mr. Li had to suffer just because he didn't have a smart-looking Western suit."

"It's not that I haven't any new clothes," said Li. "But it's so dusty and dirty on the road, I don't think it's worth getting them soiled."

Hsin-mei said quickly, "Without Mr. Li's calling card, it wouldn't have mattered how new the clothes were. Let's drink a toast to Mr. Li."

The next morning they saw Li and Ku off on the bus. Li's sole concern was for his large metal trunk. Just as the bus was about to depart, he stuck his head from the bus window to ask Hsin-mei and Hung-chien to check if his trunk was on the top of the bus or not. The porter merely shook his head and said that with all the luggage that day, there was no room for that cumbersome piece. It would be sure to arrive the next day, and in any case the baggage-checker would not mishandle it. Miss Sun hurriedly reported this to Li. He frowned and was about to give instructions when the bus, which had been idling noisily for some time, suddenly worked up enough power and started off. Li's head jerked backward, and his words seemed to have been snatched from his lips and flung into the air. Miss Sun cocked her head to one side, but could hear nothing.

Having seen all the noise and confusion of the passengers, Hung-chien, Hsin-mei, and Miss Sun grew apprehensive about the next day, but said only, "Li and Ku managed to push their way on the bus today. We shouldn't have any problem."

The next day when the three of them received their tickets, they generously tipped the porter in charge of the luggage and told him he mustn't fail to put their large pieces of luggage on that bus. They waited in the crowd for the bus, each with a small case in his hand, and urged themselves constantly not to be pushed back. When the first new bus arrived, the crowd surged forward. This wild burst of energy proved that China did possess a great number of daring storm troopers. They merely weren't up at the front lines.

Observing that the bus was too crowded for them to squeeze in, Hung-chien and his colleagues decided to rush aboard the second bus, which was just then pulling up; but before they knew it, others had scrambled up ahead of them. The three of them managed to board the bus, secure a foothold, and then catch their breaths, exchanging rueful understanding smiles, at last finding time to perspire. People still kept coming; some were rude and others were polite, pleading with a smile, "Pardon me, could you please squeeze together a little?" Still some others gave instructions based on moral principles, "When away from home or traveling, everyone must accommodate. Let's squeeze together a little. That's better! That's better!" A few bluntly said, "Make way, my friend, there's plenty of room inside. It's silly to be blocking the doorway!" And one or two others declared hotly, "I have a ticket. Why can't I get on the bus? Was this bus reserved for you? Humph!"

Finally, all those with tickets got on board. No one would have guessed that the small bus compartment could have stretched like elastic to hold so many people. The bus was like a sardine can. The people were packed in so tightly that their bodies were flattened out. But sardines' bones are set deep in their bodies, while these passengers' knees and elbows were all stuck stiffly into the bodies next to them. Moreover, sardines in a can are all laid out perfectly straight, while these passengers were coiled and twisted and bent at the waist and knee into designated geometric angles. Hsin-mei's suitcase was too long to place on the horizontal, so he just had to set it upright in the aisle between two rows of seats and sit on top of it. Behind him was a small basket on which the woman who owned it was squatting, smoking a cigarette. Hsin-mei turned his head and asked her to please be careful not to burn his clothes with her cigarette.

This only provoked the woman, who retorted, "You don't have eyes in your back. My eyes are in fine shape. I wouldn't smoke up against your

pants, but you just be careful you don't knock your behind into my cigarette."

The woman's compatriots all joined her in laughing heartily.

Hung-chien was crowded up in front close to the bus driver, sitting
on his small suitcase. Miss Sun had something of a seat on the long wooden
bench, but it too was rather uncomfortable. The two men on either side
had both shifted their thighs to make a space just big enough to fill in
the small section of a monkey's tail before the monkey had evolved into
man.

During travel, man's horizon becomes limited. After only a few hours
on a bus, the passengers seem to be planning to spend the rest of their
lives there. Once they have settled themselves, their minds and bodies
seem to have found a final resting place, and having at last achieved eternal
rest, they read books or newspapers, smoke, snack, and doze. For the time
being, anything outside the journey belongs to a world beyond the body
and in another time.

The bus driver arranged his private belongings, got into his seat, and
started the motor. After a long, hard life on the road, this bus should have
been celebrating its golden anniversary, but it obviously could not retire
during the War of Resistance.[5] A machine has no temperamental idiosyncrasies, but this bus, presuming on its old age, had developed a disposition
that was cranky and intractable, eccentric and unfathomable. Sometimes
it behaved arrogantly like a powerful official, other times pettishly like a
little girl. Don't think that the bus driver, coarse oaf that he was, understood anything about driving it.

At the time of departure, the engine coughed, then the muffler spewed
out fumes, and the bus jerked forward, sending passengers tumbling and
knocking about in all directions, screaming in unison. Miss Sun slid from
her seat; Hung-chien bumped his head painfully; and Hsin-mei nearly
fell backwards into a woman's lap. With a mighty shake, the bus moved
ten or twenty *li* in one breath, then suddenly tried to stop for a rest, but
the driver forced it to continue forward. This happened four or five times
until it finally dawned on the bus that it was not to be a leisurely stroll
during which it could tarry where it pleased, but it was actually expected
to go somewhere, and the road ahead was endless! Infuriated, it refused to
move. The driver had no choice but to step down, and after spending a
moment trying to clear matters up with the engine, picked up a ball of
mud from the side of the road and threw it at the bus. It ambled forward,
reeling and swaying as though tipsy from drink. Each time it refused to
go, the driver let out a stream of foul abuse, and at this point he cursed
it even more soundly. However he cursed, the meaning was always the

153

same: The driver wished to enter into carnal relations with the bus's mother or grandmother. While the cursing lacked variety, its force grew stronger and stronger.

Sitting behind the driver was a uniformed government employee with a fifteen- or sixteen-year-old girl, apparently father and daughter. Though a young girl, her face was made up in colors to rival the rainbow after a rain, sunlight through a prism, or a gaily arrayed flower garden in full bloom. The powder she had on wasn't imported, but seemed more like what cement masons used to plaster over walls. The bus shook so violently that particles of the powder from her face joined the dust and danced in the sunlight. As she listened to the driver's increasingly more frank invective, nature won out over artifice and the redness of disgust showed through the applied redness. She whispered something to her father. The government employee then called out to the bus driver, "Please watch your language a little, my friend. There's a lady present! Hmm?"

The bus driver paled and was about to retort, when the military officer and his wife, who were sharing the bench with the girl and her father, put in, "What's the use of all that cursing? The bus will break down anyway. That rough language of yours is offending people."

The bus driver, who had been thinking of throwing up his hands and saying, "I quit!" suddenly remembered that the government employee and the military officer had both been escorted to the garage by the stationmaster so they could get first choice of seats. Both had brand new attaché cases and were said to be on official assignments for the provincial government. Realizing he could not get the better of them, he stifled his anger and muttered under his breath, "I, your father, just like to cuss. What's it to you! If you don't like it, then plug up your ears and go deaf!"

In his irritation, the bus driver drove even more recklessly, and the bus nearly collided with an oncoming vehicle at one point. The military officer's wife, bothered by the smell of gasoline, retched whenever the bus jolted. Each time there was a smell of soured Shaohsing wine, along with the odor of rotting onions and turnips, on her thick breath. When Hung-chien, also feeling giddy and queasy, caught a whiff of this, he could stand it no longer and hurriedly pulled out his handkerchief to press against his mouth and stop the flow of vomit. As he had not had any breakfast that morning, what came up was acid, which his handkerchief could not absorb, and it seeped through his fingers, dampening his clothes. Luckily he had not vomited very much. Then he began to feel uncomfortable in his seat. The suitcase was too hard and too low to sit on. His body was so tightly wedged in the crowd of people he could neither stretch his legs nor bend his back, which made it difficult for him to change his sitting position. All he could do to adjust was shift his weight by turns from right

154

to left buttock. After leaning for less than a minute to his left, his buttock became sore, and he switched to the right, but no matter what he did, nothing proved comfortable. Each moment became harder to bear than the last, and he doubted they would ever reach the station.

But surprisingly enough, after three breakdowns, the bus arrived at a small station. The bus driver was going to eat lunch. The passengers also got off and ate at a small roadside restaurant. Hung-chien and his colleagues, as though granted a pardon, got off to stretch and move their legs. They had no appetite for lunch, and with a pot of tea they munched on some crackers they had brought along in their cases. After a brief rest when they once more had the strength to return to the bus and suffer, the bus driver said that the bus's engine had broken down, and they would have to transfer to another bus. Everyone quickly boarded the bus to get his hand luggage, and then scrambled onto the second bus. Hung-chien and his colleagues unexpectedly managed to secure good seats at the back of this bus. Those who had had seats on the first bus and now found themselves without any declared righteously that the original seating should be observed, that the Republic of China was not a land of robbers, and that people should not resort to forcible seizure. Those with seats, however, were not only physically secure but at a psychological advantage. They could dispassionately eye those without seats, while those standing merely looked out the window, not having the courage to return their gazes.

This was a sick bus, stricken with malaria. When it moved, the doors and windows all shivered. Those sitting in the back of the bus received such a shaking that their bones came loose at the joints and their entrails were turned upside down. The coarse rice they had just eaten rattled and knocked about in their stomachs like dice in the cups at a gambling casino. It was dark when they reached Chinhua. Since the checked baggage had not been transferred from the first bus, they had to wait for it to be brought on the next day's bus. Hung-chien and his colleagues wearily left the bus station and put up for the night at a small hotel nearby. Since the day's misery was over and the next day's misery was still far away, they found a temporary ease of mind and body, an escape into a neutral zone belonging neither to that day nor the next day.

The name of the hotel was "The Grand Eurasian Hotel." Though no Europeans had ever stopped there, the name served well as a kind of prophecy and not as an empty boast. The two Chinese-style, single-storied buildings in the back were divided by wooden panels into five or six bedrooms. A tent, which served as a dining room, was erected on the bare earth in the front. The hotel relied on the aroma of wine and meat, the banging of knives on pans when the food was ready, and the cries of the waiters to draw travelers in to spend the night. The electric lights inside the tent were dazzlingly bright. The bamboo and mud-plastered walls were completely pasted over with red strips of paper on which were written the names of the best dishes of the house, including "steamed turtle," "famous local ham," "three-delicacy rice noodles," "milk coffee," and so on. Most of its dozen or so tables were occupied.

At the cashier's counter sat a fat woman plainly and publicly displaying her fair but not so flat bosom as she nursed a child. The milk was the child's dinner, so it too must be eaten in the dining room—proof that this hotel was scientifically operated. The woman's breasts were big and heavy enough to have been included in Baudelaire's poems on the local customs of Belgium. The child must have been sucking melted lard with sugar. The woman was not only fat on the outside, but she seemed rather thick in the head and full in the gut as well—solid flesh and no soul. If she did have one, then it must have been tiny, just large enough to keep her physical body from rotting, like a little salt sprinkled on meat, since with no soul at all a body will immediately decompose. In any case, her corpulence was an indication of the restaurant's wholesome food. Sitting up against the counter she made an excellent living advertisement.

Hung-chien and his colleagues checked into their rooms and washed their faces, then came out to eat, found a table, and sat down. The table top looked like Fan Chin's face in *The Scholars*[6] after Butcher Hu had given him a slap. Nearly a catty of lard could have been scraped from it. They gave their order. Hung-chien and Miss Sun both said they didn't have much appetite and wanted something bland, so each ordered a serving of rice noodles. Hsin-mei did not care for rice noodles and ordered a dish of three-delicacy mixed noodles.

Suddenly noticing the pink strip of paper saying "milk coffee," Hung-chien said in surprise, "I never expected to find that here. It really lives up to its name 'Grand Eurasian Hotel'! Why don't we start off with a cup to whet our appetites and have another one after dinner European-style?"

Miss Sun was neither for nor against the idea. Hsin-mei said, "I don't think it could be very good. Call the waiter over and ask him about it."

The waiter assured them at once that it was good stuff from Shanghai with the original seal intact. Hung-chien asked what the brand was. This the waiter didn't know, but in any case it was sweet, fragrant, and top quality, for one paper bag made one cup of coffee.

"That's coffee candy to cajole children with," said Hsin-mei, suddenly understanding.

"Don't be so particular," said Hung-chien in high spirits. "Bring us three cups and then we'll see. At least it should have a little coffee flavor."

The waiter nodded and left. Miss Sun said, "That coffee candy has no milk in it. How could it be called milk coffee? Milk powder must have been added to it."

Hung-chien jerked his mouth in the fat woman's direction and said, "As long as it's not her milk, anything'll do."

Miss Sun frowned and pouted in a rather charming expression of disgust.

Reddening, Hsin-mei restrained a laugh and said, "You! Your remarks are disgusting."

The coffee came; surprisingly enough it was both black and fragrant with a layer of white froth floating on the top. Hung-chien asked the waiter what it was. The waiter said that it was milk, and when asked what sort of milk, he replied that it was the cream.

Hsin-mei remarked, "It looks to me like human spit."

Hung-chien, who was about to take a drink, brusquely shoved the cup away, saying, "I won't drink it!"

Miss Sun also refused to drink it. Hsin-mei smiled and apologized, but he didn't drink any either, and playfully spat into the cup. It did in fact look very much like the white froth floating there. Hung-chien berated him for spoiling things. Miss Sun only smiled indulgently like a mother looking on while her children fuss.

The waiter brought the dishes and Hsin-mei's noodles. The noodles were overcooked, greasy, and sticky like a bowl of paste. Some chicken neck bones and ham skin were heaped on the top. Hsin-mei lost his appetite.

Smiling, Hung-chien said, "You say there's spit in the coffee. Well, it looks to me like there's snot in that bowl of noodles of yours."

Hsin-mei pushed the bowl toward him, saying, "You eat it then," and asked the waiter to take it away and bring another. The waiter, however, refused, and Hsin-mei had to order a bowl of rice noodles instead.

When they settled the bill after dinner, Hsin-mei said, "Lucky for us Li Mei-t'ing and Ku Er-chien weren't along today. They would have scolded us for ordering things and not eating them. I really couldn't have eaten those noodles; I didn't even dare to look at those rice noodles too closely."

Their rooms, lit by oil lamps, weren't as bright as it was outside, so the three of them sat and talked for a while before going in. They were all feeling a little keyed up from exhaustion. Miss Sun herself was full of spirits, but compared to the way Hung-chien and Hsin-mei carried on, she was much less boisterous.

Just then a three- or four-year-old little girl, her hands wildly scratching in her hair, ran screaming to the fat proprietress. The fat woman patted the child sleeping soundly at her bosom with one hand while with the other she scratched the little girl's itch. The five sausage-like fingers were quite nimble. With one pluck she seized a louse, squeezed it, and telling the girl to spread out her palm, laid out the louse corpses one after another. Pointing at the dead lice with her other hand, the little girl counted them haphazardly, "One, two, five, eight, ten—"

After Miss Sun had seen and told Hsin-mei and Hung-chien about this, they all began to itch before returning to their rooms to sleep. The preceding scene, however, had put them on guard against their bedding. Miss Sun lent them her flashlight to shine on their beds, but just at that moment the battery went dead and they had to stop.

Hsin-mei said, "Don't worry. Fatigue will conquer all the little pains and itches. Let's get a good night's sleep first."

Hung-chien climbed into bed, and when after a long while, nothing happened, he relaxed and was about to fall asleep when suddenly he began to itch, an itch impossible to ignore. First one place, then another, and his whole body itched. There was a strange itching sensation on his chest. It seemed the Montmartre Flea Market and the International Louse Alliance of the Temple of Palestine were all being held at this Grand Eurasian Hotel. He was bitten till there wasn't one piece of skin left whole, and he plucked till his fingers went limp. His fingers came down with the speed of thunder and lightning on each fresh, well-defined itch, then picked it up carefully and gingerly, only to find that he hadn't caught the biting little pest after all but had wasted his energy and had nothing between his fingers but a small piece of skin. When he did finally manage to pinch one bedbug to death, he felt the sweet joy of revenge, and now having found his peace of mind, he could go to sleep. Who could have known that by killing one he had not deterred a hundred more, and his whole body still itched. Eventually, overcome with exhaustion, his consciousness began to shrink smaller and smaller till he could only push his body outside of himself. Imitating the example of Our Buddha[7] sacrificing himself to the tigers, he gave himself up to the lice. The Germans say that a person with a keen sense of hearing can hear a louse cough (*Er hört die Flohe husten*). That night a pair of sharp ears could have picked up the belching of feasting fleas.

Waking the next morning, Hung-chien found to his surprise that the lice had not completely devoured him, there was still enough to make a man, though not to become a Buddha. He heard Hsin-mei cry wrathfully from his bed, "Ha! Another one! Enjoying your meal off me, aren't you?"

"Are you talking to the fleas or catching them?"

"I'm committing suicide," replied Hsin-mei. "I caught two bedbugs and one flea, and when I crushed them, there were little specks of red—all my own blood. If that's not committing suicide—Ai! Another one! Uh oh, it got away—Hung-chien, I can't understand how that cashier woman can still be so fat with all the blood-sucking animals they have around this hotel."

"Maybe all these lice are raised by the cashier to suck the guests' blood and give it to her. You'd better not catch anymore. She'll demand that you pay with a life for every last one of them. Then there'll be real trouble. Let's get up quickly and find another hotel."

Both got out of bed and stripped off their underclothes; while standing there in the cold, stark naked and laughing, they squeezed and pressed along the seams of their clothes with their fingers. They shook them out again and again, then put them back on. On their way out of their room they met Miss Sun, who had red spots on her face and smelled of cologne. She too had itched all night, she said. The three of them went to the bus station where they saw a note on the message board left by Li and Ku saying that they had stayed at a hotel next to the train staion and had moved out. While settling the bill with the cashier, Hung-chien remarked that there were too many fleas in the hotel. The cashier disagreed, arguing that the beds in her hotel were the cleanest, and that those bedbugs and fleas must have been brought in by Hung-chien and his friends.

The baggage arrived piece by piece. One day a trunk came; another day, a bedroll. Every afternoon they went to the bus station to pick them up. When by the fifth day there was still no trace of Li's metal trunk, Li grew so upset that he began yelling and jumping about. After two long distance telephone calls, it finally arrived. Li hurriedly opened it up to see if anything had been lost. Happy for Li, everyone crowded around to look at the inside of the trunk, which was filled with tiny drawers like a dresser. When a drawer was pulled out, there were white cards neatly arranged inside like a library catalogue. They gasped in wonder.

"This is my stock in trade," explained Li, looking pleased with himself. "As long as I have this, even if all the books in China were burned, I could still go on giving courses as usual in the Chinese Literature Department."

The cards were arranged according to the four-corner system,[8] divided by both name and subject matter. Curious, Hung-chien pulled out a drawer and opened one of the cards. At the top of one card he saw the two characters "Tu Fu"[9] written lengthwise in red ink. Underneath a heading was written in purple ink followed by the text in tiny characters in blue ink. Sensing that Li's white eyes behind his dark glasses were fixed on him, Hung-chien said, "How exquisite! Amazing—" Aware that his tone was not emphatic enough to deceive Li, he quickly added, "Mr. Ku, Hsin-mei, would you like to come take a look? A truly scientific method!"

159

Ku Er-chien said, "I'd like to broaden my perspective, but I could never learn all that!" and without fear of tiring his mouth or parching his tongue, he began heaping on the praises. "Mr. Li, your fountain pen calligraphy is quite impressive, and you can write in so many different styles with such endless variations. How admirable!"

Li said with a laugh, "My calligraphy is very bad. These cards were all written under my direction by my students, so there are a dozen or so different styles of handwriting."

Shaking his head, Ku said, "Ai! As they say, 'A great teacher produces outstanding students!'" With that he pulled out a few drawers from the top, bottom, and both sides.

Li Mei-t'ing said, "The others are all the same. There's nothing to see."

"It's so comprehensive!" exclaimed Ku. "I really wish I could steal it"—and before Li could stop him, he had opened two drawers near the bottom of the trunk—"Ai! These aren't cards—"

Miss Sun came closer to look and said uncertainly, "It looks like Western medicine."

Li said icily, "It is Western medicine, for use on the road."

Too overcome by curiosity at this point to notice Li's expression, Ku opened two more drawers and saw bottle after bottle tightly packed in cotton with the soft cork stoppers exposed. Wasn't it Western medicine? he wondered.

Li could not keep from pushing Ku aside as he said, "Nothing's been lost. Let me close the trunk."

"Nobody would have stolen anything," said Hung-chien maliciously, "but the porter might have been careless in handling the trunk and broken some of the glass bottles. You should make a careful check."

"I don't think so. I stuffed everything carefully with cotton," replied Li, as he began instinctively opening the drawers. Half the trunk was filled with Western medicine, including yatron, cinchona, sulfate of quinine, and formamint,[10] all in their original wrappers. Nothing had been left out.

"Mr. Li, you couldn't use all that by yourself!" exclaimed Hsin-mei. "Did Kao Sung-nien ask you to bring it for the school?"

Like a drowning man suddenly given a rope, Li said gratefully, not letting go, "Yes, that's right! You can't get Western medicine in the interior. If by chance someone should get sick, then he'll appreciate what I, Li Mei-t'ing, have done."

Smiling, Hsin-mei said, "Let me thank you in advance! With the cards in the upper half of the trunk if all the books in China were burned, Mr. Li alone could teach Chinese literature. And with the medicine in the bottom half, if the Chinese all died of disease, Mr. Li could still stay alive."

"Nonsense!" said Ku. "Mr. Li is not only the school's benefactor, but also our savior."

Just as curiosity cost Adam and Eve their paradise, so Ku Er-chien lost the paradise Li had settled him in because of his curiosiy. No amount of flattery could ever bring back Li's good will, and Ku's next few sentences nearly sent Ku straight to hell. "I've run a temperature these last couple of days, and my throat's a little sore—but never mind. When it gets really bad, I'll ask you for three or four formamints to suck on."

Hsin-mei said that the several days' delay in Chinhua had cost them quite a bit of money. If every one would take out the money he was carrying, they could see how much they had altogether. As he had surmised on the boat, Li and Ku had not brought with them the entire amount of the travel allowance provided by the school; the two of them also probably held back a few dollars for cigarettes. The rest of them each had about eighty dollars left, and they hadn't yet paid their hotel bill. In any case, they could not make it to the school and decided to send a telegram to Kao Sung-nien asking him to wire them some money to the Central Bank at Chian. Hsin-mei said that until they got to Chian they would have to pool all their money for general use. Not a copper could be wasted. When Li asked about cigarettes, he replied that from then on no one was to buy cigarettes and would just have to give up smoking.

Hung-chien said, "I've already given it up, and Miss Sun doesn't smoke at all."

Hsin-mei said, "I smoke a pipe and have tobacco with me, so I won't need to buy any on the way. But I won't smoke any more from now on, so you won't get envious watching me."

Li was silent, then suddenly said, "I just bought two cans of tobacco yesterday, so of course we can still smoke on the way as long as we don't buy any more."

That evening the five of them bought third-class sleeping car tickets and boarded the train at Chinhua, due to arrive in Yingt'an early the next morning. A few amorous lice who were willing to brave the dangers of the long journey accompanied them all the way.

The train arrived at Yingt'an early in the morning. By the time they picked up their baggage, the bus had already left. The only decent hotel in town had hung out a "Full House" sign, so their only choice was to put up at a small inn. People stayed on the top floor of the inn, while tea and rice were sold on the ground floor. With houses on either side of the narrow street, the sun rarely shone into the teahouse on the ground floor. Rice bowls were piled on a table at the entrance along with a few pieces of half-cooked fat meat on a large plate, meat which turned out to be red-cooked pork. Now cold and black, the pork was like a once prosperous man who was down on his luck and had lost his formerly ruddy complexion. Next to this was a plate of steamed bread which, from a distance, looked like a once pure-white virgin who has been soiled. It was covered with black specks and streaks. When one came closer, the black specks flew off and disappeared in the surrounding shadows. In fact, they were flies. These, along with mosquitoes and bedbugs, are considered the "three companions of winter"[11] at small inns. As it was now just late autumn, their steadfastness in winter was not yet apparent.

The only access to the second floor was by a bamboo ladder, and it was impossible to move Li's metal trunk upstairs. The innkeeper, however, patted his chest and assured Li that it would be quite safe to leave it on the ground floor. Li consoled himself, "When the trunk was mishandled on the train and didn't get here, didn't someone else look after it for me in the same way? I don't think anything will get lost. Wasn't it several days before it finally arrived in Chinhua?"

Everyone praised him for being able to see his way out of the problem. Hsin-mei went up with the waiter to look at the rooms. The floor creaked under their footsteps, and dust came fluttering down.

Ku said with a laugh, "Mr. Chao is quite heavy!"

As Miss Sun took out her handkerchief to wipe away the dust, the innkeeper said, "Don't worry. The floor is very sturdy. A creaking floor is good. If a thief comes during the night, the guests will wake up. We've never had any thieves in our inn. They wouldn't dare come because of the way our floor creaks. Why, even if a mouse makes a move our floor will report it."

The waiter came down the ladder to ask the guests to go up. With great reluctance Li entrusted his metal trunk to the innkeeper. There were only three vacant rooms upstairs, all with single beds. The waiter added a bamboo cot to Chao and Fang's room, which was to be charged at the double rate.

Hsin-mei said, "Our room is the best. It faces the street and gets the most light. There's a net on the bed too, but I don't want to sleep in the inn's bedding. We'll have to think of something else later on."

"Why not let Miss Sun have the good room?" asked Hung-chien.

Pointing to the wall, Hsin-mei said, "Take a look."

There on the peeling white plaster wall, in crookedly written pale black characters were the lines, "Written in everlasting memory of the love shared with Miss Wang Wei-yü while passing through Yingt'an. Hsü Ta-lung of Chinan." The month, day, and year of the Republic were recorded. It reckoned out to have been written the night before. Next to

162

this, in what also appeared to be Hsü Ta-lung's hand was the poem:

Liquor does not intoxicate; one intoxicates oneself.
Lust does not blind; one blinds oneself.
This morning we met by fate.
Tomorrow you go east and I head west.

To this were added the words, "Off I go!" The exclamation mark made one imagine Mr. Hsü mimicking the style of the dialogue in Peking opera and the actor gallantly flourishing his whip.[12] In addition there were some smaller characters in pencil all on the subject of Wang Mei-yü, which must have been written prior to the night of Mr. Hsü's intoxication with liquor and blindness from lust by someone else, since Mr. Hsü's poem had been written over them. They read: "The lone prince became drunk in Yingt'an palace; Wang Mei-yü has a face so fair." There were also three lines of penciled characters with the new-style punctuation: "Attention! Wang Mei-yü is infected! During the War of Resistance, my compatriots, you must all make hygiene a basis for the strengthening of the nation. You must not spread infection! Furthermore, she recognizes money only and has no love! From one who knows!" Next to this was Hsü Ta-lung's comment in pale ink: "What sort of crime is it to defame someone else?"

Hung-chien said with a laugh, "That Hsü fellow is a man of passion and honor!"

Hsin-mei also laughed and said, "Is such a room fit for Miss Sun? It's even less fit for Li Mei-t'ing—"

Just as he spoke they heard shouts coming from Li and Ku's direction. Ku was quarreling with a waiter. Hsin-mei and Hung-chien ran out to see. Since the inn's bamboo cots had all been used to make extra beds, the waiter had placed a door plank across two unpainted wooden benches to serve as Ku's bed.

When Ku Er-chien saw Hsin-mei and Hung-chien, he became bold. Exposing his teeth and claws, he said, "Don't you find this disgusting? This is for laying out a dead man's remains. Is he trying to bully me?"

The waiter replied, "This plank is all the inn has. You civilized men in Western suits must be reasonable."

Patting a greasy spot on the breast of his blue cotton Chinese robe, Ku demanded, "Are you saying people like me who don't wear Western suits aren't reasonable? Why do other people get a bamboo cot to sleep on while I don't? Don't I pay just the same as everyone else? I'm not superstitious, but when a person travels away from home, he hopes for good omens. A rascal like you doesn't know the proper way to behave."

Since the discovery of his Western medicine the day before, Li Mei-t'ing had ceased to be Ku's protector and had been coolly watching throughout the quarrel. He now interrupted, "Just take the plank away. What're you arguing for? Find a way to move my trunk up here, and it can serve as a bed. I'll offer you a cigarette," and he stuck out his left index finger and waved it about as though it were a sample cigarette.

When the waiter saw it was not a cigarette but a yellow tobacco-stained finger, he stared at him and asked, "Where's the cigarette?"

"Humph, stupid fool!" said Li, shaking his head. "Naturally I have the cigarette. You think I'd cheat you? Move my trunk up here, and I'll give you one."

"If you have any, then give me one," said the waiter, "but if it's the trunk you want moved, that's out of the question."

Li was so angry that all he could do was laugh. Ku triumphantly asked everyone to note how utterly unreasonable this waiter was. In the end the bamboo bed Hung-chien was to sleep on was exchanged for the door plank.

Miss Sun came up and Hsin-mei asked where they should go for breakfast. Li said, "Why not right here in the inn? It'll save us the trouble of finding a place. It might even be a little cheaper."

Hsin-mei was not in a position to offer his opinion, and just at that moment the waiter arrived with tea, so he asked the waiter what was to eat at the inn. The waiter replied there was large white steamed bread, four-happiness pork, eggs, and ham. Hung-chien suggested slicing up a plate of ham and sticking it inside the steamed bread to eat. Li, Ku, and Chao all approved of the idea, calling it a "Chinese sandwich," and were all set to have the waiter go down and fix it.

Miss Sun said, "I noticed when I came in that this inn is full of flies. It's probably not very sanitary."

Li said with a smile, "Miss Sun, you've had a very sheltered and pampered upbringing. You don't know the hardships of the road. If you want to find an inn without flies you'll have to go abroad. I assure you, you won't get sick from eating it. And even if you do, I have plenty of medicine in my trunk." He contorted his features as he spoke; his twisted face, rather than his original, looked more appropriate for him.

Hsin-mei just then took a drink of the freshly boiled water in Li's room. After taking one swallow, he frowned. "I get thirstier the more I drink this. It tastes smoky. It could be used instead of kerosene to light the lamp—if you ask me, the stuff in this inn isn't dependable. You usually don't have ham until winter, and now it is only autumn. Who knows how old an antique their ham is. Instead of ordering first, let's go down and look around a bit before we decide."

From the wall the waiter took a pitch black, greasy object and offered it for their inspection, repeatedly saying, "How delicious!" his own mouth watering as he spoke, fearful only that the fat meat would waste away under the greedy stares of the guests. Wriggling and squirming from its greasy slumber, a maggot on the meat awoke. Li saw it and was repulsed by the sight; from a distance his mouth pointed toward it and he exclaimed, "We can't have it."

The waiter quickly stuck his finger over the tender, soft, white object and pressing down lightly, drew a shiny, black, oily streak like a freshly poured asphalt road across the filthy surface of the meat. At the same time he said, "It's nothing!"

Infuriated, Ku asked the waiter, "You think we're blind?"

"Outrageous," they cried.

Ku prattled away, even dragging in the bed plank incident. The commotion brought in the innkeeper. Meanwhile two other maggots in the meat also heard the noise and poked their heads out for a look. The waiter, no longer able "to do away with the corpse and destroy the evidence," merely retorted, "If you won't eat it, then other people will. I'll eat it to show you—"

The innkeeper took the pipe from his mouth and remonstrated, "Those aren't bugs. They don't hurt anything. Those are 'meat sprouts'—'meat sprouts.' "

Hung-chien's reply was, "All the food in this place sprouts, not just the meat."

The innkeeper didn't catch on, but seeing everyone laugh, he also became upset and muttered something to the waiter in the local dialect. In the end, the five of them went out to eat at the one and only respectable-looking hotel in town.

Li's cards had little effect on the stationmaster, who said there was nothing he could do for them. They must register for the buses like everyone else and they would certainly have tickets in three days. The five of them grew alarmed. Room and board for three days would be a considerable expense. If they were to go on delaying like that, their money would probably never get them to Chian. In low spirits they returned to the inn. Opposite the inn they saw a woman leaning against a door smoking a cigarette. The woman had prominent cheekbones and a thin face. Her hair, waved by some unidentifiable instrument, resembled a plum tree in full bloom in a Chinese impressionist painting. Around her neck she wore a white silk scarf and was dressed in a green silk Chinese dress which was dazzlingly resplendent, but shiny like the material high-class girls used for lining. Hsin-mei nudged Hung-chien's arm and said, "It must be 'there's a beautiful gem here.' "[13]

Hung-chien said with a laugh, "I was thinking the same thing."

Hearing them recite from the Confucian *Analects* and not understanding what it was about, Ku Er-chien asked, "What?"

Li Mei-t'ing was more clever. "Er-chien," he asked, "how do you suppose there could be a woman dressed like that in a place like this?—What are you reciting from the *Analects* for?"

"Come to our room and see," replied Hung-chien.

When Ku heard she was a prostitute, he gawked at her, unable to take his eyes off her. When the woman, who had been giving Miss Sun a careful scrutiny from head to toe, suddenly discovered she had Ku's attention, she flashed him a big smile, revealing a mouthful of fresh red gums, which bulged like a hero's chest. Sparsely studded with a few yellowed teeth, the upper jaw was too bashful to show itself. Ku blushed in confusion, and thankful that no one had noticed, hurried into the inn after Miss Sun.

Hsin-mei and Hung-chien hadn't slept well the whole night on the train, so they returned to their rooms to rest. Li knocked on the door and entered, asking them what wonderful things they had to show him. Neither of them felt like getting up, so they let him look at the wall graffiti by himself.

Li glanced out the window, then turned and cried, "You young men are up to no good! No wonder you wanted to take this room. It must be because Wang Mei-yü's bedroom is opposite yours, just four or five feet away, close enough to jump across. Get up and take a look. There's a red blanket on her bed and a large mirror on the table with perfume bottles on it—Ai! You bachelors are really sneaky. This is no joking matter—Ai, she's come up!"

Hsin-mei and Hung-chien craned their necks to see from their beds. Sure enough, the woman who had just been leaning against the door smoking a cigarette was standing at the window. They hastily drew their heads back and lay down. Li casually leaned against the window smoking a cigarette and gazing upward, taking in the view of the roofs opposite with his dark glasses. Hsin-mei and Hung-chien waited impatiently on their beds and were just about to ask him to leave when suddenly they heard the woman say, "Where did you all come from?"

Li started as though roused from a dream and said, "Are you talking to me? We're from Shanghai."

There was nothing funny about these remarks, but Hsin-mei and Hung-chien broke out laughing so hard that they pulled the covers over their heads, then quickly lifted them off in order to catch what followed.

"I'm from Shanghai, too," the woman said. "I came here as a refugee. What do you all do?"

Li subconsciously reached into his pocket to pull out a card, then caught himself and replied with dignity, "We're university professors."

"Oh, you teach?" said the woman. "There's no money in teaching. Why not set yourself up in a business?"

The two pulled up the covers again. Li merely grunted in response.

The woman said, "My father was a teacher too—"

The two were laughing so hard under the covers they cried out in pain.

"Who's that woman with you? Does she teach, too?"

"Yes."

"I've been to school myself. Hou much does she make?"

Afraid she would make fun of Miss Sun for not earning as much as she did, Hsin-mei coughed loudly.

Li merely replied, "Quite a lot, quite a lot—Care for a cigarette? Here, take one"—Hsin-mei and Hung-chien were so tense they didn't dare breathe, and when they heard Li's next remarks, they could hardly believe their ears—"Tell me, bus tickets are very hard to get. You—you know quite a few people. Can you think of any way? We will thank you properly."

The woman let out a long stream of words, spoken quickly and crisply, like a steel knife slicing up a turnip, the gist of which was that if one could not get bus tickets, one could get a ride on a military convoy. She knew a Major Hou who would be coming to see her in a while, and Li could come over then and negotiate with him directly. Li thanked her profusely. After the woman had left, Li turned to Chao and Fang, and with a triumphant swirl of his head, stood and looked at them without saying a word. They both commended him for having hit upon such a brilliant idea and for being so very skillful.

Li wished he could have jumped out of his body and patted himself on the shoulder, saying, "Li, ol' boy, you really are something!" He then bragged openly, "I know that sort of women have many of their own special ways of doing things and can sometimes be useful. That's what Meng Ch'ang-chün had in mind when he befriended men who could crow like a cock or steal like a dog."[14]

After Li had left, Hsin-mei and Hung-chien fell asleep. In his dreams, Hung-chien sensed something hitting against the dense casing of his sleep. It poked a tiny hole through, and his entire sleep dispersed like boiling water injected through an icy surface. When he awoke all he heard was "Hey! Hey!" He stepped groggily from bed and saw Wang Mei-yü yelling toward them from across the way. He was about to close the window and ignore her, when he suddenly remembered Li's negotiations with her. Hsin-mei also woke up.

Wang Mei-yü said, "Where's the one in the dark glasses? Major Hou is here."

When Li Mei-t'ing was informed, he quickly took out his Western trousers and tie which lay pressed under his mattress. He had already shaved and though his skin was cut in several places, his whole face shone with a ruddy glow. On his way out, he said that he couldn't go to a prostitute's room empty-handed and would have to spend some money. How was this social expense to be reckoned? He had just doled out one cigarette already. Everyone assured him that as long as the negotiations went off smoothly, not only would the expenses be shared, but there would be a reward for his service as well. Li asked if they would like to go to Hsin-mei's room to listen in through the window. "After all, there's nothing secretive about this," he insisted.

The others said they were not interested. Since it was now four o'clock, they would go out for a stroll and meet at six for dinner at the restaurant where they had had breakfast.

At the appointed time Li came, brimming with excitement. They quickly asked him how it had turned out. He replied that the truck would leave the next day at noon. As they plied him with more questions, he explained that Major Hou would come at nine o'clock that evening to check the luggage, and if they had any questions, they could ask him directly. The military transports were going to Shaokuan and each could take one passenger and one or two pieces of luggage. Once they got to Shaokuan, they could take a train into Hunan. The cost would be twice that of a bus. "But," said Li, "we have to wait everywhere for bus tickets and each wait takes a few days. This way we'll save on room and board."

Hsin-mei said hesitantly, "It sounds very good, but what about the money the school wired to Chian?"

"That's easy," replied Li. "All we have to do is send a telegram to President Kao asking him to wire it to Shaokuan instead."

Hung-chien said, "If we go to Shaokuan and then double back to Hunan, won't that make the trip longer?"

Li replied hotly, "There's a limit to my ability. I can only manage this much. If you have so much influence, maybe Major Hou will dispatch a special car to take you right up to the school."

Ku hurriedly put in, "I'm sure Mr. Li couldn't have made a mistake. We'll send a telegram the first thing tomorrow morning, and at noon we can board the trucks and get the hell out of here. If I have to wait around this hideous place five more days, my hair will all turn grey."

Still vexed, Li said, "I'll take care of the money for the tea today at Wang Mei-yü's myself."

Controlling his anger, Hung-chien said, "Even if we don't take the trucks, everyone ought to chip in for the social expenses. Those are two separate matters."

Hsin-mei kicked Hung-chien under the table, while he babbled on about something else. In the end Li and Fang did not start a quarrel, and

Miss Sun's bulging eyes returned to their normal state.

Shortly after they returned to the inn, the waiter yelled from the foot of the ladder with his mouth full of food, "Major Hou is here!" and they all hurried downstairs.

Major Hou had a large orange-peel nose with a face appended to it. The face was complete in every detail and the space for the eyebrows and the nose had not been squeezed out. There were a few pimples on the tip of his nose which looked like unripe strawberries. He talked and laughed loudly. One could tell at a glance that he was a heroic type.

When Major Hou saw Li, he said with a smile, "What happened? When I came back to Little Wang's you'd already run off. Where did you go?"

Li Mei-t'ing made some excuses and quickly introduced his three colleagues. Miss Sun had not yet come down.

"Our trucks can't carry private passengers," said Major Hou, launching into a long declamation. "Taking passengers is against military regulations. Understand? But it seems to me as teachers at a national university you are after all government employees, so I take a chance and try to accommodate you. Understand? I don't want a cent of your money. You get by on little enough as it is. I'm not interested in those few extra dollars. Understand? But the drivers under me and the escort soldiers need a little cigarette money. And if it's too little, you won't want to bother taking it out. Understand? I don't want any money. You don't have much luggage, do you? You don't have any contraband from Shanghai, do you? Ha, ha. You educated people sometimes go for petty advantages."

When he laughed, his cheek muscles pulled his nostrils out even larger. They replied in unison that they had no contraband.

Li indicated his large metal trunk and said, "This is one piece. There's more upstairs—"

Major Hou's eyes suddenly grew nearsighted, and he stared at the trunk squint-eyed for a long time before he finally seemed to get it into focus. As though firing a machine gun he said, "The devil! Whose is that? What's in it? I can't take that—"

Suddenly he grew nearsighted again as he gazed wide-eyed at Miss Sun who had just come down the ladder.

"Is she traveling with you too? I can't take her along either. I was called away just now before I had a chance to say more than a few words to you. I didn't make it clear. Women can't come along. If we could take women, I'd have taken Little Wang One, Two, and Three and set off long ago. Ha, ha."

Miss Sun was so furious she uttered a shrill screech. Hung-chien waited until Major Hou had entered the door opposite before he let out a curse at his already vanished broad back, "You dirty bastard!"

Hsin-mei and Ku urged Miss Sun not to get upset, "Men like that never have anything nice to say."

Miss Sun said, "I'm the only one preventing you from taking the truck—"

"Along with Mr. Li's treasure chest," put in Hung-chien. Mr. Li, you—"

Li Mei-t'ing apologized to Miss Sun, "I failed to handle things properly and subjected you to insults."

With that said Hung-chien could no longer disparage him.

When the plan fell through, Li was the first to say, "Thank God," adding, "It may be a blessing in disguise. People who carry guns don't listen to reason anyway. With Miss Sun along, we have to be especially careful. Besides, going to Hunan via Shaokuan would have added too many extra miles and made the trip too costly. Mr. Fang was quite right."

During the few days in Yingt'an, Li treated Hung-chien with new respect and was especially polite to him. Hung-chien, however, despised him all the more and behind Li's back said laughingly to Hsin-mei, "He's afraid I'll dispute with him over those few dollars he spent on that woman. That's how low he is. If I were him, I'd have paid it myself."

At night when he couldn't fall asleep, Hung-chien would feel sorry for himself, regretting more and more that he had come. Associating with people like Li Mei-t'ing and Ku Er-chien was such a shameful debasement. The last ten or fifteen days of travel had been wearing enough to sap his will.

One day, strolling with Hsin-mei, he heard a peanut vendor speaking in his native dialect. When he questioned the vendor, he found that the vendor was in fact a fellow villager who had ended up there as a refugee. The vendor simply stated on which street he lived in the county seat, neither complaining to him of the hardships he had suffered nor asking to borrow money to go home. Both relieved and moved, Hung-chien said, "He must have met with so many rebuffs from his fellow villagers that he's stopped talking about it. I really don't care to think how many setbacks I'll have to go through before I become hardened into such a state of utter despair as that."

Hsin-mei laughed at him for getting so downhearted and said, "If you can't take a blow any better than that, you'll never have a successful love affair."

Hung-chien said, "Who's willing to spend something like twenty years on Miss Su like you did?"

"I've been feeling depressed lately myself," admitted Hsin-mei. "I woke up in the middle of the night last night and suddenly started wondering if Su Wen-wan ever thought of me."

Reminded of himself and T'ang Hsiao-fu, Hung-chien's heart suddenly flared up like a tongue of flame, and he asked, "Think about you or miss you? We must think about any number of people in one day—relatives, friends, enemies, and even people who have nothing to do with us that we've met before. To really miss someone, keep him constantly in mind, and wish to be close to him is pretty rare. Life keeps people too busy. It doesn't allow us to focus our full attention and yearn for someone without interruption. The time we spend in a whole lifetime thinking about the person we love most probably wouldn't add up to one whole hour. Beyond that our thoughts just brush past him. We're only thinking about him."

Smiling, Hsin-mei said, "Well, I hope you can spare me a few seconds of your time in the future. I'll tell you one thing. After that first time I met you, I was always thinking about you and never stopped hating you for a moment. Too bad I never checked my watch and added up the time."

"You see," said Hung-chien, "love rivals think about each other more often than lovers do. Maybe Miss Su really was dreaming of you then, which is why you suddenly thought of her."

"How does anyone have time to dream about lost lonely souls like us? Besides, she belongs to Ts'ao Yüan-lang now. If she's dreaming of me, then she's being unfaithful to her husband."

Seeing how serious he was, Hung-chien doubled up with laughter. "You politician, you really are a tyrant! Whoever becomes your wife won't even be free to dream. You'll send secret agents out to spy on her unconscious."

As usual, the bus to Nanch'eng three days later was so crowded that there was barely footroom. The five of them stood in the pack of people, consoling one another, "We'll be in Nanch'eng in half a day. It won't matter if we have to stand up for a while."

A greasy-faced fellow in a short jacket spread his knees out as in the fourth boxing position and settled into his seat as though he were a permanent fixture of the bus. In front of him he placed a smoothly rounded burlap sack, which was apparently filled with rice. The sack was about as high as a seat and was right next to Miss Sun. Hsin-mei said to her, "Why don't you sit down? It'd be a lot more comfortable than a seat."

Miss Sun was also getting tired of being jostled and tossed about while standing, and so, with a word of apology to the greasy-faced fellow, she prepared to sit down. Instead, the man immediately jumped to his feet and held out both hands to stop her.

"This is rice," he bellowed, his eyes rolling. "Do you know that? Rice for eating!"

Miss Sun was too stunned to speak.

"So what if it is ricce?" asked Hsin-mei glaring at him angrily. "If a girl like her sits down for a while, it won't crush your rice."

"You're a man and don't even understand that," said the fellow. "Rice goes in the mouth to be eaten—"

Miss Sun indignantly stamped her foot and said, "I won't sit! Mr. Chao, don't pay any attention to him."

Hsin-mei would not agree, and Fang, Li, and Ku all joined in the quarrel, berating the man for being so rude as to occupy a seat himself while obstructing others with his sack of rice. Since he wouldn't let anyone sit on the rice sack, he should give up his own seat immediately. Outnumbered, he softened his manner and said, "If one of you men sits there, fine, but for the lady to sit down, that's out of the question! This is rice. It goes in the mouth and is eaten."[15]

Miss Sun declared for the second time that she wanted to stand up all the way to Nanch'eng.

Hsin-mei and the others said, "We don't want to sit down. It's the young lady who wants to. So what do you have to say to that?"

Without any other choice, the fellow sized Miss Sun up for a moment with his red eyes, then took out a small bag of clothes he had been sitting upon, picked out an old pair of cotton trousers, and covered the rice sack with them, providing as it were a gas mask for the rice. He then said gruffly, "Sit down, then!"

Miss Sun wouldn't sit at first, but unable to take the jolting of the bus and at the insistence of her companions, she sat down. Sitting diagonally across from Miss Sun was a young, very fair-skinned woman dressed in mourning, but with lips and eyelids painted a bright red. She had delicate eyebrows, tiny eyes, and a small nose. Her facial features were so dull and colorless that it seemed they could have been wiped away with a hot towel. When she spoke she twisted her head around and exposed her decayed teeth. She had been watching the fracas and chose this moment to strike up a conversation with Miss Sun. She asked in her Soochow dialect if Miss Sun were from Shanghai and cursed the people of the interior, calling them a rude and impossible breed. She explained that her husband had been working as a clerk for the Chekiang provincial government and had fallen ill and died a short time ago. She was on her way to Kweilin to seek the protection of her brother-in-law. When she learned that Miss Sun had four traveling companions, she was filled with envy, wailing in self-pity, "I am alone and friendless with only one servant to accompany me. I don't have your good fortune!" She also indicated that she would like to go with them to Hengyang, so as to have someone to look after her.

Their conversation was just getting lively when the bus stopped for a morning snack, and most passengers got off to eat breakfast. The widow, staying on the bus, opened her basket and pressed Miss Sun to have some of the rice cakes she had brought along. Afraid the widow would have trouble dividing up her cakes, Chao and Fang also got off the bus for a walk. Seeing them get off, Ku pulled out half a cigarette and puffed away in earnest.

Li glanced around, and noticing there were few people about, said to the widow, "You shouldn't have said you were a widow traveling alone. There are many bad people on the road, and lots of eyes and ears on the bus. Your remarks may give people wrong ideas."

The widow threw him a glance and, giving her mouth a tug at the corners, said, "You are such a good man." Then to the man in his twenties sitting on her left, she said, "Ah Fu, let this gentleman sit down."

With his slick, greasy hair and shiny face, Ah Fu looked like an oil-soaked loquat seed. As he was dressed in a blue cotton robe and was sitting next to the woman, one would not have guessed that he was a servant. Now that the woman had exposed his status, and he was made to give up his seat besides, he pressed his lips together and reluctantly stood up. After a show of politeness, Li squeezed his way into the seat. Sickened by what she saw, Miss Sun also got off the bus. By the time everyone had returned to the bus and it started off, Li was munching away on rice cakes and the widow and Ah Fu were smoking cigarettes. Hung-chien said to Hsin-mei in English, "Guess whose cigarettes those are."

Hsin-mei said with a laugh, "As if I didn't know! That guy is an expert liar. I really don't believe those two cans of tobacco of his haven't been used up by now."

"His tobacco stinks," said Hung-chien, "and now with three mouths puffing away at once, it's really unbearable. I should have worn a face mask. Why don't you smoke your pipe a little to dispel the stench of his tobacco?"

When they arrived in Nanch'eng, the widow and her servant put up in the same hotel as the five of them. According to Li, Miss Sun should share a room with the widow while Ah Fu slept in a room by himself. Miss Sun made it clear from her tone that she would not stay with the widow, despite the fact that Li repeatedly hinted that there was not much money left and they should save on the hotel expenses as much as possible. Without even asking Li's permission, the widow went ahead and took one room for herself and her servant. They all noted this with surprise, but Li, overcome with indignation, muttered to himself, "There must be a separation of the sexes and distinctions by rank."

Ku borrowed a current newspaper, and after reading no more than a few lines cried out, "Bad news. Mr. Chao, Mr. Li, bad news! Miss Sun."

The Japanese had invaded Ch'angsha. The situation was critical. The five of them conferred for a while and decided that since the money they had would never be enough for them to return to Shanghai, they would just have to get to Chian as quickly as possible, pick up the remittance, and then see how matters stood before further plans were made. Li wasted no time telling the widow the urgent news about Ch'angsha, embellishing it with details and painting such a vivid picture of the action it seemed as if the Japanese War Ministry had briefed him with a special intelligence report. The woman was so terrified that she said over and over in a delicate voice, "Ai ya! Mr. Li, what should I do!"

Li Mei-t'ing said that superior people such as himself could always find a way and knew how to manage in a crisis and extricate themselves from desperate situations. "Servants are unreliable. They have no know-how—if they did they wouldn't be servants! If you go with him, you're sure to meet with disaster."

Shortly after Li had left the widow, Ah Fu could be heard speaking gruffly in her room, "Chief P'an sent me to accompany you. Along the way you take up with everyone you set eyes on. Who knows what sort of man he is? How am I going to report to Chief P'an?"

"What right have you to be jealous?" asked the widow. "Did I ask you to interfere? I give you a little dignity and you turn around and act like a king! You don't appreciate the honor, you ungrateful rotten egg!"

Ah Fu laughed scornfully and said, "Who made me a cuckold? It's not enough for you to make your late husband a cuckold. Now you have to make me into one—Ai ya ya—" and he ran out the door.

The widow raged in her room, "I'll give you a good smack and teach you to show respect to me. Impertinent wretch. Take that. Next time don't think—"

Catching the insinuations behind their remarks, Li's heart turned as sour as the juice from a green plum. He wished he could have demanded clarification from the widow and given Ah Fu another good smack. He peered anxiously outside. Ah Fu was lurking in front of the widow's room, rubbing his swollen red cheek with his left hand. Catching sight of Li, he muttered, "Why don't you take a look at yourself in a piss-pot? You think you can sweet-talk your way in and take liberties—"

Losing his patience, Li burst from his room, demanding, "You swine, whom are you cursing?"

Ah Fu replied, "I'm cursing you, you swine."

"The swine is cursing me," said Li.

"I'm cursing the swine," said Ah Fu.

Their "chicken produces the egg," and "egg produces the chicken" sentence practice had no end to it, but in any case, whoever shouted the loudest spoke the truth. Afraid there'd be trouble, Ku pulled Li inside, saying, "What's the use of picking a quarrel with a mean rascal like that?"

"Come out here if you have the guts!" shouted Ah Fu with exaggerated authority. "Don't hide in a cave like a turtle. You think I'm afraid of you—"

Li was all set to burst out the door again, when Hsin-mei and Hung-chien, unable to put up with the quarrel any more, also came out and began shouting at Ah Fu, "He's not paying any attention to you. What are you running your mouth off for?"

Somewhat unnerved, Ah Fu nevertheless kept on, "Rubbish! I'll curse anyone I want to. What's it to you?"

His pipe sticking up like a cannon on an old-fashioned battleship, Hsin-mei rubbed his palms together and clapped them crisply; then clenching his fists, he said, "What if I don't like what I see?"

Ah Fu's eyes were filled with terror, but before Hsin-mei had finished speaking, the widow sprang from her room and demanded, "How dare you bully my servant? Two ganging up against one. How shameless! What kind of men are you, bullying a widow like me? You good-for-nothings!"

Hsin-mei and Hung-chien quickly made off. The widow, laughing scornfully in triumph, flung forth a few curses, then pulled Ah Fu back into her room. After Hsin-mei had admonished Li Mei-t'ing, Hung-chien said to Hsin-mei in private, "When that tigress came springing out, Miss Sun should have gone out for our side. She'd have been a match for her."

The rest of that day whenever the widow encountered the five of them she pretended not to notice them, while Ah Fu, despite his bulging face, narrowed his eyes and curled his lips at Li Mei-t'ing. Whenever the widow called "Ah Fu," her voice dripped with honey. Li sighed half the night.

They stayed another day at the hotel. Whenever Miss Sun ran into the widow that day she would nod and smile, and if Hsin-mei and the others were not with her, they might even exchange a few remarks about how difficult it was to get bus tickets, or how bored they were waiting at the hotel. Hsin-mei and the others, however, seemed to have just mastered the art of making themselves invisible. Whenever the widow met them on the street, she did not acknowledge their existence.

The next day when they boarded the bus, Hsin-mei and his colleagues checked all their luggage; with little luggage in their hands, they were all able to push their way aboard and grab a seat. The widow had brought several small unchecked pieces with her. When Ah Fu boarded the bus, he looked just like a VIP shaking hands with the guests at a reception who wished he could have borrowed a few arms from the thousand-armed Goddess of Mercy. Seeing the two of them without seats, Hsin-mei said with a grin, "Good thing we quarreled with them yesterday. Otherwise we'd now have to give up our seats, and I don't want to." The word "I" was spoken with special emphasis.

Li Mei-t'ing crimsoned, and they all suppressed a smile. The widow gazed over at Miss Sun, reminding Miss Sun of the wide-eyed beseeching look of a cow or horse, since the eyes are the tongue in a dumb animal. Miss Sun's heart softened and she dropped her eyes, but still felt uncomfortable sitting there. It was not until the bus started off and a furtive glance told her the widow had also found a seat that she relaxed.

The bus arrived at Ningtu in the afternoon. Hsin-mei and the others quickly went to pick up the luggage. There was some for everyone, but two pieces had not yet arrived. "What rotten luck!" they cried in unison. "Heaven knows how many days we'll have to wait this time." Inwardly they were all worrying about the money. When they inquired at the hotel opposite the bus station, they found that only two double rooms were left.

"How will that do?" said Hsin-mei. "Miss Sun should have a room by herself. A single would be enough. The four of us have to have two rooms."

Without hesitation Miss Sun said, "It doesn't matter to me. Just add a bamboo cot to Mr. Chao and Mr. Fang's room. Won't that save trouble and money?"

They checked into the rooms, put down their things, and totaled up the expenses for the day. They all agreed they would have to make do with something simple for dinner, and they were just about to call the waiter when suddenly they heard someone shouting from another room, "Waiter! Waiter!" accompanied by coughing and gasping noises. It was the widow's voice. A loud quarrel ensued. By listening carefully, they learned that the widow had ordered the hotel food and became nauseated after taking a few bites. They then learned that the food had been fried in wood oil. Ah Fu, that coarse creature, had gulped down two bowls of rice in one breath without even noticing the odor. Rice and vegetables all came up. "He even threw up last night's dinner!" exclaimed the widow, as if he were supposed to have taken the meal eaten in Nanch'eng all the way to Kweilin.

Li Mei-t'ing clapped his hands and said, "It must be heaven's punishment. Now we'll see whether that rascal gets out of hand again. We don't need to try the food in this hotel any more. Those two have already acted as guinea pigs for us."

The door of the widow's room was wide open when the five of them left the hotel. Ah Fu was moaning and groaning on the bed, while she was leaning on the table retching into a spittoon. The waiter held a glass of water in one hand and was patting her on the back with the other.

"Ai, she's throwing up, too!" said Li.

"Throwing up is like yawning," said Hsin-mei. "It's contagious. Especially when I feel seasick, I can't stand watching someone else vomiting."

A smile tugged at the corners of Miss Sun's eyes and she said, "Mr.

Li, you have medicine for settling the stomach. If you gave her some, she'd certainly—"

Li Mei-t'ing pretended to scream and jump about on the street, crying, "Miss Sun, you're really horrible! Now you're making fun of me, too. I'm going to tell your Uncle Chao."

That evening Hsin-mei, Hung-chien, and Miss Sun made a polite pretense of yielding to each other for a while over who was to sleep on the bamboo cot. Miss Sun was compelled by Hsin-mei and Hung-chien to sleep on the bed, not as if this was a privilege a woman should enjoy, but a duty she should fulfill. Hsin-mei was too big for a bamboo cot, so Hung-chien ended up sleeping on it, sandwiched between the beds. He felt so cramped that when he lay down all he wanted to do was toss and turn, yet he was so restricted he didn't dare make a move.

After a short while Hung-chien heard Hsin-mei's breathing become regular and assumed he had already fallen asleep. *That guy got off easy,* he thought. *Here I am wedged between these two beds without nets acting as a screen separating him from Miss Sun.* He then found the oil lamp on the table too bright. He put up with it for a while, but then unable to bear it any longer, he stepped softly from his bed thinking he'd get a drink of cold tea and blow out the lamp before getting back in. While making his way along the edge of the bed to the table, he inadvertently glanced at Miss Sun and noticed how clean and fresh her face was in sleep. A shock of loose hair had somehow covered her face, giving it a seductive look of abandon. The tips of her hair over the top of her nose rose and fell with her breathing. Watching it made his face itch for her, and he wished he could have reached out and brushed the hair aside. Her eyelashes seemed to flutter slightly in the lamplight. He gave a start, thinking his eyes must have been mistaken. Then her breathing seemed suddenly to become short. When he looked again, her face, immobile in sleep, appeared to redden. He hastily blew out the light and slipped back into bed but remained apprehensive for a long time.

They rose early the next morning. Li saw the previous day's newspaper on the cashier's counter. The first item of news was that Ch'angsha had been burned to the ground.[16] It gave him such a shock that he completely lost his voice. It wasn't until a minute later that he regained it and could speak. They were all so upset they had no time to feel hungry, which saved them the expense of breakfast. Hung-chien didn't know what to do, but it was as though this weren't his affair alone. With others along, there was always a way.

Li sighed woefully and said, "What bad luck! This trip has really had more than its share of bad luck! There were plenty of places in Shanghai wanting to keep me on or offering me a job, but I just let myself get carried away. I couldn't refuse an old friend like Kao Sung-nien. Now after putting up with so much hardship, I have to give up halfway and go back! But who is to pay for the trip?"

Hsin-mei said, "Even if we wanted to go back, there's no money. I say we go on to Chian and pick up the remittance from the school, then assess the situation from there. There's no use making plans this early."

Everyone breathed a sigh of relief and relaxed. Ku suddenly said brightly, "What a mess it'll be if the money from the school hasn't been sent."

The four of them all replied impatiently that he worried too much, but his remarks had called up an echo in their consciousness, and the reasons they gave one another weren't meant to refute Ku so much as to assure themselves. Ku immediately tried to retract his remark, like a snake trying to draw its tail back into its hole after it has been pulled, and he said, "I know such a thing is impossible. I was just mentioning it."

Hung-chien said, "I think the problem could be easily solved. One of us should go there first. If Chian has the money, it'll save all five of us from going there for nothing and wasting a lot of money on bus fare."

"Good idea!" said Hsin-mei. "We can divide the work. Some of us can wait for the luggage while others can pick up the money. That'll liven things up a bit, and we won't all be stuck in one place waiting. The money was remitted to me. I'll take my luggage and go to Chian first. Hung-chien can come along to help me out."

Miss Sun said gently but firmly, "I'll go with Mr. Chao too. My baggage has also arrived."

Giving Hsin-mei a sharp x-ray glance, Li Mei-t'ing said, "All right. That leaves just me and Mr. Ku. But all our money has gone into the general funds. How much are you going to leave us?"

Ku smiled apologetically at Li and said, "My luggage is all here. I think I'll go with them. There's no point staying here any longer."

Li's face flushed with anger as he said, "So you're all going off and leaving me here alone. All right. I don't care. So much for the 'comradeship of the road!' When the going gets tough, isn't it every man for himself? To tell you the truth, once you get to Chian and pick up the money, if you don't give me a cent, it won't bother Li Mei-t'ing at all! If I were to sell the medicine in my trunk, I could easily get about a thousand dollars for it in the interior. Just see if I can't beg my way to Shanghai."

Hsin-mei said in surprise, "Why, Mr. Li, how could you arrive at such a gross misunderstanding?"

Ku said soothingly, "Mr. Mei-t'ing, I won't go. I'll wait for the luggage here with you."

178

Hsin-mei said, "Just what should we do, then? How about if I go first by myself? Mr. Li, you wouldn't suspect me of embezzling the general funds—you want me to leave my luggage behind as security?" He finished with a laugh to lighten the severity of his tone, but the smile was stiff and obstinate as though stuck on with dried paste.

"Nonsense! Nonsense!" repeated Li. "I'm certainly not judging others with a petty man's mind."

"The hell you aren't!" muttered Hung-chien.

"I just don't think Mr. Fang's suggestion is entirely practical—forgive me, Mr. Fang, but I always speak frankly. I mean, for example, Mr. Chao, after you get to Chian and pick up the money, will you go on ahead or turn around and go back? You can't decide that by yourself. We all have to learn the news on the spot and come to a common decision—"

"So," continued Hung-chien, "we four will go on first, following the majority's decision. Aren't we the majority?"

Li Mei-t'ing was without words. Chao and Ku hastily intervened, "As friends in adversity, we'll all stick together."

After lunch Hung-chien returned to his room, complaining that Hsin-mei was too soft in the way he had given in to Li at every turn. "Your tendency to concede in order to accommodate everyone is really getting us nowhere! A leader sometimes has to be ruthless."

Miss Sun said with a laugh, "It was so funny to see Mr. Fang and Mr. Li glaring at each other and panting. It looked like they were about to swallow each other up."

Hung-chien laughed and said, "Damn! You saw the whole disgraceful scene. I had no intention of swallowing him. Swallowing something like that Li Mei-t'ing would wreck my stomach. And anyway, was I panting? I don't think so."

Miss Sun said, "Mr. Li was blowing hot air, while you were snorting cold air."

Hsin-mei showed the whites of his eyes and stuck out his tongue in mock terror at Hung-chien from behind Miss Sun's back.

On their way to Chian, they wished the bus wasn't so clumsy and slow, dragging back their hearts, which were so eagerly straining to go forward. At the same time they were afraid that once they reached Chian, they'd find nothing there; they wanted the bus to keep going on and on forever without ever reaching its destination just to keep their hope alive.

After settling in a hotel, they found they had only about ten dollars left, but said laughingly, "No matter. In a short time we'll be rich."

Upon inquiry at the cashier's office in the hotel, they learned that out of fear of air raids, the bank did not open until four o'clock in the afternoon and so was now doing business. The five of them went off to the bank, keeping an eye on the way for any good restaurants, for it had been a long time since they had had a good meal.

The clerk at the bank said that the money had arrived several days ago and gave them a form to fill out. Hsin-mei asked the clerk for a brush to fill it in. Li and Ku wedged him in on either side as though afraid he didn't know how to write. The brush was worn to a bald stump and was more in need of an application of hair tonic than ink. It left a large smudge every time Hsin-mei touched it to the paper. Li and Ku looked on disapprovingly.

The clerk said, "That brush is hard to write with. You might as well take the form back with you and fill it out. In any case you'll have to find a shop guarantor to affix his seal[17]—but I must tell you, a hotel can't act as a shop guarantor."

This gave them a terrible fright, and they began entreating with the clerk, saying they were new to the area and had no way of finding a shop guarantor and wondering if the rules could be made more flexible. The clerk expressed his sympathy and regrets, but insisted it was official business, and he had to go by the rules. He urged them to try finding someone first. They left the bank, roundly cursing the senseless rules. When they were through their cursing, they consoled one another, "Well, in any case, the money is here."

The next morning Hsin-mei and Li Mei-t'ing ate some stale peanuts, drank half a pot of tea from the night before, and set out together to look for local educational institutions. Some time after two o'clock in the afternoon they returned dispirited and exhausted, saying that the high and grade schools had all disbanded and resettled in the countryside. They had found no one. "Let's worry about it after you eat. You're dizzy from hunger." After a few mouthfuls of food, their spirits picked up, and they suddenly recalled how courteous the bank clerk had been, and to judge from his tone, it seemed that if they really couldn't find a shop guarantor, he might just give them the money anyway. They wanted to go that evening and gently negotiate the matter with the clerk again. At five o'clock while Miss Sun stayed at the hotel, the four men set off again for the bank. The clerk from the day before had already forgotten who they were. When the matter was explained to him, he still said they would have to have a guarantor and told them to try the Bureau of Education. He had heard that it hadn't moved away. After returning to the hotel, they went to bed without food to save money.

Hung-chien was too hungry to fall asleep. His body felt like an attaché case with no papers in it and his back and stomach were nearly stuck to-

180

gether. He then realized that what the French call "long like a day without bread" (*long comme un jour sans pain*) was nowhere near as bad as a night without sleep because of no bread.

Before dawn, Hsin-mei also awoke; clicking his tongue, he said, "How maddening. There's not even anything to eat in my dreams, let alone when I'm awake."

He had dreamed he was in the Capitol Restaurant Grill Room for lunch and had ordered a hamburger and a lemon cake but had waited and waited and they never came; then he awoke from hunger.

Hung-chien said, "Please don't talk about food. It'll make me even hungrier. You selfish rascal, did I get anything to eat in your dream?"

Hsin-mei laughed. "I didn't have time to let you know. At any rate I didn't eat anything! What if I roast Li Mei-t'ing for you? You won't object to that, will you?"

Hung-chien said, "Li Mei-t'ing has no meat on him, but you look fair and plump. I'll roast you to a turn, dip you in sweet sauce, sprinkle on some salt—"

Through laughter interspersed with groans, Hsin-mei said, "You shouldn't laugh when you're hungry. Laughing makes your stomach hurt even worse. Wow! It's like having teeth biting at you from inside. Ai ya ya—"

Hung-chien said, "The more I lie here, the more I suffer. I'm getting up. If I go out and take a stroll, move around some, I can forget my hunger. It's quiet on the streets in the morning. I'm going out for a whiff of fresh air."

"Nonsense," said Hsin-mei. "Fresh air stimulates the appetite. You're really asking for it. I'm saving my strength for going to the Bureau of Education. You'd better"—as he spoke he began to laugh so much he yelped in pain —"not go to the bathroom. Hold out and save something to maintain your stomach."

Before Hung-chien went out, Hsin-mei asked him for a large glass of water and drank it up to fill his stomach. He lay face up on his bed without moving, but the moment he turned, there was the sound of rushing waves from inside his body. Hung-chien took some spare coins from the general funds to buy some unshelled peanuts for their breakfast. Hsin-mei warned him not to eat anything on the sly.

The shopfronts along the street, like faces of people huddling under the bedcovers, hadn't shown themselves yet. The general store selling peanuts was also closed. Hung-chien walked on a few paces and then caught a whiff of the fragrant smell of roasted sweet potatoes. He breathed in as though quenching a powerful thirst, and his hunger immediately constricted his stomach even tighter. Roasted sweet potatoes are like illicit sex in the old Chinese saying, "Having it isn't as good as not having it." The smell is better than the taste. When you smell it, you feel you must have one, but once you actually sink your teeth into it, you find it's not really anything special.

Seeing a sweet potato stand and thinking this was much better than peanuts, Hung-chien decided to get some for breakfast. He suddenly noticed someone near the stand who closely resembled Li Mei-t'ing in dress and build. After taking a closer look, he found that indeed it was Li. Li had bought a sweet potato and was eating it, standing with his face toward the wall. Not wanting to surprise Li in the act, Hung-chien quickly went into a small alley. He waited until Li had gone before he bought some sweet potatoes and walked back. As he entered the hotel, he took care to keep them concealed from the contemptuous glance of the cashier or waiter, lest they catch on to their distressed circumstances and demand payment of their bill and pack them off.

When Hsin-mei saw Hung-chien had gotten sweet potatoes, he lauded Hung-chien for his purchasing ability. After Hung-chien relayed what had just happened, Hsin-mei said, "I knew he hadn't handed over all his money. The way he stuffed himself frantically on the sly, let's just hope he didn't choke to death. If a sweet potato is eaten too quickly, it'll get stuck in the throat, and when it's piping hot besides—I really have to give him credit for his appetite."

Miss Sun, Ku, and Li appeared, exclaiming, "Ai! Where did you get those? Wonderful!"

Ku went along with them to the Bureau of Education, saying it would give a better impression to have an additional person along. Hung-chien wanted to go, but Hsin-mei, arguing that he hadn't combed his hair or shaved his beard for more than ten days and that his face looked like a porcupine and his hair as though it was fit for a hen to roost on, wouldn't let him.

Around noon, Miss Sun said, "They're not back yet. I wonder if there's any hope?"

Hung-chien said, "Since they're not back by this time, I think it has probably been settled. If they'd received a flat refusal, they'd have been back by now. The Bureau of Education isn't that far away."

When Hsin-mei returned to the hotel, he drank half a pitcher of water, gasped for breath, and cursed the Bureau Chief, calling him a stupid idiot. Li and Ku also declared it "outrageous." The Bureau Chief had arrived at the office very late. Having taken his time to get there, he still would not see them right away, and when he did his mouth gave no information and was tighter than a tin can. Not only would he not act as guarantor, he even suspected them of being confidence men. Distastefully, he had taken Li Mei-t'ing's card with three fingers as though it were a piece of trash off the ground, and glancing at the writing on it, said, "I'm an old Shanghai hand. I know every trick of the Shanghai waterfront. These kinds of journalism schools all put up phony signposts—don't get me wrong, gentlemen, I'm speaking in general. National San Lü University? The name's quite new to me! I've never heard of it. Just established? Then I should know about it."

Poor things. They didn't dare eat much that day and what they did eat couldn't keep them from feeling hungry. It only nourished and fostered their hunger, prolonging it indefinitely in their bodies so they never reached the point of starvation, which could have put an end to it.

Hsin-mei remarked, "If we go on like this, we'll all be dead by the time we get hold of the money and will just have enough to buy a coffin for the body."

Ku's eyes suddenly lit up and he said, "Did either of you see the 'Women's Association' along the way? I did. I think women are softhearted. If we ask Miss Sun to go over, maybe she'd have some influence. Of course, it's only a last resort."

Miss Sun agreed immediately. "I'll go right now."

With a look of dismay Hsin-mei turned to Miss Sun and said, "How can we have that? Your father entrusted you to me. If I can't handle things properly, how can I bring you into it?"

Miss Sun replied, "You've already looked after me all the way—"

Not wishing to hear her thank him, Hsin-mei said quickly, "All right, you give it a try. I hope you'll have better luck than we did."

Miss Sun found no one at the Women's Association and said she would try again the next morning. Applying his knowledge of psychology, Hung-chien said, "There's no use going to see anyone again. Women are very suspicious and petty by nature. If you ask one woman to appeal to another, she's bound to get a refusal."

Since the hotel regulations specified that the bill was to be paid every third day, Hsin-mei began to worry that they would not be able to pay the bill the next day.

Li said gallantly, "If by tomorrow we still haven't found a way out, and the hotel demands payment, I'll just sell the medicine."

The next day less than an hour after Miss Sun had departed, she returned with a woman comrade in a gray cotton army uniform. After they had chattered in her room for a while, Miss Sun came out and asked Hsin-mei and the others to come in. The woman was closely examining Miss Sun's diploma (on which was a pretty photograph of Miss Sun in her mortarboard). Miss Sun introduced them one by one, and Li gave her his card. She was very impressed and said she had a friend working in the Bureau of Transportation who might be able to help a little. She would bring them word in the afternoon. They thanked her profusely but didn't dare ask her for lunch. When they saw her respectfully to the door, Miss Sun went with her arm in arm, being especially affectionate. During lunch Miss Sun received so much praise from her traveling companions that her face shone like the sun rising in the eastern sky.

By five o'clock in the afternoon there was still no sign of the woman. Hungry and anxious, everyone questioned Miss Sun several times, but could get no explanation from her. Hung-chien felt it was a bad omen. They'd never get the money, and it would drag on and on uncertainly, while they were helpless to do anything about it. It was like running into a revolving door and having nothing to push against.

By eight o'clock that evening their hearts had all gone numb from waiting, and in a state of calm despair, they decided they might as well stop worrying and get ready for bed. At that moment the woman comrade and her boy friend, like the wonderful lines from the poem that go, "Search all day and never find him, then sometimes he comes on his own," suddenly appeared. The five of them were as overjoyed as a person meeting a long-lost lover and as affectionate as a dog greeting its homecoming master. The man sat down very pompously. Whenever he asked a question, each one tried to outdo the others in answering him, which prompted him to hold up his hand and say, "One person answering is enough." He asked Miss Sun for her diploma and carefully compared the photograph with Miss Sun herself. Miss Sun had a vague suspicion he wasn't comparing her with a photograph but was looking her over and began to feel embarrassed. He then questioned Chao Hsin-mei for a moment and reproved them for not bringing any supporting documents along with them. His girl friend put in some kind words for them, and his manner at last softened. He said he didn't suspect them and would like very much to become their friend, but he didn't know if the Bureau of Transportation could act as a shop guarantor. He asked them to go find out at the bank first and let him know, then he'd affix his seal. So they stayed on another day to make another trip to the bank. That evening everyone felt hungry even in his sleep, as though hunger had declared its independence, taken on a form of its own, and separated from the body.

Two days later they drew out the money. Their shoes had by this time become so familiar with the route from hotel to bank that the shoes could have made the trip by themselves. The bank also gave them a telegram, which had just arrived from Kao Sung-nien, telling them not to worry about getting to the school since there were no effects from the Ch'angsha incident.

That evening in order to express their thanks and celebrate the occasion, they invited the woman comrade and her friend out to a restaurant for a grand meal. After downing three cups of wine, Ku opened his mouth and, with his gold teeth sparkling in a lavish smile and his face, which shone brightly from the wine, beaming all around the table like a searchlight, said, "When our Mr. Li here left Shanghai, he had his fortune told. It was said that some 'noble person' would come to his aid and turn bad luck to good fortune along the way. Sure enough, we met the two of you quite by accident and you acted as our guarantors. In the future both of you will surely be rich and important beyond all bounds. Mr. Chao, Mr. Li, let's all five of us drink a toast to them. Miss Sun, you, you drink a swallow too."

Miss Sun, who had thought for sure that the "noble person" referred to herself, had lowered her head, blushing red. When subsequently she heard the remark had nothing to do with her, like breath puffed against a pane of glass on a warm day, the redness vanished before forming a mist. As citizens of a democratic republic the woman comrade and her friend knew the doctrine of "the people are noble," but when they heard this feudalistic flattery, their wine-flushed faces beamed happily like crimson flowers in full bloom.

Hsin-mei said mischievously, "If you're going to talk about a 'noble person,' our Miss Sun is also a 'noble person.' If it hadn't been for her—"

Without waiting for him to finish, Li immediately drank a toast to Miss Sun.

Hung-chien said, "I'm the biggest disgrace. I didn't do a thing this time. I was just a 'rice-bucket.' "

"That's right," said Li Mei-t'ing. "Little Fang is the real noble one. He sat in the hotel without stirring, while we did all the running around for him. Hsin-mei, we didn't get anywhere, but we sure ran our legs off, didn't we?"

That evening just before turning in, Hsin-mei said, "Today we can go to sleep in comfort. Hung-chien, did you notice how ugly that woman is? After she'd had some wine, she was ugly enough to frighten one to death."

Hung-chien replied, "I know she's ugly, but since she's our benefactress I couldn't bear to take a close look at her. Taking a close look at someone ugly is a form of cruelty—unless it's an evil person you want to punish."

The next morning they arrived at Chiehhualung, on the border between the provinces of Kianghsi and Hunan. The Kianghsi bus did not cross over, so they had to transfer to the Hunan bus, which departed at noon. Of all the buses they had taken on the way, none had arrived at a station as promptly as this one; so rather than quarrel about the short distance they felt that they'd come out a good half-day ahead and decided to take a night's rest instead of catching the bus that day.

It was a remote mountain region. There were seven or eight small inns backed by the mountains along the highway on either side of the bus station. In the inn where they stayed, the kitchen was set up at the entrance. The front room served as the guests' dining room during the day and as the bed-chamber of the innkeeper and his wife at night. The back room was divided into two guest rooms which were shut off from the sunlight; exposed to the wind and rain, the rooms were hot in summer, cool in winter, and reflected the times and the changing seasons. All around the inn was the heavy stench of urine and excrement, as though the inn were a plant for which it was the guests' duty to provide fertilizer and irrigation. The innkeeper was frying food on the street, which sent Hsin-mei and the others into sneezing fits in their rooms. Hung-chien thought he had caught a chill, while Li said, "Someone at home must be worrying about me!" Only later did they realize it was from the fumes given off by hot peppers in the food.

After eating, the four men took an afternoon nap. Miss Sun, sharing a room with Hsin-mei and Hung-chien, said she wasn't sleepy and went outside to sit on a bamboo reclining chair and read, but she too fell asleep. She awoke with a headache and chills and couldn't eat anything at dinner. It was late autumn, and deep in the mountains the days were short. A ray of moonlight showed through the clouds like a squinting, nearsighted eye. After a moment the moon, too round and smooth for anything to stick to it and too light and nimble to be held down, floated out unencumbered from the mass of tousled, fluff-like clouds. One side was not yet full, like a face swollen up on one side from a slap. Since her stomach was bothering her, Miss Sun suggested they go for a moonlight stroll. They walked along the highway in an area of dried grass with no trees in sight and not even one respectable shadow. The moonlight had stripped away the night's masks and covers, depriving it of any dignity.

That night the cold mountain air froze and contracted the lodgers' sleep but was not enough to wrap them up mind and body, so the five of them slept fitfully until daybreak. As usual Hsin-mei and Hung-chien slipped out early from the room, so Miss Sun could get dressed at her leisure. When they returned to the room to get their towels and toothbrushes, they found her still in bed, moaning and groaning with her head under the covers. When they quickly asked her what was the matter, she said she felt so dizzy that she didn't dare shift her position or even open her eyes wide.

Hsin-mei felt her forehead and said, "You don't seem to have a fever. It must be you're tired and have caught a slight chill. Relax and get a good day's rest. The three of us will go tomorrow."

Saying that wouldn't be necessary, Miss Sun tried to raise her head, then sank back down. She let out a long, drawn-out breath, then asked them to put a spittoon next to her bed. When Hung-chien asked the innkeeper for a spittoon, the innkeeper answered, "You mean you can't find room enough to spit in a big place like this? What do you need a spittoon for?"

After a long search, they finally found a broken wooden basin for washing feet. Miss Sun threw up again and again into the basin. When she was through, she lay back down. Hung-chien went out to get some drinking water. Hsin-mei said it was sunny outside and since the pillow of the reclining chair was high, it would be a little more comfortable to lie there. He told her to try getting dressed, while he spread a blanket over the chair for her. She wouldn't let them help her. With her head down and her eyes closed, she felt her way along the wall to the reclining chair and collapsed into it. Hung-chien filled Hsin-mei's rubber water bottle and gave it to her to warm her stomach, asking her if she'd care for some water to drink. She took a swallow, then threw it up. Both of them grew worried, and thinking there might be some *Jen-tan*[18] pills among the medicine Li Mei-t'ing had brought, asked him for a packet through the door.

Since the bus didn't leave until noon, Li Mei-t'ing was lounging on his bed. He was actually bringing the medicine to the school so he could sell it at a high price. With the seals left intact, he was planning to sell his medicine at ten times the original price to the poor, remote school infirmary. Even if a packet were opened just to take a few pills, once the wrapper was torn, he couldn't get anything for the rest of it, but then he couldn't very well ask Miss Sun to pay him for it. While *Jen-tan* wasn't worth more than a few dollars, he didn't feel her manner toward him during the trip merited the friendship of one packet of *Jen-tan*. On the other hand, not to give her any medicine would just show how stingy he was. When they were in Chian and not eating three full meals every day, he had worried about getting some disease of malnutrition, and had secretly opened a bottle of Japanese cod liver oil. Every day after a meal he took three capsules as a dietary supplement. Cod liver oil capsules were of course more expensive than *Jen-tan*, but then an opened bottle was like a woman who'd been married before—its market value dropped. Li threw on some clothes and came out to ask about Miss Sun. When he learned that she had suffered a chill in her stomach, something which would get better by itself after she lay down for a while, he decided it wouldn't make any difference if she took cod liver oil capsules, so he said, "You go ahead and have breakfast. I'll see that Miss Sun gets the medicine."

Not wishing Li Mei-t'ing to accuse them of trying to steal his glory, Hung-chien and Hsin-mei did go eat breakfast to avoid suspicion. Li went back to his room to get a capsule and asked for a glass of drinking water. Miss Sun languidly opened her eyes and swallowed it as he directed. When Hung-chien went to see Miss Sun after he had eaten breakfast, he smelled a fishy odor. He was just about to ask her about it, when suddenly her cheeks turned completely wet. Some of the tears from the corners of her tightly shut eyes trickled past her ears and dampened the pillow. He was so stunned he didn't know what to do. It was as though he had inadvertently come upon some secret he wasn't supposed to know. Quickly he confided to Hsin-mei about it. Hsin-mei also thought this sort of crying was something that should be kept from strangers and did not dare question her closely about it. The two of them consulted their entire stock of learning on the subject of women for an explanation as to why she was crying. In the end, it was a case of "heroes seeing eye to eye." Her crying, they both agreed, was mostly due to mental anguish. When a girl finds herself hundreds of miles from home, falls ill in mid-journey, and hasn't a single relative to turn to, it's only natural for her to cry. What especially aroused their pity was that she didn't dare cry out loud. Both agreed they should be nicer to her and quietly went to her bed. She seemed to have fallen asleep; the tearstains and dust on her face had congealed into several black streaks. Fortunately, a young girl's tears aren't yet like the raindrops of autumn or winter. They don't bring destruction and ruin to the face, but are more like the steady rains of early April, which soak and swell the ground, making it muddier.

The four or five days of their journey from Chiehhualung to Shaoyang were as smooth as satin. On their lips was the newly discovered truth: "Money is an absolute necessity." As the way from Shaoyang to the school consisted entirely of mountain roads, they had to switch to sedan chairs. Tired of riding buses, they were delighted with the novelty of sedan chairs, but after riding for a while, they realized that these were harder to endure than a bus. Their toes ached from the cold, and they preferred getting down and walking a while. The whole way was rugged and winding over endless mountains and fields, as though time had already forgotten this route. After traveling more than seventy *li*, time seemed nonexistent. Mountain mists gradually rose, darkness turned to dusk, and dusk congealed into blackness.

The thick, black clump was a hamlet where they were to stay that evening. When they got into the lodge, the sedan-chair bearers and rickshaw pullers lit a fire, and they gathered around to warm themselves while vegetables were fried and the rice was cooked. No lamps were lit at night in the lodge. Instead, a long piece of firewood was burned at one end and stuck in the pile. As the slender flames swayed and bobbed, the shadows of objects in the room also came alive. They all slept in an unpartitioned room. There were no beds, just five piles of straw. They preferred the rice straw to hotel beds, which sometimes felt like a relief map and sometimes like the chest of a tuberculosis patient.

Hung-chien was extremely tired and sleepy, but his mind would not settle down. Sleep gathered in on all sides but did not close up, like two halves of a window curtain that are about to join when suddenly the cord becomes stuck, letting through a thread of the outside world. After he had finally fallen asleep, a small voice began crying plaintively, from deep within his dreams, "Get off my clothes! Get off my clothes!" Hung-chien instinctively rolled aside and then was immediately wide-awake. He heard a sigh by his head, very faint like a suppressed emotion escaping as a furtive breath. He was so frightened his hair stood on end. He could not make out anything in the darkness and thought of lighting a match, but he was afraid he really would see something. Hsin-mei was snoring; far away a dog was barking. He paused for a moment to collect his wits and laughed at himself for imagining things. He relaxed and was about to drift off to sleep, but it was as though some force were preventing him from sleeping, propping up his whole being, propping him up and not letting him settle down. In a semiconscious state, he had a dim sense that when awake one is suspended loosely in space but he becomes heavy the moment he falls asleep.

As he was struggling to go to sleep, he heard Miss Sun next to him breathing unsteadily as though she wanted to cry but couldn't. When he roused himself and focused his attention, his sleep vanished again, and he very distinctly heard a sigh close to his ear, like a breath let out when work is finished. Hung-chien turned his head away to escape that sighing mouth. His throat and tongue had gone dry and stuck together in fright, so he couldn't call out, "Who is it?" Afraid that the mouth would press close to his ear and tell him who it was, he quickly pulled the covers over his head. His heart was pounding so hard that it seemed his breast could not contain it. Through the covers he heard Hsin-mei grinding his teeth in sleep. The sound dispelled his fright and made him feel he had returned to the human world. When he stuck his head out, something scurried past his head and he heard a mouse squeak. He lit a match. The jittery flame leaped up and then died out, but he had glimpsed his watch, which read exactly twelve o'clock. Awakened by the flash of light, Miss Sun turned over. He asked her if she had had a bad dream. She told him she had dreamt that a pair of child's hands were pushing at her body and wouldn't let her sleep. He told him of his own impressions and urged her not to be afraid.

Before five in the morning, the sedan bearers washed and cooked rice. Hung-chien and Miss Sun, neither of whom had slept the rest of the night, also rose and went outside for a breath of fresh air. They then discovered that nothing but graves were behind the house. It looked as though the house had been built on top of the graves. Not far behind the lodge a broken door frame stuck up sharply. The main part of the building had burned down, leaving only this entrance. The two door panels had also been carted away.

Pointing to the coarse steamed bread, Hung-chien asked, "Miss Sun, do you believe in ghosts?"

Miss Sun, who since her nightmare had become much closer to Hung-chien, replied with a smile, "It's hard to say. Sometimes I do and sometimes I definitely don't. Like last night, for instance, I thought ghosts were really scary. But now, even though there are graves all around, I don't feel there's such a thing as a ghost."

Hung-chien said, "That's a very fresh thought. There's definitely a time factor involved in the existence of ghosts, like certain flowers of spring that are gone by summer."

Miss Sun said, "You said the voice you heard was like a child's, and the hands in my dream were like a child's, too. It's just too strange."

"Maybe the place where we were sleeping was once a child's grave. See how small those graves are. They don't seem like adults'."

"Why don't ghosts grow up?" asked Miss Sun innocently. "Children who've been dead for decades are still children."

Hung-chien replied, "That's why separation or death is preferred to 'spending a lifetime together.' It can keep people from aging. Not only do ghosts not grow old, but friends we haven't seen for a long time remain just as dashing in our mind's eye as they were then, even though we ourselves have already grown old—Hey, Hsin-mei."

Hsin-mei laughed loudly and asked, "What did you two come to this godforsaken place to talk about so early in the morning?"

They both related what had happened during the night. Hsin-mei said sardonically, "So you really had a communion of souls in your dreams. How wonderful! I didn't feel a thing myself. But of course I'm too vulgar. No ghost would bother to pay me a visit. By the way, the sedan bearers say we can get to the school by this afternoon."

In his sedan chair Fang Hung-chien wondered what it would be like when they reached the school that day. In any case he no longer entertained any hopes. That broken-down door behind the lodge was a good symbol. It was like an entrance, concealing behind it deep palaces and high towers. One was lured inside only to find nothing there: an entrance into nothing, a place that went nowhere. "All hope abandon, ye who enter here!" In spite of this, an irrepressible curiosity and anticipation, like water boiling on the stove, pushed up against the lid of the kettle. He hated the way the sedan bearers meandered along and preferred to get off the chair and walk by himself.

Stirred by a similar feeling, Hsin-mei had also grown restless in his chair and began to walk. "Hung-chien," he said, "we've really gained a lot of experience during this trip. Ultimately everything came out well, and we reached the Western Paradise [Buddhist heaven]. At least from now on we can keep a respectful distance from Li Mei-t'ing and Ku Er-chien. In the case of Li it goes without saying, but Ku's fawning obsequiousness is really unbearable."

Hung-chien said, "I've found that flattery is just like love. It doesn't allow a third party to look on disinterestedly. Next time we start praising someone, we should be careful that no one else is around."

Hsin-mei said, "A trip like this really tests a person's character. Traveling is so exhausting and vexing; it's apt to show a person's true self. People who go through a long hard journey together without incurring each other's dislike can become good friends—but hold on, let me finish. The honeymoon trip after marriage is an exception. People should take a month's trip together first and then after a month of the rigors of travel, if neither one has seen through the other and doesn't detest the other, if they haven't quarreled and fallen out and still want to stick to the original marriage agreement, then such a couple is sure never to divorce."

"Why don't you tell that to Mr. and Mrs. Ts'ao Yüan-lang?"

"Sorry, but I'm saying this to you alone. Now that you've made this trip, Miss Sun doesn't annoy you, does she?"

As he spoke, Hsin-mei took a look back at Miss Sun's sedan chair, then turned around and laughed heartily.

"Don't talk rubbish. Tell me, now that you've made this trip, what do you think of me? Do you find me annoying?"

"You're not annoying, but you're completely useless."

Hung-chien had not expected such a blunt answer from Hsin-mei and was so enraged that he could do no more than smile bitterly. His high spirits completely destroyed, he walked on in silence for a few more steps; then with a wave at Hsin-mei, he said, "I'm going to go ride in the chair." Once in the sedan chair he sat dejectedly, not knowing why it was considered a virtue to speak frankly.

6

꘡꘡

KAO SUNG-NIEN, the president of San Lü University, was an "old science scholar." The word "old" here is quite bothersome. It could describe science or it could just as well be describing a scientist. Unfortunately, there is a world of difference between a scientist and science. A scientist is like wine. The older he gets, the more valuable he is, while science is like a woman. When she gets old, she's worthless. Once Mandarin grammar reaches its full development, the time will come when "old science scholar" can be clearly distinguished from "scholar of old science" or one will say "science old scholar" or "old science scholar." But as it's still too early for that yet, a general term of reference will have to do in the meantime.

Kao Sung-nien's fat but firm face was like an unleavened millet-flour steamed bread. "Voracious time" (*Edax vetustas*) could not make a dent on it. There was not a single tooth mark or crease. If a coed who had violated a school rule were extremely pretty, President Kao would only want her to beg for mercy and admit her mistake before him; then perhaps he would not carry out the law to the fullest extent but would let her off with a light punishment. This proves that this scientist wasn't old yet. Twenty years ago he studied entomology abroad. Apparently the insects of twenty years ago had evolved into university students and professors, and so he had been invited to act as an "example to scholars." As a university president, his prospects were unlimited.

University presidents fall into two categories—those from the liberal arts and those from the natural sciences. Those from liberal arts rarely accede to this position, and when they do they don't look upon it as an honor, since they probably came to it after having been turned out of public office.

Failing as an official, they turn to scholarly pursuits, cultivating mind and body with the riches of the classics and the sounds of music and chanting. For those from the natural sciences, the situation is quite different. China is the greatest promoter of science of any country in the world; no other governmental body is so willing to offer high posts to scientists. As Western science moves forward, Chinese scientists move upward. In the West, scholarship devoted to the study of human sentiments and to the study of nature's laws have always been kept separate. In China, however, one need only have a knowledge of hydroelectrics, civil engineering, mechanics, plant and animal technology, and so on, to be able to run public affairs and govern people. That is the greatest triumph of the "uniform law of nature." For someone from the natural sciences to be a university president is merely the beginning of a career in government. Heretofore, the Way of Great Learning[1] lay in ruling the country and pacifying the land; now ruling the country and pacifying the land lies in the Way of the University (literally, great learning), which in addition is wide and open. For the former category, a university is a rocking chair for resting; for the latter, it is a cradle for nurturing—as long as the person takes care not to rock himself to sleep.

Kao Sung-nien worked furiously day and night without rest. He was so keen he literally slept with his eyes wide open and his glasses on, so that he was never hazy even in his dreams. The cradle had been very well chosen. It was the garden of a local millionaire, in the countryside of the P'ing-ch'eng district; it faced a stream with mountains in the background. This country town was definitely not strategically important. The one thing that the Japanese were generous and unsparing with—bombs—would be wasted there. Thus the town, no more than half a *li* from the school, was prospering every day, featuring photo shops, restaurants, bathhouses, theaters, a police station, and high and grade schools.

That spring when Kao Sung-nien received his appointment to set up the school, a few old friends in Chungking gave him a farewell party. During the dinner they remarked on the large number of universities and the scarcity of professors in the interior, and since San Lü was a new and as yet unknown university in a remote area, they wondered if he could recruit any prominent professors.

Kao Sung-nien replied with a smile, "My view is quite different from yours, gentlemen. Of course, it'd be nice to have a well-known professor. With his prestige, the school would gain from his affiliation, while he himself would not be dependent on the school. If he were haughty or temperamental, he would not devote himself fully to the school nor obey absolutely the commands of his superior. If he threatened to quit, you'd have a hard time finding a replacement, and the students would find some excuse to make trouble. I think a school shouldn't merely train its students but should train its faculty as well. If unknowns are brought in, they will have to look to the school for favors and depend on the school for their status, while the school will not be beholden to them. They can really work with the school and be willing to work hard for the good of everyone. The school is also an organization, and as such it certainly requires scientific management. There are never any special persons in a sound organization, only individual units dutifully carrying out orders. So, there is nothing difficult about recruiting professors."

His listeners were overcome with admiration. Kao had not always held this view but had merely spouted it out on the spur of the moment. After receiving the adulation of his friends, he gradually believed it to be the gospel truth and was overcome with self-admiration. From then on he was constantly expounding this idea, giving it an added sanction by saying, "I'm a student of biology, and a school is an organism, too. The faculty should be to the school as the cells are to the organism—" This gospel truth was transformed into scientific law.

Thanks to this scientific law, Li Mei-t'ing, Ku Er-chien, and Fang Hung-chien were all honored with professorial appointments. They arrived at the school that afternoon after two. After he learned of their arrival, Kao hurried over to the faculty dormitory to greet them, then returned to his office, no longer able to dismiss the matter that had been troubling him for the past month. Since the crisis at Ch'angsha, nine out of ten professors he hired had sent telegrams canceling their contracts on one pretext or another. Everything was topsy-turvy and many classes had to be canceled; fortunately, the war had affected the students also, and only 158 of them had shown up. Having four professors arrive all at once was a real boost to his morale, and it would look a little better when he wrote a report to the Ministry of Education.

But how was he to explain things to Li Mei-t'ing and Fang Hung-chien? Vice-minister Wang of the Ministry of Education had recommended Wang Ch'u-hou to be chairman of the Department of Chinese Literature. Meanwhile he had already written and appointed Li Mei-t'ing to the post—but Wang Ch'u-hou was Vice-minister Wang's uncle and for that reason was better qualified than Li Mei-t'ing. The succession of telegrams from professors declining appointments at that time had put his head in a spin. Afraid that the group from Shanghai would turn back halfway, he decided he had better humor Vice-minister Wang first. He felt Wang Ch'u-hou could not be easily handled, while Li Mei-t'ing was an old friend and as such could always be brought around. He was worried that Li's temper would be hard to deal with. Very hard indeed! That young Fang fellow, on the other hand, should be easy to handle. Fang was a friend of Chao

Hsin-mei. Not wanting to come himself, Hsin-mei had at first recommended Fang, saying Fang was a returned student with a doctorate from Germany. What absolute nonsense that was! According to the resumé sent by Fang himself, Fang had no degree at all and was nothing but a student drifter who had led a life of dissipation in one country after another. Furthermore, Fang had never even studied political science. To hire Fang as a professor would be an injustice! At the most Fang could start as an associate professor and work his way up step by step. Young people shouldn't climb too high in their jobs. He could have Hsin-mei tell Fang that. The difficulty still lay with Li Mei-t'ing. In any case, Li had been through hell and high water to get here, so Li certainly wouldn't just break off and leave immediately. Since getting here had been so difficult, leaving wouldn't be so easy either. He would make Li some empty promises and let it go at that. After all, wasn't it through his influence that Li had made it from a private school to a national university in one leap? One had to show some gratitude. In any case, all this could wait till the next day. No use worrying about it now. Meanwhile, there was dinner at the police chief's house that night. The dinner was the usual social affair. The great banquets in the small village always came down to the same few dishes. Kao had had his fill of them, but it was now past four, and he was getting a little hungry. At the thought of dinner, his mouth watered.

When travelers reach their destination, they disperse like the wave splashing in all directions upon reaching shore. But that day Hung-chien and the other three men still went to the village together to get a haircut and take a bath. When they returned to the school, they saw on the bulletin board an announcement written on a piece of pink paper stating that the Chinese literature students were holding a tea in the social room at seven-thirty that evening to welcome Mr. Li Mei-t'ing.

"What a nuisance! What a nuisance!" said Li in delight. "I'm so tired; I was planning to go to bed early today! Those kids are too enthusiastic for their own good. Mr. Chao, aren't they quick at getting the news!"

"Of all the nerve!" said Hsin-mei. "Why don't the Political Science Department students throw a party to welcome me?"

Li said, "What's your hurry? Why don't you take my place at today's reception? I'd rather sleep."

Ku Er-chien nodded and said with a sigh, "People in Chinese studies know the proper etiquette, all right. I don't think the students in any other department would ever pay their teacher such honor and respect." With that he smiled sweetly at Li. God must have regretted at that moment not having appended a waggable dog's tail to man's body, thereby reducing by no one knows how much man's power of expression.

Hung-chien said, "All of you are affiliated with one department or another. I still don't know which department I will be teaching in. President Kao didn't make it clear in his telegram."

"That doesn't matter," said Hsin-mei quickly. "You can teach philosophy, Chinese—"

Li Mei-t'ing said with a sly smile, "You'll have to get my permission to teach Chinese, Mr. Fang. Do a good job of currying favor with me, and we can come to terms on anything."

While he was speaking, Miss Sun came up and said she was living in the women's dormitory and sharing a room with the women's adviser, Miss Fan. She too flattered Li Mei-t'ing about the reception. Li smiled flippantly and said, "Miss Sun, you should change your field. Don't go to the Foreign Languages Department office. Be my teaching assistant instead, and tonight we can go to the party together."

While the five of them had dinner at a small restaurant near the university's main gate, Li Mei-t'ing listened without hearing and ate without noticing the taste. They all teased him, saying he was preparing his speech for the reception. Li emphatically denied it, saying, "Nonsense! Why do I need to prepare for that!"

At about nine o'clock that evening Fang Hung-chien was talking with Hsin-mei in the latter's room and yawning repeatedly. He was about to return to his room to sleep, when Li knocked on the door and came in. They were both about to tease him when they noticed by his face that something was wrong and asked, "Why did the reception end so early?"

Without a word, Li sat down on a chair, his nostrils blowing out air like a locomotive getting ready to pull out. They quickly asked him what had happened. He pounded the table, calling Kao Sung-nien a scoundrel, and declared that even if he had to take his case all the way to the Ministry of Education he would never lose. He also said that the president had gone off to have dinner with someone and wasn't back yet, and there wasn't a sign of him anywhere, maintaining that anyone that negligent of his duties should be damned to hell. As it turned out, the reception had been arranged by Wang Ch'u-hou in accordance with the famous precept from *The Art of War*:[2] "Launch a frontal assault before the enemy has a chance to catch his breath." The four lecturers and the teaching assistants in the Department of Chinese Literature who had arrived at the school some time ago had already become his friends, and the students, in general, had also been obedient. Knowing that Kao Sung-nien had made a prior agreement with Li Mei-t'ing, he had taken advantage of Li's absence and usurped Li's position. Being a department chairman is just like getting married: "The one installed three days earlier becomes the wife." The party for Li turned out to be more like the new concubine's First Meeting ceremony than a reception.

196

The moment Li Mei-t'ing walked in the meeting room with a student representative, he sensed something was wrong, and when he heard his colleagues and the students say "Chairman Wang" once or twice, Li grew suspicious and alarmed.

When Wang Ch'u-hou saw him, he fervently took Li's hand in both of his, rubbing it for some time without letting go as though clasping the hand of a mistress. At the same time he said with mixed fear and admiration, "Mr. Li, you really kept us waiting on tenterhooks. We've been expecting you every day—Mr. Chang, Mr. Hsüeh, weren't we just this morning talking about him—we were just this morning talking about you. Did you have a rough journey? Rest up for the next two days before going to classes. There's no rush. I've arranged all your courses. Mr. Li, we've really been soul-brothers for a long time. When President Kao called me in Ch'engtu asking me to organize the Chinese Literature Department, I thought to myself, I'm getting old, and the journey is a difficult one. Much better to stick with the old rather than try something new. That's why I really didn't want to come at first. But President Kao really could go on! He asked my nephew—"

Mr. Chang, Mr. Hsüeh, and Mr. Huang all said at once, "Mr. Wang is Vice-minister Wang's uncle."

"He asked my nephew to keep persuading me, and I couldn't refuse an old friend. My wife's health isn't very good, and she felt like getting a change of air. When I arrived here and learned you were coming, I was quite overjoyed. I think the department will certainly be well run. . . ."

Li Mei-t'ing's speech to have been delivered as chairman was locked up inside and left unsaid. Controlling his anger, he made a few offhand remarks, drank a cup of tea, then left the party early, complaining of a headache.

Hsin-mei and Hung-chien consoled him for a while and urged him to go back to his room and get some sleep. The next day he could go to Kao Sung-nien and speak his piece.

On his way out, Li remarked, "If in spite of our friendship Old Kao can still deceive me like this, he must have some tricks up his sleeve for you two as well. Just watch. As long as we adopt a unified stance, we have nothing to fear from him!"

After Li left, Hung-chien turned to Hsin-mei and declared, "That's outrageous!"

Hsin-mei replied with a frown, "I think there must be some misunderstanding. I don't know the story behind it. Maybe Li's love is all one-sided. Otherwise, it's ridiculous! But then for someone like Li Mei-t'ing to be chairman is a joke in itself. Those fancy cards of his with the printed titles can't help him now. Ha, ha."

Hung-chien said, "This is my unlucky year in any case. I'm prepared to be disappointed wherever I go. Probably tomorrow Kao Sung-nien won't even recognize this lousy professor."

"There you go again!" said Hsin-mei impatiently. "It's as if you couldn't really be happy unless you were unlucky. Well, let me tell you something. You can't believe everything Li Mei-t'ing says. And besides, you came on my recommendation. Whatever happens, I'm here."

Although Hung-chien was determined to be pessimistic, when he heard this, he decided it wouldn't hurt to put off his pessimism for another day.

Next morning Hsin-mei told Hung-chien that he would see the president the first thing and get Hung-chien's case straightened out, instructing Hung-chien to wait until he came back before going to see Kao Sung-nien.

After more than an hour, Hung-chien became impatient. *I am really being oversensitive*, he thought. *Kao Sung-nien cabled me directly. Could someone who is the head of an organization be so flippant with his promises? Hsin-mei has already done his duty as a reference. Now I'll have to pay Kao a formal call myself. That would be the most straightforward way.*

When Kao saw Fang Hung-chien's pleasant, smiling face, he thought Fang was either a very good-natured or conniving sort of fellow. He quickly asked, "Did you see Mr. Chao?"

"Not yet. I thought I should come see you. It is only appropriate." Fang Hung-chien was certain that he had spoken very properly.

Hell! thought Kao Sung-nien, *Hsin-mei must have gotten tied up with Li Mei-t'ing and been unable to get away. Now I'll have to do a lot of fast talking with this Fang fellow.* "Mr. Fang, Mr. Chao was going to talk with you—there are several things I've already spoken to him about—"

Hung-chien sensed something was wrong from the way Kao spoke, but for the moment he could not withdraw the smile from his face, and so it lingered on rather awkwardly. Looking at Fang's face, Kao wished he could have picked off the smile with his fingers.

"Mr. Fang, did you get my letter?"

When most people lie, their eyes and mouth will not cooperate. While the mouth is boldly prattling on, the eyes are timidly avoiding the other's gaze. Kao Sung-nien was skilled at dealing with people, and furthermore, while studying biology, he had learned the wisdom handed down in the West: If your gaze meets that of a lion or tiger and you glare at each other, the wild beast will be so hypnotized by your stare he won't dare attack. Of course, before he starts eating you, a wild beast won't necessarily dart bewitching glances at you, but then Fang Hung-chien wasn't a wild beast either. At the most he could be called a house pet.

Kao Sung-nien's three-hundred-watt glare made Fang so uncomfortable that Fang began to feel as though not having received the letter was his own fault and that he had been too presumptuous in coming here. Trusting Kao Sung-nien had in fact written a letter retracting his appointment, Fang, at the same time, felt a certain expected satisfaction and exclaimed in agitation, "No, I didn't! I really didn't get it! Was it important? When did you send it?" as though he were the one lying and had received the letter but was now denying it.

"Ai! How could you not have gotten it?" Kao sat up straight, his look of feigned surprise carried to perfection and far more natural than Fang's genuine dismay. That Kao hadn't become an actor was a misfortune for the stage and a blessing for the actors. "That letter was very important. Ai! Wartime postal service is simply abominable. But now that you're here, splendid. I can tell you everything directly."

Hung-chien relaxed somewhat and said obligingly, "There's always trouble with mail between the interior and Shanghai. The incident in Ch'ang-sha probably affected it too. A lot of mail could have gotten lost. If your letter to me was sent early—"

Kao Sung-nien made a gesture of not attaching any importance to the letter, grandly forgiving the letter which he had never written and which Fang Hung-chien had never received. "No use talking about the letter. I'm very much afraid that if you had read the letter, you would not have condescended to accept the appointment. But now that you're here, don't start thinking about running off. Ha, ha! It's this way. I'll explain everything. Though I'd never met you before, when I heard Hsin-mei speak of your scholarship, character, and so on, I was quite delighted and immediately sent you a telegram asking you to come help. The telegram stated that—"

Kao Sung-nien paused a moment to see how good a negotiator Hung-chien was, for a good negotiator would never at this point recite the promised terms for him. But like a fish swallowing bait, Fang Hung-chien was hooked at once, and quickly went on, "Your telegram appointed me professor, but didn't say in which department I was to teach, so I'd like to ask about that."

"I originally intended to ask you to be a professor in the Political Science Department since you had been recommended by Hsin-mei, who said you had a doctorate from Germany. But according to your own resumé, you have no degree—"

Hung-chien's face flushed as red as a sick man with a temperature of one hundred three degrees.

"And you hadn't even studied political science. Hsin-mei was completely wrong. Your friendship with Hsin-mei isn't really very deep, is it?"

The temperature registered on Hung-chien's face rose another degree Fahrenheit, and he was unable to answer. Seeing this, Kao Sung-nien grew even bolder.

"Of course, I won't quibble about a degree. I'm only concerned with true talent and learning. But the regulations set down by the Ministry of Education are very strict. According to your academic credentials, you could at the most be a full-time lecturer. If I petitioned for a professorial salary, it would be denied for sure. I'm confident Hsin-mei's recommendation couldn't be wrong, and so I'm making an exception and appointing you as an associate professor with a salary of two hundred eighty dollars a month and a raise next school year. This was all explained in the express letter I sent you. I assumed you had received it."

Hung-chien could only declare for the second time that he had not received the letter, feeling at the same time that his demotion to associate professor was already a blessing from above.

"As for your contract, I just asked Hsin-mei to take it with him. What you teach is now the problem. We still have no philosophy department for the time being, and there are already enough professors in the Chinese department. There's just one class of logic required of all freshmen in the College of Letters and Law and that is three hours. That seems a bit too little. I'll think of something else later on."

Hung-chien left the president's office feeling as if his soul had been run over by a steamroller. Not a breath of spirit left in him, he felt like some poor abandoned creature to whom Kao Sung-nien had given shelter in an act of great mercy. Filled with shame and hate, he had no one on whom to vent his feelings. When he got back to his room, Hsin-mei hurried over, saying that he had more or less helped Kao Sung-nien solve Li Mei-t'ing's case and was ready to discuss Hung-chien's. When he learned that Hung-chien had already spoken with Kao Sung-nien, he said quickly, "You didn't flare up with him, did you? It's all my fault. I was under the impression you had your doctorate. When I first recommended you, I was just hoping to get it settled quickly—"

"So you could have Miss Su all to yourself—"

"You don't have to bring that up. I had my salary—all right, all right, I won't, I won't." Clasping his hands and smiling apologetically, Hsin-mei praised Hung-chien for his forbearance, and told him how Li Mei-t'ing had come barging in, blustering disgracefully while he was talking in the president's office. Hung-chien asked what happened with Li.

Hsin-mei smiled sardonically and said, "Kao Sung-nien asked me to try to reason with him, so after prattling on about it for a long time, he said that unless the school buys the Western medicine he brought at his price—

Ai, and I still have to go give Kao Sung-nien the reply. Your case was weighing on my mind, so I hurried back to see you."

Hung-chien had calmed down by then, but when he heard that Kao Sung-nien was to buy for the school the contraband goods that Li had brought at the price Li was asking, his anger surfaced again. Now that Li had received compensation, he thought, he was the only real loser. When Kao Sung-nien gave a party that evening in honor of the newly arrived professors, Hung-chien fussed and refused to go but was unable to withstand Hsin-mei's earnest entreaties, and when early that evening Kao Sung-nien came by to pay a call, he felt he had sufficiently recovered face and went after all.

While Hsin-mei had no extracts of elixirs like Li Mei-t'ing, who traveled with the essence of Chinese literature all stored up in his cards, he had brought along a dozen or so reference books. Fang Hung-chien, on the other hand, never had any idea he would be teaching logic, and none of the books on the history of Western society, primitive culture, the collected books of historiography, and so on, which he had brought along, was of any use to him. When he seriously thought about his teaching assignment, he became so nervous that he had no time to stay angry and just hoped Kao Sung-nien would let him teach the history of comparative cultures or the history of Chinese literature instead. But there was no need for the former course now, and someone was already teaching the latter. A beggar has to take what he gets; it's not up to him to choose the dishes.

Hsin-mei consoled him, "Students nowadays aren't as advanced as they used to be—"

It seems that in this great age of rubber tires, the level of the students and the moral standards of the times are the only two things that have regressed.

"Don't panic. You'll manage somehow."

Hung-chien went to the library to look for books. The library had fewer than one thousand books, most of which were old, battered, torn textbooks of Chinese, relics of schools that had been suspended during the war. A thousand years hence these books would be as priceless as the manuscripts from the Tun-huang caves. Now they were ancient without being rare. Shortsighted, shallow-minded book collectors still did not have sense enough to buy them up. All libraries, like the brains of a drudge at examination time, are graveyards of learning. This library, however, was like an old-fashioned charitable organization which cherished the written word. If heaven knew of it, those in charge in this generation would never be struck by lightning and in the next life would surely all be intelligent and influential.

Hung-chien browsed around for a long time, then to his surprise found a Chinese translation of *An Outline of Logic*. He checked it out and went back to his room, as happy as T'ang San-tsang returning to Ch'angan with the sutras.[3] After reading a few pages of *An Outline of Logic*, it occurred to him that since no textbooks were available, perhaps he should make this one available to all, by mimeographing and distributing it to students. Then he reflected that wouldn't be necessary. Professors used to keep other reference books, which served as "secret pillow treasures," and so they were willing to use textbooks. Now that there were no reference books, and he was solely dependent on this one textbook to instill knowledge and spread culture, he could not possibly share it with everyone. He'd better let the students remain mystified by it all and take notes on his lectures. After all, he was nothing more than an associate professor. It wasn't worth knocking himself out for that. At the first meeting of the class he would express his sympathy for the students, lament the difficulty of finding books in the unoccupied area, and say that under such circumstances the professor was no longer a useless appendage. Having a professor lecture was an emergency measure instituted in the days before the invention of printing, he would go on, and since it was no longer the Middle Ages, everybody had books to read and logically speaking shouldn't have to come to class and waste each other's time. He was sure these comments would be very well received and at the thought of how the students would react, he was so elated that he could hardly sit still.

Hung-chien and the rest of the group arrived at the school on Wednesday. Kao Sung-nien let them rest until the following Monday before starting classes. During those few days, Hsin-mei was the president's man of the hour, having received the most calls from his colleagues, while Hung-chien was seldom so honored. Small in size, the school had been put together haphazardly. Except for the women students and a small number of faculty members with families, everyone lived in a large compound. This arrangement clearly showed each person's status at the school.

On Sunday afternoon Hung-chien was busily preparing his lecture material when Miss Sun came, looking more ruddy than she had on the trip. Hung-chien was about to get Hsin-mei, but she said she had just come from Hsin-mei's place, that the professors in the Political Science Department were holding a conference there, and the room was filled with smoke. When she saw that they were all busy, she did not sit down.

Fang Hung-chien said with a grin, "Whenever politicians congregate, there's bound to be heavy pollution."

Miss Sun laughed and then said, "I came today to thank you and Mr. Chao. Yesterday afternoon the comptroller's office reimbursed me for the traveling expenses."

"It was Mr. Chao who got that for you. I had nothing to do with it."

"No, I know otherwise." Miss Sun was gently stubborn. "It was you who reminded Mr. Chao about it. When you were on the boat—" She realized she had said half a sentence too much and blushed. The sentence was chopped at midpoint.

Hung-chien suddenly remembered the conversation on the boat. So the girl really had heard everything. Seeing her like this, he too felt embarrassed. Blushing from shyness, like yawning or stuttering, can be infectious. It's sticky, like walking through mud in rubbers. You can't set your foot down; then when you do you can't pull it out.

He covered up with a joke, "Well, now that you have your traveling expenses for the trip home, you'd better go home while you still can. This place is a bore."

Pouting like a child, Miss Sun said, "I really do feel like going home! I miss home every day. I even wrote my father saying how much I missed home. Next summer vacation is so far away; I get nervous just thinking about it."

"It's always like that the first time away from home. You'll get over it after a while. Have you talked with your department chairman yet?"

"I'm scared to death! Mr. Liu wants me to teach a section of English. I really can't do it! Mr. Liu said four classes of English have to be held concurrently, and since there are only three teachers in the department including himself, I'll have to take over one section. I really don't know how to teach. The students are all older than I, and they all look so tough."

"Just try teaching a little and you'll learn. I've never taught before either. The students can't be very advanced. Prepare your lessons thoroughly, and when you start teaching, you'll find your preparation is more than enough."

"The section I'm to teach had the worst scores on the English entrance examination. But, Mr. Fang, you don't know how miserable I am myself. I thought I'd come here and study hard for a year or two. They won't let the foreigner here teach and instead they want me to teach and lose face!"

"Who's the foreigner here?"

"You mean you didn't know? The wife of Mr. Han, who is the chairman of the History Department. I've never seen her, but Miss Fan says she's so thin she's nothing but bones and very ugly. Some people say she's a White Russian, but others insist she's a Jew who became a refugee after Austria was annexed to Germany. Her husband claims she's American. Mr. Han wanted her to be a professor in the Department of Foreign Languages, but Mr. Liu refused. Liu says she's not qualified because she can't speak any English, and now there's no need to teach German or Russian. Mr. Han was furious and said Mr. Liu isn't qualified and can't speak English either, saying further that Liu had put out a few middle school textbooks and muddled his way through a summer session abroad to get a certificate. He wondered who Liu thinks he is—the remarks really get nasty. Mr. Kao finally managed to break it up, but now Mr. Han is threatening to resign."

"No wonder he didn't show up the other day when the president had his party. Ai! You're really good. Where'd you get all that news?"

Miss Sun said with a laugh, "Miss Fan told me. This school is like a big family. Unless you live off campus you can't keep anything secret. And there's so much bickering going on. Yesterday Mr. Liu's sister arrived from Kweilin. Apparently she has a B.A. in history. Everyone's saying now Mr. Liu and Mr. Han can come to terms by trading a teaching assistant in the History Department for a professor in the Foreign Languages Department."

"But a sister is not as close as a wife, nor a teaching assistant as high as a professor," declaimed Hung-chien. "If I were your Mr. Liu, I would never accept such a rotten deal."

While he was speaking, Hsin-mei came in and said, "OK, I've seen those people out—Miss Sun, I knew you wouldn't leave right away."

He had meant nothing by this remark, but Miss Sun blushed. Hung-chien quickly told him about the affair involving Mrs. Han, adding, "Why are there so many political intrigues in a school? It's not even as straightforward as officialdom."

"Wherever you have a group of people living together, you'll have politics," said Hsin-mei, as though propagating a doctrine.

Miss Sun stayed for a while longer, then left.

Hsin-mei remarked, "I'll write her father declaring that I've turned my responsibility as guardian over to you, OK?"

"I think that subject has been 'worked to death' as the composition teachers would say," replied Hung-chien. "There's nothing more to be said about it. How about finding some new topic for a joke?"

Hsin-mei laughed at him for talking nonsense.

After the first week of classes, Hung-chien gradually became acquainted with some of his colleagues who lived in the same wing. Lu Tzu-hsiao of the History Department had paid him a very cordial, neighborly visit, so one afternoon Hung-chien returned the call. Lu was very meticulous about his clothes and always kept his hair slick and shiny. Afraid of having his hair buried by a hat, he would not "share the same sky with a hat"[4] and went bareheaded even in the dead of winter. His nose was short and wide, as though it had originally come straight downward but had received a head-on punch in the nostrils and, unable to come down further, had retreated by fanning out on both sides. Because he had never married, his attitude toward his age inevitably fell behind the times. At first he would give his full age according to the Western way of reckoning, but as the years went by, he secretly bought a translation of the book *Life Begins at Forty* and would simply not tell anyone his age nor give the animal sign of the year of his birth,[5] merely saying, "Oh, quite young! Still just a little kid!" and then acting lively and mischievous the way a little kid should. He liked to mutter furtively under his breath as though every remark he made were a military secret. Of course, he did know a few military secrets, for didn't he have a relative in the Executive Yüan[6] and a friend in the Ministry of Foreign Affairs? His relative had once sent him a letter. On the large envelope with "Executive Yüan" printed in the upper left-hand corner was written "Mr. Lu Tzu-hsiao" in large letters, making it look as though the Executive Yüan was all set to give him the major position at the center. Though the envelope for the letter he wrote to his friend in the Ministry of Foreign Affairs was not very big, the seven words "Ministry of Foreign Affairs, European-American Bureau" of the address were written in such bold, black, neatly penned characters that an illiterate should have been able to make them out at a single glance in the depths of night. These two pieces of incoming and outgoing mail alternately adorned his desk. Two days ago that morning the damned errand boy, while straightening up his room, had accidentally knocked over the ink bottle, making a blackened mess of the Executive Yüan. Too late to save it, Lu had jumped about screaming curses. Meanwhile, preoccupied with the nation, the relative forgot about his family and never wrote again. Caught up with foreign affairs, the friend had no time for domestic matters, and never sent a single reply. From then on, Lu could only write to the Executive Yüan, so the two letters on his desk were both outgoing mail. That day was the day for the letter to the Ministry of Foreign Affairs. Lu waited until Hung-chien had seen the envelope on his desk, then hurriedly put it away in his drawer, saying, "It's nothing. A friend is asking me to work at the Ministry of Foreign Affairs, and so I'm answering his letter."

Assuming this to be true, Hung-chien could not but express his reluctance to see him go and urge him to stay, saying, "Oh! So you're moving up! Will the president be willing to let you go?"

Lu repeatedly shook his head, saying, "None of that! I'm not interested in being an official. I'm replying with a flat refusal. The president treats people very well. He sent several telegrams urging me to come. Now that you all are here, and the school is gradually getting on its feet, how could I pull out and leave him in the lurch?"

Recalling his own talk with Kao Sung-nien, Hung-chien said with a sigh, "The president of course gives you special treatment. People like myself—"

Lu spoke so softly there was air produced but no sound, as though his thoughts were breathing. "Yes, the president does have that shortcoming.

He doesn't keep his word. I know your case was very unfair." This was said confidentially as though all four walls had ears secretly listening in.

Hung-chien had never thought that other people already knew about his case. Coloring slightly, he said, "My case was nothing special, but, Mr. Kao—I guess I learned a lesson."

"You can't say that! Associate professor is a little low, of course, but among associate professors, your salary is the highest."

"What? You mean the rank of associate professor is divided into grades?" Hung-chien was of a mind with Dr. Johnson of England in not distinguishing between the rank of a louse and a flea.

"It's divided into several grades. Take your traveling companion and our department colleague Ku Er-chien, for example. He's two grades lower than you. Or our department chairman, Mr. Han. He's a grade higher than Mr. Chao, while Mr. Chao is a grade higher than Liu Tung-fang of the Foreign Languages Department. There are quite a number of grades. This is your first job since returning from abroad, so you're not familiar with it."

It all suddenly became clear to Hung-chien. When he heard that he was higher than Ku Er-chien, he felt somewhat better and asked casually, "Why's your department chairman's salary so high?"

"Because he's a doctor, a Ph.D. I've never been to America, so I've never heard of the university he graduated from, but it's supposed to be quite famous. It's in New York, called Carleton University or something."

Hung-chien sat up in astonishment. It was as though someone had uncovered a secret of his, and he cried out, "Which university?"

"Carleton University. Do you know Carleton University?"

"Yes, I do! Humph, I also—" Hung-chien wished he could have bitten down on his tongue, but two words had already slipped out.

When Lu Tzu-hsiao realized that there was something more behind all this, like bamboo sprouts just barely revealing their pointed tips in the earth, he wanted to get right to the bottom of it. When Hung-chien wouldn't say, he grew even more suspicious and just wished he could have adopted the torture tactics of the special services to force out a confession.

Hung-chien returned to his room, angry and amused. Ever since the time Miss T'ang had interrogated him about buying a diploma, he had refused to think about his negotiations with the Irishman. He kept it firmly in mind that he was going to forget the whole matter. Whenever his thoughts veered off in that direction, he would hurriedly change his line of thinking, though not before he felt a twinge of shame. Lu's remarks just now, however, had been like a dose of medicine half easing the shame in his heart. Han Hsüeh-yü was telling his lie, and while they were not in collusion, it was as if having Han there lightened the charges of deception against himself.

Of course, this added a new uneasiness, but this kind of uneasiness was out in the open and exposed to the sunlight, not like the business of the bought diploma, every trace of which, like a corpse in a murder case, had to be hidden even from himself. The only way to lie and deceive was as Han Hsüeh-yü had done it. One had to have the courage to carry it all the way through. He was just no good at it. What a big fool—to have lied and still tried to maintain his honesty. If he had just gone boldly and brazenly ahead, he could at least have avoided Kao Sung-nien's bullying. Instead, he had ended up having to bear all at once the two opposite miseries of suffering wrong for his honesty and being humiliated by exposure as a cheat. He suddenly thought that lately he hadn't even been able to tell a lie. Then it struck him that lying was often a manifestation of joy and happiness as well as a form of creativity, like make-believe in the play of a child. When a person has a sense of well-being and his spirits are overflowing, he can ignore stubborn facts and joke about his present circumstances. When one really has fallen on hard times, he's not much good at lying.

A day later Han Hsüeh-yü came especially to pay a call. When he gave his name, Fang Hung-chien felt uneasy but was at the same time pleasantly disappointed. He had pictured Han Hsüeh-yü as arrogant and sly, but to his surprise Han was quiet and reticent. He thought perhaps Lu Tzu-hsiao had been mistaken or that Miss Sun must have put too much stock in rumor.

Slow-witted honesty was Han Hsüeh-yü's specialty. Modern man has two popular myths: first, that homeliness in a girl is a virtue, so that pretty girls do not have half as much intelligence or honor as ugly girls; and second, that if a man lacks eloquence, he must be virtuous, making deaf-mutes the most sincere and honest people. Perhaps because he has been taken in too often by speeches and propaganda, modern man has overreacted to the point where he thinks only those who never talk speak the truth upon opening their mouths, prompting all newly appointed officials to say in their homily, "Statesmanship does not lie in excessive talk," wishing they could just point to their mouth, their heart, and heaven and settle it all with these three gestures. Though Han Hsüeh-yü was not a deaf-mute, he did have a slight stutter. In order to cover his stuttering, he spoke little, slowly and with great effort, as though each word carried with it the weight of his entire personality. People who don't talk readily are apt to give others the impression that they are packed with wisdom, just as a locked, tightly sealed chest is assumed to be crammed with treasure.

When Kao Sung-nien saw Han in Kunming for the first time, Kao felt Han to be sincere and serene like a gentleman. Moreover, it was obvious from Han's premature baldness that his brain was so filled with knowledge it was bursting forth and crowding out his hair. When Kao took a look at Han's vitae and saw besides his doctoral degree the item: "Articles have appeared in such major American journals as *The Journal of History* and the *Saturday Review of Literature*," Kao could not help but give Han respect. Several people coming to Kao with letters of introduction had resumés stating that they had "lectured" abroad many times. Having studied in a small European country himself, Kao knew that often when one thought one was lecturing [literally, speaking on learning], the audience assumed he was learning to speak—a good chance to practice the foreign language. But to publish articles in major journals abroad—that took real talent and scholarship. When he asked Han if he could take a look at his works, the latter had replied calmly that the journals had been left at his old home in the occupied area, that any Chinese university should subscribe to these two journals, and that Kao should be able to find them easily nearby, unless some of the old issues in the library had been lost during the escape. Kao Sung-nien never thought a liar could be so calm and unruffled. The books of all universities were in disarray, and he wouldn't necessarily be able to find the particular issues. But there didn't seem to be any doubt that they did contain Han Hsüeh-yü's articles. Han Hsüeh-yü had in fact submitted articles to these journals, but Kao Sung-nien did not know that his articles had been published in the "Personals" column of the *Saturday Review of Literature*: "Well-educated Chinese youth wishes to assist Sinologists. Low rates"; and in the "Correspondence" column of *The Journal of History*: "Han Hsüeh-yü is seeking back issues of this journal from twenty years ago. Anyone wishing to sell please write to such and such an address." Finally when Kao heard that Mrs. Han was an American, he simply regarded Han with newfound respect. One had to be very well versed in Western learning to marry a foreign woman. Hadn't he himself tried without success to marry a Belgian girl in his youth? This man could be department chairman. He never thought at the time that the foreign wife was a White Russian that Han had wed in China.

Talking with Han Hsüeh-yü was like watching a movie in slow motion. You would never expect a terse remark could take so much preparation to mobilize such a complex physical machinery. His words brought time to a halt and it just had to drag itself slowly along. Han had an ashy complexion, which on a cloudy day could blend in perfectly with the color of the surrounding sky and make him invisible—a first-rate camouflage. The only distinctive feature about him was a large lump in his throat. When he spoke, the lump went up and down. Watching it, Hung-chien felt his own throat begin to itch. When Han stopped to swallow saliva, the lump would nearly disappear and then reappear again, reminding Hung-chien of a frog swallowing flies. Noticing how little Han spoke and how much effort it took, Hung-chien wished Han could have pulled out the Adam's apple like a stopper from a bottle and let the rest of his speech flow more freely.

Han invited Hung-chien over for dinner, and when Hung-chien had thanked him, Han still sat stiffly in his seat saying nothing.

Hung-chien was obliged to carry on the conversation. He asked, "I heard you married Mrs. Han in America."

Han nodded, stretched his neck, and swallowed some saliva. The saliva went down, and up floated a sentence from beneath the lump in his throat, "Have you ever been to America?"

"No, I've never been there—" *might as well test him out*—"but I once thought of going. I corresponded with a Dr. Mahoney." *Am I being oversensitive?* Han seemed to redden slightly, like the sun suddenly showing through on a cloudy day.

"The fellow's a swindler." Han's tone was in no way agitated. Nor did he say more.

"I know. What Carleton University? I was nearly taken in by him." Hung-chien was thinking, *if Han's willing to admit the Irishman is a "swindler," Han must know he can't put anything over on me.*

"You weren't taken in by him, were you? Carleton University is a good school. He was a junior employee who had been discharged. He used the name to cheat money out of ignorant people abroad. You really weren't taken in? Well, that's good, then."

"You mean there really is a school called Carleton? I thought it was all the work of that Irishman." Hung-chien sat up, surprised.

"A very serious, strict school, though very few people know about it—ordinary students have a hard time getting in."

"Mr. Lu said that you had graduated from that school."

"Yes."

Hung-chien was filled with suspicions and would really have liked to question Han in detail, but as it was their first meeting, he could not very well pin him down on it. That would only make it look as though he didn't believe Han. Besides, the man was so sparing with words, he'd never get anything out of him. The best thing would be to take a look at Han's diploma when he had the chance. Then he'd know for sure whether or not Han's Carleton University and his own Carleton University were one and the same.

On his way home Han Hsüeh-yü's legs felt slightly limp. Lu Tzu-hsiao's report was quite correct, he thought. This Fang fellow had had dealings with the Irishman. Luckily Fang had never been to America. He wished he knew whether Fang really hadn't bought a diploma. Fang could be lying.

Fang Hung-chien found the dinner at the Hans quite satisfactory. Though Han Hsüeh-yü did not say much, he was a thoughtful host. Mrs.

Han was very homely with her red hair and freckled face, which looked like flyspecks on a cake, but her manner was so lively that she seemed electrifying. Hung-chien had found from close study that Westerners are ugly in a different way from Chinese: Chinese ugliness seems to be the result of the Creator's having skimped on time and materials. It is a slapdash, perfunctorily put together ugliness. Westerners' ugliness seems a mark of the Creator's spite. He has purposely set out to play jokes with the facial features. The ugliness thus has a plan and a motive behind it.

Mrs. Han declared repeatedly how much she loved China, but then at the same time she would say that daily life in China was not as convenient as in New York. Hung-chien felt in the end that her accent was not genuine. He himself had never been to America, but if Chao Hsin-mei were there, he could have detected it. Maybe she had immigrated to New York. No one had been so attentive toward him since he came to the school.

His depression of the last few days gradually disappeared. Why should he care whether Han Hsüeh-yü's diploma was fake or not? he thought. In any case Han and he were good friends, and that was all that mattered. One thing bothered him, however. When Mrs. Han was talking about New York, Han Hsüeh-yü had signaled her with his eyes, which had not escaped his notice. It was as though he had overheard someone talking about him behind his back. Maybe he was just being oversensitive, and he'd better forget about it. In high spirits, he went straight over to see Hsin-mei.

"Old Chao, I'm back. Sorry about today—making you eat by yourself."

Since Han Hsüeh-yü had not invited him, Hsin-mei had eaten a cold, hard meal of the day by himself. The food he'd eaten soured his stomach, while what he hadn't eaten soured his thoughts. He said, "So our international VIP is back! Did you have a good dinner? Was it Chinese or Western food? Was the foreign wife a good hostess?"

"It was Chinese food that their maid cooked. Mrs. Han sure is ugly! You can find such an ugly wife in China, too. Why go abroad to search for such a treasure! Hsin-mei, I wish you'd been there today—"

"Humph, thanks. Who else was there today? Just you? Well, isn't that something! Han Hsüeh-yü ignores everyone else all the way from the president down to his own colleagues just to cater to you. Are you a relative of the foreign wife or something?" Hsin-mei couldn't stop laughing at his own jokes.

Inwardly pleased with all this, Hung-chien pretended to take umbrage, saying, "So an associate professor is a nobody, is he? Only you big department heads and professors are eligible to make friends with each other, are you? Seriously, Hsin-mei, if you'd been there today, we could have solved the question of Mrs. Han's nationality. You're an old America hand. If you'd

210

heard her speak and put a few questions to her, then the truth would have been out."

Though Hsin-mei found these remarks very agreeable, he still wasn't ready to look pleased.

"You really have no sense of gratitude. After eating their food, you still have to poke your nose around and try to pry into their secrets. As long as she's a woman, she can be a wife. What difference does it make if she's American or Russian? Are you trying to tell me if she were an American she'd be twice as much a woman? More efficient than others at having children?"

Hung-chien said with a smile, "I'm interested in Han Hsüeh-yü's academic credentials. I just have a feeling that if his wife's nationality is fake, then his academic credentials are open to question, too."

"Why don't you save yourself the trouble? Look, you can't get away with a lie. Ever since you pulled that trick, you've been oversuspicious of other people. I know the whole thing was a joke, but a joke can end up causing a lot of trouble! People like us who behave ourselves properly don't get so suspicious of everything."

"Oh, doesn't that just sound beautiful?" said Hung-chien crossly. "When I first told you Han Hsüeh-yü's salary was a grade higher than yours, why did you get so mad you wanted to throw away your cone-shaped hat?"[7]

"I'm not that small-minded. It's all your fault. You come to me with all these rumors you've heard. Otherwise, I have peace of mind and no reason to pick a quarrel with anybody."

Hsin-mei had learned a new pose. While listening to someone, he would recline in his chair with his eyes closed; only the smoke curling from the pipe at the corner of his mouth indicated he was not asleep. Hung-chien was already peeved at seeing him this way, and these last few remarks were more than he could take.

"All right, all right! I'd sooner die than argue with you."

Sensing that Hung-chien was really aroused, Hsin-mei quickly opened his eyes and said, "I was only joking. Don't get so mad that you upset your stomach. Here, have a cigarette. Later you probably won't be able to go to someone's house for dinner! Didn't you see the notice? Oh, of course, you couldn't have. There's a school administrative meeting the day after tomorrow to discuss the implementation of the tutorial system. I've heard the tutors will have to eat with the students."

Hung-chien returned dejectedly to his room. A rare moment of high spirits had to be ruined by a friend. Man was created to be lonely. Each one has to keep to himself and never have anything to do with anyone else to his dying day. When the body can't hold something, whether it be digested or eliminated, it is the individual's own business. So why does one have to seek out a companion to share the emotions his heart can't contain? When he's with other people, he is forever offending or being offended. As with porcupines, each one just has to keep a distance from the others. If they get close, this one will be sticking that one's flesh, or that one will be scraping this one's skin. Hung-chien really felt like unburdening these emotions to someone who could understand. Miss Sun seemed to understand him better than Hsin-mei. At least she listened with great interest to what he had to say—but then, if as he had just said, people should avoid contact with each other, how could he go seeking out a woman! Maybe when men are together they are like a herd of porcupines, while men together with women are like—Hung-chien couldn't think what they were like, and he opened his notebook to prepare for the next day's class.

Hung-chien was still teaching three hours of class. Whenever other faculty members began talking about his teaching load, they never failed to tell him to his face how much they envied his leisure. It seemed Kao Sung-nien had his own motives for giving him special treatment. Hung-chien had never studied logic before and had no reference books handy. Though he worked hard at preparing, he found no interest in it, and the students in his class were there for the credits only. According to the school regulations, students in the College of Letters and Law had to choose one course among Physics, Chemistry, Biology, and Logic. Most of them swarmed like bees to Logic, because it was the easiest—"It's all rubbish"—and not only did they not have to conduct experiments, but when it was cold, they could stick their hands in their sleeves and not take notes. They chose it because it was easy, and because it was easy, they looked down on it the way men look down on easy-to-get women. Logic was "rubbish," and so naturally the person teaching logic was a piece of "trash." He was "nothing but an associate professor," who belonged to no department besides. In their eyes, Hung-chien's position was not much higher than that of instructors of party ideology or military drill. But those teaching party ideology and military drill had been sent by a government agency. Hung-chien didn't have as much status as they did. "I've heard he's Chao Hsin-mei's cousin. He came with him. Kao Sung-nien just hired him as a lecturer, but Chao Hsin-mei wangled an associate professorship for him." No wonder Hung-chien always had the feeling that the students in his class did not take his lectures very seriously. In that kind of atmosphere teaching could hardly be very exciting. What made it worse was that logic was so dry and tasteless at the start. It wasn't until he got to the third stage of dialectics that he could spice it up with a few jokes. In the meantime there was no way to make it more palatable.

Besides this there were two other things which disturbed Hung-chien.

One was calling the roll. He recalled that among the prominent professors he had had, none of them ever called roll or reported student absences. This was how a great scholar went about it: "If you want to listen, then come listen. It's all the same to me." Overcome with admiration, he could not but imitate them. At the first class Hung-chien was like Adam in the *Book of Genesis* calling out the names of the newly created animals. After that, he didn't even bring his roll book. By the second week he discovered that of the fifty-odd students, seven or eight were absent. Those empty seats were like the empty gaps in a mouth after several teeth have been lost. They gave one an uncomfortable feeling. The next time he noticed that while the women students were holding firmly to their original seats in the first row, the men students seemed to have taken the seats starting from the back, leaving the second row empty. One student sat all by himself in the third row. As Hung-chien was surveying this formation, the men students all grinned mischievously and lowered their heads. Following his glance the women students turned and glanced back, then looked around at him and smiled. He at least managed to refrain from commenting, "Obviously my power to repel you is greater than the women's power to attract you." After that he decided he would just have to take roll. At this rate there'd be no one left to listen to him but the desks and chairs, which had feet but were without the power to run away. But then, how humiliating it was suddenly to go from the permissiveness of a great scholar to the tediousness of a grade school teacher! These students were not to be outfoxed. They had seen through his intention.

The other thing was the lectures. It was like trying to make clothes out of a piece of material that is not big enough. He thought he had prepared sufficient material, only to find when he got to class that as he spoke, it shrank away faster than he could stop it. When he had just about reached the end of his notes, the dismissal bell was still a long way off. An empty stretch of time in which there was nothing to say approached like a white torrent of rushing water heading toward a car driven at full throttle. He stood watching in panic with no place to escape. His thoughts in turmoil, he searched desperately for something to say to fill in, but after a few sentences it was all finished. He stole a glance at his watch and found that he had delayed only half a minute. At that point he turned hot all over, his face flushed slightly, and he began to stutter, certain that the students were all secretly laughing at him. Once, just like a man given a laxative after going hungry for a few days, he could not even squeeze anything out no matter how hard he tried, and he just had to dismiss class a quarter of an hour early. When he talked to Hsin-mei about it, he found that Hsin-mei had the same problem and said that after all, someone just starting to teach had no experience. Hsin-mei added, "Now I understand why foreigners say 'kill time' to mean beat the few moments of misery before the bell! I really wish I could chop it in two with one blow."

Hung-chien had just recently hit upon a way, if not to kill time instantly, at least to inflict it with a few mortal wounds. He was forever writing on the blackboard. It took as much time to write one word on the blackboard as it did to speak ten. His face and hands would be covered with chalk dust, and his arm would be sore for a while, but it was all worth it. At least he wouldn't have to dismiss class early any more. The students, however, did not put much effort into taking notes. Often when he threw all his energy into lecturing, some of them just sat there without writing down a word. Only after he began to stare at them menacingly did they finally take pen in hand and reluctantly draw a few characters in their notebooks. This annoyed him, though he didn't think he could be as bad as Li Mei-t'ing. But next door in Li Mei-t'ing's class on "The History of Social Customs of the Ch'in and Han," the students' laughter never ceased, while his own class was always dull and lifeless.

When he was in school, he thought, he wasn't such a bad student. So why was he so undistinguished as a teacher? Surely teaching wasn't something like writing poetry, which required a "special talent"? He regretted not having picked up an expert's title while studying abroad. Then when he came back, he could awe everyone with his authority, giving a few courses from his collection of notes taken in all his foreign professors' classes. He wouldn't have to hang around doing odd jobs the way he was now, taking charge of the leftover subjects. People like Li Mei-t'ing, who had been teaching for years, had ready-made lecture notes. He himself had no experience or even any preparation, and was teaching a course that was not of his own choice. If he wanted to consult references, there were no books available, so of course he couldn't teach very well. If he could just make it through this year and Kao Sung-nien kept his promise to promote him to professor, then in the summer when he returned to Shanghai, he could get some foreign books to look over and by next school year he could surely do just as well as Li Mei-t'ing. With these thoughts in mind, Hung-chien regained his self-confidence.

In the year since Hung-chien had come back, he had drifted away from his father. In the old days he would always report every last detail to his father. Now he could just imagine what that reply would be. If his father were in a good mood, he would console him with such words as "Sometimes a foot is too short and an inch is too long. A scholar doesn't necessarily make a good teacher." It was enough to make one cringe with shame. If his father were in a bad mood, he would undoubtedly rebuke him for not having studied harder before and only cramming everything in at the last minute. There might even be admonitions about "Repairing the fold after the sheep are lost," or "One learns as one teaches." This was what the students had to listen to during the weekly Commemoration Assembly.[8] He had heard enough of it already as a faculty member. There was no need to have it sent in from hundreds of miles away.

The day before the administrative meeting was to be held, Hung-chien and Hsin-mei decided to go to town for dinner, afraid that once the tutorial system was put into effect they would no longer have that time. That afternoon Lu Tzu-hsiao dropped by for a chat and asked Hung-chien if he heard about Miss Sun. When Hung-chien asked him what had happened, Lu replied, "If you don't know about it, then never mind."

Knowing Lu's ways, Hung-chien didn't press him. After a moment Lu Tzu-hsiao stared sharply at Hung-chien as though trying to peer through him and said, "You really don't know? How could that be?" Then enjoining him to keep it strictly confidential, he told him the whole story. As soon as the Office of Instruction had announced that Miss Sun was going to teach Section Four English, the Section Four students had called an emergency meeting and sent a representative to the president and the dean to protest it. Their reason was this: Since they were all students, those in charge should not discriminate. Why were the other sections taught by associate professors while Section Four was assigned to a teaching assistant? They knew their level wasn't very high, and that was why, they argued with righteous indignation, they deserved a good professor to teach them. Thanks to Kao Sung-nien's skill, the turmoil had been quelled. The students had no fear of Miss Sun, however, the discipline in the classroom was rather poor, and the compositions they wrote for her were simply atrocious. Miss Sun asked the Foreign Languages Department Chairman Liu for permission to have the Section Four students practice writing sentences instead of compositions. When the students learned of that, they fussed and asked Miss Sun why when other people were writing compositions, they were making sentences and being treated like high school students. She had said, "Because you can't write compositions," to which they replied, "We can't write compositions, so we should be learning how to." She could get nowhere with them and had to ask Chairman Liu to come explain things to them before the matter was finally settled.

It was composition day. When Miss Sun entered the classroom, she saw written on the board [in English]: "*Beat down Miss S. Miss S. is Japanese enemy!*" The students were all waiting expectantly with grins on their faces. Miss Sun asked them to make sentences, but they all said they hadn't brought any paper and would only do oral exercises. When she asked one student to make a sentence in each of the three persons singular and plural, the student rattled off in one breath as if reciting, *"I am your husband you are my wife he is also your husband we are your many husbands—"* The whole class roared with laughter, and Miss Sun stalked out in a rage. There was no knowing how the matter would end. Lu Tzu-hsiao further declared, "That student is in the Chinese Literature Department. I gave the students in our History Department a private talk, urging them not to make trouble in Miss Sun's class. It might make people think Mr. Han wanted his wife to teach that section and was inciting the students to chase Miss Sun out."

"I didn't know anything about it," said Hung-chien. "I haven't seen Miss Sun for a long time. So that's what's been happening."

Lu threw Hung-chien another sharp glance and said, "I thought you saw a lot of each other."

Just as Hung-chien was saying, "Who told you that?" Miss Sun walked in. Lu quickly got up and offered her his seat. On his way out, he cocked his head to one side and gave Hung-chien a nod to show that he had caught him in his lie. Hung-chien, who didn't take the time to pay attention, quickly asked Miss Sun how she'd been lately. Abruptly turning her face away, she covered her mouth with her handkerchief. Her shoulders heaved and she burst into sobs. Hung-chien rushed out to call Hsin-mei, but when they came in, she had stopped crying. When Hsin-mei had gotten the matter straight, he comforted her for a long time with kind words, which were echoed by Hung-chien.

"Students like that must be dealt with severely," said Hsin-mei vehemently. "I'll go talk to the president about it this evening. Have you reported this to Mr. Liu?"

Hung-chien said, "It's not just a question of reprimanding the students. Miss Sun can't go on teaching that class. You should ask the president to find someone else to take over her class and declare that the school has been unfair to Miss Sun."

Miss Sun said, "I'd rather die than teach that class. I really want to go home," she sobbed.

Hsin-mei quickly said it was a small matter and invited her and Hung-chien to join him for dinner. While she was thinking about the invitation, a messenger came from the president's office asking for Hsin-mei. Kao Sung-nien was giving a reception for the inspector from the Ministry of Education. All department chairmen had to attend, and he was asking Hsin-mei to go to the reception immediately.

"What a nuisance!" said Hsin-mei. "We won't be able to have our dinner today," and he left with the messenger.

Hung-chien unenthusiastically invited Miss Sun out for dinner. She suggested they go some other day, as she wanted to return to the dormitory. When Hung-chien noticed how pale she was and that her eyes were puffy and bore all the telltale marks of crying, he asked her if she wanted to wash her face. Without waiting for her to reply, he took out a fresh towel and pulled out the stopper from the thermos bottle. While she was washing her face, Hung-chien gazed out the window, thinking how Hsin-mei would misconstrue this if he knew about it. When he had given her what he thought was ample time to wash her face, he turned around and discovered that she had opened her purse and was looking in the mirror and putting on powder and lipstick. He gave a start. He had never thought she went around so well equipped with makeup; he had always thought that her unadorned face was a work of art by itself.

When Miss Sun had finished fixing her face, her eyelids, reddened from crying and set off by the color on her cheeks and mouth, looked as though they too had been touched with rouge. It lent an air of unexpected wantonness to her innocent face. As he was seeing her out, Hung-chien passed by Lu Tzu-hsiao's room. Lu was sitting in his room smoking with his door half opened. When Lu caught sight of the two of them, he quickly stood up and nodded, then sat back down again as though he were attached to a spring. They had not gone more than a few steps when they heard someone calling them from behind. They turned around and saw Li Mei-t'ing, beaming triumphantly. He told them that Kao Sung-nien had just asked him to serve as dean of students, and the appointment would be formally announced the next day. He was now on his way to the social room to welcome the inspector from the Ministry of Education. Giving Miss Sun a close scrutiny with his dark glasses as though surveying her through a telescope, he said laughingly, "Miss Sun is getting prettier and prettier! Why don't you come see me instead of just going to see Mr. Fang? When are you two getting engaged—"

Hung-chien hissed at him, and he ran off laughing.

Hung-chien had just returned to his room, when Lu Tzu-hsiao came in and said, "Why, I thought you and Miss Sun had gone out for dinner together. What happened?"

Hung-chien replied, "It's beyond my means. I'm not like you big professors. I'll wait for you to do the inviting."

Lu said, "I'll invite her if I want to. What difference does it make? I'm afraid she might not do me the honor."

"Who? Miss Sun? I can see you're quite concerned about her. Taken a liking to her, have you? Ha, ha. Let me introduce you."

"Don't be silly! If I wanted to get married, I'd have done so a long time ago. Ai, 'He who has seen a great ocean is not easily content with a pond!'"

Hung-chien said with a laugh, "Who told you to be so choosy? Miss Sun's very nice. I made the trip here with her, and I can vouch for her disposition."

"If I wanted to get married, I'd have done so a long time ago," he repeated, like a record player with its needle stuck in a groove.

"No harm in just meeting her."

Lu peered suspiciously at Hung-chien and said, "Aren't you on pretty close terms with her yourself? Taking away someone else's girl is something I wouldn't do. Nor would I pick up what someone else has let go."

"Of all the nerve! You are really low."

Lu quickly said he was only kidding and promised to invite Hung-chien out for dinner in a few days. After Lu Tzu-hsiao left, Hung-chien began to think how funny it was. Miss Sun would certainly be happy if she knew someone was adoring her. The news might cheer her up. But then Lu didn't seem worthy of her. She wouldn't go for someone like him. It'd be best if she went ahead and got married. All the frustrations she had to put up with in her job just weren't worth it. Those students really were impossible— enough to give you a headache. The slogans they had written on the board were quite grammatical, though. She should take that as a consolation. When she'd calmed down, he'd tease her about it.

Hsin-mei returned from dinner reeking of alcohol and asked Hung-chien, "Did you ever go to Oxford or Cambridge when you were in England? What's their tutorial system like?"

Hung-chien replied that he had taken a trip to Oxford and spent a day there, but didn't know in detail how the tutorial system worked. He asked Hsin-mei why he wanted to know.

Hsin-mei replied, "Today's guest of honor, the inspector, is an expert on the tutorial system. Last year he was sent to England by the Ministry of Education to study it and stayed at both Oxford and Cambridge."

Hung-chien said with a laugh, "How can there be an expert on the tutorial system? Wouldn't any student at Oxford or Cambridge know a lot more about it? All those people in charge of education can ever do is try to impress everyone with fancy names. By the same token, there should be experts on studying abroad and experts on being a university president."

"I don't agree with you," said Hsin-mei. "I think the educational system is just as worth studying as the bureaucratic system. For instance, not all the government officials are necessarily informed of its strengths and weaknesses."

"All right, I won't argue with you. We all know you teach political science. Tell me, what did this expert have to say? Does his visit have something to do with the meeting tomorrow?"

"The tutorial system is a new policy of the Ministry of Education.

218

They're telling every university to put it into effect, but apparently the response hasn't been very good. Our President Kao here is most enthusiastic about carrying it out—Oh, I forgot to tell you. 'Blind Man Li' is now the dean of students. Ai, you knew it already. The inspector will advise us on it while he's here. He's going to attend tomorrow's meeting, but what he said today wasn't especially brilliant. According to him, the tutorial system at Oxford and Cambridge has a lot of weaknesses. It's a long way off from the ideal of having students and teachers sharing a community life. The plan we put in effect will be one which has undergone his improvements and the ministry's approval. At Oxford and Cambridge each student has two tutors, an academic tutor and a morals tutor. He thinks that goes against educational principles. A teacher should be a 'learned scholar and a man of virtue' with character and scholarship both. Therefore each person is assigned one tutor who is a professor in his own department. That way scholarship and moral virtue can be combined. The British morals tutor is a tutor in name only. If the student gets into trouble on the street and is hauled away by the police, the tutor goes to the police station and bails him out. If the student owes a shop money and can't pay it, he acts as guarantor for him. The responsibility of our kind of tutor is much greater. He has to investigate, correct, and report to the authorities on the student's thinking anytime, anywhere. That's how the regulations go. We can skip that, but there's another point he's very proud of. British tutors talk with the students while smoking their pipes. This goes completely against the spirit of the New Life Movement, so we are absolutely forbidden to smoke in front of the students and we should give up smoking altogether—and yet he hasn't himself. He smoked merrily away on all the cigarettes provided by the restaurant, and even pocketed a box of matches on his way out. British teachers take their meals with the students but sit at separate tables. They sit on a platform while eating so that students and teachers are cut off from each other. That too has to be changed. From now on we're to eat all three meals a day at the same table with the students—"

"Why not just go ahead and sleep in the same bed with the students!"

Hsin-mei said with a laugh, "I nearly suggested that at the time. You still haven't heard what 'Blind Man Li' had to say! He began by flattering the inspector, then said something about how the civilized nations of China and the West are all very strict about keeping the sexes separate. Love between student and teacher undermines the authority of the teacher and the student's respect for him. Since this is so deplorable, in order to prevent any such thing from happening, unmarried teachers should not be tutors for women students. It was so annoying, and they all looked at me and laughed —you see, of all those deans and department chairmen I'm the only one who isn't married."

"Ha, ha, that's great! But if there's danger of a love affair between an unmarried teacher and the woman student he's tutoring, then there's just as much likelihood of adultery when a married teacher tutors a woman student. He didn't mention that."

"I asked him whether married men who hadn't brought their wives along could tutor women students or not. He mumbled something and told me not to get him wrong. That 'Blind Man' is a real bastard. One of these days I'm going to spread around the stories about Wang Mei-yü and that Soochow widow who traveled with us. Oh, and there's another thing. He said that men and women faculty members should not have too much contact with each other. It would give the students a bad impression."

"That clearly refers to Miss Sun and me," exclaimed Hung-chien. " 'Blind Man' just saw us together."

Hsin-mei said, "It doesn't necessarily refer to you. I noticed Kao Sung-nien's expression changed at that moment. There must be something behind it. But I think you should propose, get engaged, and married as soon as possible. That way 'Blind Man' won't be able to gossip. And—" he raised his hand, grinning broadly as he spoke—"you'll have the chance to commit adultery if you want."

To stop him from uttering any more nonsense, Hung-chien asked if he had talked with Kao Sung-nien about the student who had insulted Miss Sun. Hsin-mei said that Kao knew all about it and was planning to expel the student. Hung-chien then told him that Lu Tzu-hsiao was interested in Miss Sun. Hsin-mei replied that as her "uncle" he approved only of Hung-chien. They joked for a while; then as Hsin-mei was leaving, he said, "Oh, I forgot the most interesting part. There's one item in the proposed tutorial system promulgated by the ministry that states that after the student has graduated, if he commits any criminal act in society, the tutor will be held responsible!"

Hung-chien was dumbfounded. Hsin-mei went on, "Just think, the tutorial system is turning into that sort of thing. When the Ming Emperor Ch'eng-tsu executed ten branches of Fang Hsiao-ju's clan,[9] it's said that even Fang Hsiao-ju's teacher was put to death. Will there be anyone who still dares teach in the future? I'm certainly going to oppose it at tomorrow's meeting."

"Hell! What I saw of the Nazi Party's educational system when I was in Germany wasn't even that bad. Is that supposed to be part of the Oxford-Cambridge tutorial system?"

"Humph, Kao Sung-nien even wants me to write an article in English and submit it to a foreign journal, so Westerners can see that we have the Oxford-Cambridge atmosphere, too. For some reason all the good things from abroad always go out of whack when they come to China."

220

Hsin-mei sighed, not knowing that this is China's special talent, something for which she is unrivaled. Anything coming from abroad is always destroyed.

Hung-chien said, "You were always telling me how smart your former teacher Kao was. Now that I've come and seen him in action, I don't find him so brilliant at all."

Hsin-mei said, "Maybe I was too young and inexperienced then to judge him correctly. But I think Kao Sung-nien has come up in the world these last few years. When a person gets in a high position, he's apt to get carried away." He didn't realize that a person's shortcomings are just like a monkey's tail. When it's squatting on the ground, its tail is hidden from view, but as soon as it climbs a tree, it exposes its backside to everyone. Nevertheless, the long tail and red bottom were there all the time. They aren't just a mark of having climbed to a higher position.

The Chinese Literature major who had made trouble for Miss Sun was dealt with in this manner: Chairman Liu of the Foreign Languages Department favored dismissing him, but Chairman Wang Ch'u-hou of the Chinese Department was opposed to it. Chao Hsin-mei, because of his personal relationship with Miss Sun, was willing to help out but not to act on her behalf, and had merely supported Liu Tung-fang's position from behind the scenes. Li Mei-t'ing, the Dean of Students, stepped in to break the deadlock. Li held that the student's rudeness resulted from not having received a tutor's guiding influence, and he had therefore remained in ignorance. One who did not know any better was blameless and should be excused. The case could be settled by giving him a demerit. Li called the student in to his room and thoroughly lectured the student for some time, telling him how everyone had wanted to dismiss him, that Wang Ch'u-hou could do nothing for him, and that thanks entirely to Li, he was not dismissed. With moist eyes, the student expressed his gratitude.

Meanwhile there was no one to take over Miss Sun's class, and so Liu Tung-fang, afraid that Mrs. Han might seize the chance to step in, took over the class himself, deploring that at a national university, unlike a private one, the salary was fixed and bore no relationship to the number of hours a person taught. After taking over the class for a week, he grew tired of it, thinking how foolish he had been. His time and energy were being wasted and would never earn him a single kind word. If the school really could not find a substitute, then it would have been obvious that as department chairman he was acting for the sake of the students in taking the extra course and all the chores himself. But now when there was a Mrs. Han around, for him to take over the class himself, thereby occupying two seats with one posterior, everyone could see it was a selfish act. No one would give him credit even if he worked himself to death. Chao Hsin-mei was known among the faculty members for his English, and Chao had only six hours of class. If he had a friendly chat with Chao and asked Chao to take over Miss Sun's class, mightn't Chao agree? After all, hadn't Miss Sun come on Chao's recommendation? If she was so incompetent as a teacher, shouldn't the one who had recommended her take the responsibility? Of course Chao Hsin-mei's English was apparently better than his own—Liu Tung-fang could not but admit that—but then the English of the Section Four students was too poor to tell the difference, and they were all students from other departments anyway. His prestige in his own department would not be affected. His mind made up, Liu first put the suggestion to Kao Sung-nien, who then asked Chao Hsin-mei to come in for a conference. Because of his relationship with Miss Sun, Hsin-mei could not very well give a flat refusal, but then in a sudden inspiration he recommended Fang Hung-chien.

The president said, "Hmm, that's a good idea. Mr. Fang has too few hours to begin with. How is his English? I wonder."

"Oh, very good," said Hsin-mei confidently, thinking that Hung-chien would be more than qualified to teach these students.

Hung-chien had felt his position in the school was not very secure, and so after Hsin-mei had explained it all to him and Liu Tung-fang had earnestly asked him, he screwed up his courage, braced himself, and cautiously prepared to teach English. As soon as this was announced, Han Hsüeh-yü went to see Kao Sung-nien, declaring that his wife had no wish to teach English, that he bore Liu Tung-fang no ill will, and that he would like to hire Miss Liu as a teaching assistant in the History Department.

Kao Sung-nien was delighted and said, "Faculty members should unite and help each other. We'll certainly hire your wife to help us next school year."

Han Hsüeh-yü replied haughtily, "Whether I stay on next year or not is still a question. I've had five or six letters from T'ung-i University asking me and my wife to go there."

Kao Sung-nien quickly urged him to stay, saying that next school year he would work out something for his wife.

When Hung-chien went to the Foreign Languages Department office to discuss the classwork, he saw Miss Sun there and said jokingly in a low tone, "You're the one who got me into all this. Want me to avenge you?"

Miss Sun smiled but made no reply. Lu Tzu-hsiao did not mention his dinner invitation again.

At the meeting on the tutorial system the inspector from the ministry opened with an elegant ten-minute speech in which the phrase "When I was in England" came up on the average of one and a half times per minute. When he was through speaking, he glanced at his watch and left. The audience let out various-sized coughs that they had been holding in their

222

throats, making a continuous *ahem, ke, ke, ke*. At Chinese meetings, after three minutes of silence and after the chairman has made his announcements, one usually hears this burst of coughing. Besides letting out a few token coughs, everyone shifted to a slightly more comfortable position. Kao Sung-nien was the next speaker and inevitably elaborated on the relationship between the cell and the organism for the umpteenth time, expressing his hope that everyone would sacrifice his own personal convenience for the sake of the group at large. Next Li Mei-t'ing read the general outline promulgated by the ministry along with the detailed regulations he had drafted. He offered them for discussion.

Very little of what is said at meetings is related to the approval of or opposition to a particular motion. Some oppose the resolution because of a difference of opinion with the person making it. Others approve the resolution because they do not get along with those opposing it. Some go along because of their connections with the people opposing or approving it. That day's discussion, however, was different from the usual, even to the extent that both Liu Tung-fang and Han Hsüeh-yü opposed the resolution. The rule regarding tutors and students dining together was unanimously protested, those with families voicing the strongest opposition. The Physics Department chairman, who had not brought his family with him, said that they would not even consider the resolution unless the school paid for the tutors' meals. Wang Ch'u-hou, whose home cooking was famous, said that even if the school did pay for the tutors' meals, their families had to cook just the same, and that one less person eating made no difference in the cost of fuel and rice. Han Hsüeh-yü said that with his stomach trouble he could eat only noodles and bread. If he had to eat rice with the students, was the school ready to guarantee his health? Li Mei-t'ing insisted that this was the regulation as promulgated by the ministry and that, at the most, Saturday dinner and all three meals on Sunday could be exempted. The chairman of the Mathematics Department then asked Li how the tutors were to be divided among the tables. This had Li stymied.

There were more than forty professors, associate professors, and lecturers qualified to be tutors, while the 130-odd male students were not enough to make up twenty tables. If there were one tutor and six students at each table, that would leave twenty tutors unable to eat with the students. If there were one tutor and seven students at each table, the tutor would be too far outnumbered to maintain proper respect and would gradually incur the students' contempt. If they tried having two tutors and four students per table, considering that the food was said to be inadequate for the present eight to a table, decreasing the number of people and increasing the number of tables would only make matters worse. Was the school prepared to subsidize the food costs? With the help of figures, they became even more convinced of the righteousness of their cause, getting Li Mei-t'ing so flustered that he couldn't speak. He took off his black glasses, then put them back on, then took them off, looking over wide-eyed at Kao Sung-nien. At this juncture Chao Hsin-mei gave his view that the students too should have freedom in how they ate, and they should unite with other universities to protest the tutorial system.

In the end the original draft was considerably revised. It was decided that each tutor would eat at least two meals with the students every week according to a schedule drawn up by the office of the Dean of Students. Because the inspector from the ministry had said that at Oxford and Cambridge the teachers gave a blessing in Latin before and after each meal, Kao Sung-nien felt they should do the same. But since China, unlike England, had no Christian god to hear the prayers of the world below, there was nothing to say before and after meals. Li Mei-t'ing racked his brains, but could only come up with the line, "Give thought to the toil behind each bowl of rice and gruel." Everyone roared with laughter at this.

The chairman of the Economics Department, the father of a large brood of children, muttered, "Just say what my son says: 'Before eating, don't run about. After eating, don't jump and shout.' "

Kao Sung-nien fixed him with a cold stare and said solemnly, "I think that before everyone sits down to eat, if the Dean of Students led the students in a minute of silence to reflect on the hardships of the people during the War of Resistance and what we could do to repay the country and the society for enjoying our fill, that would be a very meaningful gesture."

The Economics Department chairman said quickly, "I'd like to move the president's suggestion."

Li Mei-t'ing seconded the motion. Kao Sung-nien put it to a vote and it was passed unanimously. Li Mei-t'ing, whose mind was always busily at work, anticipated that many of the professors would put down their chopsticks after eating half a bowl of rice with the students and slip out of the dining hall to go home and eat in comfort, so he made the following dining hall regulations: The tutors' bowls were to be filled with rice by the students first, and the students were to wait for the tutors to finish eating before tutors and students left the dining hall together. To all appearances this was done out of respect for the tutors. In addition, no one was to speak while eating. Eating in silence, a person had to keep his grievances to himself.

As soon as Li Mei-t'ing became dean of students, he had given up smoking and made a rule prohibiting smoking, but when he saw that the faculty members continued to smoke as much as ever and set a poor example for the students, he thought up a new scheme to assure the collective observance of the rule by teachers and students. Knowing that smoking was done mostly in the bathrooms, under the pretext that the bathrooms were too small for the large number of students, yet too big for the small number of faculty members living in the dormitories, he ruled that henceforth the bathrooms could be used by both students and faculty. He thought that under these circumstances students and faculty would both be less apt to smoke as they pleased, in order to keep up appearances. The result, however, was that the professors did not use the students' bathrooms, while the students crowded into the professors' bathrooms, brazenly smoking to dispel the odor, for they knew that this was a place more tightly guarded than the Forbidden City[10] itself. It was a place where, as Westerners say, His Majesty the Emperor must go in person and cannot send a representative (*Ou les rois ne peuvent aller qu'en personne*). Here everyone kept to himself, and no one would be meddlesome or put on tutorial airs.

The tutors dutifully talked with their tutees once a week. Some professors, such as Wang Ch'u-hou, Han Hsüeh-yü, and others, took the opportunity to invite them over for tea or dinner. Chao Hsin-mei found it all quite disgusting, and told Hung-chien he had been a fool to come, and that next school year he'd quit for sure.

Hung-chien said, "Before coming, you said something to me about teaching being the beginning of political activity, and in teaching one was training cadres. Now somehow you've lost interest."

Hsin-mei denied ever having said such things, but at Hung-chien's insistence, he said, "Well, maybe I did say that, but what I wanted to train was people, not machines. Besides, what was true then isn't true now. I didn't have any teaching experience then, so I said things like that. Now that I know what Chinese wartime higher education is all about, I've learned my lesson. Of course, my progress has been in learning to sail with the wind. Talk is talk, and man can change. Man should never be restricted by what he says. Rather, what he says should change with him. If he makes a statement and acts accordingly without deviating in any way, then there'd be no such things as breaking a contract, reneging, or apologizing."

Hung-chien said, "No wonder your esteemed teacher Mr. Kao sent me a telegram appointing me as professor, then gave me only an associate professorship when I got here."

"But don't forget," said Hsin-mei, "at first he only agreed to give you three hours, and now it's been increased to six. Sometimes a person doesn't mean to lie, but after he's spoken, the situation changes, giving him no other choice but to modify his original intention. Administrators especially find it hard to keep their word. You need only read in the newspaper every day what government spokesmen of all nations say, to see that. For instance, if I agree on something with somebody and even go so far as to sign a contract with him, no matter whether it says ten or twenty years in the contract, my motive in making it is based on my present hopes, understanding, and needs. But 'the present' is so unreliable. If that 'present' has already fallen behind the times, even if the contract clearly states, 'until the last day of the world,' it's all useless. We can renege on it any time. During the First World War, what's his name?—the German prime minister—said, as you know, that treaties are waste paper. My impression is that everything we say in society is just like a theater ticket. It has the words 'Invalid after date,' printed on the edge, but there's no date marked on it. It can be changed to whatever date we want."

Hung-chien said, "Wow! And you seemed like a real gentleman, someone who'd be a true friend. I never thought you were so unethical. From now on I'll have to watch what you say."

When Hsin-mei heard this backhanded compliment, he swung his head around in triumph and said, "That's what you call learning! I graduated first in my class in political science. Huh, I know all the tricks politicians play. I just don't care to do them now, that's all." From the way he spoke it sounded as if the spirit of Machiavelli had taken hold of him.

Hung-chien said with a smile, "Don't brag. Your politics seems to be nothing but theory. If you were really asked to put aside your conscience and do that, you wouldn't. You're like the dog described by foreigners: It's all bark and no bite."

Hsin-mei opened his mouth, and assuming a ferocious expression, bared two rows of strong, even teeth at Hung-chien. Hung-chien quickly stuffed a cigarette into Hsin-mei's mouth.

After his teaching load had been increased, Hung-chien regained much of his enthusiasm. When he discovered that in his Section Four English class there were three Section One auditing students who were always diligently asking questions, he was quite pleased with the fact and told Hsin-mei about it. The hard work, he felt, was in correcting the sentences. It is like washing dirty clothes. As soon as one batch is cleaned, in comes the next one just as dirty as the first. Most of the students took a look at their score, then threw away the assignment. The headache he had gotten from correcting them was all in vain.

Despite their poor command of English, the students had impressive foreign names. There was an Alexander, an Elizabeth, a Dick, a "Florrie." One called himself "Bacon" because his Chinese name was "P'ei-ken." Another student, whose family name was Huang and given name Po-lun, had the poet's name "Byron" as his English name. When Hsin-mei saw this, he said with a smile, "If his family name had been Chang, he would have given himself the name Chamberlain, the English prime minister. And if his name had been Chi, he could have become the German plane Zeppelin, or even called himself Napoleon if there had just been a Chinese family name close to 'Na.'" Hung-chien said that the way Chinese adopted foreign names always reminded him of the British sow and cow. As soon as their meat got on a menu, they went under a French name.

The New Year holidays were already over and the final examinations were to be held a week later. One evening Hsin-mei and Hung-chien discussed plans for a trip to Kweilin together during the winter vacation. They talked on until quite late in the night. When Hung-chien looked at his watch and saw that it was already past one o'clock, he hurriedly got ready for bed. First he went out of the dormitory to go to the toilet. Upstairs and downstairs in the dormitory everyone was sound asleep. His footsteps seemed to be treading on these sleepers' dreams. The metal-plated heels of his leather shoes were so heavy that they could have broken their brittle dreams to pieces. The ground outside was frost covered. Only a few bamboo leaves remained, and every now and then a chill wind blew, wasting so much useless energy just to blow a few small leaves around for people. Though there was no moon, the bare branches of a few plane trees[11] were as sharp and clean as fish spines. Only one vegetable oil lamp hung in front of the toilet. Its muddy light dotted the clear winter night with a speck of grime. The toilet's breath seemed to be afraid of the cold too, shrinking inside the room not daring to come out; while in the summer it kept sentries posted far away.

Before he entered, Hung-chien heard people talking inside. One said, "What's the matter? You've had the runs several times tonight!"

Another groaned, "It's from something I ate today at the Hans."

Hung-chien recognized the voice as that of one of the auditors in his English class.

The first speaker said, "How come Han Hsüeh-yü is always having you guys over for dinner! Is it because of Fang Hung-chien—"

The one with the stomach trouble let out a hiss.

Hung-chien's heart jumped with fright, but he could not bring his feet to a halt. The two students were completely still. Feeling like a guilty thief, Hung-chien crept along stealthily and returned to his room filled with suspicions. Han Hsüeh-yü was undoubtedly plotting against him, but how he didn't know. The next day he'd just have to publicly rip the cover from Han's little peep show. Having made this heroic resolution, he went to sleep.

The next morning before he awoke, the school messenger came with a letter. He tore it open and found that it was from Miss Sun. It said that she had heard a rumor that he was pointing out Liu Tung-fang's errors to the students in his English class. Liu Tung-fang already knew about it. Would he please be careful? Hung-chien let out a cry of astonishment.

Where did such talk come from? How could he have made himself an enemy over nothing? He suddenly remembered that those three auditors were all from the History Department and in Liu Tung-fang's Section One English class. No doubt the questions they asked him contained traps which he had fallen into. Ultimately it was all the work of that scoundrel Han Hsüeh-yü. And all along he had thought Han wanted to be friends with him, and he was keeping Han's secret! The more Hung-chien thought about it, the more disgusted he became. He deliberated for a long time how he should first explain everything to Liu Tung-fang.

When Hung-chien arrived at the Foreign Languages Department office, Miss Sun was sitting there reading a book. She looked at him with eyes full of unspoken words. A small patch of Hung-chien's throat felt parched and his hands trembled slightly. He exchanged a few pleasantries with Liu Tung-fang, then screwing up his courage, said, "A colleague is going around saying—I myself was told about this—that you are very dissatisfied with the English I teach, that in the Section One class you often point out mistakes I make to the students—"

"What?" Liu sat up with a start. "Who said that?"

The expression on Miss Sun's face became even more all-inclusive, and she even forgot to pretend to be reading.

"My English is no good to begin with. I'm teaching this time partly at your order. Of course, it's inevitable that I make mistakes. I only hope that you will point them out to me directly. But then I've heard this colleague has a slight difference of opinion with you, so I don't put too much stock in the rumors I've heard. He also says that those three auditors in my class are spies sent in by you."

"Ah? What three students—Miss Sun, would you go to the library and borrow a copy of uh—uh, the Commercial Press's *College English Selections* for me and then go to the supplies office and get—get a hundred sheets of draft paper."

Miss Sun swiftly departed.

When Hung-chien gave the names of the three students, Liu Tung-fang said, "Hung-chien, you need only realize that those three students are in the History Department. How could they be at my beck and call? Isn't the one spreading those rumors the man in charge of the History Department? If you put all the facts together, you'll understand."

Hung-chien's venture was a success. His hands stopped trembling, and acting as though he were suddenly waking from a dream, he said, "Han Hsüeh-yü, he—"

He then spilled out the whole story like rice from a gunny-sack of Han Hsüeh-yü's buying the diploma.

Surprised and delighted, Liu Tung-fang repeatedly sighed, and when he had heard everything, said, "Let me tell you frankly. My sister works in the History Department office, and she often hears the History Department students telling Han Hsüeh-yü that you abuse me in class."

Hung-chien swore that he had not.

Liu said, "Do you think I would believe that? His purpose in making all this trouble is not just to get rid of you, but to have his wife take your place. He thinks that since he's already hired my sister, when there's no one to take over the class, I'll be too embarrassed not to ask his wife for help. Well, I'm fair and impartial in hiring people and my sister isn't under his personal employ. Even if she does lose her job, I'll certainly do all I can to support her as her elder brother. By the way, let me show you something that came yesterday from the president's office."

He pulled open a drawer and took out a sheaf of papers which he gave to Hung-chien. It was a petition from the Section Four English students which read as follows: "Subject: Replacement with a Better Teacher for the Good of Our Studies." From start to finish it stated that Hung-chien was not qualified to teach English and detailed his various slips of the pen and oversights in correcting assignments to prove his incompetence in English. When he read it, Hung-chien's face turned scarlet to his ears.

Liu Tung-fang said, "Don't pay any attention to it. Section Four students aren't up to doing that. It's undoubtedly the idea of those three auditors, and very likely Han Hsüeh-yü had a hand in it. The president sent it over with a note for me to look into it. I'll certainly clear it all up for you."

Hung-chien thanked Liu profusely. Before he left, Liu asked if he had told Han Hsüeh-yü's secret to anyone else and enjoined him not to let it out. As he was leaving the office, Hung-chien ran into Miss Sun on her way back from the supplies office. She complimented him on the way he had seized the initiative in his talk with Liu. He was pleased at hearing this, but when he thought that she may have seen that petition, he was deeply mortified. It stuck firmly in his consciousness like a piece of sticky flypaper.

Liu proved to be quite skillful. The next day when Hung-chien went to class, the three auditors were not there. All went well right up until final examination time. Liu instructed Hung-chien to be lenient in grading the bad papers and strict with the good ones, for if there were many failures, it would rouse the students' ill will, while if there were too many with good marks, it could diminish the teacher's authority. In sum, when marking one should "send coal when it snows," that is, provide that which is most needed, and never be stingy—as Liu put it: "One cent can buy nothing, let alone one tenth of a cent!" Nor on the other hand should one gild the lily, letting the students regard grades as too cheap or their schoolwork as too easy—as Liu put it: "A beggar must be given at least one dollar, that is, one hundred cents, but to give a student one hundred percent was out of the question."

The day after the examinations, Wang Ch'u-hou ran into Hung-chien and told him that Mrs. Wang wanted to see him and Hsin-mei to ask them what day they'd be free during winter vacation, so she could invite them over for dinner. When Wang heard that they were going to Kweilin during winter vacation, he stroked his beard and said with a laugh, "What for? My wife is planning to make matches for both of you."

7

A MUSTACHE usually consists of two downward strokes. Wang Ch'u-hou's mustache was just a single strip. He had grown a mustache twenty years ago, at a time when officials all groomed bushy upper lips. Anything less than that would have been inadequate to mark their status; it was like the ancient philosophers of the West who always wore a long beard under their chin as a sign of wisdom. When he was a secretary at the office of the provincial military governor, the marshal's caltrop mustache was so impressive that it looked like it had been transplanted from a *Jen-tan* medicine advertisement. He didn't dare grow that kind of mustache for fear the marshal would consider him presumptuous. While the marshal's was a round-horned black caltrop mustache, he desired no more than a small sharp-horned red caltrop mustache. For some reason people who don't bear arms can never really grow a proper-looking mustache; it is either too sparse or limp or droops downward from either side of the mouth like commas in Western-style punctuation, neither arching upward nor curling gracefully. On the other hand, Wang's heavy black eyebrows could have competed strand for strand with the eyebrows of the God of Longevity.[1] It was as though he had accidentally sheared off his mustache and eyebrows all at once the first time he shaved and had tried desperately to press them back on, only to get eyebrows and mustache mixed up, so that on his mouth were the eyebrows which would never grow, while on his forehead was the mustache which always flourished. With a mustache like that he might just as well not grow one at all, and so his marriage to his present wife five years ago had been a good excuse to shave it off.

However, like all officials, bandits, professional gamblers, and speculators, Wang believed in fate. Astrologers all said he was "wood-fated" and "wood-shaped."[2] Hair and mustache are like the branches and leaves of a tree. When they are missing, it means the tree has withered. People over forty are of course half bald anyway, so they must depend entirely on these few strands of mustache to show that the old tree is still in blossom and hasn't lost its lease on life. But for his twenty-five-year-old bride, he could not be so stingy as to begrudge a single hair, so he shaved off both ends, leaving only a pinch in the middle. Then, because this pinch wasn't thick enough, he had trimmed it into a single line, movie-star style. This may have ruined the geomantic layout of his face, for after that misfortunes happened to him one after another. His new wife fell ill as soon as she became his, and he himself was impeached and forced out of office. Fortunately, when officials take a tumble, like cats which always land on all fours, they never end up in any great distress. He consoled himself with the thought that to begin with he had never relied on his salary. Moreover, he was a scholar of the old school with the ways and habits of the former Manchu dynasty. As an official he had been highly cultured, so when he retired, he was able to discourse on scholarly subjects. His wife's condition remained the same as ever without getting any worse. Perhaps this was due to that single line of mustache. His luck hadn't completely turned sour.

If those few remaining strands of mustache were able to retain part of his luck, it goes without saying that he enjoyed great fortune when he had not shaved off any. For instance, his wretched first wife did her part and died, allowing him to take a beautiful wife in a second marriage. After twenty years of marriage and his one son had graduated from college, it was high time she died. Having one's wife die is most economical. A funeral does cost a certain amount of money, but then doesn't a divorce require alimony? And if he keeps a mistress, doesn't he have to support two households? Many people have wives who really ought to die; they just don't have Wang Ch'u-hou's luck with timely bereavements. Moreover, in the case of a bereavement, people will at least send gifts. The meager gifts for a divorce or a second marriage bring in nothing, and then there are still the legal fees to be paid. Moreover, Wang Ch'u-hou, though he had been an official, was really a man of letters at heart, and men of letters always love having someone die, so they can have a subject for a memorial essay. Coffinmakers and morticians deal only in the newly dead, while men of letters can write on the stale dead of one year, tens of years, or even hundreds of years ago. "A Commemoration on the First Anniversary of Death," or "A Three-Hundred-Year Memorial Elegy," are both good topics. At the death of a wife or husband—since there are women writers—this makes an especially good topic. No matter how much literary talent someone else might have, your wife or husband is solely your topic. It's a topic with a registered patent on it. While Wang Ch'u-hou was writing a memorial essay and a biographical sketch of his deceased wife during his mourning, he thought of the line from an ancient poem, "Before me is a new wife and new children. A second chapter of my life begins," and wished he could have used it. He hoped his second wife would have children, then he would write one titled, "Written Sadly on the Anniversary of the Death of my Former Wife," with these two lines revised and inserted.

As of now this poem still remained to be written. Since being installed in her new home, the second Mrs. Wang had not given birth but merely taken sick. She had begun by nursing her illness at home only to end up making a home for her illness. It would never leave her, and she remained quite weak and delicate all year round, which made her middle-aged husband go from pity to fear. She had been to college for a year, but then because of anemia had withdrawn to nurse her health and stayed at home for four or five years. Whenever she wasn't dizzy or aching or having pains and discomfort in the rest of her body, she would amuse herself by studying Chinese painting with her husband or playing the piano. Chinese painting and the piano were the part of her dowry representing culture, equivalent to the college diploma (in a varnished wood frame) and the photograph in mortarboard (sixteen-inch color print in a painted wood frame) of other women. Wang Ch'u-hou, who could not understand Western music but should have known a little about Chinese painting, felt, nevertheless, that his wife's painting was pretty good. He would always say to guests, "She enjoys such things as music and painting, endeavors which require much mental effort. So how can she ever get well!" Mrs. Wang would then say modestly to the guests, "Since my health is poor, I can't do these things very often, so I don't paint or play very well."

Since moving to this small village, Mrs. Wang had become so lonesome she often quarreled with her husband. Because of her own self-importance, she looked down on the wives of her husband's colleagues, finding them much too impoverished. Her husband felt rather uneasy about having his bachelor colleagues often drop by his house, finding them much too young. Knowing how bored she was at home, Kao Sung-nien wanted to give her a job at the school. Clever woman that she was, Mrs. Wang refused the offer at once. For one thing she knew she was not well qualified and could be nothing more than a petty clerk, which would have been an affront to her dignity. For another, she knew it was a man's world. Even in countries like England or America where women's rights were well advanced, it was still a man who served as God, being referred to as He and never She. When women went out to work, no matter how high their position, they were still used by men. Only by remaining hidden behind the scenes could a woman use her qualifications as wife or mistress to direct or manipulate men.

Miss Fan, the women's adviser and a lecturer in the Education Department, was her admirer, and they often visited each other. Liu Tung-fang's sister, a former student of Wang Ch'u-hou, also dropped in sometimes to see her, calling her "Teacher's Wife." Liu Tung-fang had once asked Mrs. Wang to act as matchmaker for his sister. Now, being a matchmaker and a mother are the two basic desires of a woman, so when Mrs. Wang, who had become quite bored, received this commission, it was like the unemployed finding work. Wang Ch'u-hou saw no danger in being a matchmaker, since the matchmaker herself would never be given away. Mrs. Wang had already been planning to match Miss Fan with Chao Hsin-mei and Miss Liu with Fang Hung-chien. Miss Fan was older and homelier than Miss Liu, but then she was a lecturer. Her mate should be a rather high-ranking department chairman. Miss Liu was a teaching assistant, so marrying an associate professor should be quite enough. As for Miss Sun, she had never paid a call on Mrs. Wang. Mrs. Wang had met her once or twice while visiting with Miss Fan and had not had a very good impression of her.

Two days after returning from Kweilin, Hung-chien and Hsin-mei received an invitation from Wang Ch'u-hou. Ordinarily neither of them ever had any contact with Wang and had never met Mrs. Wang, so when they saw the invitation, they recalled the talk about matchmaking.

Hung-chien said, "Old Wang is a big snob. Kao Sung-nien and the three college deans are the only ones qualified to eat at his house. And of course the people in the Chinese Department. Maybe you rate, but why drag me in? If it's to make a match, there aren't any women around here. That old guy is really too much!"

Hsin-mei said, "I don't mind going to get a look at Mrs. Wang. Maybe Old Wang has a niece on his or his wife's side—Mrs. Wang is supposed to be quite a beauty—whom he wants to give to you. It was you he talked to, not me. He was referring to you alone. You feel awkward about going so you produce a phony imperial edict to drag me along with you, even saying he's making a match for both of us! Well, I don't want anyone making a match for me."

After bickering about it for a while, they decided to visit the Wangs first and find out what it was all about before the joke became a reality.

The one-story, dark brick, semi-Western style house the Wangs rented was the best building in the area except for the school dormitory. It was separated from the dormitory by a stream. The stream dried up in the winter, leaving the stream bed filled with a pile of rocks like a nest of eggs in assorted sizes newly laid by the stream. When the stream was dried up, everyone stepped over the rocks instead of crossing by the wooden bridge, which just shows that as long as no danger is present, people are always ready to take the unconventional way.

The Wangs' living room was very spacious and had a mat spread on the brick floor. The big, solid, old-fashioned redwood tables and chairs had been bought by Wang Ch'u-hou from an army officer in town. If he should ever find better prospects elsewhere, Wang could sell them to the school.

Smiling radiantly, Wang came out first and asked Hsin-mei and Hung-chien if they found it cold in the living room, then ordered the maid to bring the brazier. They remarked in unison how nice his house was, how even more elegantly it was furnished, and that of all the houses they had seen in the last six months this was by far the best.

Wang heaved a long satisfied sigh and said, "Oh, this doesn't amount to anything! I used to have some things, but now they've all been lost. You never saw my house in Nanking—fortunately, it wasn't burned down by the Japanese, but heaven knows what became of all the things I had collected in it. Fortunately, I'm not one to be affected by such things; otherwise, I'd really be heartbroken."

Hsin-mei and Hung-chien had not only become quite used to hearing this sort of talk lately; they had even gotten in the habit of saying it themselves. To be sure, the ravages of the war had left many people with wealth and property homeless and destitute, but at the same time it gave an untold number of the destitute an opportunity to hark back to their days as millionaires. The Japanese had burned so many nonexistent houses with towers in the sky, taken possession of so many nonexistent properties, and destroyed so many one-sided romances made in heaven! Lu Tzu-hsiao, for instance, often let it be known that before the war two or three girls had vied to marry him, sighing at the same time, "Now of course it's all out of the question!" Li Mei-t'ing had suddenly put up a Western-style house in the Chapei section of Shanghai. And now? Such a pity! Those wretched Japanese had set it on fire. The damage was simply inestimable. Fang Hung-chien had also enlarged by several times the old house in his village, which had fallen to the enemy. Amazingly enough, the house had been expanded without in any way encroaching on the neighbor's land. Living as he did in the concession area, Chao Hsin-mei could not work any sleight of hand on his house, but as the dashing young man he considered himself to be, he did not have to sigh over the many women who had fancied him before. He merely said that if the war had never erupted, and the Office of the Negotiator had not withdrawn to the interior, he could have gone on—no, gone up, as an official.

Wang Ch'u-hou's prewar style of living was perhaps not as lavish as he claimed, but his colleagues believed him anyway, for his day-to-day life

235

now was certainly more comfortable than anyone else's, and besides, everyone knew that he was a discharged corrupt official—"It's rare indeed for the government to be so strict. But then he had already raked in all he wanted!"

Pointing to some calligraphy scrolls on the wall by well-known contemporaries, Wang remarked, "These are ones friends gave me after I escaped. Now I've lost heart. I won't ever collect antiques again. There's nothing worth collecting in the interior anyway—those two scrolls my wife painted."

Hsin-mei and Hung-chien quickly stood up and took a close look at the two small landscape paintings. Fang Hung-chien remarked that he didn't know Mrs. Wang could paint and was quite surprised. Chao Hsin-mei remarked that he had long heard how good a painter Mrs. Wang was and that her fame was well deserved. These two remarks were both contradictory and complementary.

Wang delightedly stroked his mustache, saying, "Unfortunately, my wife is not in good health. She finds painting and music—"

Before he could finish, Mrs. Wang herself came out. She was well proportioned without being thin but had no blood in her cheeks and was not wearing any rouge, only face powder. Her lips, however, were painted a bright red, and her Chinese dress was lavender, which made her face look unusually pale. She had long eyelashes, and eyes which slanted upward at the corners. Her hair was unwaved and put up in a bun, probably because she found the local hairdressers too inept. She was holding a leather hot water bottle in her hand. Her fingernails were completely red, not the color she had stained herself with while painting since her paintings were all blue and green landscapes.

Mrs. Wang said that she had wanted for a long time to invite them over, but her health had disappointed her, so she had put off the invitation until now. They immediately asked if she were better, then said they had never ventured to come pay a visit earlier and dinner wasn't necessary. Mrs. Wang said that she was stronger in spring and summer than in autumn and winter, and they must certainly come for dinner.

Mr. Wang said with a chuckle, "This dinner invitation of ours isn't for nothing. After the matches have been made, we expect our rewards. Your party in honor of the matchmaker should have eighteen plus eighteen—thirty-six tables!"

"How can we afford that!' exclaimed Hung-chien. "We don't even have enough money to reward the matchmaker, let alone get married."

Hsin-mei said, "In times like these, who has the spare money for getting married? I'm barely able to take care of myself! Thank you, Mr. and Mrs. Wang, for your offer of dinner and matchmaking, but we'll just have to say no thanks."

Mr. Wang said, "The world has changed! Why don't young people have the slightest enthusiasm? Not the slightest bit of romance? They refuse marriage and even feign poverty! All right, we don't want any reward. We'll do it all for nothing, won't we, Hsien?"

Mrs. Wang said, "Well, for heaven's sake! The way you two go on! I don't know much about Mr. Fang, but the abilities you returned students carry around with you are inexhaustible assets. We know all about Mr. Chao's family background and future prospects. The only worry is that the young lady wouldn't be worthy—there, you think I have enough of the matchmaking spirit?"

They all joined her in laughter.

"If someone took a fancy to me, I'd have gotten married by now," said Hsin-mei.

"I'm afraid you're just too choosy," said Mrs. Wang. "You'll pick and choose without ever finding anyone to your liking. You newly returned single students are like baked sesame buns fresh out of the oven. For people with young daughters, there aren't enough of you to go around. Oh, I've seen plenty of them. The richer they are, the less they want to get married. If they can be independent, they don't care about a wife's dowry or her father's influence. They'd rather have girl friends and lead a life of profligacy; for that, they do have the money. If you're worried about not having enough money to get married, it's a lot more economical to take a wife than having girl friends right and left. Your excuse isn't good enough."

They were both horrified at hearing this and were about to reply when Wang Ch'u-hou, pretending to be angry, said, "I would like it known that I did not marry you in order to be 'economical' and save money. When I was young, I was known for proper conduct; I never carried on. A fine thing it would be if your remarks were misinterpreted!" With that he gave Hung-chien and Hsin-mei a mischievous wink.

Mrs. Wang snorted contemptuously. "When you were young? I—I don't believe you were ever young."

Wang turned red in the face, and Hung-chien quickly said that they did not mean to be ungrateful to Mr. and Mrs. Wang for their good intentions, but they would like to know who the girls were.

Mrs. Wang clapped her hands and said, "Ah ha! So Mr. Fang would like to know. The identities of the two young women are heaven's secrets and not to be revealed. Ch'u-hou, don't tell them."

Having been given this affectionate order by his wife, Wang, regaining his composure, said, "You will find out when you come tomorrow. Don't take it too seriously. It's just a chance for everyone to get together. If you are completely uninterested, what difference will it make to have a meal together? It's not something the other could hold against you or take you to court for. Ha, ha. But I have some earnest advice for you. It doesn't look as though this war will be over in a year or two; it's apt to drag on for a long, long time. If you wait for peace to come before getting married, your own youth will slip by. As they say, 'Don't put off what is best done now.' That's quite right. Once you two get married, your careers and your personal lives will both benefit. Our school has a great future, though it's not easy to hire people right away. In the case of talented men like your-selves—Hsien, haven't I always been telling you about these two?—who are willing to condescend to come here, the school certainly won't let you go. If you got married and settled down here permanently, the school would benefit greatly. As for me—don't mention this to anyone—next semester I may be in charge of the College of Letters. The Department of Education is going to split off from the College of Letters and become a Teacher's College. The present chairman of the Department of Education, Mr. K'ung, certainly can't serve as dean of the College of Letters. For my own sake, I'm ready to go to great lengths to keep you here. Besides, with your spouses working at the school too, husband and wife would both have their own income. Your obligations wouldn't be any greater—"

"How shameless!" exclaimed Mrs. Wang, cutting him short. "It's just exactly what you were saying a moment ago: 'Not the slightest bit of romance.' Everything is figured out to the last nickel!"

"Look how impatient you are!" said Wang. "Romance will come at once. Marriage is the happiest event of one's life. My wife and I both know what it is. If marriage weren't happy, we should be exhorting you not to marry. Do you think we'd still want to be matchmakers? She and I—"

Frowning, Mrs. Wang waved her hand and said, "Oh, stop. It's so sickening." She suddenly remembered an incident a year ago when her hus-band and she visited a temple in Ch'engtu and a monk had talked about transmigration, upon which her husband had whispered to her, "When I die, I'll try to be born again as soon as possible so I can marry you a second time." The recollection disgusted her. Meanwhile, Hung-chien and Hsin-mei dutifully flattered them by saying that a happy couple like the Wangs were one in a thousand.

On the way back to the school, the two of them discussed Mrs. Wang in great detail. Both felt she was remarkable, but wondered why she had married someone twenty years older than herself. They reasoned that her family must have been poor and had admired Wang because he was a local official. Furthermore, they felt her paintings were not bad, but the charac-ters inscribed on them seemed to have been written by Wang himself.

Pretending to be an expert on the subject, Hung-chien said, "Charac-ters can't be drawn. It's not like painting where you can touch up. Lots of women can draw a few impressionistic landscapes but when it comes to writing characters they really have a hard time. Mrs. Wang's calligraphy is probably abominable."

Hung-chien had reached the door of his room and was just pulling out his key to open it when Hsin-mei suddenly blurted, "Did you notice that there is something about Mrs. Wang that resembles—Su Wen-wan?" And before he'd finished speaking, he bounded up the stairs two at a time. Hung-chien stared after him in astonishment.

After the guests had left, Wang went back into the bedroom with his wife and asked, "I didn't say anything improper today, did I?" This was a customary question. After every social occasion, Mrs. Wang, who loved nit-picking, would always correct her husband.

Mrs. Wang said, "Why, no. Anyway, I didn't pay much attention, but why did you have to tell them about being dean of the College of Letters? You just love to brag about things beforehand."

Wang did in fact regret it a little at this point, but he insisted, "That doesn't matter. Let them know their jobs are partly in my hands. Why did you humiliate me today?" As he recalled it, his anger flared. "I mean those remarks about being young or not." He added this explanation because of his wife's puzzled look.

Mrs. Wang, who was critically examining her face in the round mirror of her dressing table, said, "Oh, that. Just look at your face in the mirror. It's so frightening; it looks as if you were about to gobble someone up! I don't want to look at you!"

Instead of pushing away her husband, who was standing beside her, Mrs. Wang merely picked up the silk powder puff from her powder box and dabbed a few times at his livid face in the mirror, blurring his features.

Liu Tung-fang had recently become preoccupied with personal matters. As his mother and father were both dead, his younger sister's marriage was now his responsibility. Last year at Kunming someone with every good intention had been introduced to her, but nothing had come of it. Of course, having her around the house meant extra help for Mrs. Liu. The sweaters the two children wore, for example, were all knitted by her, and the eldest daughter still shared the same bed with her. But as the years slipped by in this manner, he and his wife began to fear that she would never be married off and would become a lifelong burden. Two years ago when she escaped to the interior she was to have begun her senior year in college. Seniors were not allowed to transfer to another school, and his wife was then about to give birth. For the moment they were unable to hire a servant, and with everything at home in a mess, he had no time to find a way out for her. She postponed her schooling, and she never graduated. He felt very bad about it and would justify himself by saying that while there were any number of women graduates, how many of them could really make a living for themselves? His wife reproached him for having had his sister enter a woman's university in the first place. If she had gone to a coeducational school, the marriage problem would have been solved long ago.

Flustered, Liu countered, "Miss Fan graduated from a coeducational school. Why hasn't she been married off?"

Mrs. Liu said, "There you go again. She is much better than Miss Fan." Anyone who could talk like this about her husband's sister wasn't such a bad sister-in-law.

"Maybe it's just a matter of fate," said Liu with a sigh. "My mother used to say that Sister was born with her face down and her back up, which meant she would die in her mother's home. We often teased her about it when she was little. Now it looks like she really will be an old maid."

Mrs. Liu hurriedly put in, "How can we have that? If she really does get old, she can do just as well to marry a widower, like Mrs. Wang. Didn't that work out very nicely?" implying that human endeavor could turn back the tides of fate.

Last year when Liu had cleared up the misunderstanding for Fang Hung-chien, it had suddenly occurred to him that Fang wouldn't make a bad brother-in-law. As he was Hung-chien's protector, Fang ought to be grateful and appreciate the honor. Furthermore, by forming this family tie with him, Fang could consolidate his own position. Unless Fang were a perfect fool he would never let such a wonderful opportunity as this slip by, he reasoned. Mrs. Liu also approved of her husband's keen reasoning, her only qualm being that Fang was so inept and would need her husband to keep his job for him. Later, when she heard her husband say Fang was smart enough, she stopped worrying and made plans for the newlyweds to live in her house after their marriage. In any case there was an empty room, but a formal lease would have to be drawn up; otherwise, if the two households were not kept separate, when the Fangs had children, they would take all the good fortune and intelligence away from the Liu children.

When Mrs. Wang agreed to act as matchmaker, the Lius joyfully revealed the news to Miss Liu, fully expecting her to be shy and happy. To their surprise she merely flushed scarlet and said nothing.

The outspoken Mrs. Liu asked, "Have you ever met this Fang fellow? Your brother says that compared to the one in Kunming—"

Liu quickly gave his wife a vigorous kick under the table. Miss Liu broke her silence and had quite a bit to say. First, she did not want to get married. Who asked Mrs. Wang to be a matchmaker? Besides, were women so cheap? All this about "matchmaking" and "introducing" sounded so wonderful! But the way women got all dolled up for men to come pick and choose, wasn't it just like selling chickens or ducks at the market? And if they didn't suit the men's fancy, once the meal was over, nothing more was ever heard about it again. It was so humiliating! Furthermore, it wasn't as though she were eating off them for nothing. With all the things she did around the house, she more than made up for a servant, so why were they chasing her out? She became angrier the more she talked and even dragged out the business about not graduating from college. Afterwards, Mr. Liu reproved his wife for provoking all his sister's pent-up resentment by bringing up the Kunming matchmaking affair.

"That stubborn Liu temperament!" said Mrs. Liu, fuming. "Whoever marries her certainly will be out of luck."

Early the next morning the eldest daughter, who slept with Miss Liu, reported to her parents that her aunt had cried half the night. That day Miss Liu paced up and down the riverbank behind the house by herself, going without breakfast or lunch. Mr. and Mrs. Liu were frightened out of their wits, certain that the sight of the clear current below would lead her to thoughts of suicide. Even if she did not go so far as to take her own life, it would never do to have the whole school learn of it, so they quickly sent the eldest daughter out to follow her. Fortunately, she returned to eat dinner and even had two bowls of rice. After this the matter was never mentioned again. When the invitation arrived from the Wangs, she accepted it without a word. Mr. and Mrs. Liu did not venture to feel her out on the matter. After talking it over between themselves they decided that if on the morning of the dinner there was still no sign of action, they would go ask Mrs. Wang to come and entreat with her. That morning Miss Liu told the maid to get the iron ready so she could press some clothes. The Lius then exchanged glances and smiled surreptitiously.

Miss Fan discovered that when she had a secret, the itch to tell it was as hard to bear as a cough in the throat. To want people to know one has a secret while not letting them know what it is, however much they may ask or guess, is human vanity. Miss Fan lacked such an interrogator with whom she could whisper intimately. She and Miss Sun were roommates and, as was usually the case, were not very close. She had been living happily by herself in a large room, when for no reason at all half of it was portioned off for Miss Sun. If Miss Sun had been pretty or extravagant, perhaps Miss Sun could have been forgiven, but of all things Miss Sun was such an ordinary sort of girl. And even if Miss Sun were from Shanghai, except for her Chinese dress being a little shorter, she failed to see that Miss Sun was any more stylish than she. Thus, while the two of them often went out shopping together, they were not bosom companions. Ever since Mrs. Wang had said she wanted to introduce her to Chao Hsin-mei, she had become even more wary of Miss Sun, because Miss Sun was always saying she was going to the faculty dormitory to see Hsin-mei. Of course, Miss Sun had told her before that she always called Hsin-mei Uncle Chao, but then girls nowadays often forget to make distinctions of rank. So Miss Fan kept the invitation from the Wangs strictly secret.

Miss Fan's one hobby was reading plays, especially tragedies. As there were no theaters there yet, she bought all the well-known plays by modern Chinese playwrights that she could find and read them over carefully. She would underline in red pencil such lines in the dialogue as "We must be brave, brave, brave!" or "Enjoy life to the full and die unflinchingly," or "When the night is so dark, can day be far behind?" then read them over silently as though they held the very answer to life's riddles. Only at unhappy moments, such as when a beautiful moon aroused personal thoughts, or when she was carrying out her duties as "women's adviser," and the women students, instead of accepting her advice, muttered, "She's nothing more than a college graduate herself. What makes her qualified to be our adviser? About all she can do is watch over the maids or issue toilet paper," she discovered at such times that these pithy epigrams were of little help. Life was not in fact so enjoyable, and dying wasn't so easy either. Love in tragedies was for the most part loftily romantic. She also felt that before marriage there must be great mental traumas. But there was one matter she could not resolve. She had heard that the more experience in love a woman had, the more charm she had over men. She had also heard that men would only marry a woman whose heart was still chaste and pure. If Chao Hsin-mei courted her, which approach should she take? The day before the dinner, in a moment of "inspiration on the eve of good fortune," she conceived of a perfect attitude to take. She would let it be known that many people had been madly in love with her, but she herself had never loved anyone, so this was still her first love.

By a stroke of good luck, when she went shopping that day, the shop's cashier asked her, "Are you a student, Miss?" This one question made her feel six or seven years younger. She walked gaily along as though she had springs on her feet. When she got back to the school, she told Miss Sun about being mistaken for a student.

Miss Sun said, "I could have asked the same thing. You are just like a schoolgirl."

Miss Fan chided her for being less than honest.

Miss Fan was a bit nearsighted, and though she didn't know the American poetess' words of wisdom: "Men seldom make passes/ At girls who wear glasses," she didn't wear glasses. In her student days, when she was copying from the blackboard in class, she had to wear glasses, because among her classmates there was no one she knew well enough from whom she could borrow a notebook to copy. Women classmates who had the help of men students would never freely lend out those original and complete, revised and enlarged editions of their notes, which were the result of joint efforts. As for the women students who hadn't had the services of men students—humph! Despite being a woman herself, Miss Fan did not have a very high regard for the transcribing abilities of other members of her sex. Like all women who were very studious and concerned about their looks as well, she wore rimless glasses with platinum temple pieces. Rimless glasses seem to "make no distinctions." They blend in with the face so that wearing them or not wearing them is all the same. They aren't like rimmed glasses with a clearly demarcated border. Putting such glasses on is like hanging out the sign of the female pedant. Now the only time she needed to wear glasses was when she watched a play. Beyond this, when she went out to a dinner party such as the one that day, she would put them on only to take a close look at herself while combing her hair and putting on her makeup and, when she had finished her toilet and changed her clothes, especially to get a general view of herself from a distance in the half-length mirror. She felt her eyes looked much too listless. It was from being too excited to sleep well the night before. Mrs. Wang had some mascara to put on her eyelashes. It wouldn't hurt to go over early and borrow some to bring out a hazy, dreamlike expression in her eyes. She could ask Mrs. Wang for comments on her overall attire and make the corrections ahead of time. Miss Fan, who was the women students' adviser, looked upon Mrs. Wang as the adviser of the women students' adviser.

She arrived at the Wangs shortly after five o'clock, saying she had come early to help. Mr. Wang said that since there weren't many guests that evening, they had ordered the dishes from the best restaurant in town, so there was no need for help. He lamented that their wonderful family cook had died during the escape, and that their present servant's cooking was not up to serving to guests.

Mrs. Wang said, "Don't tell me you believe her! She didn't come here to help. She came here to show off her talents, so Chao Hsin-mei will know she isn't just well educated and attractive but can manage the house as well."

Miss Fan stopped her from saying any more nonsense and asked in a whisper for her comments. Mrs. Wang felt she hadn't put on enough red and, saying she should add a little more gay coloring, pulled her into her room to apply some more rouge for her. In the end Miss Fan went to the party looking as triumphantly red as American Indians on the warpath. She then asked Mrs. Wang if she could borrow her mascara, explaining that she did not have pink eye, so there was no danger of infection. From outside Wang Ch'u-hou heard nothing but uninterrupted laughter. If he had known English, no doubt he would have thought of the saying, "Where there are chickens and ducks, there is plenty of manure, and where there are young women, there is plenty of laughter."

Miss Liu was the last to arrive. She had a warm frank-looking face and an ample figure. Her clothes were quite tight so that creases appeared at her slightest movement. When Hsin-mei and Hung-chien saw that these were the two to be introduced, they were so disappointed they wanted to laugh. They had all met before but never spoken.

Miss Fan seemed to have drawn an invisible circle around herself and Hsin-mei and kept up such a tight conversation that not even water could have been splashed through. Hsin-mei began by saying the town was boring and that there were no places for entertainment.

"Isn't it though?" said Miss Fan. "I don't find many people I can talk to around here either. It really is dull."

Hsin-mei asked her how she amused herself. She told him she liked reading plays and asked if he did too.

Hsin-mei said, "I like plays very much. Unfortunately, I haven't read— uh—very many."

Miss Fan asked him about Ts'ao Yü.[3]

"I consider him the—uh—the greatest playwright," said Hsin-mei, taking a wild guess.

"Oh, I'm so glad, Mr. Chao," said Miss Fan, clapping her hands in delight. "We share exactly the same opinion. Which of his plays do you think is best?"

Hsin-mei had never expected there would be an examination of this sort waiting for him after his final examinations in college were over with. The ability to answer questions ambiguously or equivocally that a dozen years of quizzes and examinations had trained in him was now completely rusted, and without thinking he replied, "Didn't he write one called—uh—it was—"

The expression of shock on Miss Fan's face prevented him from saying whether it was "Spring," "Summer," "Fall," or "Winter." Her shock was like a dentist's probe, which kept her mouth open so wide that for a long moment her upper and lower jaws were unable to join together. How infuriating it would be if her husband turned out to be such a complete ignoramus! Fortunately, marriage was still a long way off; there was still time to teach him. After Hsin-mei had admitted his ignorance, she immediately put some art into her natural expression of shock and she gave him a complete two-minute course in "The History of Contemporary Chinese Drama," adding that if Hsin-mei wished to read any plays, she had some on hand. Hsin-mei hurriedly thanked her.

She suddenly said with a laugh, "Oh, I can't lend you any of my plays. If you want to read some, I'll find some other way to get them for you."

Hsin-mei asked why not. Miss Fan explained that many of the plays she had were presents from the authors. Hsin-mei assured her he would not damage or lose anything so valuable.

"Oh, it's not that," said Miss Fan guilelessly, "but playwrights are so silly. They write all kinds of nonsense on the books they give me. I couldn't let you see them. Of course, it wouldn't really matter if I did."

It was then Hsin-mei's duty to say he definitely had to see them.

Miss Liu did not say much, and Hung-chien, who had come solely for the purpose of food, made only a few stabs at polite conversation. It was rather Mrs. Wang who led the conversation, plying Miss Liu with questions. Wang-Ch'u-hou stepped inside for a moment, then came out and said to his wife, "I've made the rounds of inspection."

Hung-chien asked him what he was inspecting.

Wang said with a laugh, "It's actually a funny story. We employ two servants. The girl has been with us since we came—over half a year. I've changed maids several times, but none of them has worked out. The first one I hired asked for leave every day to spend the night at home. After dinner was over she'd disappear, and the dirty dishes would pile up. We can't have this, I thought, so I hired another one who was very quiet. She stayed here for more than ten days without going back home once. My wife and I were quite pleased. Well, one day in the small hours of the morning someone all but knocked the gate down. It turned out this woman had a lover who always sneaked in here for a secret tryst, which is why she never went home. When her husband got wind of it, he came over to seize her, the adulteress, in the act. I was furious. We finally replaced her with the present one. She's rather clever, so we taught her how to make a few simple dishes, which she does well enough, but sometimes it seems the amount she makes is too small. I thought maybe she was pocketing some of the food money for herself. Everyone's always out for a little extra, and as they say, 'Unless you're deaf or obtuse, you'll never do as head of the house,' so I might as well just forget it. Having to keep replacing servants is a nuisance! My wife and I gave her a few words of admonishment, and let it go at that.

"Then once a friend of President Kao's came from far away and brought thirty sparrows with him. The president asked me to cook them for him, and he came to dinner. You know, the president likes to come here for dinner. My wife said that sparrows are tasteless when they're fried. According to her hometown method, the sparrow's stomach is stuffed with ground pork and then fried in soy sauce. We didn't have many people for dinner that evening, just President Kao, my wife and me, and Mr. Wang, chairman of the Math Department—he's an interesting chap. Mr. Kao and Mr. Wang both agreed this was the best way to cook sparrows. After we'd eaten, Mr. Wang suddenly asked if there hadn't been thirty sparrows altogether. We thought he hadn't had enough, but he said, no, according to his calculations, we had eaten only twenty—Hsien, twenty-what?—twenty-five, so there should have been five left. I said surely he didn't think I'd taken some on the sly, and President Kao said how ridiculous. My wife went into the kitchen to look into it, and sure enough she saw half a bowl of gravy and four—not five—sparrows! And do you know what the servant said? She said she had laid them aside to put in my noodles in the morning. We were angry and amused at the same time. No one would eat those four extra sparrows—"

"What a pity! Why didn't you give them to me!" interjected Hsin-mei, like someone about to suffocate suddenly bursting out from a cloud of gas and taking in a breath of fresh air.

Mrs. Wang said with a laugh, "Who told you not to come over then? In the end they were given to President Kao to go with his noodles."

"In that case, that servant of yours is an honest fool," said Hung-chien. "She acts without considering carefully, but she has a good heart."

Wang stroked his mustache and roared with laughter.

" 'An honest fool?' " said Mrs. Wang. "She's neither honest nor a fool! We were taken in by her from the very start. In the most recent case she served some chicken broth, which was as thin as plain drinking water. I said to Mr. Wang, 'This isn't broth from boiling a chicken. It's more like a chicken has had a dip in it.' He heard it wrong and thought I'd said, 'A chicken has had its feet in it,' so he said as a joke, 'You think you're so quick and clever, yet you drank the foot-wash water.' "

They all laughed, and Mr. Wang delightedly savored his own witticism. "I called her in and questioned her about it, but she kept on denying it. Later by means of threats and cajolery, I finally got to the bottom of it. The old maidservant has a son. Every time we have company, she calls him over and picks out the best pieces for him, which she hides in the rice. I asked the girl why she hadn't told me earlier, and whether she wasn't in on the stolen food. She refused to say. It finally came out that the old maidservant wanted her as daughter-in-law and had promised her her son in marriage. Now, don't you think that's a clever one? So every time we have company, we make an inspection of the whole house first. I don't think we can keep those two much longer. I'm going to replace them as soon as I get a chance."

The guests all spoke at once. Hsin-mei and Hung-chien said, "Servants are a real problem."

Miss Fan said, "It scares me to death. Luckily with just myself, I don't need a servant."

Miss Liu said, "The maid at our house is always up to tricks, too."

Mrs. Wang said laughingly to Miss Fan, "You won't be by yourself for long—Miss Liu, your brother and sister-in-law are much beholden to you."

The servant brought in the food, and everyone rushed to grab a seat. The host said that with a round table there were no distinctions of rank in seating but they mustn't get too mixed up. He then urged everyone to eat a little more since there were so few dishes. The guests, of course, said the food was too plentiful and that with so few of them, they could not possibly eat so much.

Mr. Wang said, "Oh, I forgot to get Miss Fan's roommate Miss Sun to come. She's never been here before."

Miss Fan shot a sidelong glance at Hsin-mei who was sitting next to her. At the mention of Miss Sun's name, Hung-chien's heart began pounding and his face burned. *How funny*, he thought, *what does Miss Sun have to do with me?*

Mrs. Wang remarked, "At first when Mr. Chao came with that young woman, we all guessed she was Mr. Chao's sweetheart. It wasn't until later that we realized there was nothing to it."

Hsin-mei laughed and said to Hung-chien, "See how frightful rumors can be!"

Miss Fan said, "Miss Sun has a sweetheart now, and that's no rumor. As her roommate I know all about it."

Hsin-mei asked who it was. Fully expecting her to say it was him, Hung-chien forced himself to remain composed.

Miss Fan said, "I can't divulge her secret."

Alarmed, Hung-chien began eating for all he was worth, trying to keep his facial muscles from settling into their true expression.

Throwing a glance at Hung-chien, Hsin-mei said with a grin, "I may know who it is without your telling me."

His mouth full of food, Hung-chien nearly blurted out, "Don't talk nonsense."

Misinterpreting Hsin-mei's grin, Miss Fan relaxed and said, "You know about it too? You certainly are quick to get the news! Lu Tzu-hsiao's been after her since the winter vacation, writing to her everyday and just getting on with her wonderfully. You were in Kweilin then, so how could you have known about it?"

Hung-chien's emotions were like a whirlpool. He hadn't been dragged in himself, and so he could relax, but when he heard that Miss Sun was close to someone else, it stung him painfully. *I'm not in love with Miss Sun, so why should I object to her being on close terms with Lu Tzu-hsiao? Miss Sun is cute in her own way, but her charm is unnatural and contrived and she isn't a true beauty. Of course, she does have a likeable disposition. It's all Hsin-mei's fault, because his joking put ideas in my head. She can never see anything in someone like Lu Tzu-hsiao. But Miss Fan said they are writing each other every day, and Miss Fan wouldn't lie for no reason.* Suddenly his spirits fell.

Mr. and Mrs. Wang and Miss Liu all listened with astonishment. Hsin-mei adopted the attitude of a great statesman who, upon receiving a piece of intelligence, acts as though he has known about it all along. Assuming a grave expression, he replied, "I have my reports. Lu Tzu-hsiao once asked Mr. Fang to introduce him to Miss Sun. I don't approve of Lu; he is too old."

"You mind your own business," interrupted Mrs. Wang. "You're not her real 'uncle,' after all. And even if you were, so what? If I'd known this were the case, we'd have invited the two of them today, too. But Tzu-hsiao is a little impish. I am not very fond of him."

Mr. Wang shook his head, saying, "That won't do. With the history people, the less contact the better. Tzu-hsiao is the star professor in the History Department, so of course he's no little imp. He's worse than a little imp; he's small-minded, ha, ha! He likes to gossip. Han Hsüeh-yü is a very suspicious person. If you invite one of his subordinates for dinner without inviting him, he'll suspect you of colluding with someone in a conspiracy. The school is already rife with the 'Canton Clique,' the 'Stalwarts Clique,' and the 'Returned Students from Japan Clique.' Mr. Chao and Mr. Fang, aren't you two afraid people will say you're in the 'Wang Clique' if you eat dinner at my place? People are already saying Miss Liu's brother is in the 'Wang Clique.' "

Hsin-mei said, "I'm aware several small groups of faculty members often get together for dinner, but Hung-chien and I've never joined any of them, however much they may be criticizing us."

Mr. Wang said, "You two are in the 'Dragon Follower Clique' of President Kao—comprised of Mr. Kao's relatives or students and old friends. Mr. Fang, of course, was not originally acquainted with Mr. Kao, but because of his indirect connection through Mr. Chao, he's considered to be on the fringe of the 'Dragon Follower Clique,' or the dragon's tail, ha, ha—I know that's all hearsay; otherwise, I would never have dared ask the two of you over."

Miss Fan, without the slightest interest in the school cliques, merely felt it incumbent upon her to attack Miss Sun. "All this business about factions in the school is so silly. Miss Sun is a very nice person, but she's so messy. She has her things all over the room—Oh, I'm sorry, Mr. Chao, I forgot she is your 'niece,' " and with that she laughed in great embarrassment.

Hsin-mei said, "Oh, that doesn't matter. But, Hung-chien, we didn't think she was so bad when we traveled with her, did we?"

Surprised and angered because someone had said he was on the fringe of the "Dragon Follower Clique," Hung-chien was like the crab described by William James. Classified as a crustacean by biologists, it wanted to wave its claws about in protest and say, "I'm just me. A true gentleman comes and goes of his own accord without belonging in any category." To Hsin-mei's question he replied with an offhand "Yes."

Mrs. Wang said, "I've heard Mr. Fang is a great conversationalist. Why are you so quiet today?"

Fang Hung-chien replied hastily that the food was so good he'd even swallowed his tongue along with it.

Halfway through the meal, the subject of the lack of recreation came up again. Mrs. Wang said that she had a mahjong set, but living as they did so close to the school—

Without letting her finish, Wang interposed, "My wife's nerves are very weak and playing mahjong is so noisy that we never play—" just then there was a knock at the door—"Who could that be?"

"Well, Mrs. Wang, why didn't you invite me to your party? Mr. Wang, I made my way over here just by following the aroma of food," said Kao Sung-nien, as he walked in.

Everyone stood to attention, rising from his seat to greet Kao, except for Mrs. Wang, who, leaning indolently against the back of her chair in a position halfway between sitting and standing, asked, "Have you had dinner? Come and have something." At the same time she instructed the servant to bring a chair and set another place with a bowl and chopsticks. Hsin-mei quickly offered him his place as the seat of honor, so he was no longer sitting next to Miss Fan.

President Kao went through the motions of saying no, then sat down serenely, and was just picking up the chopsticks when he glanced around the table and cried, "Why, I can't sit here! Your seats are specially arranged. How stupid of me! How could I break you apart? Hsin-mei, you sit here."

Hsin-mei refused. Kao then offered his seat to Miss Fan, but she could only giggle, her body glued to the chair like a piece of sticky candy. In resignation, the president said, "All right, then! In all great events under heaven, what is long together must come apart, and what is long apart must come together," and laughed heartily. He then told Miss Fan how pretty she looked and took a swallow of wine. With that his smoothly shaven yellow face shone like a pair of freshly polished leather shoes.

Because of the business over his becoming an associate professor, Hung-chien had always regarded Kao Sung-nien with a certain rancor and so had as little to do with him as possible. He had never expected Kao to be so congenial. As a student of biology, Kao knew that "the survival of the fittest" was ordained by nature. He was quite confident of his own ability to adapt to the environment and to know what to say to whom on which occasion. Like the head instructor of the 200,000 imperial troops referred to in ancient novels as "an expert in all eighteen of the military arts," Kao Sung-nien, as president, was "fluent" in the disciplines of all three colleges and all ten departments of the school. "Fluent," that is, in the sense of flowing smoothly, as in "the free flow of trains" or "a smooth intestinal flow." A few "brief remarks" would go in through the ears and flow directly out of the mouth without stopping for a moment in the brain. One day the Political Science Association held its inaugural meeting and had asked him to give a speech. He could speak volubly on international relations, comparing Fascism with Communism, but maintaining that, in the final analysis, China's present political system was the best. The next day the Literary Study Group was having a social gathering. In his hortatory speech, besides saying poetry and songs were "the soul of the people," and literature was a "tool for psychological reconstruction," he encouraged the audience to become India's Tagore, England's Shakespeare, France's—uh—France's Rousseau (also pronounced 'loso'),[4] Germany's Goethe, and America's—American writers were too numerous. The day after at the Physics Club's meeting to welcome new members, having no atomic bomb to talk about yet, he could only call out a few times to the theory of relativity, making Einstein, all the way on the other side of the ocean, run a fever in his right ear and even sneeze. Besides this, he could even say "Shit" once or twice during a chat with the military instructor. Surprised and delighted, the instructor looked at him with new respect and considered him one of his own. Today Kao was having an informal meal with a few close friends with women present besides, so of course he adapted differently by cracking jokes and poking fun.

Mrs. Wang said, "We were just now taking you to task for choosing such a wretched place to set up a school. Everyone is bored to death."

"Well, if you die of boredom, I won't pay with my life! If it were someone else's, I could probably manage. Mrs. Wang's life is too precious. I couldn't pay with that, could I, Mr. Wang?"

With the boss in such high good humor, they all tried to do their duty by laughing respectfully once, twice, or whatever.

"It'd be all right if there were a radio to listen to," said Chao Hsin-mei.

Miss Fan said she too enjoyed listening to the radio.

Wang Ch'u-hou said, "A remote place has its advantages. With no other way to amuse themselves, people can visit one another and become close friends. Friends are made, and from being friends perhaps they'll go a step further and—Mr. Chao, Mr. Fang, you two young ladies, eh?"

The president called out "Hooray!" in the tone of one singing a school song, giving a party cheer, or yelling a slogan, and toasted everyone.

Hung-chien said, "Just now Mrs. Wang was talking about playing mahjong for recreation."

"Who plays mahjong?" interrupted the president.

"Didn't Mr. Wong borrow our set to play everyday?" asked Mrs. Wang, ignoring Kao Sung-nien's warning look.

Hung-chien said, "Hsin-mei and I aren't interested in mahjong anyway. We were going to buy a deck of cards to play bridge, but we couldn't find one anywhere in the town, so we ended up buying a Chinese chess set.[5] When Hsin-mei lost, he banged the chess pieces against the table so hard that several of them were busted to pieces. For the last couple of days, we haven't been able to play any more."

With Kao sitting between them, Miss Fan smiled at Hsin-mei and said she had never thought Hsin-mei could be so childish. Miss Liu then asked Hsin-mei to tell what Hung-chien did when he lost at chess.

President Kao said, "Playing chess is fine. It's just as well you couldn't find a deck of cards. It's a gambling device all the same. Though cards don't make any noise, it wouldn't be very good if the students found out about it. Li Mei-t'ing has prohibited them from playing cards. According to the principle of 'life in common' among students and teachers—"

For a while there Kao Sung-nien had acted like a human being, thought Hung-chien. *Why had Kao changed back into a president?* He wished he could say: "Open the Wongs' mahjong game to the public and invite the students to come gamble too. That'd be 'life in common.' "

Mrs. Wang impatiently interrupted President Kao, "I get a headache every time I hear those words 'life in common.' It's all Li Mei-t'ing's fancy ideas. His own family isn't here, in any case, so he doesn't feel the hardships other people with families do. At first I was afraid of the noise, so I didn't play. But now I will play. If you want to punish me, Mr. President, you can go ahead. It's none of Li Mei-t'ing's business."

President Kao sensed a coquettish attitude in the way Mrs. Wang challenged him to punish her, and it made his heart flutter and his body grow hot. "I wouldn't do that!" he said, "but running a school has its own difficulties—you need only ask Mr. Wang about that—colleagues should be amiable and tolerant toward one another."

Mrs. Wang said with a scornful laugh, "Well, I'm not Li Mei-t'ing's colleague. Mr. President, when did you ever hire me to work in your school as—as a maid? I'm not qualified to be a faculty member."

Kao clucked comfortingly in his throat.

"Today is Wednesday," said Mrs. Wang. "Saturday evening I'll get the set back and play the whole night through. We'll just see what Li Mei-t'ing is going to do about it. Mr. Chao, Mr. Fang, do you have the courage to come?"

Kao sighed, "I wasn't going to say anything, but since you're being like this, Mrs. Wang, I'll just have to tell everyone. It's because of Li Mei-t'ing that I broke in uninvited on the party today. I came to talk with Mr. Wang. I didn't know you had company."

The guests all said, "We're glad you came. Usually we can't get you to come."

Mr. Wang asked calmly, "What is it about Li Mei-t'ing?"

Mrs. Wang looked thoroughly disgusted, indicating she didn't care to hear what Kao had to say.

The president said, "Li came just as I was leaving the office and asked me who was going to speak at next Monday's assembly. I told him I hadn't thought of anyone yet. He said that in the dean's report he would like to say something about proper recreation for university faculty and students during the War of Resistance."

Mrs. Wang snorted.

"I said very well," Kao continued. "Li said if after he had spoken, the students asked him whether the mahjong games and gambling at the Wongs were considered proper recreation or not, how should he answer?"

Everyone sighed in sudden realization.

"Of course, I covered up for you by saying there couldn't be such a thing. Li said, 'All the faculty know about it. You, Mr. President, are the only one who does not know.' "

Hsin-mei and Hung-chien said, "What nonsense! We didn't know about it!"

"Li said it was all clear from his investigation. The winnings and losses were very high, the set was yours, such and such people were always playing, and you, Mr. Wang, were one of them—"

Mr. Wang's face turned scarlet, and the guests all stared uncomfortably at their bowls and chopsticks. For several seconds the room was so quiet that ants could have been heard crawling on the floor—except that at the time there were no ants.

The president laughed unnaturally and went on, "There was one thing funny. Mrs. Wang, you're sure to laugh when you hear this. Li had heard from somewhere that your set was an American one made of rubber and made no noise when played."

The room rocked with laughter. The hilarity relieved the tension of a moment ago. Hung-chien asked Mrs. Wang if it really was noiseless. Mrs. Wang laughed at him for being as much of a country bumpkin as Li

252

Mei-t'ing and added, " 'Blind Man Li' must have gone deaf. Whoever heard of an American-made, noiseless mahjong set!"

President Kao, however, did not agree with this frivolousness; he sat tight-lipped and unsmiling to show his disapproval.

Wang said, "What does Li think we should do? Announce the games to the students?"

Mrs. Wang said, "Why not just let the whole thing out? Have everyone play in the open and stop all this furtive business of covering the table with a blanket, covering the blanket with a plastic tablecloth."

Miss Fan noted brightly, "That's what you call 'noiseless mahjong!' "

"I'm sick and tired of staying here," said Mrs. Wang. "Let Li Mei-t'ing raise a fuss, let the students drive you out, and let President Kao dismiss you. I couldn't wish for anything more than to leave this place."

"Tut! tut! tut!" the president clucked.

Wang said, "It's because he couldn't be chairman of the Chinese Department that he can't get along with me. But I really didn't want to take the job. I turned the president down several times, didn't I, Mr. Kao? But then, my resignation must be entirely on my own. No one can force me out. I just won't go. Li Mei-t'ing's got me wrong. And as for his own behavior, humph, I know all about that too, such as visiting brothels in town."

Wang stopped dramatically, the others gasped in astonishment; Hsin-mei and Hung-chien immediately thought of Wang Mei-yü.

After a long pause President Kao said, "Surely he doesn't go that far?"

Seeing how partial the president was, Hung-chien blurted out indignantly, "I think what Mr. Wang said is quite possible. Mr. Li pulled all kinds of shenanigans when he was traveling with us. Ask Hsin-mei if you don't believe me."

His disapproval showing all over his face, the president said, "A gentleman hides the bad and makes known the good.[6] That sort of private business between men and women is better left ignored."

Miss Fan, who was just about to ask Hsin-mei what sort of shenanigans, took such a fright that she scooped up a spoonful of chicken soup and swallowed her question down with it.

Realizing his remarks might offend Wang Ch'u-hou, President Kao hastily added, "Don't get me wrong, Hung-chien. Li Mei-t'ing is an old colleague of mine, so naturally I know his character. But there's no point in Mr. Wang having a quarrel with him. I'll find some way to deal with Li later."

Mrs. Wang said with great magnanimity, "I'm the one to blame in any case. Ch'u-hou really wanted to humor him, but I was so disgusted from the very first time I set eyes on him that I've never invited him over. We're not like Han Hsüeh-yü and his foreign wife who treat the History Department faculty and students to a simple meal every three days and a banquet every five. And what's so amazing is they invite the students over for dinner and the faculty over for tea."

Hung-chien remembered the History Department student who had had the runs four or five times in one night.

"The expense is a trivial matter. I just don't have the energy, and I'm not so capable as that foreign woman. She's a Western lady, and she can handle all this socializing, entertaining, keeping up contacts, and she can even sing. I'm just a Chinese countrywoman. I'll keep to my place and not make a fool of myself. As I always say, if you have the ability, then be a professor. If not, then get out. Don't go telling your ugly old wife to be a hostess for your students and colleagues."

Hung-chien couldn't help exclaiming, "Bravo, bravo!"

Although Wang Ch'u-hou knew his wife wasn't referring to him, he was burning all over.

Mrs. Wang said, "Mr. Kao needn't talk to Li Mei-t'ing nor does Ch'u-hou have to have a showdown with him. All we have to do is think of some way to entice him over to the Wongs for a game of mahjong. Won't that put an end to it all?"

"Mrs. Wang, you really are—really are a clever one!" President Kao patted the table in admiration, since he could not pat Mrs. Wang's head or shoulder. "Only you could have thought up that scheme! How did you know Li Mei-t'ing loves to play mahjong?"

Mrs. Wang had made the remark in jest; when taken seriously by the president she came back with, "I know."

Mr. Wang also stroked his mustache and repeated Su Tung-p'o's famous line, " 'Most certainly! Most certainly!' "

Chao Hsin-mei's gaze seemed glued to Mrs. Wang's face. Left abandoned on the sidelines, Miss Liu was filled with resentment. She hated Mrs. Wang, she hated her brother and sister-in-law, and she despised Miss Fan. She regretted having come that day only to be ignored. Suddenly noticing Hsin-mei's expression and then glancing at Miss Fan from the corner of her eye, she smiled scornfully to herself, feeling much better.

Miss Fan had noticed it too and aroused Hsin-mei with the remark, "Mr. Chao, Mrs. Wang sure is sharp!"

Face turning red, Hsin-mei mumbled, "She sure is!" avoiding Miss Fan's gaze.

Hung-chien said, "That's a great idea. But Li Mei-t'ing is always out for petty gains. You'll have to let him win. He'll still raise a fuss if he loses."

They all laughed. Thinking how talkative and indiscreet Hung-chien was, Kao merely said, "I hope you'll all keep everything said today strictly confidential."

After dinner the host invited them to sit in the living room. The women's rouged and powdered faces, unable to withstand the perspiration steamed out by the food and wine and the vibrations from the exercise of chewing, resembled the walls during the rainy season. No wonder Byron hated sharing a table with women and having to watch them eat themselves into ugliness during the course of a meal. Although Miss Fan was so refined and elegant, yet even she would have liked to spit out the dregs of her meat, and after half a cup of wine too much, the unrouged portion of her face was as pink as the veal displayed in foreign butcher shops.

Mrs. Wang asked her women guests, "Would you like to come to my room and wash your hands?"

The two women followed after her. Kao Sung-nien and Wang Ch'u-hou talked confidentially in low tones.

Hsin-mei said to Hung-chien, "We'll leave together in a little while. Don't forget."

Hung-chien said with a grin, "What if I want to see Miss Liu home by myself?"

"Whatever happens," said Hsin-mei sternly, "let me accompany you just this once while you take her home. Isn't Mrs. Wang just trying to play a joke on us?"

Hung-chien said, "Actually no one has to take anyone home. We can go our way, and they can go theirs."

"We can't do that," insisted Hsin-mei. "We're returned students. We're supposed to know that much etiquette at least."

They both bewailed their misfortune at being young, unmarried returned students.

Miss Liu forced herself to stay for a while longer; then she said she was going home.

Hsin-mei quickly stood up and said, "Hung-chien, we should be going, too. We can see the two ladies home on our way."

Miss Liu said she could go home by herself. There was no need for anyone to accompany her.

"No, no, no," insisted Hsin-mei. "We'll see Miss Fan to the women's dormitory first, then take you home. I've never been to your place."

Hung-chien laughed to himself at the way Hsin-mei cozied up to Miss Liu in order to get rid of Miss Fan, only to leave himself open to another kind of misunderstanding. Mrs. Wang whispered something in Miss Fan's ear; Fan then pushed Mrs. Wang away with a smile mixed with a trace of annoyance.

Mr. Wang said, "Well, then, 'once you're gone, you're on your own.' The ladies' safety is now in your hands."

President Kao said he would like to stay a little longer, indicating at the same time how extremely envious he was of his young friends. With such lovely weather, it was a spring evening just right for a stroll. And as the four of them were all young, they made good companions for a spring evening stroll.

The four of them walked abreast with Miss Fan and Miss Liu in the middle and Chao and Fang on either side. When they came near a wooden bridge, Miss Fan said it would only hold two people and wanted to walk across the stream bed instead. Just as Hung-chien and Miss Liu reached the middle of the bridge, they heard Miss Fan suddenly cry out sharply, "Oooh!" They quickly stopped and asked what had happened. Miss Fan laughed, and in a scolding tone Hsin-mei urged her to go by the bridge since the rocks in the stream bed were so slippery. They then realized that Miss Fan had nearly fallen down and had luckily been caught by Hsin-mei. Miss Liu crossed the bridge and stood impatiently waiting for them. Hung-chien waited until Miss Fan had come across, then asked solicitously if she had twisted a muscle. Miss Fan thanked him and said she hadn't—it was twisted a little—but it didn't matter. It'd be all right—but she couldn't walk very fast, and she asked Miss Liu not to wait. Miss Liu uttered a murmur of consent, but Hung-chien said that Miss Liu and he could walk slowly. They had gone no more than a dozen steps when Miss Fan again called out, "Oooh!" Her handbag was missing. They all asked her if she had dropped it in the stream bed when she fell. She said she could have.

Hsin-mei said, "No one will pick it up now. We'll go back to the dormitory first and get a flashlight."

Miss Fan then remembered that she had left her handbag at Mrs. Wang's. Cursing her stupidity, she wanted to hurry back and fetch it, saying, "How can I ask you all to wait? You go on ahead. In any case Mr. Chao can go with me—Mr. Chao, you'll certainly scold me."

Whenever women go out, they usually forget something, which means that going out once actually amounts to going out twice. Anna will say, "Oh, darn it, I forgot my handkerchief." At that point her companion Mary will remember she didn't bring her compact, and Julia, reminded by the other two, will say, "I'm even more stupid. I didn't bring any money"— and the three of them will laugh as if it were the funniest thing in the world and return arm in arm to get the handkerchief, the compact, and the money. But the contagion of forgetting things had no effect on Miss Liu. It set Chao Hsin-mei to complaining to himself, *Don't tell me all this today was arranged by fate?*

256

Hung-chien suddenly felt his head and asked, "Hsin-mei, did I wear a hat today?"

Hsin-mei was puzzled for a moment; then suddenly catching on, he said, "It seems you did wear one. I can't remember clearly—yes, you did wear one, I—I didn't though."

Hung-chien said that Miss Fan's mentioning her handbag had reminded him of his hat. Since Miss Fan was having trouble walking, and he had to go back to the Wangs for his hat anyway, he'd get her handbag for her while he was at it.

"I'll be quick. You all wait here for me," and he bounded off before he'd finished speaking. He returned with only the handbag in his hand and no hat on his head, saying, "I didn't wear a hat. Hsin-mei, you fooled me."

Hsin-mei said indignantly, "Miss Liu, Miss Fan, you see how unreasonable he is. He's the big muddlehead, and yet he acts as though I'm the one who's supposed to look after his hat."

In the darkness he gratefully squeezed Hung-chien's hand. Miss Liu gave a short grating laugh. Miss Fan's thanks to Hung-chien were unnecessarily cold, and she had little else to say the rest of the way.

Despite Miss Liu's refusal, Hung-chien and Hsin-mei saw her home anyway. She of course invited them in to sit for a while. The eldest daughter who slept with her was still sitting at the dining table, having refused to go to bed until she returned, yawning again and again and rubbing her eyes with her little fists. When she saw her aunt had brought two guests home, she ran inside yelling, "Papa, Mama," waking up her three-month-old baby brother as well. Liu Tung-fang hurried out to greet the guests with Mrs. Liu behind him carrying the baby. Hung-chien and Hsin-mei dutifully remarked on how nice and well-fed the baby was and discussed whether he resembled his mother or his father. These are the sort of remarks parents never tire of hearing. Hung-chien went up close to its face and snapped his fingers. This was his only skill in amusing a child.

Mrs. Liu said, "Let's get to know your—uh—Uncle Fang.[7] Let Mr. Fang hold you." She wished she could have said "Paternal Uncle Fang."[8] "We've just had our diapers changed, so there won't be any accident!"

Hung-chien, with a rueful smile, had no choice but to take the child. It had just been sucking its thumb, and when given to another to hold, the jostling caused saliva from its hand to foam all over Hung-chien's nose and the side of his face. Since he'd been entrusted with the child by Mrs. Liu, Hung-chien had to keep his disgust to himself. Hsin-mei, having rid himself of Miss Fan, was in high spirits, and seeing an exposed area of the child's thigh, which was clean, he put his mouth up close to kiss it. This made all four Lius laugh merrily, thinking how wonderful this Mr. Chao was. Annoyed at the way Hsin-mei was putting on, Hung-chien asked Hsin-mei if he wanted to hold the baby. Seeing how uncomfortable the baby was in Hung-chien's arms, and thinking that since Hsin-mei had a senior position at the university and was an infrequent guest besides, Mrs. Liu decided she should not inconvenience Hsin-mei. She reached out her arms, saying, "We're so heavy. Uncle Fang is tired from holding us."

Hung-chien handed the child back, and while no one was watching, pulled out his handkerchief and wiped the already dried saliva from his face.

"Such a good boy," said Hsin-mei. "He's not afraid of strangers."

As though reciting an "Epitaph for a Child," Mrs. Liu began singing its praises, saying how clever it was, how well-behaved, how it slept till dawn the moment it was put to bed. Since no one was paying any attention to her, the boy's older sister opened her eyes wide and having heard all she could stand, put in, "He does too cry. He wakes me up at night with his crying."

Miss Liu said, "Who does the crying? Who's so big and still grabs things to eat? When she can't beat up little brother, who screams at the top of her lungs? Aren't you ashamed?"

Upset, the girl pointed exultantly at Miss Liu and cried, "Auntie is a grown-up, and she cries, too. I know, that day—"

Her parents hushed her and scolded her for not being in bed yet. Miss Liu pulled her inside, certain the guests had not seen the color of her face. After that, trying to carry on the conversation was like using artificial respiration to save a drowning victim. No life could be brought back into it. Miss Liu did not show her face again.

When they had said goodbye and left, Hsin-mei remarked, "Children sure are frightening! They'll tell everything. Miss Liu is so quiet and happy on the outside. Who'd have thought she ever cried. I guess everyone has his own troubles. Ai!"

Hung-chien said, "It doesn't matter about you and Miss Fan. I'm indebted to Liu Tung-fang for having helped me once, but I've no intention of getting married here. Mrs. Wang really wasted her time and effort. I'm sure to have a misunderstanding with Liu over this some day."

"It won't be that bad," said Hsin-mei, brushing it off lightly. He often asked Hung-chien what he thought of Mrs. Wang and wanted Hung-chien to help figure out how old she was.

Miss Sun's correspondence with Lu Tzu-hsiao weighed on Hung-chien's mind like a rat gnawing on something in the walls. He was disturbed by it all evening and couldn't stop thinking about it. He almost wrote Miss Sun a letter advising her as a friend to be careful about whom she made friends with. In the end he convinced himself to let her get close to Lu. He wasn't in love with her, so why should he be looking on jealously and meddling in her business? It was all Chao Hsin-mei's fault. His joking had put the idea in his head, like someone in a hypnotic state who has been given a suggestion. What usually happened in such cases was that other people kept on joking until the person involved really did fall in love. He'd seen it happen many times and certainly would never be that foolish himself. Still, he felt in the end as though he'd been wronged somehow. He hated Miss Sun and despised her besides.

That afternoon, much to his surprise, there was a knock on his door and in she came. At the sight of her all the ill will in Hung-chien's heart dissolved like the nighttime mist under the morning sun. She had come several times before but never made him so happy as now. Hung-chien remarked that he hadn't seen her since returning from Kweilin and asked her how she had been spending her winter vacation. She said she had been meaning to come thank them for the things he and Hsin-mei had brought her from Kweilin but had had two bouts of fever and chills. Today she had come over with Miss Fan to deliver some books. Hung-chien asked with a smile if they were plays for Hsin-mei. Miss Sun replied with a smile that they were.

"Have you gone up to see Uncle Chao?" Hung-chien asked.

"I wouldn't make a nuisance of myself!" said Miss Sun. "I didn't go up at all. She wanted to come see Mr. Chao and asked me whether he lived upstairs or down and what the room number was. She didn't want me to guide her. I agreed not to go up with her and told her I had something to do here, too."

"Hsin-mei won't necessarily be grateful for your guidance."

"It's all so hard!" The smile on Miss Sun's face as she said this indicated that she did not find it very hard at all to know what to do. "I didn't know until she came back last night that Mrs. Wang had had a party." This was a commonplace remark, but being oversensitive, she felt it was quite beside the point and quickly changed the subject by asking, "You'd seen the famous beauty Mrs. Wang before, hadn't you?"

"The business last night was all Mr. and Mrs. Wang's nonsense—I'd seen her twice before. She carries herself well. Is she a famous beauty? This is the first time I've ever heard of it."

Hung-chien felt rather nervous when he saw her, and his hands were continuously toying with the four-colored *supernorma* pencil on his desk which he had brought back from Germany. Miss Sun asked for the pencil, pushed out the red lead, and drew a red mouth on a blank spot of the ink blotter. About an inch away she drew ten oblong, pointed red dots, five in a group, to represent fingernails. Beyond this there were no other facial features or body. When she had finished, she said, "These are Mrs. Wang's— main points."

Hung-chien thought for a moment, then burst out laughing. "It really does bear a resemblance. I have to hand it to you for thinking that up!"

The significance of a remark in the listener's mind is often like a strange cat, which enters the room without making a sound. You don't notice its presence until it gives a "mew." When Miss Sun said at the beginning that she had something to do at the faculty dormitory, Hung-chien hadn't paid any attention to it. The remark now awoke in his consciousness as though from sleep. Maybe she had come to see Lu Tzu-hsiao and just dropped in to see him on her way. The pang of jealousy he felt inside was like a chestnut roasting on a fire about to burst from its shell in the extreme heat. Anxious to get at the truth, but afraid his personal questioning might leave a trail, he remarked, "That Miss Fan is an interesting one, all right. Yesterday was the first time I got to know her. You're roommates. Are you very close?"

"She only respects Mrs. Wang. Now of course there's Uncle Chao. Mr. Fang, did you offend Miss Fan yesterday?"

"No, why?"

"She came back cursing you—oh, goodness, I'm gossiping."

"That's strange! What did she curse me about?"

Miss Sun said with a laugh, "Oh, it wasn't anything special. She just said you wouldn't say anything, paid no attention to anyone, and did nothing but eat."

"What nonsense," said Hung-chien, reddening. "That's not true. I did speak, though not much. I just went yesterday to make up the number for the dinner party. It didn't involve me, so naturally all I did was eat."

Miss Sun threw him a quick glance, and toying with the pencil said, "What Miss Fan said was nothing really. She also called you a blockhead and said you didn't even know whether you wore a hat or not."

Hung-chien guffawed and said, "I deserve a scolding for that! It's a long story. I'll tell you about it some day. But that Miss Fan of yours—"

Miss Sun protested that Miss Fan was not hers.

"OK, OK, that roommate of yours, I don't think she's very good. All she does is criticize other people behind their backs. If Hsin-mei really did marry her, he'd have to break off with all his old friends. She mentioned you last night, too."

"She couldn't have had anything good to say. What did she say?"

Hung-chien hesitated, and Miss Sun said, "I've got to know. Tell me, Mr. Fang." All suggestion of a smile faded, and she was sweetly stubborn.

Hung-chien had seen this expression on her face once before. It aroused all his tender feelings of protectiveness, and he said, "She didn't say much. She didn't criticize you or anything. I don't remember exactly. She just said something about someone writing you letters. That's common enough. She just likes to make a big fuss over nothing."

Such an expression of rage came over Miss Sun's face that Hung-chien did not dare look at her. Her face turned completely red as quickly as a bucket of gasoline when a spark is dropped into it. Pounding the pencil against the table, she exclaimed, "Shit! I can't stand him, and she even spreads rumors around for him! I'll have to get even with her for this."

The knot in Hung-chien's throat loosened; he said quickly, "It's my fault. Don't pay any attention to her. Let her spread rumors if she wants. No one's going to believe them anyway. I for one don't believe them."

"The whole thing's so annoying, but I can't figure out what to do about it. That Lu Tzu-hsiao—" Miss Sun was so revolted by these three words, she seemed almost unwilling to allow them in her mouth. "Last year around the time of the final examinations he suddenly wrote me a letter. I didn't write a single word in reply, but he still kept on writing me letter after letter. During the winter vacation he came to the women's dormitory to see me and insisted on inviting me out to eat—"

Hung-chien asked nervously, "You didn't go, did you?"

The question made her lower her head involuntarily. "Of course, I wouldn't go. That guy is really crazy. He kept on writing letters. The more he wrote, the more ridiculous they got. The first letter said that to save me the trouble of answering, he had enclosed a sheet of paper with a question written on it." She flushed again. "Never mind what the question was. He said if my answer to the question was—was affirmative, I was to write a plus sign and send him back the paper. Otherwise I was to write a minus sign. In the last letter he simply wrote out a plus and a minus sign, and I was supposed to cross one out. Now isn't that ridiculous and infuriating?" As she spoke, her eyes were mirthful, while her lips pouted.

Hung-chien couldn't help observing with a smile, "That's a professor's—a professor's letter, all right. When we took tests in 'General Knowledge' class in junior high school, the teacher always gave us questions like that. But Lu at least is sincere in his feelings toward you."

Miss Sun's eyes flashed angrily and she said, "Who wants him to be sincere toward me! He keeps on sending those letters. If other people find out about them, it'll make me look ridiculous, too."

"Miss Sun, I have an idea for you," said Hung-chien as though mulling it over carefully in his mind. "You haven't thrown out any of the letters he's written you during all this, have you? It'd be best if you haven't. Tie them all up in one bundle and have the errand boy return them to him. Don't write a single word."

"Should I write his name and everything on the outside of the package?"

"No, don't. He'll understand well enough when he opens it up. . . ."

If a psychoanalyst heard all this, he'd know at once that the subconscious was up to tricks. Hung-chien was avenging himself on someone else by using T'ang Hsiao-fu's method of sending back his own letters.

"Simply rip up the letters before wrapping them up—no, don't. That would be too hard on him."

Miss Sun said gratefully, "I'll do just as you say. It couldn't be wrong. I really do appreciate it. I don't understand anything, and there's no one I can talk it over with. I'm so afraid of doing the wrong thing. I just don't know how I should behave. It's all such a nuisance! Would you teach me how, Mr. Fang?"

It was all too much like the poor, ignorant, weak, little girl. Maybe Hsin-mei was right when he said she was playing the fool. Hung-chien's suspicion flitted by without stopping like a swallow over water. Miss Sun not only sought his advice, but was ready to follow his every word as well. This pleased him so much; it left no room in his mind for suspicion. They talked a bit more; then Miss Sun said she wouldn't be going to Hsin-mei's that day. She wanted to return directly to the dormitory and told Hung-chien not to see her out. Hung-chien had not wanted to see her out in the first place for fear of attracting undue attention, but when she said this, he could only reply, "I'll walk you back—just halfway—to the door of the dormitory."

Miss Sun stood staring down at the floor and said, "All right, but you don't have to be so polite. There are—uh—lots of rumors going around. It's so annoying!"

Hung-chien gave a start. "What rumors?" he asked. He immediately regretted having asked the question.

"If you—if you haven't heard," said Miss Sun haltingly, "then never mind. Goodbye. I'll do what you told me to," and shaking hands, she smiled and left.

Hung-chien collapsed weakly into his chair. He felt cold and hot all over as though stricken with malaria. *Damn!* he thought. *Damn! What is this "rumor" all about? Whenever two people get together, somebody always starts a rumor just like the way a spider spins a web whenever two tree branches meet. I was too talkative today and said too many things I needn't and shouldn't have said. Wasn't I just substantiating the "rumor"? Maybe I'm wrong, but it seemed Miss Sun's parting remark was said with special emphasis. So now her marriage is all my responsibility. Isn't that just great!* He became so fidgety that he could neither sit nor stand still and began pacing around his room. *If I don't love Miss Sun, why don't I just mind my own business? Or am I in love with her—just a little bit?*

A peal of feminine laughter along with footsteps clattering on the stairs like a greenhouse collapsing interrupted Hung-chien's thoughts. It was immediately followed by Hsin-mei's voice, "Watch your step. Don't fall down again like yesterday." Then there was another peal of feminine laughter along with the sound of several doors upstairs and down suddenly opening, then closing softly. *Miss Fan really can do it up,* thought Hung-chien. *Those two peals of laughter all but amount to an announcement on the president's bulletin board to the entire school that she and Chao Hsin-mei are sweethearts. Poor Hsin-mei. How angry he must be.* Though sorry for Hsin-mei, he was relieved at the same time, feeling as though the "rumor" about himself had lost some of its gravity. He was just picking up a cigarette when Hsin-mei came in without knocking and took it away from him.

"Didn't you see Miss Fan home?" Hung-chien asked him.

Ignoring him, Hsin-mei lit the cigarette and took a few furious drags, then cried, "Damn that little jerk Sun Jou-chia! Why'd she have to bring Fan Yi along when she had a date with Lu Tzu-hsiao! Next time I see her I'm going to give her a cussing out."

Hung-chien said, "Don't make blind accusations. Remember? Didn't you say on the boat that lending books is the first step in a romance? Now what about it? Ha, ha. Heaven's will is being done."

Hsin-mei couldn't restrain a smile and said, "Did I say that on the boat? In any case I'm not going to read a single word of either play she brought."

Hung-chien asked who the playwrights were.

Hsin-mei replied, "If you want to look at them, you can go get them yourself. They're on my desk. Please open my windows for me while you're at it. I'm afraid of the cold. I even had the charcoal brazier on today. The minute she walked in, the room was filled with the smell of her cosmetics. I couldn't take it. I wanted to smoke, but she said smoke bothered her. I opened all the windows along one side, and then she immediately began sneezing, which scared me into closing them. I was afraid that if she did catch a cold, I'd never have any peace."

Hung-chien said with a laugh, "I'm afraid I'll faint, too, so I'm not going up either," and he told the errand boy to run up, open the windows, and bring down the books. In order to avoid the possibility of making any mistake, the errand boy brought down all six or seven of the Chinese and Western books on Hsin-mei's desk, including the two plays. Hung-chien opened one of them and found on the flyleaf the words, "For Yi—the author." Underneath a seal was stamped.

"Such an affectionate form of address!" remarked Hung-chien. He casually opened to the flyleaf of the other book and exclaimed, "Hey, Hsin-mei, did you see this one?"

Hsin-mei replied, "She wouldn't let me look at it right then, and now I don't want to." So saying, he reached out and took the book. There were two lines in English: "*To my precious darling. From the author.*" Hsin-mei let out an exclamation and closed the cover to see who the author was.

"Do you know this guy?" he asked Hung-chien.

"Never heard of him. You want to challenge him to a duel?"

Hsin-mei snorted and muttered, "How ridiculous! How despicable! How disgusting!"

Hung-chien said, "Are you speaking to me or cursing Fan Yi? She's really strange. Why'd she give you books to read with all this written in them?"

Hsin-mei's American vocabulary came out, "*You baby!* You mean you can't figure out what she's up to?"

"It's so obvious it makes a person wonder if she could be that obvious."

"Never mind her," said Hsin-mei. "Mrs. Wang is the one who started it all. 'Whoever ties the bell around the tiger's neck must untie it.' I'm going to go see her tomorrow."

"Please speak up for me, too."

"You aren't going with me?"

"No. I can see you're a little infatuated with Mrs. Wang. I think you'd better not go there very often. People like us lead dull lives. Shut up in this valley with no normal recreation, we are apt to get carried away the moment our feelings are aroused. We'd better avoid stimulating them."

His face reddening, Hsin-mei said, "Don't talk nonsense. That's your own confession. You've probably taken a fancy to someone yourself."

Touched on his sensitive spot, Hung-chien said, "All right, go then. Are you going to give Mrs. Wang those two plays to pass on to Miss Fan?"

"No, that wouldn't do," said Hsin-mei. "I couldn't give them back to her today. She won't come tomorrow in the hope that I'll return her visit. I won't go, of course. The day after tomorrow in the afternoon I'll have the errand boy return them to her directly."

Today's a bad day, thought Hung-chien. *This is the second person to be sending something back.* Taking a sheet of paper, he wrapped up the two books and handed them solemnly to Hsin-mei. "I'm wasting one sheet of paper. These books have the handwriting of celebrities on them, so tell the boy to be careful not to lose them."

"Celebrities!" snorted Hsin-mei. "Every last one of those writers considers himself a celebrity. It seems that when a person's fame gets so great he can't manage it, he'll divide it up among several pen names. Well, I didn't do anything today, but I've suffered enough. I've got to cheer myself up a little. Let's go out for dinner together."

Hung-chien said, "Today's my turn to eat with the students. But that doesn't matter. You go on ahead to the restaurant and order. I'll humor them with a bowl of rice and hurry over."

Hung-chien felt that during that semester of teaching he had gradually gotten the knack of things through practice. The students' impression of him seemed to have improved a little, too. The four advisees assigned to him by the office of the Dean of Students came occasionally to chat and supplied him with all kinds of insights. He discovered that while it had not been many years since he graduated, once he became a teacher, he belonged to the older generation and could no longer share the views of the present students. First, he did not have their enthusiasm. Second, he considered himself more discreet than they. He wondered why those of his colleagues who went around with students never felt the generation gap. Or did they feel it and just not let it show? Though science has advanced, man still isn't the master of his own fate. Age is an insurmountable fact in the natural course of things, like eating, drinking, sex, and death. At times this kind of generation consciousness is even sharper than class consciousness. No matter how similar your political views, theories, and tastes are to your students', there are subtle differences between you and them just like cracks in pottery. Under ordinary circumstances they don't mean much, but once given a jolt, the cracks will widen into fissures. Maybe if he were another ten or fifteen years older, he would want to mingle with young people and share their vitality in order to warm his own decrepitude, like a vampire sucking the essence of the young and strong. Such was old Professor Lu of the Physics Department, who never missed a single student activity, or Wang Ch'u-hou, who had married such a young wife. In any case, the students could be pitifully blind on the one hand and frighteningly perceptive on the other. This wasn't necessarily true of their approval; sometimes they were actually fooled by their teachers. But as for their censure, this was truly just and absolute, amounting to the "Final Judgment" of the last day of the world and leaving no room for appeal. Their loathing for Li Mei-t'ing went without saying, and they never really gave Han Hsüeh-yü their love and respect. When Hung-chien became a teacher, he realized that the way Westerners looked down on Orientals or the way the rich looked down on the poor—no, the way the poor looked down on the rich—was not half so bad as the way students looked down on professors. Fairness, not mercy, was their virtue. They refused to forgive. Perhaps because they themselves had no need for forgiveness, or at least didn't know they needed it, so Hung-chien thought.

As for Hung-chien's relations with his colleagues, they were worse than they were the first semester. Han Hsüeh-yü's nod was so perfunctory that it looked as though Han had twisted a shoulder, and Mrs. Han stared off in the distance at the scene behind Hung-chien. While Hung-chien did not care, he was somewhat perturbed by all this since it meant something else to worry about whenever he was out walking along the street, and if he saw them coming from afar he would duck out of the way. Lu Tzu-hsiao had grown very aloof, a tacit understanding having been reached between them. What disturbed him most was that Liu Tung-fang seemed to have considerably cooled toward him. What a fine matchmaker Mrs. Wang had turned out to be! His one consolation was that Wang Ch'u-hou was very much concerned about his affairs. He knew that Old Wang was going to be dean of the College of Letters and so was courting junior faculty members. People who harbored such administrative ambitions were the least reliable, and there wasn't necessarily anything he himself could gain by helping Old Wang to succeed. It was like the rickshaw boy who pulls his passenger up to a restaurant after much pain and effort, and then is still left to drag along his empty rickshaw, feeding on the west wind, with never a thought of going in to eat with him. But if someone as inconsequential as himself was worthy of patronage, then obviously he shouldn't underestimate himself. The last time Old Wang saw him, Old Wang joked that he, the matchmaker, had completely lost face. Why had neither of the fated romances come out successfully?

Hung-chien merely said, "I'm not worthy. I wouldn't dare aspire to it."

Wang Ch'u-hou said, "There's no point in your doing part-time work in the Foreign Languages Department. Next semester I'm planning to add a philosophy department and ask you to take care of courses solely within the department."

Hung-chien said gratefully, "At present I really have no place to call home. I just go begging from door to door, scorned by both faculty and students."

"Nonsense!" said Wang Ch'u-hou. "But I'm now busy planning all this. Your salary must, of course, be adjusted."

Not wishing to be too beholden to him, Hung-chien said, "The president also promised me at the beginning that next semester I would be promoted to full professor."

"The weather is very nice today," said Wang Ch'u-hou. "Why don't we take a walk around the fields? Or would you care to come to my place for a chat and have something to eat?"

Hung-chien of course said that he would like to take a walk with him.

After crossing the stream and passing by the Wang's house, they came upon a clump of ten or fifteen thin cedar trees, one of which had recently fallen and lay lengthwise on the ground. They sat down on the trunk. Wang Ch'u-hou took the cigarette from his mouth, and pointing with it all around him like a compass, said, "The scenery here isn't bad. 'Living at the foot of the tall pines,/Studying by the roots of the autumn trees.' When my wife feels up to it, I'll ask her to paint those two lines of poetry."

Hung-chien expressed his admiration.

Mr. Wang said, "Just now you were saying that the president promised you a promotion. How did he put it exactly?"

"He didn't make it definite, but that was the idea," replied Hung-chien.

"That means nothing," said Mr. Wang, shaking his head. "That sort of thing can be very exasperating! Hung-chien, you've just come back from abroad to teach, so you don't understand much about the way a university works. People with big names or special connections are of course exceptions, but for most faculty promotions, one can say this: It's easy to be promoted from lecturer to associate professor, but it's twice as hard to be promoted from associate professor to full professor. When I was at Hua Yang University they used to make this analogy: A lecturer is like a maid, a professor is like a wife, and as for an associate professor, he's no more than a concubine."—at this Hung-chien burst out laughing—"The difference of one word[9] can't be measured in terms of miles. For a maid to become a concubine is quite common—at least it used to be so. But for a concubine to gain legitimate status as a wife goes against all moral principles and obligations. It just can't be done. Wasn't there a couplet in the Ch'ing dynasty which went: 'I washed my concubine's feet,/And was given an honorary degree to start out.'[10] One of my colleagues in our department, also an associate professor, changed it to 'I win face for my concubine,/And wait for the honorable associate professor to make good.' Ha, ha—"

"Damn!" said Hung-chien. "Even an associate professor has to suffer insult!"

"But there's a way out: what is vulgarly known as 'jumping the manger.' If you can't get promoted to professor in your own school, transfer to another one where you will. If this school won't agree to your leaving, while another one will hire you as professor, then this school has no choice but to promote you. When another school gives you formal contracts or informal letters of appointment, the more you turn them down, the more you have to let the authorities here know about it. That way you'll get your salary raised. Leave things to me. After the spring vacation I'll have a friend in the Philosophy Department at Hua Yang University write a letter asking me to invite you there for him. I'll then show the letter to President Kao and sing a few rounds of praise for you on the side. He'll certainly promote you; this requires no effort on your part."

Now, if someone is willing to help you out in this way, and you don't rouse yourself to action, then you really are a worthless sort. So, from then on Hung-chien made it a point to put extra effort into preparing his lessons and gradually began to dream of being a "star professor." Just as getting a degree is a matter of duping one's professors with a thesis, so teaching is a matter of duping the students with the lecture material. Hung-chien had not duped his professors, and so he had not received his degree. Now that he wanted to dupe his students, he found he lacked a model to go by. There are two stages a professor must go through to become a star professor. First, he must make his lecture notes into a book, and second, he must use the book as his lectures. It is much like an apprentice barber who sharpens his skills by practicing on the heads of idiots or poor people. Thus, if a professor's lectures went off smoothly when tried out in the classroom, they could be published in a book. After publication, it would of course become a required textbook. Since Hung-chien was putting so much effort into his teaching, it was only natural that he should begin to have wild dreams of glory. He saw Miss Sun a few times but did not talk with her much, learning only that she had done just exactly as he had advised, no more and no less.

Hsin-mei often went to the Wangs. Hung-chien teased him about it, saying, "Be careful Wang Ch'u-hou doesn't get jealous."

Hsin-mei replied gravely, "He's not so petty as you—besides he's never home when I go. I've only seen him once or twice. The old fellow likes to gamble and always goes over to the Wongs."

Hung-chien remarked that Li Mei-t'ing must have won some money, since he'd stopped raising a fuss about mahjong games.

The evening of the fourth day of spring vacation was as warm as the previous evenings had been. Kao Sung-nien was returning from an engagement in town, strolling along drunk and sated, when on a sudden impulse he decided to detour around to the Wangs. As his family was not with him, it was very lonely returning to his bedroom. By staying out, it would seem the night was not yet over. Returning would only spell the end of it. It was nine o'clock by his watch, but there was not a sign of anyone on the field by the main gate of the campus. This was because during vacations the students returned home, went on trips, or in some cases stayed in the dormitories preparing for midterm examinations after the spring break. The sounds of frogs testing their voices could be heard scattered throughout the open countryside. He thought how early spring came in this region and at the same time was reminded of the spicy frog he had eaten last year. He knocked twice on the Wangs' gate, but no one answered. He remembered that the Wangs had recently hired a new maid. Perhaps it was her day off, but the girl servant could not have gone out. He then pulled at the bell

268

rope. This bell was connected with the servants' bedroom and had been installed for the master to use when he came back late at night. The girl opened the door with sleepy eyes and slippers on her feet. When she saw it was the president, she stifled her yawn and said that the master was not at home but had gone to the Wongs. President Kao's heart skipped a beat, and he asked about Mrs. Wang. The girl said she was home and led President Kao into the living room. She was just about to go in and call Mrs. Wang when, rubbing her head, she said it seemed Mrs. Wang had gone out too and had wakened her to shut the gate.

A wave of anger swept over Kao Sung-nien. *Playing mahjong!* he thought. *Still playing mahjong! One of these days the students will hear of it. I'll have to warn Old Wang and the rest of them.* He told the girl to shut the gate and rushed over to the Wongs.

When Wang Ch'u-hou and the others saw the president, they were all greatly embarrassed and hurriedly put away the mahjong set. Mrs. Wong herself served tea and offered the president some midnight snacks, which had been laid out for the gamblers. As soon as Kao Sung-nien saw that Mrs. Wang was not among them, he said, "Sorry to disturb you," but did not urge them to continue playing. "Mr. Wang, I'd like to speak to you about something. Let's go now."

When they were out of the house, Kao asked, "Where's Mrs. Wang?"

"She's home," replied Wang Ch'u-hou.

"I went to your house first. The girl told me she'd gone out, too."

"She couldn't have. She absolutely couldn't have," said Wang Ch'u-hou quickly, partly to answer Kao and partly to reassure himself, but his throat had gone hoarse with anxiety.

Despite his stubbornness, Chao Hsin-mei knew in his heart that Hung-chien was quite right and that he should avoid rousing any suspicions. He liked Mrs. Wang very much because she was attractive, she understood things, and she was the only woman there who had anything in common with him. He considered himself much too high-minded ever to get himself involved in a scandal. Lonely and bored during the spring vacation, he had gone over to the Wangs to chat after dinner. No one answered his knock, and he was about to leave, when suddenly Mrs. Wang opened the door herself. She said, "When I heard a knock at this hour, I didn't think it could be anyone else."

"Why did you answer it yourself?" Hsin-mei asked.

"One of the two servants has gone home, and the other one is just like a bird. She gets sleepy the moment it becomes dark. It was easier for me to open it myself than wake her up to do it."

"The weather is so nice; I came out for a walk. I was passing your house and decided to drop in to see you and Mr. Wang."

Mrs. Wang said with a smile, "Ch'u-hou has gone off to play mahjong. He won't be back until eleven. I was thinking of taking a walk myself. We can go together. You go to the gate and pull the bell to wake the girl. I'll tell her to shut the gate. Is it cold outside? I don't need an extra wrap, do I?"

Standing in the dark outside the gate, Hsin-mei heard her tell the maid, "I'm going to the Wongs, too. I'll be back with Mr. Wang in a while, so don't sleep too soundly!"

As they strolled along, Mrs. Wang asked Hsin-mei about his home, why he hadn't married, and if he'd ever had a sweetheart. "You must have had a girl friend. You can't fool me."

Hsin-mei gave her a brief account of his involvement with Su Wen-wan, but under Mrs. Wang's goading and probing, it became more and more detailed. They were chatting merrily when they found themselves back at the Wangs' gate.

Mrs. Wang said with a smile, "I got all carried away listening to you. How did I manage to come back again! Well, I'm tired now, anyway. I don't think I'll go to the Wongs. Thank you, Mr. Chao, for taking a walk with me, and thanks especially for telling me so many interesting things."

Hsin-mei grew somewhat ill at ease at this point and regretted having been so forthright and having told her everything. He then said, "You must be sick of hearing about it. A love story like that is of great interest to the person telling it, but only sounds common or funny to others. I know from experience."

Mrs. Wang said, "Well, I found it very interesting. But there's one thing I must tell you, Mr. Chao."

Hsin-mei urged her to tell him, but she refused and was going to knock on the door and go in, when Hsin-mei held her back with his hand and begged her to tell him. Kicking aside a pebble near her foot, she said, "Just remember this: Never say nice things about one woman to another."

Hsin-mei was so stunned that it was as if someone had struck him on the head. All he could do was gasp.

"Especially to someone as ill-tempered and rash as I am, to go on about how tender and refined this young lady of yours is—"

"Mrs. Wang, don't be so sensitive!" cried Hsin-mei. "I didn't mean that at all. To tell you the truth, I think you're quite like her in some ways."

Mrs. Wang half pushed aside his restraining arm and said, "Nonsense! Nonsense! No one could be like me—"

Suddenly they heard voices nearby and quickly separated.

Wang Ch'u-hou was not as young or quick-limbed as Kao Sung-nien and had run himself out of breath. Neither of them said a word. Just before reaching the Wangs, the sharp-eyed Kao Sung-nien caught sight of two figures entwined in the semitransparent evening light and rushed up to them. Wang Ch'u-hou also heard his wife talking with another man, and a red cloud came before his eyes. Hsin-mei was just about to turn around when someone grabbed him roughly by the shoulder, and he heard Mrs. Wang's horrified gasp. He turned his head and saw Kao Sung-nien's face with teeth bared less than an inch from his own. Frightened and abashed, he quickly shrugged off Kao Sung-nien's grasp.

When he saw it was Chao Hsin-mei, Kao released his hand and said, "What impertinence! How disgraceful!"

Wang Ch'u-hou seized his wife and wouldn't let go. Panting, he cursed in genteel tones, "Well! Well! Chao Hsin-mei, you scoundrel, you shameless wretch, seducing a married woman. Don't try to deny it. With my own eyes I saw you—saw you embracing—"

Mr. Wang was too enraged to finish. Hsin-mei straightened himself up to reply, then thought better of it.

Understanding what her husband had left unsaid, Mrs. Wang shook herself free of his grasp and said, "If you have something to say, then let's talk inside. My legs are getting sore from standing," and she reached out and pulled the bell rope. Her voice was pitched unusually low to suppress the quaver.

No one had expected her to say this, and taken by surprise they all followed her meekly inside. As soon as Hsin-mei stepped through the doorway, he suddenly came to his senses and was about to slip off, when Kao Sung-nien stopped him, saying, "Oh, no you don't. We're going to clear this up."

Mrs. Wang went in the living room, picked out the most comfortable chair, and sat down, telling the maid to pour her a cup of tea. None of the three men sat down. Mr. Wang paced back and forth, sighing again and again. Chao Hsin-mei stood stupidly with his head down. President Kao held his hands behind his back and pretended to be looking at the scrolls on the wall.

When the maid had brought in the tea, Mrs. Wang said, "Go on to bed. This is none of your business." After taking a sip of tea, she said deliberately, "Now, what was it you wanted to ask? It's getting late. I don't have my watch. Hsin-mei, what time is it?"

Hsin-mei pretended not to have heard. Kao darted a fierce glance in his direction and was about to take a look at his own watch, when Wang Ch'u-hou strode over to the round table, pounded it with his hand the way judges once used the wooden court gavel, and bellowed, "I won't permit you to speak to him. Tell me the truth, what is your relationship with him?"

"My relationship with him—I've forgotten myself. Hsin-mei, what's our relationship?"

Hsin-mei was so dismayed he did not know how to respond. Kao angrily clenched his fists and shook them at the floor. Wang pounded the table again and demanded, "You—speak up!" furtively rubbing his injured palm against his thigh.

"You want me to tell the truth?" asked Mrs. Wang. "All right. But mind you, don't ask any questions. You already saw everything with your own eyes. Since you understand everything, what's there to ask? In any case it's nothing to glory in. Why look for trouble by asking a lot of questions? Really!"

Mr. Wang dashed at his wife as though crazed. Fortunately, President Kao caught hold of him in time and cautioned, "Don't lose your temper. Ask him. Ask him."

At the same time Hsin-mei pressed his hands together and beseeched Mrs. Wang, "Mrs. Wang, don't talk nonsense, please—Mr. Wang, don't misunderstand. There's absolutely nothing between your wife and me. What happened today is all my fault. Let me explain—"

Mrs. Wang burst into hysterical laughter and said, "Your courage is no bigger than a mustard seed," and she indicated the size with her thumb pressed against the tip of her forefinger. "So you're as frightened as all that! Well, you can't clear yourself now, ha, ha! President Kao, what are you urging him to 'speak up' for? It's not for you to be jealous. Let's just get this all out in the open today, hmm? How about it, Mr. Kao?"

Hsin-mei stared wide-eyed at the cringing Kao Sung-nien and with a "Humph" turned and departed. With Wang Ch'u-hou's attention now shifted to Kao, there was no one to stop Hsin-mei. Only Mrs. Wang's peals of hysterical laughter followed him out the gate.

Hung-chien had not gone to bed yet. Hsin-mei came in as though drunk, his face flushed a bright red and staggering on his feet. Without waiting for Hung-chien to speak, he said, "Hung-chien, I'm leaving this school at once. I can't stay here any longer."

Hung-chien pressed Hsin-mei's shoulder in amazement and asked him why. When Hsin-mei told him what had happened, Hung-chien thought, "What a mess!" but could only ask, "You're leaving tonight? Where do you plan to go?"

Hsin-mei replied that a friend of his in Chungking had written several times asking him to go there. He would stay at a hotel in town for the night and set off early the next morning. Hung-chien knew there was no use trying to stop him, and with his mind in a turmoil, followed him upstairs to pack. Hsin-mei gave the dozen or so books he had brought with him to Hung-chien, saying, "Later on if you find you can't take these with you, donate them to the library for me." He also left his winter bedding.

When he had finished packing, Hsin-mei said, "Ai ya! I haven't written a letter to Kao Sung-nien. You think I should ask him for a leave of absence or resign? I guess I'll ask for a long-term leave of absence."

When he had written the letter, he gave it to Hung-chien to have it delivered the next day. Hung-chien woke the errand boy to come carry the baggage, and with a heavy heart, accompanied Hsin-mei to the hotel. Hsin-mei said with a rueful smile, "I'll welcome you to Chungking in the latter part of the year. This is the best way to part—very abruptly. You go on back to campus and go to bed—Oh, by the way, when you go home for summer vacation, take Miss Sun back to her father; that is, if she wants to return to Shanghai."

Hung-chien returned to the school, feeling as though his whole world had suddenly gone dark. The errand boy asked him why Mr. Chao had left, and he replied offhandedly that someone in Mr. Chao's family was ill. The errand boy asked if it was Mr. Chao's mother, and Hung-chien suddenly woke with a start. *While Mrs. Chao is alive*, he thought, *better not bring her any bad luck*, and he said, "No, it's his father."

Hung-chien rose quite late the next morning. He was just washing his face when a messenger from the president came to summon him. He gave Hsin-mei's letter to the messenger to take over first. Shortly afterwards he arrived at the president's bedroom. When Kao Sung-nien heard that he was there, Kao arranged his expression. The dignity was piled so thickly on his face it could have been scraped off with a knife.

"When did Hsin-mei leave?" Kao asked. "Did he talk it over with you before he left?"

Hung-chien said, "He just told me he was going. He left town early this morning."

"The school wants to ask you to go after him and bring him back."

"He was quite firm about leaving. Even if you yourself went after him, I don't think he'd come back."

"Do you know the reason for his leaving?"

"I have some idea about it."

Kao's face looked like a shrimp or crab after being dipped in hot water. "Then I hope you'll keep it a secret for him. If you were to let it out, it wouldn't be too good for him—uh—for the school."

Hung-chien bowed politely, and saying goodbye, he left, letting out a long-drawn-out "Phew."

Since the incident of the previous evening, Kao Sung-nien's ears had been particularly sharp. Hung-chien had let out his sigh too early, and it reached his ears. He did not utter the curse, "Scoundrel." It was expressed on his face instead.

Since the school was still on vacation, the dean's office did not make any announcements, but many faculty members, having learned that Hsin-mei had requested a long-term leave of absence, came over to ask Hung-chien about it. Hung-chien merely said that Hsin-mei had received an urgent telegram from home and that someone was ill. It was not until early evening that Hung-chien finally had time to go tell Miss Sun. On the way to her dormitory he met Miss Sun, who said she was just coming to ask about Uncle Chao.

Hung-chien said, "You sure are quick to get the news. No wonder they like to hire women as military spies."

Miss Sun said, "I'm not a spy. Miss Fan told me about it. She also said that Mrs. Wang had something to do with Uncle Chao's departure."

"How did she know?" asked Hung-chien, stamping his foot.

"She seems to have had a quarrel with Mrs. Wang over Uncle Chao's returning her books and wouldn't go to the Wangs any more. This noon a note came from Mr. Wang saying that Mrs. Wang was sick and asking her to come. She came back just now bitterly cursing Uncle Chao. She says he flirted with Mrs. Wang and got her upset. She also says that she herself had long ago realized that Uncle Chao was no good, and so was going to ignore him."

"Humph. Your Uncle Chao never called her 'Precious darling' is what's bothering her. You know the source of that phrase?"

When she heard Hung-chien mention "source," she mused, "You can't depend on that. I'm afraid she wrote that herself. She once asked me whether the word was 'author' or 'writer' in English."

"How shameless!" said Hung-chien, spitting out a mouthful of saliva.

Miss Sun walked on for a bit, then said softly, "Now Uncle is gone! That leaves just the two of us."

Hung-chien stammered, "He said to me before he left, if I go back home and you want to go too, we can go together. But I'm a good-for-nothing, you know. I can't look after you."

"Thank you, Mr. Fang. I'm afraid I'll just be a burden to you," said Miss Sun, lowering her head and her voice.

"Nonsense!" said Hung-chien politely.

"People will gossip even more now." Miss Sun kept her head and voice down as before.

Feeling uneasy, Hung-chien said with feigned nonchalance, "Let them talk. As long as you don't care, I'm not bothered by it."

"Some rat—I suspect it was Lu Tzu-hsiao—wrote my father an anonymous letter, spreading—spreading a rumor about you and me. My father wrote asking me about it—"

When Hung-chien heard this, it seemed the sky had half fallen in on him. Just at that moment he heard a voice calling him from behind, "Mr. Fang, Mr. Fang!"

He turned and saw Li Mei-t'ing and Lu Tzu-hsiao hurrying toward them. Miss Sun gave a screech like an ambulance siren reduced several thousand times in magnitude and reached out to grab Hung-chien's right arm as though seeking his protection. Hung-chien knew Li and Lu's gazes were directed at his right arm and thought, *It's all over. Since the rumor has reached the Suns anyway, what's the use of denying it?*

Lu Tzu-hsiao kept his gaze fixed on Miss Sun and breathed in short gasps.

Li Mei-t'ing said with a sly smile, "You sure were having a cozy talk. I called you several times but you didn't even hear me. I wanted to ask you, when did Hsin-mei leave—excuse me, Miss Sun, for interrupting your lovers' talk."

"If you knew it was lovers' talk, then you shouldn't have interrupted," said Hung-chien recklessly.

"Well, you certainly are at the forefront of fashion, even walking about arm in arm in broad daylight, setting a good example for the students."

"We can't follow the dean of student's example of visiting houses of ill repute."

Li Mei-t'ing paled, and sensing a change in the wind, said, "You do love cracking jokes. Now stop talking nonsense and be serious. When are you going to invite us to the wedding dinner?"

"We won't forget you when the time comes," replied Hung-chien.

Miss Sun said hesitantly, "Then let's tell Mr. Li—"

Li Mei-t'ing gave a shout, and Lu Tzu-hsiao shrieked, "Tell what? That you're engaged? Is that it?"

Miss Sun clasped Hung-chien more tightly and did not reply.

The two of them exclaimed, "Congratulations! Miss Sun, congratulations! Did he propose today? Treat us!" and they forced him to shake hands and made all kinds of jesting remarks.

Hung-chien felt as though he were in a cloud and had completely lost touch with himself, letting them shake his hand and pat his shoulder at will. Only after he had freely promised to invite them out would they leave. When they had gone some distance away, Miss Sun said apologetically, "I just panicked when I saw the two of them. I didn't know what to do. Please forgive me, Mr. Fang—what I just said wasn't meant seriously."

Hung-chien suddenly felt mentally and physically too exhausted to cope. Taking her hand, he said, "Well, I meant every word of it. Maybe it's just what I was asking for."

Miss Sun was silent for a long while, then said, "I hope you won't ever regret it," and lifted her face as though expecting him to kiss her, but he forgot about kissing her and said only, "I hope you don't regret it."

By the last day of spring vacation, everyone on the faculty knew that Fang Hung-chien was engaged and would be giving a party the next week. Li Mei-t'ing's whispered remarks during those few days far outnumbered all his earnest exhortations to the students during the entire year. Like Leonardo da Vinci, he just wished there were more muscles in his tongue, so it could withstand all the exercise. As he spread the news around, he added, "There must have been an accident; otherwise they never would have gotten engaged. Just look at it. They're getting married right after the engagement. Actually why do they have to go through the trouble twice? They might as well just go ahead and live together. Why should we care? After all, we're getting an extra meal off him. As I see it, children's clothes would make the most useful wedding presents, ha, ha! But then this affair touches on the moral standards of the school. I'll have to call the president's attention to this. I have my duties as dean of students to think of; I can't just consider my personal friendship with Fang Hung-chien now, can I? Last year when I came here with them I thought something was not right. Lu Tzu-hsiao is the big fool! Ha, ha!"

Thus, on the day of the engagement party, many of the guests studied Miss Sun's figure. When dessert was served, some women guests maliciously forced Miss Sun to eat more, especially Mrs. Han, who kept saying, "*Sweets to the sweet.*" There was the inevitable proposal that they describe the story of their love affair, which of course they refused.

Under cover of the wine, Li Mei-t'ing said, "I'll tell it for them."

Hung-chien shot him a warning glance and said in the Shanghai dialect, "Mr. Li, you are such a nice man."

Li stopped short, suddenly remembering the Soochow widow. He laughed loudly and said, "You see, everyone, he's so nervous he calls me a 'nice man.' Well then, I will be a nice man and won't tell it for him. Tzu-hsiao, now it's your turn to treat everyone to a wedding feast."

Tzu-hsiao said, "It's better to get married a little late. If a person marries early, he'll be wanting a divorce before he reaches middle age."

Everyone agreed his remarks were very inauspicious and fined him a glass of wine. Hung-chien and Miss Sun also became drunk on all the wine they were served.

Among those who had been invited but did not attend that day were Mr. and Mrs. Wang and Mr. and Mrs. Liu. Liu Tung-fang blamed Hung-chien for his sister's unsuccessful marriage bid. He had also planned to hold an exhibit of the students' achievements in English composition after the spring vacation, intending to make public Hung-chien's errors in correcting the papers. He had not anticipated, however, that most of the students would want to keep their papers modestly hidden away, refusing to take them out and lay bare their weaknesses. Then, too, since Hsin-mei had already left, if Hung-chien became angry and refused to teach English, there wouldn't be anyone to replace him. A gentleman must be flexible. He decided he would let Hung-chien teach for the remainder of the semester. If the shirt and shoes Mrs. Han gave his eldest daughter had not been delivered just before the end of the semester, he could have made his peace with the Hans already and not have had to wait till next semester to give Hung-chien's classes to her in return. Wang Ch'u-hou did not invite his colleagues or the president over for dinner again. Liu Tung-fang complained that he had not done his best as matchmaker. Now that Chao Hsin-mei had left and his clique had dissolved, Mr. Wang was ready to resign and return to Ch'engtu. Though President Kao had acted as a witness for Hung-chien's engagement, he was not at all pleased with him. Li Mei-t'ing's prediction about the marriage was not confirmed either. Lu Tzu-hsiao happened to see in Fang Hung-chien's room a small "Home University Library" edition of [Harold] Laski's *Communism*, one of the books Hsin-mei had left behind. Though Lu Tzu-hsiao's understanding of English was no sharper than the nose of a man with a bad cold, he did recognize the word "communism" on the cover, and secretly told Li Mei-t'ing, who then reported it to President Kao.

President Kao said, "I was planning to promote him. Who would have known his thought was open to question? Next semester I'll just have to dismiss him. The man has potential. Such a pity! Such a pity!"

Thus even as a "concubine" Hung-chien was not secure and just had to "leave the house." Before he left he gave all of Hsin-mei's books to the library, including that one small volume. When Han Hsüeh-yü heard that Hung-chien's contract was not to be renewed, he grabbed his White Russian wife and they hopped around the house like a frog and a flea. Henceforth his secret could not be divulged by any insider.

On the evening of July fourth, the last day of the final examinations, Han threw a big party for his colleagues with his wife's name appearing on the invitations. The occasion was American Independence Day. This of course proved that his wife was indeed a genuine, full-fledged American; for otherwise, how could she always be thinking about her mother country? Patriotism is not something that can be simulated. If the wife's nationality were real, could the husband's academic credentials then be fake?

8

IN THE WEST whenever a mule driver has a mule that refuses to move and won't respond to the whip, he will dangle a carrot on a string in front of the mule just above its lips. The stupid mule thinks that, if it takes a step forward, it can get a bite out of the carrot, so it keeps going forward step by step. The more it hankers for a bite, the faster it goes, and before the mule realizes it, it will have reached the next station. Whether or not it then gets the carrot depends on the whim of the mule driver. The heads of organizations always use this kind of ploy to "drive" their subordinates, such as the way Kao Sung-nien had promised Hung-chien a full professorship for the next semester.

Since Hsin-mei's departure, Hung-chien had seen enough of this promotion business and his mouth no longer watered for it. He decided he would look for other prospects after summer vacation. When the contract came, he was prepared to send it back untouched with a letter attached roundly criticizing the administration—his parting words of advice. It would be a good chance to let out the year's pent-up frustration. He had not yet decided on the exact wording of the letter, since he did not know what sort of contract the president's office would be sending him. Sometimes he hoped it would still be for associate professor. Then he could write back in righteous indignation, denouncing the president for breach of promise. Sometimes he hoped the contract would promote him to full professor. In that case, his letter could be even more beautifully phrased, indicating that his dissatisfaction arose not from any private grievance, but as a matter of principle.

Hung-chien never anticipated that Kao would save him the trouble of drafting or writing a letter by simply not sending him any contract at

278

all. On the other hand, Miss Sun received a contract and was even raised a step on the salary scale. Some people said this was Kao's prank—a deliberate attempt to break them apart. Kao himself asserted that he was only acting out of fairness and would not make the woman suffer because of her fiancé. "It's not just a question of their not being married yet. Even if they were married and had a child, if the husband's thought is under question, one cannot implicate wife and children in the crime! In running an institution of higher learning in the twentieth-century Republic of China, one should at least have that much democratic spirit."

When Hung-chien learned that Miss Sun had received a contract, he quickly made a detailed check among his colleagues and found that next year's contracts had all been issued. Even Han Hsüeh-yü's wife was among those hired. He stood out as uniquely ridiculous as the fox with no tail in Aesop's fables. It so enraged him that his brain ran a fever while his body went cold. All his well-thought-out words and actions were useless. They just had to stay pent up inside him to ferment. This is comparable to the student who had prepared well for his examination only to find it postponed.

Whenever Hung-chien met Kao, Kao always smiled broadly and acted as though nothing were amiss. Administrators have their own methods of social intercourse. Among close friends, you can put on airs or blow your temper all you want, but with others, the more intimate the smile and the more courteous the treatment, the deeper the suspicion and hatred become. Kao had not quite perfected his skills. His smile and politeness were like poorly copied antiques. The flaws showed all over, and one could tell at a glance that they were fakes. Hung-chien considered questioning Kao several times but then thought better of it and refrained. In a quarrel the one who speaks first doesn't necessarily hold the upper hand; having the last word is what counts as the victory. Since Kao Sung-nien never changed his expression, Kao must have a plan already worked out. If he risked going in to start a quarrel and found himself out on a limb, he'd just be laughed at. If the story got out, people would say that when Fang lost his job, his shame turned into resentment. The best way to regain face was to put on a show of indifference, to let people know he wasn't worried about his job.

It was his colleagues' attitude that Hung-chien couldn't take. They all seemed to know that he had been dismissed, but since it hadn't been made public yet, all they could do was stuff their sympathy in an envelope and send it to him under cover. People who were ordinarily very distant toward him would suddenly come for a visit. He knew they came to feel him out, so he never mentioned a word about his contract. But the pity in their words and expression was like the gifts Santa Claus puts in the Christmas stockings: They wouldn't leave till they had been delivered. This sort of sympathy was harder to take than reproach or ridicule. As soon as the guest was out of earshot, Hung-chien ground his teeth and let out a bilingual curse: "*Go to hell*, your mother's egg!"

Before their engagement, Sun Jou-chia often came to see Hung-chien. Once they were engaged, it was Hung-chien who went to see her, while she was very reluctant to come see him. At first he thought she was just a girl who had to ask him for advice in everything. After their engagement, however, he gradually realized that not only did she have her own opinions, but she was very firm about them. When she heard him say he was going to turn down the contract, she disagreed, saying that it wasn't easy to find a job and unless he had something else in mind, he shouldn't let his emotions get the better of him.

"Don't tell me you like staying in this place?" Hung-chien asked her. "Haven't you been saying all along that you wanted to go home?"

"It's different now," she said. "As long as the two of us are together, any place is all right."

Naturally when he saw how sensible and loving his fiancée was, Hung-chien was pleased, but he had no intention of doing as she said. He felt that, though they were already engaged, she was still quite a stranger to him. Never having been engaged before—the business with the Chous didn't count—he didn't know what sort of emotional state was to follow the engagement, whether it was supposed to be as dull as it was now. The way he explained it to himself was that passionate love usually reached its peak by the time of the engagement and was all over after marriage. In the case of their engagement now, there was still room left between them for their feelings to develop, and that was a very good thing. He remembered what the philosopher with a goatee had said in a class on moral philosophy in London, "There are but two kinds of people in the world. If given a bunch of grapes, for example, one kind will eat the best ones first, while the other kind will leave the best for last. In principle, the first kind of person should be an optimist, since with each grape he eats he is eating the best of the remaining grapes, while the second kind should be a pessimist, since with each grape he eats he is eating the worst of the remaining grapes. But in actual fact, it's just the opposite, the reason being that the second kind of person still has hope while the first kind has only memories." From first falling in love to growing old together it's like a bunch of grapes: There is always just one best grape remaining at the end to provide hope. Isn't that wonderful? When Hung-chien rashly recounted all this to her, she said nothing. When he spoke to her, she answered only with "oh's" and "um's." When he asked her why she was so unhappy, she said she wasn't unhappy at all.

He said, "You can't fool me."

She said, "As long as you know it, then that's enough. I want to go back to the dormitory now."

He said, "No, you can't go until you've explained it to me."

She said, "I just want to go."

He coaxed and pleaded with her all the way. Finally she said, "Since the good grape you're hoping for is at the end, I must be a bad grape, so don't ruin your appetite."

He jumped about excitedly and said she was being silly.

She said, "I know you don't really love me; otherwise, you wouldn't come up with such weird ideas."

After he had spent a long time carefully explaining everything to her, her expression softened, and smiling sweetly, she said, "I'm very stubborn. Later on you won't like it."

He kissed her, effectively cutting off her sentence, and said, "You sure are a sour grape today."

She made him tell all about his past love affairs. He refused, but after she had pressed him over and over again, he reluctantly told her a little about them. She complained it wasn't enough, and so like a rich man being tortured by a robber into confessing his assets, he disclosed them bit by bit. She still found it wasn't detailed enough, saying, "Why be so wishy-washy? You think I could be jealous over something that old and stale? I just get a kick out of hearing about it."

Hung-chien noticed a slight redness in her cheeks and a forced smile about her mouth. Thankful he'd seen them in time, he kept most of the details to himself. She asked to see Su Wen-wan's and T'ang Hsiao-fu's pictures and was not easily convinced that he really did not have any pictures of them with him.

She said, "You must have kept a diary at least. That should be very interesting. Do you have it with you?"

"How ridiculous!" he exclaimed. "I'm not one of those writers or literary types Fan Yi knows. Why should I have kept a diary when I was in love? If you don't believe me, go to my room and search for yourself."

She said, "Don't talk so loud. Everyone will hear you. If you have something to say, say it properly. I'm the only one who can put up with your rudeness! Just ask this Miss Su or Miss T'ang to try."

Angered, he kept silent. She looked at him closely and said with a smile, "Mad at me? Why do you look away? It's my fault for teasing you. Sorry."

Thus, after being engaged for one month, Hung-chien seemed to have acquired a boss, and though he hadn't been brought to heel by her, he admired her training skills. He remembered Chao Hsin-mei saying the girl was sharp. How right Chao was. Six years her senior and much more experienced in life than she, he felt he was a whole generation ahead of her. He merely found her amusing and let her do whatever she wanted, never seriously disputing with her over anything.

When the issue of his contract came up, she said gallantly, "Of course I'll send my contract back. But why don't you ask Kao Sung-nien about it directly? Maybe he inadvertently left yours out. If you feel uncomfortable about asking him yourself, you could have someone else ask him for you."

He wouldn't listen to her, and later when she learned that his contract had not been inadvertently left out, she didn't press him.

He remarked jokingly, "I'm out of work for the rest of the year. We can't get married now. If you marry me, you'll have to go hungry."

She said, "I didn't want you to support me in the first place. When I go home and see Papa, I'll ask him to think of something for you."

He suggested that they not return home at all but go to Chungking and look up Chao Hsin-mei. Hsin-mei worked for the National Defense Committee and his letters indicated he was doing quite well. He seemed to have recovered from the distress he felt at the time he had left the school.

To Hung-chien's surprise, she was strongly opposed to this, saying that Hsin-mei was no more than his equal, and that asking Hsin-mei to recommend him for a post would be too humiliating. Furthermore, she said, in the position at San Lü University, for which Hsin-mei had recommended him, he had only done odd jobs for various departments and never made it to full professor. Even as an associate professor he wasn't secure. She asked whether the job Hsin-mei recommended was any good.

"When you put it that way," said Hung-chien uneasily, "it makes me look even worse. How about leaving me a little room for self-respect?"

She said that, in any case, she wanted to go back and see her parents, and he too should meet his future in-laws. He suggested they get married there at the school. It would save money and effort for one thing and make their traveling arrangements easier for another.

She stopped to reflect, saying, "I haven't even received Mama and Papa's consent to the engagement. Luckily they like me, so there won't be any problem. But we can't get married that casually. I'll have to let them make the decisions. Don't be alarmed. Papa isn't mean. He'll like you."

Hung-chien suddenly remembered something and said, "It was that letter of your father's that hastened our engagement. I'd like to see it. When are you going to get it out?"

She looked at him, puzzled. He lightly pinched her nose and said, "How could you have forgotten? The one about the anonymous letter."

She shook herself free from his hand and said, "Obnoxious! You made my nose all red. That letter? I was so mad when I read it, I tore it up—hmm,

I really should have kept it. Now we're not afraid of rumors any more." At this she squeezed his hand.

In Chungking when Hsin-mei received news of Hung-chien's engagement, he sent an airmail express letter congratulating them. Hung-chien showed the letter to Miss Sun. When she came to the last line, "P.S. My remarks on the boat have come true. Ha, ha," she asked Hung-chien what Hsin-mei had said on the boat. Now that Hung-chien was engaged, he had of course become a little distant from his friend, so he gave her a full account of Hsin-mei's comments.

An angry look flashed over her face as she listened, but instead of flaring up, she merely said, "You men are shameless. You always say how crazy women are about you. Why don't you just look at yourselves in the mirror? Aren't you ashamed? Lu Tzu-hsiao is probably going around telling everybody how crazy I was about him! It's my lousy luck. Hsin-mei must have said bad things about me, too. Tell me."

Hung-chien quickly spouted some nonsense to end the discussion. This may have been the reason why she was against asking Hsin-mei to help him find a job.

Hung-chien suggested that for their return trip, instead of taking the old route back, they should simply fly straight from Kweilin to Hong Kong and avoid all the hardships. They could ask Hsin-mei to help them get plane tickets. Miss Sun was all in favor of this. Hsin-mei wrote back saying that his mother was going to Hong Kong from Tientsin at the end of July, and he was going to Hong Kong to meet her and take her back to Chungking. The time would be just right for them to get together in Hong Kong. When Miss Sun read the letter, she frowned and said, "I don't want to see him. He'll just make jokes. You mustn't let him."

Hung-chien said with a laugh, "The first time we meet he's bound to joke, but after that he won't. What are you afraid of him now for? You've now become his equal and no longer his niece. He'll have to address you as sister-in-law."[1]

Before Hung-chien left the school, none of his colleagues gave him a farewell party. Since the school itself was unhappy with him, the colleagues were all reluctant to have anything to do with him. He didn't seem like someone who would advance rapidly up the ladder of success. "Sun Jou-chia is really blind to marry him. She'll regret it some day. . . ." A dinner for him would probably not be like bread thrown in the Nile, which floats back to its original owner a few days later doubled in size. Inviting someone for dinner is like sowing seeds. Among the guests there would be some who would not return the invitation, such as one's superiors or low-ranking clerks, and some who most certainly would, such as one's peers with the same rank and income. Thus, for every meal sown, a harvest of several could be reaped. Hung-chien's position was not important, and he didn't belong to any department. Ordinarily no one tried to make friends with him, while he himself, being close only to Hsin-mei, hadn't scattered any dinner seeds among his colleagues.

Still, although Hung-chien never actually ate any dinners, he thanked people for them many times. Having asked his departure date, people would say regretfully, "What? Leaving so soon! Why, there's not even time for a farewell party. Damn! And right during finals, when I'm so busy I haven't a moment to spare. Miss Sun, try to persuade him to leave a few days later, so we can all have a leisurely get-together—all right, all right, whatever you say. Well then, I'll just have to dispense with courtesy. When you go home and have the wedding, let us know as soon as possible. Don't keep it from us! You mustn't forget all your old friends here once you're happily married! Ha, ha."

President Kao had been summoned by the provincial government to its capital for a meeting and didn't return to the school until time for final examinations. Throughout this period Kao never formally brought up the matter of the contract with Hung-chien. The day before he left, Hung-chien went to the president's office to ask that travel documents be issued to him in order to avoid trouble with the military police during the trip and bid goodbye to the president. Kao wasn't in his office. In the afternoon when Hung-chien went to the office again to pick up the documents, he was told that the president had already left. In the office hours they keep, heads of organizations are like the midwinter sun or that once-in-a-lifetime stroke of luck: they come late and leave early. Since Kao had always been a hard worker, Hung-chien guessed Kao had purposely avoided him, and despite his indignation, he did derive a certain perverse satisfaction from not seeing Kao.

A few of his student advisees, having finished their examinations that day, came over in the evening when they were free to chat and say goodbye. In his grateful delight Hung-chien understood the psychology of the corrupt official, who on leaving office still wants the local populace to try to make him stay, present him with a "Ten Thousand People" umbrella,[2] and put up a "Virtuous Rule" tablet[3] in his honor. Leaving a place is like death, and while a dying man knows death is inevitable, he still hopes people will show that they want him to live on. A person's postdeparture reputation is just like posthumous honors: One can be concerned for it but do nothing about it, fearing that one's departure or death, like a wax candle, will leave nothing behind but a bad odor when it goes out. Being seen off is like a man on his deathbed having filial sons and grandsons around to escort him to his grave. At death he can close his eyes in peace. The students came and left. The temporary excitement only added to his loneliness, and he tossed and turned for half the night unable to fall asleep. As much as he hated the place, now that he was about to leave, he felt a melancholy attachment to it at the thought of never seeing it again. That is how unpredictable man can be. He came last year with so many others. Now just two of them were going back. Luckily Jou-chia was there; otherwise, having lost his job, he really wouldn't have the courage to take such a long journey by himself. When he started thinking about this, like a body that curls up into a ball on a winter night, he felt a little warmer and wished only that Jou-chia were there by his side.

Sedan-chair bearers and rickshaw pullers arrived before dawn the next day. As it was already summer, they wanted to get an early start while it was still cool. Blurry-eyed from sleep and wearing an undershirt, the servant who served Hung-chien saw Hung-chien and Miss Sun out the main gate and watched them get into the chairs. In his hand he tightly clutched Hung-chien's tip, ready to count it as soon as the chairs had left. Miss Fan, her nearsighted eyes even more dimmed from lack of sleep, thinking she might run into some male colleague saying goodbye to Fang and Miss Sun, had hastily slapped some rouge on her face. With her arm hooked in Miss Sun's, she walked Miss Sun over from the women's dormitory. Miss Sun was also loathe to say goodbye and couldn't bear to part from Miss Fan. Miss Fan watched Miss Sun get into the chair, wished Jou-chia and Hung-chien a pleasant journey, and said she would certainly forward Miss Sun's mail to Shanghai.

"But what address should I use? I'll have to use Mr. Fang's address," and with that she giggled.

Miss Sun said she would be sure to write to Miss Fan. Hung-chien laughed to himself at what natural-born politicians women were. They maligned each other behind their backs and yet were so affectionate to each other's face. Two political enemies clinking glasses at a champagne party could probably have done no better. If he hadn't heard their cutting remarks about each other with his own ears, he would have thought they were really good friends.

The sedan-chair bearers finished breakfast in town and had just lifted the chairs ready to set off when Kao Sung-nien's personal servant rushed up, his forehead bathed in sweat, and handed Hung-chien a large envelope, saying that it was delivered at the president's orders. Hung-chien thought it was a contract, and his heart beat so wildly it nearly burst from his chest. He hurriedly tore open the envelope. Inside there was but one sheet of stationery and a red paper packet. Kao's letter stated that because he had been so tied up with school business all that month, he hadn't had a chance to have a good talk with Hung-chien. When he returned from the provincial capital the day before yesterday, there were so many things to be taken care of, and Hung-chien was in such a hurry to leave that he hadn't been able to give him a farewell dinner. For this he was very sorry. The school was postponing plans for a philosophy department for the time being, so to retain Fang would have been quite unfair and he did not feel right about it. Thus, he had written to such and such well-known academic institutions to recommend Fang for a job. At first he had intended to wait for a reply before informing Fang of it formally, but no reply had come as yet. As soon as he received word, he would certainly send a telegram to Shanghai. Would Fang please accept the gift coupon as a token of his congratulations on their marriage.

Before he'd even read it through to the end, Hung-chien became so enraged he wanted to get down from the chair and jump about and curse. He restrained himself, however, until the sedan bearers had gone ten *li* and stopped to rest, then handed Miss Sun a wad of paper, saying, "Look! A letter from Kao Sung-nien. Who wants a gift from him? When we get to Hengyang, I'm going to send it back in a registered letter. Oh, this is great. I was just about to write him a letter and tell him off. I only wished I had an excuse. Now this letter of his gives me a good opportunity to write him back and really let him have it."

Miss Sun said, "I think he meant well by the letter. Why make an enemy of him for nothing? What good will it do you to curse him? What if he has really recommended you to someone?"

"You are always so full of reason," he said angrily. "You won't even let a person enjoy himself with a bit of foolishness. Well, the more reasonable you get, the less I'll listen to reason."

"It's hot out," she said, "and I'm already thirsty. Don't quarrel with me. It's still four days before we get to Hengyang. If by that time you still want to write a letter cursing Kao Sung-nien, I certainly won't stop you."

He knew very well that by that time he would probably be so influenced by her stand that he would write back thanking Kao, and this made him even more furious. Instead of pouring the water for her, he just tossed her the army thermos, saying, "What nerve sending this gift! We haven't even chosen a date for the wedding, so why did he say in his letter our 'marriage ceremony has been completed'? He meant something by that, I'll tell you. Since you and I are traveling together, he thinks—"

"Don't say it!" she interrupted. "You are so suspicious. And most of the suspicions are evil." She crumpled Kao's letter into a ball as she spoke and flung it into a pond by the fields. She had just had a drink of hot water, and the redness in her face still hadn't faded by the time she stepped back into her sedan chair.

Because of the airplane ticket, they stayed in Kweilin ten or fifteen days, enjoying themselves so much it seemed more that the days were slipping by them than that they were spending the days. They consigned their two big trunks to the shipping company Hsin-mei had introduced them to and were told that the trunks would reach Shanghai in a month or so. As they had ample traveling funds, it didn't matter if they stayed on a few days longer. The day before they were to board the airplane, the weather was still nice. That night it suddenly started to rain, but in the morning the rain stopped and there was a bit of fog. It was the first time either of them had been on an airplane, and they had a very uncomfortable time of it, throwing up like sick cats. When they landed in Hong Kong, Hsin-mei was there at the airport to greet them. With their energy all but vomited out of them, they were unable to express the joy of meeting Hsin-mei after a long separation.

Upon seeing their ashen faces, Hsin-mei said, "Did you throw up? Never mind. The first time you fly you always have to pay a toll. I'll go help you find a hotel so you can get a good rest. This evening I'll give you a welcoming party."

Once they got to the hotel, Hung-chien and Jou-chia were anxious to rest. When Hsin-mei noticed they were taking only one room, he secretly turned his face to the wall and stuck his tongue out in surprise. On his way up the Peak to his relative's home, he smiled to himself, then frowned and sighed.

After some sleep, Hung-chien regained his energy, and he changed his clothes to wait for Hsin-mei. Mahjong noise from next door and the clopping of wooden clogs on the street had kept Miss Sun awake, and she still felt nauseated. Leaning back against the sofa, she said she didn't feel like going out. Alarmed, Hung-chien urged her to rouse herself a little so as not to disappoint Hsin-mei. She told him to go by himself, adding, "The two of you have lots of things to talk about, and I couldn't get a word in anyway. I'd just sit on the sidelines like an idiot. He didn't invite any other woman, so whether I go or not won't make any difference. And I'll tell you something, the restaurant he's invited us to is sure to be a ritzy one, and I don't have anything to wear. I'd just be a disgrace."

Hung-chien said, "I didn't know you were so vain! You can wear that flowered silk dress."

Miss Sun said with a laugh, "I haven't spent any of your money on clothes yet, and already I'm getting scolded for being vain. In the future I'll make sure you pay the tailor's bill for me! That dress is too old-fashioned. On the way here I noticed the dresses the girls on the street are wearing. The sleeves and hems have all gotten much shorter. And I don't have any white shoes either. I'd go buy a pair now, but I'm afraid to move. My stomach still doesn't feel right."

When Hsin-mei arrived and learned that Miss Sun was sick, he immediately suggested they have dinner some other time. She wouldn't allow it and insisted that the two men go out and eat.

Relieved, Hsin-mei said, "Mrs.–uh–Miss Sun, how good you are! You'll certainly be a very understanding wife. If it had been another woman, she'd have kept a strict watch on Hung-chien and not allowed him to have any freedom. Hung-chien, can you bear to part from her for a little while? Tell the truth. Don't complain behind my back that Old Chao kept you apart."

Hung-chien looked pleadingly at Miss Sun and said, "You really don't need me to keep you company?"

Noticing his expression, Miss Sun forced a smile and said, "You go ahead. I'm not seriously ill, after all. Mr. Chao, I'm very sorry—"

"Not at all," said Hsin-mei. "Today's invitation was nothing special. In a few days when you've recovered, I'll invite you out properly. Well then, I'll take him away. I'll bring him back to you safe and sound within an hour and a half. Ha, ha! Hung-chien, let's go! Oh, wait, maybe you have a simple ceremony for parting lovers. I'll wait for you by the elevator—"

Hung-chien pulled him away, saying, "Cut the nonsense."

When Hsin-mei was a political science major at an American university, he had once audited a course in "The Psychology of Diplomacy." The professor, who had held several posts as an embassy attaché, once said in class that when Americans invited someone out for dinner to conduct negotiations, they came straight to the point and began talking seriously the moment they sat down, even before the food was served. Europeans only talked irrelevant nonsense during the meal and didn't get down to business until they were having their coffee after the meal was over. He asked Hsin-mei how it was with the Chinese, but Hsin-mei had only given a silly smile and been unable to answer. Hsin-mei also had serious matters to discuss with Hung-chien, but that day's dinner was to be a happy get-together for two good friends. If any serious matters were brought up at the dinner table, it would only spoil the atmosphere.

After leaving the hotel, Hsin-mei said, "You haven't had any Western food for almost a year, so I'm taking you to an Austrian restaurant. It's not too far, and since it's still early, let's walk over slowly. We can have more time to talk."

Hung-chien merely said, "Actually you don't need to waste your money," and was about to comment, "You're looking even better than you did then. You'll be an official some day!" when Hsin-mei coughed dryly and without turning his gaze said, "Why didn't you get married before you took the trip?"

Hung-chien suddenly remembered how they had been registering at hotels under the name of Mr. and Mrs. Fang all along the way. Today when he got off the plane, he had been too dizzy to pay any attention to this. He was secretly glad Hsin-mei was walking beside him and couldn't see his burning face. He said hastily, "I wanted it that way myself, but she was dead set against it. She insists on returning to Shanghai to get married. She said her father—"

"Then, you're too *weak*." Hsin-mei felt this English word was inserted quite fittingly and made a very good diplomatic term: If Hung-chien and Miss Sun had had no relations, then the word meant he couldn't make up his mind whether to get married or not and was completely under her thumb. If they had done as he expected, then needless to say the word held a subtler implication, as in *"But the flesh is weak,"* and couldn't have been better chosen.

Like an already convicted criminal, Hung-chien was unable to deny Hsin-mei's accusation and decided just to give up and let his face redden away. "I regret it now, too," he said haltingly. "But we have to go home anyway. All the ceremonies and procedures are a big nuisance. Might as well let the family take care of it."

"Has Miss Sun been vomiting and not been able to eat?"

When Hung-chien heard Hsin-mei change the course of the conversation, he relaxed and said, "Yes! The plane jolted terribly today. Last night she did all the packing. Hsin-mei, do you remember that time we had dinner at the Wangs and Fan Yi started gossiping about how she couldn't clean up her things—"

"She should be all right from the plane's jolting by now. During our trip together last year the buses were shaking as much, yet she never threw up. Could there be some other reason? I've heard that throwing up—" Hsin-mei quickly added, "Of course, I've no experience," and laughed a forced, mirthless laugh.

Hung-chien hadn't expected Hsin-mei to return to this question again. Like someone escaping an air raid who thinks the planes have flown off only to find they have circled overhead and begun thunderously bombing away, he was so startled he forgot his shame and just said, "That couldn't be. It just couldn't be." At the same time he was filled with dread, knowing it very well could be.

Chewing on his pipe stem, Hsin-mei said, "Hung-chien, we're close friends. I'm not Miss Sun's legal guardian, but I did more or less accept her father's charge. I urge you to get married as soon as possible by the simplest method. You don't need to go to Shanghai to have the ceremony. In any case you won't be able to buy your steamer tickets for a week. You might as well stay an extra four or five days as a honeymoon and then take the next ship home. Other matters aside, if you return home to get married, you can't avoid inviting lots of friends and relatives over to celebrate. That will be no small expense. I know Miss Sun's circumstances, and your old man is not exactly well off either, so if you can save, why not do so? Why must you let them take charge of your wedding?"

Apart from the economic reasons, Hsin-mei brought up a succession of other pros and cons to prove that the sooner Hung-chien got married the better. Hung-chien was soon persuaded, and as though a major impasse had been broken, Hung-chien said, "I'll tell all this to Jou-chia later. Could you please find out for me whether there's a registration type of *civil wedding* here and how complicated the procedure is?"

Feeling his mission had been accomplished, Hsin-mei was jubilant. During dinner he ordered a bottle of wine and said, "Remember that time I got you drunk? Ha, ha! If I got you drunk today, I wouldn't be doing right by Miss Sun."

Hsin-mei asked several questions about the school, then said with a sigh, "It was like a bad dream—how is she?"

Hung-chien said, "Who? Mrs. Wang? I heard she recovered from her illness. I never went to the Wangs."

Hung-chien said, "I really feel sorry for her." Noticing a smile brewing on Hung-chien's face, he quickly added, "I feel sorry for everyone, for Wang Ch'u-hou, for myself, for Miss Sun, and for you, too."

Hung-chien said with a laugh, "I can understand why you feel sorry for Mr. and Mrs. Wang. Their marriage will never make it. Unless Wang Ch'u-hou dies pretty soon, there's bound to be a divorce. But what's so pitiful about you? Your family has money, and you yourself are very successful in your job. It's your own fault you haven't gotten married. It's not Fan Yi's or even Mrs. Wang's—"

Having had a drink, Hsin-mei was already quite red in the face. When he heard this, it got no redder, but his eyes blinked as if to dodge.

"All right, I won't say anything more. I've lost my job, so of course I'm pitiful. Do you feel sorry for Miss Sun because she's mismatched to me?"

"No, no," said Hsin-mei. "You don't understand."

"Why don't you say it?"

"No, I won't."

"I think you must have a new girl friend."

"What do you mean by that?"

"Because you talk in a coquettish manner just like a little girl. You must have come under someone's influence."

"Rubbish!" said Hsin-mei. "All right then, I'll tell you, OK? Didn't I say once before that Miss Sun was conniving? As a third party, it seems to me that she went through all kinds of trouble—"

An obscure thought which had lain dormant deep down in Hung-chien's consciousness seemed to be suddenly roused by Hsin-mei's remark.

"No, no, I'm drunk. I'm just talking nonsense. Hung-chien, you mustn't tell your wife. How stupid of me. I forgot the present you isn't the same as the old you. From now on when your old buddy talks to you, he should draw a boundary line," and as he spoke, he drew a line in the air about an inch from the table with the knife in his hand.

Hung-chien said, "You make marriage sound so awful. It's like being denounced by the people and deserted by your friends."

Hsin-mei said with a smile, "It's not being denounced by the people and deserted by your friends; it's that you yourself desert your friends and denounce the people. But enough of that. Tell me, what are your plans after the summer vacation?"

Hung-chien told him he was looking for a job. Hsin-mei said that the international situation was in a mess. Europe was bound to get into the war, and since Japan was an Axis Power, she'd be dragged in sooner or later, too. Shanghai, Tientsin, and Hong Kong were all unstable, which was why he was taking his mother to Chungking. "But you'll probably have to stay in Shanghai for a while this time. Would you like to work a few months at my old newspaper office? The head of the Office of Information is going to the interior. I'll recommend you to take his place. The pay isn't very good, but you could take another job on the side."

Hung-chien thanked him warmly. When Hsin-mei asked him if he had enough money with him, Hung-chien replied that his wedding would cost a bit, and he wasn't sure if he had enough or not. Hsin-mei offered to lend him some.

Hung-chien said, "What's borrowed must be returned."

Hsin-mei said, "The day after tomorrow I'll give you a sum as my wedding gift. You must accept it."

Hung-chien protested fervently, and Hsin-mei cut him off. "You mustn't refuse it. If I were married myself, I wouldn't have the freedom to lend money to friends."

Hung-chien was so moved his eyes became moist, while inwardly he despised himself for it. He owed Hsin-mei so much, he thought, yet it was over this measly sum of money that he was shedding tears. Knowing Hsin-mei didn't want his gratitude, he said, "From the way you talk, it sounds as though you're going to get married yourself. Don't try to keep it from me."

Without responding, Hsin-mei told the waiter to bring him his suit jacket, took out his wallet, and looked around for a long time as though digging a mine, then solemnly drew out a small photograph of a bright-eyed girl with a very serious expression on her face.

Hung-chien took one look and exclaimed, "Wonderful! Wonderful! Who is she?"

Hsin-mei took back the photograph, looked it over carefully and said with a grin, "Don't praise her so enthusiastically. You'll make me jealous. We had a misunderstanding once before. When you look at the picture of a friend's girl friend, a polite show of approval is enough. You don't have to get enthusiastic."

"How ridiculous!" said Hung-chien. "Who is she?"

"Her father is a Szechwanese friend of my late father's. I stayed at his home, when I first went to Szechwan."

"The way you do it, the older generation is tied by friendship while the younger is united through marriage. The friendship continues from one generation to another. Well, our future sons and daughters—" Miss Sun's condition came to mind and he felt he had misspoken. "Uh—she looks quite young to me. Is she still in school?"

Hsin-mei said, "She wouldn't study liberal arts the way she's supposed to but had to be fashionable and study electrical engineering or something. She complained about it all day. Then when school let out for summer vacation and her report card came, it turned out she had flunked two subjects and couldn't be promoted. She wanted to save face and wouldn't transfer to another department or school. So she quit school and wants to marry me. Ha, ha. Such a silly girl. I'd like to thank the two professors who flunked her. I won't ever teach again myself, but if you do, be sure to mark the women students a little more strictly. This way you may find yourself contributing to the making of many a happy marriage."

Hung-chien said with a smile that it was no wonder Hsin-mei wanted to take his mother to the interior. Hsin-mei gave the picture one last look and put it back in his wallet; then, glancing at his watch, he exclaimed, "Oh, no, it's past time. Hurry! Miss Sun will be furious!" After he paid the bill in a rush, he asked Hung-chien, "Do you want me to go back with you and hand you over to her?"

It had been dusk when they entered the restaurant, still an exploratory shade of night. When they left the restaurant, it had already settled properly into night. But it was a pleasant, semitropical summer night. Night had fallen openly and plainly with no deep, unfathomable recesses, as if to provide the director of Shakespeare's *A Midsummer Night's Dream* with a model backdrop.

Looking at the sky, Hsin-mei said, "What beautiful weather! I wonder if there are any air raids in Chungking this evening. My mother will be too frightened to go there. I'm going home to turn on the radio and listen to the news."

Hung-chien felt very full. He couldn't speak Cantonese and was afraid of getting in an argument with a rickshaw boy, so he strolled leisurely back to the hotel by himself. His talk with Hsin-mei had set him thinking. He realized that people should be successful. Successful people always had interesting things to talk about, like Hsin-mei, for example. All year he had been full of complaints, which could be set off at the slightest aggravation. Since he had never liked hearing other people complain, he assumed other people didn't care to hear him complain either. He was therefore careful to control himself; so like a dog with a muzzle, he could never speak out freely. According to Hsin-mei the war would only deteriorate and drag out. Now that he had a family to worry about, if Hsin-mei had really guessed right about Jou-chia's illness—he felt so ashamed and alarmed—he broke out in a light sweat all over.

He started to think about something else: Hsin-mei liked that girl very much. One could tell that at a glance. But it didn't seem to be a very passionate affair. Otherwise, Hsin-mei wouldn't have talked about her in such a humorous vein. Maybe the way Hsin-mei felt about his girl friend was just the way he himself felt about Jou-chia. Apparently marriage didn't require a very great love. Not detesting each other was already foundation enough for marriage. Was it all because there was too great an age gap between the man and the woman? But what about his feelings for T'ang Hsiao-fu last year. Maybe all his feelings had been exhausted on her and could no longer take control of him. That sort of feeling did seem rather frightening now when he thought back on it. It threw him into such a state that he lost all desire to eat or sleep, and it wouldn't spare him for a moment. It was just crazy, really too much! But then the sickness did have its moments. Sometimes he'd just as soon get it again. He heaved a sigh and thought how much he felt like an old man. Only a person with a healthy state of mind could get that sort of disease, just as only a big fat man could get congestion of the brain and suffer a stroke. An anemic, undernourished, thin individual never gets it. If he were ten or fifteen years older and reached the moment of "twilight brightness," maybe he could fall foolishly and madly in love. An old man's love was said to be like an old house set ablaze. Once it started burning, there was no saving it. In the dull state he was in now, his emotions did not constitute a burden on his mind, which was just as well. At least it was quite comfortable. Better to get the marriage procedures over with as quickly as possible. . . .

Hsin-mei had said Jou-chia had "gone to all kinds of trouble," and since she had obliged him by showing him her respect, he ought to feel more compassionate toward her. Hung-chien then realized he'd left her all alone for too long and hurried back to the hotel. On his way past a fruit store he stopped and bought some fresh lichee and dragon's eyes.

There was no light in the room when Hung-chien pushed open the door, only a beam of light from the corridor shining into the room. He pulled the door closed. Not hearing a sound from Jou-chia, he assumed she was asleep and stepped softly, intending to place the fruit on the table, but he failed to watch out for the chair he had sat in earlier. It was off by itself a few feet from the table, not having been put back into place. He upset it with his foot, bruising the top of his foot and his knee. "Damn it," he cursed. "Who didn't put the chair back after sitting in it?" At the same time he was thinking, "Oh, hell, I woke her up."

When Hung-chien left, loneliness was added to Jou-chia's discomfort, and she was filled with resentment. After she waited and waited and he still hadn't come, her resentment grew with interest at seemingly usurious rates, and she waited for his return just so she could settle accounts. When she heard him open the door, she spitefully refused to speak first. Then when he tipped over the chair, she nearly burst out laughing, but one laugh would have dissolved her anger. Fortunately, she had no trouble restraining herself. For a moment she could not decide which would be more righteously indignant: to say that all this time she had been anxiously waiting for him or that she had just fallen asleep only to have him wake her up.

When Hung-chien saw no sign of life after knocking over the chair, he lost his nerve and, afraid she had fainted, hurriedly switched on the light. When Jou-chia, who had been lying in darkness for over an hour, was suddenly confronted with the light, she couldn't open her eyes. She raised her eyelids, then closed them, turned away from the light, and let out a long breath. Relieved, he then discovered that his silk shirt was soaked with sweat. As he took off his jacket, he said solicitously, "I'm sorry I woke you up, Did you sleep well? How do you feel?"

"I was just dozing off when all your racket woke me in a fright. You're the one who sat in the chair, so what did you curse other people for?"

These remarks were made with her face to the wall. Hung-chien, who was then hanging his clothes up and did not hear her clearly, turned his head and asked, "What?"

She rolled over and said, "Ai! I'm tired. I don't have the energy to raise my voice to speak to you. Why don't you save me the strength?" But she did in fact raise her voice by one key—"You're the one who moved the chair over there. As soon as Hsin-mei got here as though he were a messenger sent by the King of Hades,[4] you became oblivious to everything else. Now you act recklessly and blame me."

The edge in her voice made him apologize. "It's my fault. I scraped some skin off my leg—" This sympathy-getting ploy produced no effect. "I was out for a long time. You really didn't get any sleep? Have you eaten anything? These fresh lichee—"

"So you yourself know you were out for a long time, do you? In any case, when you're eating, drinking, and enjoying yourself with a good friend, whether you stay out all night is up to you. I could die in the hotel all by myself without anyone noticing it." She began to sob, turned her face away again, and lay down.

He hurriedly sat down on the edge of the bed and reached out to turn her head back. "I've been gone too long. Please forgive me. Hey, don't be angry. I didn't go out until you told me to."

She lifted off his hand and said, "Well, now I'm telling you not to touch me with your sweaty hand. You hear me? Huh, I told you to go out? Deep down, didn't you want to go yourself? Could I have kept you here? There wouldn't have been any point to it anyway. If you'd stayed here in the hotel, you'd certainly have found some excuse to get angry at me."

He released his hand and sat down in the chair, fuming.

"So now aren't we quarreling just the same! If you'd wanted me to stay at the hotel with you, why didn't you honestly say so at the time? I'm not a tapeworm in your stomach. How do I know what you're thinking?"

She turned her head around and whimpered, "If you really loved me, you'd know without my having to tell you. It's not something that can be forced. If you can't understand unless I tell you, then forget it! Even a stranger traveling with me wouldn't have left me alone for such a long time if he saw I wasn't feeling very good today. Humph, and you're supposed to be the one who loves me!"

He snickered. "If a stranger were willing to do all that for you, he wouldn't have been a stranger. He'd have been your sweetheart at least."

"Don't try to trip me up with words. What if it were a woman? I'd rather be with women. All you men are no good. You do nothing but coax us into letting you get what you want and don't care about anything else."

These last remarks touched off Hung-chien's private thoughts, and walking to the edge of the bed he said, "All right, don't quarrel. Next time I won't go out even if you beat me or pull me. I won't stray an inch from your side. That should fix it."

A slight smile appearing on her face, she said, "Don't make it sound so pitiful. Your friend already says I hooked you. If I don't let you go out with him anymore, heaven knows how bad a name I'll get then. Let me tell you something. This is the first time I've ever been mad at you. From now on I'll be more discreet and keep my mouth shut even if you stay out till the small hours of the morning. That way I won't annoy you."

"You're too prejudiced against Hsin-mei. He means well and is very concerned about us. Have you calmed down now? I have something serious to discuss with you. Are you ready to listen?"

"Go ahead. Whether I listen or not is up to me. What's so serious that you have to pull such a long face for?" She burst into laughter.

"Could it be you're with child, and that's what's making you feel so uncomfortable?"

"What? Rubbish!" she snapped. "If I really did have a child, I wouldn't forgive you. I wouldn't forgive you. I don't want a child."

"Whether you forgive me or not is another matter. We've got to be prepared. Now Hsin-mei has urged me to get married as soon as possible."

She sat up in a flash, her eyes bulging, and her face gone completely pale. "You mean you told Hsin-mei about us? You rat! You rat! You must have bragged to him—" She pounded furiously on the bed as she spoke.

In fright he retreated a few steps from the bed. "Jou-chia, don't misunderstand. Let me explain—"

"I don't want to hear your explanation. You're bullying me. I'll never be able to face people again. You bully!" She then fell back down, put her hands over her eyes, and heaved with sobs.

Not being made of raincoat material, his heart was soaked by her tears, and he hurriedly sat down by her head, pulled her hands away and wiped her tears for her, coaxing and entreating her. When she had tired herself out from crying, she finally stopped and let him explain. After hearing him through, she said hoarsely, "I don't want him meddling in our affairs. After all, he's not my guardian. Why do you have to take everything he says as an imperial edict? If you want to do what he says, then go get married by yourself. Don't force me into it."

"We needn't talk about it any more," he said. "I won't do what he says. I'll leave everything up to you. You haven't eaten the lichee I bought for you yet. Want some? All right. Just lie there and don't move. I'll peel them for you." He moved the tea table and wastepaper basket up close to the head of the bed as he spoke. "I didn't take a rickshaw either way today. These were bought with the money I saved. Of course, I have enough money to buy fruit, but saving money to buy it makes it seem more like something I really gave you."

Her tear-stained face softening into a smile, she said, "What's the use of saving those few measly cents? If you exhaust yourself by walking, it's not worth it. The few cents you saved from the rickshaw wouldn't be enough to buy this much fruit anyway."

"The price they asked for them wasn't that much. I bargained and got them for even less," he said.

"You've never been a sharp shopper. You'll buy something expensive and still think you got it cheap. Have some yourself. Don't give them all to me."

"Since I'm so incompetent, I'm marrying a worthy wife like you!"

She shot him a glance and said, "A wife's not as good as a friend."

296

"Ai yo! There you go again. I might as well cut off my friends. Since you refuse to get married, I don't even have a wife. It's a true case of 'Losing a wife, and having one's friendship destroyed.'"[5]

"Don't talk nonsense. It's getting late. I didn't get any sleep this afternoon, and then this evening I was waiting for you. Are my eyes swollen from crying? I won't be fit for company tomorrow! Give me my mirror."

Hung-chien noticed her eyelids were in fact puffed, but unwilling to tell her the truth, he merely said, "Just a tiny bit. It doesn't matter. Get a good sleep and the swelling will disappear. Ai, you don't have to get up to look in the mirror!"

"I still have to wash my face and rinse my mouth."

When he returned to the room after taking a bath, she was already in bed. He asked, "Are you sleeping on the pillow you had just now? It's sopping wet from your tears. It won't be comfortable. Sleep on mine. Let me sleep on your damp one."

Jou-chia said gratefully, "Silly boy, I don't need a new pillow. I've already turned it over. I'll sleep on the other side. Does your leg still hurt where you scraped it? I'll get up and bandage it for you."

He had soaked his leg in the soapy water while taking a bath, and now the injured spot stung painfully, but he said, "It's all right. It doesn't hurt at all. Relax and go to sleep."

She said, "Hung-chien, what you said has really started me worrying. Do whatever you think best about the wedding."

He had washed his hair and was just then combing it. When he heard this, he put his comb down, bent over, and kissed her on the forehead. "I knew you were the most reasonable and obedient of all people."

She sighed happily, and turning her face away, fell into a deep sleep.

During the next week they were busy to the point of distraction. As soon as they were half finished with one thing, they remembered something else which had to be taken care of. Thanks to the help of Hsin-mei's relatives, the civil wedding went off without a hitch. Besides this, there were letters to be written informing their families and asking for money, the wedding ring to be ordered, and new clothes to be made. When the registration procedures were completed, they went to a photo studio and had their picture taken in rented wedding clothes, invited guests out to celebrate, and moved to a better hotel. At the last minute they sent the pictures home, even though they were hard-pressed for money. Although it had saved a great deal of trouble, they had spent all the money they had with them. Fortunately they received a generous gift from Hsin-mei.

Because he had not yet found a job for the rest of the year and had no income during the summer, Hung-chien was reluctant to spend any money at first and was against having any new clothes made, or if they were, insisted they needn't be very good. Jou-chia, on the other hand, said she wasn't a vain, wasteful woman, but since marriage was the "major ceremony" of a lifetime and took place only once, it should be done properly. It was already so cheap and simple it couldn't get any more so. If they had clothes made of good material, they could wear them next year. They were so rushed that tempers flared, and arguments followed.

Jou-chia said angrily, "I didn't want to get married here in the first place. That was your idea. You want me to dress up that day like a beggar woman? I don't have a single relative to turn to here, so I have to take care of everything myself. There's no one around to talk things over with, let alone help me! I'm fed up with all the nuisance! There're plenty of people at home to help out, and we can always find some way to make ends meet. Papa and Mama have put aside some money for me. You can write and ask your father for money, too. If we'd gotten married in Shanghai, you think your family wouldn't have to spend a cent? We've already saved the family quite a bit of trouble by getting engaged the way we did."

As a returned student, Hung-chien knew about the three P movement popular in the West (*Poor Pop Pays*): The son usually cries out for "independence and autonomy," but when it comes time to spend money, he'd make the old man fork over. Hung-chien did as she said and wrote to his father. When Jou-chia saw the draft of his letter, she objected that the wording was not clear or sincere enough and wanted him to write it over, adding, "Why are you and your father so formal with each other, and why don't you show the least bit of affection? I never write a draft when I write to my father!"

Like a writer being criticized for his first work, Hung-chien was so furious that he was all set to throw down his pen, burn the draft, and not write anything more.

"Don't write him then," she said. "I don't need your family's money; I can write to my own father."

When she had finished the letter, she asked him if he cared to look at it. He took it from her and read it over. The tone was indeed affectionate. One could almost hear all the "Papa's" and "Mama's" written on the page. In the end he too sent a letter, this time without letting her read it.

Later when she found out she wasn't pregnant, she complained to him that it was all because he had listened to Hsin-mei. This kind of slapdash wedding would only arouse the family's suspicions. But the letters home had already been sent, and everything had been prepared. There could be no last-minute cancellations. During the few days following the wedding, they eagerly awaited their families' replies. It was a far cry from the carefree days they had spent in Kweilin.

The money the Fangs and Suns wired arrived in succession. Hsin-mei reserved steamship tickets back to Shanghai for them. Mrs. Chao also arrived in Hong Kong and would shortly fly on to Chungking. Two days before the steamship was to sail, Hung-chien and his wife went up the Peak to see Hsin-mei: first, to pay their respects to Mrs. Chao; second, to give them a send-off; third, to say goodbye; and fourth, to reimburse him for the tickets and other expenses.

When they arrived at the home of the relatives with whom Hsin-mei was staying and sent in their card, Hsin-mei came running out with the doorkeeper behind him, saying, "Sister-in-law,[6] how nice of you to come. I'm honored."

Jou-chia protested with a smile, "Uncle Chao, you mustn't call me that. I'm not worthy."

Hsin-mei said, "Nothing of the sort. Hung-chien, you've chosen a bad time to come. Su Wen-wan is inside. She's been in Hong Kong for the last two days, and when she learned my mother was here, she came to see her today. I thought maybe you didn't want to see Su Wen-wan, so I hurried out to say hello. But she knows you're out here."

Hung-chien flushed scarlet and turning to Jou-chia said, "Well, I guess we won't go in then. We'll just ask Hsin-mei to give our regards to Auntie.[7] Hsin-mei, here's the money for the steamship tickets."

Hsin-mei was just refusing it when Jou-chia said, "Since we're here, we should see Auntie."

Jou-chia was wearing her new clothes today, and her courage was high. Besides, she was a little curious. Though Hung-chien was afraid of meeting Su Wen-wan, his curiosity too was aroused. Hsin-mei led them inside. Before they entered the living room and while Hung-chien was hanging his straw hat on the rack, Jou-chia opened her purse and looked at herself in her mirror.

Su Wen-wan was even more fashionably dressed than she was the year before, and her face was much fuller. Her dress, partly Western in style, was close-fitting and smart. It was in a design of pale red and light green horizontal stripes with white stripes in between, as colorful as the flags of small European countries. The large, wide-brimmed straw hat on the tea table by her side was of course hers and made the small parasol in Jou-chia's hand seem an age behind the times.

As soon as Hung-chien entered, he bowed deeply from a distance. Mrs. Chao stood up to greet him. Su Wen-wan, who remained calmly seated, said brightly, "I haven't seen you for a long time, Mr. Fang. How are you?"

Hsin-mei said, "This is Mrs. Fang."

Wen-wan had already noticed Jou-chia, but now, as though only just discovering her at Hsin-mei's mention, she nodded to her while at the same time whipping a quick glance over her from head to toe. Unable to withstand her "once-over," Jou-chia felt awkward and ill at ease.

Wen-wan asked Hsin-mei, "Is this Mrs. Fang still that bank? banking house?—Ai! My memory is really dreadful—manager's daughter?"

Hung-chien and his wife heard it all very clearly and blushed simultaneously, but could not easily refute it, since Wen-wan's question was spoken in an undertone as though not meant for their ears.

Hsin-mei, for the moment unaware of Miss Su's references to Hung-chien's past, merely said, "She's the daughter of a colleague of mine. They were married here in Hong Kong last week."

Wen-wan woke as though from a dream and sighing to herself in surprise, said, "Oh, so it's another one—Mrs. Fang, have you been in Hong Kong all this time, or were you just passing through after returning from abroad?"

Hung-chien tightly gripped the armrest of his chair to keep himself from jumping up. Hsin-mei secretly shook his head. Jou-chia could only admit that she was not returning from abroad but merely exiting from the interior. Wen-wan's interest in Jou-chia immediately vanished, and she resumed her conversation with Mrs. Chao. Mrs. Chao said that this was the first time in her life she had ever flown and was terrified at the thought.

Wen-wan said with a laugh, "Auntie, with Hsin-mei along, what are you afraid of! I've flown back and forth by myself five or six times."

Mrs. Chao said, "How can your husband feel easy about your coming and going by yourself?"

Wen-wan said, "Oh, but he has official business keeping him here! He's flown with me to Chungking twice. The first time was when we went to see my father just after we were married. He was going to come with me today to pay you a visit and see Hsin-mei while he was here."

Hsin-mei said, "I'm honored. I saw Mr. Ts'ao the day you were married. He hasn't put on any more weight, has he? He seems a head shorter than I, which makes him easily look fat. It doesn't matter in Hong Kong, but in Chungking if the official in charge of supplies and provisions got fat, people would start poking fun at him."

This was the first time since he'd arrived that Hung-chien felt like laughing.

Wen-wan flushed slightly, but before she could say anything, Mrs. Chao said, "Hsin-mei, you silly child, over thirty years old and still you like to talk nonsense. In times like these, isn't it a good thing to be fat? I wish you weren't so thin. Miss Wen-wan, a mother always thinks her son isn't fat enough. You have a very nice complexion. I feel very comfortable looking at you. It must gladden your old mother's heart to see you. Give our best to Mr. Ts'ao when you go back. He's tied up with official business, so he mustn't come over."

Wen-wan said, "It doesn't matter if he occasionally skips half a day of work, but today he asked for leave from the office. He got drunk last night."

"Alcohol is such a harmful thing," Mrs. Chao fussed. "You must urge him not to drink so much next time."

Wen-wan darted a glance at Hsin-mei and replied, "He can't drink. He's not like Hsin-mei, who has such a great capacity and will finish off a bottle of whiskey every time he drinks."

Hsin-mei secretly made a face at Hung-chien when he heard the first remark and so was too late to protest the next one.

"Someone got him drunk. The local members of our college class had a party yesterday. It said on the invitation 'Spouse Invited,' and since he's considered my 'spouse,' I took him along. Someone gave him too much to drink."

Hung-chien couldn't help asking, "How many people from our class are in Hong Kong?"

Wen-wan said, "Oh, Mr. Fang, I forgot you were in our class, too. Didn't they send you an invitation? Yesterday I was the only one from liberal arts. All the rest were in science, engineering, law, or business."

Hsin-mei said, "You see how important you are! Now it's only the ones in science, engineering, law, and business who've been lucky. The ones in liberal arts are too poor to show their faces. They're afraid to be seen by their classmates. Fortunately, you're around to uphold the dignity of the liberal arts."

Wen-wan said, "I can't believe old classmates could be that snobbish. Aren't you from the law department? If you're going to talk about being lucky, you've been pretty lucky yourself." With that she laughed triumphantly.

Hsin-mei said, "I don't come anywhere near your Mr. Ts'ao. Alumni meetings are always attended by the well-fed ones with nothing to do but shake hands with their rich classmates. When they see a classmate who hasn't made it, they ask, 'Where are you working?' and then without waiting for an answer they prick their ears up to catch what the rich classmates are saying. For students, social gatherings provide a chance for men and women to meet. When I was in America, people used to call the Foreign Students Summer Club the 'Big Three Conference': the show-offs, the suckers, and the—uh—the girl-snowers."

They all laughed. Mrs. Chao laughed till she began to cough and forbade Hsin-mei to utter any more nonsense. Wen-wan laughed more tersely than the rest and said, "You were in the Summer Club yourself. Don't deny it. I saw that picture. Which of the Big Three were you?"

Hsin-mei was unable to answer.

Wen-wan clapped her hands and said, "Well, so you can't say it. Auntie, I don't think Hsin-mei's as honest as he used to be, and he's become much more small-minded. It must have something to do with the friends he made this year."

Jou-chia stared hard at Hung-chien. Hung-chien again tightly gripped the armrest of the chair.

"Auntie, I won't see you off tomorrow. We'll meet in Chungking next month. I'll send the servant over with that little bundle of things later on. If it's inconvenient for you to carry, just let him take it back as it is."

Wen-wan stood up and picked up the straw hat by the tassel like the Greek huntress Diana taking up her shield. She enjoined Mrs. Chao not to see her out, then said to Hsin-mei, "I'm going to punish you by having you take those two cartons and see me to the door."

Hsin-mei noticed Hung-chien and his wife standing and, to prevent Wen-wan from rudely ignoring them, said, "Mr. and Mrs. Fang are saying goodbye to you."

Only then did Wen-wan nod to Hung-chien and hold her hand out for Jou-chia to shake as one might stick a finger into hot water to see if it were scalding or not. From the expression on her face it appeared she was shaking hands with someone a head taller than Jou-chia since her gaze went over Jou-chia's head. She then said warmly, "Goodbye, Auntie," and threw a half-pleased, half-vexed glance at Hsin-mei. Hsin-mei quickly picked up the boxes and followed her out.

Hung-chien and Jou-chia conversed politely with Mrs. Chao, and when Hsin-mei came back in, they rose to say goodbye. Mrs. Chao made them stay a little longer, complaining to Hsin-mei, "You acted so silly again. Why did you have to disparage her husband?"

Hung-chien thought to himself, *Su Wen-wan may think Hsin-mei has not gotten over his feelings for her and was reacting out of jealousy.*

"Don't worry," said Hsin-mei. "She wouldn't get angry. As long as we take her contraband for her, it'll be all right."

Hsin-mei wanted to walk them to the bus stop. When they had left the house, he said, "Su Wen-wan sure had her nerve today, being so rude to you that way."

Purposely putting on a show of great magnanimity, Hung-chien said, "Oh, it's nothing. She's a rich girl and a rich wife. It's only right that she put on those little airs." He didn't notice Jou-chia eyeing him. "You said 'take her contraband.' What's that all about?"

"Every time she flies to Chungking," explained Hsin-mei, "she takes some of the latest cosmetics, medicines, high-heeled shoes, fountain pens, and such to give away. Or maybe she sells them, I'm not sure."

Hung-chien nearly cried out in astonishment; then it dawned on him that the vast and lofty blue sky above was not the province of God and heaven, but was provided exclusively for the sake of dropping bombs and operating petty business ventures. "Strange!" he remarked. "I'd never have expected it of her! So she is even in business. I thought it was only people like Li Mei-t'ing who carried contraband! Isn't she a poet? Does she still write new-style poetry?"

"I don't know," said Hsin-mei with a smile. "She sure knows money business! She was just urging my mother to hurry up and buy foreign currency. It seems women are all good schemers."

Jou-chia kept a blank face, pretending not to have heard.

Hung-chien said, "I'll say something silly. She seems very—uh—very intimate with you."

Reddening, Hsin-mei said, "She knows I'm in Chungking too, so every time she goes, she always looks me up. She's just nicer to me now than she was before she got married."

Hung-chien sniffed and felt like saying, "No wonder you need a self-protective photograph," but didn't.

Hsin-mei paused a moment, then gazing off in the distance said, "Just now when I saw her to the door, she said she still kept a lot of my letters— I'd forgotten all about them. I don't know what sort of nonsense is in them. She said next month when she comes to Chungking, she's going to bring the letters along to return to me. But she won't return all of them. She said some things in the letters she can still accept. She wants to take them out in front of me one by one and pick out the ones she can't accept any more to return to me. Isn't that ridiculous?" He laughed unnaturally.

Jou-chia asked coolly, "Doesn't she know you're about to get engaged, Uncle Chao?"

Hsin-mei said, "No, I haven't told her. I'm rather distant with her."

After Hung-chien and Jou-chia had boarded the cable car down the mountain and Hsin-mei was on his way back home, it suddenly became clear to him, and he said with a sigh, "It takes a woman to see through a woman."

Hung-chien got gloomily into the car. He knew he had wronged Su Wen-wan before and deserved to be slighted by her today. But what annoyed him was that even Jou-chia had suffered her abuse. Why hadn't he poked fun at Su Wen-wan a little instead of just lowering his head, suppressing his anger, and letting her carry on at will? It was so distasteful. But then it wasn't so much getting the cold shoulder from her, it was the contrast between the past and the present which hurt so much. Two years ago, no, one year ago, he was completely her equal. Now she was as high above him as the clouds were from the mud. Why, look at Hsin-mei even. Hsin-mei showed him respect by treating him as a friend, but Hsin-mei too was gradually advancing in his career, so that now he had to look up to Hsin-mei too. It wasn't like before when they were equals. His anxious frame of mind was like a wild animal caged in a dark room, frantically ramming, clawing, beating against the walls, trying to find a way out. Noticing his silence, Jou-chia restrained herself and kept quiet. When they returned to the hotel and after the bellboy opened their door, Hung-chien took off his jacket, turned on the electric fan, and stretching his arms out before the breeze, said, "We're back. Ai!"

"Your body is back, but I'm afraid your soul has been carried off by your lover," added Jou-chia expressionlessly.

He of course said she was "being silly."

"I'm not being silly," she replied with a sardonic laugh. "You got into the car like a man of wood, not saying a word and completely forgetting I was there next to you. I was very discreet and didn't disturb you, just to see when you'd speak to me."

"Well, am I not speaking to you now? I'm not at all vexed about what happened today."

"How could you be vexed? You could only be pleased."

"That's not so. What would I be pleased about?"

"Watching your former sweetheart insult your present wife, and in front of your close friend—that doesn't make you pleased?" Jou-chia dropped her derisive tone and spoke with outright indignation, "I told you before. I don't like seeing Chao Hsin-mei. But what good did it do? You wanted to go, so could I say, 'No?' We went only to be scorned and laughed at."

"You are absolutely unreasonable. Weren't you the one who wanted to go in? When the thing is done you blame it all on me! And anyway, she didn't insult you. She even shook hands with you on her way out."

She flared with anger, then said with a laugh, "I am so honored! I was touched by the great lady's imperial hand. This lowly hand of mine will remain forever fragrant. I don't dare ever wash it! 'Didn't insult me!' Humph, if someone attacked me outright, you'd act as if you hadn't seen it. Anyway, your wife deserves being bullied by some strange woman. Well, if I ever saw my husband being ridiculed and abused, I certainly wouldn't be able to put up with it. I'd feel as if I had been stripped bare. When she said Hsin-mei's friends were no good, wasn't she referring to you?"

"Let her abuse. If I gave it back to her, she couldn't take it."

"Why didn't you give it back to her?"

"Why should I quarrel with her? I just think she's pathetic."

"How kind of you! Why don't you leave some of your sweet temper and generosity home for me to enjoy for a change? Whenever you meet someone outside, you bow your head and smile, but when you come home, if one thing I say doesn't suit you, you get hostile and start quarreling. People think Fang Hung-chien is so polite and so patient. They don't know how much I have to put up with from you. And I'm the only one who would. If it were that great lady, just try venting your anger on her." She paused a moment, then added, "Of course, if you'd married such a perfect wife as that, you'd never have to lose your temper."

What she said was partly true, although with a few spices added for seasoning. Unable to deny it and seething with rage, he just stood gazing out the window. His silence made her assume her last remark had struck home, and she was too overcome with jealousy to keep still. Controlling the agitation in her voice, she muttered sneeringly, "I see it all now. It was all a bunch of empty boasts. All—empty—boasts."

He turned and asked, "Who's boasting?"

"You. You were saying how much she used to love you, how she wanted to marry you. Today it was quite obvious she's on close terms with Hsin-mei while she never gave you so much as a straight look in the face. You went after her and didn't get her is what! Men always brag like that."

Hung-chien could come up with no counterevidence to refute this *Discussions of Ancient History*[8] sort of historical reinterpretation, and could only say, "All right, all right, so I was boasting. You've seen through it. So I was boasting."

"Isn't she wonderful!" said Jou-chia. "She's pretty, her father's rich, she has money, and she's a returned student. If I were you, even if she hadn't taken a liking to me, I'd have gotten down on my knees and pleaded, but when she actually showed favor—"

Hung-chien's eyes went red, and he roughly cut her short, "Yes, that's right, she really didn't want me. But surprisingly enough a woman like you tried every trick and scheme to marry me."

Eyes bulging, she bit her lower lip so hard it left a blood mark. In a trembling voice, she said, "I was blind! I was blind!"

Four or five hours later, Jou-chia hadn't gone blind, but both of them had gone mute. They ate and went about their business completely ignoring each other. Hung-chien knew he had spoken too harshly and inwardly regretted it, but for the moment he was not willing to give in. In the afternoon he suddenly remembered that he had to go the next day to the ship company with the receipt to pick up the tickets. Hsin-mei had given him the receipt two days before, but he'd forgotten where he'd put it and would not ask Jou-chia. He hurriedly went through his suitcases and pulled out his pockets but could find it nowhere. In his anxiety, he broke out in wave after wave of sweat, which rolled over each other like waves on the Yangtze River.

Watching him scratch his sweat-dampened head and twist his flushed ears, Jou-chia then asked, "What're you looking for? The ship company receipt?"

Hung-chien gave her a shocked look. Hope suddenly arose, and with a genial smile, he asked, "How did you guess? Did you see it?"

"You put it in the pocket of that white suit."

"Damn it!" he exclaimed, stamping his foot. "I gave that suit to the bellboy yesterday to send to the dry cleaners. What should I do now? I'll hurry over there right away."

Jou-chia opened her purse and said, "You got your clothes out to be cleaned and then just handed them over to the bellboy without first checking through them yourself! Luckily I took the receipt out for you. There was an old bill in there too."

Overwhelmed with gratitude, Hung-chien said, "Thank you, thank you."

"After trying every 'trick and scheme' to get myself married to a husband like you, you think I wouldn't look after him carefully?" As she spoke, the rims of her eyes reddened a little.

Hung-chien bowed and genuflected, admitting he was wrong and insisted on taking her out for a cold soft drink.

"I'm not a child. Don't try cajoling me with food. Those words 'every trick and scheme' I'll never forget as long as I live," she said.

He put his hand over her mouth to keep her from sighing. In the end she went out with him for a cold soft drink. As she sat sipping her orange juice, she asked if Su Wen-wan had dressed like that before.

He said, "She's a thirty-year-old married woman, and her clothes are getting more and more flamboyant. It's enough to make anyone want to laugh to himself. I don't think she's anywhere near as cute as you."

She shook her head and smiled to show that she couldn't believe her husband's remark but would like to.

"You heard Hsin-mei say how vulgar she's become. I don't know what became of her old refinement. I never expected her to turn so mercenary in one year. She's not like a well-bred girl at all," he remarked.

"Maybe she hasn't changed. Who knows what kind of corrupt official her father is? The daughter naturally takes after the father in some ways. Her real nature has been hidden underneath all along, and now that she's married and reached her full mental development, her true face finally shows itself. It doesn't matter if she's vulgar. I just think she's too low. She already has a husband, yet she still tries to make up to Hsin-mei. What kind of well-bred girl is that! I'd say she is a concubine's daughter. Take an ugly, poor wife like me. I may annoy you, but I know my place and wouldn't ever disgrace you. If you'd married that girl, you might very well have ended up keeping a mistress for Hsin-mei," she said.

He knew her remarks were very nasty, but could only nod and agree. By thus besmirching Su Wen-wan, the two made up.

This quarrel was like a summer rainstorm—severe while it lasted but over very quickly. From then on, however, each determined to control himself and avoid saying anything that would start a conflict.

The first night on the ship they were out on the deck enjoying the cool air.

"Last year when we first went to the interior on the same ship together, I never thought this year we'd be coming back on the same ship as man and wife," Hung-chien commented.

Jou-chia took his hand in lieu of a reply.

"How much did you hear of what Hsin-mei and I said on the deck that time? Tell the truth."

She withdrew her hand and said, "Who wants to listen to your conversation! You men never say anything worth listening to when you're together. Later I suddenly heard my name mentioned and was so scared I just wanted to run away."

He said with a smile, "Why didn't you?"

"Well, it was my name. Of course I had the right to hear the rest."

"We didn't say anything bad about you then, did we?"

Throwing him a glance, she said, "Which is why I was so taken in by you. I thought you were a nice person. How was I to know you're the nastiest of all people?"

In lieu of a reply, Hung-chien took her hand. She asked what day it was, and he told her it was the second of August. She sighed, "In five more days it'll be the anniversary!"

He asked what anniversary it was, and she replied disappointedly, "How could you have forgotten! Didn't we meet each other on the morning of August the seventh when Hsin-mei invited us out?"

Hung-chien was more ashamed than if he'd forgotten National Day[9] and National Humiliation Day[10] both, and he said quickly, "Oh, I remember now. I even remember what dress you were wearing that day."

Much consoled, Jou-chia said, "I wore a dress with blue flowers on a white background that day, didn't I? I don't remember anything about you that day though. It didn't leave any impression. But of course I remember the date. Isn't that what they call 'affinity'—when two strangers meet by chance and slowly become close?"

"Take all the people with us here on this ship, for instance," he said, launching forth. "We don't have a single acquaintance among them. We don't know where they came from or why they took this particular ship, and we assume it's just an accident that brought us all here together. But if we got to know their circumstances and destinations, then we'd realize that their taking this boat wasn't accidental at all, that they have reasons for taking this one just like us. It's like turning on the radio. You give the dial a turn and catch a phrase of Peking opera from this radio station, a phrase of an announcement from that one, and then suddenly a phrase of a foreign song, a melody—bits and pieces which make no sense when all brought together. But each broken fragment has a context in the program being broadcast on that radio station and isn't just nonsense. All you have to do is tune in to one particular station, and you'll understand its meaning. Dealing with other people is just like that. Strangers we don't know very well—"

She let out a big yawn a full inch square in area. Like all people he hated having someone yawn while listening to him. A year's experience in the classroom with hypnosis in disguise had only increased this hatred. He immediately stopped.

She said apologetically, "I'm tired. Go on talking."

"If you're tired," he said, "then go to bed. I won't talk anymore."

"We were having a nice talk about ourselves," she complained. "Why did you have to get off onto everyone on the ship and the whole of humanity?"

"All you women can ever talk about is yourselves," he said in exasperation. "Beyond that you don't understand a thing! You go on to bed first. I want to sit here for a while longer."

Jou-chia went off, pretending to ignore him. After Hung-chien had had a cigarette, he calmed down and began thinking how funny it was. That discourse really was like a lecture from a podium. He hadn't even taught a full year and already he'd developed this habit. Next time he'd have to be more careful and correct himself. No wonder after being a professor for so many years Lu Tzu-hsiao proposed as though he were giving an oral examination to his students. But then Jou-chia was too unrestrained. She always criticized him for having so much to say to other people while having nothing to say to her when he came back. Well, today when he launched into a long discourse with her, she just yawned. And to think he'd even praised her for being so submissive in his letter home!

For the last couple of days Hung-chien had begun to feel apprehensive as he neared home, and his mind was filled with all kinds of thoughts. *Returning home*, he felt, *is not as simple as it was made out to be. While a long separation doesn't amount to a temporary death, one at least becomes a stranger to his family. Returning home is just like returning something half-cooked to the pot. It has to be stewed a little longer before it becomes tender. Now that I am bringing Jou-chia home with me, I'll need even more time to adapt to the family.* Thinking about it made him uneasy, and he was afraid to go to bed. Sleep is such a fickle thing. When not wanted, it comes, and when it is invited, coaxed, and enticed along by every available trick, it puts on airs and conceals itself. Rather than toss and turn on his warm pillow, Hung-chien would just as soon sit for a while longer on the deck.

Jou-chia waited for her husband to come and make up, but when after a long while he didn't appear, she put away her resentment and went to sleep.

9

IT WAS IN his letter home announcing his engagement that Hung-chien had praised his wife for being submissive. When Fang Tun-weng finished reading the letter, he cackled like a hen that has just laid an egg, and within one minute the whole family had learned the news. After the old couple got over their initial surprise, vexation followed. Mrs. Fang especially reviled her son for being too rash, wondering why he hadn't asked for his parents' consent before getting engaged.

Tun-weng said, "We fulfilled our parental responsibilities by arranging a match for him with the Chous' daughter. This time he made the decision himself. If it turns out well, then so much the better. If not, then he can't complain about it to Mother and Father. Why worry about them?"

"I wonder what that Miss Sun is like," said Mrs. Fang. "Hung-chien is such a muddlehead. He didn't even send a picture!"

Tun-weng asked for the letter back from his Second Daughter-in-law, and reading it over said, "He says here in his letter she's 'submissive by nature.' "

Like all those with little education, Mrs. Fang was very superstitious about black words written on white paper, but she then raised a question of social geography, "Is she from another province? Outsiders are always a bit rough in their ways. They never get along with us."

Second Daughter-in-law said, "She's not from another province. She's from another county."

"As long as Hung-chien thinks she's submissive," said Tun-weng, "it's all right. Ai, the way daughters-in-law are nowadays, how can you still expect her to be filial? That could never be."

Second Daughter-in-law and Third Daughter-in-law exchanged glances, simultaneously wiping the genial expressions from their faces.

310

Mrs. Fang said, "I wonder if the Suns have money."

Tun-weng said with a smile, "Her father works in a newspaper office. Newspapermen are good extorters, so they must have money, ha, ha! Our Eldest seems to have the luck of a fool. The Chous of his first engagement were quite well off. Then he took a fancy to Su Hung-yeh's daughter, whose family is also rich and powerful. Now these Suns I don't think could be too bad. In any case, this girl is a college graduate and has a job. She can probably support herself."

These remarks of Tun-weng's unwittingly made two enemies for Jou-chia: Third Daughter-in-law and her sister-in-law, whose family circumstances were very ordinary and who had only high school education.

Then a letter came from Hung-chien in Hong Kong announcing his marriage and asking his father for money. Shocked and angered upon reading it, Tun-weng immediately grew very pensive. He and Mrs. Fang closed their bedroom door and studied the letter for a long time. Mrs. Fang blamed Jou-chia for seducing her son; Tun-weng also expressed some rather disrespectful views on the subject of free courtship and modern women. But he was the head of the family, and as such he felt that when one family member lost face, he lost face as well. Not only must the family disgrace not be spread abroad, it must not be spread within the family either. He must cover up for his eldest son and daughter-in-law among his sons and daughters-in-law. He sighed, "Sons and daughters certainly are 'seeds of retribution.' One has to worry about them all one's life. Mother, what's the use of getting upset about it? At least they knew enough to get married. That's all."

During dinner Tun-weng smiled easily and said, "We had a letter from Hung-chien today. They've arrived in Hong Kong. One of his friends traveling with them decided to get married in Hong Kong. Hung-chien went red-eyed with envy and wants to have the wedding ceremony with Miss Sun at the same time. The way the young people do things they are like a swarm of bees; they all like to get in on the excitement. He also mentioned that he'd be saving me money and effort. Well, he is being considerate toward Mother this way, isn't he?"

He waited till everyone had finished exclaiming, then continued, "When P'eng-t'u and Feng-i were married, I took care of all the expenses. If we were to have a wedding now on just as grand a scale as they were before in our village, I couldn't afford it. Hung-chien is saving me from having to take out my pocketbook, so how can I not be pleased? Nevertheless, P'eng-t'u, I want you to wire him some money for me tomorrow. That'll show that I treat you three brothers alike and keep him from accusing his parents of being unfair in the future."

After dinner, as Tun-weng was leaving the table, he said, "He's chosen a good way. Whenever there's a marriage, the two involved never worry about a thing. It's always the others around them who are kept on the go. If he'd gotten married in Shanghai, it wouldn't have been just Mother and me, but even you and your wives who'd have been worked to death. This way it's to the benefit of all."

He was confident these remarks had clearly pointed out all the advantages in such a way that his sons and daughters-in-law would never become suspicious. That day he wrote in his diary: "A letter came from son Hung-chien in Hong Kong stating that he planned to marry Miss Sun Jou-chia there. In consideration of the unusual times and the family's straitened circumstances, he had decided to economize and save trouble. It is a commendable idea, and so I have wired some money to help arrange it."

Third Daughter-in-law had returned to her room and was just washing her face when Second Daughter-in-law came in and whispered, "Did you hear that? I think something funny is going on. Couldn't they even wait the three or four days from Hong Kong to Shanghai?"

Not to be outdone, Third Daughter-in-law said, "When they suddenly got engaged in the interior, I thought it was too abrupt. Something was wrong even then."

"Precisely!" said Second Daughter-in-law. "I thought so too. Let's see, when did they get engaged?"

The two of them counted it out on their fingers, looked at each other and smiled. Feng-i, a simple-hearted soul, was so astounded that his eyes grew big and his jaw dropped.

Second Daughter-in-law said with a laugh, "Third Uncle, I'm afraid our First Sister-in-law will be the record-breaker among the Fang daughters-in-law."

A few days later the wedding pictures arrived. Jou-chia's face in the photographs very nearly matched the ideal she had of herself. Tun-weng was delighted when he saw them. Mrs. Fang put on her needlework glasses several times for a closer look. Feng-i said to his wife in private, "Sun Jou-chia is rather pretty. A lot better than the Chou girl who died."

Third Daughter-in-law said with a scornful laugh, "Photographs aren't dependable. You can't be sure until you see her. Some people are photogenic, and some are not. Very ugly people sometimes take good pictures, so don't be taken in. Why'd they take only a bust photo? It must be because they couldn't take the whole body. Draping it in silk and covering it up with flowers wouldn't help either, I'll bet. Huh, I was married into your family in proper, formal manner. Now I have to call a girl like that Eldest Sister-in-law. Of all the rotten luck! I really don't like it one bit. You see. That's a college graduate!"

Second Daughter-in-law expressed her feelings to her husband in this way, "Did you notice? There's an overly made-up look about Sun Jou-chia's face. You can tell at a glance she's an immoral woman, which is why she could do such a shameless thing. Your mother and father are two old fools to be praising her beauty! I don't mean to brag, but the sisters in my family were so clean and proper that our father wouldn't even let us write letters to our fiancés after we'd gotten engaged, to say nothing of ever having a boy friend."

P'eng-t'u said, "I'm afraid these in-laws of Eldest Brother's can't compare with the Chous. Chou Hou-ch'ing sure knows how to speculate and do business. His Golden Touch Bank has really prospered. Eldest Brother was a fool to break with him! The day before yesterday I ran into Chou Hou-ch'ing's son, who used to study with Hung-chien. He's seventeen or eighteen, and already he's assistant manager of the bank and can drive a car. I'm thinking of making friends with his father and restoring relations between the Chou and Fang families. Later we can pool our capital and invest. But don't tell anyone about this."

Jou-chia wouldn't go straight to her husband's home as soon as she got off the ship, but insisted on going back to her own home first. Hung-chien understood her shyness and didn't force her. He knew they couldn't set aside a room for him to stay in at home. The room he had lived in after breaking with the Chous was dark and narrow, just big enough for a small bed. Jou-chia had also made it clear that she would not be a daughter-in-law in a big family, so for the time being they would just have to stay in their own homes while they looked for rooms.

They went ashore, paid protection money to the policemen and detectives in the French Concession, and claimed their luggage. Hung-chien went with his wife to the Suns first. Since the taxi was waiting and each second was being counted, his courtesy call to his in-laws was brief to the extreme. He returned home alone. When his parents saw that the bride had not come with him, they were quite displeased, but at the same time relieved. The small room Hung-chien had occupied before was now given over to the two old maidservants to sleep in and had not yet been vacated. If the bride really had come, there wouldn't even have been room for changing clothes.

The old couple plied their son with all sorts of questions. Besides asking about the bride, they also wanted to know about his job for the rest of the year. To keep up a good front, Hung-chien said that the newspaper office had asked him to head the Office of Information.

Tun-weng said, "Then, you'll be staying in Shanghai for a while. It's so crowded here at home. Now I suppose I'll have to try finding you rooms nearby. Ai!"

Since one doesn't thank a close relative, Hung-chien had nothing to say. Tun-weng instructed his son to go that evening and invite Jou-chia over for lunch the next day. At the same time Hung-chien was to ask his mother- and father-in-law to decide upon a convenient day, so he could pick a restaurant and invite his relatives out in proper style.

Confident that he was well versed in the art of dealing with people, Tun-weng said with a smile to Mrs. Fang, "In the old-fashioned marriage, a sedan chair would carry the bride over whether she was shy or not. But not so nowadays. I'm thinking of asking Second Daughter-in-law or Third Daughter-in-law to go to the Suns with Hung-chien to invite her over and express their welcome. That way she won't feel like such a stranger."

Third Daughter-in-law remained expressionless. Second Daughter-in-law beamed with delight and said, "Wonderful! I'd like to go over and welcome Eldest Sister-in-law. I'll go with you tomorrow, Eldest Brother."

Hung-chien hurriedly thanked her but declined. When everyone had dispersed, Third Daughter-in-law said to Second Daughter-in-law, "Sister, you sure are good-natured! Who does Sun Jou-chia think she is, putting on those smelly airs and expecting us to go meet her! I certainly won't go!"

Second Daughter-in-law said, "She wouldn't come today because she can't. My guess is she's about to give birth and wouldn't dare show her face at her in-laws' home. Today she'll put it off till tomorrow. Tomorrow she'll put it off till the day after. We might as well await the arrival of a 'double blessing.' I knew Eldest Brother would never let me go. You saw how nervous he got then."

Humbled at being bested, Third Daughter-in-law said, "He may be the eldest son, but your Ah Ch'ou is still the Fangs' eldest grandson. If Sun Jou-chia has a son in a hurry, it won't do her any good."

Second Daughter-in-law tapped her with her finger and said, "Goodness! What wealth do the Fangs have to divide up? Can you even talk about eldest son or grandson in times like these? Aren't Ah Ch'ou and your Ah Hsiung both Fang grandsons? What little money the old man has is about used up. They didn't get a cent last year for winter rent, and Eldest Brother hasn't paid his share of the family expenses for three or four months. It looks to me as though the old man'll still have to support him from now on."

Third Daughter-in-law sighed. "As parents their hearts are tipped way over toward their armpits! Eldest Brother is the only one who graduated from college and studied abroad. He spent quite a bit of money, and now he still wants to spend the old man's money. I just don't understand what good it did him to study abroad. He can't even compare with our Third Brother, let alone Second Brother."

Second Daughter-in-law said, "We'll just see how 'independent' the woman college graduate is."

All their old ill will was forgotten, and they became as close as sworn sisters (natural-born sisters being jealous of each other). Never would Sun Jou-chia have dreamed she had become an angel of peace between the two sisters-in-law.

After lunch Tun-weng took a nap, while Mrs. Fang escorted the two disgruntled maids out of the room. Second Daughter-in-law and Third Daughter-in-law both went to sleep with the children. With no one watching them, Ah Ch'ou and Ah Hsiung went into the living room to get the attention of Hung-chien. Ah Ch'ou told Eldest Uncle he wanted to see Eldest Aunt, asking mischievously, "Eldest Uncle, who is Sun Jou-chia?"

"Good boy," said Hung-chien absentmindedly.

Ah Ch'ou asked for some wedding food to eat.

Hung-chien said, "Don't fuss. Tomorrow Grandpa will give you some."

Ah Ch'ou said, "Then give me a piece of candy now."

"You just ate. What do you want candy for? You're not as good a boy as Ah Hsiung."

Ah Hsiung again took his thumb from his mouth and said, "I want a piece of candy, too."

Hung-chien shook his head in exasperation and said, "What a nuisance. There isn't any candy."

Ah Ch'ou climbed up on the chair next to the window to see if there was anyone out on the street. Ah Hsiung was too small to climb up and wanted Eldest Uncle to lift him up. When Hung-chien, who was doing some calculations, ignored him, he assumed a tearful look and began yelling that he had to pee. Having never been a father, Hung-chien was unable to cope and putting down his pencil said, "Hold it. I'll take you upstairs to find Mama Chang. But once you've gone upstairs, you're not to come down again."

Ah Hsiung didn't want to go up and pointed to the spittoon next to the table. Hung-chien said, "Suit yourself."

Ah Ch'ou turned his head and said, "Somebody just went by with a popsicle in his hand. He had two of them, and he was eating one and then the other. Eldest Uncle, he had two popsicles."

When Ah Hsiung heard this, he forgot all about peeing and said, "I want to see him, too. Let me get up and see."

Ah Ch'ou said gleefully, "He's gone off somewhere. You can't see him—Eldest Uncle, have you ever had a popsicle?"

Ah Hsiung said earnestly, "I want a popsicle."

Ah Ch'ou hurriedly jumped down from the table and also said earnestly, "I want a popsicle."

Hung-chien replied that when Mama Chang or Mama Sun had straightened up the room, he'd send one of them out to buy some, but now they were not to make a fuss. Whoever did would lose his popsicle. Ah Ch'ou asked how long it would take to straighten up the room. Hung-chien replied that it would be at least half an hour.

"I won't make a fuss," said Ah Ch'ou. "I'll watch you write."

Having had enough of his right thumb, Ah Hsiung tried the ring finger of his left hand for something new. Before Hung-chien had written as many as ten words, Ah Ch'ou asked, "Eldest Uncle, has it been half an hour yet?"

"Nonsense!" said Hung-chien impatiently. "It's still a long way off."

Ah Ch'ou endured a while longer, then said, "Eldest Uncle, your pencil is so pretty. Let me write a word."

Hung-chien knew once he got his hands on the pencil it was condemned to death by decapitation and refused to give it to him. Ah Ch'ou searched from one end of the living room to the other and finally found a half-inch long pencil and an old invitation card. Giving the tip of the pencil a lick, he wrote out the characters "big" and "Fang," nearly boring through the paper with his pencil in the process. The characters resembled a pile of matchsticks.

"OK, OK," said Hung-chien, "go up and see if Mama Chang has finished yet."

Ah Ch'ou left and then came back down, saying she hadn't.

"You'll just have to wait a little longer," said Hung-chien.

Ah Ch'ou asked, "Eldest Uncle, when the bride comes, is she going to stay in that room?"

"It's none of your concern."

"Eldest Uncle, what does 'relations' mean?"

Hung-chien didn't understand.

Ah Ch'ou said, "Did you have 'relations' with Eldest Aunt at school?"

Hung-chien pounded the table and sat up straight, demanding, "What kind of talk is that? Who taught you to say that?"

Ah Ch'ou was so frightened his face turned redder than Hung-chien's, and he stammered out, "I—I heard Mama and Papa say it."

"Damn your mother!" Hung-chien raged. "No popsicle for you. You've lost your popsicle!"

When Ah Ch'ou saw Hung-chien was serious and realized he was to get no popsicle, he pretended to a spiritual victory; retreating to a relatively safe distance, he said, "I don't want your popsicle. My mama will buy me one. Eldest Uncle is bad. Bad Eldest Uncle. Dead Eldest Uncle."

"You say any more nonsense," said Hung-chien, gesturing at him, "and I'll give you a spanking."

Ah Ch'ou cocked his head to one side and puffed out his cheeks in defiance. Ah Hsiung sidled up to the table and said, "Eldest Uncle, I'm a good boy. I didn't say it."

Hung-chien said, "You'll get a popsicle. Don't be like him!"

When Ah Ch'ou heard that Ah Hsiung was still to get a popsicle, he went up to him, grabbed hold of his arm with one hand and held out the other, saying, "You lost my ball yesterday. Give it back. I want my ball. I want to bounce it now."

In fright Ah Hsiung yelled for Eldest Uncle to rescue him. Hung-chien pulled at Ah Ch'ou, who then gave Ah Hsiung a cuff on the ear. Ah Hsiung burst into tears and wet the floor. Just as Hung-chien was scolding Ah Ch'ou, Second Daughter-in-law came down and rebuked them, "You two have wakened baby brother with your racket!"

When Third Daughter-in-law heard her son crying, she too hurried downstairs. Both children were then pulled upstairs by their mothers, with Ah Ch'ou demanding all the way, "How come Eldest Uncle's giving him a popsicle and not me?"

Hung-chien pulled out his handkerchief to wipe the sweat away and heaved a sigh. How could Jou-chia ever get used to living in a family like this, he wondered. He had never thought his sister-in-law would malign him and his wife like that behind their backs. She undoubtedly had all kinds of other unpleasant things to say, which he simply did not care to know. He now even regretted having heard Ah Ch'ou's remark. Having heard their judgments of him behind his back, he'd be prepared to defend himself after death when interrogated by the King of Hades about his sins. He'd been too accustomed to his family all along to realize how much enmity and meanness lay underneath. Now because of Jou-chia he could observe it a little from an outsider's vantage point, and he suddenly realized what had really been going on all these years among his brothers and sisters-in-law and even between father and son. He had been living in a dream world.

That night Mrs. Fang went through her trunks and chests trying to find a couple of pieces of jewelry salvaged from the war to present to her daughter-in-law the next day as a First Meeting gift.[1]

Tun-weng laughed at her, saying, "You think these modern women still want to wear those old antiques of yours? You may as well forget it. 'A gift of a cart is not as good as a gift of words.' Tomorrow I'll give her a few words of advice."

In the more than thirty years since Mrs. Fang had been married, she had long since lost any curiosity about unlocking the storehouse of wisdom contained in her husband's quotations. She understood only the last sentence and said quickly, "You'd better be careful what you say tomorrow. Don't you dare bring up anything about their past affairs."

"Unless I'm as stupid as you!" replied Tun-weng hotly. "I've dealt in society for over twenty years. You think I don't know that much about the ways of the world?"

At noon the next day Hung-chien went to fetch Jou-chia.

"Your family is more tradition-minded than we are," said Jou-chia. "What's the etiquette involved in today's visit? I don't understand it and I'm not going."

Hung-chien said it was just an occasion for everyone to get acquainted, and there was no special etiquette. His father just wanted them to pay respects to their ancestors.

Jou-chia said peevishly, "Oh, so you Fangs have ancestors, while we just dropped from the sky and have none! Why don't you pay respects to the Sun ancestors? Tomorrow I'll have Papa make you kneel three times and kowtow nine times before photographs of my grandparents as a penalty. I want revenge!"

Hearing her lighthearted tone, Hung-chien smiled and said, "For my sake, suffer a little injustice."

"If it weren't for you," said Jou-chia, "I really wouldn't be willing to go today. I'm not a new puppy or kitten to be initiated in front of the Kitchen God, you know!"

When they arrived at the Fangs and Mrs. Fang saw Jou-chia wasn't as beautiful as her picture, she was secretly disappointed. She also felt her clothes weren't red enough for a bride and was especially disapproving of her shoes, which were an inauspicious white. Second Daughter-in-law and Third Daughter-in-law had done thorough makeup jobs which, because they had perspired so much in the heat, looked like the half-melted "happiness" character on wedding cakes. When they saw their new sister-in-law's face, they relaxed and forgot their worries. As for her figure, however, they were not without disappointment. Though Jou-chia could not compare with Sarah Bernhardt, the French actress, who was so slim-waisted that swallowing one quinine pill would have made her look pregnant, she was undeniably slim. The prophecy of a "double blessing" was not to be fulfilled.

Tun-weng was delighted and plied his new daughter-in-law with questions, saying with a smile, "From now on Hung-chien's mother and I won't be looking after him. We're entrusting him entirely to you—"

"Oh, yes!" Mrs. Fang put in. "Hung-chien has been incompetent since he was little. He couldn't dress himself even by the time he was seven. Even now you can see he doesn't know when to dress for warm or cool weather, and he recklessly eats sweet and salty things, just like a child. Dear, you'll have to watch out for him. Hung-chien, you won't listen to

318

what I say, but now that you're married, you must listen to what your wife says."

Jou-chia said, "He won't listen to me either—Hung-chien, did you hear that? From now on if you don't listen to what I say, I'll tell your mother."

Hung-chien replied with a silly grin. Second Daughter-in-law and Third Daughter-in-law exchanged secret looks of disdain.

When Tun-weng learned Jou-chia was going to work, he said, "I have a word of advice for you. To be sure, it's very good to have a job, but if both husband and wife work, 'the home is without master, and the broom is left upturned.' With everything at sixes and sevens, it's a family in name only. I'm not a stubborn man, but I do feel taking care of the house is the woman's responsibility. I have no dreams about your being filial toward us now, but you must make sure that your husband is kept content. Unfortunately, I'm here as a refugee. Our house is too crowded for you to stay with us. Otherwise, you could learn how to keep house from your mother-in-law." Jou-chia nodded reluctantly.

When it was time for them to pay respects, a red carpet was spread before the sacrificial table, obviously intended for Hung-chien and his wife to kneel down before the souls of the Fangs' departed ancestors. Jou-chia stepped stiffly onto the carpet without showing the least intention of kneeling down. Hung-chien, together with Jou-chia, bowed three times and was done. The onlookers were unable to express their shock and disapproval. Ah Ch'ou was more rash and asked his mother and father, "Why don't Eldest Uncle and Eldest Aunt kneel down and kowtow?" Like a telephone ringing in an empty house, the remark was unanswered. Hung-chien was so embarrassed he wanted to hide. Fortunately Ah Ch'ou and Ah Hsiung scrambled onto the red carpet to kneel and made obeisance and nearly got into a fight, which diverted everyone's attention. Mrs. Fang fully expected that after making obeisance to their ancestors, they would perform a formal kneeling ceremony of First Meeting before her and her husband. Hung-chien knew nothing of this rite, however, and thought that they were considered to have met the rules of etiquette the moment they walked in the house and that was all there was to it.

Thus the meal went anything but harmoniously. Ah Ch'ou insisted on sitting next to Jou-chia and telling Eldest Aunt to take some of this and some of that dish, giving orders right and left. By the time half of the dishes were served, Jou-chia had grown tired of humoring this pesky little nephew. Ah Ch'ou then kneeled on his chair and reached out to pick the food up by himself. While doing so, he accidentally knocked over Jou-chia's wine glass. With a cry, she quickly stood up and jumped aside, but not before her new dress had been dyed with a trail of wine stains. Grandfather and Grand-mother scolded Ah Ch'ou. Jou-chia quickly said that it didn't matter. P'eng-t'u and his wife also gave their son a severe scolding and forbade him to eat any more. With a woeful look, Ah Ch'ou sulked and refused to get down from his chair. Meanwhile P'eng-t'u and his wife hoped Hung-chien and Jou-chia would put in some kind words to save their son's face. To their surprise Hung-chien merely asked Jou-chia solicitously, "Can the wine stains be washed out? Luckily the meat ball he picked up didn't roll onto your clothes. That was a close one!"

With a long face, Second Daughter-in-law pulled Ah Ch'ou upstairs. Everyone's entreaties were too late. All that could be heard were Ah Ch'ou's sharp cries of pain from half way up the stairs, shrill and prolonged like the whistle of an express train passing through a small station without stopping. These were followed by loud wails and bawling. P'eng-t'u listened in pain and said through clenched teeth, "That child deserves a good spank-ing. I'll give it to him later when I go up."

In the afternoon as Jou-chia was about to leave, Second Daughter-in-law, her face wreathed with smiles, said, "Don't go. Why not stay here tonight?—Third Sister, let's take custody of her—Eldest Brother, only you can take her back home! You don't want to make her stay?"

His eyes puffy from crying, Ah Ch'ou stood by ignoring everyone. Because her son and daughter-in-law had failed to kowtow to her, Mrs. Fang had not given them any jewelry. After she had seen them out, she returned to her room and grumbled to her husband.

"It's not surprising that Sun Jou-chia's manners are so wanting," said Tun-weng. "People coming out of the schools are all rude and ignorant of the rules of etiquette. I don't know much about her family, but she must not have received any training at home."

"I carried him in me for ten months and raised him to manhood," grumbled Mrs. Fang. "Now that he's taken a wife, don't I deserve a kowtow from the two of them? So maybe Sun Jou-chia doesn't know any better, but then our Eldest should teach her. The more I think about it the angrier I get."

"Don't get upset," urged Tun-weng. "After a while when our Eldest comes back, I'll talk to him. He is such a muddlehead; I can see he's going to be henpecked. But Sun Jou-chia does seem to be quite a sensible woman. Did you notice how she nodded in agreement just now when I told her not to go out and work?"

As soon as she had left the house, Jou-chia said, "A perfectly good dress, and now it's ruined! I don't know if the stains will ever come out. Never have I seen such unruly children!"

Hung-chien said, "I hate them myself. Luckily we won't ever be living

320

together. I realize the meal today completely turned your stomach. By the way, speaking of the children, it just occurred to me. I think you're supposed to give them some First Meeting money, and tips to the two servants."

Jou-chia stamped her foot and cried, "Why didn't you tell me earlier? We don't do that in our family. I'm just out of school. I don't know all those silly old rules. What a nuisance! I don't like being your Fang family daughter-in-law any more!"

"Never mind," he comforted her. "I'll go buy some red envelopes and give them out for you. That'll settle it."

"Whatever you think," she said. "In any case, I can't please your family. Those two sisters-in-law of yours aren't easy to deal with, and your father's remarks were pretty weird, too. I, Sun Jou-chia, a college graduate, going to your family as an unpaid maidservant! Humph, your family isn't so well off as all that."

Hung-chien could not help defending his father, "He wasn't asking you to be a maidservant, merely urging you not to go out and work."

"Who doesn't want to stay home and enjoy herself?" she argued. "I don't like going out to work. Tell me, how much money do you earn a month that you can afford to keep me at home? Or do you Fangs have some family property? And as for your own job for the rest of the year, I have yet to see a single sign of it! Isn't it a good thing if I earn my own money? All you can do is make flippant remarks!"

"That's another matter," he said crossly. "There's some sense to what he says."

She replied with a scornful laugh, "You and your father's ideas are antiques from several thousand years back, and you of all people are a returned student."

Also smiling scornfully, he said, "What do you know about antiques! Let me tell you something. My father's idea is quite fashionable abroad. You lost out in not having studied abroad. When I was in Germany, I learned about the German women's Three K Movement: *Kirche, Küche, Kinder*—"

"I don't want to hear whatever you have to say," she said. "But I did learn today what a filial son you are. You're so obedient to your father. . . ."

The quarrel never became serious because they couldn't go to the Suns to quarrel, neither could they return to the Fangs to quarrel, and they couldn't very well quarrel there on the street. Thus there was no place for them to match wits and clash tongues. Sometimes not having a home to return to is a real blessing.

The families had met, invited each other out, visited back and forth, and even exchanged looks of disdain in their hearts. Neither was satisfied with the other. The Fangs despised the Suns for their rudeness; the Suns detested the Fangs for their outmoded ways. And behind each others' backs, each hated the other for not being rich.

One day after hearing his wife criticize Mrs. Sun, Tun-weng in a sudden inspiration added a splendid passage to his diary stating that now at last he understood why two families seeking a marriage alliance called it "joining together as Ch'in and Tsin. In the Spring and Autumn Period, the two states of Ch'in and Tsin were allied through marriage, and yet every generation thereafter took up arms. The mutual hatred between in-laws being at its fiercest today, to call it Ch'in and Tsin is quite fitting."[2] He was extremely pleased when he had finished and only wished he could have sent it over to Mr. Sun for him to enjoy.

Faced with difficulties from both families, when Hung-chien and Jou-chia had taken all the frustration they could hold, they just had to take out their frustration on each other. While he was made to suffer because of his wife, he discovered at the same time the convenience of having a wife when one is made to suffer. When he had been frustrated before, he had had to keep his feelings pent up inside, unable to release them as he pleased. There was no one to serve as an outlet for him. Now it was different. There is no one on whom a person can vent his anger with as much all-out relish as on his wife. Friends will break off and servants will go on strike, not to mention parents and brothers. Only a wife, like the Wind God's leather bag in Homer's epic poem, has such a tremendous capacity for taking in hot air, for divorce after all is not easy.

Jou-chia also discovered that one needn't have as many scruples toward one's husband as toward parents. But she had more forbearance than Hung-chien. Whenever Hung-chien began to get really angry, she would simply stop and not say another word. It was as if she and Hung-chien were having a tug of war with a piece of rope, each pulling with all his might on one end. When the rope grew so taut it was about to snap, she would take a few steps closer and let the rope go slack.

Though in the heat of anger they might find quarreling a great relief, when the quarrel was over they both felt exhausted and empty, the feeling one gets at the end of the opera or when one wakes from a drunken sleep. Before they returned to Shanghai, they would make up a quarrel soon afterward, like a rich family's food which isn't kept overnight. But now Hung-chien's hostility toward his wife after a quarrel lingered until the next day. And sometimes when no one seemed to be the winner, he would speak to her even before making up.

After one fight, Jou-chia said half in earnest and half in jest, "When you get angry, it's like a wild beast biting someone. You not only won't

322

listen to reason, you don't even have any feeling. You're the eldest son, but I can see your father and mother never spoiled you in any way. Why are you so unrestrained?"

Hung-chien laughed shamefacedly. He had just won a round of name-calling; victory had made him magnanimous. He didn't have to retort, "Your mother and father favored the male over the female and never doted on you, yet you're pretty hard to please yourself."

After he'd been to the Suns twice he could see that while Jou-chia was always full of "Papa this" and "Mama that," her parents were cool toward her affairs to the point of indifference. Mr. Sun was a nice man in the bad sense of the term—a useless fellow, who worked as chief accountant at the newspaper office and had no influence. Mrs. Sun had given birth to a son quite late in life. Having had only one male descendent continuously for three generations, the Suns made a religion out of raising their son, keeping his hair slick and his clothes starched like a high-class hairdresser in a beauty salon or a waiter in a Western restaurant. They had fulfilled their responsibility of supporting their daughter through college and had no more interest in managing her affairs. Perhaps if their son-in-law were rich, they might have taken a little more interest in their daughter.

The person closest to Jou-chia was her aunt, a returned student from America, the kind who called one's child "your baby," and one's wife "your Mrs." This kind of aunt Jou-chia of course called "Auntie." She had been quite popular in her youth and still hadn't forgotten it. She was quite harsh in her judgment of the younger generation of women students. Jou-chia loved hearing her reminisce, so Jou-chia became the sole recipient of her affection. Mr. and Mrs. Sun stood in great awe of this aunt and had to bring her in on most of the family affairs. Her husband, Mr. Lu, who always had an unforgivably smug expression on his face, enjoyed discussing current events. Because he was slightly deaf in both ears, people didn't have the energy to argue with him, and the fact that he could only hear his own voice made it even harder to reason with him. Husband and wife both held important positions in a large textile factory. He was chief engineer, and she was head of the personnel department. Thus Jou-chia also found a position in personnel.

The aunt felt her niece was mismatched and was openly contemptuous of Hung-chien's abilities and qualifications. Whenever Hung-chien met her, his feelings of inferiority rose like wartime commodity prices. The aunt, who was childless, kept a little Pekingese dog named Bobby, which was as dear to her as life itself. The dog would bark at Hung-chien whenever it saw him. Its mistress's oft-repeated remark, "Dogs are quite clever the way they can tell good from bad," only irritated Hung-chien more. But alas, dogs are made noble by dint of their master's own status, just as husbands are ennobled by their wives or wives by their husbands, and Hung-chien didn't dare beat the dog. Jou-chia tried to get her aunt to like her husband more by always having Hung-chien take the dog out to relieve itself, something which did nothing to improve Hung-chien's feelings for it.

Once Hung-chien remarked maliciously to Jou-chia, "Your aunt loves her dog more than she does you."

"Don't talk rubbish," said Jou-chia—adding the senseless remark—"That's just the way she is."

Hung-chien said, "The way she likes a dog's companionship just shows she is not fit for human company."

Eyes blazing, Jou-chia said, "It seems to me dogs can sometimes be nicer than people. At least Bobby is nicer than you. He has a sense of loyalty and doesn't bite just anyone. Someone like you deserves to be bitten."

Hung-chien said, "You're sure to be just like your aunt some day and keep a dog. Why, a poor devil like me should keep a dog. My relatives look down on me, I have no friends; my wife—uh—my wife gets mad easily and ignores me. If I had a dog around to wag its tail at me, at least there'd be something in the world lower than myself anxious to curry favor. That aunt of yours has the factory employees all catering to her wishes, while at home her niece is so obedient and dutiful, to say nothing of the other people there! You'd think she'd be satisfied, and yet she still has to keep a running dog to nod its head and wag its tail at her. Obviously there's no limit to the amount of flattery a person wants."

Controlling her voice, Jou-chia said, "Would you mind not talking so much? I can't have three days of peace. We'd just been getting along fine for the last few days, and now you have to stir up trouble over nothing."

Hung-chien spouted out with a laugh, "Oh, so fierce, so fierce!"

Hung-chien's lament over the Pekingese was partly true. Just as last year he had regretted going to the interior, so now he regretted having listened to Jou-chia and returned to Shanghai. While in the small town, he was afraid of getting pushed out in a power struggle; now that he was in a big city, he hated the callousness of people and felt instead that getting pushed out was at least an indication that people had some respect for him. Even a germ could go about smug in the expectation that it might be put under a microscope and looked at. The loneliness in the crowds and the desolateness amidst all the excitement made him feel like many other people living on this solitary island. His mental state too was like a solitary, isolated island.

Shanghai this year was quite different from what it was last year. The situation in Europe was rapidly deteriorating, and because of this the Japanese in the two large concessions were getting more out of hand every day. Britain and America, which were later to "fight side by side" with China, at that time thought only of maintaining a neutral stand. Since neither neutrality nor a stand could be maintained, their "neutral stand" eventually became a mere attempt to keep a foothold in China. Beyond this foothold the Japanese were allowed to run rampant. John Bull only "shot the bull," and Uncle Sam proved to be none other than Uncle Sham. As for Marx's clever analogy of the so-called "crowing French Chantecler," it did indeed have a Chantecler's instinct—to turn to the East and crow long and loud, the only trouble being that it mistook the sun flag [of Japan] for the real sun. America shipped load after load of scrap iron to Japan, while Britain considered blockading the Burma Road. Though France still had not cordoned off the Yünnan-Vietnamese border, it had already impounded a batch of Chinese munitions.

In Shanghai, commodity prices, like a kite with its string broken in the wind, soared high above the ground as though they had achieved Nirvana and immortality. Public workers struck again and again. Trams and buses wished they could have hung out "Full House" signs like movie theaters and hotels. Copper and nickel coins were all confiscated. Stamps were temporarily put to a new use as supplementary currency. If only people could have been sent like mail, then the painfully crowded conditions on public buses could have been avoided. The struggle for survival was gradually stripped of mask and ornament to reveal a primitive brutality. A reasonable sense of shame was not cheap at all; many could not afford it.

The number of people profiting and the number going bankrupt from the national crisis increased simultaneously. Neither interfered with the other since the poor begged only in the major thoroughfares and bustling marketplaces and stayed away from the quiet residential areas of the rich. They asked for money only from those on foot, unable to catch up with the rich in their sleek cars. Slums gradually spread like ringworm over the face of the city. Political terrorist incidents occurred nearly every day. Men of good will were so depressed that, like the transportation lines in major Western cities, they slowly began to go underground, while the dark, insidious reptiles in human form, which had been underground all along, boosted their prestige by latching on to them. Newspapers promoting "Sino-Japanese Peace" every day published lists of new comrades who had joined their ranks, while at the same time in another newspaper these "Japanese collaborators" were often declaring themselves "apolitical."

Five days after returning to Shanghai, Hung-chien went to the Sino-American News Agency to see the editor-in-chief. Hsin-mei had already made an appointment for him by mail from Hong Kong. Not wanting to ask his father-in-law to act as guide, he went by himself to the building in which the newspaper office was located. The office was on the third floor. A sign on the elevator stated that it stopped only at the fourth floor. Though he knew the lovely T'ang poem, "For a thousand *li* view, ascend another flight of stairs," he did not take the elevator. And though he didn't know Dante's melancholy line, "How hard the passage to descend and climb/By other's stairs," by the time he had climbed the two flights, he was already feeling so downcast and disheartened he wished another few steps could have been added to the stairs so he could delay a little longer.

He pushed open the swinging door and walked in. A long counter separated the people in the office from those outside. The mere addition of a copper railing on the counter would have made it look no different from a bank, pawnshop, or post office. The newspaper agency was divided into an inner and outer room. At a desk facing the door in the outer room sat a young woman filing her red fingernails with her curled third finger, on which was a diamond ring. When someone pushed the door open and entered, she did not so much as lift her head. Ordinarily Hung-chien might have wondered how someone in an office could have had red polish on her fingernails without any ink stains on her fingers, but in his haste, it never crossed his mind. From the other side of the counter he removed his hat and made his inquiry. She raised her head, her face filled with an expression of solemn unapproachability, as though having been wronged by men in a previous life, she was still keeping her guard up in this one. She looked him over a moment, shot her red lips over toward the left, then lowered her head and continued filing away at her nails.

Looking in the direction indicated by her lips, Hung-chien saw something which resembled the small, square ticket seller's booth at a train station with the words "Messages Transmitted" written on it and quickly went over to it. Inside a sixteen- or seventeen-year-old boy was sorting mail. Hung-chien called his attention by saying, "Pardon me, I'm looking for Mr. Wang, the editor-in-chief."

The boy kept on sorting his mail and answered absently, "He's not here." He had used the most economical movement of the mouth muscles to utter these three words—just enough for Hung-chien to hear and no more. Not a single nerve was twitched nor a single breath of sound emitted unnecessarily.

Hung-chien was so alarmed his legs went limp and he exclaimed, "Ai, how could he not be here! Why, he must be. Would you please go in and check?"

Having been a messsenger for two years, the boy was an old hand at dealing with people and knew that callers fell into two categories: the un-important ones who requested meekly, "Excuse me, would you please do such and such," and the big customers who ordered gruffly, "Kid, here's my card. Go get so-and-so." The one here today belonged to the former category. As he himself was now busy, he had no time to pay attention to the caller.

Hung-chien thought to himself that if he did get the job, he would certainly find some way to have this little punk dismissed. Screwing up his courage, he said, "I have an appointment with Mr. Wang at this time."

At this the boy finally turned to the woman and asked, "Miss Chiang, is Mr. Wang in?"

She shook her head impatiently and said, "How should I know!"

The boy sighed, grudgingly rose to his feet and asked Hung-chien for his card. Hung-chien had no card and just gave his name. The boy was just about to carry out his transmitting duty when someone came by, and the boy asked him, "Is Mr. Wang in?"

"I guess not," the other replied. "I haven't seen him today. He proba-bly won't be in till this afternoon."

The boy spread out his hands to indicate that he could not produce Mr. Wang. Hung-chien suddenly spotted his father-in-law working at a far-off desk by a window. His delight was akin to meeting an old friend in a strange place at a time of distress. He was immediately shown in by his father-in-law, met Mr. Wang, and had a warm talk with him. Because it was Hung-chien's first visit there, Mr. Wang insisted on seeing him out past the counter. The woman was no longer filing her nails but was busily working the Chinese typewriter, the finger with the diamond ring curling upward as before. Mr. Wang instructed Hung-chien to go up to the fourth floor and take the elevator down, and when he came to work the next day to take the elevator up to the fourth floor, then walk down. This would save him from walking one flight of stairs. Having learned his lesson, Hung-chien was as happy as could be, already feeling like an old hand at the newspaper office.

That evening he wrote a letter to Hsin-mei, thanking him for his kind-ness in recommending him for the job. In a postscript he added jokingly that to judge from his experience with the message counter that day, the newspaper's other stories and news reports probably weren't too accurate either.

Housing proved harder to find than a job. The streets were filled with houses, but none was available for Hung-chien. Shanghai seemed to expect every newcomer to bring his own house with him the way a snail carries its shell. Hung-chien and his wife grew tired and discouraged looking for a place to stay, and to this were added pointless arguments. Finally, relying on Tun-weng's good offices, they managed, without paying any commission to a housing agent, to rent two small rooms in the home of a relative. Part of this relative's family were returning to their village, and since the Fangs' large house was vacant, they wanted to live there. Tun-weng suggested that these two rooms be given in exchange. The matter was settled at once, and Tun-weng had good reason to vaunt his accomplishment in front of his son and daughter-in-law. His son, of course, docilely went along.

When his daughter-in-law went home and told her mother, Mrs. Sun, however, said, "How ridiculous! He should have provided you with housing long ago. Why is it Hung-chien's sisters-in-law all have proper places to live? The Fangs should have provided you with housing when you married into their family. They didn't and did you an injustice by keeping you newlyweds apart. So now they've managed to find two rooms. Well, what's so wonderful about that? I've always said one should never blunder into a marriage. You should have found out such things as whether the family provided housing or not."

Fortunately, Jou-chia did not repeat these remarks to her husband; otherwise, there would surely have been a row. She had discovered that while Hung-chien very much disliked his family, he would never let anyone else criticize it in any way.

They also had arguments over the buying of furniture. Hung-chien felt they need only borrow enough from his family to get by. She asserted that as a woman she placed more importance than he on the territory under her jurisdiction and wanted to acquire some family possessions. When he accompanied her to a furniture store, he was all set to buy the first table he saw. She, on the other hand, merely asked the price, gave the table a close scrutiny inside and out, and made a mental note of everything. She then wanted to go around to several other furniture stores to compare prices and quality. He lost patience and after one trip refused to go with her again. She didn't want him along anyway and went off to ask for her aunt's advice.

When the furniture was nearly all in, Mr. and Mrs. Lu came over to see their niece's new living quarters. Mr. Lu said the stairs were too dark, and the landlord should put in a light. Mrs. Lu found the rooms too small, commenting that Hung-chien's father should have insisted that at least one of the two rooms be a large one. Not deaf to what his wife said, Mr. Lu put in, "Quite true. Hung-chien, I don't think that house of yours in the country is very big. Otherwise, for them to rent your large house while you rent their small rooms is a pretty rotten deal, heh, heh."

328

Bobby barked along with him as he laughed. He then asked Hung-chien what the news was at the newspaper office for the last couple of days.

Hung-chien replied, "There've been no special reports."

"What?" he asked, not hearing clearly.

Hung-chien put his mouth up close to his ear and said loudly, "There've been no—"

Mr. Lu jumped. Frowning and rubbing his ear, he said, "Ai, your breath pierced right into my ear. Gave me an awful itch!"

When Mrs. Lu, who had given her niece the furniture to furnish one room, saw how disrespectful her nephew-in-law was toward her husband, she said, "I've never read the *Sino-American News*. Does it have a wide circulation? I don't read Chinese newspapers, only English ones."

Hung-chien replied, "In the last couple of days Poland fell. Germany and Russia's power and prestige have become immense, while England has gone down. In the future there may not be any English newspapers to read. Auntie had better study German or Russian."

Angered at this, Mrs. Lu said she didn't care to learn any German, and Russian was spoken by clerks in general stores. Understanding the point at issue, Mr. Lu gave his own views, proclaiming that with America there they had nothing to fear, and England had never amounted to anything in the first place.

After they had gone, Jou-chia complained to Hung-chien.

Hung-chien said, "This is my home, and they're not welcome here."

Jou-chia said, "The chair you're sitting in was a gift from them."

Hung-chien hurriedly stood up. When he then looked around and found that chairs and sofa were all gifts from Mrs. Lu, he sat down on the bed and said, "Who asked them for it? We can just give it back. I'd rather sit on the floor."

Half angered and half amused, Jou-chia said, "Only a child could ever make such a nonsensical remark. It's not funny at all when you say it."

No one who hears himself being called a child by the opposite sex can fail to grow docile. Though Jou-chia had not called Hung-chien this, the effect was the same.

Mr. and Mrs. Fang also came over one morning to see the newly furnished rooms. Jou-chia had already gone to work. Usually Hung-chien didn't go to the newspaper office until after breakfast.

His mother came up the stairs first and said, "Papa is at the door. He's brought something for you. Hurry down and bring it up. Don't send the maid. If she's clumsy she might break the glass."

Hung-chien hurried down to meet his father and brought an old-fashioned pendulum wall clock into the room. Tun-weng asked him if he remembered the clock. Hung-chien shook his head.

Tun-weng said generously, "It'd be a dream all right to expect your generation to protect the riches of your ancestors and keep them intact from generation to generation! Wasn't this the clock Grandfather bought and hung in the back room of the old house?"

Hung-chien then remembered. It was one of the surviving relics his two brothers had gone back to collect from their village last spring and brought out on a rented night boat.

Tun-weng said, "When you were little you liked to listen to its chimes. Grandfather said he'd give it to you when you grew up. Ai, you've completely forgotten it! I paid the watch and clock shop to repair it last week. The mechanism isn't broken at all. Old things are the sturdiest. Where can you find a clock that durable nowadays?"

Mrs. Fang put in, "That watch Jou-chia wears is so tiny; the mechanism inside can't possibly be complete."

Hung-chien said with a smile, "Mother, you're talking like you don't know anything. 'The sparrow may be small, but its five organs are complete.' Of course, the mechanism has everything it should. It's not too sturdy, that's all."

"That's just what I was saying," said his mother.

Tun-weng chose a good spot to hang the clock and told the maid to borrow a ladder from the landlord. As he watched Hung-chien climb up and hang it, he broke into a cold sweat on the clock's behalf. When the ladder had been removed, he scrutinized the clock on the wall and with great satisfaction said to his son, "Actually it could be a little higher—no, leave it there. Don't move it again. That clock is extremely accurate. I tested it yesterday. It's only seven minutes slow every hour. Remember that—seven minutes slow."

Mrs. Fang took a look at the furniture and said, "This kind of wood furniture isn't very sturdy. Redwood is the best kind of furniture. How much did you pay for it?"

When she heard Jou-chia's aunt had given it to them, she asked, "Did Jou-chia's family give her anything?"

"Her parents bought the sitting room-dining room combination," Hung-chien fibbed. Then seeing his mother's face failed to show any satisfaction, he added, "And her family took care of all the utensils under the stove."

Mrs. Fang's expression remained dissatisfied, but Hung-chien could not for the moment think of any other valuable item to save the face of his in-laws.

Mrs. Fang pointed to the iron bed and said, "This clearly you bought yourselves. Her aunt didn't give you this."

330

"You can't expect someone to give you a bed," said Hung-chien impatiently.

Mrs. Fang suddenly remembered that half the responsibility for furnishing a new home rested on the husband's family and said no more. They then asked what time Jou-chia came home every day, what dishes they usually had, whether the maid was a good cook, how much the daily expenses were, how many loads of coal they used each month, and so on. Most of the questions Hung-chien was unable to answer. Tun-weng shook his head, and Mrs. Fang said, "It's quite thoughtless to entrust the running of the entire household to the maid. Is this Mama Li dependable?"

Hung-chien said, "She used to be Jou-chia's wet nurse. She's very loyal. She wouldn't cheat us."

Tun-weng snorted and said, "What does a muddlehead like you know?"

Mrs. Fang said, "It's no good for a household to be without a mistress. I will persuade Jou-chia not to go out and work. How much can she earn in a month? If she looked after the house, she'd be able to save those few dollars from the four necessities of life."[3]

Hung-chien could not keep from speaking out honestly, "She gets good pay at the factory, twice as much as I earn."

The old couple fell into a hostile silence. Mrs. Fang felt her son sided too much with his wife, while Mr. Fang felt that his son was a complete disgrace to all husbands in the world.

When they returned home, Tun-weng said, "Our Eldest must certainly be henpecked. How can he let a woman earn more than he does? Could a husband like that establish his supremacy?"

Mrs. Fang said, "I just can't believe Jou-chia has any ability. How could our Eldest after studying abroad not be as good as she? She should let our Eldest have her job at the factory."

Tun-weng heaved a long sigh and said, "Our son is a no-account. Just leave him be!"

When Jou-chia returned home, the clock greeted her just as she entered the room. With a rattle and a click the spring turned, and it chimed five times.

"Where did that come from?" she asked in surprise. "Hey, that's not right! By my watch it's nearly six o'clock."

Mama Li explained everything.

"Did Mrs. Fang take a look under the stove?" asked Jou-chia.

Mama Li replied that she hadn't. Jou-chia then asked her what food she had bought that day and said with relief, "Oh, very good, but you should have let Mrs. Fang take a look at them so she wouldn't think we are starving her son."

Mama Li said, "I just fried a pork chop for Master. There are several raw ones left over that are marinating in wine and soy sauce. I'll fry them in a moment for your dinner."

Jou-chia said with a smile, "I've told you over and over again not to do that. You just won't change. How can I eat that many? You should give him as many as possible. Men have bigger appetites, and they're hungrier. If they don't get enough to eat, they'll get irritable."

"Don't they, though," said Mama Li. "My husband Old Li also—"

Jou-chia had never expected her to compare Hung-chien to Old Li and quickly cut her short. "I know. I've heard you talk about it since I was little. When he ate rice dumplings during the Dragon Boat Festival, he'd eat all the tips with the red beans in them and give you the bottom parts, right?"

"And the bottom parts are big and not well cooked," Mama Li elaborated. "When I ate the raw rice, my stomach swelled up for days on end!"

That evening when Hung-chien came home, he explained the history of the clock.

Jou-chia said, "So it's a real Fang family heirloom going back three generations. Hey, how can it still be seven o'clock?"

He then told her that it lost seven minutes every hour.

"In that case," said Jou-chia with a laugh, "when the short hand points to seven it's probably still seven o'clock yesterday or even the day before. What's the use of having that?"

She then remarked that when Hung-chien got angry and pulled a long face he looked a lot like the face of the clock. Hung-chien had had a cold for the last couple of days and his throat was filled with phlegm. She clapped her hands and said, "The rattling in your throat before you speak sounds just like the spring turning when it strikes. You're a monster produced by the clock."

The two of them talked and laughed together, as though there were no such thing as a quarrel between husband and wife.

One Saturday afternoon Second Daughter-in-law and Third Daughter-in-law came over for their first visit. Hung-chien was still at the newspaper office. Jou-chia hurriedly made tea and bought some refreshments to entertain them, asking, "Why didn't you bring along the two children? You can take some candy home for them later."

Third Daughter-in-law said, "Ah Hsiung made a big fuss and wanted to come with me, but I was afraid he'd get into trouble, so I didn't bring him."

Second Daughter-in-law said, "I told Ah Hsiung, Eldest Aunt's house is clean. You can't just pee any old place you want like at home. Eldest Uncle will spank you."

Jou-chia lied, "You shouldn't say that! It'd be nice to have him come."

Third Daughter-in-law, feeling her son had lost face, said to avenge him, "Our Ah Hsiung has no intelligence. Ah Ch'ou's no more than a few years older than he, but he really thinks about things. Don't think he's just a child! Like that time he got your dress dirty, for example. After he'd had a spanking, he remembered from then on never to misbehave around you."

After momentary differences on account of their respective sons, the two were immediately reunited, praising in unison the coziness of Jou-chia's small apartment and telling her how lucky she was.

Third Daughter-in-law remarked longingly, "I wonder when we'll be able to set up our own home! Of course, now I benefit so much from living with Second Sister."

"Since the Fangs only have one house to trade," said Second Daughter-in-law, "our turn will never come."

Jou-chia said quickly, "I'd like very much to live in a big family, too. It saves trouble and expense. Running a household has many headaches. All the things like fuel, rice, oil, and salt, as well as water and electricity you have to take care of yourself. And Hung-chien's not as capable as Second Brother or Third Brother."

"That's right," said Second Daughter-in-law, "I'm not like Third Sister. I know I'm useless. I'd never manage if I had to run my own household. Better to muddle along in a large family. Someone like you knows how to deal with all the various problems inside and outside the home. You have a dependable servant, and Eldest Brother can earn money. We couldn't begin to compare ourselves with you."

Afraid they'd go home and gossip, Jou-chia didn't dare answer every jab.

They gave the furnishings in both rooms a careful scrutiny, asked the price, and praised Jou-chia in unison for being so able and clever and such a good shopper, though every once in a while they put in, "I saw a table (or chair) like this one somewhere, but it was a little cheaper, I think. Too bad I didn't buy it."

Third Daughter-in-law asked Jou-chia, "Do you have a room to store your trunks?"

"No, I haven't many trunks," said Jou-chia. "They're all in the bedroom."

Second Daughter-in-law said, "The alley houses in Shanghai are so small. Even when there is a room for storing chests, it won't hold very many. When I married into the Fang family, there was something of a back room behind the bridal chamber, but there was just no way I could fit in all the chests, basins, buckets, and tables from my trousseau. I ended up filling the bridal chamber with them. It really made me sick to look at them."

"Wasn't it just the same for me?" said Third Daughter-in-law. "Those rotten Japanese robbed us clean of all those things. I get so sad whenever I think about it. Now all the things I want are gone, and I have to buy them all over again. I had seven or eight pieces of fur, including a pearled leather dress and a coat with a gray backing. Now I don't have a thing worth wearing!"

Second Daughter-in-law also drew up a partial list of a fictitious trousseau and added, "Eldest Sister's way is best. There's a war abroad, and we don't know what'll happen to Shanghai! We just might have to flee again. If you have a lot of things, you won't be able to take them along when the time comes, and you'd hate to leave them. Third Sister, you still have some things, but I have nothing. Being empty-handed is more cleancut, ha, ha! We should be going back."

At that point Jou-chia realized they had merely come to investigate her trousseau and was so infuriated that she lost all appetite for dinner. When Hung-chien came home and noticed how unresponsive she was, he teased her, "What happened? Did you get a rebuff from your aunt at the office today?"

"I'm burning mad," she flared up. "What are you joking about? Everybody in my family is very nice to me. It's only the people from your family who come over here and make me miserable."

Hung-chien was alarmed, thinking it must have been his mother who had come over to admonish her. He had kept from her everything his mother had said last time.

"Who?" he asked quickly.

"Who else but those two dear sisters-in-law of yours!"

"What a pain, what a pain," said Hung-chien, feeling relieved.

Jou-chia said, "This is your home, and so of course people in your family can come and go as they please. I don't have any sovereignty over it. Since I'm not one of your family, it's lucky I wasn't kicked out."

Hung-chien patted her on the head and said, "Don't bring up old scores. So I was wrong to have said that. Tell me how they bullied you. I think you're pretty sharp yourself. Were you no match for the two of them?"

"I'm sharp," said Jou-chia. "Well, I'm not as sharp as you Fangs! All of you are three-headed, six-armed, and have an extra heart with a few more openings and an intestine all tied in knots. I was killed, cooked, and eaten by them while asleep and dreaming. I still haven't waked up."

"How could it be that bad?" asked Hung-chien with a laugh. "But it's a sound sleep all right. I came home a little late from the newspaper office and couldn't even rouse you."

"You're just spouting nonsense," said Jou-chia sullenly. "I'm not going to pay you any attention."

Hung-chien apologized, and when he'd learned the reason, said hotly, "If I'd been home then, I'd really have very rudely exposed them. What sort of trousseau did they bring? They were giving you a lot of bull!"

"You shouldn't make unfounded accusations against them," said Jou-chia. "You were abroad when they got married. You didn't see how elaborate everything was."

Hung-chien said, "I wasn't there at the time, but I know all about their family circumstances. Second Sister-in-law's family was especially poor. When I was in college, they were thinking of having their daughter marry into our family, but my father opposed an early marriage. It was discussed for a while, then put off for several years."

Jou-chia sighed and said, "Call it my rotten luck! Now I'm forced to call people like that my sisters and even have to put up with their insults. They looked over the furniture and made remarks implying that we had paid too much for it. Since they're such capable mistresses and so concerned about me, why didn't they come over before and help me buy it!"

Hung-chien asked nervously, "Did you tell them we'd bought the furnishings for that room?"

"Yes, why?"

Hung-chien slapped himself on the back of his head and cried, "Damn! Damn it all! I should have told you that day," and he explained how his mother had asked what the in-laws had given them.

Jou-chia also became upset and said, "Why didn't you tell me before? How can I face your family now! They're certain to gossip and compare notes on everything when they get back; they'll even think we bought the furniture my aunt gave us. You are so stupid. If you're going to lie, you should at least tell me about it. Ever since that business with our marriage, you always like to show how smart you are and then end up making a mess of it every time."

He knew he was in the wrong, but wouldn't submit to a scolding and argued instead, "I had good intentions in telling that lie. I didn't tell you about it later because I was afraid you'd get mad."

"Well, you were right," she said. "Now that I know about it, I am mad. Thanks for your good intentions in lying in order to save my family's face. You should have told your mother truthfully that I bought it with an advance on my salary at the factory. We Suns are poor. When a daughter gets married, there's not much to give her. Did you Fangs pay out any betrothal money when their son got married? Did they give their son and daughter-in-law anything? Huh, these two rooms, which we still pay rent for—oh, and I forgot, there's that clock—" She noticed his long face and gave him a mirror. "Take a look at yourself. Isn't your face just like that clock? I wasn't the least bit mistaken."

He couldn't refrain from smiling.

All these unpleasant little incidents eventually made Jou-chia afraid to go to her in-laws' home, often lamenting, "We haven't even lived with them yet, and already so many disputes have started. It takes training to live in a big family. One has only to see how quick-witted, keen-eyed, and sharp-tongued your two sisters-in-law are. I could never get the better of them, nor have I any interest in trying. Let them be little filial daughters-in-law. What I can't figure out is why someone like you, who grew up in a big family, know nothing about all the scheming and plotting that go on there."

"A bachelor would never know about such things," he explained. "Your eyes aren't opened until you get married. Sometimes I think a family is really just a nest of scandal like San Lü University. Maybe if I'd been married for a few years before going there, the training would have made me more sensitive, and I wouldn't have been plotted against."

Jou-chia said quickly, "What good does it do to talk about that? If you'd gotten married before, you wouldn't have married me, unless you're sorry you married me."

Hung-chien, in no mood to pander to Jou-chia, merely muttered to himself, "A School for Scandal, it's all a School for Scandal. Whether it is a family or a school, it's all the same."

Though they both considered the family a "school for scandal," it wasn't so easy to play hooky. The day Tun-weng brought the clock over he gave his son a list of the anniversaries of the deaths of the ancestors and indicated that during those days of family sacrifices both son and daughter-in-law should return home to take part in the ceremonies. When Jou-chia saw it, she screwed up her lips. Fortunately, she had her work as an excuse, since she couldn't make it home in time during her lunch hour. Some of the anniversaries, however, fell on Sundays. If she decided to forget on purpose, Tun-weng would tell his Second or Third Daughter-in-law to telephone the landlord and ask her to come. What was particularly annoying was that every time a relative came to the Fangs and happened to mention that he hadn't met their Eldest Daughter-in-law, Mr. or Mrs. Fang would immediately call up and summon Jou-chia, no matter whether it was six o'clock in the evening when she had just returned from the office, Saturday when she wanted to go out and have a good time, or Sunday when she was prepared to go to her aunt's or parents' home.

Dead ancestors along with living relatives ran Jou-chia ragged, and she often groused to Hung-chien, "You Fangs sure are an old family with all those ancestors! Why don't you include the anniversaries of the Yellow Emperor's birth and death?"[4] Or, "You Fangs sure are a big family! What's the use of having so many relatives?"

After politely complying with them a few times, she could no longer be bothered and told Mama Li to answer the phone and say she wasn't home. After refusing to go four or five times, she gradually began to feel guilty and didn't dare go for fear of having to face their ugly looks.

While Hung-chien sympathized with his wife, he dared not offend his parents, and so he just had to return home alone. From their faces, however, it seemed as if the family blamed him for not bringing his wife under escort as in the opera *Yu-t'ang-ch'un*.[5] Unable to hand her over, he only offered lame excuses and was unwilling to come home very often.

If the definition passed down from the T'ang and Sung dynasties, "Loyalty means the heart is in the middle," is correct, then Mama Li was not loyal because her heart was too one-sided. Whenever Hung-chien told her to do something, she would always have to get Jou-chia's approval first. For example, if Hung-chien told her to buy vegetables, she would say, "Young Lady likes spinach, so I'll have to ask her about it first." Jou-chia would of course tell her to do what Hung-chien said.

Once Hung-chien said to her, "The weather's turned colder and I won't be wearing my unpadded clothes any more. It's sunny today so would you take them out and sun them for me? You can store them up later for the mistress." She insisted that Jou-chia's unpadded clothes hadn't been put away yet, and he needn't be in such a hurry, that it would warm up again. When Jou-chia sunned her clothes, she argued, they could all be done at once. Jou-chia had already left, and there was no way he could get Mama Li to understand that young women dressed differently from men. Women had only to put on a heavier overcoat and could then wear unpadded clothes on into winter.

Mama Li then said, "Master, sunning clothes is woman's business. You needn't worry about it. Young Lady left early this morning to go to work. Why don't you go out? Wouldn't it be nice if you left now and came back a little earlier this evening?"

Incidents of this sort exasperated and amused him. When amused, he would call her "Madame Li" or "Her Majesty"; when exasperated, he wished he could just ask her to leave. If she overheard a quarrel between them, her face would tense up just as tightly as her master's and mistress's, and she would not look Hung-chien directly in the face. If she gave him something, she would merely shove it at him. Afterwards he would grumble to Jou-chia, "This is absurd! With the mistress and servant joining forces, you'll both torment me to death."

Jou-chia said with a smile, "I've spoken to her about it several times. If she wants to help me, what can I do? She says all women suffer wrong from their husbands. She herself suffered from Old Li's wrongs—from the raw rice dumplings. But then, I'm alone and helpless in your family. Now you have a taste of what it's like."

Jou-chia's father treated his son-in-law with polite reserve. When her brother discovered his brother-in-law had neither the athletic prowess to play soccer or basketball nor the scholarly refinement to fix a radio or drive a car, he felt his sister had married the wrong man. In an effort to fulfill his duty as son-in-law, Hung-chien paid occasional visits to the Suns. Fortunately, Jou-chia seldom went to her parents' home, going only to her aunt's house every second or third day.

One day more than a month after moving into their apartment, the couple went to the Lus for lunch. When they had finished and were about to leave, Mrs. Lu smiled stiffly and said, "Hung-chien, I'm going to incur your dislike by giving you a word of advice. You must not bully Jou-chia any more." And then as if the force of her native language were not enough, like one drawing up a diplomatic treaty, she gave both a Chinese and an English version: "I won't allow you to *bully* her any more."

When Hung-chien heard her say she had something unpleasant to say to him, he bristled up like a porcupine at the sight of an enemy. When she had finished, however, he didn't understand what she meant, and was just about to ask, when Jou-chia said quickly, "Hung-chien is very nice to me. Who said he bullies me? I'm not so easily bullied after all."

Mrs. Lu said, "Hung-chien, you see how good Jou-chia is. She still sticks up for you!"

Fuming with rage, Hung-chien said, "How do you know I bully her? I—"

Jou-chia pulled him along, saying, "Come on, let's go! It's getting late. The movie's about to start. Auntie is only teasing you."

When they had left the house, Hung-chien said, "I don't feel like going to the movies. Why don't you go by yourself?"

Jou-chia said, "Well, for heaven's sake. I didn't offend you. At least you must know I wouldn't tell her anything."

"That's why I don't want to go to the Lus with you," he exploded. "As if I don't suffer enough at my own home, I have to go out and be lectured by your family! I bully you! Humph. If I'm not bullied to death by your aunt or wet nurse, I should live a long life! And you talk about us Fangs being hard to deal with! Every last one of you Suns is just like that goddamned little turtle-egg of a Pekingese. My reputation is bad anyway. I might as well bully you a little today. I'm going my way and you can go yours. See the movie or go back to your parents, whichever you want!" and he pushed away Jou-chia's arm, which was crooked around his.

She had not actually cared about seeing the movie, but when her husband acted so rudely as to ignore all biological impossibilities by making a dog into a crustacean in order to compare it with members of her family, she too was incensed. As she could not very well start a quarrel right there on the street, she said, "What's wrong if I do go to the movies by myself? I don't care for your company," and with a toss of her head, she abandoned her husband and crossed the street to the tram stop alone.

Hung-chien stood there by himself, feeling lost and forlorn. As he watched her back, so helplessly delicate, appear and disappear in the crowds on the street, from somewhere arose a feeling of pity and protectiveness, and he ran after her.

As she was walking along, Jou-chia felt a tap on the shoulder and jumped with fright. When she turned her head and saw it was Hung-chien, she felt a mixture of surprise and delight and asked, "Why did you come?"

"I was afraid you'd run off with someone, so I came to keep an eye on you."

Jou-chia said with a smile, "The way you quarrel, the day is bound to come when I do run away, but I'd never run off with someone. You think I don't put up with enough from you? I'd really be a fool to go looking for another man."

"One thing I'm not mistaken about today is that your aunt accused me unfairly."

"OK, so someone in my family accused you falsely. I apologize. Today's movie will be on me."

Hung-chien groped around with both hands in the various pockets of his overcoat, vest, and pants for his money.

"The tram's about to come," said Jou-chia, laughing at him. "Don't try to catch lice here in the street. Since you have a wallet, why don't you put all your money together? You don't have much anyway. When I straighten out your clothes for you, I find a dollar bill in one pocket and a postage stamp in another."

"Before I got married," he explained, "I used to put my money in my wallet when I took a friend out to eat. When I paid the bill I'd pull it out to make a good impression. Now my wallet's gotten old, and I threw it somewhere."

"It makes me mad just to talk about it. Before we got married, you never invited me out properly for one single meal. Now that I'm your wife, I may as well forget about your ever inviting me out to have a decent meal."

He said, "I can't afford to take you out today. I gave this month's pay to my father the day before yesterday. I have enough left to treat you to a snack. After the movie we can find a place to have some tea."

"We didn't have lunch at home today, and Mama Li is expecting us to come back for dinner. If we have a snack, we won't be able to eat dinner, and everything left over will be wasted. Let's skip the snack—ha, ha, you see how frugal I am, how well I take care of the house. Your mother is the only one who says I don't look after the domestic chores."

Halfway through the movie, Hung-chien suddenly distracted her attention by whispering, "Now I get it. It must have been that old devil Mama Li who told tales. Didn't you send her over to the Lus with something the other day?"

She had already guessed as much but had kept it to herself. She merely said, "I'll ask her about it when we get home. Don't you go quarreling with her on any account. I'll talk to her myself. If we dismiss her, we won't be able to find a replacement. A small family like ours which doesn't play mahjong or give parties[6] and pays low wages can't keep a servant very long. As for my aunt, naturally I'll explain to her. Now watch the movie and don't worry about all that. I'm not going to talk any more. We've already missed some of the movie."

As soon as Hung-chien was out of the way, Jou-chia questioned Mama Li. Mama Li denied it at once. "I didn't say anything. I just said that Master has a very quick temper."

"That's enough," said Jou-chia and warned her not to say anything again. For the next couple of days, Mama Li obeyed Hung-chien's every word. Jou-chia had considered telling her aunt everything about the Fangs herself. Fortunately, she hadn't let anything out; otherwise, Hung-chien really would have raised cain. He was so concerned about saving face. As for her own family's trifles, she knew Hung-chien would never speak of them to the Fangs. Of that she could be sure. After marrying Hung-chien, she had remained a Sun at heart. After Hung-chien married her, on the other hand, he gradually grew away from the Fangs. Obviously girls are better. It is just that fathers are so stupid that they side with their sons.

From then on Hung-chien refused to go with her to the Lus, and Jou-chia didn't dare force him. Whenever she returned from a visit there and mentioned meeting someone or hearing about something, Hung-chien, feeling envious and left out, would make sarcastic remarks.

One Sunday morning after breakfast Jou-chia said, "I want to go out. Will you permit me, Hung-chien?"

Hung-chien said, "Are you going to your aunt's? Humph, if I don't permit you, won't you go all the same? What's the point of asking me? Can't you go in the afternoon?"

"I'm free to come and go as I please. I show you a little respect by asking you, and you turn around and get angry. Winter days are short. There's no point going in the afternoon. Now the sun's nice. I want to take some yarn along to knit a wool vest for you and discuss with her how it should be."

Hung-chien snorted. "You won't of course be coming home to eat. We finally have a Sunday when both of us are home at noon, and you have to leave me and go out for lunch."

"Oh! How pitiful you make it sound! It's as if you can't live without me for a minute! Do you have anything to say to me when I'm home? You pace up and down heaving sighs, and when I ask you what's on your mind, you don't even pay any attention—Today is Sunday, so let's not quarrel, OK? I'll be back soon," and without waiting for a reply, she turned and went into the bedroom to change her clothes. When she had changed her clothes and come out, Hung-chien was sitting completely still in the chair with a newspaper over his face.

She stroked his hair and asked, "Why so lazy? You didn't even comb your hair when you got up this morning. You can go get a haircut today. I'm going."

Hung-chien ignored her. Jou-chia threw him a glance, but it didn't penetrate the newspaper. She then turned and left.

In the afternoon as soon as she came in, she asked Mama Li, "Did Master go out?"

"He just got back from a haircut," said Mama Li. "He hasn't gone to the newspaper office yet."

She went upstairs and said, "Hung-chien, I'm back. Papa and my broth-r, as well as two cousins, were all there today. They wanted to take me ,hopping, but I was afraid you'd get impatient waiting, so I came home as soon as I could."

Hung-chien gave the clock on the wall a meaningful look, then hurriedly held out his arm to look at his watch, saying, "It's getting late. It's almost four o'clock. Let me think. You left at nine this morning, didn't you? I've been waiting for you to eat. . . ."

Jou-chia said with a smile, "What a shameless rat you are! You knew perfectly well I wouldn't come home to eat. Besides, when I left the house, I told Mama Li to serve your lunch at twelve—not twelve by that precious heirloom of yours, but twelve by the alarm clock."

Hung-chien had no answer to this, and having lost the first round, he tried another tack, "Have you finished knitting the wool vest yet? I want to put it on and go out now."

"No, I haven't," she said impatiently. "If you want to wear one, go

341

out and buy one yourself. I've never seen anyone as nasty as you! I'm busy six days a week, yet you won't allow me half a day of fun. When I come back, I have to see your long face."

"Oh, so you're the only one who's busy six days a week," said Hung-chien. "I'm not! Of course, you have your rewards for being busy. You have great ability and good connections. You earn more money than I do—"

"Thank goodness I am able to earn a little money; otherwise, you'd really bully me to death. My aunt wasn't a bit unjust when she said you bullied me."

He fiercely pounded the table and said, "Then call your family representative Madame Li up here and tell her to run over and report to your auntie."

"One of these days I'll report it myself. I don't think there's another man in all the world as unfeeling as you. Since they annoy you, it should be enough that they don't come over here. But you won't even let me go see them. You really want me to sever ties with all my close relatives? With that loner temperament of yours, you should never have married me. What a pity that women can't pop up out of the mud or drop down from the sky, because no one but a person like that with neither father nor mother could ever suit your temperament so well. Huh, I can see it all now. We Suns have no power or influence, so we incur your dislike. If you ran into Su Wen-wan's or T'ang Hsiao-fu's father, I can't believe you wouldn't crawl over on your hands and knees to pay respects."

Hung-chien shook with rage, "If you say any more nonsense, I'll hit you."

Seeing his livid face and reddened ears, Jou-chia realized her remarks had gone too far and kept silent.

After a moment's pause, Hung-chien said, "You've gotten me to the point where I don't even dare go to my own family! Seeing your aunt every day in your office isn't enough? Since your aunt is so wonderful, you might as well just go over there and stay."

Jou-chia muttered, "She's nicer to me than you are. And the people in my family are nicer than the ones in yours."

Hung-chien replied with a hiss.

"You can hiss all you like," said Jou-chia. "My family is nicer than yours, and I happen to want to go home often. You can't stop me."

Without any recourse against his wife's obstinacy, he glared at her for a long time, then flung open the door to go out and ran smack into Mama Li. The push nearly sent her reeling down the stairs. "Have you overheard enough?" he asked. "Go gossip. I'm not afraid of you."

When he returned from the newspaper office, Jou-chia was already in

342

bed, and neither of them spoke. The next day was the same. On the third day Hung-chien could stand it no longer, and during breakfast he knocked his bowl and chopsticks noisily around on the table. Jou-chia ignored him as before. Acknowledging defeat, Hung-chien broke the silence first: "Are you dead?"

"You speaking to me?" asked Jou-chia. "No, I'm not dead yet. I wouldn't give you the peace and quiet! I was watching you pound the chopsticks and slam your bowl around in such a display of skill!"

Hung-chien sighed, "Sometimes I really wish I could sock you one."

Jou-chia threw him a glance and said, "I can see it's only a matter of time before you let go and hit me."

In this way the two more or less made up. But often when making up after a major quarrel people will still go back and pick out little points to argue over. The man will say, "I wouldn't have gotten mad if you hadn't said such and such," and the woman will say, "Then why did you have to bring it up first?" If they can't clear it up, there'll be another tiff.

After Hung-chien had begun working at the newspaper office, he met an old acquaintance, Mrs. Shen, with whom he had had tea at Su Wen-wan's. She was still editing the *Family and Women* section for which Chao Hsin-mei had then recommended her to the agency. Now she was editing the *Culture and Arts* section as well. She was as plump as ever and smelled just the same. Only her style of dress was not as Gallic as when she had first returned from abroad, and the French in her speech had dropped off. She had met too many people in the past year and had long since forgotten Hung-chien. After he introduced himself, she said feelingly in a sweet girlish voice, "Oh, yes! Now I remember! How time does fly! You look just the same, which is why I thought your face was so familiar. As for me, I've aged so much in this last year! Mr. Fang, you just don't know what I've been through!"

Hung-chien dutifully assured her that she hadn't aged. She then asked him if he'd seen Mrs. Ts'ao lately, and he told her he had seen her in Hong Kong.

"My goodness!" she said, slapping her forehead. "See how stupid I am! I got a letter from Wen-wan last week. She wrote that she'd seen you and had a good talk. She also asked me to do something for her, but I've been so busy I haven't had time. There're just so many little things I have to do every day!"

Hung-chien chuckled to himself over her lies and asked her the whereabouts of Mr. Shen. She raised her eyebrows, rounded her eyes, and put a finger to her lips in a thoroughly French expression; then taking a look around to see that no one was paying attention, she came up close and whispered, "He's gone into hiding. He's too well known. The Japanese and the puppet government in Nanking[7] are all trying to get him to come out and work for them. Don't tell anyone!"

Hung-chien held his breath, nearly suffocating in the process, and hurriedly took a few steps backward, repeatedly assuring her he wouldn't. He mentioned it to Jou-chia when he got home, marveling at what a small world it was. Of all things, after running into Su Wen-wan, now he had seen Mrs. Shen too.

Jou-chia said coldly, "Yes, the world is small. Just wait. You'll run into someone else too."

Not understanding, Hung-chien asked whom she meant.

Jou-chia said with a smile, "Need I say it? You know whom I mean. Hey, don't blush."

He then realized she was referring to T'ang Hsiao-fu and said with a sneer, "What rubbish! It never even crossed my mind in a dream. So what if I did meet her?"

"Ask yourself."

He sighed, "You, you little fool, are the only one who can't get her out of your mind! I've long since forgotten her. She's probably married, become a mother, and doesn't even remember me any more. Now when I think how serious I used to be about love before I got married, it really seems naïve. The fact is, no matter whom you marry, after you're married, you'll find it's not the same person but someone else. If people knew that before marriage they could skip all that stuff about courtship, romance, and so on. When two people get to know each other and fall in love, they both conceal their true faces so that the whole time up until they get married they still don't know each other. It's the old-fashioned marriages that are more straightforward. Neither party gets to know the other before marriage."

Jou-chia said, "Are you through declaiming? I just have two things to say: First, you have absolutely no heart. To this very day I still take love seriously. Second, you really are your father's son, getting more and more obstinate."

He said, "What do you mean 'have absolutely no heart'? Don't I treat you pretty well? Besides, I was only speaking in general. You're so small-minded that you have to apply everything to yourself. You could say you hadn't discovered my real self before you got married either, and now you know me in my true colors."

"Of all the drivel you've been spouting," said Jou-chia, "that's the one thing worth hearing."

"You're very young," said Hung-chien. "When you get to be my age, you'll understand all that."

"Don't go flaunting your age," said Jou-chia. "You're just over thirty! Flaunt your age and you must not have much longer to live. I'm not even thirty yet, and you've infuriated me to death already."

He laughed. "Jou-chia, you're so civilized in everything else, but that remark is backward. That's like an old-fashioned woman who threatens her husband with suicide. Instead of using a knife, a rope, or arsenic, you use an abstraction like fury. What's that—spiritual civilization?"

Jou-chia said, "Phooey! If I want to die, I'll die. Whom would I want to threaten or frighten? But don't get so happy. I won't forgive you."

"There you go, taking it seriously again," said Hung-chien. "If we keep up, we'll end up quarreling. Go to sleep. You have to get up early tomorrow to go to work. Close your eyes, such lovely eyes. If you don't get enough sleep, they'll be swollen tomorrow, and your aunt will come over and question me about it." As he spoke, he patted her a few times as though patting a child to sleep.

When his wife had fallen asleep, he began reflecting on how cold and indifferent he felt now at the thought of possibly meeting T'ang Hsiao-fu again. If he really did meet her, it would be just the same. That was because the self, which had loved her a year ago, had long since died. The selves which had loved her, which had been afraid of Su Wen-wan, and which had been seduced by Miss Pao, had all died one after another. He had buried some of his dead selves in his memory, erected a monument to them, and occasionally paid them homage, such as by a moment of feeling for T'ang Hsiao-fu. Others seemed to have died by the wayside and been left there to rot and decompose or be devoured by birds and beasts—but never to be completely obliterated, such as the self which had bought the diploma from the Irishman.

More than two months after Hung-chien had begun working at the newspaper office, he saw a notice in the newspaper one morning placed by Mrs. Shen under her usual pen name. The general purport of it was that she had always devoted herself to journalism and placed herself above politics. All the tales being circulated about her abroad were but wild and unfounded rumor, and so on and so forth. Filled with apprehension, he asked around at the newspaper office and then learned that her husband had taken a post with the puppet government, and she too had gone to Nanking. He remembered the warning Hsin-mei had given him in Hong Kong and wrote to tell Hsin-mei about the incident, asking if he had gotten married and why he hadn't written for so long.

When Hung-chien discussed the matter with his wife on his return home, she too was distressed by it, but said, "It's just as well Mrs. Shen's gone. The section she edited wasn't very exciting. The things she herself wrote were always the same old stuff, shifted around from one day to the next. At least it saved trouble. Newspaper readers throw them out when they're through anyway. They wouldn't pull out an old paper to compare. I guess she didn't want to publish a collection, because the several dozen articles only amounted to one. It would really have been a big joke. At that rate I could edit *Family and Women* myself. You can take her place and edit *Culture and Arts*."

Hung-chien said, "I'm not so sure of myself as you, dear wife. You don't know how hard it is to solicit manuscripts. Let me just confess something to you: That column 'What Every Housewife Should Know' in the *Family and Women* section, stuff like 'Sesame oil sprinkled on soy sauce will keep it from becoming moldy, etc.' was written by me."

Jou-chia doubled up with laughter and said, "That kills me! What do you know about sesame oil added to soy sauce! Did you get that from Mama Li? I'd never noticed it."

Hung-chien said, "Which is why you can't run the house properly. Mama Li should take me as her teacher! Mrs. Shen didn't have any manuscripts, so she came complaining to me, saying that my Information Office ought to furnish some material. I was afraid of getting a whiff of her, so to get rid of her faster I agreed. I found an old copy of the *Housewife's Handbook* and copied out six or seven lines every week, then gave them to her before she came. You don't have her body odor. If you wanted manuscripts, I'd be the first one to ignore you."

Jou-chia frowned and said, "Your remarks are nasty; they make me sick. If she heard what you said, she'd certainly have you arrested and taken to 76 West Hu Street for a beating."[8]

His wife's jest immediately made him turn serious as he said, "I don't think we can stay here any longer. Now you understand why I didn't want to come here in the first place."

One Saturday three weeks later, Hung-chien returned home very early. Jou-chia said, "There was an air mail express letter from Chao Hsin-mei. I thought it was something important, so I opened it and read it. Sorry."

Changing into his slippers, Hung-chien said, "Oh, a letter from him! Let me have it. What did he say?"

"What's the big hurry? Nothing important. He wrote an express letter and requested a receipt. I had to take forever to find your chop [his seal to stamp the receipt], the mailman downstairs yelling for me to hurry up, getting me all flustered! Next time don't leave your chop just anywhere. Keep it in one place so it can be found easily. Is this the first time he's written you since we returned to Shanghai? I don't think there's any need to send an express letter but to write more often."

Hung-chien knew she was somewhat hostile toward Hsin-mei, and so he ignored what she said. The letter was very simple: It said that he had received all his letters, and that he knew all about Mrs. Shen's affair, that Shanghai was going steadily downhill, that Hung-chien had best come to Chungking as soon as possible, and that Hung-chien might work in the same organization. Moreover, Hung-chien could go to the Shanghai office of the company that transported their luggage last time and see Manager Hsüeh to discuss the details of the itinerary and find traveling companions. The letter ended with the line: "My wife has asked me to send regards to yours."

Like a man groping about in the dark who suddenly sees the light, Hung-chien was inwardly pleased, but didn't show his pleasure on his face. He merely said, "That devil! He never said a word about getting married or even sent a wedding picture. I'd really like you to see this Mrs. Chao."

"I can imagine what she's like without seeing her. I've had the honor of meeting all the women Hsin-mei has fallen for, like Mrs. Wang and Miss Su. She's probably the same type."

"That's not so, which is why I hope he'll send a picture for you to see."

"We gave him our wedding pictures. I don't mean to sow discord, but it seems to me this great friend of yours doesn't hold you very dear. You've written him four or five letters, haven't you? Now finally he half-heartedly sends you a letter like this, not even letting you know he got married. He's rich and has lots of friends. If I were you and hadn't gotten a single reply from him, I wouldn't ever have written him a second time."

She had touched on a sore point, and he said evasively, "You always have to exaggerate. I've never written him more than three letters. He didn't let me know that he'd gotten married, because he was afraid I'd send a gift. He understands that I'm poor and realizes that since we received a generous wedding gift from him, we'd want to give him something in return."

Jou-chia laughed drily and said, "Oh, so that's it! Only you understand what he means. So you're good friends after all, with mutual understanding! Still, a wedding isn't like a funeral. You can always send something later. He should simply have left out the words 'my wife' in the letter. There's still time if you want to send him something."

Having been bested in the argument, Hung-chien could only say grouchily, "Then you take care of it for me."

"I've no time," said Jou-chia, brushing her hair.

"You were still human when you went out this morning," said Hung-chien. "How did you manage to turn into a porcupine?"

"I'm a porcupine. Don't talk to the porcupine."

After a moment of silence, the porcupine herself spoke, "Hsin-mei urged you to go to Chungking in his letter. How are you going to answer him?"

"I'd like to go all right," said Hung-chien hesitantly, "but I'll have to give it some careful thought."

"What about me?" she said, her face expressionless. It was like a window with the Venetian blinds drawn. Hung-chien knew this was the lull before the storm.

"It's because of you that I'm so hesitant. As for Shanghai, I really don't want to stay here any longer, and there's no future for me at the newspaper office. Half of the support for this family comes from you. . . ." He thought this remark would ease the atmosphere. "Since Hsin-mei has been nice enough to make the offer, I'd like very much to go try my luck in the interior again, but the matter isn't decided. There'd be a lot of trouble involved in settling a family in a new place. You remember, of course, the job we had finding a place when we came back to Shanghai this time. Hsin-mei's a married man. It won't be like it was before. My plan is for me to go to Chungking first by myself, and once I've settled things to come and get you. What do you think? Of course, it'll require deliberation. I haven't decided yet. It wouldn't hurt if you tell me what you think."

During all this, he was waiting for her to interrupt him at any moment; he hadn't expected her to keep silent and let him speak his piece. Her silence made him feel more apprehensive as he kept talking.

"I've listened to all your fancy talk. Let's just come right out with it. After four months of marriage, you're tired of your ugly, mean old wife—whom you never loved in the first place—and now that you have a chance to go far away, why not get a change of air? Your good friend is your savior. He's the one who pushed you to get married—it galls me to think about it—and now he's the one who helps you regain your freedom. Go on then! He's making you a high official, and he just may even find you an official's wife! I'm not worthy."

Hung-chien clucked and said, "Where'd you get such nonsense! You really are hypersensitive."

"I'm not the least bit hypersensitive. You go right ahead. I certainly won't stand in your way. If you think for a minute I'll let your friend say that after using 'every trick and scheme' to get you, now I won't let you out of my sight, or that I'll let you say your family burdens got in the way of your future, humph, I won't! I eat out of my own pocket, and I've never asked you to support me. I'm not your burden. Once you leave, whether you come back or not is entirely up to you."

He sighed, "Well, then—" Jou-chia was expecting him to say "I won't go," and was not prepared when he said, "I'll take you along. That'll settle it."

"I have a perfectly good job here. Why should I give it up for no reason and go with you? Once we get there, if neither of us finds a job, can we ask Hsin-mei to support us? If you get a job and I don't, heaven knows how much you'll bully me then! Hsin-mei's letter said nothing about finding a high position for me. What am I supposed to do there? Be a socialite? I'm too ugly, I've no qualifications—except to serve the official's wife as a maid."

"How ridiculous! How absolutely ridiculous! I haven't bullied you. You yourself are always saying how much more capable you are than I am, how much more money you earn. Now you know yourself that you're dependent on your relatives' connection here. You mean once you get into the interior you might not find a job?"

"I depend on my relatives? And what about you? You have no relatives to depend on, so you depend on your friend. Isn't it just the same thing? Anyway, I've never said I am more capable than you. It's just that you're so small-minded you can't swallow the fact that I earn more money than you do. As for the interior, I've been there before too. Don't forget it wasn't me whose contract wasn't renewed at San Lü University. For whom did I sacrifice a job in the interior in order to come to Shanghai? You really have no conscience!"

"Since you brought up San Lü University," said Hung-chien with an ugly sneer, "I'd just like to settle some old scores with you. I wish I'd never listened to you. Kao Sung-nien must have died laughing at that thank-you letter I wrote him from Hengyang. I'll never listen to you again. You think Kao offered you a contract because he really wanted to keep you? Don't be so smug. He was making trouble for me, you fool!"

"In any case you listen to everybody. What Chao Hsin-mei says especially is more divine than an imperial edict. It's what I say that you won't listen to. All I know is that I got a contract and you didn't, whether Kao was 'making trouble' or not. Did Kao tell you he was making trouble? How do you know he was? Aren't you just covering up your shame with your one finger [evading the truth]?"

"You're right. He really did want to keep you, so he could let the students 'Beat down Miss Sun' again."

Her face flushed as red as the comb on a fighting cock, and the rims of her eyes also turned red. She stopped to collect herself, then said, "I was a young girl, just out of college on my first job. Getting bullied by those men-student dogs is nothing to feel ashamed of. It's not like a returned student who turned into a teacher whose dismissal was demanded by the students. It was the information I passed along that saved his job."

349

A torrent of words rushed to Hung-chien's tongue all at once, but he couldn't utter a single one. Without waiting for him to speak, she announced, "I'm going to bed," and went into the bathroom to rinse her mouth and wash her face, pulling the door closed behind her. When she came out, he wanted to continue the argument, but she said, "I'm not going to quarrel with you. When feelings have gotten this bad, what good does it do to say any more? Better to be quiet and leave a little leeway. If you want to quarrel, then go ahead. I've rinsed my mouth, and I'm not going to talk any more."

With that she hopped into bed, pulled up the covers, then got up again, opened a drawer and picked out two wads of cotton which she stuffed in her ears. She then lay down and closed her eyes. Presently her breathing became regular as though she had fallen asleep. Her husband wished he could have yanked her up and forced her to quarrel with him, but all he could do was shake his fist at her. She saw it all clearly from underneath her eyelashes and was both angered and secretly amused.

The following evening when Hung-chien returned home, she was waiting for him with baked oranges she had cooked. Hung-chien spitefully refused to eat them, but his greediness won out, and he ate them anyway, all the while cursing himself for being unable to do any better.

"Did you write Hsin-mei?" she asked.

"No, my dear wife, I haven't answered his letter," he said.

"It's not that I won't let you go. I'm just urging you not to act impulsively. Hsin-mei is very warmhearted by nature, I know. But he has one shortcoming. He often makes promises that he can't keep. You've had experience with that before. San Lü Universtiy sent you a telegram directly, then ended up discounting it. Now this time it's his own letter, and yet he is vague about the possibility of getting you a job."

Hung-chien said with a grin, "You really are full of 'a thousand tricks and a hundred schemes,' and so wise and resourceful in every way, shape, and form. Luckily, he's a man. If he were a woman, I can't imagine how you could be any more jealous."

Jou-chia was somewhat abashed by this, but laughed lightheartedly and said, "Isn't it a good thing I'm jealous over you? If he were a woman, would he pay any attention to you? Would he have anything to do with you? You're really dreaming! I'm the only one who would still try to ingratiate myself with you today after all the abuse I took from you yesterday."

The newspaper office was receiving terrorist letters and warnings from the Concession authorities over its radical views. In the office it was being bruited about that the American lawyer who acted as the nominal publisher was no longer willing to give his name to the newspaper agency; that Mr.

Wang, the editor-in-chief, had fallen out of favor with the stockholders; and that Mrs. Shen was linked up with the puppet government acting to buy people out. Hung-chien got on rather well with Mr. Wang, so when he heard all these rumors, he went to ask him about them, and while he was there he showed him Hsin-mei's letter. Mr. Wang thought it was a very good idea but urged Hung-chien not to resign just yet. He was in the midst of a struggle with the management over editorial policy and it would soon be decided whether he stayed on or quit.

Hung-chien said gallantly, "I'll leave the day you do."

Mr. Wang said, "If it's agreeable, then stay; if not, then leave. It's up to each individual. I don't dare force you. But Hsin-mei entrusted you to me. Whatever action I take I'll certainly let you know, I won't keep anything from you."

On his return home, Hung-chien did not mention a word of all this to Jou-chia. It seemed to him that in the last six months whenever he talked anything over with her, he could never do as he had originally intended and always ended up feeling frustrated. This time he had made up his mind by himself and was as happy as a child who has secretly done something naughty behind the backs of grown-ups. Knowing he hadn't replied to Hsin-mei's letter, Jou-chia assumed she had won him over.

On the morning of the day of winter solstice by the lunar calendar, just as Jou-chia was about to leave the apartment, Hung-chien said, "Don't forget. We have to go to my parents today for winter solstice dinner. My father telephoned himself yesterday to tell us. You can't back out this time."

Wrinkling her nose in an expression of disgust, she said, "All right, I'll go, I'll go! 'The ugly wife will visit her in-laws!' If I really wanted to argue with you, then I would not go today. After all, you didn't go with me to my aunt's house for Christmas dinner. Why do I have to go with you today?"

Hung-chien laughed at her for being such a sourpuss.

She said, "I just thought I'd mention it to you. Otherwise, having taken advantage of me, you'd even think you were in the right. I'll come back here and wait for you so we can go together. Ask me to go by myself, and I'll refuse."

Hung-chien said, "It's not as if you're a bride entering her new home for the first time. Why ask me to make an extra trip?"

Jou-chia left without answering him. Shortly after that, Mr. Wang telephoned and asked him to come at once. He guessed that something major had happened, and his heart fluttered with excitement. He was eager and yet at the same time afraid to find out what it was.

When Wang saw him, he smiled ruefully and said, "Last night the

Board of Directors gave me permission to resign. I can leave anytime I wish. They've already found a replacement. The resignation is effective tomorrow, so I'm letting you know beforehand."

Hung-chien said, "Then I'll resign today. I'm your appointee. Should I submit it in writing?"

"Why don't you talk it over with your father-in-law?" suggested Wang.

Hung-chien said, "This is my own business."

Wang was an upright man. Now that he was being forced out because of his principles, he liked having a little excitement attendant on his leaving to lessen the dreariness of his departure and didn't want to slip off alone as though eloping. He'd been in the working world long enough to know that in any organization replacements can always be found, and positions refilled. When one resigns out of spite, it is only the resignee who suffers. The position itself never suffers. If a person refuses to take a seat, it is only his own legs which suffer. The chair won't go hungry if left empty or get sore legs if left standing. But if a few more chairs are left empty, an impression of want will be created. Though Hung-chien wasn't Wang's man, the more people who quit the better. It wouldn't hurt to get up a good number. Thus, at the same time Wang mentioned his resignation to the domestic news editor, the international news editor, the economics news editor, and two feature editors. The newspaper management had already prepared for this and had plenty of people waiting in the wings. Furthermore, knowing that these resignations were of a political nature, the management hoped they would depart as quickly as possible in order to avoid further complications. In any case, salaries for the month had already been paid. Except for efforts to retain the economics news editor, the management approved one after another of all the letters of resignation Wang submitted to them. Since the Office of Information was least important, and a replacement could be found at any time, Hung-chien was the first to go jobless by being allowed to resign before anyone else.

That afternoon when his father-in-law heard the news, his father-in-law hurried over to ask him whether he had gotten Jou-chia's consent in the matter or not. Hung-chien replied offhandedly that he had. His father-in-law looked unhappy at this and didn't seem to believe him. Since Hung-chien would not be coming the next day, and there were several matters which he had to take care of, he called Jou-chia to tell her he didn't have time to return home and get her, so would she please go directly over without waiting for him. He could tell over the phone that she was quite displeased, but as his father-in-law suddenly appeared, he could not explain to her.

He did not get to his parents' home until almost seven o'clock. All the way there he regretted not having called up to see if Jou-chia had gone over or not. She might very well refuse to go alone. When his parents saw him, they asked why he had come by himself.

His mother, her face livid, said, "That wife of yours certainly is 'too noble to set foot on lowly turf.' She won't even come when invited."

Hung-chien was just about to explain when Jou-chia entered. Second Daughter-in-law and Third Daughter-in-law went to greet her, saying with a smile, "Such a rare visitor!"

Mrs. Fang barely put on a forced smile, as though the act were painful to her face. Jou-chia gave the excuse that she was very busy.

Third Daughter-in-law said, "Of course, people like you with jobs on the outside are much busier than we are."

Second Daughter-in-law said, "There are fixed hours for work. Eldest Brother, Third Brother, and my husband also work outside without having to stay out all day. But Eldest Sister works and takes care of the house as well, so she can't find the time to come see us."

Since they were talking as though expounding the truths of Zen with subtle jabs hidden underneath, which was enough to send one's head reeling just listening to it, Hung-chien slipped upstairs to see his father. He hadn't spoken more than three sentences when Jou-chia came in. She asked her father-in-law how he was and made a few polite remarks; then unable to contain herself any longer, she complained to her husband, "Now I know why you didn't come home to get me. Why did you quit your job without first discussing it with me? So maybe I don't understand anything, but at least you should have come here first and asked for your father's advice."

Without any inkling of the subject, old Mr. Fang cried out in astonishment.

Hung-chien said in embarrassment, "I was just about to tell Father. How—how did you find out about it?"

Jou-chia said, "Papa called me. You even deceived him! He didn't resign. Why did you have to resign in such a hurry! Wouldn't it have been better to wait and see how things worked out?"

Hung-chien quickly justified himself.

Tun-weng inwardly blamed his son for being too rash but would not humiliate him in front of his daughter-in-law, and since the die was already cast in any case, he said, "Well, if that's the case, it's just as well you did resign. People like us must never seek petty advantages at the expense of justice and righteousness. I became a refugee rather than return to our village precisely because I had a little moral integrity left. I didn't approve

353

of your joining this newspaper agency in the first place. I felt it was far inferior to teaching. Come over tomorrow and the two of us can discuss this matter together. I'll try to find a job for you."

Jou-chia had nothing more to say and pulled a face as long as a beautiful donkey's.

During dinner Mrs. Fang exhorted Hung-chien to eat more meat and vegetables, "You've grown thinner lately, and your face has lost its glow. What sort of things do you eat at home? Jou-chia is too busy with her job to look after you. Why don't you come here and eat? You've eaten the food I've cooked with my own hands since you were little, and it's never poisoned you."

Jou-chia lowered her head and did her best to control herself. She managed to get through half a bowl of rice, then would eat nothing more. Mrs. Fang could tell by her daughter-in-law's face that Jou-chia was not easy to deal with and did not dare provoke Jou-chia further, merely consoling herself that at least her daughter-in-law had not had the nerve to retort.

On the way home, Hung-chien repeatedly apologized for his mother. Jou-chia said simply, "You let her talk without saying a word in my defense. I take this as a lesson."

Once home, she complained that her stomach hurt and told Mama Li to fill the hot water bottle so she could warm her stomach.

Mama Li said quickly, "Did you eat something that made you sick?"

She replied, "No, I'm not sick from eating; I'm sick with rage."

Ordinarily Hung-chien would certainly have rebuked her for telling the servant about the master's affairs, but that day he dared not say anything. That evening Jou-chia paid no more attention to him, and the next morning husband and wife continued to maintain a stony silence.

During breakfast Mama Li asked Hung-chien what he wanted for lunch. He replied that he had business at his parents' home and probably wouldn't be back for lunch, so she needn't fix anything.

Jou-chia sneered, "Mama Li, you can save yourself the trouble from now on. Master won't be eating at home any more. His mother says your food is poisonous."

"Ai!" said Hung-chien with a frown, "Why do you have to tell her—"

"Because I happen to feel like telling her," said Jou-chia with a heavy stamp of the heel of her shoe. "Mama Li is a witness here, and I want everything made clear. From now on you can beat me to death or kill me, but I'm not going to your home ever again. If I die and your highly cultured household prepares food as sacrifices for me, my ghost won't come either."

At this the tears welled up in her eyes, and Hung-chien, moved to pity, stood up to comfort her, but she pushed him away.

354

"And another thing. From now on we'll just keep the river water separate from the well water. You needn't tell me anything about your affairs. We're all going to be Japanese collaborators. Even the dogs you Fangs keep stand by justice and righteousness."

With that she turned and left, humming an English melody on her way down the stairs to show her total unconcern.

Glum and despondent, Hung-chien was reluctant to go back to his parents' home, but Tun-weng called up to press him. He went and listened to a long lecture from his father, who offered him no concrete advice or help. He began to hate everyone in his family and refused to stay long.

After he left, he went to the moving company to see the manager about the traveling expenses. The manager wasn't in, so he made an appointment for the next day. He went next to Mr. Wang's home, but he wasn't home either. By this time the trams were filled with office workers leaving work. He could not squeeze his way on, so he walked home, all the while wondering what he could do to dispel his wife's antagonism.

At the entrance to the alley when he noticed the Lus' car, he stiffened inside. He opened the back door of the house and went in through the kitchen, which they shared with the landlord's family. Mama Li was not there. A can on the stove was chattering away. He walked halfway up the stairs. The door to the small sitting room was open a crack, and he heard Mrs. Lu talking inside in a loud voice. Rage seized him. He didn't want to go in, but his feet seemed to be nailed to the spot. He heard her say, "Hung-chien has no ability, but he does have a terrific temper. I know that without Mama Li telling me. Jou-chia, men are like kids. They mustn't be spoiled. You give in to him too much."

The blood rushed to his face, and he wished he could have burst in on them with a loud shout. Suddenly he heard the sound of Mama Li's footsteps approaching the stairs. Afraid of being caught in an embarrassing situation, he quietly slipped out the door. His rage made him oblivious to the bone-piercing chill of the wind. *When would that disgusting woman get out?* he wondered. *Might as well not go home for dinner. Having lost my job, I'm all set to go begging anyway. No use saving those few cents.*

After he had walked a few blocks, his anger somewhat subsided. He passed a Western bakery; the gleaming white light in the window shone brightly on a wide variety of cakes and pastries. Outside the window stood an old man in a tattered jacket staring fixedly at the cakes in the window. He was carrying a basket on his arm filled with crudely made clay dolls and pinwheels made with waxed paper. *City kids these days don't want such crude toys when they have so many fancy foreign goods to choose from,* Hung-chien thought. *This poor old fellow couldn't have much business.* It suddenly occurred to him that he himself was just like the toys in that basket. No one showed any interest in him these days either, which was why it was so difficult to get a job. With a sigh he took out the wallet Jou-chia had given him and gave the old man two bills. Two little beggars, who had been waiting at the bakery entrance to beg from patrons coming out, immediately scurried over and asked for a handout and followed him from a distance.

By that time he had become hungry. He chose a cheap Russian restaurant and was about to go in when he dug his hand into his pocket to feel around and found his wallet was missing. In agitation, he perspired lightly in the chill wind, so lightly it was more like emotional steam let off than sweat. *What a wretched day! I might as well return home. I don't even have the money to take a tram.* All his resentment turned on his wife. If Mrs. Lu hadn't come. he would never have gone out and had to suffer the cold wind; and if he hadn't gone out, he wouldn't have lost his wallet. Mrs. Lu was his wife's aunt and his wife had invited her over—and even if his wife hadn't invited her, he would still lay the blame on her. Furthermore, he had always put his money in bits and pieces in all his pockets, front, back, and sides. At the most a pickpocket could clean out one pocket. Now that he had a wallet, all his money was kept together, making it that much easier for a pickpocket. It was all Jou-chia's great idea.

Mama Li was washing dishes in the kitchen. When she saw him come in, she asked, "Master, have you had dinner?"

He merely pretended not to hear. Mama Li had never seen him return so stony-faced. Her eyes followed him anxiously out of the kitchen.

When Jou-chia saw him, she put down the newspaper, stood up, and said, "You're back! Is it cold outside? Where did you have dinner? We waited and waited for you, but when you didn't come back, we went ahead and ate."

He had been expecting to eat dinner as soon as he got home. Now when he learned they had already eaten, he found a certain satisfaction in his disappointment, as though a firm foundation had been set for his outburst. *Today's quarrel would be a noisy one*, he thought.

"I have no relatives to go to for a meal," said Hung-chien sullenly. "Of course I haven't eaten."

"Then, hurry and have Mama Li go buy you something," said Jou-chia in surprise. "Where'd you go? You made us wait for such a long time! Auntie came especially to see you. We waited and waited, and when you didn't come I had her stay for dinner."

Hung-chien was like a drowning man who grabs the end of a rope and hangs on for dear life.

"Oh, so she came, did she!" he said. "No wonder! She ate up all my food and now I have nothing. Well, I'm much obliged to her for coming, but I didn't invite her! I don't go to her place, so why does she have to come to mine? Your aunt is to be kept for dinner, while your husband should go hungry. All right, then, if that's the way you want it, I'll go hungry for a day. Don't ask Mama Li to buy anything."

Jou-chia sat down, picked up the newspaper, and said, "I'm always sorry when I pay any attention to you. Ungrateful wretch! If you want to go hungry, it serves you right. It makes no difference to me. You've quit your job at the newspaper agency. What grave national matters was the great man of justice and righteousness out attending to? Coming back so late! I take care of half of the expenses in this family and I have every right to invite company. It's no business of yours. Besides, the dishes Mama Li cooks are poisonous. You'd be better off not eating them."

Hung-chien's rage redoubled and he felt a stabbing pain in his stomach, but he didn't have a penny on him. He would have to wait till the next day to go to the bank to get some money, but in the meantime he was not going to ask Jou-chia for any.

"In any case," he said, "you'll be glad if I starve to death. Then your dear aunt can find a better husband for you."

"Tsui!" said Jou-chia with a scornful laugh, "I think you've gone mad. You won't die of hunger. It should clear your head a little."

Hung-chien's anger surged forth inside him like a second tide of water and he asked, "Is that a secret that dear aunt of yours passed on to you? 'Jou-chia, a man shouldn't be spoiled too much. You must starve him, freeze him, and abuse him.' "

Studying her husband's face closely, she said, "Oh, the landlord's servant did say she saw you come home. Why didn't you come up the stairs openly instead of skulking about like a thief, hiding halfway up the stairs and listening in? Only those two sisters-in-law of yours are capable of doing something like that. And you call yourself a man. Aren't you ashamed?"

He said, "I wanted to hear it; otherwise, I'd really be in the dark, not knowing how people are maligning me behind my back."

"How did we malign you? Why don't you say it?"

Hung-chien bluffed, "You know perfectly well yourself without my telling you."

Jou-chia had in fact told her aunt what had happened during the winter solstice dinner the day before. Both of them had laughed and reviled in unison. Thinking Hung-chien had heard all this, she was a little flustered and said, "It wasn't meant for your ears in the first place. Who asked you to eavesdrop? Tell me, when my aunt said she'd find you a job in the factory, did your sharp little ears pick that up?"

He gave a start and shouted, "Who wants her to find me a job? If I become a beggar, I wouldn't want to beg from her! Isn't it enough for her to raise those two running dogs, Bobby and Sun Jou-chia? You can just tell her that Fang Hung-chien, who 'has no ability, but does have a terrific temper,' will not be any running dog for a capitalist running dog."

The two stood facing each other. Eyes blazing with anger, Jou-chia said, "Not a word she said was unjust. People feel sorry for you. If you don't want the rice bowl, it won't get moldy. All right, your father can 'find a job' for you. But there's nothing great about depending on your old man. If you had any ability, you'd find your own job."

"I'm not depending on anyone. I'll tell you something. I already sent a telegram to Chao Hsin-mei today, and I just now settled everything with the moving company people. After I'm gone, you can really enjoy yourself. You can not only keep your aunt for dinner, you can even have her stay overnight. Or you can just go ahead and move in with her and let her support you like Bobby."

Jou-chia's lips parted slightly and her eyes opened wide. She let him finish, then said through clenched teeth, "All right, so we're through. Your luggage and clothes you can take care of yourself. Don't bother me about them. Last year you frittered your time away in Shanghai with no job, then went with Chao Hsin-mei to the interior. After you lost your job there, relying on Hsin-mei's pull you came to Shanghai. You lost your job in Shanghai and now you go running to Chao Hsin-mei in the interior again. Just think about it. You follow him all your life, clinging to his coattails with your teeth. If you aren't his running dog, then what are you? You not only don't have any ability, you don't even have any ambition. Don't talk to me about moral integrity. Just be careful you don't annoy this friend of yours. If he kicks you out, and you come back to Shanghai, I'd just like to see if you can face anyone then. I don't care if you go or stay."

Unable to take any more, Hung-chien said, "Then just shut up," and he reached out and gave her a strong shove in the chest. She staggered backward, crashing into the edge of the table and knocking a glass to the floor with her arm. The pieces of glass mixed with the water.

Gasping for breath she said, "You dare hit me? You dare hit me!"

Mama Li came bursting in like a cotton pellet in her thick clothing, screaming, "Master, how could you raise a hand against her? If you hit me, I'll yell and let everyone downstairs hear. Young Lady, where did he hit you? Are you hurt? Don't be frightened. I'll set my old life against his. A man hitting a woman! Your father and mother never hit you. I nursed you from the time you were a baby and never once gave you so much as a strong pat. And he hit you!"

358

Her tears came rolling down as she spoke. Jou-chia collapsed on the sofa sobbing bitterly. Hung-chien watched her crying piteously, but he would not pity her and only hated her all the more.

Mama Li stood by the sofa protecting Jou-chia and said, "Don't cry, Young Lady. If you cry, I'll cry too—" and as she spoke, she pulled her apron up to wipe her tears—"See how badly you beat her! Young Lady, I'm really thinking of telling your aunt, but I'm just afraid once I'm gone, he'll hit you again."

Hung-chien said gruffly, "Ask your mistress if I hit her or not! Run over and call her aunt. I won't hit your mistress," and with a push and a shove, he pushed Mama Li right out of the room.

Less than a minute later she came rushing back in again, saying, "Young Lady, I asked the landlord's daughter to call up your aunt for me. She's coming at once. We needn't be afraid of him anymore."

It had never occurred to Hung-chien or Jou-chia that Mama Li was serious about it. But as the two of them were now in hostile positions, they could not very well join up and reproach her for meddling. Jou-chia forgot all about crying; Hung-chien stared at the servant in amazement like a child seeing some strange creature in the zoo.

After a moment of silence, Hung-chien said, "All right, when she comes, I'm leaving. You two women ganging up isn't enough. You have to go get another one. Then you'll say how I, a man, am bullying you. I'll be back when she's gone." He went over and took his jacket from the coatrack.

Jou-chia didn't want her aunt coming over and blowing up the incident, but when she saw her husband beating a retreat like this, her hate and scorn won out over her hurt. She cried hoarsely, "You're a *coward*! *Coward*! *Coward*! I don't want to see you ever again, you *coward*!" Each word struck like a lash meant to whip up her husband's courage. Then as though feeling this weren't enough, she grabbed an ivory comb from the table and hurled it at him with all her strength. Just turning his head to reply, he did not have time to dodge. The comb struck his left cheek hard and fell to the floor with a thud, breaking in two.

Jou-chia heard him cry out "Ai ya" in pain, and when she saw the spot where the comb had struck him immediately redden and swell up from the blood underneath the skin, she regretted having gone too far, but at the same time she was frightened, expecting him to retaliate. Mama Li positioned herself between the two of them.

Appalled at Jou-chia's viciousness, and seeing her standing there stiffly holding on to the table, her tear-stained face as pale as dead ashes, her eyes all red and her nostrils flaring, swallowing saliva, he felt both pity and fear. At the same time he heard footsteps ascending the stairs and didn't dispute with her any further, saying merely, "You really are vicious! It's not enough that your own family knows about it, you have to raise such a fuss so all the neighbors know too. Now the landlord's family has heard. You've just learned to be spiteful and brazen-faced. Well, I still plan to behave like a gentleman and keep my face. I'm leaving. Learn some more new skills when your teacher comes. You're really a good student. You put them to use as soon as you've learned them. You can warn her for me that I'll forgive her this time, but if she leads you astray once more, I'll go there looking for her. Don't think I'm afraid of her. Mama Li, when Mrs. Lu comes, don't just tell her how bad I am. You saw with your own eyes who struck whom."

He went up to the door, saying in a loud voice, "I'm going out," slowly turned the knob to give the eavesdroppers on the other side of the door time to move away, and then went out. Jou-chia watched wide-eyed as he left the room, then collapsed on the sofa, put her head in her hands, and wept in anguish. It seemed the tide of tears didn't flow from her eyes only, but it was as if hot tears were being squeezed from her heart and all over her body and drained out together.

Hung-chien's nerves were too numb as he left the house to feel the cold. He was conscious only of a burning in his left cheek. His thoughts churned chaotically in his brain like snowflakes whirling about in the north wind. He let his legs carry him where they would. The all-night street lights passed his shadow along from one lamp to the next. Another self inside him seemed to be saying, "It's all over! All over!" His scattered, random thoughts immediately seemed to come together at one point, and he was beset with anguish. His left cheek suddenly tingled. He found it damp to the touch, and thinking it was blood, was so shocked his heart stood still and his legs went limp. He moved over under a lamp post to look, and when he found no traces of blood on his fingers, realized it was only tears.

At the same time he felt exhaustion all over his body and hunger inside his stomach. He reached instinctively into his pocket, thinking he'd wait for a street-hawker to come by and buy a loaf of bread, when he suddenly remembered that he had no money with him. A hungry person can burn with anger, but like a fire fed on paper, it doesn't last long. Having nowhere to go, he decided the best thing to do was to go home and sleep. If he did encounter Mrs. Lu, he wasn't afraid of her. So he was the one who had started it, but Jou-chia had retaliated so viciously, the two incidents canceled each other out. He saw by his watch that it was already past ten. He wasn't sure how long he had been out. Maybe she had already gone. Seeing no car at the entrance to the alley, he breathed a sigh of relief.

As soon as he entered, the landlady heard the noise and hurried out, saying, "Oh, it's you, Mr. Fang. Your wife wasn't feeling well. She went to the Lus with Mama Li and won't be back tonight. Here's the key to your room. She left it with me to give you. You can come over to my house for breakfast tomorrow morning. Mama Li has arranged it."

Hung-chien's heart sank irretrievably. He mechanically took the key and thanked her. The landlady seemed to have more to say, but he bounded up the stairs. He opened the door to the bedroom and turned on the light. The shattered glass and broken comb were still in the same place, and one trunk was missing from the pile. He stood there in a daze, mind and body too dulled to feel angry and upset. Jou-chia had left, but the room still retained her angry look, and the sound of her crying and her voice hadn't vanished from the air. He noticed a card on the table and went over to take a look. It was Mrs. Lu's. In a sudden fit of anger, he tore it to pieces. "All right," he said spitefully, "you're free to go off and leave me. Get the hell out, your mother's egg! All of you, get the hell out of my sight!"

This brief outburst of rage consumed all his remaining energy, and he was so weak he could have broken down and sobbed his heart out. He fell fully clothed on the bed and felt as if the room were swirling around him. He thought, *Oh, no. I just can't get sick. Tomorrow I'll have to go see the manager, and then once it's all settled, I'll have to get together the money for the traveling expenses. I may be able to spend the Chinese New Year in Chungking.* Hope rose again in his heart, like damp firewood which won't catch fire but has begun to smoke, and it seemed everything would work out. Before he knew it, dark earth and hazy sky merged and wrapped tight. He fell asleep like a night when all the lights have gone out. At first his sleep was brittle. His hunger tried to nip through his stupor like a pair of forceps, but he subconsciously blocked it. Gradually the forceps became loose and blunt, and his sleep became so sound it could not be pinched. It was a sleep devoid of dreams and sensations, the primordial sleep of mankind that is also a sample of death.

The old ancestral clock began chiming away as though it had stored up half a day's time to ring it out carefully in the still of the night, counting "One, two, three, four, five, six." It was six o'clock five hours ago. At that time Hung-chien was on his way home, intending to treat Jou-chia nicely and request her not to stir up any more unpleasantness between them over the incident of the day before. At that time Jou-chia was at home waiting for Hung-chien to come home for dinner, hoping he would make up with her aunt and go to work in her factory. The irony and disappointment of men unintentionally contained in this out-of-date timepiece went deeper than any language, than any tears or laughter.

Afterword

ꀀꀀ

Fortress Besieged, or *Wei-ch'eng*, first serialized in *Literary Renaissance* (*Wen-i fu-hsing*) and published in book form in 1947, has been acclaimed as "one of modern China's two best novels,"[1] or her "greatest novel;"[2] it has been the subject of two doctoral dissertations and one master's thesis and various scholarly papers in English and Chinese.[3] Among differing views on the merits of the novel, C. T. Hsia has highly praised the novel's comic exuberance and satire;[4] Dennis Hu, its linguistic manipulation; Theodore Huters, its relationship to modern Chinese letters; and Mai Ping-k'un has written favorably on both Ch'ien's essays and his fiction. What each critic has stressed is one aspect of the novel's multifaceted brilliance, and it is the intent of this introduction to discuss the novel as an artistic whole.

On November 21, 1910, Ch'ien Chung-shu, the author of *Fortress Besieged*, was born into a literary family in Wuhsi, Kiangsu province. His father Ch'ien Chi-po (1887–1957) was a renowned literary historian and university professor. Ch'ien was a precocious child, noted for his photographic memory and brilliance in writing Chinese verse and prose. Upon graduation from grade school, he attended St. John's University Affiliated High Schools in Soochow and Wuhsi. In high school, Ch'ien excelled in English. When he sat for the matriculation examination of the prestigious Tsing-hua University, it was said that he scored very poorly in mathematics but did so well in English and Chinese composition that he passed the examination with some éclat.

At Tsing-hua, Ch'ien was known as an arrogant young man, who cut lectures and kept much to himself. Among his few intimate friends was Achilles Fang, the "word wizard" (as Marianne Moore called him), who was then a student in the department of philosophy. There Ch'ien also met his future wife Yang Chiang. After graduating from Tsing-hua in 1933, he accepted a teaching appointment at Kuang-hua University in Shanghai.

In 1935, on a Boxer Indemnity Scholarship, Ch'ien went to Exeter College, Oxford, and majored in English literature. He read more thrillers and detective yarns than was healthy for a student devoted to serious research. He also developed a keen interest in Hegel's philosophy and Marcel Proust's fiction. Perhaps most ego-deflating was his failure to pass the probationer examination in English palaeography, and he had to sit for it a second time. Nonetheless, he did achieve his B. Litt. degree from Oxford in 1937. His thesis, composed of three meticulously researched chapters ("China in the English Literature of the Seventeenth Century" and "China in the English Literature of the Eighteenth Century"), was later published in the English edition of the *Quarterly Bulletin of Chinese Bibliography* (*Tu-shu chi-k'an*). Having taken his Oxford degree, he studied a year in Paris.

Returning to China in 1938, the second year of the second Sino-Japanese War, Ch'ien, at home in the literatures of two or three major European languages, taught at the National Southwest Associated University in Kunming;[5] the National Teachers College at Lan-t'ien in Pao-ching, Hunan province; Aurora Women's College of Arts and Sciences in Shanghai; and Chi-nan University in Shanghai. From 1946 to 1948 he was also the editor of the English language periodical *Philobiblon*, published by the National Central University Library in Nanking.

Among the small corpus of pre-Communist works by Ch'ien, the following are noteworthy. At Tsing-hua he wrote a number of short stories and vignette-type essays for *Crescent Moon* (*Hsin yüeh*) and *Literary Review* (*Wen-hsüeh tsa-chih*) magazines. In 1941 the essays were published in Shanghai as a volume entitled *Marginalia of Life* (*Hsieh tsai jen-sheng pien-shang*). Some of the short stories were anthologized in his 1946 publication entitled *Men, Beasts, and Ghosts* (*Jen, Shou, Kuei*). In 1948 he published *On the Art of Poetry* (*T'an yi lu*), composed in an elegant *wen-yen*, or classical, style.

After the Communist victory in 1949, he returned to Peking to teach at Tsing-hua University. While still in Shanghai, Ch'ien had become dissatisfied with *Fortress Besieged*, and thought he could do better. He began to write another novel to be called "Heart of the Artichoke" (Pai-ho hsin), after Baudelaire's phrase "*Le coeur d'artichaut.*" He had written some 3,000 to 4,000 words, but unfortunately the manuscript was lost in the mail when the Ch'iens moved from Shanghai to Peking. He has not worked on the novel since then.

In Peking Ch'ien first worked as a researcher in the Foreign Literature

Institute of the Academy of Sciences; then he transferred to the Chinese Literature Institute of the same academy. Since the foundation of the Institute of Literature in the Academy of Social Sciences in 1952, he has been one of its two senior fellows, the other being Yu Ping-Po, well-known for his studies on the *Dream of the Red Chamber* (*Hung-lou meng*). Ch'ien's wife Yang Chiang is a researcher in the institute.

Ch'ien seems to have abandoned the writing of his earlier vitriolic works and restricted himself to literary scholarship. His most significant post-1949 work has been *Annotated Selection of Sung Poetry* (*Sung-shih hsüan-chu*), which was published in 1958. Later he headed a team of scholars responsible for the writing of the T'ang and Sung sections of a history of Chinese literature. In 1974 it was widely rumored that he had died. The rumor prompted C. T. Hsia to write a memorial essay, "In Memory of Mr. Ch'ien Chung-shu" (Chui-nien Ch'ien Chung-shu hsien-sheng).[6] Ch'ien, however, is alive and well and has been "resurrected" after the fall of the Gang of Four. His recent activities include visits to Rome in the fall of 1978 and to the United States in the spring of 1979 as a member of Chinese academic delegations. While he was in Italy, he talked with three scholars who were translating or had translated *Fortress Besieged* into French, Czech, and Russian. Yang Chiang was a member of a Chinese delegation in Paris while her husband was in America. Her most recent publication was a Chinese translation of *Don Quixote* in 1978, and it is now in its second printing.

In 1979 Ch'ien published a book containing four studies, one on Chinese painting and Chinese poetry dating back to the 1930s and the other three essays written since 1949 (including one on Lin Shu, which was partially translated by George Kao and published in *Renditions*). Also in 1979 a new edition of *Annotated Selection of Sung Poetry* with thirty additional notes was published.

Ch'ien's most important publication in 1979, however, is a mammoth work of over one million words entitled *Kuan-chui pien*, in four volumes. Each section focuses on one major classical Chinese work: *I ching*, *Shih ching*, *Chuang-tzu*, *Lieh-tzu*, *Shih-chi*, *Tso-chuan*, and the complete pre-T'ang prose. Altogether ten studies, both philological and comparative (Western), comprising the four divisions of *ching*, *shih*, *tzu*, and *chi*, are written in a style more elegant and archaic than that of *On the Art of Poetry*. Ch'ien wanted to show the world that there is at least one person in China who can write in this style and has not broken with the old tradition; he also hoped to inspire younger Chinese everywhere to study the Chinese past. *Kuan-chui pien*, Ch'ien believes, will be his masterwork.[7]

Ch'ien's B. Litt. thesis, *On the Art of Poetry*, and *Annotated Selection of Sung Poetry* are all works of solid scholarship. The first represents meticulous research; the second contains many references to Western poetics from Plato to the Abbé Bremond and an honest evaluation of Chinese poets and their shortcomings; and the preface to the third is a masterpiece of literary analysis.[8] Apart from these works, Ch'ien is primarily a satirist in his essays and short stories. For example, the first essay in *Marginalia of Life* is "Satan Pays an Evening Visit to Mr. Ch'ien Chung-shu" (Mo-kuei yeh-fang Ch'ien Chung-shu hsien-sheng), a satire on man through the supernatural, the targets being hypocrisy and ignorance. In "On Laughter and Humor" (Shuo hsiao), he attacks those lacking humor; he mocks and scorns false champions of morality in "Those Who Moralize" (T'an chiao-hsün); he chides the hypocrites in "Men of Letters" (Lun wen-jen) and literary charlatans in "Illiteracy" (Shih wen-mang). In a similar vein, his vitriolic fire is also apparent in his short stories, most notably in "Inspiration" (Ling-kan), a satiric and harsh attack on the writing profession itself and a lampoon on a number of well-known literary figures. Lampooning as much as he does in *Men, Beasts, and Ghosts*, he is also a fine writer of psychological insight. His story "Cat" (Mao) is a good example of marital strife which mars the happiness of a certain Li family. Even finer than "Cat" is "Souvenir" (Chi-nien), often considered the best story in *Men, Beasts, and Ghosts*. A study of the seduction of a lonely married woman by an air force pilot during the Sino-Japanese War, it emphasizes the heroine's feelings of guilt, fascination, revulsion, and relief toward her extramarital affair. Also well done is the story's ironic ending. After the pilot dies in action, the woman's husband, not knowing of his wife's infidelity and impregnation by the pilot, suggests that they commemorate the dead pilot by naming the baby after him, if it is a boy.

Fortress Besieged, however, remains the best of Ch'ien's pre-1949 works. Structured in nine chapters, it is a comedy of manners with much picaresque humor, as well as a scholar's novel, a satire, a commentary on courtship and marriage, and a study of one contemporary man.

The nine chapters can be divided into four sections, or what Roland Barthes calls "functional sequences":[9] Section I (chapters 1–4); Section II (chapter 5); Section III (chapters 6–8); and Section IV (chapter 9). Section I begins with the story of Fang Hung-chien, who is returning to China from Europe in 1937; continues with his brief visit to his hometown, Wushi, and his experience in Shanghai; and concludes with his accepting a teaching appointment at the newly established San Lü University in the interior. Section II is relatively short and centers on the trials and tribulations Fang Hung-chien and others encounter in their journey to the university; Section III highlights in vivid color the true story of Chinese pseudo-intellectuals within the confines of an academic environment; and Section IV details the trivial misunderstandings between Fang Hung-chien and his bride and ends with the dissolution of their marriage.

In each of the four sections, Ch'ien Chung-shu emphasizes the hero's experiences from hope through frustration to defeat; a functional unit in itself, each section has its own curve of hope, frustration, and defeat. Furthermore, Section I serves as a microcosm for the other sections. The theme of "besiegement" is seen in Ch'ien Chung-shu's description of the various types of pressures closing in on Fang Hung-chien in Section I; the pressures are amplified in Sections II and III and concretized in Section IV. Traits of character that we are to know in excruciating detail for tens of pages are unmistakably sketched in a few. Fang's ineffectualness as a person in Section I clearly hints at the failures that are to haunt him in later sections. An inkling of the types of characters we are to meet in other sections also surfaces in Section I. For example, the comprador Jimmy Chang in Section I is to return as Mrs. Lu in Section IV; the effeminate pseudo-intellectuals in Miss Su's circle are to be reborn as gossipmongers and power grabbers in Section III, and Japanese collaborators in Section IV. Even the boat trip in Section I is to be repeated in Section II and Section III to indicate the ebbing of the protagonist's fortunes.

Even though Section I serves as a microcosm for the whole book and reveals the structural cleverness of the novel, this is not to say that the tone and mood of each section is the same; in fact, a definite pattern toward the worsening of Fang Hung-chien's fortunes can be discerned. Section I has the frivolousness of spring; Section II, the comic delights of summer; Section III, the somberness and seriousness of fall; and Section IV, the worst moments of wintry chill. By making each section a separate unit, by fashioning Section I into a sampling of the other three sections, and by showing the continuous change of tone and mood from Section I through Section IV, the author demonstrates that he is a very careful artist who fabricates and engineers every small part to fit his overall plan, down to the point of supplying us with an omniscient narrator who steers us all the way. The result of this careful engineering is a mighty singleness and a massive consistency.

Besides the careful engineering that goes into the structure of the novel, *Fortress Besieged* is a comedy of manners in its presentation of representative segments of the author's time. We meet the lowly porters, shopkeepers, innkeepers, bus drivers, countryfolk, soldiers, prostitutes, and French policemen serving their mother country in her Concessions in China; the middle-class returned students, country squires, journalists; and the rising middle-class bankers, compradors, factory managers, Japanese collaborators, and others. Each group has its own particular characteristics, somewhat exaggerated and simplified, by which they are easily comprehensible. In minute and accurate detail, Ch'ien Chung-shu shows their idiosyncrasies. What

367

results are brilliant caricatures of avaricious porters, defensive shopkeepers, superstitious countryfolk, hollow intellectuals, vulgar compradors and businessmen.

In Section II there is also a great deal of picaresque humor, resulting from the interplay of characters and their very different standards and assumptions. One brief example must suffice. After traveling for some time on the road, Fang Hung-chien and his companions check into a nondescript inn. In examining the menu, they learn that there is "milk coffee" available and they ask the waiter for more information.

> The waiter assured them at once that it was good stuff from Shanghai with the original seal intact. Hung-chien asked what the brand was. This the waiter didn't know, but in any case it was sweet, fragrant, and top quality, for one paper bag made one cup of coffee.
>
> "That's coffee candy to cajole children with," said Hsin-mei, suddenly understanding.
>
> "Don't be so particular," said Hung-chien in high spirits. "Bring us three cups and then we'll see. At least it should have a little coffee flavor."
>
> The waiter nodded and left. Miss Sun said, "That coffee candy has no milk in it. How could it be called milk coffee? Milk powder must have been added to it."
>
> Hung-chien jerked his mouth in the fat woman's direction and said, "As long as it's not her milk, anything'll do."
>
> Miss Sun frowned and pouted in a rather charming expression of disgust.
>
> Reddening, Hsin-mei restrained a laugh and said, "You! Your remarks are disgusting."
>
> The coffee came; surprisingly enough it was both black and fragrant with a layer of white froth floating on the top. Hung-chien asked the waiter what it was. The waiter said that it was milk, and when asked what sort of milk, he replied that it was the cream.
>
> Hsin-mei remarked, "It looks to me like human spit."
>
> Hung-chien, who was about to take a drink, brusquely shoved the cup away, saying, "I won't drink it!" (pp. 156–157)

Fortress Besieged is also a scholar's novel. Throughout the novel, particularly in Section I, references are made to Chinese and Western literature, philosophy, logic, customs, laws, educational systems, and other areas such as foreign languages and feminism. The author's knowledge is so wide that he is probably modern China's foremost "scholar novelist," a designation for a special class of literary men "who utilized the form of a long narrative not merely to tell a story but to satisfy their needs for all other kinds of intellectual and literary self-expression."[10] Among the works of Chinese literature that belong to this special category are *Journey to the West (Hsi yu chi)*, *Dream of the Red Chamber (Hung-lou meng)*, *The Scholars (Ju-lin wai-shih)*, *Flowers in the Mirror (Ching-hua yuan)*, *Yeh-sou p'u-yen*, *T'an-shih*, and *Yen-shan wai-shih*.[11]

However, a distinction must be drawn between *Fortress Besieged* and the others. Whereas the others are mostly episodic in nature and often digress on such subjects as astrology, arithmetic, calligraphy, gardening, medicine, and so forth for the sole purpose of displaying their authors' erudition, *Fortress Besieged* has structural unity and never burdens the reader with unnecessary or excessive information on any subject. The author's knowledge merely helps the narrative strand of the novel in supplying the reader with an observant, witty, and rhetorical narrator.

The narrator is indeed all of the above. His observations are sharp and direct. Remarking on the filth on the deck of *Vicomte de Bragelonne*, he muses: "The French are famous for the clarity of their thought and the lucidness of their prose, yet in whatever they do, they never fail to bring chaos, filth, and hubbub, as witness the mess on board the ship" (p. 4). In a second instance, the narrator's wit bubbles forth in his description of Miss Pao: "When men students saw Miss Pao, they burned with lewd desire, and found some relief by endlessly cracking jokes behind her back. Some called her a *charcuterie*—a shop selling cooked meats—because only such a shop would have so much warm-colored flesh on public display. Others called her 'Truth,' since it is said that 'the truth is naked.' But Miss Pao wasn't exactly without a stitch on, so they revised her name to 'Partial Truth'" (p. 7). Rhetorically, the narrator takes a great deal of delight in word play. His penchant for definitions is seen in the following two examples: "It is said that 'girl friend' is the scientific term for sweetheart, making it sound more dignified, just as the biological term for rose is 'rosaceae dicotyledonous,' or the legal term for divorcing one's wife is 'negotiated separation by consent'" (p. 26). In another case, he writes, "Kao Sung-nien, the president of San Lü University, was an 'old science scholar.' The word 'old' here is quite bothersome. It could describe science or it could just as well be describing a scientist. Unfortunately, there is a world of difference between a scientist and science. A scientist is like wine. The older he gets, the more valuable he is, while science is like a woman. When she gets old, she's worthless" (p. 192).

The author's knowledge of Chinese classics and pidgin English unquestionably helps him to better caricature Mr. Fang Tung-weng, the protagonist's father, and Mr. Jimmy Chang, a Shanghai comprador. In the case of the former, his every thought is an allusion, a proverb, or a quote from the classics, as evidenced in the following letter advising his son to pay more attention to school work:

> I did not begrudge the expense of sending you hundreds of miles away to study. If you devoted yourself to your studies as you should, would you still have the leisure to look in a mirror? You are not a woman, so what need do you have of a mirror? That sort of thing is for actors only. A real

man who gazes at himself in the mirror will only be scorned by society. Never had I thought once you parted from me that you would pick up such base habits. Most deplorable and disgusting!

Moreover, it is said that "When one's parents are still living, a son should not speak of getting old." You have no consideration for your parents, who hold you dearly in their hearts, but frighten them with the talk of death. This is certainly neglect of filial duties to the extreme! It can only be the result of your attending a coeducational school—seeing women around has put ideas in your head. The sight of girls has made you think of change. Though you make excuses about "autumnal melancholy," I know full well that what ails you are the "yearnings of springtime." (pp. 9–10)

Fang Tung-weng's style of writing is the man himself: allusive, self-righteous, prejudiced, traditional, and pedantic. The success of the portrait of Fang Tung-weng is due, to a large extent, to the author's understanding of the empty posturings of the traditional country squire whose ideas are those of the imperial past though he lives in the modern twentieth century.

On the other hand, Ch'ien Chung-shu's portrait of Jimmy Chang is precise. The following is a description of Fang Hung-chien's visit with Jimmy (the words in italics are in English in the original):

As Mr. Chang shook hands with Hung-chien, he asked him if he had to *go downtown* every day. When the pleasantries were over, Hung-chien noticed a glass cupboard filled with bowls, jars, and plates and asked, "Do you collect porcelain, Mr. Chang?"

"*Sure! Have a look-see.*" . . . Unable to tell whether they were genuine or fake, he [Hung-chien] merely said, "These must be quite valuable."

"*Sure!* Worth quite a lot of money, *plenty of dough.* Besides, these things aren't like calligraphy or paintings. If you buy calligraphy or paintings which turn out to be fakes, they aren't worth a cent. They just amount to *wastepaper.* If the porcelain is fake, at least it can hold food. Sometimes I invite foreign *friends* over for dinner and use this big K'ang-hsi . . . plate for a *salad dish.* They all think the ancient colors and odor make the food taste a little *old time.*"

. . . "But I have a *hunch* when I see something and a sudden—*what d'you call?*—inspiration comes to me. Then I buy it and it turns out to be quite *OK.* Those antique dealers all respect me. I always say to them, 'Don't try to *fool* me with fakes. *Oh yeah*, Mr. Chang here is no *sucker.* Don't think you can cheat me!' He closed the cupboard and said, "Oh, *headache*," then pressed an electric bell to summon the servant.

Puzzled, Hung-chien asked quickly, "Aren't you feeling well, Mr. Chang?"

Mr. Chang looked at Hung-chien in astonishment and said, "Who's not feeling well? You? Me? Why, I feel fine!"

"Didn't you say you had a headache?" asked Hung-chien.

Mr. Chang roared with laughter. . . . Turning to Hung-chien, he said with a laugh, " '*Headache*' is an American expression for 'wife,' not 'pain in the head!' I guess you haven't been to the *States*!" (pp. 43–44)

What brings this little scene so splendidly to life is the way the author captures the pidgin English around him, so that Jimmy Chang becomes not a dim personification, not a stock figure of allegory, but a genuine flesh-and-blood comprador living in the great metropolis—Shanghai. It is a subtle passage not because Jimmy is a subtle character or his shallowness hard to see through, but because the precise nature of that shallowness is revealed to us with a remarkable economy of words and without much extraneous comment.

Ch'ien Chung-shu is also thoroughly familiar with Western literary techniques. In his investigation of the linguistic and stylistic points of view in *Fortress Besieged*, Dennis Hu details Ch'ien's efficient use of imagery and symbolism and cites numerous examples of his linguistic manipulation (e.g., personification, symbolic prefiguration, plurisignation) and of his semantic manipulation (verbal paradoxes, narrator intrusion). The application of the above-mentioned techniques, in Hu's view, has contributed significantly to the sarcasm, satire, irony, and wit found in the novel.[12]

It should also be stressed that Ch'ien Chung-shu's early reading of Western fiction has significantly helped his writing of *Fortress Besieged*. Most notably his familiarity with Western points of view has allowed him to integrate successfully the omniscient narrator's point of view with that of Fang Hung-chien;[13] Ch'ien's reading of Dickens and other English novelists has perhaps sharpened his skills of caricature and made him aware of the picaresque tradition. What we have, then, in Ch'ien Chung-shu is a modern Chinese scholar-novelist who has the benefit of both Chinese and Western learning; consequently, his *Fortress Besieged* appeals to readers of both China and the West.

A comedy of manners and a scholar's novel *Fortress Besieged* may be, yet Ch'ien Chung-shu's ultimate aim is to make a statement about life by revealing the flaws of the people who live it. Ch'ien, however, does not write sermons to expose society's faults as he sees them; instead, he uses satire.

One primary target of his satire is the fad of studying abroad, which had its roots in the old Chinese concept of "reflecting glory on one's ancestors" (*k'uan-tsung yao-tsu*). In the imperial days, reflecting glory on one's ancestors meant passing all sorts of local, provincial, and state examinations. After the abolition of the examination system in 1905, the substitute was to study abroad. Fang Hung-chien himself makes that comparison: ". . . studying abroad today is like passing examinations under the old Manchu system. . . . It's not for the broadening of knowledge that one goes abroad but to get rid of that inferiority complex. It's like having smallpox or measles, or in other words, it's essential to have them. . . . Once we've studied abroad, we've gotten the inferiority complex out of the system, and our souls become strengthened, and when we do come across such germs as

Ph.D.'s or M.A.'s we've built up a resistance against them" (p. 77). And this craze of studying abroad continued until the Communist takeover of the Mainland in 1949, by which time it had pervaded all levels of society.[14] The sardonic narrator observes further that not only science students want to go abroad, but also students majoring in Chinese literature: "It may sound a bit absurd for someone majoring in Chinese to go abroad for advanced study. In fact, however, it is only for those studying Chinese literature that it is absolutely necessary to study abroad, since all other subjects such as mathematics, physics, philosophy, psychology, economics, and law, which have been imported from abroad, have already been Westernized. Chinese literature, the only native product, is still in need of a foreign trademark before it can hold its own. . . ." (p. 11).

Thus it is quite easy to understand Fang Hung-chien's desperation in seeking to acquire a foreign diploma. Pressured by his parents and his "in-laws," he muses, "This diploma, it seemed, would function the same as Adam and Eve's figleaf. It could hide a person's shame and wrap up his disgrace. This tiny square of paper could cover his shallowness, ignorance, and stupidity. Without it, it was as if he were spiritually stark naked and had nothing to bundle up in" (p. 12). Soon, he purchases a bogus Ph.D. from an Irishman in New York. Later, we learn one of his colleagues at San Lü University has also bought a bogus degree from the same place.

The importance of such a foreign degree, either real or false, is fully satirized by the author. First, Fang Hung-chien's "acquisition" of his degree prompts his "father-in-law" to place a blurb about Fang in a Shanghai newspaper which reads: "Fang Hung-chien, the gifted son-in-law of Chou Hou-ch'ing, a prominent local businessman and general manager of the Golden Touch Bank, recently received his doctorate of philosophy from Carleton University in Germany after pursuing advanced study abroad under Mr. Chou's sponsorship at the Universities of London, Paris, and Berlin in political science, economics, history, and sociology, in which he made excellent grades and ranked at the top of his class. He will be touring several countries before returning home in the fall. It is said that many major organizations are vying for him with job offers" (p. 31). Second, Fang becomes an instant hometown celebrity. Upon arrival at the hometown railway station, he is met by his father, his uncles, and two newspaper reporters who take his picture and prepare to interview him on world issues. Third, the local high school principal invites him to give a lecture to the summer school students. Though Fang is unwilling, his father, afflicted by the "reflecting glory on one's ancestors" syndrome, accepts the invitation for him.

The irony of all the hoopla about Fang's acquisition of a degree is that it becomes the butt of much satiric humor. The blurb about him in the Shanghai newspaper only makes Fang feel like a counterfeit before Miss Su, a genuine Ph.D. from Lyons; the picture published of him in the home-town paper makes him look like a thief caught in the act of stealing rather than an expert on world issues; and his lecture to the high school audience effectively transforms him into the town's laughing stock, for he misplaces his notes and ad-libs that the Western influences on China amounted to no more than the importation of opium and syphilis. The consequence of his mis-lecture is that all those families with eligible daughters immediately suspend their interest in him as a prospective son-in-law.

Perhaps the fiercest satire is directed at the intelligentsia. Ch'ien Chung-shu's satire is broad and sweeping. It begins with a humorous description of the Chinese students returning home aboard the *Vicomte de Bragelonne*:

> Meeting at a far corner of the earth, they became good friends at once, discussing the foreign threats and internal turmoil of their motherland, wishing they could return immediately to serve her. The ship moved ever so slowly, while homesickness welled up in everyone's heart and yearned for release. Then suddenly from heaven knows where appeared two sets of mahjong, the Chinese national pastime, said to be popular in America as well. Thus, playing mahjong not only had a down-home flavor to it but was also in tune with world trends. As luck would have it, there were more than enough people to set up two tables of mahjong. So, except for eating and sleeping, they spent their entire time gambling. Breakfast was no sooner over than down in the dining room the first round of mahjong was to begin. (p. 4)

No less biting is the author's description of the pseudo-intellectuals in Miss Su Wen-wan's circle. First on the list is Miss Su herself, with a doc-torate from Lyons, who is found to have plagiarized a German folk song verbatim; the American-educated pipe-smoking Chao Hsin-mei is an im-pertinent young man who makes speeches whenever possible; the French-educated Mrs. Shen, besides smelling like a goat, studs her speech with "*Tiens*" and "*O la la*," as she squirms her body into various seductive poses; the Cambridge-educated Ts'ao Yüan-lang is a new-style poet who writes un-readable poetry mixed with Chinese and Western allusions; Ch'u Sheng-ming (literally, careful and clear), a European-educated philosopher, writes complimentary letters to world-renowned philosophers such as Henri Berg-son and Bertrand Russell and uses their courtesy replies as recognition of his eminence as a philosopher; and lastly, there is the Chinese old-style poet Tung Hsieh-ch'üan, who presumptuously dismisses the famous Chinese poet Su Tung-p'o as overrated and Su's poetry as inferior. In their ludicrous dis-cussions and exchanges on every topic imaginable (e.g., women in politics, the Sino-Japanese War, feminism, "the third sex," ultramodern poetry, Chinese and Western poetics, traditional and modern Chinese and Western cuisine), they fully reveal their ignorance and bigotry.

Worse than the above group is the small coterie of professors and administrators at San Lü University. Heading the list of academic charlatans is the president himself, closely followed by his deans and star professors. In Section III, Ch'ien Chung-shu holds these pseudo-intellectuals up to the fluoroscope of his critical intelligence and finds them sterile and absurd, mean and pretentious, deceitful and corrupt, and worse. In this section, he treats with satiric humor the many machinations at work in the intellectual subculture. For instance, the interview between Fang Hung-chien and the president is highly effective in its characterization of the latter. The politician-president is perfidious as he claims he has sent a letter to Fang Hung-chien demoting him from professor to associate professor:

> "Ai! How could you not have gotten it?" Kao sat up straight, his look of feigned surprise carried to perfection and far more natural than Fang's genuine dismay. That Kao hadn't become an actor was a misfortune for the stage and a blessing for the actors. "That letter was very important. Ai! Wartime postal service is simply abominable. But now that you're here, splendid. I can tell you everything directly." . . .
>
> Kao Sung-nien made a gesture of not attaching any importance to the letter, grandly forgiving the letter which he had never written and which Fang Hung-chien had never received. "No use talking about the letter. I'm very much afraid that if you had read the letter, you would not have condescended to accept the appointment. . . ." (p. 199)

President Kao's deans are organization men of the worst kind, men who should know better, men educated in the humanities. The university is a hodgepodge where the emphasis is on compliance with the rules and regulations set forth by the Ministry of Education, and the teachers are all small-minded people armed with phony credentials and ears for gossip and eyes for personal advancement, and this wasteland of insensitivity is found in the middle of a lush, inspiring land of beauty. It is an academic exposé and much of it is humorous and fun to read.

As much as Ch'ien Chung-shu hates the intelligentsia, he is much more scornful of the "talented scholar and beautiful woman" (*ts'ai-tzu chia-jen*) theme pervading much of traditional and modern Chinese literature.[15] What he hopes to achieve in *Fortress Besieged* is to present a sober and realistic view of courtship and marriage and to counteract many of the evil influences perpetuated by that theme. Instead of a larger-than-life hero, he gives us Fang Hung-chien, neither handsome nor talented, who went abroad on the generosity of his "in-laws," and who encounters all sorts of difficulties in life. Further, instead of the faithful and beautiful maiden, Ch'ien presents a gallery of women, none of whom is desirable and some of whom occupy only a minor role in the story, ranging from the crafty Miss Fan to the testy Miss Liu in Section III. Even his heroines, those women who directly affect Fang, are de-idealized. First, he introduces Miss Pao, a woman primarily of the flesh; second, he describes Miss Su as a coquette who uses her coquetry as an instrument of power not only to attract men to herself but to control or disturb the other human relationships around her. In a sense she flirts outrageously, even though she gives lip service to a charming unconventionality. She cannot be content merely to attract one or two suitors; she must measure the degree of her success through the suspicions, jealousy, and anger she can create between Fang Hung-chien and Chao Hsin-mei and others. If Miss Pao and Miss Su are flesh and coquetry, Miss T'ang Hsiao-fu would seem to be apathy personified, despite her willingness to toy with Fang Hung-chien as long as he serves her purpose. Complementing flesh, coquetry, and apathy is the bitchiness of Miss Sun Jou-chia. The four of them form a composite picture of the liberated modern Chinese woman. There is no doubt that Ch'ien's picture of the four women is less than flattering, but this is not to suggest that he hates women; rather, it is his honest way of presenting them as he sees them, without idealization but as human beings with genuine shortcomings.

Insofar as traditional romantic fiction usually ends in a happy marriage, Ch'ien's *Fortress Besieged* ends on a discordant note. As suggested by the French proverb from which the title is taken, marriage is a "besiegement" and not to be confused with bliss. Even the "ideal" marriage between Squire Fang Tung-weng and his wife has its moments of discord, while Chou Hou-ch'ing minces no words describing his complete subjugation by his wife to keep his marriage afloat, and the marriage of Fang Hung-chien and Sun Jou-chia is honestly seen in its earthly limitations. The narrative element of Fang and Sun's "courtship" and "marriage" consists of a rapid succession of small incidents and minor crises that by the principle of accumulation determine their fate.

The disaster of their marriage is the result of a process, not a cataclysm, a process which has its origin in their characters. Both Fang and Sun are well-intentioned but undisciplined and instinctive, and their instincts usually direct them toward self-gratification. From the moment Sun eavesdrops on the conversation between Fang Hung-chien and Chao Hsin-mei in chapter four to her maneuvering Fang to propose to her, from the moment Fang agrees to be engaged to his accepting his friend Chao Hsin-mei's suggestion that he marry Miss Sun in Hong Kong instead of in Shanghai, the disintegrative pattern of their relationship is set.

The author is careful to make clear that neither Sun nor Fang is evil. They are, in fact, both relatively good when compared to the monsters we see elsewhere in the book. It is just that both are passive. Fang, in particular, is without the training, the discipline, and the strength of character necessary for initiating any positive action, which incidentally is also related to his lack of principles as seen in his easy switch from Miss Pao to Miss Su in chapter one, to Miss T'ang and Miss Sun in chapter two. In a real sense, without much thought of his own, he simply allows events to push and prod him along. Without the internal strength to withstand the strains of a shaky marriage and the added burdens of unstable times, the war, his unemployment, the lack of rapport between him and his parents and his in-laws, and the mutual animosity between him and his wife's aunt and family, his marriage has little chance of success from the very beginning.

The account of the disintegration of the Fang marriage is so quietly told, the incidents which by accretion produce the final rupture are individually so small and so normal that it is easy to underestimate the self-destructive power in the relationship from the start. In the face of Fang Hung-chien's lack of action or decisiveness and his verbal lacerations of his wife, it is easy, also, to underestimate Sun Jou-chia's responsibility for the eventual breakup. Like Fang, she is undisciplined, instinctive, and erratic, but her strongest trait, which reveals itself between her sporadic fits of jealousy, is her halfhearted willingness to get along with her husband and his family. But that willingness is too little to counterbalance her immaturity: her convulsive attempts to please her rich aunt and uncle, her compulsive disparagement of her husband, and her lack of interest in her husband's friends or family. Such faults, however, do not necessarily mean irrevocable dissension and separation, and as a matter of fact, Fang makes the necessary adjustments. Except for occasional doubts as to whether he should have married at all, he becomes reasonably content in domesticity. What is most fatal in Sun's character is her inability to accept the conditions of real life and real marriage. She tries to perpetuate the conditions of her courtship and ideal love, even when she no longer believes in them. Having perceived that Fang was not the romantic dream necessary to her marriage, she decides to force that dream upon him through her constant nitpicking. Her unwillingness or inability to see him as he is confronts his incapacity to change the makeup of his character. Consequently, the only logical conclusion possible is the breakup of their marriage.

The author is aware that given a different set of events the marriage of Fang and Sun need not have ended in disaster. Had Fang not been dismissed from San Lü University, had he held a responsible and respectable job in Shanghai or even continued in the position he had, had he lived some distance away from his posturing parents and obnoxious sisters-in-law, had he had more money, had his wife not had to deal with her snobbish relatives, had he not overheard what her aunt said about him, had any of the circumstances been slightly changed, the ending might have been different. Whether the novel could have ended differently, given the facts of the characters of Fang and Sun, we will not speculate, but what is important to the author is that marriage is not to be confused with bliss, that marriage brings lesions and grief. Despite all those who wish to enter into marriage and those who wish to get out of it, little truth about marriage has been told. *Fortress Besieged*, especially in its last section, addresses itself to the complexities of the institution of marriage.

Despite the seriousness and success of the courtship and marriage theme, the crowning achievement of *Fortress Besieged* is the creation of the hero, Fang Hung-chien. It is in Fang that Ch'ien Chung-shu is able fully to suggest the idea of besiegement, and thus make his comment on the condition of modern man. Fang is not a hero in any sense of the word. At best, he is comical, bumptious, often self-contradictory, and occasionally roguish in the first half of the novel and self-pitying in the second. As a typical twentieth-century Chinese born into a traditional family, the die has been cast for him from birth. He is expected to go to college, to study abroad, and to attain social prominence, which means official position and wealth. He finds a constant reminder of what is expected of him in his pedantic and moralistic father. Obviously his father has measured up to those standards with great vigor, having passed his academic examinations at an early age and being a much respected man in his hometown and the head of a large and traditional family in which three generations live together under one roof. No less demanding of Fang Hung-chien are his "in-laws," the Chous. They not only demand that he be a good investment for them by bringing home a diploma from abroad; they also expect him to be at their beck and call. When they find him falling below their expectations, they invite him to leave. Similarly, his wife's relatives expect the same from him, and when he fails them, his wife's aunt calls him a man of "no ability" but with a "terrific temper" (p. 355).

If his relatives are less than understanding, others are much more callous and unsympathetic. Heading the list is the president of San Lü University, who is much more menacing than his father or his "father-in-law" or his wife's aunt. While his father and "father-in-law" have not been able to probe into his false credentials, President Kao has no such difficulty. Kao first demotes him and then refuses to renew his contract for the next academic year. Moreover, Fang's colleagues at San Lü University make his life miserable; his every word and deed is monitored and misinterpreted to his disadvantage. His boss in the Shanghai newspaper office is only too willing to see him sacrifice his job as a gesture of support for the outgoing boss himself.

In short, everywhere Fang turns, he finds his options narrowing. The open space on the deck of the *Vicomte de Bragelonne* finally contracts itself to Fang's tiny apartment in Shanghai. After his wife has abandoned him, he opens the door to the bedroom, he stands there in a daze, mind and body too dulled to feel angry or upset. " 'All right,' he said spitefully, 'you're free to go off and leave me. Get the hell out, your mother's egg! All of you, get the hell out of my sight!' " (p. 361). What is left is the old ancestral clock, which begins chiming away as though it has stored up half a day's time for the still of night to carefully ring it out, counting, "one, two, three, four, five, six." Fang is alone.

The aloneness of Fang is Ch'ien Chung-shu's statement about the condition of modern man. What Fang has finally achieved out of his personal failures is debatable—perhaps nothing at all. The inability of Fang to learn much from his experience is a testament to Ch'ien's art. Had Fang learned as much as other protagonists in traditional initiation stories, this whole novel would have lost much of its credibility. Fang, to the very end, remains in character. His inability to comprehend his wife's desertion is much akin to his puzzlement over Miss Pao's behavior in chapter one. Just as he went to look for other means of pleasure in the person of Miss Su in chapter one, he will go to find Chao Hsin-mei in the interior as a means of forgetting his unpleasant past. What Fang demonstrates is insensitivity and the animal instinct to survive as best he can, while not understanding what he's trying to do.

Despite Fang's unattractiveness as a hero (having failed to achieve illumination from his own tragedy and denying us a neat analysis of his character), the author's sympathy is clearly with him, for Ch'ien Chung-shu feels a man is responsible neither for the evils the world puts in his path nor for the weak nature heredity may have given him. By portraying Fang without idealization, Ch'ien has given us a real person, one with whom many of us can identify, and it is precisely the creation of such a vulnerable, pitiable, average man that makes *Fortress Besieged* a sobering commentary on what it means to be an ordinary twentieth-century educated Chinese living in a time of war, in a time when old and new ideas and concepts clash, and besieged by forces which he cannot fully understand. Fang Hung-chien is not merely Fang Hung-chien himself, he is contemporary man. The pressures he faces are those that were faced by his contemporaries in the 1930s. In this sense, Fang is not only an individual but also a representative of his class.

Fortress Besieged is a book of many things. It makes us laugh at its dense populace of every social type imaginable. But beyond the mirth and liveliness, Ch'ien Chung-shu also wants us to see the follies, vices, and stupidities of men everywhere; and when we do, the laughter that has been evoked is abruptly silenced. The surface of the book is comic, but at its core we find a relentless satire of twentieth-century Chinese intellectuals, a sobering commentary on the true nature of courtship and marriage, and the sympathetic portrayal of one man, in whom we find a little bit of each of us.

NKM

Notes

CHAPTER ONE

1. A reference to the French Concession in Shanghai, an area outside the jurisdiction of the Chinese.

2. A game usually played by four persons with 144 dominolike pieces or tiles marked in suits, counters, and dice. The tiles are drawn and discarded until one player secures a winning combination of four sets of three tiles and a pair.

3. The Chinese dress refers to *ch'a-p'ao*, which has a high collar that usually fits close to the neck.

4. A popular saying which indicates that those destined to be married to each other, though a thousand *li* apart, are drawn together by a single thread. *Li* is a measure of length reckoned at 360 paces or about 1,890 feet English measure.

5. Su Tung-p'o (1036–1101): a celebrated Chinese poet, essayist, painter, and calligrapher of the Sung dynasty. His sister, Su Hsiao-mei, probably a legendary figure, is reputed to have been equally talented.

6. The traditional Chinese civil examination system offered three academic degrees, which were conducted at three different levels—the county (or prefecture), the province, and the national capital. Successful candidates at these three levels were known respectively as *hsiu-ts'ai*, *chü-jen*, and *chin-shih*. For a quick reference, see Y. W. Ma and Joseph S. M. Lau, eds., *Traditional Chinese Stories: Themes and Variations* (New York: Columbia University Press, 1978), p. xvi.

7. The land south of the Yangtze River in eastern China is known as the cultural and political center of China, noted for the glitter of its cities and the lush green of its countryside.

8. Literally, "Turn-to-gold-at-a-touch Bank." From the Taoist story of a man who could turn stones to gold by a touch of his finger, comparable to the "Midas touch."

9. A festival ("Clear and Bright"), usually around April 5, during which the Chinese worship at the graves.

10. Literally, to lament the autumn—to regret the passing of the summer of life. An allusion from *Songs of the South* (*Ch'u tz'u*), a collection of poems associated with the state of Ch'u to the south in the Yangtze Valley. The earliest of the Ch'u poems are probably not any older than the third century B.C.

11. Literally, to harbor the amorous thoughts of spring. An allusion from the *Book of Odes* (*Shih ching*), a collection of 305 songs dating from about 1100 to 600 B.C. The arrangement is attributed to Confucius, who considered the book a model of poetic expression.

12. Literally, "just like the old frontiersman losing a horse, who knows but that which seems a misfortune may be a blessing in disguise."

13. A huge collection of manuscripts dating from before A.D. 1000, found in rock caves near Tun-huang in China. Many of the manuscripts were acquired by the British archaeologist Aurel Stein, who took them to London in 1908. The French sinologist Paul Pelliot took another batch of them to Paris later in the same year.

14. A compendium of over 11,000 volumes containing excerpts and complete works on the Confucian canon, history, philosophy, and the arts and sciences, compiled from 1403 to 1408 under the commission of the Ming emperor Ch'eng-tsu.

15. Records related to the T'ai-p'ing rebellion in the middle of the nineteenth century. The rebellion was led by Hung Hsiu-ch'uan (1813–1864), who in 1851 proclaimed the T'ai-p'ing Heavenly Kingdom and took for himself the title of emperor. He captured Nanking on March 8, 1853, and was not defeated by the Manchu government until the summer of 1864.

16. The original incident as recorded in the *Analects* (*Lun yü*) is as follows: "Ju Pei wanted to see Master K'ung [Confucius]. Master K'ung excused himself on the ground of ill health. But when the man who had brought the message was going out through the door, he took up his zither and sang, taking good care that the messenger should hear." See *The Analects of Confucius*, translated and annotated by Arthur Waley (New York: Vintage, 1938), p. 214. The *Analects* is one of the cardinal books of Chinese literature and thought, memorized and studied for many centuries.

17. Mencius was Confucius' most famous follower and lived from 372 to 289 B.C. Mencius' sayings, entitled simply *Mencius*, concur with most of Confucius' basic ideas, such as the importance of the people and the concept of the humane and righteous king as the fundamental answer to all questions of government. Moreover, Mencius believed that human beings had a tendency to do good, and that anyone might become a Sage Yao or Shun, a perfect man. The incident referred to in the text is from *Mencius*. King Hsüan of Ch'i asked Mencius if the latter would come to see him, since the king was indisposed. Mencius said he could not, because he was not well himself (this was a lie).

18. In Manchu times (Ch'ing dynasty) government officials were selected from holders of academic degrees. But it was also possible to purchase an academic title; for those who did, the title was important because it "admitted them to gentry status and privileges and was an opening for further advancement and official position." For details, see Chung-li Chang, *The Chinese Gentry* (Seattle: University of Washington Press, 1967).

19. Miss Su's dissertation, *Eighteen Colloquial Poets of China*, is an imitation of *The Anthology of Eighteen Poets* (*Shih-ba-chia shih-ch'ao*), an impressive collection of the works of such eminent poets as Li Po, Tu Fu, Li Shang-yin, and others.

20. The author implies that the Japanese are highly imitative people, and hence the Japanese have no culture of their own to speak of.

21. A standard description of a woman who appears cold and stern. It usually describes a virtuous maiden or widow.

22. Mandarin heavily marked with the Cantonese accent. Cantonese people are known for their inability to speak Mandarin well.

23. An affectionate form of address among friends, usually older to younger.

24. Literally, "someone beautiful enough to be eaten."

25. When a person is dismissed from his employment in a shop or store, he has to pack his own bedding. Hence, "packing the bedding" is synonymous with dismissal from work.

26. Victoria Peak on Hong Kong island is noted for its spectacular view of Hong Kong harbor.

27. An area in Hong Kong noted for its sandy beaches and the old Repulse Bay Hotel. It was formerly an exclusive area for the rich.

CHAPTER TWO

1. The original reads "*p'o-p'o ma-ma*," an expression which describes a fastidious "granny-type" person, very much interested in minor or unimportant details.

2. "*Kan nü-erh*" is an adopted daughter. A daughter can be "adopted," however, without going through any of the complicated legal process, and this type of adoption carries no legal or financial obligations.

3. "*Kan-ma*": adopted mother. "Adoption" can take place as described in note 2.

4. Literally, "ears that catch the wind." Metaphorically, the expression describes someone who hears all the gossip.

5. One of the most prestigious universities in China.

6. Literally, "the throat and tongue of the people." Metaphorically, the expression refers to a newspaper that represents the best interests of the people.

7. Literally, "a straight pen counsels." A conventional phrase used to describe a newspaper.

8. *A Collection of Ambiguous Chinese Words*: a book about Chinese words by Sun Hsing-yen (1753–1818).

9. *Miscellaneous Manuscripts of Kuei-ssu*: a work by Yü Cheng-hsieh (1775–1840) printed in the Kuei-ssu year (1833), containing a selection of the author's miscellaneous works on history, anthropology, folklore, geography, and the classics.

10. *A Collection of the Seven Classic Tower*: "Seven Classic Tower" is the studio name of the Manchu scholar Chiang Hsiang-nan. Presumably, this book is a collection of his works.

11. *A Record of Talks by the Sea*: a sketch by Yüan Tzu-chih (1827–1898). After returning from Europe, Yüan wrote this record of his observations.

12. Literally, "clasp the feet of Buddha." The idiom means that when some-

one gets into trouble through lack of due preparation, he seeks help at the last critical moment.

13 Cheng Ho (1371–1433): a eunuch who distinguished himself as a military officer. In 1405 he sailed from China with a large fleet to cruise along the coasts of Cambodia and Siam. His mission was to demand tribute from those countries, but others say he undertook the journey to search for the vanished Emperor Hui Ti. In 1408 and 1412 he led expeditions to many other countries of southeastern Asia, going as far as Ceylon, and persuaded those countries to send envoys back with him to China. In 1425 he was appointed chief commandant in Nanking. In 1430 he and his lieutenants visited seventeen countries, including Hormuz in the Persian Gulf.

14. *Collected Statutes of the Ming*: a compendium of administrative lore, presented in 1510 to the Ming dynasty.

15. Hsü Chih-mo (1895–1931): generally recognized as the greatest Chinese poet of the early twentieth century. In the ten years of his productive life he espoused a total liberation of man's soul, man's pursuit of beauty and of love. He was much influenced by Swinburne, Rossetti, and Thomas Hardy.

16. Cheng-te period (1506–1521): title of the period of the reign of Emperor Wu-tsung of the Ming dynasty.

17. A campaign by Chiang Kai-shek to bring about the moral regeneration of China during the years 1934–1937 in order to oppose Communism and achieve national unity. He urged the people to practice the four traditional virtues: politeness, integrity, self-respect, and righteousness.

18. One of the fiercest battles between the Chinese and the Japanese during the second Sino-Japanese War. On August 13, 1937, the fighting began in Shanghai. The Chinese forces valiantly defended the entrenched positions until their flank was exposed by a surprise Japanese attack in Hangchow Bay in early November; the Japanese later captured Shanghai and rolled on toward Nanking.

19. Literally, "that this person should have this disease." It suggests inevitability.

20. A reference to the Japanese attack on Shanghai on January 28, 1932. Chapei, a suburb of Shanghai, was the first target, and the battle lasted for six weeks.

21. An expression which describes superlative beauty; it is equivalent to Helen of Troy in Western literature.

22. Friedrich von Logau (1604–1655): a German epigrammatist whose epigrams appeared in two collections (1638, 1654).

23. A reference to the cities in the interior of China, as distinguished from the coastal cities.

24. People noted for their righteousness and moral rectitude.

25. A broker or middleman, held in contempt by the intellectuals in Chinese society in the early part of the twentieth century.

26. English words in the original novel are italicized throughout.

27. When a person does not have a son, he may have his son-in-law live with him and his family. When such a situation occurs, he usually provides room and board and other incidental expenses to his son-in-law.

28. Ch'eng-hua (1465–1487) and Hsüan-te (1426–1435): titles of the reigns of Emperors Hsien-tsung and Hsüan-tsung of the Ming dynasty. K'ang-hsi (1662–1722): title of the reign of the second emperor of the Ch'ing dynasty. The first two reigns span a significant period in the development of Chinese porcelain.

The third, K'ang-hsi, is the period during which Chinese porcelain is considered to have reached its full glory.

29. Incantation appealing to the White Goddess of Mercy, also known as Kuan Yin, the protectress of women and children, the bestower of children, and the all-compassionate mother-goddess. There are numberless Chinese legends and stories about her origin, life, and activities.

30. Most intimate friends. In the tradition of Chinese knights-errant, those who are sworn brothers pledge loyalty and dedication to one another. Naturally, not all those who claim to be sworn brothers actually live up to these ideals.

31. A total of 32 games. Four games constitute a round. Within each round, each of the four players will have a chance to be the banker, except when the banker himself has won the game. When that happens, he remains as banker and additional games are played until another player wins the game.

32. A colloquial expression for job.

33. An expression which means a good-for-nothing, a person who does no more than consume rice.

34. A play on the expression, "Raise the tray to the eyebrows," which connotes mutual respect between husband and wife.

35. Titles of the most famous early Chinese novels. *Romance of the Three Kingdoms* (*San-kuo chih yen-i*) is probably the most popular historical narrative in China. It describes the conflicts between the kingdoms of Wei, Shu, and Wu during the Three Kingdoms period (220–280), and it is attributed to Lo Kuan-chung (1330–1400). At about the same time that the earliest surviving version of the *Romance of the Three Kingdoms* appeared, the *Tale of the Marshes* (*Shui-hu chuan*) became available. Attributed to either Lo Kuan-chung or Shih Nai-an and written in a far more colloquial language than the *Romance*, the *Tale of the Marshes* deals with the exploits of a band of outlaws of the early twelfth century. In addition to the *Romance* and the *Tale of the Marshes*, there is *Journey to the West* (*Hsi-yu chi*), known to English readers as *Monkey*. The work is attributed to Wu Ch'eng-en (1506–1582). It recounts the pilgrimage of the famous and revered monk Hsüan-tsang (596–664), also known as Tripitaka, who journeyed to India in the seventh century to bring back 657 items of Buddhist scriptures.

CHAPTER THREE

1. Sentimental *tz'u* poetry. The most familiar themes in *tz'u* poetry (popular during the T'ang dynasty, Five Dynasties, and the Sung dynasty) were romantic love, love mingled with nostalgia and regret, or groundless melancholy and ennui. For a more detailed discussion, see James J. Y. Liu, "Literary Qualities of the Lyric (Tz'u)," in *Studies in Chinese Literary Genres*, ed. by Cyril Birch (Berkeley: University of California Press, 1974), pp. 133–153.

2. Huang Shan-ku: alternative name for Huang T'ing-chien (1050–1110), distinguished poet and calligrapher of the Sung dynasty. Shen Tzu-p'ei: alternative name for Shen Tseng-chih (1850–1922), scholar and poet of Ch'ing dynasty.

3. Zen: a form of Buddhism developed in China as Ch'an, which was transplanted to Japan. It became a fad among the American Beatniks in the 1960s. It upholds the direct, mystical experiences of reality through maturing of an inner experience.

4. To be listed among successful candidates in government examinations.

385

5. *Ch'un ch'iu*: chronicles of significant events taking place during the reign of the twelve rulers of Lu, the native state of Confucius, the compiler, between the years 722 and 481 B.C. The events are recounted in extremely brief, almost cryptic style, but with subtle moral judgments passed, such as by means of selection or omission.

6. When Nanking, the Chinese capital, was lost to the Japanese in December 1937, the Nationalist Government moved its capital to Chungking, Szechwan province.

7. An allusion from *Mencius*. See note 17, Chapter One.

8. According to the ancient art of physiognomy in China, a person's fortune can be told by assessing his facial features, body build, resonance of voice, coloring, etc. The five planets designate different parts of the face. For example, the fire planet (Mars) refers to the forehead area. Body builds are divided into five primary elements: wood, water, metal, earth, and fire, i.e., "wood-shaped" is tall and thin; "earth-shaped" is thick and heavy, etc. Similarly, the eyes, ears, nose, mouth, eyebrows, etc., are classified according to shape with each shape denoted by a descriptive term. These features are all considered signs of certain designated fortunes or traits of character, such as longevity, prosperity, intelligence, suspiciousness, etc. Hsin-mei's features all point to wealth and high government position.

The Taoist in the Hemp Robe was a monk of Sung times noted for his ability as a physiognomist.

9. A *yamen* is a magistrate's office or a civil or military court, and a mandarin in premodern times wielded enormous power and came and went as he pleased.

10. Reference to the withdrawal of the Nationalist Government from Nanking in December 1937, during the second Sino-Japanese War.

11. It is customary for the Chinese to address elderly men as uncles. In the present case, Mr. Shen is a friend of Miss Su, and hence it is proper for him to refer to her father as uncle.

12. A slogan popular among the politicians and students in early twentieth-century China.

13. Founder of the Ch'ing dynasty (Manchu), which ruled China for 268 years from 1644 to 1912.

14. It is customary to call a friend, a colleague, or even a stranger of your own age "brother."

15. "Rice gruel" means sweet and flattering words. When "rice gruel is poured down the wrong ear," it means the flattery has not achieved its desired effect and has possibly backfired, or it has been said to the wrong person.

16. A legendary emperor of China (2838–2698 B.C.), supposed to have introduced agricultural and herbal medicine to China.

17. Term of address of a servant for the young mistress of the house. The daughter of the family is usually identified as "Hsiao-chieh" (young lady) to and by the servants.

18. Chia Tao (779–849): a famous poet of the T'ang dynasty. He began his life as a monk, and after a short, undistinguished political career, he spent the last years of his life as a minor government official. His body was reputed to be large and his early poetry "affected the bizarre exaggerations of the age, even more so than most, so that his poetic daring became something of a joke." See Liu Wu-chi and Irving Lo, eds., *Sunflower Splendor* (Bloomington: Indiana University Press, 1975), p. 570, for further details.

19. Excellent papers for painting or calligraphy were produced in Hsüan-ch'eng, Anhui province. The Jung-pao Printing House may still be in existence in Peking.

20. The Italian here may be a typographical error. The translators were not able to decipher what the author had in mind.

21. Li I-shan: also known as Li Shang-yin (813–858), born in Honan province. Most of his extant poems, numbering about six hundred, are ambiguous, often untitled, and deal with clandestine love.

22. Ch'ang O: the name of a legendary lady who stole the drug of immortality from her husband and fled with it to the moon, where she became the Goddess of the Moon.

23. A round diagram representing the yin (female) and yang (male) elements.

24. Literally, "unwilling even to pluck a single hair—for others."

25. Literally, "to paint the clouds and shade the moon." A technique in art to present the outstanding feature by making it contrast with everything else.

26. In correcting essays or compositions, Chinese language teachers frequently used a writing brush and starred the parts they considered excellent in red ink.

27. See note 11, Chapter One.

28. Huang Chung-tse: alternative name for Huang Chin-jen (1749–1783), one of the most famous poets of the Ch'ing dynasty. Impoverished during his lifetime, he was widely recognized for his poetic talents after his death. By 1793 there were two editions of his works in print. Kung Ting-an: alternative name for Kung Tzu-chen (1792–1841). A child prodigy, he wrote some of his poems at the age of fifteen. He was a prolific writer, but only a small amount of his prose and poetry are extant.

29. Ch'ien-lung (1736–1795) and Chia-ch'ing (1796–1820): the reign titles of the fourth and fifth emperors of the Ch'ing dynasty.

30. T'ung-chih (1862–1874) and Kuang-hsü (1875–1907): the reign titles of the eighth and ninth emperors of the Ch'ing dynasty.

31. A familiar term of address among friends. Often used with a surname in reference to a man, indicating friendship or mild affection.

32. Lu-shan: located to the south of Kiukiang county in Kianghsi province. Facing water on three sides and land on one side, it was the location of Chiang Kai-shek's summer residence during the second Sino-Japanese War.

33. Ch'en San-yüan: alternative name for Ch'en San-li (1852–1937), a well-known poet and essayist of the late Ch'ing dynasty.

34. Yang Chi (1334–1383): a Ming poet and minor painter.

35. Ch'i-chüeh: verse form of four lines with seven characters to a line which follows a very strict rhyme scheme and tonal pattern.

36. Chen-yüan (785–805): the reign title for Emperor Te-tsung of the T'ang dynasty.

37. Wine was kept in urns and sold by weight in Chinese restaurants. One catty would be equivalent to 1⅓ pounds.

38. An allusion to a T'ang poem. The poem encourages the reader to be hedonistic.

39. A brand of green tea from Hangchow.

40. From the story of Chu Mai-ch'en of the Han dynasty, whose wife left him because she could not stand his poverty. Later he rose to a high position through diligent study, and his wife, who was by then destitute, begged to re-

join him, but he replied, "If you can pick up spilt water, you may return." She then went away and hanged herself.

41. An expression meaning to retie a loose marriage knot, used to refer to a divorcée who marries the same person again.

42. A reference to a story in the *Romance of the Three Kingdoms* in which Chu-kuo Liang, left to defend a town with no soldiers, feigned nonchalance by playing music in the tower on the town walls to give the enemy commander the impression that the town was confident and well prepared for an attack.

43. Wang Yang-ming (1472–1529): a scholar, official, and influential philosopher of the Ming dynasty. A Neo-Confucianist, Wang and others severely attacked Buddhism for mistaking concrete reality for emptiness and Buddhists as unjust and cowardly, because they worked for their own interests and avoided social responsibility.

44. Su Man-shu (1884–1918): a Chinese poet, novelist, and translator, born in Japan of a Japanese mother and a Chinese father.

45. Huang Tsun-hsien (1848–1905): a Chinese poet, essayist, and diplomat. He served for a long time in London and America and brought into his poetry contemporary political and social developments.

46. Literally, "two-haired," a name given to those Chinese who associated with foreigners, who were known as the "hairy ones."

47. Most of these are well-known poets of the T'ang and Sung dynasties, the greatest eras of Chinese poetry. Their alternative names are given with their dates: Tu Shao-ling (Tu Fu, 712–770); Wang Kuang-ling (Wang Ling, 1032–1059); Mei Yüan-ling (Mei Yao-ch'en, 1002–1060); Li Ch'ang-ku (Li Ho, 791–817).

48. Huang Shan-ku: alternative name for Huang T'ing-chien (1045–1105). A native of Kianghsi province, he was a poet and calligrapher and the founder of the Kianghsi school of poetry. A victim of political dissensions, he was exiled several times and died in exile. He wrote more than two thousand poems.

49. Li I-shan (Li Shang-yin, 813–858); Wang Pan-shan (Wang An-shih, 1021–1086); Ch'en Hou-shan (Ch'en Shih-tao, 1053–1102); Yüan I-shan (Yüan Hao-wen, 1190–1257).

50. Name of a collection of the poetry of Ch'en San-yüan, published in 1909.

51. Mei Sheng-yü: alternative name for Mei Yao-ch'en (1002–1060). He was a scholar-bureaucrat and a major poet in the development of Sung poetry. Liu K'e-chuang (1187–1269) called Mei "the founding father of the poetry of this dynasty."

52. Yang Ta-yen: a general of the Later Wei dynasty who became so awesome for his sweeping victories that children would immediately stop crying at the very mention of his name.

53. Two missing words in the original have been supplied by the translators.

54. A popular brand of ointment that was thought to cure headaches, dizziness, and other ailments.

55. In English in the original.

CHAPTER FOUR

1. One of the Confucian canonical texts, the *Book of History* (*Shu ching*) is the earliest historical writing; it is a collection of statements, proclamations, and dialogues of eminent rulers and officials. It represents in general a rationalization of historical events into pseudohistory.

2. Maidservants are usually addressed as "Mama" this or that.

3. In fortunetelling a man's horoscope may be "colliding" with his fiancée's or spouse's. In such a case his fiancée or spouse may die prematurely because of the "clash" of the horoscopes.

4. The five organs are the heart, the lungs, the liver, the kidneys, and the stomach. The seven orifices in the human head are eyes, ears, nostrils, and mouth.

5. *The Book of Change*: a work of great antiquity which was used as a book of divination. It has two parts, one of which is an omen text giving rhymed interpretations of ordinary country omens and bearing some resemblance to peasant lore of other countries. The other part of the te..t is a divination manual containing formulae such as those that have been deciphered on the oracle bones and tortoise shells.

6. Hsün Tzu (298 B.C.): an early philosopher who held that the nature of man is not good but evil, that there exists the need for a firm authority.

7. "Fei-hsiang": the title of a chapter in *Hsün Tzu* (the principal work of Hsün Tzu), in which he argued against judging a man by his physical appearance, naming Confucius and other great sages as examples of men who, though ugly in appearance, achieved great success.

8. Among the writers cited by the author, the best-known are Ssu-ma Hsiang-ju and Fan Yeh. Ssu-ma Hsiang-ju (179–117 B.C.) was a noted *fu* writer. The *fu* is an essay in varied verse with prose introduction and interludes. The generic name of *fu* is "rhyme-prose." Fan Yeh (398–445) was distinguished for learning and literary ability from early youth and is best known for his compilation of the *History of the Eastern Han Dynasty* while he was serving as a mandarin in Anhui province.

9. *Feng-shen yen-i*: a Ming novel about the legendary story of the first king of the Chou dynasty and his generals. Contains many colorful exploits of demigods, Buddhas, immortals, and fabulous creatures who took one side or the other. Fang Pi and Fang Hsiang were two generals.

10. "Fei-kung" (nonaggression): the title of a chapter in *Mo Tzu*, the principal work of the philosopher Mo Tzu (470?–391? B.C.), who expounded the doctrine of universal love and whose ideas generally challenged Confucian doctrine.

11. Chiang T'ai-kung: chief counselor to King Wen of the 11th to 12th centuries B.C. The term "Fei-hsiung" (No Bear) comes from the following story. One day when King Wen was about to go out hunting, he was told by the divining stalks that his quarry would not be a dragon, leopard, tiger, or bear but a king's counselor. He later came across an old man fishing with a straight piece of iron instead of a hook upon which the fish readily allowed themselves to be hooked. He entered into conversation with him, and finding his responses wise, he brought him home and made him chief counselor.

(557–645), one of China's greatest calligraphers. "Nine-palace" is the name of

12. "Fei-yen": the title of a main character in a T'ang *ch'uan-ch'i* tale of the same name. A T'ang *ch'uan-ch'i* is a tale written in the literary language about marvelous and fantastic experiences. The genre flourished between the mid-eighth and mid-ninth centuries.

13. A play on words; because of his lack of skill, he has "killed off" the people of one of the four corners.

14. Traditionally, officialdom and medicine were held up as goals for the

389

service-minded scholars. If a scholar couldn't pass his civil examinations, the next thing he might want to do would be to become a good physician, so that he could render service to the people.

15. In the nineteen thirties in China, the subject of traditional Chinese versus Western medicine was a popular theme in fiction.

16. *Ching-hua yüan*: a satiric novel by Li Ju-chen (1763–1830), a scholar-novelist. In a number of respects its form resembles *Gulliver's Travels* in which the author, like Swift, used the travels of his protagonist to strange lands beyond the seas for criticizing and satirizing Chinese customs and institutions.

17. In English in the original.

18. Dragon Boat Festival: On the fifth day of the fifth lunar month.

19. Two oft-quoted lines from a four-line poem by Yüan Chen (779–831) of the T'ang dynasty. The clouds of Wu Mountain in Szechwan province are considered the most beautiful in the world.

20. A Western-style apartment usually has a separate living room, dining room, and bathroom, whereas individual rooms are not partitioned off in Chinese-style apartments.

21. The style of calligraphy named after its originator, Ou-yang Hsün (557–645) one of China's greatest calligraphers. "Nine-palace" is the name of a stone tablet on which is carved the most famous sample of his calligraphy.

22. Li Tung-ch'üan: alternative name for Li Shu-ku, a Ch'ing dynasty poet and painter.

23. An allusion to a poem by T'ao Yuan-ming (365–427), a celebrated poet of the Six Dynasties period. The first four lines of the poem read as follows: "I built my hut among the worlds of man,/Yet near me no noise of horse or coach was heard,/You ask how that is possible?/When the heart is detached, one's place becomes distant. . . ."

24. Since Chao is Miss Sun's father's friend, it is therefore customary for Miss Sun to address Chao as uncle, even though Chao may not be much older than Miss Sun herself.

25. A Chinese unit of area equal to 806.65 square yards.

26. Be neglected or ignored.

27. Old Lady Hsü: an attractive middle-aged woman, from the story of Lady Hsü, a concubine of Emperor Yüan of the Liang dynasty, who carried on amorous affairs even when she was quite old.

28. Po Yi and Shu Ch'i: a celebrated pair of brothers who lived in the twelfth century B.C. at the end of the Yin dynasty. When the Yin was overthrown and the new Chou dynasty established, they refused to change their allegiance and wandered away into the mountains, declaring they would not support themselves with the grain of Chou, eating wild seeds instead and eventually dying of cold and hunger. They were later extolled by Confucius for their steadfast purity of mind.

CHAPTER FIVE

1. Tseng Kuo-fang (1811–1872): a great statesman, general, and scholar of the Ch'ing dynasty.

2. Also known as Yüeh-chü (Chekiang opera) or alternately as Sheng-hsien hsi (The Theater of Sheng County), the Shaohsing opera originated in the late years of the Ch'ing dynasty. It arose in Shaohsing, in Sheng county, in Chekiang province; the plays were based entirely on folk tunes, accompanied by only a

clapper (pan). The opera became extremely popular in Shanghai. Next to the Peking opera, it is the most popular of all types of Chinese drama.

3. A composition with eight "legs" or sections. The first section has two sentences and sums up the composition's most important points. The second is an expansion of the first. The third is the introduction of the main section. The fourth and fifth provide the topic's contrasting aspects, leading to the sixth section, the body of the composition. While the seventh is a continuation of the sixth, the eighth is the conclusion. The length of the essay is usually two to three hundred words. During the Ch'ing dynasty, the ability to write an excellent "eight-legged" essay was a fundamental requirement in passing civil service examinations.

4. A fabulous ruler of ancient China, said to have discovered fire.

5. The second Sino-Japanese War, 1937–1945.

6. *Ju-lin wai-shih*: literally, the unofficial history of Confucian scholars, a satiric work of officialdom written from 1743 to 1750 by Wu Ching-tzu (1701–1754).

7. A reference to *Tathagata*, a Buddhist term, frequently used by the Buddha when referring to himself; the meaning is literally "he who has thus come or arrived."

8. A system of classifying Chinese characters is based on numbers assigned to ten different kinds of strokes. A four-digit number can be derived from the types of stroke found in the four corners of each character.

9. Tu Fu (712–770): one of China's greatest poets.

10. Yatron is the brand name for chiniofon, a medicine used for treating amebiasis; cinchona, also called Jesuits' bark or Peruvian bark, is used for treating malaria; sulfate of quinine is medicine used as a febrifuge, antimalarial, antiperiodic, and bitter tonic; formamint is a medicated drop for treating pharyngitis.

11. Pine, bamboo, and plum flower are traditionally known as the "three companions of winter."

12. The Chinese stage is normally rather bare, with no more than a carpet, table, and two chairs. The significance of the action is portrayed not by elaborate and heavy stage properties but by a highly complex set of formal, symbolic gestures and portable objects. For instance, by carrying a riding whip with heavy silk tassels, an actor indicates he is riding a horse, and a formal upward kick represents the motion of mounting a horse.

13. The saying is from the *Confucian Analects*, IX, 12. "Tse-kung said, 'There is a beautiful gem here. Should I lay it up in a case and keep it? Or should I seek a good price and sell it?' The master said, 'Sell it; sell it! But I would wait for one to offer the price.'" (James Legge's translation; New York: Dover, 1893).

14. Meng Ch'ang-chün (d. 279): a native of the state of Ch'i. When he was put in prison, one of his retainers, who could steal like a dog, was able to steal a fur robe for the King's favorite concubine. She then persuaded the King to release Meng Ch'ang-chün. Later the King changed his mind and sent a courier after him. Meng would have been stopped at the frontier gate, which was not opened until cockcrow, had not another retainer, who could crow like a cock, been able to have the gate opened for Meng.

15. To many superstitious people a woman is considered "unclean," and hence no woman should sit on any food that goes into the mouth.

16. The fire in Ch'ang-sha was one of many episodes as the war in China took a turn for the worse in 1937. There was the fall of Nanking on December 13,

and later the occupation of major cities such as Tsingtao, Hangchow, and others by the Japanese.

17. In wartime China credit was hard to establish. Hence to prove one's identity or to cash a check, a shop or store was required to affix its seal to guarantee the person's identity or the check's validity.

18. Mint-flavored sugar pellets.

CHAPTER SIX

1. From *The Great Learning* (*Ta hsüeh*), one of the Four Books read by all educated Chinese. It contains short philosophical sections from the *Book of Rites* (*Li chi*) on key Confucian ideas.

2. *Ping fa*: a compilation on the subject of war and stratagem accredited to Sun Tzu, who probably lived in the early fourth century B.C.

3. T'ang San-tsang (596–664), also known as Hsüan-tsang and Tripitaka, was a Chinese Buddhist priest who journeyed to India, where he visited its holy places, and brought back over six hundred copies of the sacred books of Buddhism. In 645, when he returned to China after an absence of seventeen years, he was received with public honors. See also note 35, Chapter Two.

4. The original expression, "not sharing the same sky," refers to irreconcilable enemies who hate each other so much they can't live under the same sky. The author is poking fun at Lu's slick hair.

5. Each year is represented by an animal (i.e., rat, ox, tiger, hare, dragon, snake, horse, sheep, monkey, cock, dog, and boar) and the complete cycle repeats itself once every twelve years. Hence it is possible to know another person's age simply by asking him what his animal sign is.

6. The most powerful executive branch of the Chinese Nationalist Government, with jurisdiction over many important ministries, such as the Ministry of Foreign Affairs, the Ministry of Defense, the Ministry of Finance, the Ministry of Education, and others.

7. The cone-shaped hat was worn by officials in ancient times. "To throw away the cone-shaped hat" means to resign one's position.

8. A commemorative meeting every Monday in memory of Sun Yat-sen (1866–1925), the founder of modern China, during which announcements are read, the national anthem is sung, and plans are made for the rest of the week.

9. Fang Hsiao-ju (1357–1402): a scholar and tutor to the sons of Emperor Hui-ti, second emperor of the Ming dynasty. When this emperor disappeared under mysterious circumstances, Fang refused to serve the new emperor, Ch'eng-tsu. For this Fang was cut to pieces in the marketplace and his family was exterminated to the last branch.

10. The palace grounds in the city of Peking.

11. *Sterculia platanifolia*: It is sometimes called the national tree of China; the trunk is straight and the leaves are beautifully green. It is said to be the only tree on which the phoenix will rest.

CHAPTER SEVEN

1. A delightful old figure, easily recognizable by his domed head, and the peach he invariably carries. His long beard and staff denote his old age, and the peach, which he holds, is culled from a miraculous tree that blossoms every

three thousand years and bears fruit three thousand years later. He is sometimes depicted as surrounded by mushrooms, which confer immortality. So far he has survived political change and enjoys enormous popularity in Chinese art.

2. Someone tall and thin in body build. See also note 8, Chapter Three.

3. Ts'ao Yü (real name Wan Chia-po), born in 1905 in Hupeh province, is considered the greatest writer of modern Chinese drama (hua-chü). His best plays were written between 1933 and 1940. His first was *Thunderstorm* (*Lei-yü*, 1933), followed by *Sunrise* (*Jih ch'u*, 1935), and others.

4. *Loso*: A transcription of the word "Rousseau," it also means to talk incessantly and tediously.

5. Chinese chess is similar to Western chess. But the game is played on the lines, not on the squares. The European pawn, castle, knight, bishop, and king are matched in their moves by the Chinese soldier, chariot, horse, minister, and king, and the object of both games is the same.

6. The Confucian ideal of the perfect gentleman.

7. The Chinese is "Fang po-po." "Po-po" generally refers to the elder brother of one's father, even though in some areas in China the term also means "father."

8. The Chinese is "Fang ku-fu." "Ku-fu" is the husband of the father's sister, and its English equivalent is "paternal uncle."

9. A wife is addressed as "fu-jen," while the word for concubine is "ju fu-jen," meaning literally, "like a 'fu-jen.'"

10. A couplet by Tseng Kuo-fang. See also note 1, Chapter Five.

CHAPTER EIGHT

1. The Chinese is "*shih-sao*," a term of address to the wife of a friend.

2. An umbrella given by the people to a popular departing official or some public benefactor.

3. A tablet commemorating a person's virtuous conduct, the first of the three imperishable qualities of a man. The other two are "to establish one's merit," and "to establish one's words, teaching. . . . ."

4. Someone bewitching enough to have "sucked away" another person's soul.

5. Losing at both ends, from a story in the *Romance of the Three Kingdoms*.

6. The Chinese is "*shao fu-jen*," a proper term of address for a friend's wife. It is similar to note 1 in this chapter.

7. The Chinese is "*lao pai-mu*," which is here translated as "auntie."

8. Ku Chieh-kang edited the *Ku-shih pien* (1926–1941), a multivolume reevaluation of China's traditional history and traditional methods of historical investigation and interpretation.

9. On October 10, 1911, a Chinese soldier killed his commanding officer and the Chinese Revolution of 1911 officially began at Wuchang, leading to the abdication of the Manchu child-emperor Hsuan-t'ung on February 12, 1912. Since then, October 10 has been commemorated as the National Day of the Republic of China.

10. On January 18, 1915, the Japanese Minister in Peking, Hioki Eki, presented to President Yüan Shih-k'ai (1859–1916) what came to be known as the

Twenty-one Demands, which would give Japan special political and economic privileges not only in Shantung province and in Manchuria but in other parts of China as well. Soon word of the demands leaked out, and Chinese student organizations in Peking met and planned to hold a mass demonstration on May 7, designated as the "National Humiliation Day." The demonstration, however, was held on May 4.

CHAPTER NINE

1. First Meeting gifts: The mother-in-law usually gives jewelry to a new member of the family, who in turn gives gifts of cash or items of small value to nephews, nieces, and servants.

2. During the Ch'un Ch'iu period (722–481 B.C.), the royal families of the states of Ch'in and Tsin formed marital alliances one generation after another. Thus the phrase, "joining together as Ch'in and Tsin," means to be allied in marriage.

3. Fuel, rice, oil, and salt are the four necessities of life.

4. Huang Ti, the Yellow Emperor (fl. 2697 B.C.): reputed founder of the Chinese empire, recognized by the historian Ssu-ma Ch'ien, who wrote the first general history of China in the first century B.C. Ssu-ma describes the Yellow Emperor as a human ruler and the Yellow Emperor's reign as the golden age when the government of the world was perfect.

5. A Peking opera which tells the story of Su San, a courtesan, and her lover, Wang Chin-lung. The scene referred to here is a very popular one in which Su San, falsely accused of murder, is taken under escort on a long journey to court for her trial with a cangue around her neck in which her hands are locked.

6. A servant receives tips from family guests when they come to the house to play mahjong and when she cleans up after them.

7. By the end of 1938 the Japanese controlled most of northern China and the eastern coastal regions extending inland as far as Hankow in the center of eastern China. To administer this vast area, the Japanese developed puppet governments. They succeeded in enticing Wang Ching-wei (1883–1944), a longtime Kuomintang leader, to defect and head a puppet government in Nanking.

8. The address of the secret police during the Japanese occupation of Shanghai.

AFTERWORD

1. See T'ang Shih's review of Shih T'o's *Marriage* (*Chieh-hun*) in *Wen-hsin*, 8, no. 3 (March 1948), p. 473. In the review, T'ang calls Mao Tun's *Midnight* (*Tzu-yeh*) and Ch'ien Chung-shu's *Fortress Besieged* the two best modern Chinese novels. See also Ping Hsi's "*Wei-ch'eng* tu hou" (After Reading *Fortress Besieged*) in *Ta-kung pao* (August 19, 1947), p. 9. Ping Hsi expresses a similar idea. Quoted by David Theodore Huters, "Traditional Innovation: Qian Zhong-shu and Modern Chinese Letters," Ph.D. dissertation, Stanford University, 1977, p. 344.

2. C. T. Hsia, *A History of Modern Chinese Fiction* (New Haven, Conn.: Yale University Press, 1961), p. 441.

3. The two doctoral dissertations are Dennis Hu's "A Linguistic-Literary Study of Ch'ien Chung-shu's Three Creative Works," University of Wisconsin at Madison, 1977; and David Theodore Huters, "Traditional Innovation: Qian Zhong-shu and Modern Chinese Letters," Stanford University, 1977. The master's thesis is Mai Ping-k'un's "Lun Ch'ien Chung-shu te san-wen ho hsiao-shuo"

(On Ch'ien Chung-shu's Essays and Fictional Writings), The Chinese University of Hong Kong, 1976. For a detailed listing of works by Ch'ien and about him, see Hu, pp. 212–217, and Huters, pp. 349–363.

4. C. T. Hsia, *A History*, p. 442.

5. Huters has written that it is doubtful that Ch'ien ever taught at the National Southwest Associated University in Kunming as claimed by Dennis Hu and C. T. Hsia. Neither Mr. George Yeh of Taipei nor Mr. Stephen Soong of Hong Kong has any recollection of Ch'ien's ever having taught there (Huters, p. 190, especially note 25). In May 1979 Ch'ien commented that there must have been a lapse of memory on the part of my old teacher Mr. George Yeh, who was the dean of the English faculty at the National Southwest Associated University when I taught there for a year under him."

6. C. T. Hsia, "Chui-nien Ch'ien Chung-shu hsien-sheng" (In Memory of Mr. Ch'ien Chung-shu), *Chung-kuo shih pao*, Overseas Edition, February 14, 1976, p. 6, and February 15, 1976, p. 7; also collected in Hsia's *Jen te wen-hsüeh* (Taipei: Ch'un Wen-hsüeh ch'u-pan she, 1977), pp. 177–194.

7. Professor C. T. Hsia of Columbia University, who talked with Ch'ien Chung-shu on April 23, 1979, in New York City, supplied many of the facts found here. On May 4–5, 1979, Leo Ou-fan Lee of Indiana University submitted the biographical part of the Introduction and the Author's Preface to Ch'ien Chung-shu for correction while he was in Chicago. A page from the original Preface was omitted in the translation at his request, several items of biographical detail were clarified, and recent information has been added.

8. C. T. Hsia, *A History*, p.433.

9. Roland Barthes, "An Introduction to the Structural Analysis of Narrative," tr. by Lionel Dusit, *New Literary History*, VI, 2 (Winter 1975), pp. 253, 255. Barthes' definition of a sequence is a "logical string of nuclei, linked together by a solidarity relation: the sequence opens when one of its germs is lacking an antecedent of the same kin, and it closes when another of its terms no longer entails any consequent function." Quoted by Huters, p. 343, note 2.

10. C. T. Hsia, "The Scholar-Novelist and Chinese Culture: A Reappraisal of *Ching-hua Yuan*," in *Chinese Narrative*, ed. by Andrew H. Plaks (Princeton, N.J.: Princeton University Press, 1977), p. 269.

11. Ibid.

12. See Dennis Hu, "Ch'ien Chung-shu's Novel *Wei-ch'eng*," *Journal of Asian Studies*, XXXVII, 3 (May 1978), pp. 427–443.

13. Huters, pp. 301–302. Huters points out that there are two narrative voices throughout the novel, but since there is a frequent overlapping between them, the reader thinks of them as one.

14. The fad of studying abroad goes on unabated in Hong Kong and especially in Taiwan even today.

15. For a full treatment of the theme in traditional Chinese fiction, see William Bruce Crawford, "'The Oil Vendor and the Courtesan' and the *Ts'ai-tzu Chia-jen* Novels," in *Critical Essays on Chinese Literature*, ed. by W. H. Nienhauser, Jr. (Hong Kong: The Chinese University Press, 1976), pp. 31–42. In the twentieth century, the Butterfly fiction (i.e., sentimental love stories) was extremely popular, despite efforts by modern writers to call for relevant themes in modern fiction. See Perry Link, "Traditional-Style Popular Urban Fiction," in *Modern Chinese Literature in the May Fourth Era*, ed. by Merle Goldman (Cambridge, Mass.: Harvard University Press, 1977), pp. 327–349 .

New *Directions* CLASSICS

Please write to the publisher for a free complete catalog of publications
(New Directions 80 Eighth Ave, New York City 10011).
Or visit our website at www.ndpublishing.com